Henry James

The Golden Bowl

e-artnow 2018

Charlotte Brontë
Jane Eyre

Anne Brontë
The Tenant of Wildfell Hall

Walter Scott
Ivanhoe

Henry James
The Wings of the Dove

Henry James
Washington Square

Henry James
The Bostonians

Jane Austen
Pride & Prejudice

Jane Austen
EMMA

Jane Austen
Mansfield Park & Emma

Anthony Trollope
Framley Parsonage

Henry James

The Golden Bowl

e-artnow, 2018
Contact: info@e-artnow.org

ISBN 978-80-273-3079-9

Contents

Book First: The Prince

Part First

I

The Prince had always liked his London, when it had come to him; he was one of the modern Romans who find by the Thames a more convincing image of the truth of the ancient state than any they have left by the Tiber. Brought up on the legend of the City to which the world paid tribute, he recognised in the present London much more than in contemporary Rome the real dimensions of such a case. If it was a question of an Imperium, he said to himself, and if one wished, as a Roman, to recover a little the sense of that, the place to do so was on London Bridge, or even, on a fine afternoon in May, at Hyde Park Corner. It was not indeed to either of those places that these grounds of his predilection, after all sufficiently vague, had, at the moment we are concerned with him, guided his steps; he had strayed, simply enough, into Bond Street, where his imagination, working at comparatively short range, caused him now and then to stop before a window in which objects massive and lumpish, in silver and gold, in the forms to which precious stones contribute, or in leather, steel, brass, applied to a hundred uses and abuses, were as tumbled together as if, in the insolence of the Empire, they had been the loot of far-off victories. The young man's movements, however, betrayed no consistency of attention — not even, for that matter, when one of his arrests had proceeded from possibilities in faces shaded, as they passed him on the pavement, by huge beribboned hats, or more delicately tinted still under the tense silk of parasols held at perverse angles in waiting victorias. And the Prince's undirected thought was not a little symptomatic, since, though the turn of the season had come and the flush of the streets begun to fade, the possibilities of faces, on the August afternoon, were still one of the notes of the scene. He was too restless — that was the fact — for any concentration, and the last idea that would just now have occurred to him in any connection was the idea of pursuit.

He had been pursuing for six months as never in his life before, and what had actually unsteadied him, as we join him, was the sense of how he had been justified. Capture had crowned the pursuit — or success, as he would otherwise have put it, had rewarded virtue; whereby the consciousness of these things made him, for the hour, rather serious than gay. A sobriety that might have consorted with failure sat in his handsome face, constructively regular and grave, yet at the same time oddly and, as might be, functionally almost radiant, with its dark blue eyes, its dark brown moustache and its expression no more sharply "foreign" to an English view than to have caused it sometimes to be observed of him with a shallow felicity that he looked like a "refined" Irishman. What had happened was that shortly before, at three o'clock, his fate had practically been sealed, and that even when one pretended to no quarrel with it the moment had something of the grimness of a crunched key in the strongest lock that could be made. There was nothing to do as yet, further, but feel what one had done, and our personage felt it while he aimlessly wandered. It was already as if he were married, so definitely had the solicitors, at three o'clock, enabled the date to be fixed, and by so few days was that date now distant. He was to dine at half-past eight o'clock with the young lady on whose behalf, and on whose father's, the London lawyers had reached an inspired harmony with his own man of business, poor Calderoni, fresh from Rome and now apparently in the wondrous situation of being "shown London," before promptly leaving it again, by Mr. Verver himself, Mr. Verver whose easy way with his millions had taxed to such small purpose, in the arrangements, the principle of reciprocity. The reciprocity with which the Prince was during these minutes most struck was that of Calderoni's bestowal of his company for a view of the lions. If there was one thing in the world the young man, at this juncture, clearly intended, it was to be much more decent as a son-inlaw than lots of fellows he could think of had shown themselves in that character. He thought of these fellows, from whom he was so to differ, in English; he used, mentally, the English term to describe his difference, for, familiar with the tongue from his earliest years, so that no note of strangeness remained with him either for lip or for ear, he found it convenient, in life, for the greatest number of relations. He found it convenient, oddly, even for his relation with himself — though not unmindful that there might still, as time went on, be others, including a more intimate degree of that one, that would seek, possibly with violence, the larger or the finer issue — which was it? — of the vernacular. Miss Verver had told him he spoke English too well — it was his only fault, and he had not been able to speak worse even to oblige her. "When I speak worse, you see, I speak French," he had said; intimating thus that there were discriminations, doubtless of the invidious kind, for which that language was the most apt. The girl had taken this, she let him know, as a reflection on her own French, which she had always so dreamed of making good, of making better; to say nothing of his evident feeling that the idiom supposed a cleverness she was not a person to rise to. The Prince's answer to such remarks — genial, charming, like every answer the parties to his new arrangement had yet had from him — was that he was practising his American in order to converse properly, on equal terms as it were, with Mr. Verver. His prospective father-inlaw had a command of it, he said, that put him at a disadvantage in any discussion; besides which — well, besides which he had made to the girl the observation that positively, of all his observations yet, had most finely touched her.

"You know I think he's a REAL galantuomo —'and no mistake.' There are plenty of sham ones about. He seems to me simply the best man I've ever seen in my life."

"Well, my dear, why shouldn't he be?" the girl had gaily inquired.

It was this, precisely, that had set the Prince to think. The things, or many of them, that had made Mr. Verver what he was seemed practically to bring a charge of waste against the other things that, with the other people known to the young man, had failed of such a result. "Why, his 'form,'" he had returned, "might have made one doubt."

"Father's form?" She hadn't seen it. It strikes me he hasn't got any."

"He hasn't got mine — he hasn't even got yours."

"Thank you for 'even'!" the girl had laughed at him. "Oh, yours, my dear, is tremendous. But your father has his own. I've made that out. So don't doubt it. It's where it has brought him out — that's the point."

"It's his goodness that has brought him out," our young woman had, at this, objected.

"Ah, darling, goodness, I think, never brought anyone out. Goodness, when it's real, precisely, rather keeps people in." He had been interested in his discrimination, which amused him. "No, it's his WAY. It belongs to him."

But she had wondered still. "It's the American way. That's all."

"Exactly — it's all. It's all, I say! It fits him — so it must be good for something."

"Do you think it would be good for you?" Maggie Verver had smilingly asked.

To which his reply had been just of the happiest. "I don't feel, my dear, if you really want to know, that anything much can now either hurt me or help me. Such as I am — but you'll see for yourself. Say, however, I am a galantuomo — which I devoutly hope: I'm like a chicken, at best, chopped up and smothered in sauce; cooked down as a creme de volaille, with half the parts left out. Your father's the natural fowl running about the bassecour. His feathers, movements, his sounds — those are the parts that, with me, are left out."

"All, as a matter of course — since you can't eat a chicken alive!"

The Prince had not been annoyed at this, but he had been positive. "Well, I'm eating your father alive — which is the only way to taste him. I want to continue, and as it's when he talks American that he is most alive, so I must also cultivate it, to get my pleasure. He couldn't make one like him so much in any other language."

It mattered little that the girl had continued to demur — it was the mere play of her joy. "I think he could make you like him in Chinese."

"It would be an unnecessary trouble. What I mean is that he's a kind of result of his inevitable tone. My liking is accordingly FOR the tone — which has made him possible."

"Oh, you'll hear enough of it," she laughed, "before you've done with us."

Only this, in truth, had made him frown a little.

"What do you mean, please, by my having 'done' with you?"

"Why, found out about us all there is to find."

He had been able to take it indeed easily as a joke. "Ah, love, I began with that. I know enough, I feel, never to be surprised. It's you yourselves meanwhile," he continued, "who really know nothing. There are two parts of me" — yes, he had been moved to go on. "One is made up of the history, the doings, the marriages, the crimes, the follies, the boundless betises of other people — especially of their infamous waste of money that might have come to me. Those things are written — literally in rows of volumes, in libraries; are as public as they're abominable. Everybody can get at them, and you've, both of you, wonderfully, looked them in the face. But there's another part, very much smaller doubtless, which, such as it is, represents my single self, the unknown, unimportant, unimportant — unimportant save to YOU — personal quantity. About this you've found out nothing."

"Luckily, my dear," the girl had bravely said; "for what then would become, please, of the promised occupation of my future?"

The young man remembered even now how extraordinarily CLEAR — he couldn't call it anything else — she had looked, in her prettiness, as she had said it. He also remembered what he had been moved to reply. "The happiest reigns, we are taught, you know, are the reigns without any history."

"Oh, I'm not afraid of history!" She had been sure of that. "Call it the bad part, if you like — yours certainly sticks out of you. What was it else," Maggie Verver had also said, "that made me originally think of you? It wasn't — as I should suppose you must have seen — what you call your unknown quantity, your particular self. It was the generations behind you, the follies and the crimes, the plunder and the waste — the wicked Pope, the monster most of all, whom so many of the volumes in your family library are all about. If I've read but two or three yet, I shall give myself up but the more — as soon as I have time — to the rest. Where, therefore" — she had put it to him again —"without your archives, annals, infamies, would you have been?"

He recalled what, to this, he had gravely returned. "I might have been in a somewhat better pecuniary situation." But his actual situation under the head in question positively so little mattered to them that, having by that time lived deep into the sense of his advantage, he had kept no impression of the girl's rejoinder. It had but sweetened the waters in which he now floated, tinted them as by the action of some essence, poured from a gold-topped phial, for making one's bath aromatic. No one before him, never — not even the infamous Pope — had so sat up to his neck in such a bath. It showed, for that matter, how little one of his race could escape, after all, from history. What was it but history, and of THEIR kind very much, to have the assurance of the enjoyment of more money than the palace-builder himself could have dreamed of? This was the element that bore him up and into which Maggie scattered, on occasion, her exquisite colouring drops. They were of the colour — of what on earth? of what but the extraordinary American good faith? They were of the colour of her innocence, and yet at the same time of her imagination, with which their relation, his and these people's, was all suffused. What he had further said on the occasion of which we thus represent him as catching the echoes from his own thoughts while he loitered — what he had further said came back to him, for it had been the voice itself of his luck, the soothing sound that was always with him. "You Americans are almost incredibly romantic."

"Of course we are. That's just what makes everything so nice for us."

"Everything?" He had wondered.

"Well, everything that's nice at all. The world, the beautiful, world — or everything in it that is beautiful. I mean we see so much."

He had looked at her a moment — and he well knew how she had struck him, in respect to the beautiful world, as one of the beautiful, the most beautiful things. But what he had answered was: "You see too much — that's what may sometimes make you difficulties. When you don't, at least," he had amended with a further thought, "see too little." But he had quite granted that he knew what she meant, and his warning perhaps was needless.

He had seen the follies of the romantic disposition, but there seemed somehow no follies in theirs — nothing, one was obliged to recognise, but innocent pleasures, pleasures without penalties. Their enjoyment was a tribute to others without being a loss to themselves. Only the funny thing, he had respectfully submitted, was that her father, though older and wiser, and a man into the bargain, was as bad — that is as good — as herself.

"Oh, he's better," the girl had freely declared "that is he's worse. His relation to the things he cares for — and I think it beautiful — is absolutely romantic. So is his whole life over here — it's the most romantic thing I know."

"You mean his idea for his native place?"

"Yes — the collection, the Museum with which he wishes to endow it, and of which he thinks more, as you know, than of anything in the world. It's the work of his life and the motive of everything he does."

The young man, in his actual mood, could have smiled again — smiled delicately, as he had then smiled at her. "Has it been his motive in letting me have you?"

"Yes, my dear, positively — or in a manner," she had said.

"American City isn't, by the way, his native town, for, though he's not old, it's a young thing compared with him — a younger one. He started there, he has a feeling about it, and the place has grown, as he says, like the programme of a charity performance. You're at any rate a part of his collection," she had explained —"one of the things that can only be got over here. You're a rarity, an object of beauty, an object of price. You're not perhaps absolutely unique, but you're so curious and eminent that there are very few others like you — you belong to a class about which everything is known. You're what they call a morceau de musee."

"I see. I have the great sign of it," he had risked —"that I cost a lot of money."

"I haven't the least idea," she had gravely answered, "what you cost"— and he had quite adored, for the moment, her way of saying it. He had felt even, for the moment, vulgar. But he had made the best of that. "Wouldn't you find out if it were a question of parting with me? My value would in that case be estimated."

She had looked at him with her charming eyes, as if his value were well before her. "Yes, if you mean that I'd pay rather than lose you."

And then there came again what this had made him say. "Don't talk about ME — it's you who are not of this age. You're a creature of a braver and finer one, and the cinquecento, at its most golden hour, wouldn't have been ashamed of you. It would of me, and if I didn't know some of the pieces your father has acquired, I should rather fear, for American City, the criticism of experts. Would it at all events be your idea," he had then just ruefully asked, "to send me there for safety?"

"Well, we may have to come to it."

"I'll go anywhere you want."

"We must see first — it will be only if we have to come to it. There are things," she had gone on, "that father puts away — the bigger and more cumbrous of course, which he stores, has already stored in masses, here and in Paris, in Italy, in Spain, in warehouses, vaults, banks, safes, wonderful secret places. We've been like a pair of pirates — positively stage pirates, the sort who wink at each other and say 'Ha-ha!' when they come to where their treasure is buried. Ours is buried pretty well everywhere — except what we like to see, what we travel with and have about us. These, the smaller pieces, are the things we take out and arrange as we can, to make the hotels we stay at and the houses we hire a little less ugly. Of course it's a danger, and we have to keep watch. But father loves a fine piece, loves, as he says, the good of it, and it's for the company of some of his things that he's willing to run his risks. And we've had extraordinary luck" — Maggie had made that point; "we've never lost anything yet. And the finest objects are often the smallest. Values, in lots of cases, you must know, have nothing to do with size. But there's nothing, however tiny," she had wound up, "that we've missed."

"I like the class," he had laughed for this, "in which you place me! I shall be one of the little pieces that you unpack at the hotels, or at the worst in the hired houses, like this wonderful one, and put out with the family photographs and the new magazines. But it's something not to be so big that I have to be buried."

"Oh," she had returned, "you shall not be buried, my dear, till you're dead. Unless indeed you call it burial to go to American City."

"Before I pronounce I should like to see my tomb." So he had had, after his fashion, the last word in their interchange, save for the result of an observation that had risen to his lips at the beginning, which he had then checked, and which now came back to him. "Good, bad or indifferent, I hope there's one thing you believe about me."

He had sounded solemn, even to himself, but she had taken it gaily. "Ah, don't fix me down to 'one'! I believe things enough about you, my dear, to have a few left if most of them, even, go to smash. I've taken care of THAT. I've divided my faith into water-tight compartments. We must manage not to sink."

"You do believe I'm not a hypocrite? You recognise that I don't lie or dissemble or deceive? Is THAT water-tight?"

The question, to which he had given a certain intensity, had made her, he remembered, stare an instant, her colour rising as if it had sounded to her still stranger than he had intended. He had perceived on the spot that any SERIOUS discussion of veracity, of loyalty, or rather of the want of them, practically took her unprepared, as if it were quite new to her. He had noticed it before: it was the English, the American sign that duplicity, like "love," had to be joked about. It couldn't be "gone into." So the note of his inquiry was — well, to call it nothing else — premature; a mistake worth making, however, for the almost overdone drollery in which her answer instinctively sought refuge.

"Water-tight — the biggest compartment of all? Why, it's the best cabin and the main deck and the engine-room and the steward's pantry! It's the ship itself — it's the whole line. It's the captain's table and all one's luggage — one's reading for the trip." She had images, like that, that were drawn from steamers and trains, from a familiarity with "lines," a command of "own" cars, from an experience of continents and seas, that he was unable as yet to emulate; from vast modern machineries and facilities whose acquaintance he had still to make, but as to which it was part of the interest of his situation as it stood that he could, quite without wincing, feel his future likely to bristle with them.

It was in fact, content as he was with his engagement and charming as he thought his affianced bride, his view of THAT furniture that mainly constituted our young man's "romance" — and to an extent that made of his inward state a contrast that he was intelligent enough to feel. He was intelligent enough to feel quite humble, to wish not to be in the least hard or voracious, not to insist on his own side of the bargain, to warn himself in short against arrogance and greed. Odd enough, of a truth, was his sense of this last danger — which may illustrate moreover his general attitude toward dangers from within. Personally, he considered, he hadn't the vices in question — and that was so much to the good. His race, on the other hand, had had them handsomely enough, and he was somehow full of his race. Its presence in him was like the consciousness of some inexpugnable scent in which his clothes, his whole person, his hands and the hair of his head, might have been steeped as in some chemical bath: the effect was nowhere in particular, yet he constantly felt himself at the mercy of the cause. He knew his antenatal history, knew it in every detail, and it was a thing to keep causes well before him. What was his frank judgment of so much of its ugliness, he asked himself, but a part of the cultivation of humility? What was this so important step he had just taken but the desire for some new history that should, so far as possible, contradict, and even if need be flatly dishonour, the old? If what had come to him wouldn't do he must MAKE something different. He perfectly recognised — always in his humility — that the material for the making had to be Mr. Verver's millions. There was nothing else for him on earth to make it with; he had tried before — had had to look about and see the truth. Humble as he was, at the same time, he was not so humble as if he had known himself frivolous or stupid. He had an idea — which may amuse his historian — that when you were stupid enough to be mistaken about such a matter you did know it. Therefore he wasn't mistaken — his future might be MIGHT be scientific. There was nothing in himself, at all events, to prevent it. He was allying himself to science, for it was science but the absence of prejudice backed by the presence of money? His life would be full of machinery, which was the antidote to superstition, which was in its turn, too much, the consequence, or at least the exhalation, of archives. He thought of these — of his not being at all events futile, and of his absolute acceptance of the developments of the coming age to redress the balance of his being so differently considered. The moments when he most winced were those at which he found himself believing that, really, futility would have been forgiven him. Even WITH it, in that absurd view, he would have been good enough. Such was the laxity, in the Ververs, of the romantic spirit. They didn't, indeed, poor dears, know what, in that line — the line of futility — the real thing meant. HE did — having seen it, having tried it, having taken its measure. This was a memory in fact simply to screen out — much as, just in front of him while he walked, the iron shutter of a shop, closing early to the stale summer day, rattled down at the turn of some crank. There was machinery again, just as the plate glass, all about him, was money, was power, the power of the rich peoples. Well, he was OF them now, of the rich peoples; he was on their side — if it wasn't rather the pleasanter way of putting it that they were on his.

Something of this sort was in any case the moral and the murmur of his walk. It would have been ridiculous — such a moral from such a source — if it hadn't all somehow fitted to the gravity of the hour, that gravity the oppression of which I began by recording. Another feature was the immediate nearness of the arrival of the contingent from home. He was to meet them at Charing Cross on the morrow: his younger brother, who had married before him, but whose wife, of Hebrew race, with a portion that had gilded the pill, was not in a condition to travel; his sister and her husband, the most anglicised of Milanesi, his maternal uncle, the most shelved of diplomatists, and his Roman cousin, Don Ottavio, the most disponible of exdeputies and of relatives — a scant handful of the consanguineous who, in spite of Maggie's plea for hymeneal reserve, were to accompany him to the altar. It was no great array, yet it was apparently to be a more numerous muster than any possible to the bride herself, having no wealth of kinship to choose from and making it up, on the other hand, by loose invitations. He had been interested in the girl's attitude on the matter and had wholly deferred to it, giving him, as it did, a glimpse, distinctly pleasing, of the kind of ruminations she would in general be governed by — which were quite such as fell in with his own taste. They hadn't natural relations, she and her father, she had explained; so they wouldn't try to supply the place by artificial, by make-believe ones, by any searching of highways and hedges. Oh yes, they had acquaintances enough — but a marriage was an intimate thing. You asked acquaintances when you HAD your kith and kin — you asked them over and above. But you didn't ask them alone, to cover your nudity and look like what they weren't. She knew what she meant and what she liked, and he was all ready to take from her, finding a good omen in both of the facts. He expected her, desired her, to have character; his wife SHOULD have it, and he wasn't afraid of her having much. He had had, in his earlier time, to deal with plenty of people who had had it; notably with the three four ecclesiastics, his great-uncle, the Cardinal, above all, who had taken a hand and played a part in his education: the effect of all of which had never been to upset him. He was thus fairly on the look-out for the characteristic in this most intimate, as she was to come, of his associates. He encouraged it when it appeared.

He felt therefore, just at present, as if his papers were in order, as if his accounts so balanced as they had never done in his life before and he might close the portfolio with a snap. It would open again, doubtless, of itself, with the arrival of the Romans; it would even perhaps open with his dining to-night in Portland Place, where Mr. Verver had pitched a tent suggesting that of Alexander furnished with the spoils of Darius. But what meanwhile marked his crisis, as I have said, was his sense of the immediate two or three hours. He paused on corners, at crossings; there kept rising for him, in waves, that consciousness, sharp as to its source while vague as to its end, which I began by speaking of — the consciousness of an appeal to do something or other, before it was too late, for himself. By any friend to whom he might have mentioned it the appeal could have been turned to frank derision. For what, for whom indeed but himself and the high advantages attached, was he about to marry an extraordinarily charming girl, whose "prospects," of the solid sort, were as guaranteed as her amiability? He wasn't to do it, assuredly, all for her. The Prince, as happened, however, was so free to feel and yet not to formulate that there rose before him after a little, definitely, the image of a friend whom he had often found ironic. He withheld the tribute of attention from passing faces only to let his impulse accumulate. Youth and beauty made him scarcely turn, but the image of Mrs. Assingham made him presently stop a hansom. HER youth, her beauty were things more or less of the past, but to find her at home, as he possibly might, would be "doing" what he still had time for, would put something of a reason into his restlessness and thereby probably soothe it. To recognise the propriety of this particular pilgrimage — she lived far enough off, in long Cadogan Place — was already in fact to work it off a little. A perception of the propriety of formally thanking her, and of timing the act just as he happened to be doing — this, he made out as he went, was obviously all that had been the matter with him. It was true that he had mistaken the mood of the moment, misread it rather, superficially, as an impulse to look the other way — the other way from where his pledges had accumulated. Mrs. Assingham, precisely, represented, embodied his pledges — was, in her pleasant person, the force that had set them successively in motion. She had MADE his marriage, quite as truly as his papal ancestor had made his family — though he could scarce see what she had made it for unless because she too was perversely romantic. He had neither bribed nor persuaded her, had given her nothing — scarce even till now articulate thanks; so that her profit-to think of it vulgarly — must have all had to come from the Ververs.

Yet he was far, he could still remind himself, from supposing that she had been grossly remunerated. He was wholly sure she hadn't; for if there were people who took presents and people who didn't she would be quite on the right side and of the proud class. Only then, on the other hand, her disinterestedness was rather awful — it implied, that is, such abysses of confidence. She was admirably attached to Maggie — whose possession of such a friend might moreover quite rank as one of her "assets"; but the great proof of her affection had been in bringing them, with her design, together. Meeting him during a winter in Rome, meeting him afterwards in Paris, and "liking" him, as she had in time frankly let him know from the first, she had marked him for her young friend's own and had then, unmistakably, presented him in a light. But the interest in Maggie — that was the point — would have achieved but little without her interest in HIM. On what did that sentiment, unsolicited and unrecompensed, rest? what good, again — for it was much like his question about Mr. Verver — should he ever have done her? The Prince's notion of a recompense to women — similar in this to his notion of an appeal — was more or less to make love to them. Now he hadn't, as he believed, made love the least little bit to Mrs. Assingham — nor did he think she had for a moment supposed it. He liked in these days, to mark them off, the women to whom he hadn't made love: it represented — and that was what pleased him in it — a different stage of existence from the time at which he liked to mark off the women to whom he had. Neither, with all this, had Mrs. Assingham herself been either aggressive or resentful. On what occasion, ever, had she appeared to find him wanting? These things, the motives of such people, were obscure — a little alarmingly so; they contributed to that element of the impenetrable which alone slightly qualified his sense of his good fortune. He remembered to have read, as a boy, a wonderful tale by Allan Poe, his prospective wife's countryman-which was a thing to show, by the way, what imagination Americans COULD have: the story of the shipwrecked Gordon Pym, who, drifting in a small boat further toward the North Pole — or was it the South? — than anyone had ever done, found at a given moment before him a thickness of white air that was like a dazzling curtain of light, concealing as darkness conceals, yet of the colour of milk or of snow. There were moments when he felt his own boat move upon some such mystery. The state of mind of his new friends, including Mrs. Assingham herself, had resemblances to a great white curtain. He had never known curtains but as purple even to blackness — but as producing where they hung a darkness intended and ominous. When they were so disposed as to shelter surprises the surprises were apt to be shocks.

Shocks, however, from these quite different depths, were not what he saw reason to apprehend; what he rather seemed to himself not yet to have measured was something that, seeking a name for it, he would have called the quantity of confidence reposed in him. He had stood still, at many a moment of the previous month, with the thought, freshly determined or renewed, of the general expectation — to define it roughly — of which he was the subject. What was singular was that it seemed not so much an expectation of anything in particular as a large, bland, blank assumption of merits almost beyond notation, of essential quality and value. It was as if he had been some old embossed coin, of a purity of gold no longer used, stamped with glorious arms, mediaeval, wonderful, of which the "worth" in mere modern change, sovereigns and half crowns, would be great enough, but as to which, since there were finer ways of using it, such taking to pieces was superfluous. That was the image for the security in which it was open to him to rest; he was to constitute a possession, yet was to escape being reduced to his component parts. What would this mean but that, practically, he was never to be tried or tested? What would it mean but that, if they didn't "change" him, they really wouldn't know — he wouldn't know himself — how many pounds, shillings and pence he had to give? These at any rate, for the present, were unanswerable questions; all that was before him was that he was invested with attributes. He was taken seriously. Lost there in the white mist was the seriousness in them that made them so take him. It was even in Mrs. Assingham, in spite of her having, as she had frequently shown, a more mocking spirit. All he could say as yet was that he had done nothing, so far as to break any charm. What should he do if he were to ask her frankly this afternoon what was, morally speaking, behind their veil. It would come to asking what they expected him to do. She would answer him probably: "Oh, you know, it's what we expect you to be!" on which he would have no resource but to deny his knowledge. Would that break the spell, his saying he had no idea? What idea in fact could he have? He also took himself seriously — made a point of it; but it wasn't simply a question of fancy and pretension. His own estimate he saw ways, at one time and another, of dealing with: but theirs, sooner or later, say what they might, would put him to the practical proof. As the practical proof, accordingly, would naturally be proportionate to the cluster of his attributes, one arrived at a scale that he was not, honestly, the man to calculate. Who but a billionaire could say what was fair exchange for a billion? That measure was the shrouded object, but he felt really, as his cab stopped in Cadogan Place, a little nearer the shroud. He promised himself, virtually, to give the latter a twitch.

II

"They're not good days, you know," he had said to Fanny Assingham after declaring himself grateful for finding her, and then, with his cup of tea, putting her in possession of the latest news — the documents signed an hour ago, de part et d'autre, and the telegram from his backers, who had reached Paris the morning before, and who, pausing there a little, poor dears, seemed to think the whole thing a tremendous lark. "We're very simple folk, mere country cousins compared with you," he had also observed, "and Paris, for my sister and her husband, is the end of the world. London therefore will be more or less another planet. It has always been, as with so many of us, quite their Mecca, but this is their first real caravan; they've mainly known 'old England' as a shop for articles in india-rubber and leather, in which they've dressed themselves as much as possible. Which all means, however, that you'll see them, all of them, wreathed in smiles. We must be very easy with them. Maggie's too wonderful — her preparations are on a scale! She insists on taking in the sposi and my uncle. The, others will come to me. I've been engaging their rooms at the hotel, and, with all those solemn signatures of an hour ago, that brings the case home to me."

"Do you mean you're afraid?" his hostess had amusedly asked.

"Terribly afraid. I've now but to wait to see the monster come. They're not good days; they're neither one thing nor the other. I've really got nothing, yet I've everything to lose. One doesn't know what still may happen."

The way she laughed at him was for an instant almost irritating; it came out, for his fancy, from behind the white curtain. It was a sign, that is, of her deep serenity, which worried instead of soothing him. And to be soothed, after all, to be tided over, in his mystic impatience, to be told what he could understand and believe — that was what he had come for. "Marriage then," said Mrs. Assingham, "is what you call the monster? I admit it's a fearful thing at the best; but, for heaven's sake, if that's what you're thinking of, don't run away from it."

"Ah, to run away from it would be to run away from you," the Prince replied; "and I've already told you often enough how I depend on you to see me through." He so liked the way she took this, from the corner of her sofa, that he gave his sincerity — for it WAS sincerity — fuller expression. "I'm starting on the great voyage — across the unknown sea; my ship's all rigged and appointed, the cargo's stowed away and the company complete. But what seems the matter with me is that I can't sail alone; my ship must be one of a pair, must have, in the waste of waters, a — what do you call it? — a consort. I don't ask you to stay on board with me, but I must keep your sail in sight for orientation. I don't in the least myself know, I assure you, the points of the compass. But with a lead I can perfectly follow. You MUST be my lead."

"How can you be sure," she asked, "where I should take you?"

"Why, from your having brought me safely thus far. I should never have got here without you. You've provided the ship itself, and, if you've not quite seen me aboard, you've attended me, ever so kindly, to the dock. Your own vessel is, all conveniently, in the next berth, and you can't desert me now."

She showed him again her amusement, which struck him even as excessive, as if, to his surprise, he made her also a little nervous; she treated him in fine as if he were not uttering truths, but making pretty figures for her diversion. "My vessel, dear Prince?" she smiled. "What vessel, in the world, have I? This little house is all our ship, Bob's and mine — and thankful we are, now, to have it. We've wandered far, living, as you may say, from hand to mouth, without rest for the soles of our feet. But the time has come for us at last to draw in."

He made at this, the young man, an indignant protest. "You talk about rest — it's too selfish! — when you're just launching me on adventures?"

She shook her head with her kind lucidity. "Not adventures — heaven forbid! You've had yours — as I've had mine; and my idea has been, all along, that we should neither of us begin again. My own last, precisely, has been doing for you all you so prettily mention. But it consists simply in having conducted you to rest. You talk about ships, but they're not the comparison. Your tossings are over — you're practically IN port. The port," she concluded, "of the Golden Isles."

He looked about, to put himself more in relation with the place; then, after an hesitation, seemed to speak certain words instead of certain others. "Oh, I know where I AM —! I do decline to be left, but what I came for, of course, was to thank you. If today has seemed, for the first time, the end of preliminaries, I feel how little there would have been any at all without you. The first were wholly yours."

"Well," said Mrs. Assingham, "they were remarkably easy. I've seen them, I've HAD them," she smiled, "more difficult. Everything, you must feel, went of itself. So, you must feel, everything still goes."

The Prince quickly agreed. "Oh, beautifully! But you had the conception."

"Ah, Prince, so had you!"

He looked at her harder a moment. "You had it first. You had it most."

She returned his look as if it had made her wonder. "I LIKED it, if that's what you mean. But you liked it surely yourself. I protest, that I had easy work with you. I had only at last — when I thought it was time — to speak for you."

"All that is quite true. But you're leaving me, all the same, you're leaving me — you're washing your hands of me," he went on. "However, that won't be easy; I won't BE left." And he had turned his eyes about again, taking in the pretty room that she had just described as her final refuge, the place of peace for a world-worn couple, to which she had lately retired with "Bob." "I shall keep this spot in sight. Say what you will, I shall need you. I'm not, you know," he declared, "going to give you up for anybody."

"If you're afraid — which of course you're not — are you trying to make me the same?" she asked after a moment.

He waited a minute too, then answered her with a question. "You say you 'liked' it, your undertaking to make my engagement possible. It remains beautiful for me that you did; it's charming and unforgettable. But, still more, it's mysterious and wonderful. WHY, you dear delightful woman, did you like it?"

"I scarce know what to make," she said, "of such an inquiry. If you haven't by this time found out yourself, what meaning can anything I say have for you? Don't you really after all feel," she added while nothing came from him —"aren't you conscious every minute, of the perfection of the creature of whom I've put you into possession?"

"Every minute — gratefully conscious. But that's exactly the ground of my question. It wasn't only a matter of your handing me over — it was a matter of your handing her. It was a matter of HER fate still more than of mine. You thought all the good of her that one woman can think of another, and yet, by your account, you enjoyed assisting at her risk."

She had kept her eyes on him while he spoke, and this was what, visibly, determined a repetition for her. "Are you trying to frighten me?"

"Ah, that's a foolish view — I should be too vulgar. You apparently can't understand either my good faith or my humility. I'm awfully humble," the young man insisted; "that's the way I've been feeling today, with everything so finished and ready. And you won't take me for serious."

She continued to face him as if he really troubled her a little. "Oh, you deep old Italians!"

"There you are," he returned —"it's what I wanted you to come to. That's the responsible note."

"Yes," she went on —"if you're 'humble' you MUST be dangerous."

She had a pause while he only smiled; then she said: "I don't in the least want to lose sight of you. But even if I did I shouldn't think it right."

"Thank you for that — it's what I needed of you. I'm sure, after all, that the more you're with me the more I shall understand. It's the only thing in the world I want. I'm excellent, I really think, all round — except that I'm stupid. I can do pretty well anything I SEE. But I've got to see it first." And he pursued his demonstration. "I don't in the least mind its having to be shown me — in fact I like that better. Therefore it is that I want, that I shall always want, your eyes. Through THEM I wish to look — even at any risk of their showing me what I mayn't like. For then," he wound up, "I shall know. And of that I shall never be afraid."

She might quite have been waiting to see what he would come to, but she spoke with a certain impatience. "What on earth are you talking about?"

But he could perfectly say: "Of my real, honest fear of being 'off' some day, of being wrong, WITHOUT knowing it. That's what I shall always trust you for — to tell me when I am. No — with you people it's a sense. We haven't got it — not as you have. Therefore —!" But he had said enough. "Ecco!" he simply smiled.

It was not to be concealed that he worked upon her, but of course she had always liked him. "I should be interested," she presently remarked, "to see some sense you don't possess."

Well, he produced one on the spot. "The moral, dear Mrs. Assingham. I mean, always, as you others consider it. I've of course something that in our poor dear backward old Rome sufficiently passes for it. But it's no more like yours than the tortuous stone staircase — half-ruined into the bargain! — in some castle of our quattrocento is like the 'lightning elevator' in one of Mr. Verver's fifteen-storey buildings. Your moral sense works by steam — it sends you up like a rocket. Ours is slow and steep and unlighted, with so many of the steps missing that — well, that it's as short, in almost any case, to turn round and come down again."

"Trusting," Mrs. Assingham smiled, "to get up some other way?"

"Yes — or not to have to get up at all. However," he added, "I told you that at the beginning."

"Machiavelli!" she simply exclaimed.

"You do me too much honour. I wish indeed I had his genius. However, if you really believe I have his perversity you wouldn't say it. But it's all right," he gaily enough concluded; "I shall always have you to come to."

On this, for a little, they sat face to face; after which, without comment, she asked him if he would have more tea. All she would give him, he promptly signified; and he developed, making her laugh, his idea that the tea of the English race was somehow their morality, "made," with boiling water, in a little pot, so that the more of it one drank the more moral one would become. His drollery served as a transition, and she put to him several questions about his sister and the others, questions as to what Bob, in particular, Colonel Assingham, her husband, could do for the arriving gentlemen, whom, by the Prince's leave, he would immediately go to see. He was funny, while they talked, about his own people too, whom he described, with anecdotes of their habits, imitations of their manners and prophecies of their conduct, as more rococo than anything Cadogan Place would ever have known. This, Mrs. Assingham professed, was exactly what would endear them to her, and that, in turn, drew from her visitor a fresh declaration of all the comfort of his being able so to depend on her. He had been with her, at this point, some twenty minutes; but he had paid her much longer visits, and he stayed now as if to make his attitude prove his appreciation. He stayed moreover — THAT was really the sign of the hour — in spite of the nervous unrest that had brought him and that had in truth much rather fed on the scepticism by which she had apparently meant to soothe it. She had not soothed him, and there arrived, remarkably, a moment when the cause of her failure gleamed out. He had not frightened her, as she called it — he felt that; yet she was herself not at ease. She had been nervous, though trying to disguise it; the sight of him, following on the announcement of his name, had shown her as disconcerted. This conviction, for the young man, deepened and sharpened; yet with the effect, too, of making him glad in spite of it. It was as if, in calling, he had done even better than he intended. For it was somehow IMPORTANT — that was what it was — that there should be at this hour something the matter with Mrs. Assingham, with whom, in all their acquaintance, so considerable now, there had never been the least little thing the matter. To wait thus and watch for it was to know, of a truth, that there was something the matter with HIM; since strangely, with so little to go upon — his heart had positively begun to beat to the tune of suspense. It fairly befell at last, for a climax, that they almost ceased to pretend — to pretend, that is, to cheat each other with forms. The unspoken had come up, and there was a crisis — neither could have said how long it lasted — during which they were reduced, for all interchange, to looking at each other on quite an inordinate scale. They might at this moment, in their positively portentous stillness, have been keeping it up for a wager, sitting for their photograph or even enacting a tableau-vivant.

The spectator of whom they would thus well have been worthy might have read meanings of his own into the intensity of their communion — or indeed, even without meanings, have found his account, aesthetically, in some gratified play of our modern sense of type, so scantly to be distinguished from our modern sense of beauty. Type was there, at the worst, in Mrs. Assingham's dark, neat head, on which the crisp black hair made waves so fine and so numerous that she looked even more in the fashion of the hour than she desired. Full of discriminations against the obvious, she had yet to accept a flagrant appearance and to make the best of misleading signs. Her richness of hue, her generous nose, her eyebrows marked like those of an actress — these things, with an added amplitude of person on which middle age had set its seal, seemed to present her insistently as a daughter of the south, or still more of the east, a creature formed by hammocks and divans, fed upon sherbets and waited upon by slaves. She looked as if her most active effort might be to take up, as she lay back, her mandolin, or to share a sugared fruit with a pet gazelle. She was in fact, however, neither a pampered Jewess nor a lazy Creole; New York had been, recordedly, her birthplace and "Europe" punctually her discipline. She wore yellow and purple because she thought it better, as she said, while one was about it, to look like the Queen of Sheba than like a revendeuse; she put pearls in her hair and crimson and gold in her tea-gown for the same reason: it was her theory that nature itself had overdressed her and that her only course was to drown, as it was hopeless to try to chasten, the overdressing. So she was covered and surrounded with "things," which were frankly toys and shams, a part of the amusement with which she rejoiced to supply her friends. These friends were in the game that of playing with the disparity between her aspect and her character. Her character was attested by the second movement of her face, which convinced the beholder that her vision of the humours of the world was not supine, not passive. She enjoyed, she needed the warm air of friendship, but the eyes of the American city looked out, somehow, for the opportunity of it, from under the lids of Jerusalem. With her false indolence, in short, her false leisure, her false pearls and palms and courts and fountains, she was a person for whom life was multitudinous detail, detail that left her, as it at any moment found her, unappalled and unwearied.

"Sophisticated as I may appear" — it was her frequent phrase — she had found sympathy her best resource. It gave her plenty to do; it made her, as she also said, sit up. She had in her life two great holes to fill, and she described herself as dropping social scraps into them as she had known old ladies, in her early American time, drop morsels of silk into the baskets in which they collected the material for some eventual patchwork quilt.

One of these gaps in Mrs. Assingham's completeness was her want of children; the other was her want of wealth. It was wonderful how little either, in the fulness of time, came to show; sympathy and curiosity could render their objects practically filial, just as an English husband who in his military years had "run" everything in his regiment could make economy blossom like the rose. Colonel Bob had, a few years after his marriage, left the army, which had clearly, by that time, done its laudable all for the enrichment of his personal experience, and he could thus give his whole time to the gardening in question. There reigned among the younger friends of this couple a legend, almost too venerable for historical criticism, that the marriage itself, the happiest of its class, dated from the far twilight of the age, a primitive period when such things — such things as American girls accepted as "good enough" — had not begun to be; — so that the pleasant pair had been, as to the risk taken on either side, bold and original, honourably marked, for the evening of life, as discoverers of a kind of hymeneal Northwest Passage. Mrs. Assingham knew better, knew there had been no historic hour, from that of Pocahontas down, when some young Englishman hadn't precipitately believed and some American girl hadn't, with a few more gradations, availed herself to the full of her incapacity to doubt; but she accepted resignedly the laurel of the founder, since she was in fact pretty well the doyenne, above ground, of her transplanted tribe, and since, above all, she HAD invented combinations, though she had not invented Bob's own. It was he who had done that, absolutely puzzled it out, by himself, from his first odd glimmer-resting upon it moreover, through the years to come, as proof enough, in him, by itself, of the higher cleverness. If she kept her own cleverness up it was largely that he should have full credit. There were moments in truth when she privately felt how little — striking out as he had done — he could have afforded that she should show the common limits. But Mrs. Assingham's cleverness was in truth tested when her present visitor at last said to her: "I don't think, you know, that you're treating me quite right. You've something on your mind that you don't tell me."

It was positive too that her smile, in reply, was a trifle dim. "Am I obliged to tell you everything I have on my mind?"

"It isn't a question of everything, but it's a question of anything that may particularly concern me. Then you shouldn't keep it back. You know with what care I desire to proceed, taking everything into account and making no mistake that may possibly injure HER."

Mrs. Assingham, at this, had after an instant an odd interrogation. "'Her'?"

"Her and him. Both our friends. Either Maggie or her father."

"I have something on my mind," Mrs. Assingham presently returned; "something has happened for which I hadn't been prepared. But it isn't anything that properly concerns you."

The Prince, with immediate gaiety, threw back his head. "What do you mean by 'properly'? I somehow see volumes in it. It's the way people put a thing when they put it — well, wrong. *I* put things right. What is it that has happened for me?"

His hostess, the next moment, had drawn spirit from his tone.

"Oh, I shall be delighted if you'll take your share of it. Charlotte Stant is in London. She has just been here."

"Miss Stant? Oh really?" The Prince expressed clear surprise — a transparency through which his eyes met his friend's with a certain hardness of concussion. "She has arrived from America?" he then quickly asked.

"She appears to have arrived this noon — coming up from Southampton; at an hotel. She dropped upon me after luncheon and was here for more than an hour."

The young man heard with interest, though not with an interest too great for his gaiety. "You think then I've a share in it? What IS my share?"

"Why, any you like — the one you seemed just now eager to take. It was you yourself who insisted."

He looked at her on this with conscious inconsistency, and she could now see that he had changed colour. But he was always easy.

"I didn't know then what the matter was."

"You didn't think it could be so bad?"

"Do you call it very bad?" the young man asked. "Only," she smiled, "because that's the way it seems to affect YOU."

He hesitated, still with the trace of his quickened colour, still looking at her, still adjusting his manner. "But you allowed you were upset."

"To the extent — yes — of not having in the least looked for her. Any more," said Mrs. Assingham, "than I judge Maggie to have done."

The Prince thought; then as if glad to be able to say something very natural and true: "No — quite right. Maggie hasn't looked for her. But I'm sure," he added, "she'll be delighted to see her."

"That, certainly" — and his hostess spoke with a different shade of gravity.

"She'll be quite overjoyed," the Prince went on. "Has Miss Stant now gone to her?"

"She has gone back to her hotel, to bring her things here. I can't have her," said Mrs. Assingham, "alone at an hotel."

"No; I see."

"If she's here at all she must stay with me." He quite took it in. "So she's coming now?"

"I expect her at any moment. If you wait you'll see her."

"Oh," he promptly declared —"charming!" But this word came out as if, a little, in sudden substitution for some other. It sounded accidental, whereas he wished to be firm. That accordingly was what he next showed himself. "If it wasn't for what's going on these next days Maggie would certainly want to have her. In fact," he lucidly continued, "isn't what's happening just a reason to MAKE her want to?" Mrs. Assingham, for answer, only looked at him, and this, the next instant, had apparently had more effect than if she had spoken. For he asked a question that seemed incongruous. "What has she come for!"

It made his companion laugh. "Why, for just what you say. For your marriage."

"Mine?" — he wondered.

"Maggie's — it's the same thing. It's 'for' your great event. And then," said Mrs. Assingham, "she's so lonely."

"Has she given you that as a reason?"

"I scarcely remember — she gave me so many. She abounds, poor dear, in reasons. But there's one that, whatever she does, I always remember for myself."

"And which is that?" He looked as if he ought to guess but couldn't.

"Why, the fact that she has no home — absolutely none whatever. She's extraordinarily alone."

Again he took it in. "And also has no great means."

"Very small ones. Which is not, however, with the expense of railways and hotels, a reason for her running to and fro."

"On the contrary. But she doesn't like her country."

"Hers, my dear man? — it's little enough 'hers.'" The attribution, for the moment, amused his hostess. "She has rebounded now — but she has had little enough else to do with it."

"Oh, I say hers," the Prince pleasantly explained, "very much as, at this time of day, I might say mine. I quite feel, I assure you, as if the great place already more or less belonged to ME."

"That's your good fortune and your point of view. You own — or you soon practically WILL own — so much of it. Charlotte owns almost nothing in the world, she tells me, but two colossal trunks-only one of which I have given her leave to introduce into this house. She'll depreciate to you," Mrs. Assingham added, "your property."

He thought of these things, he thought of every thing; but he had always his resource at hand of turning all to the easy. "Has she come with designs upon me?" And then in a moment, as if even this were almost too grave, he sounded the note that had least to do with himself. "Est-elle toujours aussi belle?" That was the furthest point, somehow, to which Charlotte Stant could be relegated.

Mrs. Assingham treated it freely. "Just the same. The person in the world, to my sense, whose looks are most subject to appreciation. It's all in the way she affects you. One admires her if one doesn't happen not to. So, as well, one criticises her."

"Ah, that's not fair!" said the Prince.

"To criticise her? Then there you are! You're answered."

"I'm answered." He took it, humorously, as his lesson — sank his previous self-consciousness, with excellent effect, in grateful docility. "I only meant that there are perhaps better things to be done with Miss Stant than to criticise her. When once you begin THAT, with anyone —!" He was vague and kind.

"I quite agree that it's better to keep out of it as long as one can. But when one MUST do it —"

"Yes?" he asked as she paused. "Then know what you mean."

"I see. Perhaps," he smiled, "*I* don't know what I mean."

"Well, it's what, just now, in all ways, you particularly should know." Mrs. Assingham, however, made no more of this, having, before anything else, apparently, a scruple about the tone she had just used. "I quite understand, of course, that, given her great friendship with Maggie, she should have wanted to be present. She has acted impulsively — but she has acted generously."

"She has acted beautifully," said the Prince.

"I say 'generously' because I mean she hasn't, in any way, counted the cost. She'll have it to count, in a manner, now," his hostess continued. "But that doesn't matter."

He could see how little. "You'll look after her."

"I'll look after her."

"So it's all right."

"It's all right," said Mrs. Assingham. "Then why are you troubled?"

It pulled her up — but only for a minute. "I'm not — any more than you."

The Prince's dark blue eyes were of the finest, and, on occasion, precisely, resembled nothing so much as the high windows of a Roman palace, of an historic front by one of the great old designers, thrown open on a feast-day to the golden air. His look itself, at such times, suggested an image — that of some very noble personage who, expected, acclaimed by the crowd in the street and with old precious stuffs falling over the sill for his support, had gaily and gallantly come to show himself: always moreover less in his own interest than in that of spectators and subjects whose need to admire, even to gape, was periodically to be considered. The young man's expression became, after this fashion, something vivid and concrete — a beautiful personal presence, that of a prince in very truth, a ruler, warrior, patron, lighting up brave architecture and diffusing the sense of a function. It had been happily said of his face that the figure thus appearing in the great frame was the ghost of some proudest ancestor. Whoever the ancestor now, at all events, the Prince was, for Mrs. Assingham's benefit, in view of the people. He seemed, leaning on crimson damask, to take in the bright day. He looked younger than his years; he was beautiful, innocent, vague.

"Oh, well, I'M not!" he rang out clear.

"I should like to SEE you, sir!" she said. "For you wouldn't have a shadow of excuse." He showed how he agreed that he would have been at a loss for one, and the fact of their serenity was thus made as important as if some danger of its opposite had directly menaced them. The only thing was that if the evidence of their cheer was so established Mrs. Assingham had a little to explain her original manner, and she came to this before they dropped the question. "My first impulse is always to behave, about everything, as if I feared complications. But I don't fear them — I really like them. They're quite my element."

He deferred, for her, to this account of herself. "But still," he said, "if we're not in the presence of a complication."

She hesitated. "A handsome, clever, odd girl staying with one is always a complication."

The young man weighed it almost as if the question were new to him. "And will she stay very long?"

His friend gave a laugh. "How in the world can I know? I've scarcely asked her."

"Ah yes. You can't."

But something in the tone of it amused her afresh. "Do you think you could?"

"I?" he wondered.

"Do you think you could get it out of her for me — the probable length of her stay?"

He rose bravely enough to the occasion and the challenge. "I daresay, if you were to give me the chance."

"Here it is then for you," she answered; for she had heard, within the minute, the stop of a cab at her door. "She's back."

III

It had been said as a joke, but as, after this, they awaited their friend in silence, the effect of the silence was to turn the time to gravity — a gravity not dissipated even when the Prince next spoke. He had been thinking the case over and making up his mind. A handsome, clever, odd girl staying with one was a complication. Mrs. Assingham, so far, was right. But there were the facts — the good relations, from schooldays, of the two young women, and the clear confidence with which one of them had arrived. "She can come, you know, at any time, to US."

Mrs. Assingham took it up with an irony beyond laughter. "You'd like her for your honeymoon?"

"Oh no, you must keep her for that. But why not after?"

She had looked at him a minute; then, at the sound of a voice in the corridor, they had got up. "Why not? You're splendid!" Charlotte Stant, the next minute, was with them, ushered in as she had alighted from her cab, and prepared for not finding Mrs. Assingham alone — this would have been to be noticed — by the butler's answer, on the stairs, to a question put to him. She could have looked at her hostess with such straightness and brightness only from knowing that the Prince was also there — the discrimination of but a moment, yet which let him take her in still better than if she had instantly faced him. He availed himself of the chance thus given him, for he was conscious of all these things. What he accordingly saw, for some seconds, with intensity, was a tall, strong, charming girl who wore for him, at first, exactly the look of her adventurous situation, a suggestion, in all her person, in motion and gesture, in free, vivid, yet altogether happy indications of dress, from the becoming compactness of her hat to the shade of tan in her shoes, of winds and waves and custom-houses, of far countries and long journeys, the knowledge of how and where and the habit, founded on experience, of not being afraid. He was aware, at the same time, that of this combination the "strongminded" note was not, as might have been apprehended, the basis; he was now sufficiently familiar with English-speaking types, he had sounded attentively enough such possibilities, for a quick vision of differences. He had, besides, his own view of this young lady's strength of mind. It was great, he had ground to believe, but it would never interfere with the play of her extremely personal, her always amusing taste. This last was the thing in her — for she threw it out positively, on the spot, like a light — that she might have reappeared, during these moments, just to cool his worried eyes with. He saw her in her light that immediate, exclusive address to their friend was like a lamp she was holding aloft for his benefit and for his pleasure. It showed him everything — above all her presence in the world, so closely, so irretrievably contemporaneous with his own: a sharp, sharp fact, sharper during these instants than any other at all, even than that of his marriage, but accompanied, in a subordinate and controlled way, with those others, facial, physiognomic, that Mrs. Assingham had been speaking of as subject to appreciation. So they were, these others, as he met them again, and that was the connection they instantly established with him. If they had to be interpreted, this made at least for intimacy. There was but one way certainly for HIM — to interpret them in the sense of the already known.

Making use then of clumsy terms of excess, the face was too narrow and too long, the eyes not large, and the mouth, on the other hand, by no means small, with substance in its lips and a slight, the very slightest, tendency to protrusion in the solid teeth, otherwise indeed well arrayed and flashingly white. But it was, strangely, as a cluster of possessions of his own that these things, in Charlotte Stant, now affected him; items in a full list, items recognised, each of them, as if, for the long interval, they had been "stored" wrapped up, numbered, put away in a cabinet. While she faced Mrs. Assingham the door of the cabinet had opened of itself; he took the relics out, one by one, and it was more and more, each instant, as if she were giving him time. He saw again that her thick hair was, vulgarly speaking, brown, but that there was a shade of tawny autumn leaf in it, for "appreciation" — a colour indescribable and of which he had known no other case, something that gave her at moments the sylvan head of a huntress. He saw the sleeves of her jacket drawn to her wrists, but he again made out the free arms within them to be of the completely rounded, the polished slimness that Florentine sculptors, in the great time, had loved, and of which the apparent firmness is expressed in their old silver and old bronze. He knew her narrow hands, he knew her long fingers and the shape and colour of her finger-nails, he knew her special beauty of movement and line when she turned her back, and the perfect working of all her main attachments, that of some wonderful finished instrument, something intently made for exhibition, for a prize. He knew above all the extraordinary fineness of her flexible waist, the stem of an expanded flower, which gave her a likeness also to some long, loose silk purse, well filled with gold pieces, but having been passed, empty, through a finger-ring that held it together. It was as if, before she turned to him, he had weighed the whole thing in his open palm and even heard a little the chink of the metal. When she did turn to him it was to recognise with her eyes what he might have been doing. She made no circumstance of thus coming upon him, save so far as the intelligence in her face could at any moment make a circumstance of almost anything. If when she moved off she looked like a huntress, she looked when she came nearer like his notion, perhaps not wholly correct, of a muse. But what she said was simply: "You see you're not rid of me. How is dear Maggie?"

It was to come soon enough by the quite unforced operation of chance, the young man's opportunity to ask her the question suggested by Mrs. Assingham shortly before her entrance. The license, had he chosen to embrace it, was within a few minutes all there — the license given him literally to inquire of this young lady how long she was likely to be with them. For a matter of the mere domestic order had quickly determined, on Mrs. Assingham's part, a withdrawal, of a few moments, which had the effect of leaving her visitors free. "Mrs. Betterman's there?" she had said to Charlotte in allusion to some member of the household who was to have received her and seen her belongings settled; to which Charlotte had replied that she had encountered only the butler, who had been quite charming. She had deprecated any action taken on behalf of her effects; but her hostess, rebounding from accumulated cushions, evidently saw more in Mrs. Betterman's non-appearance than could meet the casual eye. What she saw, in short, demanded her intervention, in spite of an earnest "Let ME go!" from the girl, and a prolonged smiling wail over the trouble she was giving. The Prince was quite aware, at this moment, that departure, for himself, was indicated; the question of Miss Stant's installation didn't demand his presence; it was a case for one to go away — if one hadn't a reason for staying. He had a reason, however — of that he was equally aware; and he had not for a good while done anything more conscious and intentional than not, quickly, to take leave. His visible insistence — for it came to that — even demanded of him a certain disagreeable effort, the sort of effort he had mostly associated with acting for an idea. His idea was there, his idea was to find out something, something he wanted much to know, and to find it out not tomorrow, not at some future time, not in short with waiting and wondering, but if possible before quitting the place. This particular curiosity, moreover, confounded itself a little with the occasion offered him to satisfy Mrs. Assingham's own; he wouldn't have admitted that he was staying to ask a rude question — there was distinctly nothing rude in his having his reasons. It would be rude, for that matter, to turn one's back, without a word or two, on an old friend.

Well, as it came to pass, he got the word or two, for Mrs. Assingham's preoccupation was practically simplifying. The little crisis was of shorter duration than our account of it; duration, naturally, would have forced him to take up his hat. He was somehow glad, on finding himself alone with Charlotte, that he had not been guilty of that inconsequence. Not to be flurried was the kind of consistency he wanted, just as consistency was the kind of dignity. And why couldn't he have dignity when he had so much of the good conscience, as it were, on which such advantages rested? He had done nothing he oughtn't — he had in fact done nothing at all. Once more, as a man conscious of having known many women, he could assist, as he would have called it, at the recurrent, the predestined phenomenon, the thing always as certain as sunrise or the coming round of Saints' days, the doing by the woman of the thing that gave her away. She did it, ever, inevitably, infallibly — she couldn't possibly not do it. It was her nature, it was her life, and the man could always expect it without lifting a finger. This was HIS, the man's, any man's, position and strength — that he had necessarily the advantage, that he only had to wait, with a decent patience, to be placed, in spite of himself, it might really be said, in the right. Just so the punctuality of performance on the part of the other creature was her weakness and her deep misfortune — not less, no doubt, than her beauty. It produced for the man that extraordinary mixture of pity and profit in which his relation with her, when he was not a mere brute, mainly consisted; and gave him in fact his most pertinent ground of being always nice to her, nice about her, nice FOR her. She always dressed her act up, of course, she muffled and disguised and arranged it, showing in fact in these dissimulations a cleverness equal to but one thing in the world, equal to her abjection: she would let it be known for anything, for everything, but the truth of which it was made. That was what, precisely, Charlotte Stant would be doing now; that was the present motive and support, to a certainty, of each of her looks and motions. She was the twentieth woman, she was possessed by her doom, but her doom was also to arrange appearances, and what now concerned him was to learn how she proposed. He would help her, would arrange WITH her to any point in reason; the only thing was to know what appearance could best be produced and best be preserved. Produced and preserved on her part of course; since on his own there had been luckily no folly to cover up, nothing but a perfect accord between conduct and obligation.

They stood there together, at all events, when the door had closed behind their friend, with a conscious, strained smile and very much as if each waited for the other to strike the note or give the pitch. The young man held himself, in his silent suspense — only not more afraid because he felt her own fear. She was afraid of herself, however; whereas, to his gain of lucidity, he was afraid only of her. Would she throw herself into his arms, or would she be otherwise wonderful? She would see what he would do — so their queer minute without words told him; and she would act accordingly. But what could he do but just let her see that he would make anything, everything, for her, as honourably easy as possible? Even if she should throw herself into his arms he would make that easy — easy, that is, to overlook, to ignore, not to remember, and not, by the same token, either, to regret. This was not what in fact happened, though it was also not at a single touch, but by the finest gradations, that his tension subsided. "It's too delightful to be back!" she said at last; and it was all she definitely gave him — being moreover nothing but what anyone else might have said. Yet with two or three other things that, on his response, followed it, it quite pointed the path, while the tone of it, and her whole attitude, were as far removed as need have been from the truth of her situation. The abjection that was present to him as of the essence quite failed to peep out, and he soon enough saw that if she was arranging she could be trusted to arrange. Good — it was all he asked; and all the more that he could admire and like her for it,

The particular appearance she would, as they said, go in for was that of having no account whatever to give him — it would be in fact that of having none to give anybody — of reasons or of motives, of comings or of goings. She was a charming young woman who had met him before, but she was also a charming young woman with a life of her own. She would take it high — up, up, up, ever so high. Well then, he would do the same; no height would be too great for them, not even the dizziest conceivable to a young person so subtle. The dizziest seemed indeed attained when, after another moment, she came as near as she was to come to an apology for her abruptness.

"I've been thinking of Maggie, and at last I yearned for her. I wanted to see her happy — and it doesn't strike me I find you too shy to tell me I SHALL."

"Of course she's happy, thank God! Only it's almost terrible, you know, the happiness of young, good, generous creatures. It rather frightens one. But the Blessed Virgin and all the Saints," said the Prince, "have her in their keeping."

"Certainly they have. She's the dearest of the dear. But I needn't tell you," the girl added.

"Ah," he returned with gravity, "I feel that I've still much to learn about her." To which he subjoined "She'll rejoice awfully in your being with us."

"Oh, you don't need me!" Charlotte smiled. "It's her hour. It's a great hour. One has seen often enough, with girls, what it is. But that," she said, "is exactly why. Why I've wanted, I mean, not to miss it."

He bent on her a kind, comprehending face. "You mustn't miss anything." He had got it, the pitch, and he could keep it now, for all he had needed was to have it given him. The pitch was the happiness of his wife that was to be-the sight of that happiness as a joy for an old friend. It was, yes, magnificent, and not the less so for its coming to him, suddenly, as sincere, as nobly exalted. Something in Charlotte's eyes seemed to tell him this, seemed to plead with him in advance as to what he was to find in it. He was eager — and he tried to show her that too — to find what she liked; mindful as he easily could be of what the friendship had been for Maggie. It had been armed with the wings of young imagination, young generosity; it had been, he believed — always counting out her intense devotion to her father — the liveliest emotion she had known before the dawn of the sentiment inspired by himself. She had not, to his knowledge, invited the object of it to their wedding, had not thought of proposing to her, for a matter of a couple of hours, an arduous and expensive journey. But she had kept her connected and informed, from week to week, in spite of preparations and absorptions. "Oh, I've been writing to Charlotte — I wish you knew her better:" he could still hear, from recent weeks, this record of the fact, just as he could still be conscious, not otherwise than queerly, of the gratuitous element in Maggie's wish, which he had failed as yet to indicate to her. Older and perhaps more intelligent, at any rate, why shouldn't Charlotte respond — and be quite FREE to respond — to such fidelities with something more than mere formal good manners? The relations of women with each other were of the strangest, it was true, and he probably wouldn't have trusted here a young person of his own race. He was proceeding throughout on the ground of the immense difference — difficult indeed as it might have been to disembroil in this young person HER race-quality. Nothing in her definitely placed her; she was a rare, a special product. Her singleness, her solitude, her want of means, that is her want of ramifications and other advantages, contributed to enrich her somehow with an odd, precious neutrality, to constitute for her, so detached yet so aware, a sort of small social capital. It was the only one she had — it was the only one a lonely, gregarious girl COULD have, since few, surely, had in anything like the same degree arrived at it, and since this one indeed had compassed it but through the play of some gift of nature to which you could scarce give a definite name.

It wasn't a question of her strange sense for tongues, with which she juggled as a conjuror at a show juggled with balls or hoops or lighted brands — it wasn't at least entirely that, for he had known people almost as polyglot whom their accomplishment had quite failed to make interesting. He was polyglot himself, for that matter — as was the case too with so many of his friends and relations; for none of whom, more than for himself, was it anything but a common convenience. The point was that in this young woman it was a beauty in itself, and almost a mystery: so, certainly, he had more than once felt in noting, on her lips, that rarest, among the Barbarians, of all civil graces, a perfect felicity in the use of Italian. He had known strangers — a few, and mostly men — who spoke his own language agreeably; but he had known neither man nor woman who showed for it Charlotte's almost mystifying instinct. He remembered how, from the first of their acquaintance, she had made no display of it, quite as if English, between them, his English so matching with hers, were their inevitable medium. He had perceived all by accident — by hearing her talk before him to somebody else that they had an alternative as good; an alternative in fact as much better as the amusement for him was greater in watching her for the slips that never came. Her account of the mystery didn't suffice: her recall of her birth in Florence and Florentine childhood; her parents, from the great country, but themselves already of a corrupt generation, demoralised, falsified, polyglot well before her, with the Tuscan balia who was her first remembrance; the servants of the villa, the dear contadini of the poder, the little girls and the other peasants of the next podere, all the rather shabby but still ever so pretty human furniture of her early time, including the good sisters of the poor convent of the Tuscan hills, the convent shabbier than almost anything else, but prettier too, in which she had been kept at school till the subsequent phase, the phase of the much grander institution in Paris at which Maggie was to arrive, terribly frightened, and as a smaller girl, three years before her own ending of her period of five. Such reminiscences, naturally, gave a ground, but they had not prevented him from insisting that some strictly civil ancestor — generations back, and from the Tuscan hills if she would-made himself felt, ineffaceably, in her blood and in her tone. She knew nothing of the ancestor, but she had taken his theory from him, gracefully enough, as one of the little presents that make friendship flourish. These matters, however, all melted together now, though a sense of them was doubtless concerned, not unnaturally, in the next thing, of the nature of a surmise, that his discretion let him articulate. "You haven't, I rather gather, particularly liked your country?" They would stick, for the time, to their English.

"It doesn't, I fear, seem particularly mine. And it doesn't in the least matter, over there, whether one likes it or not — that is to anyone but one's self. But I didn't like it," said Charlotte Stant.

"That's not encouraging then to me, is it?" the Prince went on.

"Do you mean because you're going?"

"Oh yes, of course we're going. I've wanted immensely to go." She hesitated. "But now? — immediately?"

"In a month or two — it seems to be the new idea." On which there was something in her face — as he imagined — that made him say: "Didn't Maggie write to you?"

"Not of your going at once. But of course you must go. And of course you must stay" — Charlotte was easily clear —"as long as possible."

"Is that what you did?" he laughed. "You stayed as long as possible?"

"Well, it seemed to me so — but I hadn't 'interests.' You'll have them — on a great scale. It's the country for interests," said Charlotte. "If I had only had a few I doubtless wouldn't have left it."

He waited an instant; they were still on their feet. "Yours then are rather here?"

"Oh, mine!" — the girl smiled. "They take up little room, wherever they are."

It determined in him, the way this came from her and what it somehow did for her-it determined in him a speech that would have seemed a few minutes before precarious and in questionable taste. The lead she had given him made the difference, and he felt it as really a lift on finding an honest and natural word rise, by its license, to his lips. Nothing surely could be, for both of them, more in the note of a high bravery. "I've been thinking it all the while so probable, you know, that you would have seen your way to marrying."

She looked at him an instant, and, just for these seconds, he feared for what he might have spoiled. "To marrying whom?"

"Why, some good, kind, clever, rich American."

Again his security hung in the balance — then she was, as he felt, admirable.

"I tried everyone I came across. I did my best. I showed I had come, quite publicly, FOR that. Perhaps I showed it too much. At any rate it was no use. I had to recognise it. No one would have me." Then she seemed to show as sorry for his having to hear of her anything so disconcerting. She pitied his feeling about it; if he was disappointed she would cheer him up. "Existence, you know, all the same, doesn't depend on that. I mean," she smiled, "on having caught a husband."

"Oh — existence!" the Prince vaguely commented. "You think I ought to argue for more than mere existence?" she asked. "I don't see why MY existence — even reduced as much as you like to being merely mine — should be so impossible. There are things, of sorts, I should be able to have — things I should be able to be. The position of a single woman today is very favourable, you know."

"Favourable to what?"

"Why, just TO existence — which may contain, after all, in one way and another, so much. It may contain, at the worst, even affections; affections in fact quite particularly; fixed, that is, on one's friends. I'm extremely fond of Maggie, for instance — I quite adore her. How could I adore her more if I were married to one of the people you speak of?"

The Prince gave a laugh. "You might adore HIM more —!"

"Ah, but it isn't, is it?" she asked, "a question of that."

"My dear friend," he returned, "it's always a question of doing the best for one's self one can — without injury to others." He felt by this time that they were indeed on an excellent basis; so he went on again, as if to show frankly his sense of its firmness. "I venture therefore to repeat my hope that you'll marry some capital fellow; and also to repeat my belief that such a marriage will be more favourable to you, as you call it, than even the spirit of the age."

She looked at him at first only for answer, and would have appeared to take it with meekness had she not perhaps appeared a little more to take it with gaiety. "Thank you very much," she simply said; but at that moment their friend was with them again. It was undeniable that, as she came in, Mrs. Assingham looked, with a certain smiling sharpness, from one of them to the other; the perception of which was perhaps what led Charlotte, for reassurance, to pass the question on. "The Prince hopes so much I shall still marry some good person."

Whether it worked for Mrs. Assingham or not, the Prince was himself, at this, more than ever reassured. He was SAFE, in a word — that was what it all meant; and he had required to be safe. He was really safe enough for almost any joke. "It's only," he explained to their hostess, "because of what Miss Stant has been telling me. Don't we want to keep up her courage?" If the joke was broad he had at least not begun it — not, that is, AS a joke; which was what his companion's address to their friend made of it. "She has been trying in America, she says, but hasn't brought it off."

The tone was somehow not what Mrs. Assingham had expected, but she made the best of it. "Well then," she replied to the young man, "if you take such an interest you must bring it off."

"And you must help, dear," Charlotte said unperturbed —"as you've helped, so beautifully, in such things before." With which, before Mrs. Assingham could meet the appeal, she had addressed herself to the Prince on a matter much nearer to him. "YOUR mar-riage is on Friday? — on Saturday?"

"Oh, on Friday, no! For what do you take us? There's not a vulgar omen we're neglecting. On Saturday, please, at the Oratory, at three o'clock — before twelve assistants exactly."

"Twelve including ME?"

It struck him — he laughed. "You'll make the thirteenth. It won't do!"

"Not," said Charlotte, "if you're going in for 'omens.' Should you like me to stay away?"

"Dear no — we'll manage. We'll make the round number — we'll have in some old woman. They must keep them there for that, don't they?"

Mrs. Assingham's return had at last indicated for him his departure; he had possessed him-self again of his hat and approached her to take leave. But he had another word for Charlotte. "I dine to-night with Mr. Verver. Have you any message?"

The girl seemed to wonder a little. "For Mr. Verver?"

"For Maggie — about her seeing you early. That, I know, is what she'll like."

"Then I'll come early — thanks."

"I daresay," he went on, "she'll send for you. I mean send a carriage."

"Oh, I don't require that, thanks. I can go, for a penny, can't I?" she asked of Mrs. Ass-ingham, "in an omnibus."

"Oh, I say!" said the Prince while Mrs. Assingham looked at her blandly.

"Yes, love — and I'll give you the penny. She shall get there," the good lady added to their friend.

But Charlotte, as the latter took leave of her, thought of something else. "There's a great favour, Prince, that I want to ask of you. I want, between this and Saturday, to make Maggie a marriage-present."

"Oh, I say!" the young man again soothingly exclaimed.

"Ah, but I MUST," she went on. "It's really almost for that I came back. It was impossible to get in America what I wanted."

Mrs. Assingham showed anxiety. "What is it then, dear, you want?"

But the girl looked only at their companion. "That's what the Prince, if he'll be so good, must help me to decide."

"Can't *I*," Mrs. Assingham asked, "help you to decide?"

"Certainly, darling, we must talk it well over." And she kept her eyes on the Prince. "But I want him, if he kindly will, to go with me to look. I want him to judge with me and choose. That, if you can spare the hour," she said, "is the great favour I mean."

He raised his eyebrows at her — he wonderfully smiled. "What you came back from America to ask? Ah, certainly then, I must find the hour!" He wonderfully smiled, but it was rather more, after all, than he had been reckoning with. It went somehow so little with the rest that, directly, for him, it wasn't the note of safety; it preserved this character, at the best, but by being the note of publicity. Quickly, quickly, however, the note of publicity struck him as better than any other. In another moment even it seemed positively what he wanted; for what so much as publicity put their relation on the right footing? By this appeal to Mrs. Assingham it was established as right, and she immediately showed that such was her own understanding.

"Certainly, Prince," she laughed, "you must find the hour!" And it was really so express a license from her, as representing friendly judgment, public opinion, the moral law, the margin allowed a husband about to be, or whatever, that, after observing to Charlotte that, should she come to Portland Place in the morning, he would make a point of being there to see her and so, easily, arrange with her about a time, he took his departure with the absolutely confirmed impression of knowing, as he put it to himself, where he was. Which was what he had prolonged his visit for. He was where he could stay.

IV

"I don't quite see, my dear," Colonel Assingham said to his wife the night of Charlotte's arrival, "I don't quite see, I'm bound to say, why you take it, even at the worst, so ferociously hard. It isn't your fault, after all, is it? I'll be hanged, at any rate, if it's mine."

The hour was late, and the young lady who had disembarked at Southampton that morning to come up by the "steamer special," and who had then settled herself at an hotel only to re-settle herself a couple of hours later at a private house, was by this time, they might hope, peacefully resting from her exploits. There had been two men at dinner, rather battered brothers-in-arms, of his own period, casually picked up by her host the day before, and when the gentlemen, after the meal, rejoined the ladies in the drawing-room, Charlotte, pleading fatigue, had already excused herself. The beguiled warriors, however, had stayed till after eleven — Mrs. Assingham, though finally quite without illusions, as she said, about the military character, was always beguiling to old soldiers; and as the Colonel had come in, before dinner, only in time to dress, he had not till this moment really been summoned to meet his companion over the situation that, as he was now to learn, their visitor's advent had created for them. It was actually more than midnight, the servants had been sent to bed, the rattle of the wheels had ceased to come in through a window still open to the August air, and Robert Assingham had been steadily learning, all the while, what it thus behoved him to know. But the words just quoted from him presented themselves, for the moment, as the essence of his spirit and his attitude. He disengaged, he would be damned if he didn't — they were both phrases he repeatedly used — his responsibility. The simplest, the sanest, the most obliging of men, he habitually indulged in extravagant language. His wife had once told him, in relation to his violence of speech; that such excesses, on his part, made her think of a retired General whom she had once seen playing with toy soldiers, fighting and winning battles, carrying on sieges and annihilating enemies with little fortresses of wood and little armies of tin. Her husband's exaggerated emphasis was his box of toy soldiers, his military game. It harmlessly gratified in him, for his declining years, the military instinct; bad words, when sufficiently numerous and arrayed in their might, could represent battalions, squadrons, tremendous cannonades and glorious charges of cavalry. It was natural, it was delightful — the romance, and for her as well, of camp life and of the perpetual booming of guns. It was fighting to the end, to the death, but no one was ever killed.

Less fortunate than she, nevertheless, in spite of his wealth of expression, he had not yet found the image that described her favourite game; all he could do was practically to leave it to her, emulating her own philosophy. He had again and again sat up late to discuss those situations in which her finer consciousness abounded, but he had never failed to deny that anything in life, anything of hers, could be a situation for himself. She might be in fifty at once if she liked — and it was what women did like, at their ease, after all; there always being, when they had too much of any, some man, as they were well aware, to get them out. He wouldn't at any price, have one, of any sort whatever, of his own, or even be in one along with her. He watched her, accordingly, in her favourite element, very much as he had sometimes watched, at the Aquarium, the celebrated lady who, in a slight, though tight, bathing-suit, turned somersaults and did tricks in the tank of water which looked so cold and uncomfortable to the non-amphibious. He listened to his companion to-night, while he smoked his last pipe, he watched her through her demonstration, quite as if he had paid a shilling. But it was true that, this being the case, he desired the value of his money. What was it, in the name of wonder, that she was so bent on being responsible FOR? What did she pretend was going to happen, and what, at the worst, could the poor girl do, even granting she wanted to do anything? What, at the worst, for that matter, could she be conceived to have in her head?

"If she had told me the moment she got here," Mrs. Assingham replied, "I shouldn't have my difficulty in finding out. But she wasn't so obliging, and I see no sign at all of her becoming so. What's certain is that she didn't come for nothing. She wants" — she worked it out at her leisure —"to see the Prince again. THAT isn't what troubles me. I mean that such a fact, as a fact, isn't. But what I ask myself is, What does she want it FOR?"

"What's the good of asking yourself if you know you don't know?" The Colonel sat back at his own ease, with an ankle resting on the other knee and his eyes attentive to the good appearance of an extremely slender foot which he kept jerking in its neat integument of fine-spun black silk and patent leather. It seemed to confess, this member, to consciousness of military discipline, everything about it being as polished and perfect, as straight and tight and trim, as a soldier on parade. It went so far as to imply that someone or other would have "got" something or other, confinement to barracks or suppression of pay, if it hadn't been just as it was. Bob Assingham was distinguished altogether by a leanness of person, a leanness quite distinct from physical laxity, which might have been determined, on the part of superior powers, by views of transport and accommodation, and which in fact verged on the abnormal. He "did" himself as well as his friends mostly knew, yet remained hungrily thin, with facial, with abdominal cavities quite grim in their effect, and with a consequent looseness of apparel that, combined with a choice of queer light shades and of strange straw-like textures, of the aspect of Chinese mats, provocative of wonder at his sources of supply, suggested the habit of tropic islands, a continual cane-bottomed chair, a governorship exercised on wide verandahs. His smooth round head, with the particular shade of its white hair, was like a silver pot reversed; his cheekbones and the bristle of his moustache were worthy of Attila the Hun. The hollows of his eyes were deep and darksome, but the eyes within them, were like little blue flowers plucked that morning. He knew everything that could be known about life, which he regarded as, for far the greater part, a matter of pecuniary arrangement. His wife accused him of a want, alike, of moral and of intellectual reaction, or rather indeed of a complete incapacity for either. He never went even so far as to understand what she meant, and it didn't at all matter, since he could be in spite of the limitation a perfectly social creature. The infirmities, the predicaments of men neither surprised nor shocked him, and indeed — which was perhaps his only real loss in a thrifty career — scarce even amused; he took them for granted without horror, classifying them after their kind and calculating results and chances. He might, in old bewildering climates, in old campaigns of cruelty and license, have had such revelations and known such amazements that he had nothing more to learn. But he was wholly content, in spite of his fondness, in domestic discussion, for the superlative degree; and his kindness, in the oddest way, seemed to have nothing to do with his experience. He could deal with things perfectly, for all his needs, without getting near them.

This was the way he dealt with his wife, a large proportion of whose meanings he knew he could neglect. He edited, for their general economy, the play of her mind, just as he edited, savingly, with the stump of a pencil, her redundant telegrams. The thing in the world that was least of a mystery to him was his Club, which he was accepted as perhaps too completely managing, and which he managed on lines of perfect penetration. His connection with it was really a master-piece of editing. This was in fact, to come back, very much the process he might have been proposing to apply to Mrs. Assingham's view of what was now before them; that is to their connection with Charlotte Stant's possibilities. They wouldn't lavish on them all their little fortune of curiosity and alarm; certainly they wouldn't spend their cherished savings so early in the day. He liked Charlotte, moreover, who was a smooth and compact inmate, and whom he felt as, with her instincts that made against waste, much more of his own sort than his wife. He could talk with her about Fanny almost better than he could talk with Fanny about Charlotte. However, he made at present the best of the latter necessity, even to the pressing of the question he has been noted as having last uttered. "If you can't think what to be afraid of, wait till you can think. Then you'll do it much better. Or otherwise, if that's waiting too long, find out from HER. Don't try to find out from ME. Ask her herself."

Mrs. Assingham denied, as we know, that her husband had a play of mind; so that she could, on her side, treat these remarks only as if they had been senseless physical gestures or nervous facial movements. She overlooked them as from habit and kindness; yet there was no one to whom she talked so persistently of such intimate things. "It's her friendship with Maggie that's the immense complication. Because THAT," she audibly mused, "is so natural."

"Then why can't she have come out for it?"

"She came out," Mrs. Assingham continued to meditate, "because she hates America. There was no place for her there — she didn't fit in. She wasn't in sympathy — no more were the people she saw. Then it's hideously dear; she can't, on her means, begin to live there. Not at all as she can, in a way, here."

"In the way, you mean, of living with US?"

"Of living with anyone. She can't live by visits alone — and she doesn't want to. She's too good for it even if she could. But she will — she MUST, sooner or later — stay with THEM. Maggie will want her — Maggie will make her. Besides, she'll want to herself."

"Then why won't that do," the Colonel asked, "for you to think it's what she has come for?"

"How will it do, HOW?" — she went on as without hearing him.

"That's what one keeps feeling."

"Why shouldn't it do beautifully?"

"That anything of the past," she brooded, "should come back NOW? How will it do, how will it do?"

"It will do, I daresay, without your wringing your hands over it. When, my dear," the Colonel pursued as he smoked, "have you ever seen anything of yours — anything that you've done — NOT do?"

"Ah, I didn't do this!" It brought her answer straight. "I didn't bring her back."

"Did you expect her to stay over there all her days to oblige you?"

"Not a bit — for I shouldn't have minded her coming after their marriage. It's her coming, this way, before." To which she added with inconsequence: "I'm too sorry for her — of course she can't enjoy it. But I don't see what perversity rides her. She needn't have looked it all so in the face — as she doesn't do it, I suppose, simply for discipline. It's almost — that's the bore of it — discipline to ME."

"Perhaps then," said Bob Assingham, "that's what has been her idea. Take it, for God's sake, as discipline to you and have done with it. It will do," he added, "for discipline to me as well."

She was far, however, from having done with it; it was a situation with such different sides, as she said, and to none of which one could, in justice, be blind. "It isn't in the least, you know, for instance, that I believe she's bad. Never, never," Mrs. Assingham declared. "I don't think that of her."

"Then why isn't that enough?"

Nothing was enough, Mrs. Assingham signified, but that she should develop her thought. "She doesn't deliberately intend, she doesn't consciously wish, the least complication. It's perfectly true that she thinks Maggie a dear — as who doesn't? She's incapable of any PLAN to hurt a hair of her head. Yet here she is — and there THEY are," she wound up.

Her husband again, for a little, smoked in silence. "What in the world, between them, ever took place?"

"Between Charlotte and the Prince? Why, nothing — except their having to recognise that nothing COULD. That was their little romance — it was even their little tragedy."

"But what the deuce did they DO?"

"Do? They fell in love with each other — but, seeing it wasn't possible, gave each other up."

"Then where was the romance?"

"Why, in their frustration, in their having the courage to look the facts in the face."

"What facts?" the Colonel went on.

"Well, to begin with, that of their neither of them having the means to marry. If she had had even a little — a little, I mean, for two — I believe he would bravely have done it." After which, as her husband but emitted an odd vague sound, she corrected herself. "I mean if he himself had had only a little — or a little more than a little, a little for a prince. They would have done what they could" — she did them justice — "if there had been a way. But there wasn't a way, and Charlotte, quite to her honour, I consider, understood it. He HAD to have money — it was a question of life and death. It wouldn't have been a bit amusing, either, to marry him as a pauper — I mean leaving him one. That was what she had — as HE had — the reason to see."

"And their reason is what you call their romance?"

She looked at him a moment. "What do you want more?"

"Didn't HE," the Colonel inquired, "want anything more? Or didn't, for that matter, poor Charlotte herself?"

She kept her eyes on him; there was a manner in it that half answered. "They were thoroughly in love. She might have been his —" She checked herself; she even for a minute lost herself. "She might have been anything she liked — except his wife."

"But she wasn't," said the Colonel very smokingly.

"She wasn't," Mrs. Assingham echoed.

The echo, not loud but deep, filled for a little the room. He seemed to listen to it die away; then he began again. "How are you sure?"

She waited before saying, but when she spoke it was definite. "There wasn't time."

He had a small laugh for her reason; he might have expected some other. "Does it take so much time?"

She herself, however, remained serious. "It takes more than they had."

He was detached, but he wondered. "What was the matter with their time?" After which, as, remembering it all, living it over and piecing it together, she only considered, "You mean that you came in with your idea?" he demanded.

It brought her quickly to the point, and as if also in a measure to answer herself. "Not a bit of it — THEN. But you surely recall," she went on, "the way, a year ago, everything took place. They had parted before he had ever heard of Maggie."

"Why hadn't he heard of her from Charlotte herself?"

"Because she had never spoken of her."

"Is that also," the Colonel inquired, "what she has told you?"

"I'm not speaking," his wife returned, "of what she has told me. That's one thing. I'm speaking of what I know by myself. That's another."

"You feel, in other words, that she lies to you?" Bob Assingham more sociably asked.

She neglected the question, treating it as gross. "She never so much, at the time, as named Maggie."

It was so positive that it appeared to strike him. "It's he then who has told you?"

She after a moment admitted it. "It's he."

"And he doesn't lie?"

"No — to do him justice. I believe he absolutely doesn't. If I hadn't believed it," Mrs. Assingham declared, for her general justification, "I would have had nothing to do with him — that is in this connection. He's a gentleman — I mean ALL as much of one as he ought to be. And he had nothing to gain. That helps," she added, "even a gentleman. It was I who named Maggie to him — a year from last May. He had never heard of her before."

"Then it's grave," said the Colonel.

She hesitated. "Do you mean grave for me?"

"Oh, that everything's grave for 'you' is what we take for granted and are fundamentally talking about. It's grave — it WAS — for Charlotte. And it's grave for Maggie. That is it WAS — when he did see her. Or when she did see HIM."

"You don't torment me as much as you would like," she presently went on, "because you think of nothing that I haven't a thousand times thought of, and because I think of everything that you never will. It would all," she recognised, "have been grave if it hadn't all been right. You can't make out," she contended, "that we got to Rome before the end of February."

He more than agreed. "There's nothing in life, my dear, that I CAN make out."

Well, there was nothing in life, apparently, that she, at real need, couldn't. "Charlotte, who had been there, that year, from early, quite from November, left suddenly, you'll quite remember, about the 10th of April. She was to have stayed on — she was to have stayed, naturally, more or less, for us; and she was to have stayed all the more that the Ververs, due all winter, but delayed, week after week, in Paris, were at last really coming. They were coming — that is Maggie was — largely to see her, and above all to be with her THERE. It was all altered — by Charlotte's going to Florence. She went from one day to the other — you forget everything. She gave her reasons, but I thought it odd, at the time; I had a sense that something must have happened. The difficulty was that, though I knew a little, I didn't know enough. I didn't know her relation with him had been, as you say, a 'near' thing — that is I didn't know HOW near. The poor girl's departure was a flight — she went to save herself."

He had listened more than he showed — as came out in his tone. "To save herself?"

"Well, also, really, I think, to save HIM too. I saw it afterwards — I see it all now. He would have been sorry — he didn't want to hurt her."

"Oh, I daresay," the Colonel laughed. "They generally don't!"

"At all events," his wife pursued, "she escaped — they both did; for they had had simply to face it. Their marriage couldn't be, and, if that was so, the sooner they put the Apennines between them the better. It had taken them, it is true, some time to feel this and to find it out. They had met constantly, and not always publicly, all that winter; they had met more than was known — though it was a good deal known. More, certainly," she said, "than I then imagined — though I don't know what difference it would after all have made with me. I liked him, I thought him charming, from the first of our knowing him; and now, after more than a year, he has done nothing to spoil it. And there are things he might have done — things that many men easily would. Therefore I believe in him, and I was right, at first, in knowing I was going to. So I haven't" — and she stated it as she might have quoted from a slate, after adding up the items, the sum of a column of figures — "so I haven't, I say to myself, been a fool."

"Well, are you trying to make out that I've said you have? All their case wants, at any rate," Bob Assingham declared, "is that you should leave it well alone. It's theirs now; they've bought it, over the counter, and paid for it. It has ceased to be yours."

"Of which case," she asked, "are you speaking?"

He smoked a minute: then with a groan: "Lord, are there so many?"

"There's Maggie's and the Prince's, and there's the Prince's and Charlotte's."

"Oh yes; and then," the Colonel scoffed, "there's Charlotte's and the Prince's."

"There's Maggie's and Charlotte's," she went on — "and there's also Maggie's and mine. I think too that there's Charlotte's and mine. Yes," she mused, "Charlotte's and mine is certainly a case. In short, you see, there are plenty. But I mean," she said, "to keep my head."

"Are we to settle them all," he inquired, "to-night?"

"I should lose it if things had happened otherwise — if I had acted with any folly." She had gone on in her earnestness, unheeding of his question. "I shouldn't be able to bear that now. But my good conscience is my strength; no one can accuse me. The Ververs came on to Rome alone — Charlotte, after their days with her in Florence, had decided about America. Maggie, I daresay, had helped her; she must have made her a present, and a handsome one, so that many things were easy. Charlotte left them, came to England, 'joined' somebody or other, sailed for New York. I have still her letter from Milan, telling me; I didn't know at the moment all that was behind it, but I felt in it nevertheless the undertaking of a new life. Certainly, in any case, it cleared THAT air — I mean the dear old Roman, in which we were steeped. It left the field free — it gave me a free hand. There was no question for me of anybody else when I brought the two others together. More than that, there was no question for them. So you see," she concluded, "where that puts me." She got up, on the words, very much as if they were the blue daylight towards which, through a darksome tunnel, she had been pushing her way, and the elation in her voice, combined with her recovered alertness, might have signified the sharp whistle of the train that shoots at last into the open. She turned about the room; she looked out a moment into the August night; she stopped, here and there, before the flowers in bowls and vases. Yes, it was distinctly as if she had proved what was needing proof, as if the issue of her operation had been, almost unexpectedly, a success. Old arithmetic had perhaps been fallacious, but the new settled the question. Her husband, oddly, however, kept his place without apparently measuring these results. As he had been amused at her intensity, so he was not uplifted by her relief; his interest might in fact have been more enlisted than he allowed. "Do you mean," he presently asked, "that he had already forgot about Charlotte?"

She faced round as if he had touched a spring. "He WANTED to, naturally — and it was much the best thing he could do." She was in possession of the main case, as it truly seemed; she had it all now. "He was capable of the effort, and he took the best way. Remember too what Maggie then seemed to us."

"She's very nice; but she always seems to me, more than anything else, the young woman who has a million a year. If you mean that that's what she especially seemed to him, you of course place the thing in your light. The effort to forget Charlotte couldn't, I grant you, have been so difficult."

This pulled her up but for an instant. "I never said he didn't from the first — I never said that he doesn't more and more — like Maggie's money."

"I never said I shouldn't have liked it myself," Bob Assingham returned. He made no movement; he smoked another minute. "How much did Maggie know?"

"How much?" She seemed to consider — as if it were between quarts and gallons — how best to express the quantity. "She knew what Charlotte, in Florence, had told her."

"And what had Charlotte told her?"

"Very little."

"What makes you so sure?"

"Why, this — that she couldn't tell her." And she explained a little what she meant. "There are things, my dear — haven't you felt it yourself, coarse as you are? — that no one could tell Maggie. There are things that, upon my word, I shouldn't care to attempt to tell her now."

The Colonel smoked on it. "She'd be so scandalised?"

"She'd be so frightened. She'd be, in her strange little way, so hurt. She wasn't born to know evil. She must never know it." Bob Assingham had a queer grim laugh; the sound of which, in fact, fixed his wife before him. "We're taking grand ways to prevent it."

But she stood there to protest. "We're not taking any ways. The ways are all taken; they were taken from the moment he came up to our carriage that day in Villa Borghese — the second or third of her days in Rome, when, as you remember, you went off somewhere with Mr. Verver, and the Prince, who had got into the carriage with us, came home with us to tea. They had met; they had seen each other well; they were in relation: the rest was to come of itself and as it could. It began, practically, I recollect, in our drive. Maggie happened to learn, by some other man's greeting of him, in the bright Roman way, from a streetcorner as we passed, that one of the Prince's baptismal names, the one always used for him among his relations, was Amerigo: which (as you probably don't know, however, even after a lifetime of ME), was the name, four hundred years ago, or whenever, of the pushing man who followed, across the sea, in the wake of Columbus and succeeded, where Columbus had failed, in becoming godfather, or name-father, to the new Continent; so that the thought of any connection with him can even now thrill our artless breasts."

The Colonel's grim placidity could always quite adequately meet his wife's not infrequent imputation of ignorances, on the score of the land of her birth, unperturbed and unashamed; and these dark depths were even at the present moment not directly lighted by an inquiry that managed to be curious without being apologetic. "But where does the connection come in?"

His wife was prompt. "By the women — that is by some obliging woman, of old, who was a descendant of the pushing man, the make-believe discoverer, and whom the Prince is therefore luckily able to refer to as an ancestress. A branch of the other family had become great — great enough, at least, to marry into his; and the name of the navigator, crowned with glory, was, very naturally, to become so the fashion among them that some son, of every generation, was appointed to wear it. My point is, at any rate, that I recall noticing at the time how the Prince was, from the start, helped with the dear Ververs by his wearing it. The connection became romantic for Maggie the moment she took it in; she filled out, in a flash, every link that might be vague. 'By that sign,' I quite said to myself, 'he'll conquer' — with his good fortune, of course, of having the other necessary signs too. It really," said Mrs. Assingham, "was, practically, the fine side of the wedge. Which struck me as also," she wound up, "a lovely note for the candour of the Ververs."

The Colonel took in the tale, but his comment was prosaic. "He knew, Amerigo, what he was about. And I don't mean the OLD one."

"I know what you mean!" his wife bravely threw off.

"The old one" — he pointed his effect "isn't the only discoverer in the family."

"Oh, as much as you like! If he discovered America — or got himself honoured as if he had — his successors were, in due time, to discover the Americans. And it was one of them in particular, doubtless, who was to discover how patriotic we are."

"Wouldn't this be the same one," the Colonel asked, "who really discovered what you call the connection?"

She gave him a look. "The connection's a true thing — the connection's perfectly historic, Your insinuations recoil upon your cynical mind. Don't you understand," she asked, "that the history of such people is known, root and branch, at every moment of its course?"

"Oh, it's all right," said Bob Assingham.

"Go to the British Museum," his companion continued with spirit.

"And what am I to do there?"

"There's a whole immense room, or recess, or department, or whatever, filled with books written about his family alone. You can see for yourself."

"Have you seen for YOUR self?"

She faltered but an instant. "Certainly — I went one day with Maggie. We looked him up, so to say. They were most civil." And she fell again into the current her husband had slightly ruffled. "The effect was produced, the charm began to work, at all events, in Rome, from that hour of the Prince's drive with us. My only course, afterwards, had to be to make the best of it. It was certainly good enough for that," Mrs. Assingham hastened to add, "and I didn't in the least see my duty in making the worst. In the same situation, today; I wouldn't act differently. I entered into the case as it then appeared to me — and as, for the matter of that, it still does. I LIKED it, I thought all sorts of good of it, and nothing can even now," she said with some intensity, "make me think anything else."

"Nothing can ever make you think anything you don't want to," the Colonel, still in his chair, remarked over his pipe. "You've got a precious power of thinking whatever you do want. You want also, from moment to moment, to think such desperately different things. What happened," he went on, "was that you fell violently in love with the Prince yourself, and that as you couldn't get me out of the way you had to take some roundabout course. You couldn't marry him, any more than Charlotte could — that is not to yourself. But you could to somebody else — it was always the Prince, it was always marriage. You could to your little friend, to whom there were no objections."

"Not only there were no objections, but there were reasons, positive ones — and all excellent, all charming." She spoke with an absence of all repudiation of his exposure of the spring of her conduct; and this abstention, clearly and effectively conscious, evidently cost her nothing. "It IS always the Prince; and it IS always, thank heaven, marriage. And these are the things, God grant, that it will always be. That I could help, a year ago, most assuredly made me happy, and it continues to make me happy."

"Then why aren't you quiet?"

"I AM quiet," said Fanny Assingham.

He looked at her, with his colourless candour, still in his place; she moved about again, a little, emphasising by her unrest her declaration of her tranquillity. He was as silent, at first, as if he had taken her answer, but he was not to keep it long. "What do you make of it that, by your own show, Charlotte couldn't tell her all? What do you make of it that the Prince didn't tell her anything? Say one understands that there are things she can't be told — since, as you put it, she is so easily scared and shocked." He produced these objections slowly, giving her time, by his pauses, to stop roaming and come back to him. But she was roaming still when he concluded his inquiry. "If there hadn't been anything there shouldn't have been between the pair before Charlotte bolted — in order, precisely, as you say, that there SHOULDN'T be: why in the world was what there HAD been too bad to be spoken of?"

Mrs. Assingham, after this question, continued still to circulate — not directly meeting it even when at last she stopped.

"I thought you wanted me to be quiet."

"So I do — and I'm trying to make you so much so that you won't worry more. Can't you be quiet on THAT?"

She thought a moment — then seemed to try. "To relate that she had to 'bolt' for the reasons we speak of, even though the bolting had done for her what she wished — THAT I can perfectly feel Charlotte's not wanting to do."

"Ah then, if it HAS done for her what she wished-!" But the Colonel's conclusion hung by the "if" which his wife didn't take up. So it hung but the longer when he presently spoke again. "All one wonders, in that case, is why then she has come back to him."

"Say she hasn't come back to him. Not really to HIM."

"I'll say anything you like. But that won't do me the same good as your saying it."

"Nothing, my dear, will do you good," Mrs. Assingham returned. "You don't care for anything in itself; you care for nothing but to be grossly amused because I don't keep washing my hands —!"

"I thought your whole argument was that everything is so right that this is precisely what you do."

But his wife, as it was a point she had often made, could go on as she had gone on before. "You're perfectly indifferent, really; you're perfectly immoral. You've taken part in the sack of cities, and I'm sure you've done dreadful things yourself. But I DON'T trouble my head, if you like. 'So now there!'" she laughed.

He accepted her laugh, but he kept his way. "Well, I back poor Charlotte."

"'Back' her?"

"To know what she wants."

"Ah then, so do I. She does know what she wants." And Mrs. Assingham produced this quantity, at last, on the girl's behalf, as the ripe result of her late wanderings and musings. She had groped through their talk, for the thread, and now she had got it. "She wants to be magnificent."

"She is," said the Colonel almost cynically.

"She wants" — his wife now had it fast "to be thoroughly superior, and she's capable of that."

"Of wanting to?"

"Of carrying out her idea."

"And what IS her idea?"

"To see Maggie through."

Bob Assingham wondered. "Through what?"

"Through everything. She KNOWS the Prince."

"And Maggie doesn't. No, dear thing" — Mrs. Assingham had to recognise it —"she doesn't."

"So that Charlotte has come out to give her lessons?"

She continued, Fanny Assingham, to work out her thought. "She has done this great thing for him. That is, a year ago, she practically did it. She practically, at any rate, helped him to do it himself — and helped me to help him. She kept off, she stayed away, she left him free; and what, moreover, were her silences to Maggie but a direct aid to him? If she had spoken in Florence; if she had told her own poor story; if she had, come back at any time — till within a few weeks ago; if she hadn't gone to New York and hadn't held out there: if she hadn't done these things all that has happened since would certainly have been different. Therefore she's in a position to be consistent now. She knows the Prince," Mrs. Assingham repeated. It involved even again her former recognition. "And Maggie, dear thing, doesn't."

She was high, she was lucid, she was almost inspired; and it was but the deeper drop therefore to her husband's flat common sense. "In other words Maggie is, by her ignorance, in danger? Then if she's in danger, there IS danger."

"There WON'T be-with Charlotte's understanding of it. That's where she has had her conception of being able to be heroic, of being able in fact to be sublime. She is, she will be" — the good lady by this time glowed. "So she sees it — to become, for her best friend, an element of POSITIVE safety."

Bob Assingham looked at it hard. "Which of them do you call her best friend?"

She gave a toss of impatience. "I'll leave you to discover!" But the grand truth thus made out she had now completely adopted. "It's for US, therefore, to be hers."

" 'Hers'?"

"You and I. It's for us to be Charlotte's. It's for us, on our side, to see HER through."

"Through her sublimity?"

"Through her noble, lonely life. Only — that's essential — it mustn't be lonely. It will be all right if she marries."

"So we're to marry her?"

"We're to marry her. It will be," Mrs. Assingham continued, "the great thing I can do." She made it out more and more. "It will make up."

"Make up for what?" As she said nothing, however, his desire for lucidity renewed itself. "If everything's so all right what is there to make up for?"

"Why, if I did do either of them, by any chance, a wrong. If I made a mistake."

"You'll make up for it by making another?" And then as she again took her time: "I thought your whole point is just that you're sure."

"One can never be ideally sure of anything. There are always possibilities."

"Then, if we can but strike so wild, why keep meddling?"

It made her again look at him. "Where would you have been, my dear, if I hadn't meddled with YOU?"

"Ah, that wasn't meddling — I was your own. I was your own," said the Colonel, "from the moment I didn't object."

"Well, these people won't object. They are my own too — in the sense that I'm awfully fond of them. Also in the sense," she continued, "that I think they're not so very much less fond of me. Our relation, all round, exists — it's a reality, and a very good one; we're mixed up, so to speak, and it's too late to change it. We must live IN it and with it. Therefore to see that Charlotte gets a good husband as soon as possible — that, as I say, will be one of my ways of living. It will cover," she said with conviction, "all the ground." And then as his own conviction appeared to continue as little to match: "The ground, I mean, of any nervousness I may ever feel. It will be in fact my duty and I shan't rest till my duty's performed." She had arrived by this time at something like exaltation. "I shall give, for the next year or two if necessary, my life to it. I shall have done in that case what I can."

He took it at last as it came. "You hold there's no limit to what you 'can'?"

"I don't say there's no limit, or anything of the sort. I say there are good chances — enough of them for hope. Why shouldn't there be when a girl is, after all, all that she is?"

"By after 'all' you mean after she's in love with somebody else?"

The Colonel put his question with a quietude doubtless designed to be fatal; but it scarcely pulled her up. "She's not too much in love not herself to want to marry. She would now particularly like to."

"Has she told you so?"

"Not yet. It's too soon. But she will. Meanwhile, however, I don't require the information. Her marrying will prove the truth."

"And what truth?"

"The truth of everything I say."

"Prove it to whom?"

"Well, to myself, to begin with. That will be enough for me — to work for her. What it will prove," Mrs. Assingham presently went on, "will be that she's cured. That she accepts the situation."

He paid this the tribute of a long pull at his pipe. "The situation of doing the one thing she can that will really seem to cover her tracks?"

His wife looked at him, the good dry man, as if now at last he was merely vulgar. "The one thing she can do that will really make new tracks altogether. The thing that, before any other, will be wise and right. The thing that will best give her her chance to be magnificent."

He slowly emitted his smoke. "And best give you, by the same token, yours to be magnificent with her?"

"I shall be as magnificent, at least, as I can."

Bob Assingham got up. "And you call ME immoral?"

She hesitated. "I'll call you stupid if you prefer. But stupidity pushed to a certain point IS, you know, immorality. Just so what is morality but high intelligence?" This he was unable to tell her; which left her more definitely to conclude. "Besides, it's all, at the worst, great fun."

"Oh, if you simply put it at THAT —!"

His implication was that in this case they had a common ground; yet even thus he couldn't catch her by it. "Oh, I don't mean," she said from the threshold, "the fun that you mean. Good-night." In answer to which, as he turned out the electric light, he gave an odd, short groan, almost a grunt. He HAD apparently meant some particular kind.

V

"Well, now I must tell you, for I want to be absolutely honest." So Charlotte spoke, a little ominously, after they had got into the Park. "I don't want to pretend, and I can't pretend a moment longer. You may think of me what you will, but I don't care. I knew I shouldn't and I find now how little. I came back for this. Not really for anything else. For this," she repeated as, under the influence of her tone, the Prince had already come to a pause.

"For 'this'?" He spoke as if the particular thing she indicated were vague to him — or were, rather, a quantity that couldn't, at the most, be much.

It would be as much, however, as she should be able to make it. "To have one hour alone with you." It had rained heavily in the night, and though the pavements were now dry, thanks to a cleansing breeze, the August morning, with its hovering, thick-drifting clouds and freshened air, was cool and grey. The multitudinous green of the Park had been deepened, and a wholesome smell of irrigation, purging the place of dust and of odours less acceptable, rose from the earth. Charlotte had looked about her, with expression, from the first of their coming in, quite as if for a deep greeting, for general recognition: the day was, even in the heart of London, of a rich, low-browed, weatherwashed English type. It was as if it had been waiting for her, as if she knew it, placed it, loved it, as if it were in fact a part of what she had come back for. So far as this was the case the impression of course could only be lost on a mere vague Italian; it was one of those for which you had to be, blessedly, an American — as indeed you had to be, blessedly, an American for all sorts of things: so long as you hadn't, blessedly or not, to remain in America. The Prince had, by half-past ten — as also by definite appointment — called in Cadogan Place for Mrs. Assingham's visitor, and then, after brief delay, the two had walked together up Sloane Street and got straight into the Park from Knightsbridge. The understanding to this end had taken its place, after a couple of days, as inevitably consequent on the appeal made by the girl during those first moments in Mrs. Assingham's drawing-room. It was an appeal the couple of days had done nothing to invalidate — everything, much rather, to place in a light, and as to which, obviously, it wouldn't have fitted that anyone should raise an objection. Who was there, for that matter, to raise one, from the moment Mrs. Assingham, informed and apparently not disapproving, didn't intervene? This the young man had asked himself — with a very sufficient sense of what would have made him ridiculous. He wasn't going to begin — that at least was certain — by showing a fear. Even had fear at first been sharp in him, moreover, it would already, not a little, have dropped; so happy, all round, so propitious, he quite might have called it, had been the effect of this rapid interval.

The time had been taken up largely by his active reception of his own wedding-guests and by Maggie's scarce less absorbed entertainment of her friend, whom she had kept for hours together in Portland Place; whom she had not, as wouldn't have been convenient, invited altogether as yet to migrate, but who had been present, with other persons, his contingent, at luncheon, at tea, at dinner, at perpetual repasts — he had never in his life, it struck him, had to reckon with so much eating — whenever he had looked in. If he had not again, till this hour, save for a minute, seen Charlotte alone, so, positively, all the while, he had not seen even Maggie; and if, therefore, he had not seen even Maggie, nothing was more natural than that he shouldn't have seen Charlotte. The exceptional minute, a mere snatch, at the tail of the others, on the huge Portland Place staircase had sufficiently enabled the girl to remind him — so ready she assumed him to be- of what they were to do. Time pressed if they were to do it at all. Everyone had brought gifts; his relations had brought wonders — how did they still have, where did they still find, such treasures? She only had brought nothing, and she was ashamed; yet even by the sight of the rest of the tribute she wouldn't be put off. She would do what she could, and he was, unknown to Maggie, he must remember, to give her his aid. He had prolonged the minute so far as to take time to hesitate, for a reason, and then to risk bringing his reason out. The risk was because he might hurt her — hurt her pride, if she had that particular sort. But she might as well be hurt one way as another; and, besides, that particular sort of pride was just what she hadn't. So his slight resistance, while they lingered, had been just easy enough not to be impossible.

"I hate to encourage you — and for such a purpose, after all — to spend your money."

She had stood a stair or two below him; where, while she looked up at him beneath the high, domed light of the hall, she rubbed with her palm the polished mahogany of the balustrade, which was mounted on fine ironwork, eighteenth-century English. "Because you think I must have so little? I've enough, at any rate — enough for us to take our hour. Enough," she had smiled, "is as good as a feast! And then," she had said, "it isn't of course a question of anything expensive, gorged with treasure as Maggie is; it isn't a question of competing or outshining. What, naturally, in the way of the priceless, hasn't she got? Mine is to be the offering of the poor — something, precisely, that — no rich person COULD ever give her, and that, being herself too rich ever to buy it, she would therefore never have." Charlotte had spoken as if after so much thought. "Only, as it can't be fine, it ought to be funny — and that's the sort of thing to hunt for. Hunting in London, besides, is amusing in itself."

He recalled even how he had been struck with her word. "'Funny'?" "Oh, I don't mean a comic toy — I mean some little thing with a charm. But absolutely RIGHT, in its comparative cheapness. That's what I call funny," she had explained. "You used," she had also added, "to help me to get things cheap in Rome. You were splendid for beating down. I have them all still, I needn't say — the little bargains I there owed you. There are bargains in London in August."

"Ah, but I don't understand your English buying, and I confess I find it dull." So much as that, while they turned to go up together, he had objected. "I understood my poor dear Romans."

"It was they who understood you — that was your pull," she had laughed. "Our amusement here is just that they don't understand us. We can make it amusing. You'll see."

If he had hesitated again it was because the point permitted. "The amusement surely will be to find our present."

"Certainly — as I say."

"Well, if they don't come down —?"

"Then we'll come up. There's always something to be done. Besides, Prince," she had gone on, "I'm not, if you come to that, absolutely a pauper. I'm too poor for some things," she had said — yet, strange as she was, lightly enough; "but I'm not too poor for others." And she had paused again at the top. "I've been saving up."

He had really challenged it. "In America?"

"Yes, even there — with my motive. And we oughtn't, you know," she had wound up, "to leave it beyond tomorrow."

That, definitely, with ten words more, was what had passed — he feeling all the while how any sort of begging-off would only magnify it. He might get on with things as they were, but he must do anything rather than magnify. Besides which it was pitiful to make her beg of him. He WAS making her — she had begged; and this, for a special sensibility in him, didn't at all do. That was accordingly, in fine, how they had come to where they were: he was engaged, as hard as possible, in the policy of not magnifying. He had kept this up even on her making a point — and as if it were almost the whole point — that Maggie of course was not to have an idea. Half the interest of the thing at least would be that she shouldn't suspect; therefore he was completely to keep it from her — as Charlotte on her side would — that they had been anywhere at all together or had so much as seen each other for five minutes alone. The absolute secrecy of their little excursion was in short of the essence; she appealed to his kindness to let her feel that he didn't betray her. There had been something, frankly, a little disconcerting in such an appeal at such an hour, on the very eve of his nuptials: it was one thing to have met the girl casually at Mrs. Assingham's and another to arrange with her thus for a morning practically as private as their old mornings in Rome and practically not less intimate. He had immediately told Maggie, the same evening, of the minutes that had passed between them in Cadogan Place — though not mentioning those of Mrs. Assingham's absence any more than he mentioned the fact of what their friend had then, with such small delay, proposed. But what had briefly checked his assent to any present, to any positive making of mystery — what had made him, while they stood at the top of the stairs, demur just long enough for her to notice it — was the sense of the resemblance of the little plan before him to occasions, of the past, from which he was quite disconnected, from which he could only desire to be. This was like beginning something over, which was the last thing he wanted. The strength, the beauty of his actual position was in its being wholly a fresh start, was that what it began would be new altogether. These items of his consciousness had clustered so quickly that by the time Charlotte read them in his face he was in presence of what they amounted to. She had challenged them as soon as read them, had met them with a "Do you want then to go and tell her?" that had somehow made them ridiculous. It had made him, promptly, fall back on minimizing it — that is on minimizing "fuss." Apparent scruples were, obviously, fuss, and he had on the spot clutched, in the light of this truth, at the happy principle that would meet every case.

This principle was simply to be, with the girl, always simple — and with the very last simplicity. That would cover everything. It had covered, then and there, certainly, his immediate submission to the sight of what was clearest. This was, really, that what she asked was little compared to what she gave. What she gave touched him, as she faced him, for it was the full tune of her renouncing. She really renounced — renounced everything, and without even insisting now on what it had all been for her. Her only insistence was her insistence on the small matter of their keeping their appointment to themselves. That, in exchange for "everything," everything she gave up, was verily but a trifle. He let himself accordingly be guided; he so soon assented, for enlightened indulgence, to any particular turn she might wish the occasion to take, that the stamp of her preference had been well applied to it even while they were still in the Park. The application in fact presently required that they should sit down a little, really to see where they were; in obedience to which propriety they had some ten minutes, of a quality quite distinct, in a couple of penny-chairs under one of the larger trees. They had taken, for their walk, to the cropped, rain-freshened grass, after finding it already dry; and the chairs, turned away from the broad alley, the main drive and the aspect of Park Lane, looked across the wide reaches of green which seemed in a manner to refine upon their freedom. They helped Charlotte thus to make her position — her temporary position — still more clear, and it was for this purpose, obviously, that, abruptly, on seeing her opportunity, she sat down. He stood for a little before her, as if to mark the importance of not wasting time, the importance she herself had previously insisted on; but after she had said a few words it was impossible for him not to resort again to good-nature. He marked as he could, by this concession, that if he had finally met her first proposal for what would be "amusing" in it, so any idea she might have would contribute to that effect. He had consequently — in all consistency — to treat it as amusing that she reaffirmed, and reaffirmed again, the truth that was HER truth.

"I don't care what you make of it, and I don't ask anything whatever of you — anything but this. I want to have said it — that's all; I want not to have failed to say it. To see you once and be with you, to be as we are now and as we used to be, for one small hour — or say for two — that's what I have had for weeks in my head. I mean, of course, to get it BEFORE — before what you're going to do. So, all the while, you see," she went on with her eyes on him, "it was a question for me if I should be able to manage it in time. If I couldn't have come now I probably shouldn't have come at all — perhaps even ever. Now that I'm here I shall stay, but there were moments, over there, when I despaired. It wasn't easy — there were reasons; but it was either this or nothing. So I didn't struggle, you see, in vain. AFTER — oh, I didn't want that! I don't mean," she smiled, "that it wouldn't have been delightful to see you even then — to see you at any time; but I would never have come for it. This is different. This is what I wanted. This is what I've got. This is what I shall always have. This is what I should have missed, of course," she pursued, "if you had chosen to make me miss it. If you had thought me horrid, had refused to come, I should, naturally, have been immensely 'sold.' I had to take the risk. Well, you're all I could have hoped. That's what I was to have said. I didn't want simply to get my time with you, but I wanted you to know. I wanted you" — she kept it up,

slowly, softly, with a small tremor of voice, but without the least failure of sense or sequence
—"I wanted you to understand. I wanted you, that is, to hear. I don't care, I think, whether
you understand or not. If I ask nothing of you I don't — I mayn't — ask even so much as that.
What you may think of me — that doesn't in the least matter. What I want is that it shall
always be with you — so that you'll never be able quite to get rid of it — that I DID. I won't
say that you did — you may make as little of that as you like. But that I was here with you
where we are and as we are — I just saying this. Giving myself, in other words, away — and
perfectly willing to do it for nothing. That's all."

She paused as if her demonstration was complete — yet, for the moment, without moving; as
if in fact to give it a few minutes to sink in; into the listening air, into the watching space, into
the conscious hospitality of nature, so far as nature was, all Londonised, all vulgarised, with
them there; or even, for that matter, into her own open ears, rather than into the attention of
her passive and prudent friend. His attention had done all that attention could do; his handsome,
slightly anxious, yet still more definitely "amused" face sufficiently played its part. He clutched,
however, at what he could best clutch at — the fact that she let him off, definitely let him off.
She let him off, it seemed, even from so much as answering; so that while he smiled back at
her in return for her information he felt his lips remain closed to the successive vaguenesses
of rejoinder, of objection, that rose for him from within. Charlotte herself spoke again at last
—"You may want to know what I get by it. But that's my own affair." He really didn't want
to know even this — or continued, for the safest plan, quite to behave as if he didn't; which
prolonged the mere dumbness of diversion in which he had taken refuge. He was glad when,
finally — the point she had wished to make seeming established to her satisfaction — they
brought to what might pass for a close the moment of his life at which he had had least to
say. Movement and progress, after this, with more impersonal talk, were naturally a relief; so
that he was not again, during their excursion, at a loss for the right word. The air had been,
as it were, cleared; they had their errand itself to discuss, and the opportunities of London,
the sense of the wonderful place, the pleasures of prowling there, the question of shops, of
possibilities, of particular objects, noticed by each in previous prowls. Each professed surprise
at the extent of the other's knowledge; the Prince in especial wondered at his friend's possession
of her London. He had rather prized his own possession, the guidance he could really often
give a cabman; it was a whim of his own, a part of his Anglomania, and congruous with that
feature, which had, after all, so much more surface than depth. When his companion, with the
memory of other visits and other rambles, spoke of places he hadn't seen and things he didn't
know, he actually felt again — as half the effect — just a shade humiliated. He might even
have felt a trifle annoyed — if it hadn't been, on this spot, for his being, even more, interested.
It was a fresh light on Charlotte and on her curious world-quality, of which, in Rome, he
had had his due sense, but which clearly would show larger on the big London stage. Rome
was, in comparison, a village, a family-party, a little old-world spinnet for the fingers of one
hand. By the time they reached the Marble Arch it was almost as if she were showing him a
new side, and that, in fact, gave amusement a new and a firmer basis. The right tone would
be easy for putting himself in her hands. Should they disagree a little — frankly and fairly —
about directions and chances, values and authenticities, the situation would be quite gloriously
saved. They were none the less, as happened, much of one mind on the article of their keeping
clear of resorts with which Maggie would be acquainted. Charlotte recalled it as a matter of
course, named it in time as a condition — they would keep away from any place to which he
had already been with Maggie.

This made indeed a scant difference, for though he had during the last month done few
things so much as attend his future wife on her making of purchases, the antiquarii, as he
called them with Charlotte, had not been the great affair. Except in Bond Street, really, Maggie
had had no use for them: her situation indeed, in connection with that order of traffic, was
full of consequences produced by her father's. Mr. Verver, one of the great collectors of the
world, hadn't left his daughter to prowl for herself; he had little to do with shops, and was

mostly, as a purchaser, approached privately and from afar. Great people, all over Europe, sought introductions to him; high personages, incredibly high, and more of them than would ever be known, solemnly sworn as everyone was, in such cases, to discretion, high personages made up to him as the one man on the short authentic list likely to give the price. It had therefore been easy to settle, as they walked, that the tracks of the Ververs, daughter's as well as father's, were to be avoided; the importance only was that their talk about it led for a moment to the first words they had as yet exchanged on the subject of Maggie. Charlotte, still in the Park, proceeded to them — for it was she who began — with a serenity of appreciation that was odd, certainly, as a sequel to her words of ten minutes before. This was another note on her — what he would have called another light — for her companion, who, though without giving a sign, admired, for what it was, the simplicity of her transition, a transition that took no trouble either to trace or to explain itself. She paused again an instant, on the grass, to make it; she stopped before him with a sudden "Anything of course, dear as she is, will do for her. I mean if I were to give her a pin-cushion from the Baker-Street Bazaar."

"That's exactly what *I* meant" — the Prince laughed out this allusion to their snatch of talk in Portland Place. "It's just what I suggested."

She took, however, no notice of the reminder; she went on in her own way. "But it isn't a reason. In that case one would never do anything for her. I mean," Charlotte explained, "if one took advantage of her character."

"Of her character?"

"We mustn't take advantage of her character," the girl, again unheeding, pursued. "One mustn't, if not for HER, at least for one's self. She saves one such trouble."

She had spoken thoughtfully, with her eyes on her friend's; she might have been talking, preoccupied and practical, of someone with whom he was comparatively unconnected. "She certainly GIVES one no trouble," said the Prince. And then as if this were perhaps ambiguous or inadequate: "She's not selfish — God forgive her! — enough."

"That's what I mean," Charlotte instantly said. "She's not selfish enough. There's nothing, absolutely, that one NEED do for her. She's so modest," she developed —"she doesn't miss things. I mean if you love her — or, rather, I should say, if she loves you. She lets it go."

The Prince frowned a little — as a tribute, after all, to seriousness. "She lets what —?"

"Anything — anything that you might do and that you don't. She lets everything go but her own disposition to be kind to you. It's of herself that she asks efforts — so far as she ever HAS to ask them. She hasn't, much. She does everything herself. And that's terrible."

The Prince had listened; but, always with propriety, he didn't commit himself. "Terrible?"

"Well, unless one is almost as good as she. It makes too easy terms for one. It takes stuff, within one, so far as one's decency is concerned, to stand it. And nobody," Charlotte continued in the same manner, "is decent enough, good enough, to stand it — not without help from religion, or something of that kind. Not without prayer and fasting — that is without taking great care. Certainly," she said, "such people as you and I are not."

The Prince, obligingly, thought an instant. "Not good enough to stand it?"

"Well, not good enough not rather to feel the strain. We happen each, I think, to be of the kind that are easily spoiled."

Her friend, again, for propriety, followed the argument. "Oh, I don't know. May not one's affection for her do something more for one's decency, as you call it, than her own generosity — her own affection, HER 'decency' — has the unfortunate virtue to undo?"

"Ah, of course it must be all in that."

But she had made her question, all the same, interesting to him. "What it comes to — one can see what you mean — is the way she believes in one. That is if she believes at all."

"Yes, that's what it comes to," said Charlotte Stant.

"And why," he asked, almost soothingly, "should it be terrible?" He couldn't, at the worst, see that.

"Because it's always so — the idea of having to pity people."

"Not when there's also, with it, the idea of helping them."

"Yes, but if we can't help them?"

"We CAN — we always can. That is," he competently added, "if we care for them. And that's what we're talking about."

"Yes" — she on the whole assented. "It comes back then to our absolutely refusing to be spoiled."

"Certainly. But everything," the Prince laughed as they went on — "all your 'decency,' I mean — comes back to that."

She walked beside him a moment. "It's just what *I* meant," she then reasonably said.

VI

The man in the little shop in which, well after this, they lingered longest, the small but interesting dealer in the Bloomsbury street who was remarkable for an insistence not importunate, inasmuch as it was mainly mute, but singularly, intensely coercive — this personage fixed on his visitors an extraordinary pair of eyes and looked from one to the other while they considered the object with which he appeared mainly to hope to tempt them. They had come to him last, for their time was nearly up; an hour of it at least, from the moment of their getting into a hansom at the Marble Arch, having yielded no better result than the amusement invoked from the first. The amusement, of course, was to have consisted in seeking, but it had also involved the idea of finding; which latter necessity would have been obtrusive only if they had found too soon. The question at present was if they were finding, and they put it to each other, in the Bloomsbury shop, while they enjoyed the undiverted attention of the shopman. He was clearly the master, and devoted to his business — the essence of which, in his conception, might precisely have been this particular secret that he possessed for worrying the customer so little that it fairly made for their relations a sort of solemnity. He had not many things, none of the redundancy of "rot" they had elsewhere seen, and our friends had, on entering, even had the sense of a muster so scant that, as high values obviously wouldn't reign, the effect might be almost pitiful. Then their impression had changed; for, though the show was of small pieces, several taken from the little window and others extracted from a cupboard behind the counter — dusky, in the rather low-browed place, despite its glass doors — each bid for their attention spoke, however modestly, for itself, and the pitch of their entertainer's pretensions was promptly enough given. His array was heterogeneous and not at all imposing; still, it differed agreeably from what they had hitherto seen.

Charlotte, after the incident, was to be full of impressions, of several of which, later on, she gave her companion — always in the interest of their amusement — the benefit; and one of the impressions had been that the man himself was the greatest curiosity they had looked at. The Prince was to reply to this that he himself hadn't looked at him; as, precisely, in the general connection, Charlotte had more than once, from other days, noted, for his advantage, her consciousness of how, below a certain social plane, he never SAW. One kind of shopman was just like another to him — which was oddly inconsequent on the part of a mind that, where it did notice, noticed so much. He took throughout, always, the meaner sort for granted — the night of their meanness, or whatever name one might give it for him, made all his cats grey. He didn't, no doubt, want to hurt them, but he imaged them no more than if his eyes acted only for the level of his own high head. Her own vision acted for every relation — this he had seen for himself: she remarked beggars, she remembered servants, she recognised cabmen; she had often distinguished beauty, when out with him, in dirty children; she had admired "type" in faces at hucksters' stalls. Therefore, on this occasion, she had found their antiquario interesting; partly because he cared so for his things, and partly because he cared — well, so for them. "He likes his things — he loves them," she was to say; "and it isn't only — it isn't perhaps even at all — that he loves to sell them. I think he would love to keep them if he could; and he prefers, at any rate, to sell them to right people. We, clearly, were right people — he knows them when he sees them; and that's why, as I say, you could make out, or at least *I* could, that he cared for us. Didn't you see" — she was to ask it with an insistence —"the way he looked at us and took us in? I doubt if either of us have ever been so well looked at before. Yes, he'll remember us" — she was to profess herself convinced of that almost to uneasiness. "But it was after all" — this was perhaps reassuring —"because, given his taste, since he HAS taste, he was pleased with us, he was struck — he had ideas about us. Well, I should think people might; we're beautiful — aren't we? — and he knows. Then, also, he has his way; for that way of saying nothing with his lips when he's all the while pressing you so with his face, which shows how he knows you feel it — that is a regular way."

Of decent old gold, old silver, old bronze, of old chased and jewelled artistry, were the objects that, successively produced, had ended by numerously dotting the counter, where the shopman's slim, light fingers, with neat nails, touched them at moments, briefly, nervously, tenderly, as those of a chess-player rest, a few seconds, over the board, on a figure he thinks he may move and then may not: small florid ancientries, ornaments, pendants, lockets, brooches, buckles, pretexts for dim brilliants, bloodless rubies, pearls either too large or too opaque for value; miniatures mounted with diamonds that had ceased to dazzle; snuffboxes presented to — or by — the too-questionable great; cups, trays, taper-stands, suggestive of pawn-tickets, archaic and brown, that would themselves, if preserved, have been prized curiosities. A few commemorative medals, of neat outline but dull reference; a classic monument or two, things of the first years of the century; things consular, Napoleonic, temples, obelisks, arches, tinily re-embodied, completed the discreet cluster; in which, however, even after tentative reinforcement from several quaint rings, intaglios, amethysts, carbuncles, each of which had found a home in the ancient sallow satin of some weakly-snapping little box, there was, in spite of the due proportion of faint poetry, no great force of persuasion. They looked, the visitors, they touched, they vaguely pretended to consider, but with scepticism, so far as courtesy permitted, in the quality of their attention. It was impossible they shouldn't, after a little, tacitly agree as to the absurdity of carrying to Maggie a token from such a stock. It would be-that was the difficulty — pretentious without being "good"; too usual, as a treasure, to have been an inspiration of the giver, and yet too primitive to be taken as tribute welcome on any terms. They had been out more than two hours and, evidently, had found nothing. It forced from Charlotte a kind of admission.

"It ought, really, if it should be a thing of this sort, to take its little value from having belonged to one's self."

"Ecco!" said the Prince — just triumphantly enough. "There you are."

Behind the dealer were sundry small cupboards in the wall. Two or three of these Charlotte had seen him open, so that her eyes found themselves resting on those he had not visited. But she completed her admission. "There's nothing here she could wear."

It was only after a moment that her companion rejoined. "Is there anything — do you think — that you could?"

It made her just start. She didn't, at all events, look at the objects; she but looked for an instant very directly at him. "No."

"Ah!" the Prince quietly exclaimed.

"Would it be," Charlotte asked, "your idea to offer me something?"

"Well, why not — as a small ricordo."

"But a ricordo of what?"

"Why, of 'this' — as you yourself say. Of this little hunt."

"Oh, I say it — but hasn't my whole point been that I don't ask you to. Therefore," she demanded — but smiling at him now — "where's the logic?"

"Oh, the logic —!" he laughed.

"But logic's everything. That, at least, is how I feel it. A ricordo from you — from you to me — is a ricordo of nothing. It has no reference."

"Ah, my dear!" he vaguely protested. Their entertainer, meanwhile, stood there with his eyes on them, and the girl, though at this minute more interested in her passage with her friend than in anything else, again met his gaze. It was a comfort to her that their foreign tongue covered what they said — and they might have appeared of course, as the Prince now had one of the snuffboxes in his hand, to be discussing a purchase.

"You don't refer," she went on to her companion. "I refer."

He had lifted the lid of his little box and he looked into it hard. "Do you mean by that then that you would be free —?"

"'Free' —?"

"To offer me something?"

This gave her a longer pause, and when she spoke again she might have seemed, oddly, to be addressing the dealer. "Would you allow me —?"

"No," said the Prince into his little box.

"You wouldn't accept it from me?"

"No," he repeated in the same way.

She exhaled a long breath that was like a guarded sigh. "But you've touched an idea that HAS been mine. It's what I've wanted." Then she added: "It was what I hoped."

He put down his box — this had drawn his eyes. He made nothing, clearly, of the little man's attention. "It's what you brought me out for?"

"Well, that's, at any rate," she returned, "my own affair. But it won't do?"

"It won't do, cara mia."

"It's impossible?"

"It's impossible." And he took up one of the brooches.

She had another pause, while the shopman only waited. "If I were to accept from you one of these charming little ornaments as you suggest, what should I do with it?"

He was perhaps at last a little irritated; he even — as if HE might understand — looked vaguely across at their host. "Wear it, per Bacco!"

"Where then, please? Under my clothes?"

"Wherever you like. But it isn't then, if you will," he added, "worth talking about."

"It's only worth talking about, mio caro," she smiled, "from your having begun it. My question is only reasonable — so that your idea may stand or fall by your answer to it. If I should pin one of these things on for you would it be, to your mind, that I might go home and show it to Maggie as your present?"

They had had between them often in talk the refrain, jocosely, descriptively applied, of "old Roman." It had been, as a pleasantry, in the other time, his explanation to her of everything; but nothing, truly, had even seemed so old-Roman as the shrug in which he now indulged. "Why in the world not?"

"Because — on our basis — it would be impossible to give her an account of the pretext."

"The pretext —?" He wondered.

"The occasion. This ramble that we shall have had together and that we're not to speak of."

"Oh yes," he said after a moment "I remember we're not to speak of it."

"That of course you're pledged to. And the one thing, you see, goes with the other. So you don't insist."

He had again, at random, laid back his trinket; with which he quite turned to her, a little wearily at last — even a little impatiently. "I don't insist."

It disposed for the time of the question, but what was next apparent was that it had seen them no further. The shopman, who had not stirred, stood there in his patience — which, his mute intensity helping, had almost the effect of an ironic comment. The Prince moved to the glass door and, his back to the others, as with nothing more to contribute, looked — though not less patiently — into the street. Then the shopman, for Charlotte, momentously broke silence. "You've seen, disgraziatamente, signora principessa," he sadly said, "too much" — and it made the Prince face about. For the effect of the momentous came, if not from the sense, from the sound of his words; which was that of the suddenest, sharpest Italian. Charlotte exchanged with her friend a glance that matched it, and just for the minute they were held in check. But their glance had, after all, by that time, said more than one thing; had both exclaimed on the apprehension, by the wretch, of their intimate conversation, let alone of her possible, her impossible, title, and remarked, for mutual reassurance, that it didn't, all the same, matter. The Prince remained by the door, but immediately addressing the speaker from where he stood.

"You're Italian then, are you?"

But the reply came in English. "Oh dear no."

"You're English?"

To which the answer was this time, with a smile, in briefest Italian. "Che!" The dealer waived the question — he practically disposed of it by turning straightway toward a receptacle to which he had not yet resorted and from which, after unlocking it, he extracted a square box, of some twenty inches in height, covered with worn-looking leather. He placed the box on the counter, pushed back a pair of small hooks, lifted the lid and removed from its nest a drinking-vessel larger than a common cup, yet not of exorbitant size, and formed, to appearance, either of old fine gold or of some material once richly gilt. He handled it with tenderness, with ceremony, making a place for it on a small satin mat. "My Golden Bowl," he observed — and it sounded, on his lips, as if it said everything. He left the important object — for as "important" it did somehow present itself — to produce its certain effect. Simple, but singularly elegant, it stood on a circular foot, a short pedestal with a slightly spreading base, and, though not of signal depth, justified its title by the charm of its shape as well as by the tone of its surface. It might have been a large goblet diminished, to the enhancement of its happy curve, by half its original height. As formed of solid gold it was impressive; it seemed indeed to warn off the prudent admirer. Charlotte, with care, immediately took it up, while the Prince, who had after a minute shifted his position again, regarded it from a distance.

It was heavier than Charlotte had thought. "Gold, really gold?" she asked of their companion. He hesitated. "Look a little, and perhaps you'll make out."

She looked, holding it up in both her fine hands, turning it to the light. "It may be cheap for what it is, but it will be dear, I'm afraid, for me."

"Well," said the man, "I can part with it for less than its value. I got it, you see, for less."

"For how much then?"

Again he waited, always with his serene stare. "Do you like it then?"

Charlotte turned to her friend. "Do YOU like it?" He came no nearer; he looked at their companion. "cos'e?"

"Well, signori miei, if you must know, it's just a perfect crystal."

"Of course we must know, per Dio!" said the Prince. But he turned away again — he went back to his glass door.

Charlotte set down the bowl; she was evidently taken. "Do you mean it's cut out of a single crystal?"

"If it isn't I think I can promise you that you'll never find any joint or any piecing."

She wondered. "Even if I were to scrape off the gold?"

He showed, though with due respect, that she amused him. "You couldn't scrape it off — it has been too well put on; put on I don't know when and I don't know how. But by some very fine old worker and by some beautiful old process."

Charlotte, frankly charmed with the cup, smiled back at him now. "A lost art?"

"Call it a lost art,"

"But of what time then is the whole thing?"

"Well, say also of a lost time."

The girl considered. "Then if it's so precious, how comes it to be cheap?"

Her interlocutor once more hung fire, but by this time the Prince had lost patience. "I'll wait for you out in the air," he said to his companion, and, though he spoke without irritation, he pointed his remark by passing immediately into the street, where, during the next minutes, the others saw him, his back to the shopwindow, philosophically enough hover and light a fresh cigarette. Charlotte even took, a little, her time; she was aware of his funny Italian taste for London street-life.

Her host meanwhile, at any rate, answered her question. "Ah, I've had it a long time without selling it. I think I must have been keeping it, madam, for you."

"You've kept it for me because you've thought I mightn't see what's the matter with it?"

He only continued to face her — he only continued to appear to follow the play of her mind. "What IS the matter with it?"

"Oh, it's not for me to say; it's for you honestly to tell me. Of course I know something must be."

"But if it's something you can't find out, isn't it as good as if it were nothing?"

"I probably SHOULD find out as soon as I had paid for it."

"Not," her host lucidly insisted, "if you hadn't paid too much."

"What do you call," she asked, "little enough?"

"Well, what should you say to fifteen pounds?"

"I should say," said Charlotte with the utmost promptitude, "that it's altogether too much."

The dealer shook his head slowly and sadly, but firmly. "It's my price, madam — and if you admire the thing I think it really might be yours. It's not too much. It's too little. It's almost nothing. I can't go lower."

Charlotte, wondering, but resisting, bent over the bowl again. "Then it's impossible. It's more than I can afford."

"Ah," the man returned, "one can sometimes afford for a present more than one can afford for one's self." He said it so coaxingly that she found herself going on without, as might be said, putting him in his place. "Oh, of course it would be only for a present —!"

"Then it would be a lovely one."

"Does one make a present," she asked, "of an object that contains, to one's knowledge, a flaw?"

"Well, if one knows of it one has only to mention it. The good faith," the man smiled, "is always there."

"And leave the person to whom one gives the thing, you mean, to discover it?"

"He wouldn't discover it — if you're speaking of a gentleman."

"I'm not speaking of anyone in particular," Charlotte said.

"Well, whoever it might be. He might know — and he might try. But he wouldn't find."

She kept her eyes on him as if, though unsatisfied, mystified, she yet had a fancy for the bowl. "Not even if the thing should come to pieces?" And then as he was silent: "Not even if he should have to say to me 'The Golden Bowl is broken'?"

He was still silent; after which he had his strangest smile. "Ah, if anyone should WANT to smash it —!"

She laughed; she almost admired the little man's expression. "You mean one could smash it with a hammer?"

"Yes; if nothing else would do. Or perhaps even by dashing it with violence — say upon a marble floor."

"Oh, marble floors!" But she might have been thinking — for they were a connection, marble floors; a connection with many things: with her old Rome, and with his; with the palaces of his past, and, a little, of hers; with the possibilities of his future, with the sumptuosities of his marriage, with the wealth of the Ververs. All the same, however, there were other things; and they all together held for a moment her fancy. "Does crystal then break — when it IS crystal? I thought its beauty was its hardness."

Her friend, in his way, discriminated. "Its beauty is its BEING crystal. But its hardness is certainly, its safety. It doesn't break," he went on, "like vile glass. It splits — if there is a split."

"Ah!" — Charlotte breathed with interest. "If there is a split." And she looked down again at the bowl. "There IS a split, eh? Crystal does split, eh?"

"On lines and by laws of its own."

"You mean if there's a weak place?"

For all answer, after an hesitation, he took the bowl up again, holding it aloft and tapping it with a key. It rang with the finest, sweetest sound. "Where is the weak place?"

She then did the question justice. "Well, for ME, only the price. I'm poor, you see — very poor. But I thank you and I'll think." The Prince, on the other side of the shop-window, had finally faced about and, as to see if she hadn't done, was trying to reach, with his eyes, the comparatively dim interior. "I like it," she said —"I want it. But I must decide what I can do."

The man, not ungraciously, resigned himself. "Well, I'll keep it for you."

The small quarter-of-an-hour had had its marked oddity — this she felt even by the time the open air and the Bloomsbury aspects had again, in their protest against the truth of her gathered impression, made her more or less their own. Yet the oddity might have been registered as small as compared to the other effect that, before they had gone much further, she had, with her companion, to take account of. This latter was simply the effect of their having, by some tacit logic, some queer inevitability, quite dropped the idea of a continued pursuit. They didn't say so, but it was on the line of giving up Maggie's present that they practically proceeded — the line of giving it up without more reference to it. The Prince's first reference was in fact quite independently made. "I hope you satisfied yourself, before you had done, of what was the matter with that bowl."

"No indeed, I satisfied myself of nothing. Of nothing at least but that the more I looked at it the more I liked it, and that if you weren't so unaccommodating this would be just the occasion for your giving me the pleasure of accepting it."

He looked graver for her, at this, than he had looked all the morning. "Do you propose it seriously — without wishing to play me a trick?"

She wondered. "What trick would it be?"

He looked at her harder. "You mean you really don't know?"

"But know what?"

"Why, what's the matter with it. You didn't see, all the while?"

She only continued, however, to stare. "How could you see — out in the street?"

"I saw before I went out. It was because I saw that I did go out. I didn't want to have another scene with you, before that rascal, and I judged you would presently guess for yourself."

"Is he a rascal?" Charlotte asked. "His price is so moderate. She waited but a moment. "Five pounds. Really so little."

"Five pounds?"

He continued to look at her. "Five pounds."

He might have been doubting her word, but he was only, it appeared, gathering emphasis. "It would be dear — to make a gift of — at five shillings. If it had cost you even but five pence I wouldn't take it from you."

"Then," she asked, "what IS the matter?"

"Why, it has a crack."

It sounded, on his lips, so sharp, it had such an authority, that she almost started, while her colour, at the word, rose. It was as if he had been right, though his assurance was wonderful. "You answer for it without having looked?"

"I did look. I saw the object itself. It told its story. No wonder it's cheap."

"But it's exquisite," Charlotte, as if with an interest in it now made even tenderer and stranger, found herself moved to insist.

"Of course it's exquisite. That's the danger." Then a light visibly came to her — a light in which her friend suddenly and intensely showed. The reflection of it, as she smiled at him, was in her own face. "The danger — I see — is because you're superstitious."

"Per Dio, I'm superstitious! A crack is a crack — and an omen's an omen."

"You'd be afraid —?"

"Per Bacco!"

"For your happiness?"

"For my happiness."

"For your safety?"

"For my safety."

She just paused. "For your marriage?"

"For my marriage. For everything."

She thought again. "Thank goodness then that if there BE a crack we know it! But if we may perish by cracks in things that we don't know —!" And she smiled with the sadness of it. "We can never then give each other anything."

He considered, but he met it. "Ah, but one does know. *I* do, at least — and by instinct. I don't fail. That will always protect me."

It was funny, the way he said such things; yet she liked him, really, the more for it. They fell in for her with a general, or rather with a special, vision. But she spoke with a mild despair.

"What then will protect ME?"

"Where I'm concerned *I* will. From me at least you've nothing to fear," he now quite amiably responded. "Anything you consent to accept from me —" But he paused.

"Well?"

"Well, shall be perfect."

"That's very fine," she presently answered. "It's vain, after all, for you to talk of my accepting things when you'll accept nothing from me."

Ah, THERE, better still, he could meet her. "You attach an impossible condition. That, I mean, of my keeping your gift so to myself."

Well, she looked, before him there, at the condition — then, abruptly, with a gesture, she gave it up. She had a headshake of disenchantment — so far as the idea had appealed to her. It all appeared too difficult. "Oh, my 'condition' — I don't hold to it. You may cry it on the housetops — anything I ever do."

"Ah well, then —!" This made, he laughed, all the difference.

But it was too late. "Oh, I don't care now! I SHOULD have liked the Bowl. But if that won't do there's nothing."

He considered this; he took it in, looking graver again; but after a moment he qualified. "Yet I shall want some day to give you something."

She wondered at him. "What day?"

"The day you marry. For you WILL marry. You must — SERIOUSLY — marry."

She took it from him, but it determined in her the only words she was to have uttered, all the morning, that came out as if a spring had been pressed. "To make you feel better?"

"Well," he replied frankly, wonderfully —"it will. But here," he added, "is your hansom."

He had signalled — the cab was charging. She put out no hand for their separation, but she prepared to get in. Before she did so, however, she said what had been gathering while she waited. "Well, I would marry, I think, to have something from you in all freedom."

Part Second

VII

Adam Verver, at Fawns, that autumn Sunday, might have been observed to open the door of the billiard-room with a certain freedom — might have been observed, that is, had there been a spectator in the field. The justification of the push he had applied, however, and of the push, equally sharp, that, to shut himself in, he again applied — the ground of this energy was precisely that he might here, however briefly, find himself alone, alone with the handful of letters, newspapers and other unopened missives, to which, during and since breakfast, he had lacked opportunity to give an eye. The vast, square, clean apartment was empty, and its large clear windows looked out into spaces of terrace and garden, of park and woodland and shining artificial lake, of richly-condensed horizon, all dark blue upland and church-towered village and strong cloudshadow, which were, together, a thing to create the sense, with everyone else at church, of one's having the world to one's self. We share this world, none the less, for the hour, with Mr. Verver; the very fact of his striking, as he would have said, for solitude, the fact of his quiet flight, almost on tiptoe, through tortuous corridors, investing him with an interest that makes our attention — tender indeed almost to compassion — qualify his achieved isolation. For it may immediately be mentioned that this amiable man bethought himself of his personal advantage, in general, only when it might appear to him that other advantages, those of other persons, had successfully put in their claim. It may be mentioned also that he always figured other persons — such was the law of his nature — as a numerous array, and that, though conscious of but a single near tie, one affection, one duty deepest-rooted in his life, it had never, for many minutes together, been his portion not to feel himself surrounded and committed, never quite been his refreshment to make out where the many-coloured human appeal, represented by gradations of tint, diminishing concentric zones of intensity, of importunity, really faded to the blessed impersonal whiteness for which his vision sometimes ached. It shaded off, the appeal — he would have admitted that; but he had as yet noted no point at which it positively stopped.

Thus had grown in him a little habit — his innermost secret, not confided even to Maggie, though he felt she understood it, as she understood, to his view, everything — thus had shaped itself the innocent trick of occasionally making believe that he had no conscience, or at least that blankness, in the field of duty, did reign for an hour; a small game to which the few persons near enough to have caught him playing it, and of whom Mrs. Assingham, for instance, was one, attached indulgently that idea of quaintness, quite in fact that charm of the pathetic, involved in the preservation by an adult of one of childhood's toys. When he took a rare moment "off," he did so with the touching, confessing eyes of a man of forty-seven caught in the act of handling a relic of infancy — sticking on the head of a broken soldier or trying the lock of a wooden gun. It was essentially, in him, the IMITATION of depravity — which, for amusement, as might have been, he practised "keeping up." In spite of practice he was still imperfect, for these so artlessly-artful interludes were condemned, by the nature of the case, to brevity. He had fatally stamped himself — it was his own fault — a man who could be interrupted with impunity. The greatest of wonders, moreover, was exactly in this, that so interrupted a man should ever have got, as the phrase was, should above all have got so early, to where he was. It argued a special genius; he was clearly a case of that. The spark of fire, the point of light, sat somewhere in his inward vagueness as a lamp before a shrine twinkles in the dark perspective of a church; and while youth and early middle-age, while the stiff American breeze of example and opportunity were blowing upon it hard, had made of the chamber of his brain a strange workshop of fortune. This establishment, mysterious and almost anonymous, the windows of which, at hours of highest pressure, never seemed, for starers and wonderers, perceptibly to glow, must in fact have been during certain years the scene of an unprecedented, a miraculous white-heat, the receipt for producing which it was practically felt that the master of the forge could not have communicated even with the best intentions.

The essential pulse of the flame, the very action of the cerebral temperature, brought to the highest point, yet extraordinarily contained — these facts themselves were the immensity of the result; they were one with perfection of machinery, they had constituted the kind of acquisitive power engendered and applied, the necessary triumph of all operations. A dim explanation of phenomena once vivid must at all events for the moment suffice us; it being obviously no account of the matter to throw on our friend's amiability alone the weight of the demonstration of his economic history. Amiability, of a truth, is an aid to success; it has even been known to be the principle of large accumulations; but the link, for the mind, is none the less fatally missing between proof, on such a scale, of continuity, if of nothing more insolent, in one field, and accessibility to distraction in every other. Variety of imagination — what is that but fatal, in the world of affairs, unless so disciplined as not to be distinguished from monotony? Mr. Verver then, for a fresh, full period, a period betraying, extraordinarily, no wasted year, had been inscrutably monotonous behind an iridescent cloud. The cloud was his native envelope — the soft looseness, so to say, of his temper and tone, not directly expressive enough, no doubt, to figure an amplitude of folds, but of a quality unmistakable for sensitive feelers. He was still reduced, in fine, to getting his rare moments with himself by feigning a cynicism. His real inability to maintain the pretence, however, had perhaps not often been better instanced than by his acceptance of the inevitable today — his acceptance of it on the arrival, at the end of a quarter-of-an hour, of that element of obligation with which he had all the while known he must reckon. A quarter-of-an-hour of egoism was about as much as he, taking one situation with another, usually got. Mrs. Rance opened the door — more tentatively indeed than he himself had just done; but on the other hand, as if to make up for this, she pushed forward even more briskly on seeing him than he had been moved to do on seeing nobody. Then, with force, it came home to him that he had, definitely, a week before, established a precedent. He did her at least that justice — it was a kind of justice he was always doing someone. He had on the previous Sunday liked to stop at home, and he had exposed himself thereby to be caught in the act. To make this possible, that is, Mrs. Rance had only had to like to do the same — the trick was so easily played. It had not occurred to him to plan in any way for her absence — which would have destroyed, somehow, in principle, the propriety of his own presence. If persons under his roof hadn't a right not to go to church, what became, for a fair mind, of his own right? His subtlest manoeuvre had been simply to change from the library to the billiard-room, it being in the library that his guest, or his daughter's, or the guest of the Miss Lutches — he scarce knew in which light to regard her — had then, and not unnaturally, of course, joined him. It was urged on him by his memory of the duration of the visit she had that time, as it were, paid him, that the law of recurrence would already have got itself enacted. She had spent the whole morning with him, was still there, in the library, when the others came back — thanks to her having been tepid about their taking, Mr. Verver and she, a turn outside. It had been as if she looked on that as a kind of subterfuge — almost as a form of disloyalty. Yet what was it she had in mind, what did she wish to make of him beyond what she had already made, a patient, punctilious host, mindful that she had originally arrived much as a stranger, arrived not at all deliberately or yearningly invited? — so that one positively had her possible susceptibilities the MORE on one's conscience. The Miss Lutches, the sisters from the middle West, were there as friends of Maggie's, friends of the earlier time; but Mrs. Rance was there — or at least had primarily appeared — only as a friend of the Miss Lutches.

This lady herself was not of the middle West — she rather insisted on it — but of New Jersey, Rhode Island or Delaware, one of the smallest and most intimate States: he couldn't remember which, though she insisted too on that. It was not in him — we may say it for him — to go so far as to wonder if their group were next to be recruited by some friend of her own; and this partly because she had struck him, verily, rather as wanting to get the Miss Lutches themselves away than to extend the actual circle, and partly, as well as more essentially, because such connection as he enjoyed with the ironic question in general resided substantially less in a personal use of it than in the habit of seeing it as easy to others. He was so framed by nature as to be able to keep his inconveniences separate from his resentments; though indeed if the sum of these latter had at the most always been small, that was doubtless in some degree a consequence of the fewness of the former. His greatest inconvenience, he would have admitted, had he analyzed, was in finding it so taken for granted that, as he had money, he had force. It pressed upon him hard, and all round, assuredly, this attribution of power. Everyone had need of one's power, whereas one's own need, at the best, would have seemed to be but some trick for not communicating it. The effect of a reserve so merely, so meanly defensive would in most cases, beyond question, sufficiently discredit the cause; wherefore, though it was complicating to be perpetually treated as an infinite agent, the outrage was not the greatest of which a brave man might complain. Complaint, besides, was a luxury, and he dreaded the imputation of greed. The other, the constant imputation, that of being able to "do," would have no ground if he hadn't been, to start with — this was the point — provably luxurious. His lips, somehow, were closed — and by a spring connected moreover with the action of his eyes themselves. The latter showed him what he had done, showed him where he had come out; quite at the top of his hill of difficulty, the tall sharp spiral round which he had begun to wind his ascent at the age of twenty, and the apex of which was a platform looking down, if one would, on the kingdoms of the earth and with standing-room for but half-a-dozen others.

His eyes, in any case, now saw Mrs. Rance approach with an instant failure to attach to the fact any grossness of avidity of Mrs. Rance's own — or at least to descry any triumphant use even for the luridest impression of her intensity. What was virtually supreme would be her vision of his having attempted, by his desertion of the library, to mislead her — which in point of fact barely escaped being what he had designed. It was not easy for him, in spite of accumulations fondly and funnily regarded as of systematic practice, not now to be ashamed; the one thing comparatively easy would be to gloss over his course. The billiard-room was NOT, at the particular crisis, either a natural or a graceful place for the nominally main occupant of so large a house to retire to — and this without prejudice, either, to the fact that his visitor wouldn't, as he apprehended, explicitly make him a scene. Should she frankly denounce him for a sneak he would simply go to pieces; but he was, after an instant, not afraid of that. Wouldn't she rather, as emphasising their communion, accept and in a manner exploit the anomaly, treat it perhaps as romantic or possibly even as comic? — show at least that they needn't mind even though the vast table, draped in brown holland, thrust itself between them as an expanse of desert sand. She couldn't cross the desert, but she could, and did, beautifully get round it; so that for him to convert it into an obstacle he would have had to cause himself, as in some childish game or unbecoming romp, to be pursued, to be genially hunted. This last was a turn he was well aware the occasion should on no account take; and there loomed before him — for the mere moment — the prospect of her fairly proposing that they should knock about the balls. That danger certainly, it struck him, he should manage in some way to deal with. Why too, for that matter, had he need of defences, material or other? — how was it a question of dangers really to be called such? The deep danger, the only one that made him, as an idea, positively turn cold, would have been the possibility of her seeking him in marriage, of her bringing up between them that terrible issue. Here, fortunately, she was powerless, it being apparently so provable against her that she had a husband in undiminished existence.

She had him, it was true, only in America, only in Texas, in Nebraska, in Arizona or some-where — somewhere that, at old Fawns House, in the county of Kent, scarcely counted as a definite place at all; it showed somehow, from afar, as so lost, so indistinct and illusory, in the great alkali desert of cheap Divorce. She had him even in bondage, poor man, had him in contempt, had him in remembrance so imperfect as barely to assert itself, but she had him, none the less, in existence unimpeached: the Miss Lutches had seen him in the flesh — as they had appeared eager to mention; though when they were separately questioned their descriptions failed to tally. He would be at the worst, should it come to the worst, Mrs. Rance's difficulty, and he served therefore quite enough as the stout bulwark of anyone else. This was in truth logic without a flaw, yet it gave Mr. Verver less comfort than it ought. He feared not only danger — he feared the idea of danger, or in other words feared, hauntedly, himself. It was above all as a symbol that Mrs. Rance actually rose before him — a symbol of the supreme effort that he should have sooner or later, as he felt, to make. This effort would be to say No — he lived in terror of having to. He should be proposed to at a given moment — it was only a question of time — and then he should have to do a thing that would be extremely disagreeable. He almost wished, on occasion, that he wasn't so sure he WOULD do it. He knew himself, however, well enough not to doubt: he knew coldly, quite bleakly, where he would, at the crisis, draw the line. It was Maggie's marriage and Maggie's finer happiness — happy as he had supposed her before — that had made the difference; he hadn't in the other time, it now seemed to him, had to think of such things. They hadn't come up for him, and it was as if she, positively, had herself kept them down. She had only been his child — which she was indeed as much as ever; but there were sides on which she had protected him as if she were more than a daughter. She had done for him more than he knew — much, and blissfully, as he always HAD known. If she did at present more than ever, through having what she called the change in his life to make up to him for, his situation still, all the same, kept pace with her activity — his situation being simply that there was more than ever to be done.

There had not yet been quite so much, on all the showing, as since their return from their twenty months in America, as since their settlement again in England, experimental though it was, and the consequent sense, now quite established for him, of a domestic air that had cleared and lightened, producing the effect, for their common personal life, of wider perspectives and large waiting spaces. It was as if his son-inlaw's presence, even from before his becoming his son-inlaw, had somehow filled the scene and blocked the future — very richly and handsomely, when all was said, not at all inconveniently or in ways not to have been desired: inasmuch as though the Prince, his measure now practically taken, was still pretty much the same "big fact," the sky had lifted, the horizon receded, the very foreground itself expanded, quite to match him, quite to keep everything in comfortable scale. At first, certainly, their decent little old-time union, Maggie's and his own, had resembled a good deal some pleasant public square, in the heart of an old city, into which a great Palladian church, say — something with a grand architectural front — had suddenly been dropped; so that the rest of the place, the space in front, the way round, outside, to the east end, the margin of street and passage, the quantity of over-arching heaven, had been temporarily compromised. Not even then, of a truth, in a manner disconcerting — given, that is, for the critical, or at least the intelligent, eye, the great style of the facade and its high place in its class. The phenomenon that had since occurred, whether originally to have been pronounced calculable or not, had not, naturally, been the miracle of a night, but had taken place so gradually, quietly, easily, that from this vantage of wide, wooded Fawns, with its eighty rooms, as they said, with its spreading park, with its acres and acres of garden and its majesty of artificial lake — though that, for a person so familiar with the "great" ones, might be rather ridiculous — no visibility of transition showed, no violence of adjustment, in retrospect, emerged. The Palladian church was always there, but the piazza took care of itself. The sun stared down in his fulness, the air circulated, and the public not less; the limit stood off, the way round was easy, the east end was as fine, in its fashion, as the west, and there were also side doors for entrance, between the two — large, monumental, ornamental, in their style — as for all proper great churches. By some such process, in fine, had the Prince, for his father-inlaw, while remaining solidly a feature, ceased to be, at all ominously, a block.

Mr. Verver, it may further be mentioned, had taken at no moment sufficient alarm to have kept in detail the record of his reassurance; but he would none the less not have been unable, not really have been indisposed, to impart in confidence to the right person his notion of the history of the matter. The right person — it is equally distinct — had not, for this illumination, been wanting, but had been encountered in the form of Fanny Assingham, not for the first time indeed admitted to his counsels, and who would have doubtless at present, in any case, from plenitude of interest and with equal guarantees, repeated his secret. It all came then, the great clearance, from the one prime fact that the Prince, by good fortune, hadn't proved angular. He clung to that description of his daughter's husband as he often did to terms and phrases, in the human, the social connection, that he had found for himself: it was his way to have times of using these constantly, as if they just then lighted the world, or his own path in it, for him — even when for some of his interlocutors they covered less ground. It was true that with Mrs. Assingham he never felt quite sure of the ground anything covered; she disputed with him so little, agreed with him so much, surrounded him with such systematic consideration, such predetermined tenderness, that it was almost — which he had once told her in irritation as if she were nursing a sick baby. He had accused her of not taking him seriously, and she had replied — as from her it couldn't frighten him — that she took him religiously, adoringly. She had laughed again, as she had laughed before, on his producing for her that good right word about the happy issue of his connection with the Prince — with an effect the more odd perhaps as she had not contested its value. She couldn't of course, however, be, at the best, as much in love with his discovery as he was himself. He was so much so that he fairly worked it — to his own comfort; came in fact sometimes near publicly pointing the moral of what might have occurred if friction, so to speak, had occurred. He pointed it frankly one day to the personage in question, mentioned to the Prince the particular justice he did him, was even explicit as to the danger that, in their remarkable relation, they had thus escaped. Oh, if he HAD been angular! — who could say what might THEN have happened? He spoke — and it was the way he had spoken to Mrs. Assingham too — as if he grasped the facts, without exception, for which angularity stood.

It figured for him, clearly, as a final idea, a conception of the last vividness. He might have been signifying by it the sharp corners and hard edges, all the stony pointedness, the grand right geometry of his spreading Palladian church. Just so, he was insensible to no feature of the felicity of a contact that, beguilingly, almost confoundingly, was a contact but with practically yielding lines and curved surfaces. "You're round, my boy," he had said —"you're ALL, you're variously and inexhaustibly round, when you might, by all the chances, have been abominably square. I'm not sure, for that matter," he had added, "that you're not square in the general mass — whether abominably or not. The abomination isn't a question, for you're inveterately round — that's what I mean — in the detail. It's the sort of thing, in you, that one feels — or at least I do — with one's hand. Say you had been formed, all over, in a lot of little pyramidal lozenges like that wonderful side of the Ducal Palace in Venice — so lovely in a building, but so damnable, for rubbing against, in a man, and especially in a near relation. I can see them all from here — each of them sticking out by itself — all the architectural cut diamonds that would have scratched one's softer sides. One would have been scratched by diamonds — doubtless the neatest way if one was to be scratched at all — but one would have been more or less reduced to a hash. As it is, for living with, you're a pure and perfect crystal. I give you my idea — I think you ought to have it — just as it has come to me." The Prince had taken the idea, in his way, for he was well accustomed, by this time, to taking; and nothing perhaps even could more have confirmed Mr. Verver's account of his surface than the manner in which these golden drops evenly flowed over it. They caught in no interstice, they gathered in no concavity; the uniform smoothness betrayed the dew but by showing for the moment a richer tone. The young man, in other words, unconfusedly smiled — though indeed as if assenting, from principle and habit, to more than he understood. He liked all signs that things were well, but he cared rather less WHY they were.

In regard to the people among whom he had since his marriage been living, the reasons they so frequently gave — so much oftener than he had ever heard reasons given before — remained on the whole the element by which he most differed from them; and his father-in-law and his wife were, after all, only first among the people among whom he had been living. He was never even yet sure of how, at this, that or the other point, he would strike them; they felt remarkably, so often, things he hadn't meant, and missed not less remarkably, and not less often, things he had. He had fallen back on his general explanation —"We haven't the same values;" by which he understood the same measure of importance. His "curves" apparently were important because they had been unexpected, or, still more, unconceived; whereas when one had always, as in his relegated old world, taken curves, and in much greater quantities too, for granted, one was no more surprised at the resulting feasibility of intercourse than one was surprised at being upstairs in a house that had a staircase. He had in fact on this occasion disposed alertly enough of the subject of Mr. Verver's approbation. The promptitude of his answer, we may in fact well surmise, had sprung not a little from a particular kindled remembrance; this had given his acknowledgment its easiest turn. "Oh, if I'm a crystal I'm delighted that I'm a perfect one, for I believe that they sometimes have cracks and flaws — in which case they're to be had very cheap!" He had stopped short of the emphasis it would have given his joke to add that there had been certainly no having HIM cheap; and it was doubtless a mark of the good taste practically reigning between them that Mr. Verver had not, on his side either, taken up the opportunity. It is the latter's relation to such aspects, however, that now most concerns us, and the bearing of his pleased view of this absence of friction upon Amerigo's character as a representative precious object. Representative precious objects, great ancient pictures and other works of art, fine eminent "pieces" in gold, in silver, in enamel, majolica, ivory, bronze, had for a number of years so multiplied themselves round him and, as a general challenge to acquisition and appreciation, so engaged all the faculties of his mind, that the instinct, the particular sharpened appetite of the collector, had fairly served as a basis for his acceptance of the Prince's suit.

Over and above the signal fact of the impression made on Maggie herself, the aspirant to his daughter's hand showed somehow the great marks and signs, stood before him with the high authenticities, he had learned to look for in pieces of the first order. Adam Verver knew, by this time, knew thoroughly; no man in Europe or in America, he privately believed, was less capable, in such estimates, of vulgar mistakes. He had never spoken of himself as infallible — it was not his way; but, apart from the natural affections, he had acquainted himself with no greater joy, of the intimately personal type, than the joy of his originally coming to feel, and all so unexpectedly, that he had in him the spirit of the connoisseur. He had, like many other persons, in the course of his reading, been struck with Keats's sonnet about stout Cortez in the presence of the Pacific; but few persons, probably, had so devoutly fitted the poet's grand image to a fact of experience. It consorted so with Mr. Verver's consciousness of the way in which, at a given moment, he had stared at HIS Pacific, that a couple of perusals of the immortal lines had sufficed to stamp them in his memory. His "peak in Darien" was the sudden hour that had transformed his life, the hour of his perceiving with a mute inward gasp akin to the low moan of apprehensive passion, that a world was left him to conquer and that he might conquer it if he tried. It had been a turning of the page of the book of life — as if a leaf long inert had moved at a touch and, eagerly reversed, had made such a stir of the air as sent up into his face the very breath of the Golden Isles. To rifle the Golden Isles had, on the spot, become the business of his future, and with the sweetness of it — what was most wondrous of all — still more even in the thought than in the act. The thought was that of the affinity of Genius, or at least of Taste, with something in himself — with the dormant intelligence of which he had thus almost violently become aware and that affected him as changing by a mere revolution of the screw his whole intellectual plane. He was equal, somehow, with the great seers, the invokers and encouragers of beauty — and he didn't after all perhaps dangle so far below the great producers and creators. He had been nothing of that kind before-too decidedly, too dreadfully not; but now he saw why he had been what he had, why he had failed and fallen short even in huge success; now he read into his career, in one single magnificent night, the immense meaning it had waited for.

It was during his first visit to Europe after the death of his wife, when his daughter was ten years old, that the light, in his mind, had so broken — and he had even made out at that time why, on an earlier occasion, the journey of his honeymoon year, it had still been closely covered.

He had "bought" then, so far as he had been able, but he had bought almost wholly for the frail, fluttered creature at his side, who had had her fancies, decidedly, but all for the art, then wonderful to both of them, of the Rue de la Paix, the costly authenticities of dressmakers and jewellers. Her flutter — pale disconcerted ghost as she actually was, a broken white flower tied round, almost grotesquely for his present sense, with a huge satin "bow" of the Boulevard — her flutter had been mainly that of ribbons, frills and fine fabrics; all funny, pathetic evidence, for memory, of the bewilderments overtaking them as a bridal pair confronted with opportunity. He could wince, fairly, still, as he remembered the sense in which the poor girl's pressure had, under his fond encouragement indeed, been exerted in favour of purchase and curiosity. These were wandering images, out of the earlier dusk, that threw her back, for his pity, into a past more remote than he liked their common past, their young affection, to appear. It would have had to be admitted, to an insistent criticism, that Maggie's mother, all too strangely, had not so much failed of faith as of the right application of it; since she had exercised it eagerly and restlessly, made it a pretext for innocent perversities in respect to which philosophic time was at, last to reduce all groans to gentleness. And they had loved each other so that his own intelligence, on the higher line, had temporarily paid for it. The futilities, the enormities, the depravities, of decoration and ingenuity, that, before his sense was unsealed, she had made him think lovely! Musing, reconsidering little man that he was, and addicted to silent pleasures — as he was accessible to silent pains — he even sometimes wondered what would have become of his intelligence, in the sphere in which it was to learn more and more exclusively to play, if his wife's influence upon it had not been, in the strange scheme of things, so promptly removed. Would she have led him altogether, attached as he was to her, into the wilderness of mere mistakes? Would she have prevented him from ever scaling his vertiginous Peak? — or would she, otherwise, have been able to accompany him to that eminence, where he might have pointed out to her, as Cortez to HIS companions, the revelation vouchsafed? No companion of Cortez had presumably been a real lady: Mr. Verver allowed that historic fact to determine his inference.

VIII

What was at all events not permanently hidden from him was a truth much less invidious about his years of darkness. It was the strange scheme of things again: the years of darkness had been needed to render possible the years of light. A wiser hand than he at first knew had kept him hard at acquisition of one sort as a perfect preliminary to acquisition of another, and the preliminary would have been weak and wanting if the good faith of it had been less. His comparative blindness had made the good faith, which in its turn had made the soil propitious for the flower of the supreme idea. He had had to LIKE forging and sweating, he had had to like polishing and piling up his arms. They were things at least he had had to believe he liked, just as he had believed he liked transcendent calculation and imaginative gambling all for themselves, the creation of "interests" that were the extinction of other interests, the livid vulgarity, even, of getting in, or getting out, first. That had of course been so far from really the case — with the supreme idea, all the while, growing and striking deep, under everything, in the warm, rich earth. He had stood unknowing, he had walked and worked where it was buried, and the fact itself, the fact of his fortune, would have been a barren fact enough if the first sharp tender shoot had never struggled into day. There on one side was the ugliness his middle time had been spared; there on the other, from all the portents, was the beauty with which his age might still be crowned. He was happier, doubtless, than he deserved; but THAT, when one was happy at all, it was easy to be. He had wrought by devious ways, but he had reached the place, and what would ever have been straighter, in any man's life, than his way, now, of occupying it? It hadn't merely, his plan, all the sanctions of civilization; it was positively civilization condensed, concrete, consummate, set down by his hands as a house on a rock — a house from whose open doors and windows, open to grateful, to thirsty millions, the higher, the highest knowledge would shine out to bless the land. In this house, designed as a gift, primarily, to the people of his adoptive city and native State, the urgency of whose release from the bondage of ugliness he was in a position to measure — in this museum of museums, a palace of art which was to show for compact as a Greek temple was compact, a receptacle of treasures sifted to positive sanctity, his spirit today almost altogether lived, making up, as he would have said, for lost time and haunting the portico in anticipation of the final rites.

These would be the "opening exercises," the august dedication of the place. His imagination, he was well aware, got over the ground faster than his judgment; there was much still to do for the production of his first effect. Foundations were laid and walls were rising, the structure of the shell all determined; but raw haste was forbidden him in a connection so intimate with the highest effects of patience and piety; he should belie himself by completing without a touch at least of the majesty of delay a monument to the religion he wished to propagate, the exemplary passion, the passion for perfection at any price. He was far from knowing as yet where he would end, but he was admirably definite as to where he wouldn't begin. He wouldn't begin with a small show — he would begin with a great, and he could scarce have indicated, even had he wished to try, the line of division he had drawn. He had taken no trouble to indicate it to his fellow-citizens, purveyors and consumers, in his own and the circumjacent commonwealths, of comic matter in large lettering, diurnally "set up," printed, published, folded and delivered, at the expense of his presumptuous emulation of the snail. The snail had become for him, under this ironic suggestion, the loveliest beast in nature, and his return to England, of which we are present witnesses, had not been unconnected with the appreciation so determined. It marked what he liked to mark, that he needed, on the matter in question, instruction from no one on earth. A couple of years of Europe again, of renewed nearness to changes and chances, refreshed sensibility to the currents of the market, would fall in with the consistency of wisdom, the particular shade of enlightened conviction, that he wished to observe. It didn't look like much for a whole family to hang about waiting-they being now, since the birth of his grandson, a whole family; and there was henceforth only one ground in all the world, he felt, on which the question of appearance would ever really again count for him. He cared that a work of art of price should "look like" the master to whom it might perhaps be deceitfully attributed; but he had ceased on the whole to know any matter of the rest of life by its looks.

He took life in general higher up the stream; so far as he was not actually taking it as a collector, he was taking it, decidedly, as a grandfather. In the way of precious small pieces he had handled nothing so precious as the Principino, his daughter's first-born, whose Italian designation endlessly amused him and whom he could manipulate and dandle, already almost toss and catch again, as he couldn't a correspondingly rare morsel of an earlier pate tendre. He could take the small clutching child from his nurse's arms with an iteration grimly discountenanced, in respect to their contents, by the glass doors of high cabinets. Something clearly beatific in this new relation had, moreover, without doubt, confirmed for him the sense that none of his silent answers to public detraction, to local vulgarity, had ever been so legitimately straight as the mere element of attitude — reduce it, he said, to that — in his easy weeks at Fawns. The element of attitude was all he wanted of these weeks, and he was enjoying it on the spot, even more than he had hoped: enjoying it in spite of Mrs. Rance and the Miss Lutches; in spite of the small worry of his belief that Fanny Assingham had really something for him that she was keeping back; in spite of his full consciousness, overflowing the cup like a wine too generously poured, that if he had consented to marry his daughter, and thereby to make, as it were, the difference, what surrounded him now was, exactly, consent vivified, marriage demonstrated, the difference, in fine, definitely made. He could call back his prior, his own wedded consciousness — it was not yet out of range of vague reflection. He had supposed himself, above all he had supposed his wife, as married as anyone could be, and yet he wondered if their state had deserved the name, or their union worn the beauty, in the degree to which the couple now before him carried the matter. In especial since the birth of their boy, in New York — the grand climax of their recent American period, brought to so right an issue — the happy pair struck him as having carried it higher, deeper, further; to where it ceased to concern his imagination, at any rate, to follow them. Extraordinary, beyond question, was one branch of his characteristic mute wonderment — it characterised above all, with its subject before it, his modesty: the strange dim doubt, waking up for him at the end of the years, of whether Maggie's mother had, after all, been capable of the maximum. The maximum of tenderness he meant — as the terms existed for him; the maximum of immersion in the fact of being married. Maggie herself was capable; Maggie herself at this season, was, exquisitely, divinely, the maximum: such was the impression that, positively holding off a little for the practical, the tactful consideration it inspired in him, a respect for the beauty and sanctity of it almost amounting to awe — such was the impression he daily received from her. She was her mother, oh yes — but her mother and something more; it becoming thus a new light for him, and in such a curious way too, that anything more than her mother should prove at this time of day possible.

He could live over again at almost any quiet moment the long process of his introduction to his present interests — an introduction that had depended all on himself, like the "cheek" of the young man who approaches a boss without credentials or picks up an acquaintance, makes even a real friend, by speaking to a passer in the street. HIS real friend, in all the business, was to have been his own mind, with which nobody had put him in relation. He had knocked at the door of that essentially private house, and his call, in truth, had not been immediately answered; so that when, after waiting and coming back, he had at last got in, it was, twirling his hat, as an embarrassed stranger, or, trying his keys, as a thief at night. He had gained confidence only with time, but when he had taken real possession of the place it had been never again to come away. All of which success represented, it must be allowed, his one principle of pride. Pride in the mere original spring, pride in his money, would have been pride in something that had come, in comparison, so easily. The right ground for elation was difficulty mastered, and his difficulty — thanks to his modesty — had been to believe in his facility. THIS was the problem he had worked out to its solution — the solution that was now doing more than all else to make his feet settle and his days flush; and when he wished to feel "good," as they said at American City, he had but to retrace his immense development. That was what the whole thing came back to — that the development had not been somebody's else passing falsely, accepted too ignobly, for his. To think how servile he might have been was absolutely to respect himself, was in fact, as much as he liked, to admire himself, as free. The very finest spring that ever responded to his touch was always there to press — the memory of his freedom as dawning upon him, like a sunrise all pink and silver, during a winter divided between Florence, Rome and Naples some three years after his wife's death. It was the hushed daybreak of the Roman revelation in particular that he could usually best recover, with the way that there, above all, where the princes and Popes had been before him, his divination of his faculty most went to his head. He was a plain American citizen, staying at an hotel where, sometimes, for days together, there were twenty others like him; but no Pope, no prince of them all had read a richer meaning, he believed, into the character of the Patron of Art. He was ashamed of them really, if he wasn't afraid, and he had on the whole never so climbed to the tip-top as in judging, over a perusal of Hermann Grimm, where Julius II and Leo X were "placed" by their treatment of Michael Angelo. Far below the plain American citizen — in the case at least in which this personage happened not to be too plain to be Adam Verver. Going to our friend's head, moreover, some of the results of such comparisons may doubtless be described as having stayed there. His freedom to see — of which the comparisons were part — what could it do but steadily grow and grow?

It came perhaps even too much to stand to him for ALL freedom — since, for example, it was as much there as ever at the very time of Mrs. Rance's conspiring against him, at Fawns, with the billiard-room and the Sunday morning, on the occasion round which we have perhaps drawn our circle too wide. Mrs. Rance at least controlled practically each other license of the present and the near future: the license to pass the hour as he would have found convenient; the license to stop remembering, for a little, that, though if proposed to — and not only by this aspirant but by any other — he wouldn't prove foolish, the proof of wisdom was none the less, in such a fashion, rather cruelly conditioned; the license in especial to proceed from his letters to his journals and insulate, orientate, himself afresh by the sound, over his gained interval, of the many-mouthed monster the exercise of whose lungs he so constantly stimulated. Mrs. Rance remained with him till the others came back from church, and it was by that time clearer than ever that his ordeal, when it should arrive, would be really most unpleasant. His impression — this was the point — took somehow the form not so much of her wanting to press home her own advantage as of her building better than she knew; that is of her symbolising, with virtual unconsciousness, his own special deficiency, his unfortunate lack of a wife to whom applications could be referred. The applications, the contingencies with which Mrs. Rance struck him as potentially bristling, were not of a sort, really, to be met by one's self. And the possibility of them, when his visitor said, or as good as said, "I'm restrained, you see, because of Mr. Rance, and also because I'm proud and refined; but if it WASN'T for Mr. Rance and for my refinement and my pride!" — the possibility of them, I say, turned to a great murmurous rustle, of a volume to fill the future; a rustle of petticoats, of scented, many-paged letters, of voices as to which, distinguish themselves as they might from each other, it mattered little in what part of the resounding country they had learned to make themselves prevail. The Assinghams and the Miss Lutches had taken the walk, through the park, to the little old church, "on the property," that our friend had often found himself wishing he were able to transport, as it stood, for its simple sweetness, in a glass case, to one of his exhibitory halls; while Maggie had induced her husband, not inveterate in such practices, to make with her, by carriage, the somewhat longer pilgrimage to the nearest altar, modest though it happened to be, of the faith — her own as it had been her mother's, and as Mr. Verver himself had been loosely willing, always, to let it be taken for his — without the solid ease of which, making the stage firm and smooth, the drama of her marriage might not have been acted out.

What at last appeared to have happened, however, was that the divided parties, coming back at the same moment, had met outside and then drifted together, from empty room to room, yet not in mere aimless quest of the pair of companions they had left at home. The quest had carried them to the door of the billiard-room, and their appearance, as it opened to admit them, determined for Adam Verver, in the oddest way in the world, a new and sharp perception. It was really remarkable: this perception expanded, on the spot, as a flower, one of the strangest, might, at a breath, have suddenly opened. The breath, for that matter, was more than anything else, the look in his daughter's eyes — the look with which he SAW her take in exactly what had occurred in her absence: Mrs. Rance's pursuit of him to this remote locality, the spirit and the very form, perfectly characteristic, of his acceptance of the complication — the seal set, in short, unmistakably, on one of Maggie's anxieties. The anxiety, it was true, would have been, even though not imparted, separately shared; for Fanny Assingham's face was, by the same stroke, not at all thickly veiled for him, and a queer light, of a colour quite to match, fairly glittered in the four fine eyes of the Miss Lutches. Each of these persons — counting out, that is, the Prince and the Colonel, who didn't care, and who didn't even see that the others did — knew something, or had at any rate had her idea; the idea, precisely, that this was what Mrs. Rance, artfully biding her time, WOULD do. The special shade of apprehension on the part of the Miss Lutches might indeed have suggested the vision of an energy supremely asserted. It was droll, in truth, if one came to that, the position of the Miss Lutches: they had themselves brought, they had guilelessly introduced Mrs. Rance, strong in the fact of Mr. Rance's having been literally beheld of them; and it was now for them, positively, as if their handful of flowers — since Mrs. Rance was a handful! — had been but the vehicle of a dangerous snake. Mr. Verver fairly felt in the air the Miss Lutches' imputation — in the intensity of which, really, his own propriety might have been involved.

That, none the less, was but a flicker; what made the real difference, as I have hinted, was his mute passage with Maggie. His daughter's anxiety alone had depths, and it opened out for him the wider that it was altogether new. When, in their common past, when till this moment, had she shown a fear, however dumbly, for his individual life? They had had fears together, just as they had had joys, but all of hers, at least, had been for what equally concerned them. Here of a sudden was a question that concerned him alone, and the soundless explosion of it somehow marked a date. He was on her mind, he was even in a manner on her hands — as a distinct thing, that is, from being, where he had always been, merely deep in her heart and in her life; too deep down, as it were, to be disengaged, contrasted or opposed, in short objectively presented. But time finally had done it; their relation was altered: he SAW, again, the difference lighted for her. This marked it to himself — and it wasn't a question simply of a Mrs. Rance the more or the less. For Maggie too, at a stroke, almost beneficently, their visitor had, from being an inconvenience, become a sign. They had made vacant, by their marriage, his immediate foreground, his personal precinct — they being the Princess and the Prince. They had made room in it for others — so others had become aware. He became aware himself, for that matter, during the minute Maggie stood there before speaking; and with the sense, moreover, of what he saw her see, he had the sense of what she saw HIM. This last, it may be added, would have been his intensest perception had there not, the next instant, been more for him in Fanny Assingham. Her face couldn't keep it from him; she had seen, on top of everything, in her quick way, what they both were seeing.

IX

So much mute communication was doubtless, all this time, marvellous, and we may confess to having perhaps read into the scene, prematurely, a critical character that took longer to develop. Yet the quiet hour of reunion enjoyed that afternoon by the father and the daughter did really little else than deal with the elements definitely presented to each in the vibration produced by the return of the church-goers. Nothing allusive, nothing at all insistent, passed between them either before or immediately after luncheon — except indeed so far as their failure soon again to meet might be itself an accident charged with reference. The hour or two after luncheon — and on Sundays with especial rigour, for one of the domestic reasons of which it belonged to Maggie quite multitudinously to take account — were habitually spent by the Princess with her little boy, in whose apartment she either frequently found her father already established or was sooner or later joined by him. His visit to his grandson, at some hour or other, held its place, in his day, against all interventions, and this without counting his grandson's visits to HIM, scarcely less ordered and timed, and the odd bits, as he called them, that they picked up together when they could — communions snatched, for the most part, on the terrace, in the gardens or the park, while the Principino, with much pomp and circumstance of perambulator, parasol, fine lace over-veiling and incorruptible female attendance, took the air. In the private apartments, which, occupying in the great house the larger part of a wing of their own, were not much more easily accessible than if the place had been a royal palace and the small child an heir-apparent — in the nursery of nurseries the talk, at these instituted times, was always so prevailingly with or about the master of the scene that other interests and other topics had fairly learned to avoid the slighting and inadequate notice there taken of them. They came in, at the best, but as involved in the little boy's future, his past, or his comprehensive present, never getting so much as a chance to plead their own merits or to complain of being neglected. Nothing perhaps, in truth, had done more than this united participation to confirm in the elder parties that sense of a life not only uninterrupted but more deeply associated, more largely combined, of which, on Adam Verver's behalf, we have made some mention. It was of course an old story and a familiar idea that a beautiful baby could take its place as a new link between a wife and a husband, but Maggie and her father had, with every ingenuity, converted the precious creature into a link between a mamma and a grandpapa. The Principino, for a chance spectator of this process, might have become, by an untoward stroke, a hapless half-orphan, with the place of immediate male parent swept bare and open to the next nearest sympathy.

They had no occasion thus, the conjoined worshippers, to talk of what the Prince might be or might do for his son — the sum of service, in his absence, so completely filled itself out. It was not in the least, moreover, that there was doubt of him, for he was conspicuously addicted to the manipulation of the child, in the frank Italian way, at such moments as he judged discreet in respect to other claims: conspicuously, indeed, that is, for Maggie, who had more occasion, on the whole, to speak to her husband of the extravagance of her father than to speak to her father of the extravagance of her husband. Adam Verver had, all round, in this connection, his own serenity. He was sure of his son-inlaw's auxiliary admiration — admiration, he meant, of his grand-son; since, to begin with, what else had been at work but the instinct — or it might fairly have been the tradition — of the latter's making the child so solidly beautiful as to HAVE to be admired? What contributed most to harmony in this play of relations, however, was the way the young man seemed to leave it to be gathered that, tradition for tradition, the grandpapa's own was not, in any estimate, to go for nothing. A tradition, or whatever it was, that had flowered prelusively in the Princess herself — well, Amerigo's very discretions were his way of taking account of it. His discriminations in respect to his heir were, in fine, not more angular than any others to be observed in him; and Mr. Verver received perhaps from no source so distinct an impression of being for him an odd and important phenomenon as he received from this impunity of appropriation, these unchallenged nursery hours. It was as if the grandpapa's special show of the character were but another side for the observer to study, another item for him to note. It came back, this latter personage knew, to his own previous perception — that of the Prince's inability, in any matter in which he was concerned, to CONCLUDE. The idiosyncrasy, for him, at each stage, had to be demonstrated — on which, however, he admirably accepted it. This last was, after all, the point; he really worked, poor young man, for acceptance, since he worked so constantly for comprehension. And how, when you came to that, COULD you know that a horse wouldn't shy at a brass-band, in a country road, because it didn't shy at a traction-engine? It might have been brought up to traction-engines without having been brought up to brass-bands. Little by little, thus, from month to month, the Prince was learning what his wife's father had been brought up to; and now it could be checked off — he had been brought, up to the romantic view of principini. Who would have thought it, and where would it all stop? The only fear somewhat sharp for Mr. Verver was a certain fear of disappointing him for strangeness. He felt that the evidence he offered, thus viewed, was too much on the positive side. He didn't know — he was learning, and it was funny for him — to how many things he HAD been brought up. If the Prince could only strike something to which he hadn't! This wouldn't, it seemed to him, ruffle the smoothness, and yet MIGHT, a little, add to the interest.

What was now clear, at all events, for the father and the daughter, was their simply knowing they wanted, for the time, to be together — at any cost, as it were; and their necessity so worked in them as to bear them out of the house, in a quarter hidden from that in which their friends were gathered, and cause them to wander, unseen, unfollowed, along a covered walk in the "old" garden, as it was called, old with an antiquity of formal things, high box and shaped yew and expanses of brick wall that had turned at once to purple and to pink. They went out of a door in the wall, a door that had a slab with a date set above it, 1713, but in the old multiplied lettering, and then had before them a small white gate, intensely white and clean amid all the greenness, through which they gradually passed to where some of the grandest trees spaciously clustered and where they would find one of the quietest places. A bench had been placed, long ago, beneath a great oak that helped to crown a mild eminence, and the ground sank away below it, to rise again, opposite, at a distance sufficient to enclose the solitude and figure a bosky horizon. Summer, blissfully, was with them yet, and the low sun made a splash of light where it pierced the looser shade; Maggie, coming down to go out, had brought a parasol, which, as, over her charming bare head, she now handled it, gave, with the big straw hat that her father in these days always wore a good deal tipped back, definite intention to their walk. They knew the bench; it was "sequestered" — they had praised it for that together, before, and liked the word; and after they had begun to linger there they could have smiled (if they hadn't been really too serious, and if the question hadn't so soon ceased to matter), over the probable wonder of the others as to what would have become of them.

The extent to which they enjoyed their indifference to any judgment of their want of ceremony, what did that of itself speak but for the way that, as a rule, they almost equally had others on their mind? They each knew that both were full of the superstition of not "hurting," but might precisely have been asking themselves, asking in fact each other, at this moment, whether that was to be, after all, the last word of their conscientious development. Certain it was, at all events, that, in addition to the Assinghams and the Lutches and Mrs. Rance, the attendance at tea, just in the right place on the west terrace, might perfectly comprise the four or five persons — among them the very pretty, the typically Irish Miss Maddock, vaunted, announced and now brought — from the couple of other houses near enough, one of these the minor residence Of their proprietor, established, thriftily, while he hired out his ancestral home, within sight and sense of his profit. It was not less certain, either, that, for once in a way, the group in question must all take the case as they found it. Fanny Assingham, at any time, for that matter, might perfectly be trusted to see Mr. Verver and his daughter, to see their reputation for a decent friendliness, through any momentary danger; might be trusted even to carry off their absence for Amerigo, for Amerigo's possible funny Italian anxiety; Amerigo always being, as the Princess was well aware, conveniently amenable to this friend's explanations, beguilements, reassurances, and perhaps in fact rather more than less dependent on them as his new life — since that was his own name for it — opened out. It was no secret to Maggie — it was indeed positively a public joke for her — that she couldn't explain as Mrs. Assingham did, and that, the Prince liking explanations, liking them almost as if he collected them, in the manner of book-plates or postage-stamps, for themselves, his requisition of this luxury had to be met. He didn't seem to want them as yet for use — rather for ornament and amusement, innocent amusement of the kind he most fancied and that was so characteristic of his blessed, beautiful, general, slightly indolent lack of more dissipated, or even just of more sophisticated, tastes.

However that might be, the dear woman had come to be frankly and gaily recognised — and not least by herself — as filling in the intimate little circle an office that was not always a sinecure. It was almost as if she had taken, with her kind, melancholy Colonel at her heels, a responsible engagement; to be within call, as it were, for all those appeals that sprang out of talk, that sprang not a little, doubtless too, out of leisure. It naturally led her position in the household, as, she called it, to considerable frequency of presence, to visits, from the good couple, freely repeated and prolonged, and not so much as under form of protest. She was there to keep him quiet — it was Amerigo's own description of her influence; and it would only have needed a more visible disposition to unrest in him to make the account perfectly fit. Fanny herself limited indeed, she minimised, her office; you didn't need a jailor, she contended, for a domesticated lamb tied up with pink ribbon. This was not an animal to be controlled — it was an animal to be, at the most, educated. She admitted accordingly that she was educative — which Maggie was so aware that she herself, inevitably, wasn't; so it came round to being true that what she was most in charge of was his mere intelligence. This left, goodness knew, plenty of different calls for Maggie to meet — in a case in which so much pink ribbon, as it might be symbolically named, was lavished on the creature. What it all amounted to, at any rate, was that Mrs. Assingham would be keeping him quiet now, while his wife and his father-in-law carried out their own little frugal picnic; quite moreover, doubtless, not much less neededly in respect to the members of the circle that were with them there than in respect to the pair they were missing almost for the first time. It was present to Maggie that the Prince could bear, when he was with his wife, almost any queerness on the part of people, strange English types, who bored him, beyond convenience, by being so little as he himself was; for this was one of the ways in which a wife was practically sustaining. But she was as positively aware that she hadn't yet learned to see him as meeting such exposure in her absence. How did he move and talk, how above all did he, or how WOULD he, look — he who, with his so nobly handsome face, could look such wonderful things — in case of being left alone with some of the subjects of his wonder? There were subjects for wonder among these very neighbours; only Maggie herself had her own odd way — which didn't moreover the least irritate him — of really liking them in proportion as they could strike her as strange. It came out in her by heredity, he amused himself with declaring, this love of chinoiseries; but she actually this evening didn't mind — he might deal with her Chinese as he could.

Maggie indeed would always have had for such moments, had they oftener occurred, the impression made on her by a word of Mrs. Assingham's, a word referring precisely to that appetite in Amerigo for the explanatory which we have just found in our path. It wasn't that the Princess could be indebted to another person, even to so clever a one as this friend, for seeing anything in her husband that she mightn't see unaided; but she had ever, hitherto, been of a nature to accept with modest gratitude any better description of a felt truth than her little limits — terribly marked, she knew, in the direction of saying the right things — enabled her to make. Thus it was, at any rate, that she was able to live more or less in the light of the fact expressed so lucidly by their common comforter — the fact that the Prince was saving up, for some very mysterious but very fine eventual purpose, all the wisdom, all the answers to his questions, all the impressions and generalisations, he gathered; putting them away and packing them down because he wanted his great gun to be loaded to the brim on the day he should decide to let it off. He wanted first to make sure of the whole of the subject that was unrolling itself before him; after which the innumerable facts he had collected would find their use. He knew what he was about — — trust him at last therefore to make, and to some effect, his big noise. And Mrs. Assingham had repeated that he knew what he was about. It was the happy form of this assurance that had remained with Maggie; it could always come in for her that Amerigo knew what he was about. He might at moments seem vague, seem absent, seem even bored: this when, away from her father, with whom it was impossible for him to appear anything but respectfully occupied, he let his native gaiety go in outbreaks of song, or even of quite whimsical senseless sound, either expressive of intimate relaxation or else fantastically plaintive. He might at times reflect with the frankest lucidity on the circumstance that the case was for a good while yet absolutely settled in regard to what he still had left, at home, of his very own; in regard to the main seat of his affection, the house in Rome, the big black palace, the Palazzo Nero, as he was fond of naming it, and also on the question of the villa in the Sabine hills, which she had, at the time of their engagement, seen and yearned over, and the Castello proper, described by him always as the "perched" place, that had, as she knew, formerly stood up, on the pedestal of its mountain-slope, showing beautifully blue from afar, as the head and front of the princedom. He might rejoice in certain moods over the so long-estranged state of these properties, not indeed all irreclaimably alienated, but encumbered with unending leases and charges, with obstinate occupants, with impossibilities of use — all without counting the cloud of mortgages that had, from far back, buried them beneath the ashes of rage and remorse, a shroud as thick as the layer once resting on the towns at the foot of Vesuvius, and actually making of any present restorative effort a process much akin to slow excavation. Just so he might with another turn of his humour almost wail for these brightest spots of his lost paradise, declaring that he was an idiot not to be able to bring himself to face the sacrifices — sacrifices resting, if definitely anywhere, with Mr. Verver — necessary for winning them back.

One of the most comfortable things between the husband and the wife meanwhile — one of those easy certitudes they could be merely gay about — was that she never admired him so much, or so found him heartbreakingly handsome, clever, irresistible, in the very degree in which he had originally and fatally dawned upon her, as when she saw other women reduced to the same passive pulp that had then begun, once for all, to constitute HER substance. There was really nothing they had talked of together with more intimate and familiar pleasantry than of the license and privilege, the boundless happy margin, thus established for each: she going so far as to put it that, even should he some day get drunk and beat her, the spectacle of him with hated rivals would, after no matter what extremity, always, for the sovereign charm of it, charm of it in itself and as the exhibition of him that most deeply moved her, suffice to bring her round. What would therefore be more open to him than to keep her in love with him? He agreed, with all his heart, at these light moments, that his course wouldn't then be difficult, inasmuch as, so simply constituted as he was on all the precious question — and why should he be ashamed of it? — he knew but one way with the fair. They had to be fair — and he was fastidious and particular, his standard was high; but when once this was the case what relation with them was conceivable, what relation was decent, rudimentary, properly human, but that of a plain interest in the fairness? His interest, she always answered, happened not to be "plain," and plainness, all round, had little to do with the matter, which was marked, on the contrary, by the richest variety of colour; but the working basis, at all events, had been settled — the Miss Maddocks of life been assured of their importance for him. How conveniently assured Maggie — to take him too into the joke — had more than once gone so far as to mention to her father; since it fell in easily with the tenderness of her disposition to remember she might occasionally make him happy by an intimate confidence. This was one of her rules-full as she was of little rules, considerations, provisions. There were things she of course couldn't tell him, in so many words, about Amerigo and herself, and about their happiness and their union and their deepest depths — and there were other things she needn't; but there were also those that were both true and amusing, both communicable and real, and of these, with her so conscious, so delicately cultivated scheme of conduct as a daughter, she could make her profit at will. A pleasant hush, for that matter, had fallen on most of the elements while she lingered apart with her companion; it involved, this serenity, innumerable complete assumptions: since so ordered and so splendid a rest, all the tokens, spreading about them, of confidence solidly supported, might have suggested for persons of poorer pitch the very insolence of facility. Still, they weren't insolent — THEY weren't, our pair could reflect; they were only blissful and grateful and personally modest, not ashamed of knowing, with competence, when great things were great, when good things were good, and when safe things were safe, and not, therefore, placed below their fortune by timidity which would have been as bad as being below it by impudence. Worthy of it as they were, and as each appears, under our last possible analysis, to have wished to make the other feel that they were, what they most finally exhaled into the evening air as their eyes mildly met may well have been a kind of helplessness in their felicity. Their rightness, the justification of everything — something they so felt the pulse of — sat there with them; but they might have been asking themselves a little blankly to what further use they could put anything so perfect. They had created and nursed and established it; they had housed it here in dignity and crowned it with comfort; but mightn't the moment possibly count for them — or count at least for us while we watch them with their fate all before them — as the dawn of the discovery that it doesn't always meet ALL contingencies to be right? Otherwise why should Maggie have found a word of definite doubt — the expression of the fine pang determined in her a few hours before — rise after a time to her lips? She took so for granted moreover her companion's intelligence of her doubt that the mere vagueness of her question could say it all. "What is it, after all, that they want to do to you?" "They" were for the Princess too the hovering forces of which Mrs. Rance was the symbol, and her father, only smiling back now, at his ease, took no trouble to appear not to know what she meant. What she meant — when once she had spoken — could come out well enough; though indeed it was nothing, after they had come to the point, that could serve as ground for a great defensive campaign. The waters of talk spread a little, and Maggie presently contributed an idea in saying: "What has really happened is that the proportions, for us, are altered." He accepted equally, for the time, this somewhat cryptic remark; he still failed to challenge her even when she added that it wouldn't so much matter if he hadn't been so terribly young. He uttered a sound of protest only when she went to declare that she ought as a daughter, in common decency, to have waited. Yet by that time she was already herself admitting that she should have had to wait long — if she waited, that is, till he was old. But there was a way. "Since you ARE an irresistible youth, we've got to face it. That, somehow, is what that woman has made me feel. There'll be others."

X

To talk of it thus appeared at last a positive relief to him. "Yes, there'll be others. But you'll see me through."

She hesitated. "Do you mean if you give in?"

"Oh no. Through my holding out."

Maggie waited again, but when she spoke it had an effect of abruptness. "Why SHOULD you hold out forever?"

He gave, none the less, no start — and this as from the habit of taking anything, taking everything, from her as harmonious. But it was quite written upon him too, for that matter, that holding out wouldn't be, so very completely, his natural, or at any rate his acquired, form. His appearance would have testified that he might have to do so a long time — for a man so greatly beset. This appearance, that is, spoke but little, as yet, of short remainders and simplified senses — and all in spite of his being a small, spare, slightly stale person, deprived of the general prerogative of presence. It was not by mass or weight or vulgar immediate quantity that he would in the future, any more than he had done in the past, insist or resist or prevail. There was even something in him that made his position, on any occasion, made his relation to any scene or to any group, a matter of the back of the stage, of an almost visibly conscious want of affinity with the footlights. He would have figured less than anything the stage-manager or the author of the play, who most occupy the foreground; he might be, at the best, the financial "backer," watching his interests from the wing, but in rather confessed ignorance of the mysteries of mimicry. Barely taller than his daughter, he pressed at no point on the presumed propriety of his greater stoutness. He had lost early in life much of his crisp, closely-curling hair, the fineness of which was repeated in a small neat beard, too compact to be called "full," though worn equally, as for a mark where other marks were wanting, on lip and cheek and chin. His neat, colourless face, provided with the merely indispensable features, suggested immediately, for a description, that it was CLEAR, and in this manner somewhat resembled a small decent room, clean-swept and unencumbered with furniture, but drawing a particular advantage, as might presently be noted, from the outlook of a pair of ample and uncurtained windows. There was something in Adam Verver's eyes that both admitted the morning and the evening in unusual quantities and gave the modest area the outward extension of a view that was "big" even when restricted to stars. Deeply and changeably blue, though not romantically large, they were yet youthfully, almost strangely beautiful, with their ambiguity of your scarce knowing if they most carried their possessor's vision out or most opened themselves to your own. Whatever you might feel, they stamped the place with their importance, as the house-agents say; so that, on one side or the other, you were never out of their range, were moving about, for possible community, opportunity, the sight of you scarce knew what, either before them or behind them. If other importances, not to extend the question, kept themselves down, they were in no direction less obtruded than in that of our friend's dress, adopted once for all as with a sort of sumptuary scruple. He wore every day of the year, whatever the occasion, the same little black "cut away" coat, of the fashion of his younger time; he wore the same cool-looking trousers, chequered in black and white — the proper harmony with which, he inveterately considered, was a sprigged blue satin necktie; and, over his concave little stomach, quaintly indifferent to climates and seasons, a white duck waistcoat. "Should you really," he now asked, "like me to marry?" He spoke as if, coming from his daughter herself, it MIGHT be an idea; which, for that matter, he would be ready to carry out should she definitely say so.

Definite, however, just yet, she was not prepared to be, though it seemed to come to her with force, as she thought, that there was a truth, in the connection, to utter. "What I feel is that there is somehow something that used to be right and that I've made wrong. It used to be right that you hadn't married, and that you didn't seem to want to. It used also" — she continued to make out "to seem easy for the question not to come up. That's what I've made different. It does come up. It WILL come up."

"You don't think I can keep it down?" Mr. Verver's tone was cheerfully pensive.

"Well, I've given you, by MY move, all the trouble of having to."

He liked the tenderness of her idea, and it made him, as she sat near him, pass his arm about her. "I guess I don't feel as if you had 'moved' very far. You've only moved next door."

"Well," she continued, "I don't feel as if it were fair for me just to have given you a push and left you so. If I've made the difference for you, I must think of the difference."

"Then what, darling," he indulgently asked, "DO you think?"

"That's just what I don't yet know. But I must find out. We must think together — as we've always thought. What I mean," she went on after a moment, "is that it strikes me that I ought to at least offer you some alternative. I ought to have worked one out for you."

"An alternative to what?"

"Well, to your simply missing what you've lost — without anything being done about it."

"But what HAVE I lost?"

She thought a minute, as if it were difficult to say, yet as if she more and more saw it. "Well, whatever it was that, BEFORE, kept us from thinking, and kept you, really, as you might say, in the market. It was as if you couldn't be in the market when you were married to me. Or rather as if I kept people off, innocently, by being married to you. Now that I'm married to some one else you're, as in consequence, married to nobody. Therefore you may be married to anybody, to everybody. People don't see why you shouldn't be married to THEM."

"Isn't it enough of a reason," he mildly inquired, "that I don't want to be?"

"It's enough of a reason, yes. But to BE enough of a reason it has to be too much of a trouble. I mean FOR you. It has to be too much of a fight. You ask me what you've lost," Maggie continued to explain. "The not having to take the trouble and to make the fight — that's what you've lost. The advantage, the happiness of being just as you were — because I was just as I was — that's what you miss."

"So that you think," her father presently said, "that I had better get married just in order to be as I was before?"

The detached tone of it — detached as if innocently to amuse her by showing his desire to accommodate — was so far successful as to draw from her gravity a short, light laugh. "Well, what I don't want you to feel is that if you were to I shouldn't understand. I SHOULD understand. That's all," said the Princess gently.

Her companion turned it pleasantly over. "You don't go so far as to wish me to take somebody I don't like?"

"Ah, father," she sighed, "you know how far I go — how far I COULD go. But I only wish that if you ever SHOULD like anybody, you may never doubt of my feeling how I've brought you to it. You'll always know that I know that it's my fault."

"You mean," he went on in his contemplative way, "that it will be you who'll take the consequences?"

Maggie just considered. "I'll leave you all the good ones, but I'll take the bad."

"Well, that's handsome." He emphasised his sense of it by drawing her closer and holding her more tenderly. "It's about all I could expect of you. So far as you've wronged me, therefore, we'll call it square. I'll let you know in time if I see a prospect of your having to take it up. But am I to understand meanwhile," he soon went on, "that, ready as you are to see me through my collapse, you're not ready, or not AS ready, to see me through my resistance? I've got to be a regular martyr before you'll be inspired?"

She demurred at his way of putting it. "Why, if you like it, you know, it won't BE a collapse."

"Then why talk about seeing me through at all? I shall only collapse if I do like it. But what I seem to feel is that I don't WANT to like it. That is," he amended, "unless I feel surer I do than appears very probable. I don't want to have to THINK I like it in a case when I really shan't. I've had to do that in some cases," he confessed —"when it has been a question of other things. I don't want," he wound up, "to be MADE to make a mistake."

"Ah, but it's too dreadful," she returned, "that you should even have to FEAR — or just nervously to dream — that you may be. What does that show, after all," she asked, "but that you do really, well within, feel a want? What does it show but that you're truly susceptible?"

"Well, it may show that" — he defended himself against nothing. "But it shows also, I think, that charming women are, in the kind of life we're leading now, numerous and formidable."

Maggie entertained for a moment the proposition; under cover of which, however, she passed quickly from the general to the particular. "Do you feel Mrs. Rance to be charming?"

"Well, I feel her to be formidable. When they cast a spell it comes to the same thing. I think she'd do anything."

"Oh well, I'd help you," the Princess said with decision, "as against HER — if that's all you require. It's too funny," she went on before he again spoke, "that Mrs. Rance should be here at all. But if you talk of the life we lead, much of it is, altogether, I'm bound to say, too funny. The thing is," Maggie developed under this impression, "that I don't think we lead, as regards other people, any life at all. We don't at any rate, it seems to me, lead half the life we might. And so it seems, I think, to Amerigo. So it seems also, I'm sure, to Fanny Assingham."

Mr. Verver-as if from due regard for these persons — considered a little. "What life would they like us to lead?"

"Oh, it's not a question, I think, on which they quite feel together. SHE thinks, dear Fanny, that we ought to be greater."

"Greater —?" He echoed it vaguely. "And Amerigo too, you say?"

"Ah yes"-her reply was prompt "but Amerigo doesn't mind. He doesn't care, I mean, what we do. It's for us, he considers, to see things exactly as we wish. Fanny herself," Maggie pursued, "thinks he's magnificent. Magnificent, I mean, for taking everything as it is, for accepting the 'social limitations' of our life, for not missing what we don't give him."

Mr. Verver attended. "Then if he doesn't miss it his magnificence is easy."

"It IS easy-that's exactly what I think. If there were things he DID miss, and if in spite of them he were always sweet, then, no doubt, he would be a more or less unappreciated hero. He COULD be a Hero — he WILL be one if it's ever necessary. But it will be about something better than our dreariness. *I* know," the Princess declared, "where he's magnificent." And she rested a minute on that. She ended, however, as she had begun. "We're not, all the same, committed to anything stupid. If we ought to be grander, as Fanny thinks, we CAN be grander. There's nothing to prevent."

"Is it a strict moral obligation?" Adam Verver inquired.

"No — it's for the amusement."

"For whose? For Fanny's own?"

"For everyone's — though I dare say Fanny's would be a large part." She hesitated; she had now, it might have appeared, something more to bring out, which she finally produced. "For yours in particular, say — if you go into the question." She even bravely followed it up. "I haven't really, after all, had to think much to see that much more can be done for you than is done."

Mr. Verver uttered an odd vague sound. "Don't you think a good deal is done when you come out and talk to me this way?"

"Ah," said his daughter, smiling at him, "we make too much of that!" And then to explain: "That's good, and it's natural — but it isn't great. We forget that we're as free as air."

"Well, THAT'S great," Mr. Verver pleaded. "Great if we act on it. Not if we don't."

She continued to smile, and he took her smile; wondering again a little by this time, however; struck more and more by an intensity in it that belied a light tone. "What do you want," he demanded, "to do to me?" And he added, as she didn't say: "You've got something in your mind." It had come to him within the minute that from the beginning of their session there she had been keeping something back, and that an impression of this had more than once, in spite of his general theoretic respect for her present right to personal reserves and mysteries, almost ceased to be vague in him. There had been from the first something in her anxious eyes, in the way she occasionally lost herself, that it would perfectly explain. He was therefore now quite sure.

"You've got something up your sleeve."

She had a silence that made him right. "Well, when I tell you you'll understand. It's only up my sleeve in the sense of being in a letter I got this morning. All day, yes — it HAS been in my mind. I've been asking myself if it were quite the right moment, or in any way fair, to ask you if you could stand just now another woman."

It relieved him a little, yet the beautiful consideration of her manner made it in a degree portentous. "Stand" one —?"

"Well, mind her coming."

He stared — then he laughed. It depends on who she is."

"There — you see! I've at all events been thinking whether you'd take this particular person but as a worry the more. Whether, that is, you'd go so far with her in your notion of having to be kind."

He gave at this the quickest shake to his foot. How far would she go in HER notion of it.

"Well," his daughter returned, "you know how far, in a general way, Charlotte Stant goes."

"Charlotte? Is SHE coming?"

"She writes me, practically, that she'd like to if we're so good as to ask her."

Mr. Verver continued to gaze, but rather as if waiting for more. Then, as everything appeared to have come, his expression had a drop. If this was all it was simple. "Then why in the world not?"

Maggie's face lighted anew, but it was now another light. "It isn't a want of tact?"

"To ask her?"

"To propose it to you."

"That *I* should ask her?"

He put the question as an effect of his remnant of vagueness, but this had also its own effect. Maggie wondered an instant; after which, as with a flush of recognition, she took it up. "It would be too beautiful if you WOULD!"

This, clearly, had not been her first idea — the chance of his words had prompted it. "Do you mean write to her myself?"

"Yes — it would be kind. It would be quite beautiful of you. That is, of course," said Maggie, "if you sincerely CAN."

He appeared to wonder an instant why he sincerely shouldn't, and indeed, for that matter, where the question of sincerity came in. This virtue, between him and his daughter's friend, had surely been taken for granted. "My dear child," he returned, "I don't think I'm afraid of Charlotte."

"Well, that's just what it's lovely to have from you. From the moment you're NOT — the least little bit — I'll immediately invite her."

"But where in the world is she?" He spoke as if he had not thought of Charlotte, nor so much as heard her name pronounced, for a very long time. He quite in fact amicably, almost amusedly, woke up to her.

"She's in Brittany, at a little bathing-place, with some people I don't know. She's always with people, poor dear — she rather has to be; even when, as is sometimes the case; they're people she doesn't immensely like."

"Well, I guess she likes US," said Adam Verver. "Yes — fortunately she likes us. And if I wasn't afraid of spoiling it for you," Maggie added, "I'd even mention that you're not the one of our number she likes least."

"Why should that spoil it for me?"

"Oh, my dear, you know. What else have we been talking about? It costs you so much to be liked. That's why I hesitated to tell you of my letter."

He stared a moment — as if the subject had suddenly grown out of recognition. "But Charlotte — on other visits — never used to cost me anything."

"No — only her 'keep,'" Maggie smiled.

"Then I don't think I mind her keep — if that's all." The Princess, however, it was clear, wished to be thoroughly conscientious. "Well, it may not be quite all. If I think of its being pleasant to have her, it's because she WILL make a difference."

"Well, what's the harm in that if it's but a difference for the better?"

"Ah then — there you are!" And the Princess showed in her smile her small triumphant wisdom. "If you acknowledge a possible difference for the better we're not, after all, so tremendously right as we are. I mean we're not — as satisfied and amused. We do see there are ways of being grander."

"But will Charlotte Stant," her father asked with surprise, "make us grander?"

Maggie, on this, looking at him well, had a remarkable reply. "Yes, I think. Really grander."

He thought; for if this was a sudden opening he wished but the more to meet it. "Because she's so handsome?"

"No, father." And the Princess was almost solemn. "Because she's so great."

"Great —?"

"Great in nature, in character, in spirit. Great in life."

"So?" Mr. Verver echoed. "What has she done — in life?"

"Well, she has been brave and bright," said Maggie. "That mayn't sound like much, but she has been so in the face of things that might well have made it too difficult for many other girls. She hasn't a creature in the world really — that is nearly — belonging to her. Only acquaintances who, in all sorts of ways, make use of her, and distant relations who are so afraid she'll make use of THEM that they seldom let her look at them."

Mr. Verver was struck — and, as usual, to some purpose. "If we get her here to improve us don't we too then make use of her?"

It pulled the Princess up, however, but an instant. "We're old, old friends — we do her good too. I should always, even at the worst — speaking for myself — admire her still more than I used her."

"I see. That always does good."

Maggie hesitated. "Certainly — she knows it. She knows, I mean, how great I think her courage and her cleverness. She's not afraid — not of anything; and yet she no more ever takes a liberty with you than if she trembled for her life. And then she's INTERESTING — which plenty of other people with plenty of other merits never are a bit." In which fine flicker of vision the truth widened to the Princess's view. "I myself of course don't take liberties, but then I do, always, by nature, tremble for my life. That's the way I live."

"Oh I say, love!" her father vaguely murmured.

"Yes, I live in terror," she insisted. "I'm a small creeping thing."

"You'll not persuade me that you're not as good as Charlotte Stant," he still placidly enough remarked.

"I may be as good, but I'm not so great — and that's what we're talking about. She has a great imagination. She has, in every way, a great attitude. She has above all a great conscience." More perhaps than ever in her life before Maggie addressed her father at this moment with a shade of the absolute in her tone. She had never come so near telling him what he should take it from her to believe. "She has only twopence in the world — but that has nothing to do with it. Or rather indeed" — she quickly corrected herself —"it has everything. For she doesn't care. I never saw her do anything but laugh at her poverty. Her life has been harder than anyone knows."

It was moreover as if, thus unprecedentedly positive, his child had an effect upon him that Mr. Verver really felt as a new thing. "Why then haven't you told me about her before?"

"Well, haven't we always known —?"

"I should have thought," he submitted, "that we had already pretty well sized her up."

"Certainly — we long ago quite took her for granted. But things change, with time, and I seem to know that, after this interval, I'm going to like her better than ever. I've lived more myself, I'm older, and one judges better. Yes, I'm going to see in Charlotte," said the Princess — and speaking now as with high and free expectation —"more than I've ever seen."

"Then I'll try to do so too. She WAS" — it came back to Mr. Verver more —"the one of your friends I thought the best for you."

His companion, however, was so launched in her permitted liberty of appreciation that she for the moment scarce heard him. She was lost in the case she made out, the vision of the different ways in which Charlotte had distinguished herself.

"She would have liked for instance — I'm sure she would have liked extremely — to marry; and nothing in general is more ridiculous, even when it has been pathetic, than a woman who has tried and has not been able."

It had all Mr. Verver's attention. "She has 'tried' —?"

"She has seen cases where she would have liked to."

"But she has not been able?"

"Well, there are more cases, in Europe, in which it doesn't come to girls who are poor than in which it does come to them. Especially," said Maggie with her continued competence, "when they're Americans."

Well, her father now met her, and met her cheerfully, on all sides. "Unless you mean," he suggested, "that when the girls are American there are more cases in which it comes to the rich than to the poor."

She looked at him good-humouredly. "That may be-but I'm not going to be smothered in MY case. It ought to make me — if I were in danger of being a fool — all the nicer to people like Charlotte. It's not hard for ME," she practically explained, "not to be ridiculous — unless in a very different way. I might easily be ridiculous, I suppose, by behaving as if I thought I had done a great thing. Charlotte, at any rate, has done nothing, and anyone can see it, and see also that it's rather strange; and yet no one — no one not awfully presumptuous or offensive would like, or would dare, to treat her, just as she is, as anything but quite RIGHT. That's what it is to have something about you that carries things off."

Mr. Verver's silence, on this, could only be a sign that she had caused her story to interest him; though the sign when he spoke was perhaps even sharper. "And is it also what you mean by Charlotte's being 'great'?"

"Well," said Maggie, "it's one of her ways. But she has many."

Again for a little her father considered. "And who is it she has tried to marry?"

Maggie, on her side as well, waited as if to bring it out with effect; but she after a minute either renounced or encountered an obstacle. "I'm afraid I'm not sure."

"Then how do you know?"

"Well, I don't KNOW" — and, qualifying again, she was earnestly emphatic. "I only make it out for myself."

"But you must make it out about someone in particular."

She had another pause. "I don't think I want even for myself to put names and times, to pull away any veil. I've an idea there has been, more than once, somebody I'm not acquainted with — and needn't be or want to be. In any case it's all over, and, beyond giving her credit for everything, it's none of my business."

Mr. Verver deferred, yet he discriminated. "I don't see how you can give credit without knowing the facts."

"Can't I give it — generally — for dignity? Dignity, I mean, in misfortune."

"You've got to postulate the misfortune first."

"Well," said Maggie, "I can do that. Isn't it always a misfortune to be-when you're so fine — so wasted? And yet," she went on, "not to wail about it, not to look even as if you knew it?"

Mr. Verver seemed at first to face this as a large question, and then, after a little, solicited by another view, to let the appeal drop. "Well, she mustn't be wasted. We won't at least have waste."

It produced in Maggie's face another gratitude. "Then, dear sir, that's all I want."

And it would apparently have settled their question and ended their talk if her father had not, after a little, shown the disposition to revert. "How many times are you supposing that she has tried?"

Once more, at this, and as if she hadn't been, couldn't be, hated to be, in such delicate matters, literal, she was moved to attenuate. "Oh, I don't say she absolutely ever TRIED —!"

He looked perplexed. "But if she has so absolutely failed, what then had she done?"

"She has suffered — she has done that." And the Princess added: "She has loved — and she has lost."

Mr. Verver, however, still wondered. "But how many times."

Maggie hesitated, but it cleared up. "Once is enough. Enough, that is, for one to be kind to her."

Her father listened, yet not challenging — only as with a need of some basis on which, under these new lights, his bounty could be firm. "But has she told you nothing?"

"Ah, thank goodness, no!"

He stared. "Then don't young women tell?"

"Because, you mean, it's just what they're supposed to do?" She looked at him, flushed again now; with which, after another hesitation, "Do young men tell?" she asked.

He gave a short laugh. "How do I know, my dear, what young men do?"

"Then how do I know, father, what vulgar girls do?"

"I see — I see," he quickly returned.

But she spoke the next moment as if she might, odiously, have been sharp. "What happens at least is that where there's a great deal of pride there's a great deal of silence. I don't know, I admit, what I should do if I were lonely and sore — for what sorrow, to speak of, have I ever had in my life? I don't know even if I'm proud — it seems to me the question has never come up for me."

"Oh, I guess you're proud, Mag," her father cheerfully interposed. "I mean I guess you're proud enough."

"Well then, I hope I'm humble enough too. I might, at all events, for all I know, be abject under a blow. How can I tell? Do you realise, father, that I've never had the least blow?"

He gave her a long, quiet look. "Who SHOULD realise if I don't?"

"Well, you'll realise when I HAVE one!" she exclaimed with a short laugh that resembled, as for good reasons, his own of a minute before. "I wouldn't in any case have let her tell me what would have been dreadful to me. For such wounds and shames are dreadful: at least," she added, catching herself up, "I suppose they are; for what, as I say, do I know of them? I don't WANT to know!" — she spoke quite with vehemence. "There are things that are sacred whether they're joys or pains. But one can always, for safety, be kind," she kept on; "one feels when that's right."

She had got up with these last words; she stood there before him with that particular suggestion in her aspect to which even the long habit of their life together had not closed his sense, kept sharp, year after year, by the collation of types and signs, the comparison of fine object with fine object, of one degree of finish, of one form of the exquisite with another — the appearance of some slight, slim draped "antique" of Vatican or Capitoline halls, late and refined, rare as a note and immortal as a link, set in motion by the miraculous infusion of a modern impulse and yet, for all the sudden freedom of folds and footsteps forsaken after centuries by their pedestal, keeping still the quality, the perfect felicity, of the statue; the blurred, absent eyes, the smoothed, elegant, nameless head, the impersonal flit of a creature lost in an alien age and passing as an image in worn relief round and round a precious vase. She had always had odd moments of striking him, daughter of his very own though she was, as a figure thus simplified, "generalised" in its grace, a figure with which his human connection was fairly interrupted by some vague analogy of turn and attitude, something shyly mythological and nymphlike. The trick, he was not uncomplacently aware, was mainly of his own mind; it came from his caring for precious vases only less than for precious daughters. And what was more to the point still, it often operated while he was quite at the same time conscious that Maggie had been described, even in her prettiness, as "prim" — Mrs. Rance herself had enthusiastically used the word of her; while he remembered that when once she had been told before him, familiarly, that she resembled a nun, she had replied that she was delighted to hear it and would certainly try to; while also, finally, it was present to him that, discreetly heedless, thanks to her long association with nobleness in art, to the leaps and bounds of fashion, she brought her hair down very straight and flat over her temples, in the constant manner of her mother, who had not been a bit mythological. Nymphs and nuns were certainly separate types, but Mr. Verver, when he really amused himself, let consistency go. The play of vision was at all events so rooted in him that he could receive impressions of sense even while positively thinking. He was positively thinking while Maggie stood there, and it led for him to yet another question — which in its turn led to others still. "Do you regard the condition as hers then that you spoke of a minute ago?"

"The condition —?"

"Why that of having loved so intensely that she's, as you say, 'beyond everything'?"

Maggie had scarcely to reflect — her answer was so prompt. "Oh no. She's beyond nothing. For she has had nothing."

"I see. You must have had things to be them. It's a kind of law of perspective."

Maggie didn't know about the law, but she continued definite. "She's not, for example, beyond help."

"Oh well then, she shall have all we can give her. I'll write to her," he said, "with pleasure."

"Angel!" she answered as she gaily and tenderly looked at him.

True as this might be, however, there was one thing more — he was an angel with a human curiosity. "Has she told you she likes me much?"

"Certainly she has told me — but I won't pamper you. Let it be enough for you it has always been one of my reasons for liking HER."

"Then she's indeed not beyond everything," Mr. Verver more or less humorously observed.

"Oh it isn't, thank goodness, that she's in love with you. It's not, as I told you at first, the sort of thing for you to fear."

He had spoken with cheer, but it appeared to drop before this reassurance, as if the latter overdid his alarm, and that should be corrected. "Oh, my dear, I've always thought of her as a little girl."

"Ah, she's not a little girl," said the Princess.

"Then I'll write to her as a brilliant woman."

"It's exactly what she is."

Mr. Verver had got up as he spoke, and for a little, before retracing their steps, they stood looking at each other as if they had really arranged something. They had come out together for themselves, but it had produced something more. What it had produced was in fact expressed by the words with which he met his companion's last emphasis. "Well, she has a famous friend in you, Princess."

Maggie took this in-it was too plain for a protest. "Do you know what I'm really thinking of?" she asked.

He wondered, with her eyes on him — eyes of contentment at her freedom now to talk; and he wasn't such a fool, he presently showed, as not, suddenly, to arrive at it. "Why, of your finding her at last yourself a husband."

"Good for YOU!" Maggie smiled. "But it will take," she added, "some looking."

"Then let me look right here with you," her father said as they walked on.

XI

Mrs. Assingham and the Colonel, quitting Fawns before the end of September, had come back later on; and now, a couple of weeks after, they were again interrupting their stay, but this time with the question of their return left to depend, on matters that were rather hinted at than importunately named. The Lutches and Mrs. Rance had also, by the action of Charlotte Stant's arrival, ceased to linger, though with hopes and theories, as to some promptitude of renewal, of which the lively expression, awakening the echoes of the great stone-paved, oak-panelled, galleried hall that was not the least interesting feature of the place, seemed still a property of the air. It was on this admirable spot that, before her October afternoon had waned, Fanny Assingham spent with her easy host a few moments which led to her announcing her own and her husband's final secession, at the same time as they tempted her to point the moral of all vain reverberations. The double door of the house stood open to an effect of hazy autumn sunshine, a wonderful, windless, waiting, golden hour, under the influence of which Adam Verver met his genial friend as she came to drop into the post-box with her own hand a thick sheaf of letters. They presently thereafter left the house together and drew out half-an-hour on the terrace in a manner they were to revert to in thought, later on, as that of persons who really had been taking leave of each other at a parting of the ways. He traced his impression, on coming to consider, back to a mere three words she had begun by using about Charlotte Stant. She simply "cleared them out" — those had been the three words, thrown off in reference to the general golden peace that the Kentish October had gradually ushered in, the "halcyon" days the full beauty of which had appeared to shine out for them after Charlotte's arrival. For it was during these days that Mrs. Rance and the Miss Lutches had been observed to be gathering themselves for departure, and it was with that difference made that the sense of the whole situation showed most fair — the sense of how right they had been to engage for so ample a residence, and of all the pleasure so fruity an autumn there could hold in its lap. This was what had occurred, that their lesson had been learned; and what Mrs. Assingham had dwelt upon was that without Charlotte it would have been learned but half. It would certainly not have been taught by Mrs. Rance and the Miss Lutches if these ladies had remained with them as long as at one time seemed probable. Charlotte's light intervention had thus become a cause, operating covertly but none the less actively, and Fanny Assingham's speech, which she had followed up a little, echoed within him, fairly to startle him, as the indication of something irresistible. He could see now how this superior force had worked, and he fairly liked to recover the sight — little harm as he dreamed of doing, little ill as he dreamed of wishing, the three ladies, whom he had after all entertained for a stiffish series of days. She had been so vague and quiet about it, wonderful Charlotte, that he hadn't known what was happening — happening, that is, as a result of her influence. "Their fires, as they felt her, turned to smoke," Mrs. Assingham remarked; which he was to reflect on indeed even while they strolled. He had retained, since his long talk with Maggie — the talk that had settled the matter of his own direct invitation to her friend — an odd little taste, as he would have described it, for hearing things said about this young woman, hearing, so to speak, what COULD be said about her: almost as it her portrait, by some eminent hand, were going on, so that he watched it grow under the multiplication of touches. Mrs. Assingham, it struck him, applied two or three of the finest in their discussion of their young friend — so different a figure now from that early playmate of Maggie's as to whom he could almost recall from of old the definite occasions of his having paternally lumped the two children together in the recommendation that they shouldn't make too much noise nor eat too much jam. His companion professed that in the light of Charlotte's prompt influence she had not been a stranger to a pang of pity for their recent visitors. "I felt in fact, privately, so sorry for them, that I kept my impression to myself while they were here — wishing not to put the rest of you on the scent; neither Maggie, nor the Prince, nor yourself, nor even Charlotte HERself, if you didn't happen to notice. Since you didn't, apparently, I perhaps now strike you as extravagant. But I'm not — I followed it all. One SAW the consciousness I speak of come over the poor things, very much as I suppose people at the court of the Borgias may have watched each other begin to look queer after having had the honour of taking wine with the heads of the family. My comparison's only a little awkward, for I don't in the least mean that Charlotte was consciously dropping poison into their cup. She was just herself their poison, in the sense of mortally disagreeing with them — but she didn't know it."

"Ah, she didn't know it?" Mr. Verver had asked with interest.

"Well, I THINK she didn't" — Mrs. Assingham had to admit that she hadn't pressingly sounded her. "I don't pretend to be sure, in every connection, of what Charlotte knows. She doesn't, certainly, like to make people suffer — not, in general, as is the case with so many of us, even other women: she likes much rather to put them at their ease with her. She likes, that is — as all pleasant people do — to be liked."

"Ah, she likes to be liked?" her companion had gone on.

"She did, at the same time, no doubt, want to help us — to put us at our ease. That is she wanted to put you — and to put Maggie about you. So far as that went she had a plan. But it was only AFTER — it was not before, I really believe — that she saw how effectively she could work."

Again, as Mr. Verver felt, he must have taken it up. "Ah, she wanted to help us? — wanted to help ME?"

"Why," Mrs. Assingham asked after an instant, "should it surprise you?"

He just thought. "Oh, it doesn't!"

"She saw, of course, as soon as she came, with her quickness, where we all were. She didn't need each of us to go, by appointment, to her room at night, or take her out into the fields, for our palpitating tale. No doubt even she was rather impatient."

"OF the poor things?" Mr. Verver had here inquired while he waited.

"Well, of your not yourselves being so — and of YOUR not in particular. I haven't the least doubt in the world, par exemple, that she thinks you too meek."

"Oh, she thinks me too meek?"

"And she had been sent for, on the very face of it, to work right in. All she had to do, after all, was to be nice to you."

"To — a — ME?" said Adam Verver.

He could remember now that his friend had positively had a laugh for his tone. "To you and to every one. She had only to be what she is — and to be it all round. If she's charming, how can she help it? So it was, and so only, that she 'acted'-as the Borgia wine used to act. One saw it come over them — the extent to which, in her particular way, a woman, a woman other, and SO other, than themselves, COULD be charming. One saw them understand and exchange looks, then one saw them lose heart and decide to move. For what they had to take home was that it's she who's the real thing."

"Ah, it's she who's the real thing?" As HE had not hitherto taken it home as completely as the Miss Lutches and Mrs. Rance, so, doubtless, he had now, a little, appeared to offer submission in his appeal. "I see, I see" — he could at least simply take it home now; yet as not without wanting, at the same time, to be sure of what the real thing was. "And what would it be-a — definitely that you understand by that?"

She had only for an instant not found it easy to say. "Why, exactly what those women themselves want to be, and what her effect on them is to make them recognise that they never will."

"Oh — of course never?"

It not only remained and abode with them, it positively developed and deepened, after this talk, that the luxurious side of his personal existence was now again furnished, socially speaking, with the thing classed and stamped as "real" — just as he had been able to think of it as not otherwise enriched in consequence of his daughter's marriage. The note of reality, in so much projected light, continued to have for him the charm and the importance of which the maximum had occasionally been reached in his great "finds" — continued, beyond any other, to keep him attentive and gratified. Nothing perhaps might affect us as queerer, had we time to look into it, than this application of the same measure of value to such different pieces of property as old Persian carpets, say, and new human acquisitions; all the more indeed that the amiable man was not without an inkling, on his own side, that he was, as a taster of life, economically constructed. He put into his one little glass everything he raised to his lips, and it was as if he had always carried in his pocket, like a tool of his trade, this receptacle, a little glass cut with a fineness of which the art had long since been lost, and kept in an old morocco case stamped in uneffaceable gilt with the arms of a deposed dynasty. As it had served him to satisfy himself, so to speak, both about Amerigo and about the Bernadino Luini he had happened to come to knowledge of at the time he was consenting to the announcement of his daughter's betrothal, so it served him at present to satisfy himself about Charlotte Stant and an extraordinary set of oriental tiles of which he had lately got wind, to which a provoking legend was attached, and as to which he had made out, contentedly, that further news was to be obtained from a certain Mr. Gutermann-Seuss of Brighton. It was all, at bottom, in him, the aesthetic principle, planted where it could burn with a cold, still flame; where it fed almost wholly on the material directly involved, on the idea (followed by appropriation) of plastic beauty, of the thing visibly perfect in its kind; where, in short, in spite of the general tendency of the "devouring element" to spread, the rest of his spiritual furniture, modest, scattered, and tended with unconscious care, escaped the consumption that in so many cases proceeds from the undue keeping-up of profane altar-fires. Adam Verver had in other words learnt the lesson of the senses, to the end of his own little book, without having, for a day, raised the smallest scandal in his economy at large; being in this particular not unlike those fortunate bachelors, or other gentlemen of pleasure, who so manage their entertainment of compromising company that even the austerest housekeeper, occupied and competent below-stairs, never feels obliged to give warning.

That figure has, however, a freedom that the occasion doubtless scarce demands, though we may retain it for its rough negative value. It was to come to pass, by a pressure applied to the situation wholly from within, that before the first ten days of November had elapsed he found himself practically alone at Fawns with his young friend; Amerigo and Maggie having, with a certain abruptness, invited his assent to their going abroad for a month, since his amusement was now scarce less happily assured than his security. An impulse eminently natural had stirred within the Prince; his life, as for some time established, was deliciously dull, and thereby, on the whole, what he best liked; but a small gust of yearning had swept over him, and Maggie repeated to her father, with infinite admiration, the pretty terms in which, after it had lasted a little, he had described to her this experience. He called it a "serenade," a low music that, outside one of the windows of the sleeping house, disturbed his rest at night. Timid as it was, and plaintive, he yet couldn't close his eyes for it, and when finally, rising on tiptoe, he had looked out, he had recognised in the figure below with a mandolin, all duskily draped in her grace, the raised appealing eyes and the one irresistible voice of the ever-to-beloved Italy. Sooner or later, that way, one had to listen; it was a hovering, haunting ghost, as of a creature to whom one had done a wrong, a dim, pathetic shade crying out to be comforted. For this there was obviously but one way — as there were doubtless also many words for the simple fact that so prime a Roman had a fancy for again seeing Rome. They would accordingly — hadn't they better? — go for a little; Maggie meanwhile making the too-absurdly artful point with her father, so that he repeated it, in his amusement, to Charlotte Stant, to whom he was by this time conscious of addressing many remarks, that it was absolutely, when she came to think, the first thing Amerigo had ever asked of her. "She doesn't count of course his having asked of her to marry him" — this was Mr. Verver's indulgent criticism; but he found Charlotte, equally touched by the ingenuous Maggie, in easy agreement with him over the question. If the Prince had asked something of his wife every day in the year, this would be still no reason why the poor dear man should not, in a beautiful fit of homesickness, revisit, without reproach, his native country.

What his father-in-law frankly counselled was that the reasonable, the really too reasonable, pair should, while they were about it, take three or four weeks of Paris as well — Paris being always, for Mr. Verver, in any stress of sympathy, a suggestion that rose of itself to the lips.

If they would only do that, on their way back, or however they preferred it, Charlotte and he would go over to join them there for a small look — though even then, assuredly, as he had it at heart to add, not in the least because they should have found themselves bored at being left together. The fate of this last proposal indeed was that it reeled, for the moment, under an assault of destructive analysis from Maggie, who — having, as she granted, to choose between being an unnatural daughter or an unnatural mother, and "electing" for the former — wanted to know what would become of the Principino if the house were cleared of everyone but the servants. Her question had fairly resounded, but it had afterwards, like many of her questions, dropped still more effectively than it had risen: the highest moral of the matter being, before the couple took their departure, that Mrs. Noble and Dr. Brady must mount unchallenged guard over the august little crib. If she hadn't supremely believed in the majestic value of the nurse, whose experience was in itself the amplest of pillows, just as her attention was a spreading canopy from which precedent and reminiscence dropped as thickly as parted curtains — if she hadn't been able to rest in this confidence she would fairly have sent her husband on his journey without her. In the same manner, if the sweetest — for it was so she qualified him — of little country doctors hadn't proved to her his wisdom by rendering irresistible, especially on rainy days and in direct proportion to the frequency of his calls, adapted to all weathers, that she should converse with him for hours over causes and consequences, over what he had found to answer with his little five at home, she would have drawn scant support from the presence of a mere grandfather and a mere brilliant friend. These persons, accordingly, her own predominance having thus, for the time, given way, could carry with a certain ease, and above all with mutual aid, their consciousness of a charge. So far as their office weighed they could help each other with it — which was in fact to become, as Mrs. Noble herself loomed larger for them, not a little of a relief and a diversion.

Mr. Verver met his young friend, at certain hours, in the day-nursery, very much as he had regularly met the child's fond mother — Charlotte having, as she clearly considered, given Maggie equal pledges and desiring never to fail of the last word for the daily letter she had promised to write. She wrote with high fidelity, she let her companion know, and the effect of it was, remarkably enough, that he himself didn't write. The reason of this was partly that Charlotte "told all about him" — which she also let him know she did — and partly that he enjoyed feeling, as a consequence, that he was generally, quite systematically, eased and, as they said, "done" for. Committed, as it were, to this charming and clever young woman, who, by becoming for him a domestic resource, had become for him practically a new person — and committed, especially, in his own house, which somehow made his sense of it a deeper thing — he took an interest in seeing how far the connection could carry him, could perhaps even lead him, and in thus putting to the test, for pleasant verification, what Fanny Assingham had said, at the last, about the difference such a girl could make. She was really making one now, in their simplified existence, and a very considerable one, though there was no one to compare her with, as there had been, so usefully, for Fanny — no Mrs. Rance, no Kitty, no Dotty Lutch, to help her to be felt, according to Fanny's diagnosis, as real. She was real, decidedly, from other causes, and Mr. Verver grew in time even a little amused at the amount of machinery Mrs. Assingham had seemed to see needed for pointing it. She was directly and immediately real, real on a pleasantly reduced and intimate scale, and at no moments more so than during those — at which we have just glanced — when Mrs. Noble made them both together feel that she, she alone, in the absence of the queen-mother, was regent of the realm and governess of the heir. Treated on such occasions as at best a pair of dangling and merely nominal court-functionaries, picturesque hereditary triflers entitled to the petites entrees but quite external to the State, which began and ended with the Nursery, they could only retire, in quickened sociability, to what was left them of the Palace, there to digest their gilded insignificance and cultivate, in regard to the true Executive, such snuff-taking ironies as might belong to rococo chamberlains moving among china lap-dogs.

Every evening, after dinner, Charlotte Stant played to him; seated at the piano and requiring no music, she went through his "favourite things" — and he had many favourites — with a facility that never failed, or that failed but just enough to pick itself up at a touch from his fitful voice. She could play anything, she could play everything — always shockingly, she of course insisted, but always, by his own vague measure, very much as if she might, slim, sinuous and strong, and with practised passion, have been playing lawn-tennis or endlessly and rhythmically waltzing. His love of music, unlike his other loves, owned to vaguenesses, but while, on his comparatively shaded sofa, and smoking, smoking, always smoking, in the great Fawns drawing-room as everywhere, the cigars of his youth, rank with associations — while, I say, he so listened to Charlotte's piano, where the score was ever absent but, between the lighted candles, the picture distinct, the vagueness spread itself about him like some boundless carpet, a surface delightfully soft to the pressure of his interest. It was a manner of passing the time that rather replaced conversation, but the air, at the end, none the less, before they separated, had a way of seeming full of the echoes of talk. They separated, in the hushed house, not quite easily, yet not quite awkwardly either, with tapers that twinkled in the large dark spaces, and for the most part so late that the last solemn servant had been dismissed for the night.

Late as it was on a particular evening toward the end of October, there had been a full word or two dropped into the still-stirring sea of other voices — a word or two that affected our friend even at the moment, and rather oddly, as louder and rounder than any previous sound; and then he had lingered, under pretext of an opened window to be made secure, after taking leave of his companion in the hall and watching her glimmer away up the staircase. He had for himself another impulse than to go to bed; picking up a hat in the hall, slipping his arms into a sleeveless cape and lighting still another cigar, he turned out upon the terrace through one of the long drawing-room windows and moved to and fro there for an hour beneath the sharp autumn stars. It was where he had walked in the afternoon sun with Fanny Assingham, and the sense of that other hour, the sense of the suggestive woman herself, was before him again as, in spite of all the previous degustation we have hinted at, it had not yet been. He thought, in a loose, an almost agitated order, of many things; the power that was in them to agitate having been part of his conviction that he should not soon sleep. He truly felt for a while that he should never sleep again till something had come to him; some light, some idea, some mere happy word perhaps, that he had begun to want, but had been till now, and especially the last day or two, vainly groping for. "Can you really then come if we start early?" — that was practically all he had said to the girl as she took up her bedroom light. And "Why in the world not, when I've nothing else to do, and should, besides, so immensely like it?" — this had as definitely been, on her side, the limit of the little scene. There had in fact been nothing to call a scene, even of the littlest, at all — though he perhaps didn't quite know why something like the menace of one hadn't proceeded from her stopping half-way upstairs to turn and say, as she looked down on him, that she promised to content herself, for their journey, with a toothbrush and a sponge. There hovered about him, at all events, while he walked, appearances already familiar, as well as two or three that were new, and not the least vivid of the former connected itself with that sense of being treated with consideration which had become for him, as we have noted, one of the minor yet so far as there were any such, quite one of the compensatory, incidents of being a father-inlaw. It had struck him, up to now, that this particular balm was a mixture of which Amerigo, as through some hereditary privilege, alone possessed the secret; so that he found himself wondering if it had come to Charlotte, who had unmistakably acquired it, through the young man's having amiably passed it on. She made use, for her so quietly grateful host, however this might be, of quite the same shades of attention and recognition, was mistress in an equal degree of the regulated, the developed art of placing him high in the scale of importance. That was even for his own thought a clumsy way of expressing the element of similarity in the agreeable effect they each produced on him, and it held him for a little only because this coincidence in their felicity caused him vaguely to connect or associate them in the matter of tradition, training, tact, or whatever else one might call it. It might almost have been — if such a link between them was to be imagined — that Amerigo had, a little, "coached" or incited their young friend, or perhaps rather that she had simply, as one of the signs of the general perfection Fanny Assingham commended in her, profited by observing, during her short opportunity before the start of the travellers, the pleasant application by the Prince of his personal system. He might wonder what exactly it was that they so resembled each other in treating him like — from what noble and propagated convention, in cases in which the exquisite "importance" was to be neither too grossly attributed nor too grossly denied, they had taken their specific lesson; but the difficulty was here of course that one could really never know — couldn't know without having been one's self a personage; whether a Pope, a King, a President, a Peer, a General, or just a beautiful Author.

Before such a question, as before several others when they recurred, he would come to a pause, leaning his arms on the old parapet and losing himself in a far excursion. He had as to so many of the matters in hand a divided view, and this was exactly what made him reach out, in his unrest, for some idea, lurking in the vast freshness of the night, at the breath of which disparities would submit to fusion, and so, spreading beneath him, make him feel that he floated. What he kept finding himself return to, disturbingly enough, was the reflection, deeper than anything else, that in forming a new and intimate tie he should in a manner abandon, or at the best signally relegate, his daughter. He should reduce to definite form the idea that he had lost her — as was indeed inevitable — by her own marriage; he should reduce to definite form the idea of his having incurred an injury, or at the best an inconvenience, that required some makeweight and deserved some amends. And he should do this the more, which was the great point, that he should appear to adopt, in doing it, the sentiment, in fact the very conviction, entertained, and quite sufficiently expressed, by Maggie herself, in her beautiful generosity, as to what he had suffered — putting it with extravagance — at her hands. If she put it with extravagance the extravagance was yet sincere, for it came — which she put with extravagance too — from her persistence, always, in thinking, feeling, talking about him, as young. He had had glimpses of moments when to hear her thus, in her absolutely unforced compunction, one would have supposed the special edge of the wrong she had done him to consist in his having still before him years and years to groan under it. She had sacrificed a parent, the pearl of parents, no older than herself: it wouldn't so much have mattered if he had been of common parental age. That he wasn't, that he was just her extraordinary equal and contemporary, this was what added to her act the long train of its effect. Light broke for him at last, indeed, quite as a consequence of the fear of breathing a chill upon this luxuriance of her spiritual garden. As at a turn of his labyrinth he saw his issue, which opened out so wide, for the minute, that he held his breath with wonder. He was afterwards to recall how, just then, the autumn night seemed to clear to a view in which the whole place, everything round him, the wide terrace where he stood, the others, with their steps, below, the gardens, the park, the lake, the circling woods, lay there as under some strange midnight sun. It all met him during these instants as a vast expanse of discovery, a world that looked, so lighted, extraordinarily new, and in which familiar objects had taken on a distinctness that, as if it had been a loud, a spoken pretension to beauty, interest, importance, to he scarce knew what, gave them an inordinate quantity of character and, verily, an inordinate size. This hallucination, or whatever he might have called it, was brief, but it lasted long enough to leave him gasping. The gasp of admiration had by this time, however, lost itself in an intensity that quickly followed — the way the wonder of it, since wonder was in question, truly had been the strange DELAY of his vision. He had these several days groped and groped for an object that lay at his feet and as to which his blindness came from his stupidly looking beyond. It had sat all the while at his hearth-stone, whence it now gazed up in his face.

Once he had recognised it there everything became coherent. The sharp point to which all his light converged was that the whole call of his future to him, as a father, would be in his so managing that Maggie would less and less appear to herself to have forsaken him. And it not only wouldn't be decently humane, decently possible, not to make this relief easy to her — the idea shone upon him, more than that, as exciting, inspiring, uplifting. It fell in so beautifully with what might be otherwise possible; it stood there absolutely confronted with the material way in which it might be met. The way in which it might be met was by his putting his child at peace, and the way to put her at peace was to provide for his future — that is for hers — by marriage, by a marriage as good, speaking proportionately, as hers had been. As he fairly inhaled this measure of refreshment he tasted the meaning of recent agitations. He had seen that Charlotte could contribute — what he hadn't seen was what she could contribute TO. When it had all supremely cleared up and he had simply settled this service to his daughter well before him as the proper direction of his young friend's leisure, the cool darkness had again closed round him, but his moral lucidity was constituted. It wasn't only moreover that the word, with a click, so fitted the riddle, but that the riddle, in such perfection, fitted the word. He might have been equally in want and yet not have had his remedy. Oh, if Charlotte didn't accept him, of course the remedy would fail; but, as everything had fallen together, it was at least there to be tried. And success would be great — that was his last throb — if the measure of relief effected for Maggie should at all prove to have been given by his own actual sense of felicity. He really didn't know when in his life he had thought of anything happier. To think of it merely for himself would have been, even as he had just lately felt, even doing all justice to that condition — yes, impossible. But there was a grand difference in thinking of it for his child.

XII

It was at Brighton, above all, that this difference came out; it was during the three wonderful days he spent there with Charlotte that he had acquainted himself further — though doubtless not even now quite completely — with the merits of his majestic scheme. And while, moreover, to begin with, he still but held his vision in place, steadying it fairly with his hands, as he had often steadied, for inspection, a precarious old pot or kept a glazed picture in its right relation to the light, the other, the outer presumptions in his favour, those independent of what he might himself contribute and that therefore, till he should "speak," remained necessarily vague — that quantity, I say, struck him as positively multiplying, as putting on, in the fresh Brighton air and on the sunny Brighton front, a kind of tempting palpability. He liked, in this preliminary stage, to feel that he should be able to "speak" and that he would; the word itself being romantic, pressing for him the spring of association with stories and plays where handsome and ardent young men, in uniforms, tights, cloaks, high-boots, had it, in soliloquies, ever on their lips; and the sense on the first day that he should probably have taken the great step before the second was over conduced already to make him say to his companion that they must spend more than their mere night or two. At his ease on the ground of what was before him he at all events definitely desired to be, and it was strongly his impression that he was proceeding step by step. He was acting — it kept coming back to that — not in the dark, but in the high golden morning; not in precipitation, flurry, fever, dangers these of the path of passion properly so called, but with the deliberation of a plan, a plan that might be a thing of less joy than a passion, but that probably would, in compensation for that loss, be found to have the essential property, to wear even the decent dignity, of reaching further and of providing for more contingencies. The season was, in local parlance, "on," the elements were assembled; the big windy hotel, the draughty social hall, swarmed with "types," in Charlotte's constant phrase, and resounded with a din in which the wild music of gilded and befrogged bands, Croatian, Dalmatian, Carpathian, violently exotic and nostalgic, was distinguished as struggling against the perpetual popping of corks. Much of this would decidedly have disconcerted our friends if it hadn't all happened, more preponderantly, to give them the brighter surprise. The noble privacy of Fawns had left them — had left Mr. Verver at least — with a little accumulated sum of tolerance to spend on the high pitch and high colour of the public sphere. Fawns, as it had been for him, and as Maggie and Fanny Assingham had both attested, was out of the world, whereas the scene actually about him, with the very sea a mere big booming medium for excursions and aquariums, affected him as so plump in the conscious centre that nothing could have been more complete for representing that pulse of life which they had come to unanimity at home on the subject of their advisedly not hereafter forgetting. The pulse of life was what Charlotte, in her way, at home, had lately reproduced, and there were positively current hours when it might have been open to her companion to feel himself again indebted to her for introductions. He had "brought" her, to put it crudely, but it was almost as if she were herself, in her greater gaiety, her livelier curiosity and intensity, her readier, happier irony, taking him about and showing him the place. No one, really, when he came to think, had ever taken him about before — it had always been he, of old, who took others and who in particular took Maggie. This quickly fell into its relation with him as part of an experience — marking for him, no doubt, what people call, considerately, a time of life; a new and pleasant order, a flattered passive state, that might become — why shouldn't it? — one of the comforts of the future.

Mr. Gutermann-Seuss proved, on the second day — our friend had waited till then — a remarkably genial, a positively lustrous young man occupying a small neat house in a quarter of the place remote from the front and living, as immediate and striking signs testified, in the bosom of his family. Our visitors found themselves introduced, by the operation of close contiguity, to a numerous group of ladies and gentlemen older and younger, and of children larger and smaller, who mostly affected them as scarce less anointed for hospitality and who produced at first the impression of a birthday party, of some anniversary gregariously and religiously kept, though they subsequently fell into their places as members of one quiet domestic circle, preponderantly and directly indebted for their being, in fact, to Mr. Gutermann-Seuss. To the casual eye a mere smart and shining youth of less than thirty summers, faultlessly appointed in every particular, he yet stood among his progeny — eleven in all, as he confessed without a sigh, eleven little brown clear faces, yet with such impersonal old eyes astride of such impersonal old noses — while he entertained the great American collector whom he had so long hoped he might meet, and whose charming companion, the handsome, frank, familiar young lady, presumably Mrs. Verver, noticed the graduated offspring, noticed the fat, ear-ringed aunts and the glossy, cockneyfied, familiar uncles, inimitable of accent and assumption, and of an attitude of cruder intention than that of the head of the firm; noticed the place in short, noticed the treasure produced, noticed everything, as from the habit of a person finding her account at any time, according to a wisdom well learned of life, in almost any "funny" impression. It really came home to her friend on the spot that this free range of observation in her, picking out the frequent funny with extraordinary promptness, would verily henceforth make a different thing for him of such experiences, of the customary hunt for the possible prize, the inquisitive play of his accepted monomania; which different thing could probably be a lighter and perhaps thereby a somewhat more boisterously refreshing form of sport. Such omens struck him as vivid, in any case, when Mr. Gutermann-Seuss, with a sharpness of discrimination he had at first scarce seemed to promise, invited his eminent couple into another room, before the threshold of which the rest of the tribe, unanimously faltering, dropped out of the scene. The treasure itself here, the objects on behalf of which Mr. Verver's interest had been booked, established quickly enough their claim to engage the latter's attention; yet at what point of his past did our friend's memory, looking back and back, catch him, in any such place, thinking so much less of wares artfully paraded than of some other and quite irrelevant presence? Such places were not strange to him when they took the form of bourgeois back-parlours, a trifle ominously grey and grim from their north light, at watering-places prevailingly homes of humbug, or even when they wore some aspect still less, if not perhaps still more, insidious. He had been everywhere, pried and prowled everywhere, going, on occasion, so far as to risk, he believed, life, health and the very bloom of honour; but where, while precious things, extracted one by one from thrice-locked yet often vulgar drawers and soft satchels of old oriental ilk, were impressively ranged before him, had he, till now, let himself, in consciousness, wander like one of the vague?

He didn't betray it — ah THAT he knew; but two recognitions took place for him at once, and one of them suffered a little in sweetness by the confusion. Mr. Gutermann-Seuss had truly, for the crisis, the putting down of his cards, a rare manner; he was perfect master of what not to say to such a personage as Mr. Verver while the particular importance that dispenses with chatter was diffused by his movements themselves, his repeated act of passage between a featureless mahogany meuble and a table so virtuously disinterested as to look fairly smug under a cotton cloth of faded maroon and indigo, all redolent of patriarchal teas. The Damascene tiles, successively, and oh so tenderly, unmuffled and revealed, lay there at last in their full harmony and their venerable splendour, but the tribute of appreciation and decision was, while the spectator considered, simplified to a point that but just failed of representing levity on the part of a man who had always acknowledged without shame, in such affairs, the intrinsic charm of what was called discussion. The infinitely ancient, the immemorial amethystine blue of the glaze, scarcely more meant to be breathed upon, it would seem, than the cheek of royalty — this property of the ordered and matched array had inevitably all its determination for him, but his submission was, perhaps for the first time in his life, of the quick mind alone, the process really itself, in its way, as fine as the perfection perceived and admired: every inch of the rest of him being given to the foreknowledge that an hour or two later he should have "spoken." The burning of his ships therefore waited too near to let him handle his opportunity with his usual firm and sentient fingers — waited somehow in the predominance of Charlotte's very person, in her being there exactly as she was, capable, as Mr. Gutermann-Seuss himself was capable, of the right felicity of silence, but with an embracing ease, through it all, that made deferred criticism as fragrant as some joy promised a lover by his mistress, or as a big bridal bouquet held patiently behind her. He couldn't otherwise have explained, surely, why he found himself thinking, to his enjoyment, of so many other matters than the felicity of his acquisition and the figure of his cheque, quite equally high; any more than why, later on, with their return to the room in which they had been received and the renewed encompassment of the tribe, he felt quite merged in the elated circle formed by the girl's free response to the collective caress of all the shining eyes, and by her genial acceptance of the heavy cake and port wine that, as she was afterwards to note, added to their transaction, for a finish, the touch of some mystic rite of old Jewry.

This characterisation came from her as they walked away — walked together, in the waning afternoon, back to the breezy sea and the bustling front, back to the nimble and the flutter and the shining shops that sharpened the grin of solicitation on the mask of night. They were walking thus, as he felt, nearer and nearer to where he should see his ships burn, and it was meanwhile for him quite as if this red glow would impart, at the harmonious hour, a lurid grandeur to his good faith. It was meanwhile too a sign of the kind of sensibility often playing up in him that — fabulous as this truth may sound — he found a sentimental link, an obligation of delicacy, or perhaps even one of the penalties of its opposite, in his having exposed her to the north light, the quite properly hard business-light, of the room in which they had been alone with the treasure and its master. She had listened to the name of the sum he was capable of looking in the face. Given the relation of intimacy with him she had already, beyond all retractation, accepted, the stir of the air produced at the other place by that high figure struck him as a thing that, from the moment she had exclaimed or protested as little as he himself had apologised, left him but one thing more to do. A man of decent feeling didn't thrust his money, a huge lump of it, in such a way, under a poor girl's nose — a girl whose poverty was, after a fashion, the very basis of her enjoyment of his hospitality — without seeing, logically, a responsibility attached. And this was to remain none the less true for the fact that twenty minutes later, after he had applied his torch, applied it with a sign or two of insistence, what might definitely result failed to be immediately clear. He had spoken — spoken as they sat together on the out-of-the-way bench observed during one of their walks and kept for the previous quarter of the present hour well in his memory's eye; the particular spot to which, between intense pauses and intenser advances, he had all the while consistently led her. Below the great consolidated cliff, well on to where the city of stucco sat most architecturally perched, with the rumbling beach and the rising tide and the freshening stars in front and above, the safe sense of the whole place yet prevailed in lamps and seats and flagged walks, hovering also overhead in the close neighbourhood of a great replete community about to assist anew at the removal of dish-covers.

"We've had, as it seems to me, such quite beautiful days together, that I hope it won't come to you too much as a shock when I ask if you think you could regard me with any satisfaction as a husband." As if he had known she wouldn't, she of course couldn't, at all gracefully, and whether or no, reply with a rush, he had said a little more — quite as he had felt he must in thinking it out in advance. He had put the question on which there was no going back and which represented thereby the sacrifice of his vessels, and what he further said was to stand for the redoubled thrust of flame that would make combustion sure. "This isn't sudden to me, and I've wondered at moments if you haven't felt me coming to it. I've been coming ever since we left Fawns — I really started while we were there." He spoke slowly, giving her, as he desired, time to think; all the more that it was making her look at him steadily, and making her also, in a remarkable degree, look "well" while she did so — a large and, so far, a happy, consequence. She wasn't at all events shocked — which he had glanced at but for a handsome humility — and he would give her as many minutes as she liked. "You mustn't think I'm forgetting that I'm not young."

"Oh, that isn't so. It's I that am old. You ARE young." This was what she had at first answered — and quite in the tone too of having taken her minutes. It had not been wholly to the point, but it had been kind — which was what he most wanted. And she kept, for her next words, to kindness, kept to her clear, lowered voice and unshrinking face. "To me too it thoroughly seems that these days have been beautiful. I shouldn't be grateful to them if I couldn't more or less have imagined their bringing us to this." She affected him somehow as if she had advanced a step to meet him and yet were at the same time standing still. It only meant, however, doubtless, that she was, gravely and reasonably, thinking — as he exactly desired to make her. If she would but think enough she would probably think to suit him. "It seems to me," she went on, "that it's for YOU to be sure."

"Ah, but I AM sure," said Adam Verver. "On matters of importance I never speak when I'm not. So if you can yourself FACE such a union you needn't in the least trouble."

She had another pause, and she might have been felt as facing it while, through lamplight and dusk, through the breath of the mild, slightly damp southwest, she met his eyes without evasion. Yet she had at the end of another minute debated only to the extent of saying: "I won't pretend I don't think it would be good for me to marry. Good for me, I mean," she pursued, "because I'm so awfully unattached. I should like to be a little less adrift. I should like to have a home. I should like to have an existence. I should like to have a motive for one thing more than another — a motive outside of myself. In fact," she said, so sincerely that it almost showed pain, yet so lucidly that it almost showed humour, "in fact, you know, I want to BE married. It's — well, it's the condition."

"The condition —?" He was just vague.

"It's the state, I mean. I don't like my own. 'Miss,' among us all, is too dreadful — except for a shopgirl. I don't want to be a horrible English old-maid."

"Oh, you want to be taken care of. Very well then, I'll do it."

"I dare say it's very much that. Only I don't see why, for what I speak of," she smiled —"for a mere escape from my state — I need do quite so MUCH."

"So much as marry me in particular?"

Her smile was as for true directness. "I might get what I want for less."

"You think it so much for you to do?"

"Yes," she presently said, "I think it's a great deal."

Then it was that, though she was so gentle, so quite perfect with him, and he felt he had come on far — then it was that of a sudden something seemed to fail and he didn't quite know where they were. There rose for him, with this, the fact, to be sure, of their disparity, deny it as mercifully and perversely as she would. He might have been her father. "Of course, yes — that's my disadvantage: I'm not the natural, I'm so far from being the ideal match to your youth and your beauty. I've the drawback that you've seen me always, so inevitably, in such another light."

But she gave a slow headshake that made contradiction soft — made it almost sad, in fact, as from having to be so complete; and he had already, before she spoke, the dim vision of some objection in her mind beside which the one he had named was light, and which therefore must be strangely deep. "You don't understand me. It's of all that it is for YOU to do — it's of that I'm thinking."

Oh, with this, for him, the thing was clearer! "Then you needn't think. I know enough what it is for me to do."

But she shook her head again. "I doubt if you know. I doubt if you CAN."

"And why not, please — when I've had you so before me? That I'm old has at least THAT fact about it to the good — that I've known you long and from far back."

"Do you think you've 'known' me?" asked Charlotte Stant. He hesitated — for the tone of it, and her look with it might have made him doubt. Just these things in themselves, however, with all the rest, with his fixed purpose now, his committed deed, the fine pink glow, projected forward, of his ships, behind him, definitely blazing and crackling — this quantity was to push him harder than any word of her own could warn him. All that she was herself, moreover, was so lighted, to its advantage, by the pink glow. He wasn't rabid, but he wasn't either, as a man of a proper spirit, to be frightened. "What is that then — if I accept it — but as strong a reason as I can want for just LEARNING to know you?"

She faced him always — kept it up as for honesty, and yet at the same time, in her odd way, as for mercy. "How can you tell whether if you did you would?"

It was ambiguous for an instant, as she showed she felt. "I mean when it's a question of learning, one learns sometimes too late."

"I think it's a question," he promptly enough made answer, "of liking you the more just for your saying these things. You should make something," he added, "of my liking you."

"I make everything. But are you sure of having exhausted all other ways?"

This, of a truth, enlarged his gaze. "But what other ways?"

"Why, you've more ways of being kind than anyone I ever knew."

"Take it then," he answered, "that I'm simply putting them all together for you." She looked at him, on this, long again — still as if it shouldn't be said she hadn't given him time or had withdrawn from his view, so to speak, a single inch of her surface. This at least she was fully to have exposed. It represented her as oddly conscientious, and he scarce knew in what sense it affected him. On the whole, however, with admiration. "You're very, very honourable."

"It's just what I want to be. I don't see," she added, "why you're not right, I don't see why you're not happy, as you are. I can not ask myself, I can not ask YOU," she went on, "if you're really as much at liberty as your universal generosity leads you to assume. Oughtn't we," she asked, "to think a little of others? Oughtn't I, at least, in loyalty — at any rate in delicacy — to think of Maggie?" With which, intensely gentle, so as not to appear too much to teach him his duty, she explained. "She's everything to you — she has always been. Are you so certain that there's room in your life —?"

"For another daughter? — is that what you mean?" She had not hung upon it long, but he had quickly taken her up.

He had not, however, disconcerted her. "For another young woman — very much of her age, and whose relation to her has always been so different from what our marrying would make it. For another companion," said Charlotte Stant.

"Can't a man be, all his life then," he almost fiercely asked, "anything but a father?" But he went on before she could answer. "You talk about differences, but they've been already made — as no one knows better than Maggie. She feels the one she made herself by her own marriage — made, I mean, for me. She constantly thinks of it — it allows her no rest. To put her at peace is therefore," he explained, "what I'm trying, with you, to do. I can't do it alone, but I can do it with your help. You can make her," he said, "positively happy about me."

"About you?" she thoughtfully echoed. "But what can I make her about herself?"

"Oh, if she's at ease about me the rest will take care of itself. The case," he declared, "is in your hands. You'll effectually put out of her mind that I feel she has abandoned me."

Interest certainly now was what he had kindled in her face, but it was all the more honourable to her, as he had just called it that she should want to see each of the steps of his conviction. "If you've been driven to the 'likes' of me, mayn't it show that you've felt truly forsaken?"

"Well, I'm willing to suggest that, if I can show at the same time that I feel consoled."

"But HAVE you," she demanded, "really felt so?" He hesitated.

"Consoled?"

"Forsaken."

"No — I haven't. But if it's her idea —!" If it was her idea, in short, that was enough. This enunciation of motive, the next moment, however, sounded to him perhaps slightly thin, so that he gave it another touch. "That is if it's my idea. I happen, you see, to like my idea."

"Well, it's beautiful and wonderful. But isn't it, possibly," Charlotte asked, "not quite enough to marry me for?"

"Why so, my dear child? Isn't a man's idea usually what he does marry for?"

Charlotte, considering, looked as if this might perhaps be a large question, or at all events something of an extension of one they were immediately concerned with. "Doesn't that a good deal depend on the sort of thing it may be?" She suggested that, about marriage, ideas, as he called them, might differ; with which, however, giving no more time to it, she sounded another question. "Don't you appear rather to put it to me that I may accept your offer for Maggie's sake? Somehow" — she turned it over — "I don't so clearly SEE her quite so much finding reassurance, or even quite so much needing it."

"Do you then make nothing at all of her having been so ready to leave us?"

Ah, Charlotte on the contrary made much! "She was ready to leave us because she had to be. From the moment the Prince wanted it she could only go with him."

"Perfectly — so that, if you see your way, she will be able to 'go with him' in future as much as she likes."

Charlotte appeared to examine for a minute, in Maggie's interest, this privilege — the result of which was a limited concession. "You've certainly worked it out!"

"Of course I've worked it out — that's exactly what I HAVE done. She hadn't for a long time been so happy about anything as at your being there with me."

"I was to be with you," said Charlotte, "for her security."

"Well," Adam Verver rang out, "this IS her security. You've only, if you can't see it, to ask her."

"'Ask' her?" — the girl echoed it in wonder. "Certainly — in so many words. Telling her you don't believe me."

Still she debated. "Do you mean write it to her?"

"Quite so. Immediately. To-morrow."

"Oh, I don't think I can write it," said Charlotte Stant. "When I write to her" — and she looked amused for so different a shade — "it's about the Principino's appetite and Dr. Brady's visits."

"Very good then — put it to her face to face. We'll go straight to Paris to meet them."

Charlotte, at this, rose with a movement that was like a small cry; but her unspoken sense lost itself while she stood with her eyes on him — he keeping his seat as for the help it gave him, a little, to make his appeal go up. Presently, however, a new sense had come to her, and she covered him, kindly, with the expression of it. "I do think, you know, you must rather 'like' me."

"Thank you," said Adam Verver. "You WILL put it to her yourself then?"

She had another hesitation. "We go over, you say, to meet them?"

"As soon as we can get back to Fawns. And wait there for them, if necessary, till they come."

"Wait — a — at Fawns?"

"Wait in Paris. That will be charming in itself."

"You take me to pleasant places." She turned it over. "You propose to me beautiful things."

"It rests but with you to make them beautiful and pleasant. You've made Brighton —!"

"Ah!" — she almost tenderly protested. "With what I'm doing now?"

"You're promising me now what I want. Aren't you promising me," he pressed, getting up, "aren't you promising me to abide by what Maggie says?"

Oh, she wanted to be sure she was. "Do you mean she'll ASK it of me?"

It gave him indeed, as by communication, a sense of the propriety of being himself certain. Yet what was he but certain? "She'll speak to you. She'll speak to you FOR me."

This at last then seemed to satisfy her. "Very good. May we wait again to talk of it till she has done so?" He showed, with his hands down in his pockets and his shoulders expressively up, a certain disappointment. Soon enough, none the less, his gentleness was all back and his patience once more exemplary. "Of course I give you time. Especially," he smiled, "as it's time that I shall be spending with you. Our keeping on together will help you perhaps to see. To see, I mean, how I need you."

"I already see," said Charlotte, "how you've persuaded yourself you do." But she had to repeat it. "That isn't, unfortunately, all."

"Well then, how you'll make Maggie right."

"'Right'?" She echoed it as if the word went far. And "O — oh!" she still critically murmured as they moved together away.

XIII

He had talked to her of their waiting in Paris, a week later, but on the spot there this period of patience suffered no great strain. He had written to his daughter, not indeed from Brighton, but directly after their return to Fawns, where they spent only forty-eight hours before resuming their journey; and Maggie's reply to his news was a telegram from Rome, delivered to him at noon of their fourth day and which he brought out to Charlotte, who was seated at that moment in the court of the hotel, where they had agreed that he should join her for their proceeding together to the noontide meal. His letter, at Fawns — a letter of several pages and intended lucidly, unreservedly, in fact all but triumphantly, to inform — had proved, on his sitting down to it, and a little to his surprise, not quite so simple a document to frame as even his due consciousness of its weight of meaning had allowed him to assume: this doubtless, however, only for reasons naturally latent in the very wealth of that consciousness, which contributed to his message something of their own quality of impatience. The main result of their talk, for the time, had been a difference in his relation to his young friend, as well as a difference, equally sensible, in her relation to himself; and this in spite of his not having again renewed his undertaking to "speak" to her so far even as to tell her of the communication despatched to Rome. Delicacy, a delicacy more beautiful still, all the delicacy she should want, reigned between them — it being rudimentary, in their actual order, that she mustn't be further worried until Maggie should have put her at her ease.

It was just the delicacy, however, that in Paris — which, suggestively, was Brighton at a hundredfold higher pitch — made, between him and his companion, the tension, made the suspense, made what he would have consented perhaps to call the provisional peculiarity, of present conditions. These elements acted in a manner of their own, imposing and involving, under one head, many abstentions and precautions, twenty anxieties and reminders — things, verily, he would scarce have known how to express; and yet creating for them at every step an acceptance of their reality. He was hanging back, with Charlotte, till another person should intervene for their assistance, and yet they had, by what had already occurred, been carried on to something it was out of the power of other persons to make either less or greater. Common conventions — that was what was odd — had to be on this basis more thought of; those common conventions that, previous to the passage by the Brighton strand, he had so enjoyed the sense of their overlooking. The explanation would have been, he supposed — or would have figured it with less of unrest — that Paris had, in its way, deeper voices and warnings, so that if you went at all "far" there it laid bristling traps, as they might have been viewed, all smothered in flowers, for your going further still. There were strange appearances in the air, and before you knew it you might be unmistakably matching them. Since he wished therefore to match no appearance but that of a gentleman playing with perfect fairness any game in life he might be called to, he found himself, on the receipt of Maggie's missive, rejoicing with a certain inconsistency. The announcement made her from home had, in the act, cost some biting of his pen to sundry parts of him — his personal modesty, his imagination of her prepared state for so quick a jump, it didn't much matter which — and yet he was more eager than not for the drop of delay and for the quicker transitions promised by the arrival of the imminent pair. There was after all a hint of offence to a man of his age in being taken, as they said at the shops, on approval. Maggie, certainly, would have been as far as Charlotte herself from positively desiring this, and Charlotte, on her side, as far as Maggie from holding him light as a real value. She made him fidget thus, poor girl, but from generous rigour of conscience.

These allowances of his spirit were, all the same, consistent with a great gladness at the sight of the term of his ordeal; for it was the end of his seeming to agree that questions and doubts had a place. The more he had inwardly turned the matter over the more it had struck him that they had in truth only an ugliness. What he could have best borne, as he now believed, would have been Charlotte's simply saying to him that she didn't like him enough. This he wouldn't have enjoyed, but he would quite have understood it and been able ruefully to submit. She did like him enough — nothing to contradict that had come out for him; so that he was restless for her as well as for himself. She looked at him hard a moment when he handed her his telegram, and the look, for what he fancied a dim, shy fear in it, gave him perhaps his best moment of conviction that — as a man, so to speak — he properly pleased her. He said nothing — the words sufficiently did it for him, doing it again better still as Charlotte, who had left her chair at his approach, murmured them out. "We start to-night to bring you all our love and joy and sympathy." There they were, the words, and what did she want more? She didn't, however, as she gave him back the little unfolded leaf, say they were enough — though he saw, the next moment, that her silence was probably not disconnected from her having just visibly turned pale. Her extraordinarily fine eyes, as it was his present theory that he had always thought them, shone at him the more darkly out of this change of colour; and she had again, with it, her apparent way of subjecting herself, for explicit honesty and through her willingness to face him, to any view he might take, all at his ease, and even to wantonness, of the condition he produced in her. As soon as he perceived that emotion kept her soundless he knew himself deeply touched, since it proved that, little as she professed, she had been beautifully hoping. They stood there a minute while he took in from this sign that, yes then, certainly she liked him enough — liked him enough to make him, old as he was ready to brand himself, flush for the pleasure of it. The pleasure of it accordingly made him speak first. "Do you begin, a little, to be satisfied?"

Still, however, she had to think. "We've hurried them, you see. Why so breathless a start?"

"Because they want to congratulate us. They want," said Adam Verver, "to SEE our happiness."

She wondered again — and this time also, for him, as publicly as possible. "So much as that?"

"Do you think it's too much?"

She continued to think plainly. "They weren't to have started for another week."

"Well, what then? Isn't our situation worth the little sacrifice? We'll go back to Rome as soon as you like WITH them."

This seemed to hold her — as he had previously seen her held, just a trifle inscrutably, by his allusions to what they would do together on a certain contingency. "Worth it, the little sacrifice, for whom? For us, naturally — yes," she said. "We want to see them — for our reasons. That is," she rather dimly smiled, "YOU do."

"And you do, my dear, too!" he bravely declared. "Yes then — I do too," she after an instant ungrudging enough acknowledged. "For us, however, something depends on it."

"Rather! But does nothing depend on it for them?"

"What CAN — from the moment that, as appears, they don't want to nip us in the bud? I can imagine their rushing up to prevent us. But an enthusiasm for us that can wait so very little — such intense eagerness, I confess," she went on, "more than a little puzzles me. You may think me," she also added, "ungracious and suspicious, but the Prince can't at all want to come back so soon. He wanted quite too intensely to get away."

Mr. Verver considered. "Well, hasn't he been away?"

"Yes, just long enough to see how he likes it. Besides," said Charlotte, "he may not be able to join in the rosy view of our case that you impute to her. It can't in the least have appeared to him hitherto a matter of course that you should give his wife a bouncing stepmother."

Adam Verver, at this, looked grave. "I'm afraid then he'll just have to accept from us whatever his wife accepts; and accept it — if he can imagine no better reason — just because she does. That," he declared, "will have to do for him."

His tone made her for a moment meet his face; after which, "Let me," she abruptly said, "see it again" — taking from him the folded leaf that she had given back and he had kept in his hand. "Isn't the whole thing," she asked when she had read it over, "perhaps but a way like another for their gaining time?"

He again stood staring; but the next minute, with that upward spring of his shoulders and that downward pressure of his pockets which she had already, more than once, at disconcerted moments, determined in him, he turned sharply away and wandered from her in silence. He looked about in his small despair; he crossed the hotel court, which, overarched and glazed, muffled against loud sounds and guarded against crude sights, heated, gilded, draped, almost carpeted, with exotic trees in tubs, exotic ladies in chairs, the general exotic accent and presence suspended, as with wings folded or feebly fluttering, in the superior, the supreme, the inexorably enveloping Parisian medium, resembled some critical apartment of large capacity, some "dental," medical, surgical waiting-room, a scene of mixed anxiety and desire, preparatory, for gathered barbarians, to the due amputation or extraction of excrescences and redundancies of barbarism. He went as far as the porte-cochere, took counsel afresh of his usual optimism, sharpened even, somehow, just here, by the very air he tasted, and then came back smiling to Charlotte. "It is incredible to you that when a man is still as much in love as Amerigo his most natural impulse should be to feel what his wife feels, to believe what she believes, to want what she wants? — in the absence, that is, of special impediments to his so doing." The manner of it operated — she acknowledged with no great delay this natural possibility. "No — nothing is incredible to me of people immensely in love."

"Well, isn't Amerigo immensely in love?"

She hesitated but as for the right expression of her sense of the degree — but she after all adopted Mr. Verver's. "Immensely."

"Then there you are!"

She had another smile, however — she wasn't there quite yet. "That isn't all that's wanted."

"But what more?"

"Why that his wife shall have made him really believe that SHE really believes." With which Charlotte became still more lucidly logical. "The reality of his belief will depend in such a case on the reality of hers. The Prince may for instance now," she went on, "have made out to his satisfaction that Maggie may mainly desire to abound in your sense, whatever it is you do. He may remember that he has never seen her do anything else."

"Well," said Adam Verver, "what kind of a warning will he have found in that? To what catastrophe will he have observed such a disposition in her to lead?"

"Just to THIS one!" With which she struck him as rising straighter and clearer before him than she had done even yet.

"Our little question itself?" Her appearance had in fact, at the moment, such an effect on him that he could answer but in marvelling mildness. "Hadn't we better wait a while till we call it a catastrophe?"

Her rejoinder to this was to wait — though by no means as long as he meant. When at the end of her minute she spoke, however, it was mildly too. "What would you like, dear friend, to wait for?" It lingered between them in the air, this demand, and they exchanged for the time a look which might have made each of them seem to have been watching in the other the signs of its overt irony. These were indeed immediately so visible in Mr. Verver's face that, as if a little ashamed of having so markedly produced them — and as if also to bring out at last, under pressure, something she had all the while been keeping back — she took a jump to pure plain reason. "You haven't noticed for yourself, but I can't quite help noticing, that in spite of what you assume — WE assume, if you like — Maggie wires her joy only to you. She makes no sign of its overflow to me."

It was a point — and, staring a moment, he took account of it. But he had, as before, his presence of mind — to say nothing of his kindly humour. "Why, you complain of the very thing that's most charmingly conclusive! She treats us already as ONE."

Clearly now, for the girl, in spite of lucidity and logic, there was something in the way he said things —! She faced him in all her desire to please him, and then her word quite simply and definitely showed it. "I do like you, you know."

Well, what could this do but stimulate his humour? "I see what's the matter with you. You won't be quiet till you've heard from the Prince himself. I think," the happy man added, "that I'll go and secretly wire to him that you'd like, reply paid, a few words for yourself."

It could apparently but encourage her further to smile. "Reply paid for him, you mean — or for me?"

"Oh, I'll pay, with pleasure, anything back for you — as many words as you like." And he went on, to keep it up. "Not requiring either to see your message."

She could take it, visibly, as he meant it. "Should you require to see the Prince's?"

"Not a bit. You can keep that also to yourself."

On his speaking, however, as if his transmitting the hint were a real question, she appeared to consider — and almost as if for good taste — that the joke had gone far enough. "It doesn't matter. Unless he speaks of his own movement —! And why should it be," she asked, "a thing that WOULD occur to him?"

"I really think," Mr. Verver concurred, "that it naturally wouldn't. HE doesn't know you're morbid."

She just wondered — but she agreed. "No — he hasn't yet found it out. Perhaps he will, but he hasn't yet; and I'm willing to give him meanwhile the benefit of the doubt." So with this the situation, to her view, would appear to have cleared had she not too quickly had one of her restless relapses. "Maggie, however, does know I'm morbid. SHE hasn't the benefit."

"Well," said Adam Verver a little wearily at last, "I think I feel that you'll hear from her yet." It had even fairly come over him, under recurrent suggestion, that his daughter's omission WAS surprising. And Maggie had never in her life been wrong for more than three minutes.

"Oh, it isn't that I hold that I've a RIGHT to it," Charlotte the next instant rather oddly qualified — and the observation itself gave him a further push.

"Very well — I shall like it myself."

At this then, as if moved by his way of constantly — and more or less against his own contention — coming round to her, she showed how she could also always, and not less gently, come half way. "I speak of it only as the missing GRACE — the grace that's in everything that Maggie does. It isn't my due" — she kept it up — "but, taking from you that we may still expect it, it will have the touch. It will be beautiful."

"Then come out to breakfast." Mr. Verver had looked at his watch. "It will be here when we get back."

"If it isn't" — and Charlotte smiled as she looked about for a feather boa that she had laid down on descending from her room — "if it isn't it will have had but THAT slight fault."

He saw her boa on the arm of the chair from which she had moved to meet him, and, after he had fetched it, raising it to make its charming softness brush his face — for it was a wondrous product of Paris, purchased under his direct auspices the day before — he held it there a minute before giving it up. "Will you promise me then to be at peace?"

She looked, while she debated, at his admirable present. "I promise you."

"Quite for ever?"

"Quite for ever."

"Remember," he went on, to justify his demand, "remember that in wiring you she'll naturally speak even more for her husband than she has done in wiring me."

It was only at a word that Charlotte had a demur. "'Naturally' —?"

"Why, our marriage puts him for you, you see — or puts you for him — into a new relation, whereas it leaves his relation to me unchanged. It therefore gives him more to say to you about it."

"About its making me his stepmother-inlaw — or whatever I SHOULD become?" Over which, for a little, she not undivertedly mused. "Yes, there may easily be enough for a gentleman to say to a young woman about that."

"Well, Amerigo can always be, according to the case, either as funny or as serious as you like; and whichever he may be for you, in sending you a message, he'll be it ALL." And then as the girl, with one of her so deeply and oddly, yet so tenderly, critical looks at him, failed to take up the remark, he found himself moved, as by a vague anxiety, to add a question. "Don't you think he's charming?"

"Oh, charming," said Charlotte Stant. "If he weren't I shouldn't mind."

"No more should I!" her friend harmoniously returned.

"Ah, but you DON'T mind. You don't have to. You don't have to, I mean, as I have. It's the last folly ever to care, in an anxious way, the least particle more than one is absolutely forced. If I were you," she went on —"if I had in my life, for happiness and power and peace, even a small fraction of what you have, it would take a great deal to make me waste my worry. I don't know," she said, "what in the world — that didn't touch my luck — I should trouble my head about."

"I quite understand you — yet doesn't it just depend," Mr. Verver asked, "on what you call one's luck? It's exactly my luck that I'm talking about. I shall be as sublime as you like when you've made me all right. It's only when one is right that one really has the things you speak of. It isn't they," he explained, "that make one so: it's the something else I want that makes THEM right. If you'll give me what I ask, you'll see."

She had taken her boa and thrown it over her shoulders, and her eyes, while she still delayed, had turned from him, engaged by another interest, though the court was by this time, the hour of dispersal for luncheon, so forsaken that they would have had it, for free talk, should they have been moved to loudness, quite to themselves. She was ready for their adjournment, but she was also aware of a pedestrian youth, in uniform, a visible emissary of the Postes et Telegraphes, who had approached, from the street, the small stronghold of the concierge and who presented there a missive taken from the little cartridge-box slung over his shoulder. The portress, meeting him on the threshold, met equally, across the court, Charlotte's marked attention to his visit, so that, within the minute, she had advanced to our friends with her cap-streamers flying and her smile of announcement as ample as her broad white apron. She raised aloft a telegraphic message and, as she delivered it, sociably discriminated. "Cette fois-ci pour madame!" — with which she as genially retreated, leaving Charlotte in possession. Charlotte, taking it, held it at first unopened. Her eyes had come back to her companion, who had immediately and triumphantly greeted it. "Ah, there you are!"

She broke the envelope then in silence, and for a minute, as with the message he himself had put before her, studied its contents without a sign. He watched her without a question, and at last she looked up. "I'll give you," she simply said, "what you ask."

The expression of her face was strange — but since when had a woman's at moments of supreme surrender not a right to be? He took it in with his own long look and his grateful silence — so that nothing more, for some instants, passed between them. Their understanding sealed itself — he already felt that she had made him right. But he was in presence too of the fact that Maggie had made HER so; and always, therefore, without Maggie, where, in fine, would he be? She united them, brought them together as with the click of a silver spring, and, on the spot, with the vision of it, his eyes filled, Charlotte facing him meanwhile with her expression made still stranger by the blur of his gratitude. Through it all, however, he smiled. "What my child does for me —!"

Through it all as well, that is still through the blur, he saw Charlotte, rather than heard her, reply. She held her paper wide open, but her eyes were all for his. "It isn't Maggie. It's the Prince."

"I SAY!" — he gaily rang out. "Then it's best of all."

"It's enough."

"Thank you for thinking so!" To which he added "It's enough for our question, but it isn't — is it? quite enough for our breakfast? Dejeunons."

She stood there, however, in spite of this appeal, her document always before them. "Don't you want to read it?"

He thought. "Not if it satisfies you. I don't require it."

But she gave him, as for her conscience, another chance. "You can if you like."

He hesitated afresh, but as for amiability, not for curiosity. "Is it funny?"

Thus, finally, she again dropped her eyes on it, drawing in her lips a little. "No — I call it grave."

"Ah, then, I don't want it."

"Very grave," said Charlotte Stant.

"Well, what did I tell you of him?" he asked, rejoicing, as they started: a question for all answer to which, before she took his arm, the girl thrust her paper, crumpled, into the pocket of her coat.

Part Third

XIV

Charlotte, half way up the "monumental" staircase, had begun by waiting alone — waiting to be rejoined by her companion, who had gone down all the way, as in common kindness bound, and who, his duty performed, would know where to find her. She was meanwhile, though extremely apparent, not perhaps absolutely advertised; but she would not have cared if she had been — so little was it, by this time, her first occasion of facing society with a consciousness materially, with a confidence quite splendidly, enriched. For a couple of years now she had known as never before what it was to look "well" — to look, that is, as well as she had always felt, from far back, that, in certain conditions, she might. On such an evening as this, that of a great official party in the full flush of the London spring-time, the conditions affected her, her nerves, her senses, her imagination, as all profusely present; so that perhaps at no moment yet had she been so justified of her faith as at the particular instant of our being again concerned with her, that of her chancing to glance higher up from where she stood and meeting in consequence the quiet eyes of Colonel Assingham, who had his elbows on the broad balustrade of the great gallery overhanging the staircase and who immediately exchanged with her one of his most artlessly familiar signals. This simplicity of his visual attention struck her, even with the other things she had to think about, as the quietest note in the whole high pitch — much, in fact, as if she had pressed a finger on a chord or a key and created, for the number of seconds, an arrest of vibration, a more muffled thump. The sight of him suggested indeed that Fanny would be there, though so far as opportunity went she had not seen her. This was about the limit of what it could suggest.

The air, however, had suggestions enough — it abounded in them, many of them precisely helping to constitute those conditions with which, for our young woman, the hour was brilliantly crowned. She was herself in truth crowned, and it all hung together, melted together, in light and colour and sound: the unsurpassed diamonds that her head so happily carried, the other jewels, the other perfections of aspect and arrangement that made her personal scheme a success, the PROVED private theory that materials to work with had been all she required and that there were none too precious for her to understand and use — to which might be added lastly, as the strong-scented flower of the total sweetness, an easy command, a high enjoyment, of her crisis. For a crisis she was ready to take it, and this ease it was, doubtless, that helped her, while she waited, to the right assurance, to the right indifference, to the right expression, and above all, as she felt, to the right view of her opportunity for happiness — unless indeed the opportunity itself, rather, were, in its mere strange amplitude, the producing, the precipitating cause. The ordered revellers, rustling and shining, with sweep of train and glitter of star and clink of sword, and yet, for all this, but so imperfectly articulate, so vaguely vocal — the double stream of the coming and the going, flowing together where she stood, passed her, brushed her, treated her to much crude contemplation and now and then to a spasm of speech, an offered hand, even in some cases to an unencouraged pause; but she missed no countenance and invited no protection: she fairly liked to be, so long as she might, just as she was — exposed a little to the public, no doubt, in her unaccompanied state, but, even if it were a bit brazen, careless of queer reflections on the dull polish of London faces, and exposed, since it was a question of exposure, to much more competent recognitions of her own. She hoped no one would stop — she was positively keeping herself; it was her idea to mark in a particular manner the importance of something that had just happened. She knew how she should mark it, and what she was doing there made already a beginning.

When presently, therefore, from her standpoint, she saw the Prince come back she had an impression of all the place as higher and wider and more appointed for great moments; with its dome of lustres lifted, its ascents and descents more majestic, its marble tiers more vividly overhung, its numerosity of royalties, foreign and domestic, more unprecedented, its symbolism of "State" hospitality both emphasised and refined. This was doubtless a large consequence of a fairly familiar cause, a considerable inward stir to spring from the mere vision, striking as that might be, of Amerigo in a crowd; but she had her reasons, she held them there, she carried them in fact, responsibly and overtly, as she carried her head, her high tiara, her folded fan, her indifferent, unattended eminence; and it was when he reached her and she could, taking his arm, show herself as placed in her relation, that she felt supremely justified. It was her notion of course that she gave a glimpse of but few of her grounds for this discrimination — indeed of the most evident alone; yet she would have been half willing it should be guessed how she drew inspiration, drew support, in quantity sufficient for almost anything, from the individual value that, through all the picture, her husband's son-inlaw kept for the eye, deriving it from his fine unconscious way, in the swarming social sum, of outshining, overlooking and overtopping. It was as if in separation, even the shortest, she half forgot or disbelieved how he affected her sight, so that reappearance had, in him, each time, a virtue of its own — a kind of disproportionate intensity suggesting his connection with occult sources of renewal. What did he do when he was away from her that made him always come back only looking, as she would have called it, "more so?" Superior to any shade of cabotinage, he yet almost resembled an actor who, between his moments on the stage, revisits his dressing-room and, before the glass, pressed by his need of effect, retouches his make-up. The Prince was at present, for instance, though he had quitted her but ten minutes before, still more than then the person it pleased her to be left with — a truth that had all its force for her while he made her his care for their conspicuous return together to the upper rooms. Conspicuous beyond any wish they could entertain was what, poor wonderful man, he couldn't help making it; and when she raised her eyes again, on the ascent, to Bob Assingham, still aloft in his gallery and still looking down at her, she was aware that, in spite of hovering and warning inward voices, she even enjoyed the testimony rendered by his lonely vigil to the lustre she reflected.

He was always lonely at great parties, the dear Colonel — it wasn't in such places that the seed he sowed at home was ever reaped by him; but nobody could have seemed to mind it less, to brave it with more bronzed indifference; so markedly that he moved about less like one of the guests than like some quite presentable person in charge of the police arrangements or the electric light. To Mrs. Verver, as will be seen, he represented, with the perfect good faith of his apparent blankness, something definite enough; though her bravery was not thereby too blighted for her to feel herself calling him to witness that the only witchcraft her companion had used, within the few minutes, was that of attending Maggie, who had withdrawn from the scene, to her carriage. Notified, at all events, of Fanny's probable presence, Charlotte was, for a while after this, divided between the sense of it as a fact somehow to reckon with and deal with, which was a perception that made, in its degree, for the prudence, the pusillanimity of postponement, of avoidance — and a quite other feeling, an impatience that presently ended by prevailing, an eagerness, really, to BE suspected, sounded, veritably arraigned, if only that she might have the bad moment over, if only that she might prove to herself, let alone to Mrs. Assingham also, that she could convert it to good; if only, in short, to be "square," as they said, with her question. For herself indeed, particularly, it wasn't a question; but something in her bones told her that Fanny would treat it as one, and there was truly nothing that, from this friend, she was not bound in decency to take. She might hand things back with every tender precaution, with acknowledgments and assurances, but she owed it to them, in any case, and it to all Mrs. Assingham had done for her, not to get rid of them without having well unwrapped and turned them over.

To-night, as happened — and she recognised it more and more, with the ebbing minutes, as an influence of everything about her — to-night exactly, she would, no doubt, since she knew why, be as firm as she might at any near moment again hope to be for going through that process with the right temper and tone. She said, after a little, to the Prince, "Stay with me; let no one take you; for I want her, yes, I do want her to see us together, and the sooner the better" — said it to keep her hand on him through constant diversions, and made him, in fact, by saying it, profess a momentary vagueness. She had to explain to him that it was Fanny Assingham, she wanted to see — who clearly would be there, since the Colonel never either stirred without her or, once arrived, concerned himself for her fate; and she had, further, after Amerigo had met her with "See us together? why in the world? hasn't she often seen us together?" to inform him that what had elsewhere and otherwise happened didn't now matter and that she at any rate well knew, for the occasion, what she was about. "You're strange, cara mia," he consentingly enough dropped; but, for whatever strangeness, he kept her, as they circulated, from being waylaid, even remarking to her afresh as he had often done before, on the help rendered, in such situations, by the intrinsic oddity of the London "squash," a thing of vague, slow, senseless eddies, revolving as in fear of some menace of conversation suspended over it, the drop of which, with some consequent refreshing splash or spatter, yet never took place. Of course she was strange; this, as they went, Charlotte knew for herself: how could she be anything else when the situation holding her, and holding him, for that matter, just as much, had so the stamp of it? She had already accepted her consciousness, as we have already noted, that a crisis, for them all, was in the air; and when such hours were not depressing, which was the form indeed in which she had mainly known them, they were apparently in a high degree exhilarating.

Later on, in a corner to which, at sight of an empty sofa, Mrs. Assingham had, after a single attentive arrest, led her with a certain earnestness, this vision of the critical was much more sharpened than blurred. Fanny had taken it from her: yes, she was there with Amerigo alone, Maggie having come with them and then, within ten minutes, changed her mind, repented and departed. "So you're staying on together without her?" the elder woman had asked; and it was Charlotte's answer to this that had determined for them, quite indeed according to the latter's expectation, the need of some seclusion and her companion's pounce at the sofa. They were staying on together alone, and — oh distinctly! — it was alone that Maggie had driven away, her father, as usual, not having managed to come. "'As usual' —?" Mrs. Assingham had seemed to wonder; Mr. Verver's reluctances not having, she in fact quite intimated, hitherto struck her. Charlotte responded, at any rate, that his indisposition to go out had lately much increased — even though to-night, as she admitted, he had pleaded his not feeling well. Maggie had wished to stay with him — for the Prince and she, dining out, had afterwards called in Portland Place, whence, in the event, they had brought her, Charlotte, on. Maggie had come but to oblige her father — she had urged the two others to go without her; then she had yielded, for the time, to Mr. Verver's persuasion. But here, when they had, after the long wait in the carriage, fairly got in; here, once up the stairs, with the rooms before them, remorse had ended by seizing her: she had listened to no other remonstrance, and at present therefore, as Charlotte put it, the two were doubtless making together a little party at home. But it was all right — so Charlotte also put it: there was nothing in the world they liked better than these snatched felicities, little parties, long talks, with "I'll come to you tomorrow," and "No, I'll come to you," make-believe renewals of their old life. They were fairly, at times, the dear things, like children playing at paying visits, playing at "Mr. Thompson" and "Mrs. Fane," each hoping that the other would really stay to tea. Charlotte was sure she should find Maggie there on getting home — a remark in which Mrs. Verver's immediate response to her friend's inquiry had culminated. She had thus, on the spot, the sense of having given her plenty to think about, and that moreover of liking to see it even better than she had expected. She had plenty to think about herself, and there was already something in Fanny that made it seem still more.

"You say your husband's ill? He felt too ill to come?"

"No, my dear — I think not. If he had been too ill I wouldn't have left him."

"And yet Maggie was worried?" Mrs. Assingham asked.

"She worries, you know, easily. She's afraid of influenza — of which he has had, at different times, though never with the least gravity, several attacks."

"But you're not afraid of it?"

Charlotte had for a moment a pause; it had continued to come to her that really to have her case "out," as they said, with the person in the world to whom her most intimate difficulties had oftenest referred themselves, would help her, on the whole, more than hinder; and under that feeling all her opportunity, with nothing kept back; with a thing or two perhaps even thrust forward, seemed temptingly to open. Besides, didn't Fanny at bottom half expect, absolutely at the bottom half WANT, things? — so that she would be disappointed if, after what must just have occurred for her, she didn't get something to put between the teeth of her so restless rumination, that cultivation of the fear, of which our young woman had already had glimpses, that she might have "gone too far" in her irrepressible interest in other lives. What had just happened — it pieced itself together for Charlotte — was that the Assingham pair, drifting like everyone else, had had somewhere in the gallery, in the rooms, an accidental concussion; had it after the Colonel, over his balustrade, had observed, in the favouring high light, her public junction with the Prince. His very dryness, in this encounter, had, as always, struck a spark from his wife's curiosity, and, familiar, on his side, with all that she saw in things, he had thrown her, as a fine little bone to pick, some report of the way one of her young friends was "going on" with another. He knew perfectly — such at least was Charlotte's liberal assumption — that she wasn't going on with anyone, but she also knew that, given the circumstances, she was inevitably to be sacrificed, in some form or another, to the humorous intercourse of the inimitable couple. The Prince meanwhile had also, under coercion, sacrificed her; the Ambassador had come up to him with a message from Royalty, to whom he was led away; after which she had talked for five minutes with Sir John Brinder, who had been of the Ambassador's company and who had rather artlessly remained with her. Fanny had then arrived in sight of them at the same moment as someone else she didn't know, someone who knew Mrs. Assingham and also knew Sir John. Charlotte had left it to her friend's competence to throw the two others immediately together and to find a way for entertaining her in closer quarters. This was the little history of the vision, in her, that was now rapidly helping her to recognise a precious chance, the chance that mightn't again soon be so good for the vivid making of a point. Her point was before her; it was sharp, bright, true; above all it was her own. She had reached it quite by herself; no one, not even Amerigo — Amerigo least of all, who would have nothing to do with it — had given her aid. To make it now with force for Fanny Assingham's benefit would see her further, in the direction in which the light had dawned, than any other spring she should, yet awhile, doubtless, be able to press. The direction was that of her greater freedom — which was all in the world she had in mind. Her opportunity had accordingly, after a few minutes of Mrs. Assingham's almost imprudently interested expression of face, positively acquired such a price for her that she may, for ourselves, while the intensity lasted, rather resemble a person holding out a small mirror at arm's length and consulting it with a special turn of the head. It was, in a word, with this value of her chance that she was intelligently playing when she said in answer to Fanny's last question: "Don't you remember what you told me, on the occasion of something or other, the other day? That you believe there's nothing I'm afraid of? So, my dear, don't ask me!"

"Mayn't I ask you," Mrs. Assingham returned, "how the case stands with your poor husband?"

"Certainly, dear. Only, when you ask me as if I mightn't perhaps know what to think, it seems to me best to let you see that I know perfectly what to think."

Mrs. Assingham hesitated; then, blinking a little, she took her risk. "You didn't think that if it was a question of anyone's returning to him, in his trouble, it would be better you yourself should have gone?"

Well, Charlotte's answer to this inquiry visibly shaped itself in the interest of the highest considerations. The highest considerations were good humour, candour, clearness and, obviously, the REAL truth. "If we couldn't be perfectly frank and dear with each other, it would be ever so much better, wouldn't it? that we shouldn't talk about anything at all; which, however, would be dreadful — and we certainly, at any rate, haven't yet come to it. You can ask me anything under the sun you like, because, don't you see? you can't upset me."

"I'm sure, my dear Charlotte," Fanny Assingham laughed, "I don't want to upset you."

"Indeed, love, you simply COULDN'T even if you thought it necessary — that's all I mean. Nobody could, for it belongs to my situation that I'm, by no merit of my own, just fixed — fixed as fast as a pin stuck, up to its head, in a cushion. I'm placed — I can't imagine anyone MORE placed. There I AM!"

Fanny had indeed never listened to emphasis more firmly applied, and it brought into her own eyes, though she had reasons for striving to keep them from betrayals, a sort of anxiety of intelligence. "I dare say — but your statement of your position, however you see it, isn't an answer to my inquiry. It seems to me, at the same time, I confess," Mrs. Assingham added, "to give but the more reason for it. You speak of our being 'frank.' How can we possibly be anything else? If Maggie has gone off through finding herself too distressed to stay, and if she's willing to leave you and her husband to show here without her, aren't the grounds of her preoccupation more or less discussable?"

"If they're not," Charlotte replied, "it's only from their being, in a way, too evident. They're not grounds for me — they weren't when I accepted Adam's preference that I should come to-night without him: just as I accept, absolutely, as a fixed rule, ALL his preferences. But that doesn't alter the fact, of course, that my husband's daughter, rather than his wife, should have felt SHE could, after all, be the one to stay with him, the one to make the sacrifice of this hour — seeing, especially, that the daughter has a husband of her own in the field." With which she produced, as it were, her explanation. "I've simply to see the truth of the matter — see that Maggie thinks more, on the whole, of fathers than of husbands. And my situation is such," she went on, "that this becomes immediately, don't you understand? a thing I have to count with."

Mrs. Assingham, vaguely heaving, panting a little but trying not to show it, turned about, from some inward spring, in her seat. "If you mean such a thing as that she doesn't adore the Prince —!"

"I don't say she doesn't adore him. What I say is that she doesn't think of him. One of those conditions doesn't always, at all stages, involve the other. This is just HOW she adores him," Charlotte said. "And what reason is there, in the world, after all, why he and I shouldn't, as you say, show together? We've shown together, my dear," she smiled, "before."

Her friend, for a little, only looked at her — speaking then with abruptness. "You ought to be absolutely happy. You live with such GOOD people."

The effect of it, as well, was an arrest for Charlotte; whose face, however, all of whose fine and slightly hard radiance, it had caused, the next instant, further to brighten. "Does one ever put into words anything so fatuously rash? It's a thing that must be said, in prudence, FOR one — by somebody who's so good as to take the responsibility: the more that it gives one always a chance to show one's best manners by not contradicting it. Certainly, you'll never have the distress, or whatever, of hearing me complain."

"Truly, my dear, I hope in all conscience not!" and the elder woman's spirit found relief in a laugh more resonant than was quite advised by their pursuit of privacy.

To this demonstration her friend gave no heed. "With all our absence after marriage, and with the separation from her produced in particular by our so many months in America, Maggie has still arrears, still losses to make up — still the need of showing how, for so long, she simply kept missing him. She missed his company — a large allowance of which is, in spite of everything else, of the first necessity to her. So she puts it in when she can — a little here, a little there, and it ends by making up a considerable amount. The fact of our distinct establishments — which has, all the same, everything in its favour," Charlotte hastened to declare, "makes her really see more of him than when they had the same house. To make sure she doesn't fail of it she's always arranging for it — which she didn't have to do while they lived together. But she likes to arrange," Charlotte steadily proceeded; "it peculiarly suits her; and the result of our separate households is really, for them, more contact and more intimacy. To-night, for instance, has been practically an arrangement. She likes him best alone. And it's the way," said our young woman, "in which he best likes HER. It's what I mean therefore by being 'placed.'

And the great thing is, as they say, to 'know' one's place. Doesn't it all strike you," she wound up, "as rather placing the Prince too?"

Fanny Assingham had at this moment the sense as of a large heaped dish presented to her intelligence and inviting it to a feast — so thick were the notes of intention in this remarkable speech. But she also felt that to plunge at random, to help herself too freely, would — apart from there not being at such a moment time for it — tend to jostle the ministering hand, confound the array and, more vulgarly speaking, make a mess. So she picked out, after consideration, a solitary plum. "So placed that YOU have to arrange?"

"Certainly I have to arrange."

"And the Prince also — if the effect for him is the same?"

"Really, I think, not less."

"And does he arrange," Mrs. Assingham asked, "to make up HIS arrears?" The question had risen to her lips — it was as if another morsel, on the dish, had tempted her. The sound of it struck her own ear, immediately, as giving out more of her thought than she had as yet intended; but she quickly saw that she must follow it up, at any risk, with simplicity, and that what was simplest was the ease of boldness. "Make them up, I mean, by coming to see YOU?"

Charlotte replied, however, without, as her friend would have phrased it, turning a hair. She shook her head, but it was beautifully gentle. "He never comes."

"Oh!" said Fanny Assingham: with which she felt a little stupid. "There it is. He might so well, you know, otherwise."

"'Otherwise'?" — and Fanny was still vague.

It passed, this time, over her companion, whose eyes, wandering, to a distance, found themselves held. The Prince was at hand again; the Ambassador was still at his side; they were stopped a moment by a uniformed personage, a little old man, of apparently the highest military character, bristling with medals and orders. This gave Charlotte time to go on. "He has not been for three months." And then as with her friend's last word in her ear: "'Otherwise' — yes. He arranges otherwise. And in my position," she added, "I might too. It's too absurd we shouldn't meet."

"You've met, I gather," said Fanny Assingham, "to-night."

"Yes — as far as that goes. But what I mean is that I might — placed for it as we both are — go to see HIM."

"And do you?" Fanny asked with almost mistaken solemnity.

The perception of this excess made Charlotte, whether for gravity or for irony, hang fire a minute. "I HAVE been. But that's nothing," she said, "in itself, and I tell you of it only to show you how our situation works. It essentially becomes one, a situation, for both of us. The Prince's, however, is his own affair — I meant but to speak of mine."

"Your situation's perfect," Mrs. Assingham presently declared.

"I don't say it isn't. Taken, in fact, all round, I think it is. And I don't, as I tell you, complain of it. The only thing is that I have to act as it demands of me."

"To 'act'?" said Mrs. Assingham with an irrepressible quaver.

"Isn't it acting, my dear, to accept it? I do accept it. What do you want me to do less?"

"I want you to believe that you're a very fortunate person."

"Do you call that LESS?" Charlotte asked with a smile. "From the point of view of my freedom I call it more. Let it take, my position, any name you like."

"Don't let it, at any rate" — and Mrs. Assingham's impatience prevailed at last over her presence of mind — "don't let it make you think too much of your freedom."

"I don't know what you call too much — for how can I not see it as it is? You'd see your own quickly enough if the Colonel gave you the same liberty — and I haven't to tell you, with your so much greater knowledge of everything, what it is that gives such liberty most. For yourself personally of course," Charlotte went on, "you only know the state of neither needing it nor missing it. Your husband doesn't treat you as of less importance to him than some other woman."

"Ah, don't talk to me of other women!" Fanny now overtly panted. "Do you call Mr. Verver's perfectly natural interest in his daughter —?"

"The greatest affection of which he is capable?" Charlotte took it up in all readiness. "I do distinctly — and in spite of my having done all I could think of — to make him capable of a greater. I've done, earnestly, everything I could — I've made it, month after month, my study. But I haven't succeeded — it has been vividly brought home to me to-night. However," she pursued, "I've hoped against hope, for I recognise that, as I told you at the time, I was duly warned." And then as she met in her friend's face the absence of any such remembrance: "He did tell me that he wanted me just BECAUSE I could be useful about her." With which Charlotte broke into a wonderful smile. "So you see I AM!"

It was on Fanny Assingham's lips for the moment to reply that this was, on the contrary, exactly what she didn't see; she came in fact within an ace of saying: "You strike me as having quite failed to help his idea to work — since, by your account, Maggie has him not less, but so much more, on her mind. How in the world, with so much of a remedy, comes there to remain so much of what was to be obviated?" But she saved herself in time, conscious above all that she was in presence of still deeper things than she had yet dared to fear, that there was "more in it" than any admission she had made represented — and she had held herself familiar with admissions: so that, not to seem to understand where she couldn't accept, and not to seem to accept where she couldn't approve, and could still less, with precipitation, advise, she invoked the mere appearance of casting no weight whatever into the scales of her young friend's consistency. The only thing was that, as she was quickly enough to feel, she invoked it rather to excess. It brought her, her invocation, too abruptly to her feet. She brushed away everything. "I can't conceive, my dear, what you're talking about!"

Charlotte promptly rose then, as might be, to meet it, and her colour, for the first time, perceptibly heightened. She looked, for the minute, as her companion had looked — as if twenty protests, blocking each other's way, had surged up within her. But when Charlotte had to make a selection, her selection was always the most effective possible. It was happy now, above all, for being made not in anger but in sorrow. "You give me up then?"

"Give you up —?"

"You forsake me at the hour of my life when it seems to me I most deserve a friend's loyalty? If you do you're not just, Fanny; you're even, I think," she went on, "rather cruel; and it's least of all worthy of you to seem to wish to quarrel with me in order to cover your desertion." She spoke, at the same time, with the noblest moderation of tone, and the image of high, pale, lighted disappointment she meanwhile presented, as of a creature patient and lonely in her splendour, was an impression so firmly imposed that she could fill her measure to the brim and yet enjoy the last word, as it is called in such cases, with a perfection void of any vulgarity of triumph. She merely completed, for truth's sake, her demonstration. "What is a quarrel with me but a quarrel with my right to recognise the conditions of my bargain? But I can carry them out alone," she said as she turned away. She turned to meet the Ambassador and the Prince, who, their colloquy with their Field-Marshal ended, were now at hand and had already, between them, she was aware, addressed her a remark that failed to penetrate the golden glow in which her intelligence was temporarily bathed. She had made her point, the point she had foreseen she must make; she had made it thoroughly and once for all, so that no more making was required; and her success was reflected in the faces of the two men of distinction before her, unmistakably moved to admiration by her exceptional radiance. She at first but watched this reflection, taking no note of any less adequate form of it possibly presented by poor Fanny — poor Fanny left to stare at her incurred "score," chalked up in so few strokes on the wall; then she took in what the Ambassador was saying, in French, what he was apparently repeating to her.

"A desire for your presence, Madame, has been expressed en tres-haut lieu, and I've let myself in for the responsibility, to say nothing of the honour, of seeing, as the most respectful of your friends, that so august an impatience is not kept waiting." The greatest possible Personage had, in short, according to the odd formula of societies subject to the greatest personages possible, "sent for" her, and she asked, in her surprise, "What in the world does he want to do to me?" only to know, without looking, that Fanny's bewilderment was called to a still larger application, and to hear the Prince say with authority, indeed with a certain prompt dryness: "You must go immediately — it's a summons." The Ambassador, using authority as well, had already somehow possessed himself of her hand, which he drew into his arm, and she was further conscious as she went off with him that, though still speaking for her benefit, Amerigo had turned to Fanny Assingham. He would explain afterwards — besides which she would understand for herself. To Fanny, however, he had laughed — as a mark, apparently, that for this infallible friend no explanation at all would be necessary.

XV

It may be recorded none the less that the Prince was the next moment to see how little any such assumption was founded. Alone with him now Mrs. Assingham was incorruptible. "They send for Charlotte through YOU?"

"No, my dear; as you see, through the Ambassador."

"Ah, but the Ambassador and you, for the last quarter-of-an-hour, have been for them as one. He's YOUR ambassador." It may indeed be further mentioned that the more Fanny looked at it the more she saw in it. "They've connected her with you — she's treated as your appendage."

"Oh, my 'appendage,'" the Prince amusedly exclaimed —"cara mia, what a name! She's treated, rather, say, as my ornament and my glory. And it's so remarkable a case for a mother-in-law that you surely can't find fault with it."

"You've ornaments enough, it seems to me — as you've certainly glories enough — without her. And she's not the least little bit," Mrs. Assingham observed, "your mother-inlaw. In such a matter a shade of difference is enormous. She's no relation to you whatever, and if she's known in high quarters but as going about with you, then — then —!" She failed, however, as from positive intensity of vision. "Then, then what?" he asked with perfect good-nature.

"She had better in such a case not be known at all."

"But I assure you I never, just now, so much as mentioned her. Do you suppose I asked them," said the young man, still amused, "if they didn't want to see her? You surely don't need to be shown that Charlotte speaks for herself — that she does so above all on such an occasion as this and looking as she does to-night. How, so looking, can she pass unnoticed? How can she not have 'success'? Besides," he added as she but watched his face, letting him say what he would, as if she wanted to see how he would say it, "besides, there IS always the fact that we're of the same connection, of — what is your word? — the same 'concern.' We're certainly not, with the relation of our respective sposi, simply formal acquaintances. We're in the same boat" — and the Prince smiled with a candour that added an accent to his emphasis.

Fanny Assingham was full of the special sense of his manner: it caused her to turn for a moment's refuge to a corner of her general consciousness in which she could say to herself that she was glad SHE wasn't in love with such a man. As with Charlotte just before, she was embarrassed by the difference between what she took in and what she could say, what she felt and what she could show. "It only appears to me of great importance that — now that you all seem more settled here — Charlotte should be known, for any presentation, any further circulation or introduction, as, in particular, her husband's wife; known in the least possible degree as anything else. I don't know what you mean by the 'same' boat. Charlotte is naturally in Mr. Verver's boat."

"And, pray, am *I* not in Mr. Verver's boat too? Why, but for Mr. Verver's boat, I should have been by this time" — and his quick Italian gesture, an expressive direction and motion of his forefinger, pointed to deepest depths —"away down, down, down." She knew of course what he meant — how it had taken his father-inlaw's great fortune, and taken no small slice, to surround him with an element in which, all too fatally weighted as he had originally been, he could pecuniarily float; and with this reminder other things came to her — how strange it was that, with all allowance for their merit, it should befall some people to be so inordinately valued, quoted, as they said in the stock-market, so high, and how still stranger, perhaps, that there should be cases in which, for some reason, one didn't mind the so frequently marked absence in them of the purpose really to represent their price. She was thinking, feeling, at any rate, for herself; she was thinking that the pleasure SHE could take in this specimen of the class didn't suffer from his consent to be merely made buoyant: partly because it was one of those pleasures (he inspired them) that, by their nature, COULDN'T suffer, to whatever proof they were put; and partly because, besides, he after all visibly had on his conscience some sort of return for services rendered. He was a huge expense assuredly — but it had been up to now her conviction that his idea was to behave beautifully enough to make the beauty well nigh an equivalent. And that he had carried out his idea, carried it out by continuing to lead the life, to breathe the air, very nearly to think the thoughts, that best suited his wife and her father — this she had till lately enjoyed the comfort of so distinctly perceiving as to have even been moved more than once, to express to him the happiness it gave her. He had that in his favour as against other matters; yet it discouraged her too, and rather oddly, that he should so keep moving, and be able to show her that he moved, on the firm ground of the truth. His acknowledgment of obligation was far from unimportant, but she could find in his grasp of the real itself a kind of ominous intimation. The intimation appeared to peep at her even out of his next word, lightly as he produced it.

"Isn't it rather as if we had, Charlotte and I, for bringing us together, a benefactor in common?" And the effect, for his interlocutress, was still further to be deepened. "I somehow feel, half the time, as if he were her father-inlaw too. It's as if he had saved us both — which is a fact in our lives, or at any rate in our hearts, to make of itself a link. Don't you remember" — he kept it up —"how, the day she suddenly turned up for you, just before my wedding, we so frankly and funnily talked, in her presence, of the advisability, for her, of some good marriage?" And then as his friend's face, in her extremity, quite again as with Charlotte, but continued to fly the black flag of general repudiation: "Well, we really began then, as it seems to me, the work of placing her where she is. We were wholly right — and so was she. That it was exactly the thing is shown by its success. We recommended a good marriage at almost any price, so to speak, and, taking us at our word, she has made the very best. That was really what we meant, wasn't it? Only — what she has got — something thoroughly good. It would be difficult, it seems to me, for her to have anything better — once you allow her the way it's to be taken. Of course if you don't allow her that the case is different. Her offset is a certain decent freedom — which, I judge, she'll be quite contented with. You may say that will be very good of her, but she strikes me as perfectly humble about it. She proposes neither to claim it nor to use it with any sort of retentissement. She would enjoy it, I think, quite as quietly as it might be given. The 'boat,' you see" — the Prince explained it no less considerately and lucidly —"is a good deal tied up at the dock, or anchored, if you like, out in the stream. I have to jump out from time to time to stretch my legs, and you'll probably perceive, if you give it your attention, that Charlotte really can't help occasionally doing the same. It isn't even a question, sometimes, of one's getting to the dock — one has to take a header and splash about in the water. Call our having remained here together to-night, call the accident of my having put them, put our illustrious friends there, on my companion's track — for I grant you this as a practical result of our combination — call the whole thing one of the harmless little plunges off the deck, inevitable for each of us. Why not take them, when they occur, as inevitable — and, above all, as not endangering life or limb? We shan't drown, we shan't sink — at least I can answer for myself. Mrs. Verver too, moreover — do her the justice — visibly knows how to swim."

He could easily go on, for she didn't interrupt him; Fanny felt now that she wouldn't have interrupted him for the world. She found his eloquence precious; there was not a drop of it that she didn't, in a manner, catch, as it came, for immediate bottling, for future preservation. The crystal flask of her innermost attention really received it on the spot, and she had even already the vision of how, in the snug laboratory of her afterthought, she should be able chemically to analyse it. There were moments, positively, still beyond this, when, with the meeting of their eyes, something as yet unnamable came out for her in his look, when something strange and subtle and at variance with his words, something that GAVE THEM AWAY, glimmered deep down, as an appeal, almost an incredible one, to her finer comprehension. What, inconceivably, was it like? Wasn't it, however gross, such a rendering of anything so occult, fairly like a quintessential wink, a hint of the possibility of their REALLY treating their subject — of course on some better occasion — and thereby, as well, finding it much more interesting? If this far red spark, which might have been figured by her mind as the head-light of an approaching train seen through the length of a tunnel, was not, on her side, an ignis fatuus, a mere subjective phenomenon, it twinkled there at the direct expense of what the Prince was inviting her to understand. Meanwhile too, however, and unmistakably, the real treatment of their subject did, at a given moment, sound. This was when he proceeded, with just the same perfect possession of his thought — on the manner of which he couldn't have improved — to complete his successful simile by another, in fact by just the supreme touch, the touch for which it had till now been waiting. "For Mrs. Verver to be known to people so intensely and exclusively as her husband's wife, something is wanted that, you know, they haven't exactly got. He should manage to be known — or at least to be seen — a little more as his wife's husband. You surely must by this time have seen for yourself that he has his own habits and his own ways, and that he makes, more and more — as of course he has a perfect right to do — his own discriminations. He's so perfect, so ideal a father, and, doubtless largely by that very fact, a generous, a comfortable, an admirable father-inlaw, that I should really feel it base to avail myself of any standpoint whatever to criticise him. To YOU, nevertheless, I may make just one remark; for you're not stupid — you always understand so blessedly what one means."

He paused an instant, as if even this one remark might be difficult for him should she give no sign of encouraging him to produce it. Nothing would have induced her, however, to encourage him; she was now conscious of having never in her life stood so still or sat, inwardly, as it were, so tight; she felt like the horse of the adage, brought — and brought by her own fault — to the water, but strong, for the occasion, in the one fact that she couldn't be forced to drink. Invited, in other words, to understand, she held her breath for fear of showing she did, and this for the excellent reason that she was at last fairly afraid to. It was sharp for her, at the same time, that she was certain, in advance, of his remark; that she heard it before it had sounded, that she already tasted, in fine, the bitterness it would have for her special sensibility. But her companion, from an inward and different need of his own, was presently not deterred by her silence. "What I really don't see is why, from his own point of view — given, that is, his conditions, so fortunate as they stood — he should have wished to marry at all." There it was then — exactly what she knew would come, and exactly, for reasons that seemed now to thump at her heart, as distressing to her. Yet she was resolved, meanwhile, not to suffer, as they used to say of the martyrs, then and there; not to suffer, odiously, helplessly, in public — which could be prevented but by her breaking off, with whatever inconsequence; by her treating their discussion as ended and getting away. She suddenly wanted to go home much as she had wanted, an hour or two before, to come. She wanted to leave well behind her both her question and the couple in whom it had, abruptly, taken such vivid form — but it was dreadful to have the appearance of disconcerted flight. Discussion had of itself, to her sense, become danger — such light, as from open crevices, it let in; and the overt recognition of danger was worse than anything else. The worst in fact came while she was thinking how she could retreat and still not overtly recognise. Her face had betrayed her trouble, and with that she was lost. "I'm afraid, however," the Prince said, "that I, for some reason, distress you — for which I beg your pardon. We've always talked so well together — it has been, from the beginning, the greatest pull for me." Nothing so much as such a tone could have quickened her collapse; she felt he had her now at his mercy, and he showed, as he went on, that he knew it. "We shall talk again, all the same, better than ever — I depend on it too much. Don't you remember what I told you, so definitely, one day before my marriage? — that, moving as I did in so many ways among new things, mysteries, conditions, expectations, assumptions different from any I had known, I looked to you, as my original sponsor, my fairy godmother, to see me through. I beg you to believe," he added, "that I look to you yet."

His very insistence had, fortunately, the next moment, affected her as bringing her help; with which, at least, she could hold up her head to speak. "Ah, you ARE through — you were through long ago. Or if you aren't you ought to be."

"Well then, if I ought to be it's all the more reason why you should continue to help me. Because, very distinctly, I assure you, I'm not. The new things or ever so many of them — are still for me new things; the mysteries and expectations and assumptions still contain an immense element that I've failed to puzzle out. As we've happened, so luckily, to find ourselves again really taking hold together, you must let me, as soon as possible, come to see you; you must give me a good, kind hour. If you refuse it me" — and he addressed himself to her continued reserve —"I shall feel that you deny, with a stony stare, your responsibility."

At this, as from a sudden shake, her reserve proved an inadequate vessel. She could bear her own, her private reference to the weight on her mind, but the touch of another hand made it too horribly press. "Oh, I deny responsibility — to YOU. So far as I ever had it I've done with it."

He had been, all the while, beautifully smiling; but she made his look, now, penetrate her again more. "As to whom then do you confess it?"

"Ah, mio caro, that's — if to anyone — my own business!"

He continued to look at her hard. "You give me up then?"

It was what Charlotte had asked her ten minutes before, and its coming from him so much in the same way shook her in her place. She was on the point of replying "Do you and she agree together for what you'll say to me?" — but she was glad afterwards to have checked herself in time, little as her actual answer had perhaps bettered it. "I think I don't know what to make of you."

"You must receive me at least," he said.

"Oh, please, not till I'm ready for you!" — and, though she found a laugh for it, she had to turn away. She had never turned away from him before, and it was quite positively for her as if she were altogether afraid of him.

XVI

Later on, when their hired brougham had, with the long vociferation that tormented her impatience, been extricated from the endless rank, she rolled into the London night, beside her husband, as into a sheltering darkness where she could muffle herself and draw breath. She had stood for the previous half-hour in a merciless glare, beaten upon, stared out of countenance, it fairly seemed to her, by intimations of her mistake. For what she was most immediately feeling was that she had, in the past, been active, for these people, to ends that were now bearing fruit and that might yet bear a larger crop. She but brooded, at first, in her corner of the carriage: it was like burying her exposed face, a face too helplessly exposed, in the cool lap of the common indifference, of the dispeopled streets, of the closed shops and darkened houses seen through the window of the brougham, a world mercifully unconscious and unreproachful. It wouldn't, like the world she had just left, know sooner or later what she had done, or would know it, at least, only if the final consequence should be some quite overwhelming publicity. She fixed this possibility itself so hard, however, for a few moments, that the misery of her fear produced the next minute a reaction; and when the carriage happened, while it grazed a turn, to catch the straight shaft from the lamp of a policeman in the act of playing his inquisitive flash over an opposite house-front, she let herself wince at being thus incriminated only that she might protest, not less quickly, against mere blind terror. It had become, for the occasion, preposterously, terror — of which she must shake herself free before she could properly measure her ground. The perception of this necessity had in truth soon aided her; since she found, on trying, that, lurid as her prospect might hover there, she could none the less give it no name. The sense of seeing was strong in her, but she clutched at the comfort of not being sure of what she saw. Not to know what it would represent on a longer view was a help, in turn, to not making out that her hands were embrued; since if she had stood in the position of a producing cause she should surely be less vague about what she had produced. This, further, in its way, was a step toward reflecting that when one's connection with any matter was too indirect to be traced it might be described also as too slight to be deplored. By the time they were nearing Cadogan Place she had in fact recognised that she couldn't be as curious as she desired without arriving at some conviction of her being as innocent. But there had been a moment, in the dim desert of Eaton Square, when she broke into speech.

"It's only their defending themselves so much more than they need — it's only THAT that makes me wonder. It's their having so remarkably much to say for themselves."

Her husband had, as usual, lighted his cigar, remaining apparently as busy with it as she with her agitation. "You mean it makes you feel that you have nothing?" To which, as she made no answer, the Colonel added: "What in the world did you ever suppose was going to happen? The man's in a position in which he has nothing in life to do."

Her silence seemed to characterise this statement as superficial, and her thoughts, as always in her husband's company, pursued an independent course. He made her, when they were together, talk, but as if for some other person; who was in fact for the most part herself. Yet she addressed herself with him as she could never have done without him. "He has behaved beautifully — he did from the first. I've thought it, all along, wonderful of him; and I've more than once, when I've had a chance, told him so. Therefore, therefore —!" But it died away as she mused.

"Therefore he has a right, for a change, to kick up his heels?"

"It isn't a question, of course, however," she undivertedly went on, "of their behaving beautifully apart. It's a question of their doing as they should when together — which is another matter."

"And how do you think then," the Colonel asked with interest, "that, when together, they SHOULD do? The less they do, one would say, the better — if you see so much in it."

His wife, at this, appeared to hear him. "I don't see in it what YOU'D see. And don't, my dear," she further answered, "think it necessary to be horrid or low about them. They're the last people, really, to make anything of that sort come in right."

"I'm surely never horrid or low," he returned, "about anyone but my extravagant wife. I can do with all our friends — as I see them myself: what I can't do with is the figures you make of them. And when you take to adding your figures up —!" But he exhaled it again in smoke.

"My additions don't matter when you've not to pay the bill." With which her meditation again bore her through the air. "The great thing was that when it so suddenly came up for her he wasn't afraid. If he had been afraid he could perfectly have prevented it. And if I had seen he was — if I hadn't seen he wasn't — so," said Mrs. Assingham, "could I. So," she declared, "WOULD I. It's perfectly true," she went on —"it was too good a thing for her, such a chance in life, not to be accepted. And I LIKED his not keeping her out of it merely from a fear of his own nature. It was so wonderful it should come to her. The only thing would have been if Charlotte herself couldn't have faced it. Then, if SHE had not had confidence, we might have talked. But she had it to any amount."

"Did you ask her how much?" Bob Assingham patiently inquired.

He had put the question with no more than his usual modest hope of reward, but he had pressed, this time, the sharpest spring of response. "Never, never — it wasn't a time to 'ask.' Asking is suggesting — and it wasn't a time to suggest. One had to make up one's mind, as quietly as possible, by what one could judge. And I judge, as I say, that Charlotte felt she could face it. For which she struck me at the time as — for so proud a creature — almost touchingly grateful. The thing I should never forgive her for would be her forgetting to whom it is her thanks have remained most due."

"That is to Mrs. Assingham?"

She said nothing for a little — there were, after all, alternatives. "Maggie herself of course — astonishing little Maggie."

"Is Maggie then astonishing too?" — and he gloomed out of his window.

His wife, on her side now, as they rolled, projected the same look. "I'm not sure that I don't begin to see more in her than — dear little person as I've always thought — I ever supposed there was. I'm not sure that, putting a good many things together, I'm not beginning to make her out rather extraordinary."

"You certainly will if you can," the Colonel resignedly remarked.

Again his companion said nothing; then again she broke out. "In fact — I do begin to feel it — Maggie's the great comfort. I'm getting hold of it. It will be SHE who'll see us through. In fact she'll have to. And she'll be able."

Touch by touch her meditation had completed it, but with a cumulative effect for her husband's general sense of her method that caused him to overflow, whimsically enough, in his corner, into an ejaculation now frequent on his lips for the relief that, especially in communion like the present, it gave him, and that Fanny had critically traced to the quaint example, the aboriginal homeliness, still so delightful, of Mr. Verver. "Oh, Lordy, Lordy!"

"If she is, however," Mrs. Assingham continued, "she'll be extraordinary enough — and that's what I'm thinking of. But I'm not indeed so very sure," she added, "of the person to whom Charlotte ought in decency to be most grateful. I mean I'm not sure if that person is even almost the incredible little idealist who has made her his wife."

"I shouldn't think you would be, love," the Colonel with some promptness responded. "Charlotte as the wife of an incredible little idealist —!" His cigar, in short, once more, could alone express it.

"Yet what is that, when one thinks, but just what she struck one as more or less persuaded that she herself was really going to be?" — this memory, for the full view, Fanny found herself also invoking.

It made her companion, in truth, slightly gape. "An incredible little idealist — Charlotte herself?"

"And she was sincere," his wife simply proceeded "she was unmistakably sincere. The question is only how much is left of it."

"And that — I see — happens to be another of the questions you can't ask her. You have to do it all," said Bob Assingham, "as if you were playing some game with its rules drawn up — though who's to come down on you if you break them I don't quite see. Or must you do it in three guesses — like forfeits on Christmas eve?" To which, as his ribaldry but dropped from her, he further added: "How much of anything will have to be left for you to be able to go on with it?"

"I shall go on," Fanny Assingham a trifle grimly declared, "while there's a scrap as big as your nail. But we're not yet, luckily, reduced only to that." She had another pause, holding the while the thread of that larger perception into which her view of Mrs. Verver's obligation to Maggie had suddenly expanded. "even if her debt was not to the others — even then it ought to be quite sufficiently to the Prince himself to keep her straight. For what, really, did the Prince do," she asked herself, "but generously trust her? What did he do but take it from her that if she felt herself willing it was because she felt herself strong? That creates for her, upon my word," Mrs. Assingham pursued, "a duty of considering him, of honourably repaying his trust, which — well, which she'll be really a fiend if she doesn't make the law of her conduct. I mean of course his trust that she wouldn't interfere with him — expressed by his holding himself quiet at the critical time."

The brougham was nearing home, and it was perhaps this sense of ebbing opportunity that caused the Colonel's next meditation to flower in a fashion almost surprising to his wife. They were united, for the most part, but by his exhausted patience; so that indulgent despair was generally, at the best, his note. He at present, however, actually compromised with his despair to the extent of practically admitting that he had followed her steps. He literally asked, in short, an intelligent, well nigh a sympathising, question. "Gratitude to the Prince for not having put a spoke in her wheel — that, you mean, should, taking it in the right way, be precisely the ballast of her boat?"

"Taking it in the right way." Fanny, catching at this gleam, emphasised the proviso.

"But doesn't it rather depend on what she may most feel to BE the right way?"

"No — it depends on nothing. Because there's only one way — for duty or delicacy."

"Oh — delicacy!" Bob Assingham rather crudely murmured.

"I mean the highest kind — moral. Charlotte's perfectly capable of appreciating that. By every dictate of moral delicacy she must let him alone."

"Then you've made up your mind it's all poor Charlotte?" he asked with an effect of abruptness.

The effect, whether intended or not, reached her — brought her face short round. It was a touch at which she again lost her balance, at which, somehow, the bottom dropped out of her recovered comfort. "Then you've made up yours differently? It really struck you that there IS something?"

The movement itself, apparently, made him once more stand off. He had felt on his nearer approach the high temperature of the question. "Perhaps that's just what she's doing: showing him how much she's letting him alone — pointing it out to him from day to day."

"Did she point it out by waiting for him to-night on the stair-case in the manner you described to me?"

"I really, my dear, described to you a manner?" the Colonel, clearly, from want of habit, scarce recognised himself in the imputation.

"Yes — for once in a way; in those few words we had after you had watched them come up you told me something of what you had seen. You didn't tell me very much — THAT you couldn't for your life; but I saw for myself that, strange to say, you had received your impression, and I felt therefore that there must indeed have been something out of the way for you so to betray it." She was fully upon him now, and she confronted him with his proved sensibility to the occasion — confronted him because of her own uneasy need to profit by it. It came over her still more than at the time, it came over her that he had been struck with something, even HE, poor dear man; and that for this to have occurred there must have been much to be struck with.

She tried in fact to corner him, to pack him insistently down, in the truth of his plain vision, the very plainness of which was its value; for so recorded, she felt, none of it would escape — she should have it at hand for reference. "Come, my dear — you thought what you thought: in the presence of what you saw you couldn't resist thinking. I don't ask more of it than that. And your idea is worth, this time, quite as much as any of mine — so that you can't pretend, as usual, that mine has run away with me. I haven't caught up with you. I stay where I am. But I see," she concluded, "where you are, and I'm much obliged to you for letting me. You give me a point de repere outside myself — which is where I like it. Now I can work round you."

Their conveyance, as she spoke, stopped at their door, and it was, on the spot, another fact of value for her that her husband, though seated on the side by which they must alight, made no movement. They were in a high degree votaries of the latch-key, so that their household had gone to bed; and as they were unaccompanied by a footman the coachman waited in peace. It was so indeed that for a minute Bob Assingham waited — conscious of a reason for replying to this address otherwise than by the so obvious method of turning his back. He didn't turn his face, but he stared straight before him, and his wife had already perceived in the fact of his not moving all the proof she could desire — proof, that is, of her own contention. She knew he never cared what she said, and his neglect of his chance to show it was thereby the more eloquent. "Leave it," he at last remarked, "to THEM."

"'Leave' it —?" She wondered.

"Let them alone. They'll manage."

"They'll manage, you mean, to do everything they want? Ah, there then you are!"

"They'll manage in their own way," the Colonel almost cryptically repeated.

It had its effect for her: quite apart from its light on the familiar phenomenon of her husband's indurated conscience, it gave her, full in her face, the particular evocation of which she had made him guilty. It was wonderful truly, then, the evocation. "So cleverly — THAT'S your idea? — that no one will be the wiser? It's your idea that we shall have done all that's required of us if we simply protect them?"

The Colonel, still in his place, declined, however, to be drawn into a statement of his idea. Statements were too much like theories, in which one lost one's way; he only knew what he said, and what he said represented the limited vibration of which his confirmed old toughness had been capable. Still, none the less, he had his point to make — for which he took another instant. But he made it, for the third time, in the same fashion. "They'll manage in their own way." With which he got out.

Oh yes, at this, for his companion, it had indeed its effect, and while he mounted their steps she but stared, without following him, at his opening of their door. Their hall was lighted, and as he stood in the aperture looking back at her, his tall lean figure outlined in darkness and with his crush-hat, according to his wont, worn cavalierly, rather diabolically, askew, he seemed to prolong the sinister emphasis of his meaning. In general, on these returns, he came back for her when he had prepared their entrance; so that it was now as if he were ashamed to face her in closer quarters. He looked at her across the interval, and, still in her seat, weighing his charge, she felt her whole view of everything flare up. Wasn't it simply what had been written in the Prince's own face BENEATH what he was saying? — didn't it correspond with the mocking presence there that she had had her troubled glimpse of? Wasn't, in fine, the pledge that they would "manage in their own way" the thing he had been feeling for his chance to invite her to take from him? Her husband's tone somehow fitted Amerigo's look — the one that had, for her, so strangely, peeped, from behind, over the shoulder of the one in front. She had not then read it — but wasn't she reading it when she now saw in it his surmise that she was perhaps to be squared? She wasn't to be squared, and while she heard her companion call across to her "Well, what's the matter?" she also took time to remind herself that she had decided she couldn't be frightened. The "matter"? — why, it was sufficiently the matter, with all this, that she felt a little sick. For it was not the Prince that she had been prepared to regard as primarily the shaky one. Shakiness in Charlotte she had, at the most, perhaps postulated — it would be, she somehow felt, more easy to deal with. Therefore if HE had come so far it was a different pair of sleeves. There was nothing to choose between them. It made her so helpless that, as the time passed without her alighting, the Colonel came back and fairly drew her forth; after which, on the pavement, under the street-lamp, their very silence might have been the mark of something grave — their silence eked out for her by his giving her his arm and their then crawling up their steps quite mildly and unitedly together, like some old Darby and Joan who have had a disappointment. It almost resembled a return from a funeral — unless indeed it resembled more the hushed approach to a house of mourning. What indeed had she come home for but to bury, as decently as possible, her mistake?

XVII

It appeared thus that they might enjoy together extraordinary freedom, the two friends, from the moment they should understand their position aright. With the Prince himself, from an early stage, not unnaturally, Charlotte had made a great point of their so understanding it; she had found frequent occasion to describe to him this necessity, and, her resignation tempered, or her intelligence at least quickened, by irrepressible irony, she applied at different times different names to the propriety of their case. The wonderful thing was that her sense of propriety had been, from the first, especially alive about it. There were hours when she spoke of their taking refuge in what she called the commonest tact — as if this principle alone would suffice to light their way; there were others when it might have seemed, to listen to her, that their course would demand of them the most anxious study and the most independent, not to say original, interpretation of signs. She talked now as if it were indicated, at every turn, by finger-posts of almost ridiculous prominence; she talked again as if it lurked in devious ways and were to be tracked through bush and briar; and she even, on occasion, delivered herself in the sense that, as their situation was unprecedented, so their heaven was without stars. "'Do'?" she once had echoed to him as the upshot of passages covertly, though briefly, occurring between them on her return from the visit to America that had immediately succeeded her marriage, determined for her by this event as promptly as an excursion of the like strange order had been prescribed in his own case. "Isn't the immense, the really quite matchless beauty of our position that we have to 'do' nothing in life at all? — nothing except the usual, necessary, everyday thing which consists in one's not being more of a fool than one can help. That's all — but that's as true for one time as for another. There has been plenty of 'doing,' and there will doubtless be plenty still; but it's all theirs, every inch of it; it's all a matter of what they've done TO us." And she showed how the question had therefore been only of their taking everything as everything came, and all as quietly as might be. Nothing stranger surely had ever happened to a conscientious, a well-meaning, a perfectly passive pair: no more extraordinary decree had ever been launched against such victims than this of forcing them against their will into a relation of mutual close contact that they had done everything to avoid.

She was to remember not a little, meanwhile, the particular prolonged silent look with which the Prince had met her allusion to these primary efforts at escape. She was inwardly to dwell on the element of the unuttered that her tone had caused to play up into his irresistible eyes; and this because she considered with pride and joy that she had, on the spot, disposed of the doubt, the question, the challenge, or whatever else might have been, that such a look could convey. He had been sufficiently off his guard to show some little wonder as to their having plotted so very hard against their destiny, and she knew well enough, of course, what, in this connection, was at the bottom of his thought, and what would have sounded out more or less if he had not happily saved himself from words. All men were brutes enough to catch when they might at such chances for dissent — for all the good it really did them; but the Prince's distinction was in being one of the few who could check himself before acting on the impulse. This, obviously, was what counted in a man as delicacy. If her friend had blurted or bungled he would have said, in his simplicity, "Did we do 'everything to avoid' it when we faced your remarkable marriage?" — quite handsomely of course using the plural, taking his share of the case, by way of a tribute of memory to the telegram she had received from him in Paris after Mr. Verver had despatched to Rome the news of their engagement. That telegram, that acceptance of the prospect proposed to them — an acceptance quite other than perfunctory — she had never destroyed; though reserved for no eyes but her own it was still carefully reserved. She kept it in a safe place — from which, very privately, she sometimes took it out to read it over. "A la guerre comme a la guerre then" — it had been couched in the French tongue. "We must lead our lives as we see them; but I am charmed with your courage and almost surprised at my own." The message had remained ambiguous; she had read it in more lights than one; it might mean that even without her his career was up-hill work for him, a daily fighting-matter on behalf of a good appearance, and that thus, if they were to become neighbours again, the event would compel him to live still more under arms. It might mean on the other hand that he found he was happy enough, and that accordingly, so far as she might imagine herself a danger, she was to think of him as prepared in advance, as really seasoned and secure. On his arrival in Paris with his wife, none the less, she had asked for no explanation, just as he himself had not asked if the document were still in her possession. Such an inquiry, everything implied, was beneath him — just as it was beneath herself to mention to him, uninvited, that she had instantly offered, and in perfect honesty, to show the telegram to Mr. Verver, and that if this companion had but said the word she would immediately have put it before him. She had thereby forborne to call his attention to her consciousness that such an exposure would, in all probability, straightway have dished her marriage; that all her future had in fact, for the moment, hung by the single hair of Mr. Verver's delicacy (as she supposed they must call it); and that her position, in the matter of responsibility, was therefore inattackably straight.

For the Prince himself, meanwhile, time, in its measured allowance, had originally much helped him — helped him in the sense of there not being enough of it to trip him up; in spite of which it was just this accessory element that seemed, at present, with wonders of patience, to lie in wait. Time had begotten at first, more than anything else, separations, delays and intervals; but it was troublesomely less of an aid from the moment it began so to abound that he had to meet the question of what to do with it. Less of it was required for the state of being married than he had, on the whole, expected; less, strangely, for the state of being married even as he was married. And there was a logic in the matter, he knew; a logic that but gave this truth a sort of solidity of evidence. Mr. Verver, decidedly, helped him with it — with his wedded condition; helped him really so much that it made all the difference. In the degree in which he rendered it the service on Mr. Verver's part was remarkable — as indeed what service, from the first of their meeting, had not been? He was living, he had been living these four or five years, on Mr. Verver's services: a truth scarcely less plain if he dealt with them, for appreciation, one by one, than if he poured them all together into the general pot of his gratitude and let the thing simmer to a nourishing broth. To the latter way with them he was undoubtedly most disposed; yet he would even thus, on occasion, pick out a piece to taste on its own merits. Wondrous at such hours could seem the savour of the particular "treat," at his father-inlaw's expense, that he more and more struck himself as enjoying. He had needed months and months to arrive at a full appreciation — he couldn't originally have given offhand a name to his deepest obligation; but by the time the name had flowered in his mind he was practically living at the ease guaranteed him. Mr. Verver then, in a word, took care of his relation to Maggie, as he took care, and apparently always would, of everything else. He relieved him of all anxiety about his married life in the same manner in which he relieved him on the score of his bank-account. And as he performed the latter office by communicating with the bankers, so the former sprang as directly from his good understanding with his daughter. This understanding had, wonderfully — THAT was in high evidence — the same deep intimacy as the commercial, the financial association founded, far down, on a community of interest. And the correspondence, for the Prince, carried itself out in identities of character the vision of which, fortunately, rather tended to amuse than to — as might have happened — irritate him. Those people — and his free synthesis lumped together capitalists and bankers, retired men of business, illustrious collectors, American fathers-inlaw, American fathers, little American daughters, little American wives — those people were of the same large lucky group, as one might say; they were all, at least, of the same general species and had the same general instincts; they hung together, they passed each other the word, they spoke each other's language, they did each other "turns." In this last connection it of course came up for our young man at a given moment that Maggie's relation with HIM was also, on the perceived basis, taken care of. Which was in fact the real upshot of the matter. It was a "funny" situation — that is it was funny just as it stood. Their married life was in question, but the solution was, not less strikingly, before them. It was all right for himself, because Mr. Verver worked it so for Maggie's comfort; and it was all right for Maggie, because he worked it so for her husband's.

The fact that time, however, was not, as we have said, wholly on the Prince's side might have shown for particularly true one dark day on which, by an odd but not unprecedented chance, the reflections just noted offered themselves as his main recreation. They alone, it appeared, had been appointed to fill the hours for him, and even to fill the great square house in Portland Place, where the scale of one of the smaller saloons fitted them but loosely. He had looked into this room on the chance that he might find the Princess at tea; but though the fireside service of the repast was shiningly present the mistress of the table was not, and he had waited for her, if waiting it could be called, while he measured again and again the stretch of polished floor. He could have named to himself no pressing reason for seeing her at this moment, and her not coming in, as the half-hour elapsed, became in fact quite positively, however perversely, the circumstance that kept him on the spot. Just there, he might have been feeling, just there he could best take his note. This observation was certainly by itself meagre amusement for a dreary little crisis; but his walk to and fro, and in particular his repeated pause at one of the high front windows, gave each of the ebbing minutes, none the less, after a time, a little more of the quality of a quickened throb of the spirit. These throbs scarce expressed, however, the impatience of desire, any more than they stood for sharp disappointment: the series together resembled perhaps more than anything else those fine waves of clearness through which, for a watcher of the east, dawn at last trembles into rosy day. The illumination indeed was all for the mind, the prospect revealed by it a mere immensity of the world of thought; the material outlook was all the while a different matter. The March afternoon, judged at the window, had blundered back into autumn; it had been raining for hours, and the colour of the rain, the colour of the air, of the mud, of the opposite houses, of life altogether, in so grim a joke, so idiotic a masquerade, was an unutterable dirty brown. There was at first even, for the young man, no faint flush in the fact of the direction taken, while he happened to look out, by a slow-jogging four-wheeled cab which, awkwardly deflecting from the middle course, at the apparent instance of a person within, began to make for the left-hand pavement and so at last, under further instructions, floundered to a full stop before the Prince's windows. The person within, alighting with an easier motion, proved to be a lady who left the vehicle to wait and, putting up no umbrella, quickly crossed the wet interval that separated her from the house. She but flitted and disappeared; yet the Prince, from his standpoint, had had time to recognise her, and the recognition kept him for some minutes motionless.

Charlotte Stant, at such an hour, in a shabby four-wheeler and a waterproof, Charlotte Stant turning up for him at the very climax of his special inner vision, was an apparition charged with a congruity at which he stared almost as if it had been a violence. The effect of her coming to see him, him only, had, while he stood waiting, a singular intensity — though after some minutes had passed the certainty of this began to drop. Perhaps she had NOT come, or had come only for Maggie; perhaps, on learning below that the Princess had not returned, she was merely leaving a message, writing a word on a card. He should see, at any rate; and meanwhile, controlling himself, would do nothing. This thought of not interfering took on a sudden force for him; she would doubtless hear he was at home, but he would let her visit to him be all of her own choosing. And his view of a reason for leaving her free was the more remarkable that, though taking no step, he yet intensely hoped. The harmony of her breaking into sight while the superficial conditions were so against her was a harmony with conditions that were far from superficial and that gave, for his imagination, an extraordinary value to her presence. The value deepened strangely, moreover, with the rigour of his own attitude — with the fact too that, listening hard, he neither heard the house-door close again nor saw her go back to her cab; and it had risen to a climax by the time he had become aware, with his quickened sense, that she had followed the butler up to the landing from which his room opened. If anything could further then have added to it, the renewed pause outside, as if she had said to the man "Wait a moment!" would have constituted this touch. Yet when the man had shown her in, had advanced to the tea-table to light the lamp under the kettle and had then busied himself, all deliberately, with the fire, she made it easy for her host to drop straight from any height of tension and to meet her, provisionally, on the question of Maggie. While the butler remained it was Maggie that she had come to see and Maggie that — in spite of this attendant's high blankness on the subject of all possibilities on that lady's part — she would cheerfully, by the fire, wait for. As soon as they were alone together, however, she mounted, as with the whizz and the red light of a rocket, from the form to the fact, saying straight out, as she stood and looked at him: "What else, my dear, what in the world else can we do?"

It was as if he then knew, on the spot, why he had been feeling, for hours, as he had felt — as if he in fact knew, within the minute, things he had not known even while she was panting, as from the effect of the staircase, at the door of the room. He knew at the same time, none the less, that she knew still more than he — in the sense, that is, of all the signs and portents that might count for them; and his vision of alternative — she could scarce say what to call them, solutions, satisfactions — opened out, altogether, with this tangible truth of her attitude by the chimney-place, the way she looked at him as through the gained advantage of it; her right hand resting on the marble and her left keeping her skirt from the fire while she held out a foot to dry. He couldn't have told what particular links and gaps had at the end of a few minutes found themselves renewed and bridged; for he remembered no occasion, in Rome, from which the picture could have been so exactly copied. He remembered, that is, none of her coming to see him in the rain while a muddy four-wheeler waited, and while, though having left her waterproof downstairs, she was yet invested with the odd eloquence — the positive picturesqueness, yes, given all the rest of the matter — of a dull dress and a black Bowdlerised hat that seemed to make a point of insisting on their time of life and their moral intention, the hat's and the frock's own, as well as on the irony of indifference to them practically playing in her so handsome rain-freshened face. The sense of the past revived for him nevertheless as it had not yet done: it made that other time somehow meet the future close, interlocking with it, before his watching eyes, as in a long embrace of arms and lips, and so handling and hustling the present that this poor quantity scarce retained substance enough, scarce remained sufficiently THERE, to be wounded or shocked.

What had happened, in short, was that Charlotte and he had, by a single turn of the wrist of fate —"led up" to indeed, no doubt, by steps and stages that conscious computation had missed — been placed face to face in a freedom that partook, extraordinarily, of ideal perfection, since the magic web had spun itself without their toil, almost without their touch. Above all, on this occasion, once more, there sounded through their safety, as an undertone, the very voice he had listened to on the eve of his marriage with such another sort of unrest. Dimly, again and again, from that period on, he had seemed to hear it tell him why it kept recurring; but it phrased the large music now in a way that filled the room. The reason was — into which he had lived, quite intimately, by the end of a quarter-of-an-hour — that just this truth of their safety offered it now a kind of unexampled receptacle, letting it spread and spread, but at the same time elastically enclosing it, banking it in, for softness, as with billows of eiderdown. On that morning; in the Park there had been, however dissimulated, doubt and danger, whereas the tale this afternoon was taken up with a highly emphasised confidence. The emphasis, for their general comfort, was what Charlotte had come to apply; inasmuch as, though it was not what she definitely began with, it had soon irrepressibly shaped itself. It was the meaning of the question she had put to him as soon as they were alone — even though indeed, as from not quite understanding, he had not then directly replied; it was the meaning of everything else, down to the conscious quaintness of her ricketty "growler" and the conscious humility of her dress. It had helped him a little, the question of these eccentricities, to let her immediate appeal pass without an answer. He could ask her instead what had become of her carriage and why, above all, she was not using it in such weather.

"It's just because of the weather," she explained. "It's my little idea. It makes me feel as I used to — when I could do as I liked."

XVIII

This came out so straight that he saw at once how much truth it expressed; yet it was truth that still a little puzzled him. "But did you ever like knocking about in such discomfort?"

"It seems to me now that I then liked everything. It's the charm, at any rate," she said from her place at the fire, "of trying again the old feelings. They come back — they come back. Everything," she went on, "comes back. Besides," she wound up, "you know for yourself."

He stood near her, his hands in his pockets; but not looking at her, looking hard at the tea-table. "Ah, I haven't your courage. Moreover," he laughed, "it seems to me that, so far as that goes, I do live in hansoms. But you must awfully want your tea," he quickly added; "so let me give you a good stiff cup."

He busied himself with this care, and she sat down, on his pushing up a low seat, where she had been standing; so that, while she talked, he could bring her what she further desired. He moved to and fro before her, he helped himself; and her visit, as the moments passed, had more and more the effect of a signal communication that she had come, all responsibly and deliberately, as on the clear show of the clock-face of their situation, to make. The whole demonstration, none the less, presented itself as taking place at a very high level of debate — in the cool upper air of the finer discrimination, the deeper sincerity, the larger philosophy. No matter what were the facts invoked and arrayed, it was only a question, as yet, of their seeing their way together: to which indeed, exactly, the present occasion appeared to have so much to contribute. "It's not that you haven't my courage," Charlotte said, "but that you haven't, I rather think, my imagination. Unless indeed it should turn out after all," she added, "that you haven't even my intelligence. However, I shall not be afraid of that till you've given me more proof." And she made again, but more clearly, her point of a moment before. "You knew, besides, you knew today, I would come. And if you knew that you know everything." So she pursued, and if he didn't meanwhile, if he didn't even at this, take her up, it might be that she was so positively fitting him again with the fair face of temporising kindness that he had given her, to keep her eyes on, at the other important juncture, and the sense of which she might ever since have been carrying about with her like a precious medal — not exactly blessed by the Pope suspended round her neck. She had come back, however this might be, to her immediate account of herself, and no mention of their great previous passage was to rise to the lips of either. "Above all," she said, "there has been the personal romance of it."

"Of tea with me over the fire? Ah, so far as that goes I don't think even my intelligence fails me."

"Oh, it's further than that goes; and if I've had a better day than you it's perhaps, when I come to think of it, that I AM braver. You bore yourself, you see. But I don't. I don't, I don't," she repeated.

"It's precisely boring one's self without relief," he protested, "that takes courage."

"Passive then — not active. My romance is that, if you want to know, I've been all day on the town. Literally on the town — isn't that what they call it? I know how it feels." After which, as if breaking off, "And you, have you never been out?" she asked.

He still stood there with his hands in his pockets. "What should I have gone out for?"

"Oh, what should people in our case do anything for? But you're wonderful, all of YOU — you know how to live. We're clumsy brutes, we other's, beside you — we must always be 'doing' something. However," Charlotte pursued, "if you had gone out you might have missed the chance of me — which I'm sure, though you won't confess it, was what you didn't want; and might have missed, above all, the satisfaction that, look blank about it as you will, I've come to congratulate you on. That's really what I can at last do. You can't not know at least, on such a day as this — you can't not know," she said, "where you are." She waited as for him either to grant that he knew or to pretend that he didn't; but he only drew a long deep breath which came out like a moan of impatience. It brushed aside the question of where he was or what he knew; it seemed to keep the ground clear for the question of his visitor herself, that of Charlotte Verver exactly as she sat there. So, for some moments, with their long look, they but treated the matter in silence; with the effect indeed, by the end of the time, of having considerably brought it on. This was sufficiently marked in what Charlotte next said. "There it all is — extraordinary beyond words. It makes such a relation for us as, I verily believe, was never before in the world thrust upon two well-meaning creatures. Haven't we therefore to take things as we find them?" She put the question still more directly than that of a moment before, but to this one, as well, he returned no immediate answer. Noticing only that she had finished her tea, he relieved her of her cup, carried it back to the table, asked her what more she would have; and then, on her "Nothing, thanks," returned to the fire and restored a displaced log to position by a small but almost too effectual kick. She had meanwhile got up again, and it was on her feet that she repeated the words she had first frankly spoken. "What else can we do, what in all the world else?"

He took them up, however, no more than at first. "Where then have you been?" he asked as from mere interest in her adventure.

"Everywhere I could think of — except to see people. I didn't want people — I wanted too much to think. But I've been back at intervals — three times; and then come away again. My cabman must think me crazy — it's very amusing; I shall owe him, when we come to settle, more money than he has ever seen. I've been, my dear," she went on, "to the British Museum — which, you know, I always adore. And I've been to the National Gallery, and to a dozen old booksellers', coming across treasures, and I've lunched, on some strange nastiness, at a cookshop in Holborn. I wanted to go to the Tower, but it was too far — my old man urged that; and I would have gone to the Zoo if it hadn't been too wet — which he also begged me to observe. But you wouldn't believe — I did put in St. Paul's. Such days," she wound up, "are expensive; for, besides the cab, I've bought quantities of books." She immediately passed, at any rate, to another point: "I can't help wondering when you must last have laid eyes on them." And then as it had apparently for her companion an effect of abruptness: "Maggie, I mean, and the child. For I suppose you know he's with her."

"Oh yes, I know he's with her. I saw them this morning."

"And did they then announce their programme?"

"She told me she was taking him, as usual, da nonno."

"And for the whole day?"

He hesitated, but it was as if his attitude had slowly shifted.

"She didn't say. And I didn't ask."

"Well," she went on, "it can't have been later than half-past ten — I mean when you saw them. They had got to Eaton Square before eleven. You know we don't formally breakfast, Adam and I; we have tea in our rooms — at least I have; but luncheon is early, and I saw my husband, this morning, by twelve; he was showing the child a picture-book. Maggie had been there with them, had left them settled together. Then she had gone out — taking the carriage for something he had been intending but that she offered to do instead."

The Prince appeared to confess, at this, to his interest.

"Taking, you mean, YOUR carriage?"

"I don't know which, and it doesn't matter. It's not a question," she smiled, "of a carriage the more or the less. It's not a question even, if you come to that, of a cab. It's so beautiful," she said, "that it's not a question of anything vulgar or horrid." Which she gave him time to agree about; and though he was silent it was, rather remarkably, as if he fell in. "I went out — I wanted to. I had my idea. It seemed to me important. It has BEEN — it IS important. I know as I haven't known before the way they feel. I couldn't in any other way have made so sure of it."

"They feel a confidence," the Prince observed.

He had indeed said it for her. "They feel a confidence." And she proceeded, with lucidity, to the fuller illustration of it; speaking again of the three different moments that, in the course of her wild ramble, had witnessed her return — for curiosity, and even really a little from anxiety — to Eaton Square. She was possessed of a latch-key, rarely used: it had always irritated Adam

— one of the few things that did — to find servants standing up so inhumanly straight when they came home, in the small hours, after parties. "So I had but to slip in, each time, with my cab at the door, and make out for myself, without their knowing it, that Maggie was still there. I came, I went — without their so much as dreaming. What do they really suppose," she asked, "becomes of one? — not so much sentimentally or morally, so to call it, and since that doesn't matter; but even just physically, materially, as a mere wandering woman: as a decent harmless wife, after all; as the best stepmother, after all, that really ever was; or at the least simply as a maitresse de maison not quite without a conscience. They must even in their odd way," she declared, "have SOME idea."

"Oh, they've a great deal of idea," said the Prince. And nothing was easier than to mention the quantity. "They think so much of us. They think in particular so much of you."

"Ah, don't put it all on 'me'!" she smiled.

But he was putting it now where she had admirably prepared the place. "It's a matter of your known character."

"Ah, thank you for 'known'!" she still smiled.

"It's a matter of your wonderful cleverness and wonderful charm. It's a matter of what those things have done for you in the world — I mean in THIS world and this place. You're a Personage for them — and Personages do go and come."

"Oh no, my dear; there you're quite wrong." And she laughed now in the happier light they had diffused. "That's exactly what Personages don't do: they live in state and under constant consideration; they haven't latch-keys, but drums and trumpets announce them; and when they go out in growlers it makes a greater noise still. It's you, caro mio," she said, "who, so far as that goes, are the Personage."

"Ah," he in turn protested, "don't put it all on me! What, at any rate, when you get home," he added, "shall you say that you've been doing?"

"I shall say, beautifully, that I've been here."

"All day?"

"Yes — all day. Keeping you company in your solitude. How can we understand anything," she went on, "without really seeing that this is what they must like to think I do for you? — just as, quite as comfortably, you do it for me. The thing is for us to learn to take them as they are."

He considered this a while, in his restless way, but with his eyes not turning from her; after which, rather disconnectedly, though very vehemently, he brought out: "How can I not feel more than anything else how they adore together my boy?" And then, further, as if, slightly disconcerted, she had nothing to meet this and he quickly perceived the effect: "They would have done the same for one of yours."

"Ah, if I could have had one —! I hoped and I believed," said Charlotte, "that that would happen. It would have been better. It would have made perhaps some difference. He thought so too, poor duck — that it might have been. I'm sure he hoped and intended so. It's not, at any rate," she went on, "my fault. There it is." She had uttered these statements, one by one, gravely, sadly and responsibly, owing it to her friend to be clear. She paused briefly, but, as if once for all, she made her clearness complete. "And now I'm too sure. It will never be."

He waited for a moment. "Never?"

"Never." They treated the matter not exactly with solemnity, but with a certain decency, even perhaps urgency, of distinctness. "It would probably have been better," Charlotte added. "But things turn out —! And it leaves us" — she made the point —"more alone."

He seemed to wonder. "It leaves you more alone."

"Oh," she again returned, "don't put it all on me! Maggie would have given herself to his child, I'm sure, scarcely less than he gives himself to yours. It would have taken more than any child of mine," she explained —"it would have taken more than ten children of mine, could I have had them — to keep our sposi apart." She smiled as for the breadth of the image, but, as he seemed to take it, in spite of this, for important, she then spoke gravely enough. "It's as strange as you like, but we're immensely alone." He kept vaguely moving, but there were moments when, again, with an awkward ease and his hands in his pockets, he was more directly before her. He stood there at these last words, which had the effect of making him for a little throw back his head and, as thinking something out, stare up at the ceiling. "What will you say," she meanwhile asked, "that you've been doing?" This brought his consciousness and his eyes back to her, and she pointed her question. "I mean when she comes in-for I suppose she WILL, some time, come in. It seems to me we must say the same thing."

Well, he thought again. "Yet I can scarce pretend to have had what I haven't."

"Ah, WHAT haven't you had? — what aren't you having?"

Her question rang out as they lingered face to face, and he still took it, before he answered, from her eyes. "We must at least then, not to be absurd together, do the same thing. We must act, it would really seem, in concert."

"It would really seem!" Her eyebrows, her shoulders went up, quite in gaiety, as for the relief this brought her. "It's all in the world I pretend. We must act in concert. Heaven knows," she said, "THEY do!"

So it was that he evidently saw and that, by his admission, the case, could fairly be put. But what he evidently saw appeared to come over him, at the same time, as too much for him, so that he fell back suddenly to ground where she was not awaiting him. "The difficulty is, and will always be, that I don't understand them. I didn't at first, but I thought I should learn to. That was what I hoped, and it appeared then that Fanny Assingham might help me."

"Oh, Fanny Assingham!" said Charlotte Verver.

He stared a moment at her tone. "She would do anything for us."

To which Charlotte at first said nothing — as if from the sense of too much. Then, indulgently enough, she shook her head. "We're beyond her."

He thought a moment — as of where this placed them. "She'd do anything then for THEM."

"Well, so would we — so that doesn't help us. She has broken down. She doesn't understand us. And really, my dear," Charlotte added, "Fanny Assingham doesn't matter."

He wondered again. "Unless as taking care of THEM."

"Ah," Charlotte instantly said, "isn't it for us, only, to do that?" She spoke as with a flare of pride for their privilege and their duty. "I think we want no one's aid."

She spoke indeed with a nobleness not the less effective for coming in so oddly; with a sincerity visible even through the complicated twist by which any effort to protect the father and the daughter seemed necessarily conditioned for them. It moved him, in any case, as if some spring of his own, a weaker one, had suddenly been broken by it. These things, all the while, the privilege, the duty, the opportunity, had been the substance of his own vision; they formed the note he had been keeping back to show her that he was not, in their so special situation, without a responsible view. A conception that he could name, and could act on, was something that now, at last, not to be too eminent a fool, he was required by all the graces to produce, and the luminous idea she had herself uttered would have been his expression of it. She had anticipated him, but, as her expression left, for positive beauty, nothing to be desired, he felt rather righted than wronged. A large response, as he looked at her, came into his face, a light of excited perception all his own, in the glory of which — as it almost might be called — what he gave her back had the value of what she had, given him. "They're extraordinarily happy."

Oh, Charlotte's measure of it was only too full. "Beatifically."

"That's the great thing," he went on; "so that it doesn't matter, really, that one doesn't understand. Besides, you do — enough."

"I understand my husband perhaps," she after an instant conceded. "I don't understand your wife."

"You're of the same race, at any rate — more or less; of the same general tradition and education, of the same moral paste. There are things you have in common with them. But I, on my side, as I've gone on trying to see if I haven't some of these things too — I, on my side, have more and more failed. There seem at last to be none worth mentioning. I can't help seeing it — I'm decidedly too different."

"Yet you're not" — Charlotte made the important point —"too different from ME."

"I don't know — as we're not married. That brings things out. Perhaps if we were," he said, "you WOULD find some abyss of divergence."

"Since it depends on that then," she smiled, "I'm safe — as you are anyhow. Moreover, as one has so often had occasion to feel, and even to remark, they're very, very simple. That makes," she added, "a difficulty for belief; but when once one has taken it in it makes less difficulty for action. I HAVE at last, for myself, I think, taken it in. I'm not afraid."

He wondered a moment. "Not afraid of what?"

"Well, generally, of some beastly mistake. Especially of any mistake founded on one's idea of their difference. For that idea," Charlotte developed, "positively makes one so tender."

"Ah, but rather!"

"Well then, there it is. I can't put myself into Maggie's skin — I can't, as I say. It's not my fit — I shouldn't be able, as I see it, to breathe in it. But I can feel that I'd do anything — to shield it from a bruise. Tender as I am for her too," she went on, "I think I'm still more so for my husband. HE'S in truth of a sweet simplicity —!"

The Prince turned over a while the sweet simplicity of Mr. Verver. "Well, I don't know that I can choose. At night all cats are grey. I only see how, for so many reasons, we ought to stand toward them — and how, to do ourselves justice, we do. It represents for us a conscious care —"

"Of every hour, literally," said Charlotte. She could rise to the highest measure of the facts. "And for which we must trust each other —!"

"Oh, as we trust the saints in glory. Fortunately," the Prince hastened to add, "we can." With which, as for the full assurance and the pledge it involved, their hands instinctively found their hands. "It's all too wonderful."

Firmly and gravely she kept his hand. "It's too beautiful."

And so for a minute they stood together, as strongly held and as closely confronted as any hour of their easier past even had seen them. They were silent at first, only facing and faced, only grasping and grasped, only meeting and met. "It's sacred," he said at last.

"It's sacred," she breathed back to him. They vowed it, gave it out and took it in, drawn, by their intensity, more closely together. Then of a sudden, through this tightened circle, as at the issue of a narrow strait into the sea beyond, everything broke up, broke down, gave way, melted and mingled. Their lips sought their lips, their pressure their response and their response their pressure; with a violence that had sighed itself the next moment to the longest and deepest of stillnesses they passionately sealed their pledge.

XIX

He had taken it from her, as we have seen, moreover, that Fanny Assingham didn't now matter — the "now" he had even himself supplied, as no more than fair to his sense of various earlier stages; and, though his assent remained scarce more than tacit, his behaviour, for the hour, so fell into line that, for many days, he kept postponing the visit he had promised his old friend on the occasion of their talk at the Foreign Office. With regret, none the less, would he have seen it quite extinguished, that theory of their relation as attached pupil and kind instructress in which they had from the first almost equally found a convenience. It had been he, no doubt, who had most put it forward, since his need of knowledge fairly exceeded her mild pretension; but he had again and again repeated to her that he should never, without her, have been where he was, and she had not successfully concealed the pleasure it might give her to believe it, even after the question of where he was had begun to show itself as rather more closed than open to interpretation. It had never indeed, before that evening, come up as during the passage at the official party, and he had for the first time at those moments, a little disappointedly, got the impression of a certain failure, on the dear woman's part, of something he was aware of having always rather freely taken for granted in her. Of what exactly the failure consisted he would still perhaps have felt it a little harsh to try to say; and if she had in fact, as by Charlotte's observation, "broken down," the details of the collapse would be comparatively unimportant. They came to the same thing, all such collapses — the failure of courage, the failure of friendship, or the failure just simply of tact; for didn't any one of them by itself amount really to the failure of wit? — which was the last thing he had expected of her and which would be but another name for the triumph of stupidity. It had been Charlotte's remark that they were at last "beyond" her; whereas he had ever enjoyed believing that a certain easy imagination in her would keep up with him to the end. He shrank from affixing a label to Mrs. Assingham's want of faith; but when he thought, at his ease, of the way persons who were capable really entertained — or at least with any refinement — the passion of personal loyalty, he figured for them a play of fancy neither timorous nor scrupulous. So would his personal loyalty, if need be, have accepted the adventure for the good creature herself; to that definite degree that he had positively almost missed the luxury of some such call from her. That was what it all came back to again with these people among whom he was married — that one found one used one's imagination mainly for wondering how they contrived so little to appeal to it. He felt at moments as if there were never anything to do for them that was worthy — to call worthy — of the personal relation; never any charming charge to take of any confidence deeply reposed. He might vulgarly have put it that one had never to plot or to lie for them; he might humourously have put it that one had never, as by the higher conformity, to lie in wait with the dagger or to prepare, insidiously, the cup. These were the services that, by all romantic tradition, were consecrated to affection quite as much as to hate. But he could amuse himself with saying — so far as the amusement went — that they were what he had once for all turned his back on.

Fanny was meanwhile frequent, it appeared, in Eaton Square; so much he gathered from the visitor who was not infrequent, least of all at tea-time, during the same period, in Portland Place; though they had little need to talk of her after practically agreeing that they had outlived her. To the scene of these conversations and suppressions Mrs. Assingham herself made, actually, no approach; her latest view of her utility seeming to be that it had found in Eaton Square its most urgent field. It was finding there in fact everything and everyone but the Prince, who mostly, just now, kept away, or who, at all events, on the interspaced occasions of his calling, happened not to encounter the only person from whom he was a little estranged. It would have been all prodigious if he had not already, with Charlotte's aid, so very considerably lived into it — it would have been all indescribably remarkable, this fact that, with wonderful causes for it so operating on the surface, nobody else, as yet, in the combination, seemed estranged from anybody. If Mrs. Assingham delighted in Maggie she knew by this time how most easily to reach her, and if she was unhappy about Charlotte she knew, by the same reasoning, how most probably to miss that vision of her on which affliction would feed. It might feed of course on finding her so absent from her home — just as this particular phenomenon of her domestic detachment could be, by the anxious mind, best studied there. Fanny was, however, for her reasons, "shy" of Portland Place itself — this was appreciable; so that she might well, after all, have no great light on the question of whether Charlotte's appearances there were frequent or not, any more than on that of the account they might be keeping of the usual solitude (since it came to this) of the head of that house. There was always, to cover all ambiguities, to constitute a fund of explanation for the divisions of Mrs. Verver's day, the circumstance that, at the point they had all reached together, Mrs. Verver was definitely and by general acclamation in charge of the "social relations" of the family, literally of those of the two households; as to her genius for representing which in the great world and in the grand style vivid evidence had more and more accumulated. It had been established in the two households at an early stage, and with the highest good-humour, that Charlotte was a, was THE, "social success," whereas the Princess, though kind, though punctilious, though charming, though in fact the dearest little creature in the world and the Princess into the bargain, was distinctly not, would distinctly never be, and might as well, practically, give it up: whether through being above it or below it, too much outside of it or too much lost in it, too unequipped or too indisposed, didn't especially matter. What sufficed was that the whole thing, call it appetite or call it patience, the act of representation at large and the daily business of intercourse, fell in with Charlotte's tested facility and, not much less visibly, with her accommodating, her generous, view of her domestic use. She had come, frankly, into the connection, to do and to be what she could, "no questions asked," and she had taken over, accordingly, as it stood, and in the finest practical spirit, the burden of a visiting-list that Maggie, originally, left to herself, and left even more to the Principino, had suffered to get inordinately out of hand.

She had in a word not only mounted, cheerfully, the London treadmill — she had handsomely professed herself, for the further comfort of the three others, sustained in the effort by a "frivolous side," if that were not too harsh a name for a pleasant constitutional curiosity. There were possibilities of dulness, ponderosities of practice, arid social sands, the bad quarters-of-an-hour that turned up like false pieces in a debased currency, of which she made, on principle, very nearly as light as if she had not been clever enough to distinguish. The Prince had, on this score, paid her his compliment soon after her return from her wedding-tour in America, where, by all accounts, she had wondrously borne the brunt; facing brightly, at her husband's side, everything that came up — and what had come, often, was beyond words: just as, precisely, with her own interest only at stake, she had thrown up the game during the visit paid before her marriage. The discussion of the American world, the comparison of notes, impressions and adventures, had been all at hand, as a ground of meeting for Mrs. Verver and her husband's son-in-law, from the hour of the reunion of the two couples. Thus it had been, in short, that Charlotte could, for her friend's appreciation, so promptly make her point; even using expressions from which he let her see, at the hour, that he drew amusement of his own. "What could be more simple than one's going through with everything," she had asked, "when it's so plain a part of one's contract? I've got so much, by my marriage" — for she had never for a moment concealed from him how "much" she had felt it and was finding it "that I should deserve no charity if I stinted my return. Not to do that, to give back on the contrary all one can, are just one's decency and one's honour and one's virtue. These things, henceforth, if you're interested to know, are my rule of life, the absolute little gods of my worship, the holy images set up on the wall. Oh yes, since I'm not a brute," she had wound up, "you shall see me as I AM!" Which was therefore as he had seen her — dealing always, from month to month, from day to day and from one occasion to the other, with the duties of a remunerated office. Her perfect, her brilliant efficiency had doubtless, all the while, contributed immensely to the pleasant ease in which her husband and her husband's daughter were lapped. It had in fact probably done something more than this — it had given them a finer and sweeter view of the possible scope of that ease. They had brought her in-on the crudest expression of it — to do the "worldly" for them, and she had done it with such genius that they had themselves in consequence renounced it even more than they had originally intended. In proportion as she did it, moreover, was she to be relieved of other and humbler doings; which minor matters, by the properest logic, devolved therefore upon Maggie, in whose chords and whose province they more naturally lay. Not less naturally, by the same token, they included the repair, at the hands of the latter young woman, of every stitch conceivably dropped by Charlotte in Eaton Square. This was homely work, but that was just what made it Maggie's. Bearing in mind dear Amerigo, who was so much of her own great mundane feather, and whom the homeliness in question didn't, no doubt, quite equally provide for — that would be, to balance, just in a manner Charlotte's very most charming function, from the moment Charlotte could be got adequately to recognise it.

Well, that Charlotte might be appraised as at last not ineffectually recognising it, was a re-flection that, during the days with which we are actually engaged, completed in the Prince's breast these others, these images and ruminations of his leisure, these gropings and fittings of his conscience and his experience, that we have attempted to set in order there. They bore him company, not insufficiently — considering, in especial, his fuller resources in that line — while he worked out — to the last lucidity the principle on which he forbore either to seek Fanny out in Cadogan Place or to perpetrate the error of too marked an assiduity in Eaton Square. This error would be his not availing himself to the utmost of the convenience of any artless theory of his constitution, or of Charlotte's, that might prevail there. That artless theories could and did prevail was a fact he had ended by accepting, under copious evidence, as definite and ultimate; and it consorted with common prudence, with the simplest economy of life, not to be wasteful of any odd gleaning. To haunt Eaton Square, in fine, would be to show that he had not, like his brilliant associate, a sufficiency of work in the world. It was just his having that sufficiency, it was just their having it together, that, so strangely and so blessedly, made, as they put it to each other, everything possible. What further propped up the case, moreover, was that the "world," by still another beautiful perversity of their chance, included Portland Place without including to anything like the same extent Eaton Square. The latter residence, at the same time, it must promptly be added, did, on occasion, wake up to opportunity and, as giving itself a frolic shake, send out a score of invitations — one of which fitful flights, precisely, had, before Easter, the effect of disturbing a little our young man's measure of his margin. Maggie, with a proper spirit, held that her father ought from time to time to give a really considered dinner, and Mr. Verver, who had as little idea as ever of not meeting expectation, was of the harmonious opinion that his wife ought. Charlotte's own judgment was, always, that they were ideally free — the proof of which would always be, she maintained, that everyone they feared they might most have alienated by neglect would arrive, wreathed with smiles, on the merest hint of a belated signal. Wreathed in smiles, all round, truly enough, these apologetic banquets struck Amerigo as being; they were, frankly, touching occasions to him, marked, in the great London bousculade, with a small, still grace of their own, an investing amenity and humanity. Everybody came, everybody rushed; but all succumbed to the soft influence, and the brutality of mere multitude, of curiosity without tenderness, was put off, at the foot of the fine staircase, with the overcoats and shawls. The entertainment offered a few evenings before Easter, and at which Maggie and he were inevitably present as guests, was a discharge of obligations not insistently incurred, and had thereby, possibly, all the more, the note of this almost Arcadian optimism: a large, bright, dull, murmurous, mild-eyed, middle-aged dinner, involving for the most part very bland, though very exalted, immensely announceable and hierarchically placeable couples, and followed, without the oppression of a later contingent, by a brief instrumental concert, over the preparation of which, the Prince knew, Maggie's anxiety had conferred with Charlotte's ingenuity and both had supremely revelled, as it were, in Mr. Verver's solvency.

The Assinghams were there, by prescription, though quite at the foot of the social ladder, and with the Colonel's wife, in spite of her humility of position, the Prince was more inwardly occupied than with any other person except Charlotte. He was occupied with Charlotte because, in the first place, she looked so inordinately handsome and held so high, where so much else was mature and sedate, the torch of responsive youth and the standard of passive grace; and because of the fact that, in the second, the occasion, so far as it referred itself with any confidence of emphasis to a hostess, seemed to refer itself preferentially, well-meaningly and perversely, to Maggie. It was not indistinguishable to him, when once they were all stationed, that his wife too had in perfection her own little character; but he wondered how it managed so visibly to simplify itself — and this, he knew, in spite of any desire she entertained — to the essential air of having overmuch on her mind the felicity, and indeed the very conduct and credit, of the feast. He knew, as well, the other things of which her appearance was at any time — and in Eaton Square especially — made up: her resemblance to her father, at times so vivid, and coming out, in the delicate warmth of occasions, like the quickened fragrance of a flower; her resemblance, as he had hit it off for her once in Rome, in the first flushed days, after their engagement, to a little dancing-girl at rest, ever so light of movement but most often panting gently, even a shade compunctiously, on a bench; her approximation, finally — for it was analogy, somehow, more than identity — to the transmitted images of rather neutral and negative propriety that made up, in his long line, the average of wifehood and motherhood. If the Roman matron had been, in sufficiency, first and last, the honour of that line, Maggie would no doubt, at fifty, have expanded, have solidified to some such dignity, even should she suggest a little but a Cornelia in miniature. A light, however, broke for him in season, and when once it had done so it made him more than ever aware of Mrs. Verver's vaguely, yet quite exquisitely, contingent participation — a mere hinted or tendered discretion; in short of Mrs. Verver's indescribable, unfathomable relation to the scene. Her placed condition, her natural seat and neighbourhood, her intenser presence, her quieter smile, her fewer jewels, were inevitably all as nothing compared with the preoccupation that burned in Maggie like a small flame and that had in fact kindled in each of her cheeks a little attesting, but fortunately by no means unbecoming, spot. The party was her father's party, and its greater or smaller success was a question having for her all the importance of his importance; so that sympathy created for her a sort of visible suspense, under pressure of which she bristled with filial reference, with little filial recalls of expression, movement, tone. It was all unmistakable, and as pretty as possible, if one would, and even as funny; but it put the pair so together, as undivided by the marriage of each, that the Princess il n'y avait pas a dire — might sit where she liked: she would still, always, in that house, be irremediably Maggie Verver. The Prince found himself on this occasion so beset with that perception that its natural complement for him would really have been to wonder if Mr. Verver had produced on people something of the same impression in the recorded cases of his having dined with his daughter.

This backward speculation, had it begun to play, however, would have been easily arrested; for it was at present to come over Amerigo as never before that his remarkable father-inlaw was the man in the world least equipped with different appearances for different hours. He was simple, he was a revelation of simplicity, and that was the end of him so far as he consisted of an appearance at all — a question that might verily, for a weakness in it, have been argued. It amused our young man, who was taking his pleasure to-night, it will be seen, in sundry occult ways, it amused him to feel how everything else the master of the house consisted of, resources, possessions, facilities and amiabilities amplified by the social legend, depended, for conveying the effect of quantity, on no personal "equation," no mere measurable medium. Quantity was in the air for these good people, and Mr. Verver's estimable quality was almost wholly in that pervasion. He was meagre and modest and clearbrowed, and his eyes, if they wandered without fear, yet stayed without defiance; his shoulders were not broad, his chest was not high, his complexion was not fresh, and the crown of his head was not covered; in spite of all of which he looked, at the top of his table, so nearly like a little boy shyly entertaining in virtue of some imposed rank, that he COULD only be one of the powers, the representative of a force — quite as an infant king is the representative of a dynasty. In this generalised view of his father-inlaw, intensified to-night but always operative, Amerigo had now for some time taken refuge. The refuge, after the reunion of the two households in England, had more and more offered itself as the substitute for communities, from man to man, that, by his original calculation, might have become possible, but that had not really ripened and flowered. He met the decent family eyes across the table, met them afterwards in the music-room, but only to read in them still what he had learned to read during his first months, the time of over-anxious initiation, a kind of apprehension in which the terms and conditions were finally fixed and absolute. This directed regard rested at its ease, but it neither lingered nor penetrated, and was, to the Prince's fancy, much of the same order as any glance directed, for due attention, from the same quarter, to the figure of a cheque received in the course of business and about to be enclosed to a banker. It made sure of the amount — and just so, from time to time, the amount of the Prince was made sure. He was being thus, in renewed instalments, perpetually paid in; he already reposed in the bank as a value, but subject, in this comfortable way, to repeated, to infinite endorsement. The net result of all of which, moreover, was that the young man had no wish to see his value diminish. He himself, after all, had not fixed it — the "figure" was a conception all of Mr. Verver's own. Certainly, however, everything must be kept up to it; never so much as to-night had the Prince felt this. He would have been uncomfortable, as these quiet expressions passed, had the case not been guaranteed for him by the intensity of his accord with Charlotte. It was impossible that he should not now and again meet Charlotte's eyes, as it was also visible that she too now and again met her husband's. For her as well, in all his pulses, he felt the conveyed impression. It put them, it kept them together, through the vain show of their separation, made the two other faces, made the whole lapse of the evening, the people, the lights, the flowers, the pretended talk, the exquisite music, a mystic golden bridge between them, strongly swaying and sometimes almost vertiginous, for that intimacy of which the sovereign law would be the vigilance of "care," would be never rashly to forget and never consciously to wound.

XX

The main interest of these hours for us, however, will have been in the way the Prince continued to know, during a particular succession of others, separated from the evening in Eaton Square by a short interval, a certain persistent aftertaste. This was the lingering savour of a cup presented to him by Fanny Assingham's hand after dinner, while the clustered quartette kept their ranged companions, in the music-room, moved if one would, but conveniently motionless. Mrs. Assingham contrived, after a couple of pieces, to convey to her friend that, for her part, she was moved — by the genius of Brahms — beyond what she could bear; so that, without apparent deliberation, she had presently floated away, at the young man's side, to such a distance as permitted them to converse without the effect of disdain. It was the twenty minutes enjoyed with her, during the rest of the concert, in the less associated electric glare of one of the empty rooms — it was their achieved and, as he would have said, successful, most pleasantly successful, talk on one of the sequestered sofas, it was this that was substantially to underlie his consciousness of the later occasion. The later occasion, then mere matter of discussion, had formed her ground for desiring — in a light undertone into which his quick ear read indeed some nervousness — these independent words with him: she had sounded, covertly but distinctly, by the time they were seated together, the great question of what it might involve. It had come out for him before anything else, and so abruptly that this almost needed an explanation. Then the abruptness itself had appeared to explain — which had introduced, in turn, a slight awkwardness. "Do you know that they're not, after all, going to Matcham; so that, if they don't — if, at least, Maggie doesn't — you won't, I suppose, go by yourself?" It was, as I say, at Matcham, where the event had placed him, it was at Matcham during the Easter days, that it most befell him, oddly enough, to live over, inwardly, for its wealth of special significance, this passage by which the event had been really a good deal determined. He had paid, first and last, many an English country visit; he had learned, even from of old, to do the English things, and to do them, all sufficiently, in the English way; if he didn't always enjoy them madly he enjoyed them at any rate as much, to an appearance, as the good people who had, in the night of time, unanimously invented them, and who still, in the prolonged afternoon of their good faith, unanimously, even if a trifle automatically, practised them; yet, with it all, he had never so much as during such sojourns the trick of a certain detached, the amusement of a certain inward critical, life; the determined need, which apparently all participant, of returning upon itself, of backing noiselessly in, far in again, and rejoining there, as it were, that part of his mind that was not engaged at the front. His body, very constantly, was engaged at the front — in shooting, in riding, in golfing, in walking, over the fine diagonals of meadow-paths or round the pocketed corners of billiard-tables; it sufficiently, on the whole, in fact, bore the brunt of bridge-playing, of breakfasting, lunching, tea-drinking, dining, and of the nightly climax over the bottigliera, as he called it, of the bristling tray; it met, finally, to the extent of the limited tax on lip, on gesture, on wit, most of the current demands of conversation and expression. Therefore something of him, he often felt at these times, was left out; it was much more when he was alone, or when he was with his own people — or when he was, say, with Mrs. Verver and nobody else — that he moved, that he talked, that he listened, that he felt, as a congruous whole.

"English society," as he would have said, cut him, accordingly, in two, and he reminded himself often, in his relations with it, of a man possessed of a shining star, a decoration, an order of some sort, something so ornamental as to make his identity not complete, ideally, without it, yet who, finding no other such object generally worn, should be perpetually, and the least bit ruefully, unpinning it from his breast to transfer it to his pocket. The Prince's shining star may, no doubt, having been nothing more precious than his private subtlety; but whatever the object was he just now fingered it a good deal, out of sight — amounting as it mainly did for him to a restless play of memory and a fine embroidery of thought. Something had rather momentously occurred, in Eaton Square, during his enjoyed minutes with his old friend: his present perspective made definitely clear to him that she had plumped out for him her first little lie. That took on — and he could scarce have said why — a sharpness of importance: she had never lied to him before — if only because it had never come up for her, properly, intelligibly, morally, that she must. As soon as she had put to him the question of what he would do — by which she meant of what Charlotte would also do — in that event of Maggie's and Mr. Verver's not embracing the proposal they had appeared for a day or two resignedly to entertain; as soon as she had betrayed her curiosity as to the line the other pair, so left to themselves, might take, a desire to avoid the appearance of at all too directly prying had become marked in her. Betrayed by the solicitude of which she had, already, three weeks before, given him a view, she had been obliged, on a second thought, to name, intelligibly, a reason for her appeal; while the Prince, on his side, had had, not without mercy, his glimpse of her momentarily groping for one and yet remaining unprovided. Not without mercy because, absolutely, he had on the spot, in his friendliness, invented one for her use, presenting it to her with a look no more significant than if he had picked up, to hand back to her, a dropped flower. "You ask if I'm likely also to back out then, because it may make a difference in what you and the Colonel decide?" — he had gone as far as that for her, fairly inviting her to assent, though not having had his impression, from any indication offered him by Charlotte, that the Assinghams were really in question for the large Matcham party. The wonderful thing, after this, was that the active couple had, in the interval, managed to inscribe themselves on the golden roll; an exertion of a sort that, to do her justice, he had never before observed Fanny to make. This last passage of the chapter but proved, after all, with what success she could work when she would.

Once launched, himself, at any rate, as he had been directed by all the terms of the intercourse between Portland Place and Eaton Square, once steeped, at Matcham, in the enjoyment of a splendid hospitality, he found everything, for his interpretation, for his convenience, fall easily enough into place; and all the more that Mrs. Verver was at hand to exchange ideas and impressions with. The great house was full of people, of possible new combinations, of the quickened play of possible propinquity, and no appearance, of course, was less to be cultivated than that of his having sought an opportunity to foregather with his friend at a safe distance from their respective sposi. There was a happy boldness, at the best, in their mingling thus, each unaccompanied, in the same sustained sociability — just exactly a touch of that eccentricity of associated freedom which sat so lightly on the imagination of the relatives left behind. They were exposed as much as one would to its being pronounced funny that they should, at such a rate, go about together — though, on the other hand, this consideration drew relief from the fact that, in their high conditions and with the easy tradition, the almost inspiring allowances, of the house in question, no individual line, however freely marked, was pronounced anything more than funny. Both our friends felt afresh, as they had felt before, the convenience of a society so placed that it had only its own sensibility to consider — looking as it did well over the heads of all lower growths; and that moreover treated its own sensibility quite as the easiest, friendliest, most informal and domesticated party to the general alliance. What anyone "thought" of anyone else — above all of anyone else with anyone else — was a matter incurring in these lulls so little awkward formulation that hovering judgment, the spirit with the scales, might perfectly have been imaged there as some rather snubbed and subdued, but quite trained and tactful poor relation, of equal, of the properest, lineage, only of aspect a little dingy, doubtless from too limited a change of dress, for whose tacit and abstemious presence, never betrayed by a rattle of her rusty machine, a room in the attic and a plate at the side-table were decently usual. It was amusing, in such lightness of air, that the Prince should again present himself only to speak for the Princess, so unfortunately unable, again, to leave home; and that Mrs. Verver should as regularly figure as an embodied, a beautifully deprecating apology for her husband, who was all geniality and humility among his own treasures, but as to whom the legend had grown up that he couldn't bear, with the height of his standards and the tone of the company, in the way of sofas and cabinets, habitually kept by him, the irritation and depression to which promiscuous visiting, even at pompous houses, had been found to expose him. That was all right, the noted working harmony of the clever son-inlaw and the charming stepmother, so long as the relation was, for the effect in question, maintained at the proper point between sufficiency and excess.

What with the noble fairness of the place, meanwhile, the generous mood of the sunny, gusty, lusty English April, all panting and heaving with impatience, or kicking and crying, even, at moments, like some infant Hercules who wouldn't be dressed; what with these things and the bravery of youth and beauty, the insolence of fortune and appetite so diffused among his fellow-guests that the poor Assinghams, in their comparatively marked maturity and their comparatively small splendour, were the only approach to a false note in the concert, the stir of the air was such, for going, in a degree, to one's head, that, as a mere matter of exposure, almost grotesque in its flagrancy, his situation resembled some elaborate practical joke carried out at his expense. Every voice in the great bright house was a call to the ingenuities and impunities of pleasure; every echo was a defiance of difficulty, doubt or danger; every aspect of the picture, a glowing plea for the immediate, and as with plenty more to come, was another phase of the spell. For a world so constituted was governed by a spell, that of the smile of the gods and the favour of the powers; the only handsome, the only gallant, in fact the only intelligent acceptance of which was a faith in its guarantees and a high spirit for its chances. Its demand — to that the thing came back — was above all for courage and good-humour; and the value of this as a general assurance — that is for seeing one through at the worst — had not even in the easiest hours of his old Roman life struck the Prince so convincingly. His old Roman life had had more poetry, no doubt, but as he looked back upon it now it seemed to hang in the air of mere iridescent horizons, to have been loose and vague and thin, with large languorous unaccountable blanks. The present order, as it spread about him, had somehow the ground under its feet, and a trumpet in its ears, and a bottomless bag of solid shining British sovereigns — which was much to the point — in its hand. Courage and good-humour therefore were the breath of the day; though for ourselves at least it would have been also much to the point that, with Amerigo, really, the innermost effect of all this perceptive ease was perhaps a strange final irritation. He compared the lucid result with the extraordinary substitute for perception that presided, in the bosom of his wife, at so contented a view of his conduct and course — a state of mind that was positively like a vicarious good conscience, cultivated ingeniously on his behalf, a perversity of pressure innocently persisted in; and this wonder of irony became on occasion too intense to be kept wholly to himself. It wasn't that, at Matcham, anything particular, anything monstrous, anything that had to be noticed permitted itself, as they said, to "happen"; there were only odd moments when the breath of the day, as it has been called, struck him so full in the face that he broke out with all the hilarity of "What indeed would THEY have made of it?" "They" were of course Maggie and her father, moping — so far as they ever consented to mope in monotonous Eaton Square, but placid too in the belief that they knew beautifully what their expert companions were in for. They knew, it might have appeared in these lights, absolutely nothing on earth worth speaking of — whether beautifully or cynically; and they would perhaps sometimes be a little less trying if they would only once for all peacefully admit that knowledge wasn't one of their needs and that they were in fact constitutionally inaccessible to it. They were good children, bless their hearts, and the children of good children; so that, verily, the Principino himself, as less consistently of that descent, might figure to the fancy as the ripest genius of the trio.

The difficulty was, for the nerves of daily intercourse with Maggie in particular, that her imagination was clearly never ruffled by the sense of any anomaly. The great anomaly would have been that her husband, or even that her father's wife, should prove to have been made, for the long run, after the pattern set from so far back to the Ververs. If one was so made one had certainly no business, on any terms, at Matcham; whereas if one wasn't one had no business there on the particular terms — terms of conformity with the principles of Eaton Square — under which one had been so absurdly dedicated. Deep at the heart of that resurgent unrest in our young man which we have had to content ourselves with calling his irritation — deep in the bosom of this falsity of position glowed the red spark of his inextinguishable sense of a higher and braver propriety. There were situations that were ridiculous, but that one couldn't yet help, as for instance when one's wife chose, in the most usual way, to make one so. Precisely here, however, was the difference; it had taken poor Maggie to invent a way so extremely unusual — yet to which, none the less, it would be too absurd that he should merely lend himself. Being thrust, systematically, with another woman, and a woman one happened, by the same token, exceedingly to like, and being so thrust that the theory of it seemed to publish one as idiotic or incapable — this WAS a predicament of which the dignity depended all on one's own handling. What was supremely grotesque, in fact, was the essential opposition of theories — as if a galantuomo, as HE at least constitutionally conceived galantuomini, could do anything BUT blush to "go about" at such a rate with such a person as Mrs. Verver in a state of childlike innocence, the state of our primitive parents before the Fall. The grotesque theory, as he would have called it, was perhaps an odd one to resent with violence, and he did it — also as a man of the world — all merciful justice; but, assuredly, none the less, there was but one way REALLY to mark, and for his companion as much as for himself, the commiseration in which they held it. Adequate comment on it could only be private, but it could also at least be active, and of rich and effectual comment Charlotte and he were fortunately alike capable. Wasn't this consensus literally their only way not to be ungracious? It was positively as if the measure of their escape from that danger were given by the growth between them, during their auspicious visit, of an exquisite sense of complicity.

XXI

He found himself therefore saying, with gaiety, even to Fanny Assingham, for their common, concerned glance at Eaton Square, the glance that was so markedly never, as it might have been, a glance at Portland Place: "What WOULD our cari sposi have made of it here? what would they, you know, really?" — which overflow would have been reckless if, already, and surprisingly perhaps even to himself, he had not got used to thinking of this friend as a person in whom the element of protest had of late been unmistakably allayed. He exposed himself of course to her replying: "Ah, if it would have been so bad for them, how can it be so good for you?" — but, quite apart from the small sense the question would have had at the best, she appeared already to unite with him in confidence and cheer. He had his view, as well — or at least a partial one — of the inner spring of this present comparative humility, which was all consistent with the retraction he had practically seen her make after Mr. Verver's last dinner. Without diplomatising to do so, with no effort to square her, none to bribe her to an attitude for which he would have had no use in her if it were not sincere, he yet felt how he both held her and moved her by the felicity of his taking pity, all instinctively, on her just discernible depression. By just so much as he guessed that she felt herself, as the slang was, out of it, out of the crystal current and the expensive picture, by just so much had his friendship charmingly made up to her, from hour to hour, for the penalties, as they might have been grossly called, of her mistake. Her mistake had only been, after all, in her wanting to seem to him straight; she had let herself in for being — as she had made haste, for that matter, during the very first half-hour, at tea, to proclaim herself — the sole and single frump of the party. The scale of everything was so different that all her minor values, her quainter graces, her little local authority, her humour and her wardrobe alike, for which it was enough elsewhere, among her bons amis, that they were hers, dear Fanny Assingham's — these matters and others would be all, now, as nought: five minutes had sufficed to give her the fatal pitch. In Cadogan Place she could always, at the worst, be picturesque — for she habitually spoke of herself as "local" to Sloane Street whereas at Matcham she should never be anything but horrible. And it all would have come, the disaster, from the real refinement, in her, of the spirit of friendship. To prove to him that she wasn't really watching him — ground for which would have been too terribly grave — she had followed him in his pursuit of pleasure: SO she might, precisely, mark her detachment. This was handsome trouble for her to take — the Prince could see it all: it wasn't a shade of interference that a good-natured man would visit on her. So he didn't even say, when she told him how frumpy she knew herself, how frumpy her very maid, odiously going back on her, rubbed it into her, night and morning, with unsealed eyes and lips, that she now knew her — he didn't then say "Ah, see what you've done: isn't it rather your own fault?" He behaved differently altogether: eminently distinguished himself — for she told him she had never seen him so universally distinguished — he yet distinguished her in her obscurity, or in what was worse, her objective absurdity, and frankly invested her with her absolute value, surrounded her with all the importance of her wit. That wit, as discriminated from stature and complexion, a sense for "bridge" and a credit for pearls, could have importance was meanwhile but dimly perceived at Matcham; so that his "niceness" to her — she called it only niceness, but it brought tears into her eyes — had the greatness of a general as well as of a special demonstration.

"She understands," he said, as a comment on all this, to Mrs. Verver —"she understands all she needs to understand. She has taken her time, but she has at last made it out for herself: she sees how all we can desire is to give them the life they prefer, to surround them with the peace and quiet, and above all with the sense of security, most favourable to it. She can't of course very well put it to us that we have, so far as she is concerned, but to make the best of our circumstances; she can't say in so many words 'Don't think of me, for I too must make the best of mine: arrange as you can, only, and live as you must.' I don't get quite THAT from her, any more than I ask for it. But her tone and her whole manner mean nothing at all unless they mean that she trusts us to take as watchful, to take as artful, to take as tender care, in our way, as she so anxiously takes in hers. So that she's — well," the Prince wound up, "what you may call practically all right." Charlotte in fact, however, to help out his confidence, didn't call it anything; return as he might to the lucidity, the importance, or whatever it was, of this lesson, she gave him no aid toward reading it aloud. She let him, two or three times over, spell it out for himself; only on the eve of their visit's end was she, for once, clear or direct in response. They had found a minute together in the great hall of the house during the half-hour before dinner; this easiest of chances they had already, a couple of times, arrived at by waiting persistently till the last other loiterers had gone to dress, and by being prepared themselves to dress so expeditiously that they might, a little later on, be among the first to appear in festal array. The hall then was empty, before the army of rearranging, cushion-patting housemaids were marshalled in, and there was a place by the forsaken fire, at one end, where they might imitate, with art, the unpremeditated. Above all, here, for the snatched instants, they could breathe so near to each other that the interval was almost engulfed in it, and the intensity both of the union and the caution became a workable substitute for contact. They had prolongations of instants that counted as visions of bliss; they had slow approximations that counted as long caresses. The quality of these passages, in truth, made the spoken word, and especially the spoken word about other people, fall below them; so that our young woman's tone had even now a certain dryness. "It's very good of her, my dear, to trust us. But what else can she do?"

"Why, whatever people do when they don't trust. Let one see they don't."

"But let whom see?"

"Well, let ME, say, to begin with."

"And should you mind that?"

He had a slight show of surprise. "Shouldn't you?"

"Her letting you see? No," said Charlotte; "the only thing I can imagine myself minding is what you yourself, if you don't look out, may let HER see." To which she added: "You may let her see, you know, that you're afraid."

"I'm only afraid of you, a little, at moments," he presently returned. "But I shan't let Fanny see that."

It was clear, however, that neither the limits nor the extent of Mrs. Assingham's vision were now a real concern to her, and she gave expression to this as she had not even yet done. "What in the world can she do against us? There's not a word that she can breathe. She's helpless; she can't speak; she would be herself the first to be dished by it." And then as he seemed slow to follow: "It all comes back to her. It all began with her. Everything, from the first. She introduced you to Maggie. She made your marriage."

The Prince might have had his moment of demur, but at this, after a little, as with a smile dim but deep, he came on. "Mayn't she also be said, a good deal, to have made yours? That was intended, I think, wasn't it? for a kind of rectification."

Charlotte, on her side, for an instant, hesitated; then she was prompter still. "I don't mean there was anything to rectify; everything was as it had to be, and I'm not speaking of how she may have been concerned for you and me. I'm speaking of how she took, in her way, each time, THEIR lives in hand, and how, therefore, that ties her up today. She can't go to them and say 'It's very awkward of course, you poor dear things, but I was frivolously mistaken.'"

He took it in still, with his long look at her. "All the more that she wasn't. She was right. Everything's right," he went on, "and everything will stay so."

"Then that's all I say."

But he worked it out, for the deeper satisfaction, even to superfluous lucidity. "We're happy, and they're happy. What more does the position admit of? What more need Fanny Assingham want?"

"Ah, my dear," said Charlotte, "it's not I who say that she need want anything. I only say that she's FIXED, that she must stand exactly where everything has, by her own act, placed her. It's you who have seemed haunted with the possibility, for her, of some injurious alternative, something or other we must be prepared for." And she had, with her high reasoning, a strange cold smile. "We ARE prepared — for anything, for everything; and AS we are, practically, so she must take us. She's condemned to consistency; she's doomed, poor thing, to a genial optimism. That, luckily for her, however, is very much the law of her nature. She was born to soothe and to smooth. Now then, therefore," Mrs. Verver gently laughed, "she has the chance of her life!"

"So that her present professions may, even at the best, not be sincere? — may be but a mask for doubts and fears, and for gaining time?"

The Prince had looked, with the question, as if this, again, could trouble him, and it determined in his companion a slight impatience. "You keep talking about such things as if they were our affair at all. I feel, at any rate, that I've nothing to do with her doubts and fears, or with anything she may feel. She must arrange all that for herself. It's enough for me that she'll always be, of necessity, much more afraid for herself, REALLY, either to see or to speak, than we should be to have her do it even if we were the idiots and cowards we aren't." And Charlotte's face, with these words — to the mitigation of the slightly hard ring there might otherwise have been in them — fairly lightened, softened, shone out. It reflected as really never yet the rare felicity of their luck. It made her look for the moment as if she had actually pronounced that word of unpermitted presumption — so apt is the countenance, as with a finer consciousness than the tongue, to betray a sense of this particular lapse. She might indeed, the next instant, have seen her friend wince, in advance, at her use of a word that was already on her lips; for it was still unmistakable with him that there were things he could prize, forms of fortune he could cherish, without at all proportionately liking their names. Had all this, however, been even completely present to his companion, what other term could she have applied to the strongest and simplest of her ideas but the one that exactly fitted it? She applied it then, though her own instinct moved her, at the same time, to pay her tribute to the good taste from which they hadn't heretofore by a hair's breadth deviated. "If it didn't sound so vulgar I should say that we're — fatally, as it were — SAFE. Pardon the low expression — since it's what we happen to be. We're so because they are. And they're so because they can't be anything else, from the moment that, having originally intervened for them, she wouldn't now be able to bear herself if she didn't keep them so. That's the way she's inevitably WITH us," said Charlotte over her smile. "We hang, essentially, together."

Well, the Prince candidly allowed she did bring it home to him. Every way it worked out. "Yes, I see. We hang, essentially, together."

His friend had a shrug — a shrug that had a grace. "Cosa volete?" The effect, beautifully, nobly, was more than Roman. "Ah, beyond doubt, it's a case."

He stood looking at her. "It's a case. There can't," he said, "have been many."

"Perhaps never, never, never any other. That," she smiled, "I confess I should like to think. Only ours."

"Only ours — most probably. Speriamo." To which, as after hushed connections, he presently added: "Poor Fanny!" But Charlotte had already, with a start and a warning hand, turned from a glance at the clock. She sailed away to dress, while he watched her reach the staircase. His eyes followed her till, with a simple swift look round at him, she vanished. Something in the sight, however, appeared to have renewed the spring of his last exclamation, which he breathed again upon the air. "Poor, poor Fanny!"

It was to prove, however, on the morrow, quite consistent with the spirit of these words that, the party at Matcham breaking up and multitudinously dispersing, he should be able to meet the question of the social side of the process of repatriation with due presence of mind. It was impossible, for reasons, that he should travel to town with the Assinghams; it was impossible, for the same reasons, that he should travel to town save in the conditions that he had for the last twenty-four hours been privately, and it might have been said profoundly, thinking out. The result of his thought was already precious to him, and this put at his service, he sufficiently believed, the right tone for disposing of his elder friend's suggestion, an assumption in fact equally full and mild, that he and Charlotte would conveniently take the same train and occupy the same compartment as the Colonel and herself. The extension of the idea to Mrs. Verver had been, precisely, a part of Mrs. Assingham's mildness, and nothing could better have characterised her sense for social shades than her easy perception that the gentleman from Portland Place and the lady from Eaton Square might now confess, quite without indiscretion, to simultaneity of movement. She had made, for the four days, no direct appeal to the latter personage, but the Prince was accidental witness of her taking a fresh start at the moment the company were about to scatter for the last night of their stay. There had been, at this climax, the usual preparatory talk about hours and combinations, in the midst of which poor Fanny gently approached Mrs. Verver. She said "You and the Prince, love," — quite, apparently, without blinking; she took for granted their public withdrawal together; she remarked that she and Bob were alike ready, in the interest of sociability, to take any train that would make them all one party. "I feel really as if, all this time, I had seen nothing of you" — that gave an added grace to the candour of the dear thing's approach. But just then it was, on the other hand, that the young man found himself borrow most effectively the secret of the right tone for doing as he preferred. His preference had, during the evening, not failed of occasion to press him with mute insistences; practically without words, without any sort of straight telegraphy, it had arrived at a felt identity with Charlotte's own. She spoke all for their friend while she answered their friend's question, but she none the less signalled to him as definitely as if she had fluttered a white handkerchief from a window. "It's awfully sweet of you, darling — our going together would be charming. But you mustn't mind us — you must suit yourselves we've settled, Amerigo and I, to stay over till after luncheon."

Amerigo, with the chink of this gold in his ear, turned straight away, so as not to be instantly appealed to; and for the very emotion of the wonder, furthermore, of what divination may achieve when winged by a community of passion. Charlotte had uttered the exact plea that he had been keeping ready for the same foreseen necessity, and had uttered it simply as a consequence of their deepening unexpressed need of each other and without the passing between them of a word. He hadn't, God knew, to take it from her — he was too conscious of what he wanted; but the lesson for him was in the straight clear tone that Charlotte could thus distil, in the perfect felicity of her adding no explanation, no touch for plausibility, that she wasn't strictly obliged to add, and in the truly superior way in which women, so situated, express and distinguish themselves. She had answered Mrs. Assingham quite adequately; she had not spoiled it by a reason a scrap larger than the smallest that would serve, and she had, above all, thrown off, for his stretched but covered attention, an image that flashed like a mirror played at the face of the sun. The measure of EVERYTHING, to all his sense, at these moments, was in it — the measure especially of the thought that had been growing with him a positive obsession and that began to throb as never yet under this brush of her having, by perfect parity of imagination, the match for it. His whole consciousness had by this time begun almost to ache with a truth of an exquisite order, at the glow of which she too had, so unmistakably then, been warming herself — the truth that the occasion constituted by the last few days couldn't possibly, save by some poverty of their own, refuse them some still other and still greater beauty. It had already told them, with an hourly voice, that it had a meaning — a meaning that their associated sense was to drain even as thirsty lips, after the plough through the sands and the sight, afar, of the palm-cluster, might drink in at last the promised well in the desert. There had been beauty, day after day, and there had been, for the spiritual lips, something of the pervasive taste of it; yet it was all, none the less, as if their response had remained below their fortune. How to bring it, by some brave, free lift, up to the same height was the idea with which, behind and beneath everything, he was restlessly occupied, and in the exploration of which, as in that of the sun-chequered greenwood of romance, his spirit thus, at the opening of a vista, met hers. They were already, from that moment, so hand-in-hand in the place that he found himself making use, five minutes later, of exactly the same tone as Charlotte's for telling Mrs. Assingham that he was likewise, in the matter of the return to London, sorry for what mightn't be.

This had become, of a sudden, the simplest thing in the world — the sense of which moreover seemed really to amount to a portent that he should feel, forevermore, on the general head, conveniently at his ease with her. He went in fact a step further than Charlotte — put the latter forward as creating his necessity. She was staying over luncheon to oblige their hostess — as a consequence of which he must also stay to see her decently home. He must deliver her safe and sound, he felt, in Eaton Square. Regret as he might, too, the difference made by this obligation, he frankly didn't mind, inasmuch as, over and above the pleasure itself, his scruple would certainly gratify both Mr. Verver and Maggie. They never yet had absolutely and entirely learned, he even found deliberation to intimate, how little he really neglected the first — as it seemed nowadays quite to have become — of his domestic duties: therefore he still constantly felt how little he must remit his effort to make them remark it. To which he added with equal lucidity that they would return in time for dinner, and if he didn't, as a last word, subjoin that it would be "lovely" of Fanny to find, on her own return, a moment to go to Eaton Square and report them as struggling bravely on, this was not because the impulse, down to the very name for the amiable act, altogether failed to rise. His inward assurance, his general plan, had at moments, where she was concerned, its drops of continuity, and nothing would less have pleased him than that she should suspect in him, however tempted, any element of conscious "cheek." But he was always — that was really the upshot — cultivating thanklessly the considerate and the delicate: it was a long lesson, this unlearning, with people of English race, all the little superstitions that accompany friendship. Mrs. Assingham herself was the first to say that she would unfailingly "report"; she brought it out in fact, he thought, quite wonderfully — having attained the summit of the wonderful during the brief interval that had separated her appeal to Charlotte from this passage with himself. She had taken the five minutes, obviously, amid the rest of the talk and the movement, to retire into her tent for meditation — which showed, among several things, the impression Charlotte had made on her. It was from the tent she emerged, as with arms refurbished; though who indeed could say if the manner in which she now met him spoke most, really, of the glitter of battle or of the white waver of the flag of truce? The parley was short either way; the gallantry of her offer was all sufficient.

"I'll go to our friends then — I'll ask for luncheon. I'll tell them when to expect you."

"That will be charming. Say we're all right."

"All right — precisely. I can't say more," Mrs. Assingham smiled.

"No doubt." But he considered, as for the possible importance of it. "Neither can you, by what I seem to feel, say less."

"Oh, I WON'T say less!" Fanny laughed; with which, the next moment, she had turned away. But they had it again, not less bravely, on the morrow, after breakfast, in the thick of the advancing carriages and the exchange of farewells. "I think I'll send home my maid from Euston," she was then prepared to amend, "and go to Eaton Square straight. So you can be easy."

"Oh, I think we're easy," the Prince returned. "Be sure to say, at any rate, that we're bearing up."

"You're bearing up — good. And Charlotte returns to dinner?"

"To dinner. We're not likely, I think, to make another night away."

"Well then, I wish you at least a pleasant day,"

"Oh," he laughed as they separated, "we shall do our best for it!" — after which, in due course, with the announcement of their conveyance, the Assinghams rolled off.

XXII

It was quite, for the Prince, after this, as if the view had further cleared; so that the half-hour during which he strolled on the terrace and smoked — the day being lovely — overflowed with the plenitude of its particular quality. Its general brightness was composed, doubtless, of many elements, but what shone out of it as if the whole place and time had been a great picture, from the hand of genius, presented to him as a prime ornament for his collection and all varnished and framed to hang up — what marked it especially for the highest appreciation was his extraordinarily unchallenged, his absolutely appointed and enhanced possession of it. Poor Fanny Assingham's challenge amounted to nothing: one of the things he thought of while he leaned on the old marble balustrade — so like others that he knew in still more nobly-terraced Italy — was that she was squared, all-conveniently even to herself, and that, rumbling toward London with this contentment, she had become an image irrelevant to the scene. It further passed across him, as his imagination was, for reasons, during the time, unprecedentedly active — that he had, after all, gained more from women than he had ever lost by them; there appeared so, more and more, on those mystic books that are kept, in connection with such commerce, even by men of the loosest business habits, a balance in his favour that he could pretty well, as a rule, take for granted. What were they doing at this very moment, wonderful creatures, but combine and conspire for his advantage? — from Maggie herself, most wonderful, in her way, of all, to his hostess of the present hour, into whose head it had so inevitably come to keep Charlotte on, for reasons of her own, and who had asked, in this benevolent spirit, why in the world, if not obliged, without plausibility, to hurry, her husband's son-in-law should not wait over in her company. He would at least see, Lady Castledean had said, that nothing dreadful should happen to her, either while still there or during the exposure of the run to town; and, for that matter, if they exceeded a little their license it would positively help them to have done so together. Each of them would, in this way, at home, have the other comfortably to blame. All of which, besides, in Lady Castledean as in Maggie, in Fanny Assingham as in Charlotte herself, was working; for him without provocation or pressure, by the mere play of some vague sense on their part — definite and conscious at the most only in Charlotte — that he was not, as a nature, as a character, as a gentleman, in fine, below his remarkable fortune.

But there were more things before him than even these; things that melted together, almost indistinguishably, to feed his sense of beauty. If the outlook was in every way spacious — and the towers of three cathedrals, in different counties, as had been pointed out to him, gleamed discernibly, like dim silver, in the rich sameness of tone — didn't he somehow the more feel it so because, precisely, Lady Castledean had kept over a man of her own, and that this offered a certain sweet intelligibility as the note of the day? It made everything fit; above all it diverted him to the extent of keeping up, while he lingered and waited, his meditative smile. She had detained Charlotte because she wished to detain Mr. Blint, and she couldn't detain Mr. Blint, disposed though he clearly was to oblige her, without spreading over the act some ampler drapery. Castledean had gone up to London; the place was all her own; she had had a fancy for a quiet morning with Mr. Blint, a sleek, civil, accomplished young man — distinctly younger than her ladyship — who played and sang delightfully (played even "bridge" and sang the English-comic as well as the French-tragic), and the presence — which really meant the absence — of a couple of other friends, if they were happily chosen, would make everything all right. The Prince had the sense, all good-humouredly, of being happily chosen, and it was not spoiled for him even by another sense that followed in its train and with which, during his life in England, he had more than once had reflectively to deal: the state of being reminded how, after all, as an outsider, a foreigner, and even as a mere representative husband and son-in-law, he was so irrelevant to the working of affairs that he could be bent on occasion to uses comparatively trivial. No other of her guests would have been thus convenient for their hostess; affairs, of whatever sorts, had claimed, by early trains, every active, easy, smoothly-working man, each in his way a lubricated item of the great social, political, administrative engrenage — claimed most of all Castledean himself, who was so very oddly, given the personage and the type, rather a large item. If he, on the other hand, had an affair, it was not of that order; it was of the order, verily, that he had been reduced to as a not quite glorious substitute.

It marked, however, the feeling of the hour with him that this vision of being "reduced" interfered not at all with the measure of his actual ease. It kept before him again, at moments, the so familiar fact of his sacrifices — down to the idea of the very relinquishment, for his wife's convenience, of his real situation in the world; with the consequence, thus, that he was, in the last analysis, among all these so often inferior people, practically held cheap and made light of. But though all this was sensible enough there was a spirit in him that could rise above it, a spirit that positively played with the facts, with all of them; from that of the droll ambiguity of English relations to that of his having in mind something quite beautiful and independent and harmonious, something wholly his own. He couldn't somehow take Mr. Blint seriously — he was much more an outsider, by the larger scale, even than a Roman prince who consented to be in abeyance. Yet it was past finding out, either, how such a woman as Lady Castledean could take him — since this question but sank for him again into the fathomless depths of English equivocation. He knew them all, as was said, "well"; he had lived with them, stayed with them, dined, hunted, shot and done various other things with them; but the number of questions about them he couldn't have answered had much rather grown than shrunken, so that experience struck him for the most part as having left in him but one residual impression. They didn't like les situations nettes — that was all he was very sure of. They wouldn't have them at any price; it had been their national genius and their national success to avoid them at every point. They called it themselves, with complacency, their wonderful spirit of compromise — the very influence of which actually so hung about him here, from moment to moment, that the earth and the air, the light and the colour, the fields and the hills and the sky, the blue-green counties and the cold cathedrals, owed to it every accent of their tone. Verily, as one had to feel in presence of such a picture, it had succeeded; it had made, up to now, for that seated solidity, in the rich sea-mist, on which the garish, the supposedly envious, peoples have ever cooled their eyes. But it was at the same time precisely why even much initiation left one, at given moments, so puzzled as to the element of staleness in all the freshness and of freshness in all the staleness, of innocence in the guilt and of guilt in the innocence. There were other marble terraces, sweeping more purple prospects, on which he would have known what to think, and would have enjoyed thereby at least the small intellectual fillip of a discerned relation between a given appearance and a taken meaning. The inquiring mind, in these present conditions, might, it was true, be more sharply challenged; but the result of its attention and its ingenuity, it had unluckily learned to know, was too often to be confronted with a mere dead wall, a lapse of logic, a confirmed bewilderment. And moreover, above all, nothing mattered, in the relation of the enclosing scene to his own consciousness, but its very most direct bearings.

Lady Castledean's dream of Mr. Blint for the morning was doubtless already, with all the spacious harmonies re-established, taking the form of "going over" something with him, at the piano, in one of the numerous smaller rooms that were consecrated to the less gregarious uses; what she had wished had been effected — her convenience had been assured. This made him, however, wonder the more where Charlotte was — since he didn't at all suppose her to be making a tactless third, which would be to have accepted mere spectatorship, in the duet of their companions. The upshot of everything for him, alike of the less and of the more, was that the exquisite day bloomed there like a large fragrant flower that he had only to gather. But it was to Charlotte he wished to make the offering, and as he moved along the terrace, which rendered visible parts of two sides of the house, he looked up at all the windows that were open to the April morning, and wondered which of them would represent his friend's room. It befell thus that his question, after no long time, was answered; he saw Charlotte appear above as if she had been called by the pausing of his feet on the flags. She had come to the sill, on which she leaned to look down, and she remained there a minute smiling at him. He had been immediately struck with her wearing a hat and a jacket — which conduced to her appearance of readiness not so much to join him, with a beautiful uncovered head and a parasol, where he stood, as to take with him some larger step altogether. The larger step had been, since the evening before, intensely in his own mind, though he had not fully thought out, even yet, the slightly difficult detail of it; but he had had no chance, such as he needed, to speak the definite word to her, and the face she now showed affected him, accordingly, as a notice that she had wonderfully guessed it for herself. They had these identities of impulse — they had had them repeatedly before; and if such unarranged but unerring encounters gave the measure of the degree in which people were, in the common phrase, meant for each other, no union in the world had ever been more sweetened with rightness. What in fact most often happened was that her rightness went, as who should say, even further than his own; they were conscious of the same necessity at the same moment, only it was she, as a general thing, who most clearly saw her way to it. Something in her long look at him now out of the old grey window, something in the very poise of her hat, the colour of her necktie, the prolonged stillness of her smile, touched into sudden light for him all the wealth of the fact that he could count on her. He had his hand there, to pluck it, on the open bloom of the day; but what did the bright minute mean but that her answering hand was already intelligently out? So, therefore, while the minute lasted, it passed between them that their cup was full; which cup their very eyes, holding it fast, carried and steadied and began, as they tasted it, to praise. He broke, however, after a moment, the silence.

"It only wants a moon, a mandolin, and a little danger, to be a serenade."

"Ah, then," she lightly called down, "let it at least have THIS!" With which she detached a rich white rosebud from its company with another in the front of her dress and flung it down to him. He caught it in its fall, fixing her again after she had watched him place it in his buttonhole. "Come down quickly!" he said in an Italian not loud but deep.

"Vengo, vengo!" she as clearly, but more lightly, tossed out; and she had left him the next minute to wait for her.

He came along the terrace again, with pauses during which his eyes rested, as they had already often done, on the brave darker wash of far-away watercolour that represented the most distant of the cathedral towns. This place, with its great church and its high accessibility, its towers that distinguishably signalled, its English history, its appealing type, its acknowledged interest, this place had sounded its name to him half the night through, and its name had become but another name, the pronounceable and convenient one, for that supreme sense of things which now throbbed within him. He had kept saying to himself "Gloucester, Gloucester, Gloucester," quite as if the sharpest meaning of all the years just passed were intensely expressed in it. That meaning was really that his situation remained quite sublimely consistent with itself, and that they absolutely, he and Charlotte, stood there together in the very lustre of this truth. Every present circumstance helped to proclaim it; it was blown into their faces as by the lips of the morning. He knew why, from the first of his marriage, he had tried with such patience for such conformity; he knew why he had given up so much and bored himself so much; he knew why he, at any rate, had gone in, on the basis of all forms, on the basis of his having, in a manner, sold himself, for a situation nette. It had all been just in order that his — well, what on earth should he call it but his freedom? — should at present be as perfect and rounded and lustrous as some huge precious pearl. He hadn't struggled nor snatched; he was taking but what had been given him; the pearl dropped itself, with its exquisite quality and rarity, straight into his hand. Here, precisely, it was, incarnate; its size and its value grew as Mrs. Verver appeared, afar off, in one of the smaller doorways. She came toward him in silence, while he moved to meet her; the great scale of this particular front, at Matcham, multiplied thus, in the golden morning, the stages of their meeting and the successions of their consciousness. It wasn't till she had come quite close that he produced for her his "Gloucester, Gloucester, Gloucester," and his "Look at it over there!"

She knew just where to look. "Yes — isn't it one of the best? There are cloisters or towers or some thing." And her eyes, which, though her lips smiled, were almost grave with their depths of acceptance; came back to him. "Or the tomb of some old king."

"We must see the old king; we must 'do' the cathedral," he said; "we must know all about it. If we could but take," he exhaled, "the full opportunity!" And then while, for all they seemed to give him, he sounded again her eyes: "I feel the day like a great gold cup that we must somehow drain together."

"I feel it, as you always make me feel everything, just as you do; so that I know ten miles off how you feel! But do you remember," she asked, "apropos of great gold cups, the beautiful one, the real one, that I offered you so long ago and that you wouldn't have? Just before your marriage" — she brought it back to him: "the gilded crystal bowl in the little Bloomsbury shop."

"Oh yes!" — but it took, with a slight surprise on the 'Prince's part, some small recollecting. "The treacherous cracked thing you wanted to palm off on me, and the little swindling Jew who understood Italian and who backed you up! But I feel this an occasion," he immediately added, "and I hope you don't mean," he smiled, "that AS an occasion it's also cracked."

They spoke, naturally, more low than loud, overlooked as they were, though at a respectful distance, by tiers of windows; but it made each find in the other's voice a taste as of something slowly and deeply absorbed. "Don't you think too much of 'cracks,' and aren't you too afraid of them? I risk the cracks," said Charlotte, "and I've often recalled the bowl and the little swindling Jew, wondering if they've parted company. He made," she said, "a great impression on me."

"Well, you also, no doubt, made a great impression on him, and I dare say that if you were to go back to him you'd find he has been keeping that treasure for you. But as to cracks," the Prince went on —"what did you tell me the other day you prettily call them in English?-'rifts within the lute'? — risk them as much as you like for yourself, but don't risk them for me." He spoke it in all the gaiety of his just barely-tremulous serenity. "I go, as you know, by my superstitions. And that's why," he said, "I know where we are. They're every one, today, on our side."

Resting on the parapet; toward the great view, she was silent a little, and he saw the next moment that her eyes were closed. "I go but by one thing." Her hand was on the sun-warmed stone; so that, turned as they were away from the house, he put his own upon it and covered it. "I go by YOU," she said. "I go by you."

So they remained a moment, till he spoke again with a gesture that matched. "What is really our great necessity, you know, is to go by my watch. It's already eleven" — he had looked at the time; "so that if we stop here to luncheon what becomes of our afternoon?"

To this Charlotte's eyes opened straight. "There's not the slightest need of our stopping here to luncheon. Don't you see," she asked, "how I'm ready?" He had taken it in, but there was always more and more of her. "You mean you've arranged —?"

"It's easy to arrange. My maid goes up with my things. You've only to speak to your man about yours, and they can go together."

"You mean we can leave at once?"

She let him have it all. "One of the carriages, about which I spoke, will already have come back for us. If your superstitions are on our side," she smiled, "so my arrangements are, and I'll back my support against yours."

"Then you had thought," he wondered, "about Gloucester?"

She hesitated — but it was only her way. "I thought you would think. We have, thank goodness, these harmonies. They are food for superstition if you like. It's beautiful," she went on, "that it should be Gloucester; 'Glo'ster, Glo'ster,' as you say, making it sound like an old song. However, I'm sure Glo'ster, Glo'ster will be charming," she still added; "we shall be able easily to lunch there, and, with our luggage and our servants off our hands, we shall have at least three or four hours. We can wire," she wound up, "from there."

Ever so quietly she had brought it, as she had thought it, all out, and it had to be as covertly that he let his appreciation expand. "Then Lady Castledean —?"

"Doesn't dream of our staying."

He took it, but thinking yet. "Then what does she dream —?"

"Of Mr. Blint, poor dear; of Mr. Blint only." Her smile for him — for the Prince himself — was free. "Have I positively to tell you that she doesn't want us? She only wanted us for the others — to show she wasn't left alone with him. Now that that's done, and that they've all gone, she of course knows for herself —!"

"'Knows'?" the Prince vaguely echoed.

"Why, that we like cathedrals; that we inevitably stop to see them, or go round to take them in, whenever we've a chance; that it's what our respective families quite expect of us and would be disappointed for us to fail of. This, as forestieri," Mrs. Verver pursued, "would be our pull — if our pull weren't indeed so great all round."

He could only keep his eyes on her. "And have you made out the very train —?"

"The very one. Paddington — the 6.50 'in.' That gives us oceans; we can dine, at the usual hour, at home; and as Maggie will of course be in Eaton Square I hereby invite you."

For a while he still but looked at her; it was a minute before he spoke. "Thank you very much. With pleasure." To which he in a moment added: "But the train for Gloucester?"

"A local one — 11.22; with several stops, but doing it a good deal, I forget how much, within the hour. So that we've time. Only," she said, "we must employ our time."

He roused himself as from the mere momentary spell of her; he looked again at his watch while they moved back to the door through which she had advanced. But he had also again questions and stops — all as for the mystery and the charm. "You looked it up — without my having asked you?"

"Ah, my dear," she laughed, "I've seen you with Bradshaw! It takes Anglo-Saxon blood."

"'Blood'?" he echoed. "You've that of every race!" It kept her before him. "You're terrible."

Well, he could put it as he liked. "I know the name of the inn."

"What is it then?"

"There are two — you'll see. But I've chosen the right one. And I think I remember the tomb," she smiled.

"Oh, the tomb —!" Any tomb would do for him. "But I mean I had been keeping my idea so cleverly for you, while there you already were with it."

"You had been keeping it 'for' me as much as you like. But how do you make out," she asked, "that you were keeping it FROM me?"

"I don't — now. How shall I ever keep anything — some day when I shall wish to?"

"Ah, for things I mayn't want to know, I promise you shall find me stupid." They had reached their door, where she herself paused to explain. "These days, yesterday, last night, this morning, I've wanted everything."

Well, it was all right. "You shall have everything."

XXIII

Fanny, on her arrival in town, carried out her second idea, despatching the Colonel to his club for luncheon and packing her maid into a cab, for Cadogan Place, with the variety of their effects. The result of this for each of the pair was a state of occupation so unbroken that the day practically passed without fresh contact between them. They dined out together, but it was both in going to their dinner and in coming back that they appeared, on either side, to have least to communicate. Fanny was wrapped in her thoughts still more closely than in the lemon-coloured mantle that protected her bare shoulders, and her husband, with her silence to deal with, showed himself not less disposed than usual, when so challenged, to hold up, as he would have said, his end of it. They had, in general, in these days, longer pauses and more abrupt transitions; in one of which latter they found themselves, for a climax, launched at midnight. Mrs. Assingham, rather wearily housed again, ascended to the first floor, there to sink, overburdened, on the landing outside the drawing-room, into a great gilded Venetian chair — of which at first, however, she but made, with her brooding face, a sort of throne of meditation. She would thus have recalled a little, with her so free orientalism of type, the immemorially speechless Sphinx about at last to become articulate. The Colonel, not unlike, on his side, some old pilgrim of the desert camping at the foot of that monument, went, by way of reconnoissance, into the drawing-room. He visited, according to his wont, the windows and their fastenings; he cast round the place the eye, all at once, of the master and the manager, the commandant and the rate-payer; then he came back to his wife, before whom, for a moment, he stood waiting. But she herself, for a time, continued to wait, only looking up at him inscrutably. There was in these minor manoeuvres and conscious patiences something of a suspension of their old custom of divergent discussion, that intercourse by misunderstanding which had grown so clumsy now. This familiar pleasantry seemed to desire to show it could yield, on occasion, to any clear trouble; though it was also sensibly, and just incoherently, in the air that no trouble was at present to be vulgarly recognised as clear.

There might, for that matter, even have been in Mr. Assingham's face a mild perception of some finer sense — a sense for his wife's situation, and the very situation she was, oddly enough, about to repudiate — that she had fairly caused to grow in him. But it was a flower to breathe upon gently, and this was very much what she finally did. She knew he needed no telling that she had given herself, all the afternoon, to her friends in Eaton Square, and that her doing so would have been but the prompt result of impressions gathered, in quantities, in brimming baskets, like the purple grapes of the vintage, at Matcham; a process surrounded by him, while it so unmistakably went on, with abstentions and discretions that might almost have counted as solemnities. The solemnities, at the same time, had committed him to nothing — to nothing beyond this confession itself of a consciousness of deep waters. She had been out on these waters, for him, visibly; and his tribute to the fact had been his keeping her, even if without a word, well in sight. He had not quitted for an hour, during her adventure, the shore of the mystic lake; he had on the contrary stationed himself where she could signal to him at need. Her need would have arisen if the planks of her bark had parted — THEN some sort of plunge would have become his immediate duty. His present position, clearly, was that of seeing her in the centre of her sheet of dark water, and of wondering if her actual mute gaze at him didn't perhaps mean that her planks WERE now parting. He held himself so ready that it was quite as if the inward man had pulled off coat and waistcoat. Before he had plunged, however — that is before he had uttered a question — he perceived, not without relief, that she was making for land. He watched her steadily paddle, always a little nearer, and at last he felt her boat bump. The bump was distinct, and in fact she stepped ashore. "We were all wrong. There's nothing."

"Nothing —?" It was like giving her his hand up the bank.

"Between Charlotte Verver and the Prince. I was uneasy — but I'm satisfied now. I was in fact quite mistaken. There's nothing."

"But I thought," said Bob Assingham, "that that was just what you did persistently asseverate. You've guaranteed their straightness from the first."

"No — I've never till now guaranteed anything but my own disposition to worry. I've never till now," Fanny went on gravely from her chair, "had such a chance to see and to judge. I had it at that place — if I had, in my infatuation and my folly," she added with expression, "nothing else. So I did see — I HAVE seen. And now I know." Her emphasis, as she repeated the word, made her head, in her seat of infallibility, rise higher. "I know."

The Colonel took it — but took it at first in silence. "Do you mean they've TOLD you —?"

"No — I mean nothing so absurd. For in the first place I haven't asked them, and in the second their word in such a matter wouldn't count."

"Oh," said the Colonel with all his oddity, "they'd tell US."

It made her face him an instant as with her old impatience of his short cuts, always across her finest flower-beds; but she felt, none the less, that she kept her irony down. "Then when they've told you, you'll be perhaps so good as to let me know."

He jerked up his chin, testing the growth of his beard with the back of his hand while he fixed her with a single eye. "Ah, I don't say that they'd necessarily tell me that they ARE over the traces."

"They'll necessarily, whatever happens, hold their tongues, I hope, and I'm talking of them now as I take them for myself only. THAT'S enough for me — it's all I have to regard." With which, after an instant, "They're wonderful," said Fanny Assingham.

"Indeed," her husband concurred, "I really think they are."

"You'd think it still more if you knew. But you don't know — because you don't see. Their situation" — this was what he didn't see —"is too extraordinary."

"'Too'?" He was willing to try.

"Too extraordinary to be believed, I mean, if one didn't see. But just that, in a way, is what saves them. They take it seriously."

He followed at his own pace. "Their situation?"

"The incredible side of it. They make it credible."

"Credible then — you do say — to YOU?"

She looked at him again for an interval. "They believe in it themselves. They take it for what it is. And that," she said, "saves them."

"But if what it 'is' is just their chance —?"

"It's their chance for what I told you when Charlotte first turned up. It's their chance for the idea that I was then sure she had."

The Colonel showed his effort to recall. "Oh, your idea, at different moments, of any one of THEIR ideas!" This dim procession, visibly, mustered before him, and, with the best will in the world, he could but watch its immensity. "Are you speaking now of something to which you can comfortably settle down?"

Again, for a little, she only glowered at him. "I've come back to my belief, and that I have done so —"

"Well?" he asked as she paused.

"Well, shows that I'm right — for I assure you I had wandered far. Now I'm at home again, and I mean," said Fanny Assingham, "to stay here. They're beautiful," she declared.

"The Prince and Charlotte?"

"The Prince and Charlotte. THAT'S how they're so remarkable. And the beauty," she explained, "is that they're afraid for them. Afraid, I mean, for the others."

"For Mr. Verver and Maggie?" It did take some following. "Afraid of what?"

"Afraid of themselves."

The Colonel wondered. "Of THEMSELVES? Of Mr. Verver's and Maggie's selves?"

Mrs. Assingham remained patient as well as lucid. "Yes — of SUCH blindness too. But most of all of their own danger."

He turned it over. "That danger BEING the blindness —?"

"That danger being their position. What their position contains — of all the elements — I needn't at this time of day attempt to tell you. It contains, luckily — for that's the mercy — everything BUT blindness: I mean on their part. The blindness," said Fanny, "is primarily her husband's."

He stood for a moment; he WOULD have it straight. "Whose husband's?"

"Mr. Verver's," she went on. "The blindness is most of all his. That they feel — that they see. But it's also his wife's."

"Whose wife's?" he asked as she continued to gloom at him in a manner at variance with the comparative cheer of her contention. And then as she only gloomed: "The Prince's?"

"Maggie's own — Maggie's very own," she pursued as for herself.

He had a pause. "Do you think Maggie so blind?"

"The question isn't of what I think. The question's of the conviction that guides the Prince and Charlotte — who have better opportunities than I for judging."

The Colonel again wondered. "Are you so very sure their opportunities are better?"

"Well," his wife asked, "what is their whole so extraordinary situation, their extraordinary relation, but an opportunity?"

"Ah, my dear, you have that opportunity — of their extraordinary situation and relation — as much as they."

"With the difference, darling," she returned with some spirit, "that neither of those matters are, if you please, mine. I see the boat they're in, but I'm not, thank God, in it myself. To-day, however," Mrs. Assingham added, "today in Eaton Square I did see."

"Well then, what?"

But she mused over it still. "Oh, many things. More, somehow, than ever before. It was as if, God help me, I was seeing FOR them — I mean for the others. It was as if something had happened — I don't know what, except some effect of these days with them at that place — that had either made things come out or had cleared my own eyes." These eyes indeed of the poor lady's rested on her companion's, meanwhile, with the lustre not so much of intenser insight as of a particular portent that he had at various other times had occasion to recognise. She desired, obviously, to reassure him, but it apparently took a couple of large, candid, gathering, glittering tears to emphasise the fact. They had immediately, for him, their usual direct action: she must reassure him, he was made to feel, absolutely in her own way. He would adopt it and conform to it as soon as he should be able to make it out. The only thing was that it took such incalculable twists and turns. The twist seemed remarkable for instance as she developed her indication of what had come out in the afternoon. "It was as if I knew better than ever what makes them —"

"What makes them?" — he pressed her as she fitfully dropped.

"Well, makes the Prince and Charlotte take it all as they do. It might well have been difficult to know HOW to take it; and they may even say for themselves that they were a long time trying to see. As I say, today," she went on, "it was as if I were suddenly, with a kind of horrible push, seeing through their eyes." On which, as to shake off her perversity, Fanny Assingham sprang up. But she remained there, under the dim illumination, and while the Colonel, with his high, dry, spare look of "type," to which a certain conformity to the whiteness of inaccessible snows in his necktie, shirt-front and waistcoat gave a rigour of accent, waited, watching her, they might, at the late hour and in the still house, have been a pair of specious worldly adventurers, driven for relief, under sudden stress, to some grim midnight reckoning in an odd corner. Her attention moved mechanically over the objects of ornament disposed too freely on the walls of staircase and landing, as to which recognition, for the time, had lost both fondness and compunction. "I can imagine the way it works," she said; "it's so easy to understand. Yet I don't want to be wrong," she the next moment broke out "I don't, I don't want to be wrong!"

"To make a mistake, you mean?"

Oh no, she meant nothing of the sort; she knew but too well what she meant. "I don't make mistakes. But I perpetrate — in thought — crimes." And she spoke with all intensity. "I'm a most dreadful person. There are times when I seem not to mind a bit what I've done, or what I think or imagine or fear or accept; when I feel that I'd do it again — feel that I'd do things myself."

"Ah, my dear!" the Colonel remarked in the coolness of debate.

"Yes, if you had driven me back on my 'nature.' Luckily for you you never have. You've done every thing else, but you've never done that. But what I really don't a bit want," she declared, "is to abet them or to protect them."

Her companion turned this over. "What is there to protect them from? — if, by your now so settled faith, they've done nothing that justly exposes them."

And it in fact half pulled her up. "Well, from a sudden scare. From the alarm, I mean, of what Maggie MAY think."

"Yet if your whole idea is that Maggie thinks nothing —?"

She waited again. "It isn't my 'whole' idea. Nothing is my 'whole' idea — for I felt today, as I tell you, that there's so much in the air."

"Oh, in the air —!" the Colonel dryly breathed.

"Well, what's in the air always HAS — hasn't it? — to come down to the earth. And Maggie," Mrs. Assingham continued, "is a very curious little person. Since I was 'in,' this afternoon, for seeing more than I had ever done — well, I felt THAT too, for some reason, as I hadn't yet felt it."

"For 'some' reason? For what reason?" And then, as his wife at first said nothing: "Did she give any sign? Was she in any way different?"

"She's always so different from anyone else in the world that it's hard to say when she's different from herself. But she has made me," said Fanny after an instant, "think of her differently. She drove me home."

"Home here?"

"First to Portland Place — on her leaving her father: since she does, once in a while, leave him. That was to keep me with her a little longer. But she kept the carriage and, after tea there, came with me herself back here. This was also for the same purpose. Then she went home, though I had brought her a message from the Prince that arranged their movements otherwise. He and Charlotte must have arrived — if they have arrived — expecting to drive together to Eaton Square and keep Maggie on to dinner there. She has everything there, you know — she has clothes."

The Colonel didn't in fact know, but he gave it his apprehension. "Oh, you mean a change?"

"Twenty changes, if you like — all sorts of things. She dresses, really, Maggie does, as much for her father — and she always did — as for her husband or for herself. She has her room in his house very much as she had it before she was married — and just as the boy has quite a second nursery there, in which Mrs. Noble, when she comes with him, makes herself, I assure you, at home. Si bien that if Charlotte, in her own house, so to speak, should wish a friend or two to stay with her, she really would be scarce able to put them up."

It was a picture into which, as a thrifty entertainer himself, Bob Assingham could more or less enter. "Maggie and the child spread so?"

"Maggie and the child spread so."

Well, he considered. "It IS rather rum,"

"That's all I claim" — she seemed thankful for the word. "I don't say it's anything more — but it IS, distinctly, rum."

Which, after an instant, the Colonel took up. "'More'? What more COULD it be?"

"It could be that she's unhappy, and that she takes her funny little way of consoling herself. For if she were unhappy" — Mrs. Assingham had figured it out — "that's just the way, I'm convinced, she would take. But how can she be unhappy, since — as I'm also convinced — she, in the midst of everything, adores her husband as much as ever?"

The Colonel at this brooded for a little at large. "Then if she's so happy, please what's the matter?"

It made his wife almost spring at him. "You think then she's secretly wretched?"

But he threw up his arms in deprecation. "Ah, my dear, I give them up to YOU. I've nothing more to suggest."

"Then it's not sweet of you." She spoke at present as if he were frequently sweet. "You admit that it is 'rum.'"

And this indeed fixed again, for a moment, his intention. "Has Charlotte complained of the want of rooms for her friends?"

"Never, that I know of, a word. It isn't the sort of thing she does. And whom has she, after all," Mrs. Assingham added, "to complain to?"

"Hasn't she always you?"

"Oh, 'me'! Charlotte and I, nowadays —!" She spoke as of a chapter closed. "Yet see the justice I still do her. She strikes me, more and more, as extraordinary."

A deeper shade, at the renewal of the word, had come into the Colonel's face. "If they're each and all so extraordinary then, isn't that why one must just resign one's self to wash one's hands of them — to be lost?" Her face, however, so met the question as if it were but a flicker of the old tone that their trouble had now become too real for — her charged eyes so betrayed the condition of her nerves that he stepped back, alertly enough, to firmer ground. He had spoken before in this light of a plain man's vision, but he must be something more than a plain man now. "Hasn't she then, Charlotte, always her husband —?"

"To complain to? She'd rather die."

"Oh!" — and Bob Assingham's face, at the vision of such extremities, lengthened for very docility. "Hasn't she the Prince then?"

"For such matters? Oh, he doesn't count."

"I thought that was just what — as the basis of our agitation — he does do!"

Mrs. Assingham, however, had her distinction ready. "Not a bit as a person to bore with complaints. The ground of MY agitation is, exactly, that she never on any pretext bores him. Not Charlotte!" And in the imagination of Mrs. Verver's superiority to any such mistake she gave, characteristically, something like a toss of her head — as marked a tribute to that lady's general grace, in all the conditions, as the personage referred to doubtless had ever received.

"Ah, only Maggie!" With which the Colonel gave a short low gurgle. But it found his wife again prepared.

"No — not only Maggie. A great many people in London — and small wonder! — bore him."

"Maggie only worst then?" But it was a question that he had promptly dropped at the returning brush of another, of which she had shortly before sown the seed. "You said just now that he would by this time be back with Charlotte 'if they HAVE arrived.' You think it then possible that they really won't have returned?"

His companion exhibited to view, for the idea, a sense of her responsibility; but this was insufficient, clearly, to keep her from entertaining it. "I think there's nothing they're not now capable of — in their so intense good faith."

"Good faith?" — he echoed the words, which had in fact something of an odd ring, critically.

"Their false position. It comes to the same thing." And she bore down, with her decision, the superficial lack of sequence. "They may very possibly, for a demonstration — as I see them — not have come back."

He wondered, visibly, at this, how she did see them. "May have bolted somewhere together?"

"May have stayed over at Matcham itself till tomorrow. May have wired home, each of them, since Maggie left me. May have done," Fanny Assingham continued, "God knows what!" She went on, suddenly, with more emotion — which, at the pressure of some spring of her inner vision, broke out in a wail of distress, imperfectly smothered. "Whatever they've done I shall never know. Never, never — because I don't want to, and because nothing will induce me. So they may do as they like. But I've worked for them ALL" She uttered this last with another irrepressible quaver, and the next moment her tears had come, though she had, with the explosion, quitted her husband as if to hide it from him. She passed into the dusky drawing-room, where, during his own prowl, shortly previous, he had drawn up a blind, so that the light of the street-lamps came in a little at the window. She made for this window, against which she leaned her head, while the Colonel, with his lengthened face, looked after her for a minute and hesitated. He might have been wondering what she had really done, to what extent, beyond his knowledge or his conception, in the affairs of these people, she COULD have committed herself. But to hear her cry, and yet try not to, was, quickly enough, too much for him; he had known her at other times quite not try not to, and that had not been so bad. He went to her and put his arm round her; he drew her head to his breast, where, while she gasped, she let it stay a little — all with a patience that presently stilled her. Yet the effect of this small crisis, oddly enough, was not to close their colloquy, with the natural result of sending them to bed: what was between them had opened out further, had somehow, through the sharp show of her feeling, taken a positive stride, had entered, as it were, without more words, the region of the understood, shutting the door after it and bringing them so still more nearly face to face. They remained for some minutes looking at it through the dim window which opened upon the world of human trouble in general and which let the vague light play here and there upon gilt and crystal and colour, the florid features, looming dimly, of Fanny's drawing-room. And the beauty of what thus passed between them, passed with her cry of pain, with her burst of tears, with his wonderment and his kindness and his comfort, with the moments of their silence, above all, which might have represented their sinking together, hand in hand, for a time, into the mystic lake where he had begun, as we have hinted, by seeing her paddle alone — the beauty of it was that they now could really talk better than before, because the basis had at last, once for all, defined itself. What was the basis, which Fanny absolutely exacted, but that Charlotte and the Prince must be saved — so far as consistently speaking of them as still safe might save them? It did save them, somehow, for Fanny's troubled mind — for that was the nature of the mind of women. He conveyed to her now, at all events, by refusing her no gentleness, that he had sufficiently got the tip, and that the tip was all he had wanted. This remained quite clear even when he presently reverted to what she had told him of her recent passage with Maggie. "I don't altogether see, you know, what you infer from it, or why you infer anything." When he so expressed himself it was quite as if in possession of what they had brought up from the depths.

XXIV

"I can't say more," this made his companion reply, "than that something in her face, her voice and her whole manner acted upon me as nothing in her had ever acted before; and just for the reason, above all, that I felt her trying her very best — and her very best, poor duck, is very good — to be quiet and natural. It's when one sees people who always ARE natural making little pale, pathetic, blinking efforts for it — then it is that one knows something's the matter. I can't describe my impression — you would have had it for yourself. And the only thing that ever CAN be the matter with Maggie is that. By 'that' I mean her beginning to doubt. To doubt, for the first time," Mrs. Assingham wound up, "of her wonderful little judgment of her wonderful little world."

It was impressive, Fanny's vision, and the Colonel, as if himself agitated by it, took another turn of prowling. "To doubt of fidelity — to doubt of friendship! Poor duck indeed! It will go hard with her. But she'll put it all," he concluded, "on Charlotte."

Mrs. Assingham, still darkly contemplative, denied this with a headshake. "She won't 'put' it anywhere. She won't do with it anything anyone else would. She'll take it all herself."

"You mean she'll make it out her own fault?"

"Yes — she'll find means, somehow, to arrive at that."

"Ah then," the Colonel dutifully declared, "she's indeed a little brick!"

"Oh," his wife returned, "you'll see, in one way or another, to what tune!" And she spoke, of a sudden, with an approach to elation — so that, as if immediately feeling his surprise, she turned round to him. "She'll see me somehow through!"

"See YOU —?"

"Yes, me. I'm the worst. For," said Fanny Assingham, now with a harder exaltation, "I did it all. I recognise that — I accept it. She won't cast it up at me — she won't cast up anything. So I throw myself upon her — she'll bear me up." She spoke almost volubly — she held him with her sudden sharpness. "She'll carry the whole weight of us."

There was still, nevertheless, wonder in it. "You mean she won't mind? I SAY, love —!" And he not unkindly stared. "Then where's the difficulty?"

"There isn't any!" Fanny declared with the same rich emphasis. It kept him indeed, as by the loss of the thread, looking at her longer. "Ah, you mean there isn't any for US!"

She met his look for a minute as if it perhaps a little too much imputed a selfishness, a concern, at any cost, for their own surface. Then she might have been deciding that their own surface was, after all, what they had most to consider. "Not," she said with dignity, "if we properly keep our heads." She appeared even to signify that they would begin by keeping them now. This was what it was to have at last a constituted basis. "Do you remember what you said to me that night of my first REAL anxiety — after the Foreign Office party?"

"In the carriage — as we came home?" Yes — he could recall it. "Leave them to pull through?"

"Precisely. 'Trust their own wit,' you practically said, 'to save all appearances.' Well, I've trusted it. I HAVE left them to pull through."

He hesitated. "And your point is that they're not doing so?"

"I've left them," she went on, "but now I see how and where. I've been leaving them all the while, without knowing it, to HER."

"To the Princess?"

"And that's what I mean," Mrs. Assingham pensively pursued. "That's what happened to me with her today," she continued to explain. "It came home to me that that's what I've really been doing."

"Oh, I see."

"I needn't torment myself. She has taken them over."

The Colonel declared that he "saw"; yet it was as if, at this, he a little sightlessly stared. "But what then has happened, from one day to the other, to HER? What has opened her eyes?"

"They were never really shut. She misses him."

"Then why hasn't she missed him before?"

Well, facing him there, among their domestic glooms and glints, Fanny worked it out. "She did — but she wouldn't let herself know it. She had her reason — she wore her blind. Now, at last, her situation has come to a head. To-day she does know it. And that's illuminating. It has been," Mrs. Assingham wound up, "illuminating to ME."

Her husband attended, but the momentary effect of his attention was vagueness again, and the refuge of his vagueness was a gasp. "Poor dear little girl!"

"Ah no — don't pity her!"

This did, however, pull him up. "We mayn't even be sorry for her?"

"Not now — or at least not yet. It's too soon — that is if it isn't very much too late. This will depend," Mrs. Assingham went on; "at any rate we shall see. We might have pitied her before — for all the good it would then have done her; we might have begun some time ago. Now, however, she has begun to live. And the way it comes to me, the way it comes to me —" But again she projected her vision.

"The way it comes to you can scarcely be that she'll like it!"

"The way it comes to me is that she will live. The way it comes to me is that she'll triumph."

She said this with so sudden a prophetic flare that it fairly cheered her husband. "Ah then, we must back her!"

"No — we mustn't touch her. We mayn't touch any of them. We must keep our hands off; we must go on tiptoe. We must simply watch and wait. And meanwhile," said Mrs. Assingham, "we must bear it as we can. That's where we are — and serves us right. We're in presence."

And so, moving about the room as in communion with shadowy portents, she left it till he questioned again. "In presence of what?"

"Well, of something possibly beautiful. Beautiful as it MAY come off."

She had paused there before him while he wondered. "You mean she'll get the Prince back?"

She raised her hand in quick impatience: the suggestion might have been almost abject. "It isn't a question of recovery. It won't be a question of any vulgar struggle. To 'get him back' she must have lost him, and to have lost him she must have had him. "With which Fanny shook her head. "What I take her to be waking up to is the truth that, all the while, she really HASN'T had him. Never."

"Ah, my dear —!" the poor Colonel panted.

"Never!" his wife repeated. And she went on without pity. "Do you remember what I said to you long ago — that evening, just before their marriage, when Charlotte had so suddenly turned up?"

The smile with which he met this appeal was not, it was to be feared, robust. "What haven't you, love, said in your time?"

"So many things, no doubt, that they make a chance for my having once or twice spoken the truth. I never spoke it more, at all events, than when I put it to you, that evening, that Maggie was the person in the world to whom a wrong thing could least be communicated. It was as if her imagination had been closed to it, her sense altogether sealed, That therefore," Fanny continued, "is what will now HAVE to happen. Her sense will have to open."

"I see." He nodded. "To the wrong." He nodded again, almost cheerfully — as if he had been keeping the peace with a baby or a lunatic. "To the very, very wrong."

But his wife's spirit, after its effort of wing, was able to remain higher. "To what's called Evil — with a very big E: for the first time in her life. To the discovery of it, to the knowledge of it, to the crude experience of it." And she gave, for the possibility, the largest measure. "To the harsh, bewildering brush, the daily chilling breath of it. Unless indeed" — and here Mrs. Assingham noted a limit "unless indeed, as yet (so far as she has come, and if she comes no further), simply to the suspicion and the dread. What we shall see is whether that mere dose of alarm will prove enough."

He considered. "But enough for what then, dear — if not enough to break her heart?"

"Enough to give her a shaking!" Mrs. Assingham rather oddly replied. "To give her, I mean, the right one. The right one won't break her heart. It will make her," she explained —"well, it will make her, by way of a change, understand one or two things in the world."

"But isn't it a pity," the Colonel asked, "that they should happen to be the one or two that will be the most disagreeable to her?"

"Oh, 'disagreeable' —? They'll have had to be disagreeable — to show her a little where she is. They'll have HAD to be disagreeable to make her sit up. They'll have had to be disagreeable to make her decide to live."

Bob Assingham was now at the window, while his companion slowly revolved; he had lighted a cigarette, for final patience, and he seemed vaguely to "time" her as she moved to and fro. He had at the same time to do justice to the lucidity she had at last attained, and it was doubtless by way of expression of this teachability that he let his eyes, for a minute, roll, as from the force of feeling, over the upper dusk of the room. He had thought of the response his wife's words ideally implied.

"Decide to live — ah yes! — for her child."

"Oh, bother her child!" — and he had never felt so snubbed, for an exemplary view, as when Fanny now stopped short. "To live, you poor dear, for her father — which is another pair of sleeves!"

And Mrs. Assingham's whole ample, ornamented person irradiated, with this, the truth that had begun, under so much handling, to glow. "Any idiot can do things for her child. She'll have a motive more original, and we shall see how it will work her. She'll have to save HIM."

"To 'save' him —?"

"To keep her father from her own knowledge. THAT" — and she seemed to see it, before her, in her husband's very eyes —"will be work cut out!" With which, as at the highest conceivable climax, she wound up their colloquy. "Good night!"

There was something in her manner, however — or in the effect, at least, of this supreme demonstration that had fairly, and by a single touch, lifted him to her side; so that, after she had turned her back to regain the landing and the staircase, he overtook her, before she had begun to mount, with the ring of excited perception. "Ah, but, you know, that's rather jolly!"

"'Jolly' —?" she turned upon it, again, at the foot of the staircase.

"I mean it's rather charming."

"'Charming' —?" It had still to be their law, a little, that she was tragic when he was comic.

"I mean it's rather beautiful. You just said, yourself, it would be. Only," he pursued promptly, with the impetus of this idea, and as if it had suddenly touched with light for him connections hitherto dim —"only I don't quite see why that very care for him which has carried her to such other lengths, precisely, as affect one as so 'rum,' hasn't also, by the same stroke, made her notice a little more what has been going on."

"Ah, there you are! It's the question that I've all along been asking myself." She had rested her eyes on the carpet, but she raised them as she pursued — she let him have it straight. "And it's the question of an idiot."

"An idiot —?"

"Well, the idiot that I'VE been, in all sorts of ways — so often, of late, have I asked it. You're excusable, since you ask it but now. The answer, I saw today, has all the while been staring me in the face."

"Then what in the world is it?"

"Why, the very intensity of her conscience about him — the very passion of her brave little piety. That's the way it has worked," Mrs. Assingham explained "and I admit it to have been as 'rum' a way as possible. But it has been working from a rum start. From the moment the dear man married to ease his daughter off, and it then happened, by an extraordinary perversity, that the very opposite effect was produced —!" With the renewed vision of this fatality, however, she could give but a desperate shrug.

"I see," the Colonel sympathetically mused. "That WAS a rum start."

But his very response, as she again flung up her arms, seemed to make her sense, for a moment, intolerable. "Yes — there I am! I was really at the bottom of it," she declared; "I don't know what possessed me — but I planned for him, I goaded him on." With which, however, the next moment, she took herself up. "Or, rather, I DO know what possessed me — for wasn't he beset with ravening women, right and left, and didn't he, quite pathetically, appeal for protection, didn't he, quite charmingly, show one how he needed and desired it? Maggie," she thus lucidly continued, "couldn't, with a new life of her own, give herself up to doing for him in the future all she had done in the past — to fencing him in, to keeping him safe and keeping THEM off. One perceived this," she went on —"out of the abundance of one's affection and one's sympathy." It all blessedly came back to her — when it wasn't all, for the fiftieth time, obscured, in face of the present facts, by anxiety and compunction. "One was no doubt a meddlesome fool; one always IS, to think one sees people's lives for them better than they see them for themselves. But one's excuse here," she insisted, "was that these people clearly DIDN'T see them for themselves — didn't see them at all. It struck one for very pity — that they were making a mess of such charming material; that they were but wasting it and letting it go. They didn't know HOW to live — and "somehow one couldn't, if one took an interest in them at all, simply stand and see it. That's what I pay for" — and the poor woman, in straighter communion with her companion's intelligence at this moment, she appeared to feel, than she had ever been before, let him have the whole of the burden of her consciousness. "I always pay for it, sooner or later, my sociable, my damnable, my unnecessary interest. Nothing of course would suit me but that it should fix itself also on Charlotte — Charlotte who was hovering there on the edge of our lives, when not beautifully, and a trifle mysteriously, flitting across them, and who was a piece of waste and a piece of threatened failure, just as, for any possible good to the WORLD, Mr. Verver and Maggie were. It began to come over me, in the watches of the night, that Charlotte was a person who COULD keep off ravening women — without being one herself, either, in the vulgar way of the others; and that this service to Mr. Verver would be a sweet employment for her future. There was something, of course, that might have stopped me: you know, you know what I mean — it looks at me," she veritably moaned, "out of your face! But all I can say is that it didn't; the reason largely being — once I had fallen in love with the beautiful symmetry of my plan — that I seemed to feel sure Maggie would accept Charlotte, whereas I didn't quite make out either what other woman, or what other KIND of woman, one could think of her accepting."

"I see — I see." She had paused, meeting all the while his listening look, and the fever of her retrospect had so risen with her talk that the desire was visibly strong in him to meet her, on his side, but with cooling breath. "One quite understands, my dear."

It only, however, kept her there sombre. "I naturally see, love, what you understand; which sits again, perfectly, in your eyes. You see that I saw that Maggie would accept her in helpless ignorance. Yes, dearest" — and the grimness of her dreariness suddenly once more possessed her: "you've only to tell me that that knowledge was my reason for what I did. How, when you do, can I stand up to you? You see," she said with an ineffable headshake, "that I don't stand up! I'm down, down, down," she declared; "yet" she as quickly added —"there's just one little thing that helps to save my life." And she kept him waiting but an instant. "They might easily — they would perhaps even certainly — have done something worse."

He thought. "Worse than that Charlotte —?"

"Ah, don't tell me," she cried, "that there COULD have been nothing worse. There might, as they were, have been many things. Charlotte, in her way, is extraordinary."

He was almost simultaneous. "Extraordinary!"

"She observes the forms," said Fanny Assingham.

He hesitated. "With the Prince —?"

"FOR the Prince. And with the others," she went on. "With Mr. Verver — wonderfully. But above all with Maggie. And the forms" — she had to do even THEM justice —"are two-thirds of conduct. Say he had married a woman who would have made a hash of them."

But he jerked back. "Ah, my dear, I wouldn't say it for the world!"

"Say," she none the less pursued, "he had married a woman the Prince would really have cared for."

"You mean then he doesn't care for Charlotte —?" This was still a new view to jump to, and the Colonel, perceptibly, wished to make sure of the necessity of the effort. For that, while he stared, his wife allowed him time; at the end of which she simply said: "No!"

"Then what on earth are they up to?" Still, however, she only looked at him; so that, standing there before her with his hands in his pockets, he had time, further, to risk, soothingly, another question. "Are the 'forms' you speak of — that are two-thirds of conduct — what will be keeping her now, by your hypothesis, from coming home with him till morning?"

"Yes — absolutely. THEIR forms."

"'Theirs' —?"

"Maggie's and Mr. Verver's — those they IMPOSE on Charlotte and the Prince. Those," she developed. "that, so perversely, as I say, have succeeded in setting themselves up as the right ones."

He considered — but only now, at last, really to relapse into woe. "Your 'perversity,' my dear, is exactly what I don't understand. The state of things existing hasn't grown, like a field of mushrooms, in a night. Whatever they, all round, may be in for now is at least the consequence of what they've DONE. Are they mere helpless victims of fate?"

Well, Fanny at last had the courage of it, "Yes — they are. To be so abjectly innocent — that IS to be victims of fate."

"And Charlotte and the Prince are abjectly innocent —?"

It took her another minute, but she rose to the full height. "Yes. That is they WERE — as much so in their way as the others. There were beautiful intentions all round. The Prince's and Charlotte's were beautiful — of THAT I had my faith. They WERE — I'd go to the stake. Otherwise," she added, "I should have been a wretch. And I've not been a wretch. I've only been a double-dyed donkey."

"Ah then," he asked, "what does our muddle make THEM to have been?"

"Well, too much taken up with considering each other. You may call such a mistake as that by what ever name you please; it at any rate means, all round, their case. It illustrates the misfortune," said Mrs. Assingham gravely, "of being too, too charming."

This was another matter that took some following, but the Colonel again did his best. "Yes, but to whom? — doesn't it rather depend on that? To whom have the Prince and Charlotte then been too charming?"

"To each other, in the first place — obviously. And then both of them together to Maggie."

"To Maggie?" he wonderingly echoed.

"To Maggie." She was now crystalline. "By having accepted, from the first, so guilelessly — yes, so guilelessly, themselves — her guileless idea of still having her father, of keeping him fast, in her life."

"Then isn't one supposed, in common humanity, and if one hasn't quarrelled with him, and one has the means, and he, on his side, doesn't drink or kick up rows — isn't one supposed to keep one's aged parent in one's life?"

"Certainly — when there aren't particular reasons against it. That there may be others than his getting drunk is exactly the moral of what is before us. In the first place Mr. Verver isn't aged."

The Colonel just hung fire — but it came. "Then why the deuce does he — oh, poor dear man! — behave as if he were?"

She took a moment to meet it. "How do you know how he behaves?"

"Well, my own love, we see how Charlotte does!" Again, at this, she faltered; but again she rose. "Ah, isn't my whole point that he's charming to her?"

"Doesn't it depend a bit on what she regards as charming?"

She faced the question as if it were flippant, then with a headshake of dignity she brushed it away. "It's Mr. Verver who's really young — it's Charlotte who's really old. And what I was saying," she added, "isn't affected!"

"You were saying" — he did her the justice —"that they're all guileless."

"That they were. Guileless, all, at first — quite extraordinarily. It's what I mean by their failure to see that the more they took for granted they could work together the more they were really working apart. For I repeat," Fanny went on, "that I really believe Charlotte and the Prince honestly to have made up their minds, originally, that their very esteem for Mr. Verver — which was serious, as well it might be! — would save them."

"I see." The Colonel inclined himself. "And save HIM."

"It comes to the same thing!"

"Then save Maggie."

"That comes," said Mrs. Assingham, "to something a little different. For Maggie has done the most."

He wondered. "What do you call the most?"

"Well, she did it originally — she began the vicious circle. For that — though you make round eyes at my associating her with 'vice' — is simply what it has been. It's their mutual consideration, all round, that has made it the bottomless gulf; and they're really so embroiled but because, in their way, they've been so improbably GOOD."

"In their way — yes!" the Colonel grinned.

"Which was, above all, Maggie's way." No flicker of his ribaldry was anything to her now. "Maggie had in the first place to make up to her father for her having suffered herself to become — poor little dear, as she believed — so intensely married. Then she had to make up to her husband for taking so much of the time they might otherwise have spent together to make this reparation to Mr. Verver perfect. And her way to do this, precisely, was by allowing the Prince the use, the enjoyment, whatever you may call it, of Charlotte to cheer his path — by instalments, as it were — in proportion as she herself, making sure her father was all right, might be missed from his side. By so much, at the same time, however," Mrs. Assingham further explained, "by so much as she took her young stepmother, for this purpose, away from Mr. Verver, by just so much did this too strike her as something again to be made up for. It has saddled her, you will easily see, with a positively new obligation to her father, an obligation created and aggravated by her unfortunate, even if quite heroic, little sense of justice. She began with wanting to show him that his marriage could never, under whatever temptation of her own bliss with the Prince, become for her a pretext for deserting or neglecting HIM. Then that, in its order, entailed her wanting to show the Prince that she recognised how the other desire — this wish to remain, intensely, the same passionate little daughter she had always been — involved in some degree, and just for the present, so to speak, her neglecting and deserting him. I quite hold," Fanny with characteristic amplitude parenthesised, "that a person can mostly feel but one passion — one TENDER passion, that is — at a time. Only, that doesn't hold good for our primary and instinctive attachments, the 'voice of blood,' such as one's feeling for a parent or a brother. Those may be intense and yet not prevent other intensities — as you will recognise, my dear, when you remember how I continued, tout betement, to adore my mother, whom you didn't adore, for years after I had begun to adore you. Well, Maggie" — she kept it up —"is in the same situation as I was, PLUS complications from which I was, thank heaven, exempt: PLUS the complication, above all, of not having in the least begun with the sense for complications that I should have had. Before she knew it, at any rate, her little scruples and her little lucidities, which were really so divinely blind — her feverish little sense of justice, as I say — had brought the two others together as her grossest misconduct couldn't have done. And now she knows something or other has happened — yet hasn't heretofore known what. She has only piled up her remedy, poor child — something that she has earnestly but confusedly seen as her necessary policy; piled it on top of the policy, on top of the remedy, that she at first thought out for herself, and that would really have needed, since then, so much modification.

Her only modification has been the growth of her necessity to prevent her father's wondering if all, in their life in common, MAY be so certainly for the best. She has now as never before to keep him unconscious that, peculiar, if he makes a point of it, as their situation is, there's anything in it all uncomfortable or disagreeable, anything morally the least out of the way. She has to keep touching it up to make it, each day, each month, look natural and normal to him; so that — God forgive me the comparison! — she's like an old woman who has taken to 'painting' and who has to lay it on thicker, to carry it off with a greater audacity, with a greater impudence even, the older she grows." And Fanny stood a moment captivated with the image she had thrown off. "I like the idea of Maggie audacious and impudent — learning to be so to gloss things over. She could — she even will, yet, I believe — learn it, for that sacred purpose, consummately, diabolically. For from the moment the dear man should see it's all rouge —!" She paused, staring at the vision.

It imparted itself even to Bob. "Then the fun would begin?" As it but made her look at him hard, however, he amended the form of his inquiry. "You mean that in that case she WILL, charming creature, be lost?"

She was silent a moment more. "As I've told you before, she won't be lost if her father's saved. She'll see that as salvation enough."

The Colonel took it in. "Then she's a little heroine."

"Rather — she's a little heroine. But it's his innocence, above all," Mrs. Assingham added, "that will pull them through."

Her companion, at this, focussed again Mr. Verver's innocence. "It's awfully quaint."

"Of course it's awfully quaint! That it's awfully quaint, that the pair are awfully quaint, quaint with all our dear old quaintness — by which I don't mean yours and mine, but that of my own sweet countrypeople, from whom I've so deplorably degenerated — that," Mrs. Assingham declared, "was originally the head and front of their appeal to me and of my interest in them. And of course I shall feel them quainter still," she rather ruefully subjoined, "before they've done with me!"

This might be, but it wasn't what most stood in the Colonel's way. "You believe so in Mr. Verver's innocence after two years of Charlotte?"

She stared. "But the whole point is just that two years of Charlotte are what he hasn't really — or what you may call undividedly — had."

"Any more than Maggie, by your theory, eh, has 'really or undividedly,' had four of the Prince? It takes all she hasn't had," the Colonel conceded, "to account for the innocence that in her, too, so leaves us in admiration."

So far as it might be ribald again she let this pass. "It takes a great many things to account for Maggie. What is definite, at all events, is that — strange though this be-her effort for her father has, up to now, sufficiently succeeded. She has made him, she makes him, accept the tolerably obvious oddity of their relation, all round, for part of the game. Behind her there, protected and amused and, as it were, exquisitely humbugged — the Principino, in whom he delights, always aiding — he has safely and serenely enough suffered the conditions of his life to pass for those he had sublimely projected. He hadn't worked them out in detail — any more than I had, heaven pity me! — and the queerness has been, exactly, in the detail. This, for him, is what it was to have married Charlotte. And they both," she neatly wound up, 'help.'"

"'Both' —?"

"I mean that if Maggie, always in the breach, makes it seem to him all so flourishingly to fit, Charlotte does her part not less. And her part is very large. Charlotte," Fanny declared, "works like a horse."

So there it all was, and her husband looked at her a minute across it. "And what does the Prince work like?"

She fixed him in return. "Like a Prince!" Whereupon, breaking short off, to ascend to her room, she presented her highly — decorated back — in which, in odd places, controlling the

162

complications of its aspect, the ruby or the garnet, the turquoise and the topaz, gleamed like faint symbols of the wit that pinned together the satin patches of her argument.

He watched her as if she left him positively under the impression of her mastery of her subject; yes, as if the real upshot of the drama before them was but that he had, when it came to the tight places of life — as life had shrunk for him now — the most luminous of wives. He turned off, in this view of her majestic retreat, the comparatively faint little electric lamp which had presided over their talk; then he went up as immediately behind her as the billows of her amber train allowed, making out how all the clearness they had conquered was even for herself a relief — how at last the sense of the amplitude of her exposition sustained and floated her. Joining her, however, on the landing above, where she had already touched a metallic point into light, he found she had done perhaps even more to create than to extinguish in him the germ of a curiosity. He held her a minute longer — there was another plum in the pie. "What did you mean some minutes ago by his not caring for Charlotte?"

"The Prince's? By his not 'really' caring?" She recalled, after a little, benevolently enough. "I mean that men don't, when it has all been too easy. That's how, in nine cases out of ten, a woman is treated who has risked her life. You asked me just now how he works," she added; "but you might better perhaps have asked me how he plays."

Well, he made it up. "Like a Prince?"

"Like a Prince. He is, profoundly, a Prince. For that," she said with expression, "he's — beautifully — a case. They're far rarer, even in the 'highest circles,' than they pretend to be-and that's what makes so much of his value. He's perhaps one of the very last — the last of the real ones. So it is we must take him. We must take him all round."

The Colonel considered. "And how must Charlotte — if anything happens — take him?"

The question held her a minute, and while she waited, with her eyes on him, she put out a grasping hand to his arm, in the flesh of which he felt her answer distinctly enough registered. Thus she gave him, standing off a little, the firmest, longest, deepest injunction he had ever received from her. "Nothing — in spite of everything — WILL happen. Nothing HAS happened. Nothing IS happening."

He looked a trifle disappointed. "I see. For US."

"For us. For whom else?" And he was to feel indeed how she wished him to understand it. "We know nothing on earth —!" It was an undertaking he must sign.

So he wrote, as it were, his name. "We know nothing on earth." It was like the soldiers' watchword at night.

"We're as innocent," she went on in the same way, "as babes."

"Why not rather say," he asked, "as innocent as they themselves are?"

"Oh, for the best of reasons! Because we're much more so."

He wondered. "But how can we be more —?"

"For them? Oh, easily! We can be anything."

"Absolute idiots then?"

"Absolute idiots. And oh," Fanny breathed, "the way it will rest us!"

Well, he looked as if there were something in that. "But won't they know we're not?"

She barely hesitated. "Charlotte and the Prince think we are — which is so much gained. Mr. Verver believes in our intelligence — but he doesn't matter."

"And Maggie? Doesn't SHE know —?"

"That we see before our noses?" Yes, this indeed took longer. "Oh, so far as she may guess it she'll give no sign. So it comes to the same thing."

He raised his eyebrows. "Comes to our not being able to help her?"

"That's the way we SHALL help her."

"By looking like fools?"

She threw up her hands. "She only wants, herself, to look like a bigger! So there we are!" With which she brushed it away — his conformity was promised. Something, however, still held her; it broke, to her own vision, as a last wave of clearness. "Moreover NOW," she said,

"I see! I mean," she added — what you were asking me: how I knew today, in Eaton Square, that Maggie's awake." And she had indeed visibly got it. "It was by seeing them together."

"Seeing her with her father?" He fell behind again. "But you've seen her often enough before."

"Never with my present eyes. For nothing like such a test — that of this length of the others' absence together — has hitherto occurred."

"Possibly! But if she and Mr. Verver insisted upon it —?"

"Why is it such a test? Because it has become one without their intending it. It has spoiled, so to speak, on their hands."

"It has soured, eh?" the Colonel said.

"The word's horrible — say rather it has 'changed.' Perhaps," Fanny went on, "she did wish to see how much she can bear. In that case she HAS seen. Only it was she alone who — about the visit — insisted. Her father insists on nothing. And she watches him do it."

Her husband looked impressed. "Watches him?"

"For the first faint sign. I mean of his noticing. It doesn't, as I tell you, come. But she's there for it to see. And I felt," she continued, "HOW she's there; I caught her, as it were, in the fact. She couldn't keep it from me — though she left her post on purpose — came home with me to throw dust in my eyes. I took it all — her dust; but it was what showed me." With which supreme lucidity she reached the door of her room. "Luckily it showed me also how she has succeeded. Nothing — from him — HAS come."

"You're so awfully sure?"

"Sure. Nothing WILL. Good-night," she said. "She'll die first."

Book Second: The Princess

Part Fourth

XXV

It was not till many days had passed that the Princess began to accept the idea of having done, a little, something she was not always doing, or indeed that of having listened to any inward voice that spoke in a new tone. Yet these instinctive postponements of reflection were the fruit, positively, of recognitions and perceptions already active; of the sense, above all, that she had made, at a particular hour, made by the mere touch of her hand, a difference in the situation so long present to her as practically unattackable. This situation had been occupying, for months and months, the very centre of the garden of her life, but it had reared itself there like some strange, tall tower of ivory, or perhaps rather some wonderful, beautiful, but outlandish pagoda, a structure plated with hard, bright porcelain, coloured and figured and adorned, at the overhanging eaves, with silver bells that tinkled, ever so charmingly, when stirred by chance airs. She had walked round and round it — that was what she felt; she had carried on her existence in the space left her for circulation, a space that sometimes seemed ample and sometimes narrow: looking up, all the while, at the fair structure that spread itself so amply and rose so high, but never quite making out, as yet, where she might have entered had she wished. She had not wished till now — such was the odd case; and what was doubtless equally odd, besides, was that, though her raised eyes seemed to distinguish places that must serve, from within, and especially far aloft, as apertures and outlooks, no door appeared to give access from her convenient garden level. The great decorated surface had remained consistently impenetrable and inscrutable. At present, however, to her considering mind, it was as if she had ceased merely to circle and to scan the elevation, ceased so vaguely, so quite helplessly to stare and wonder: she had caught herself distinctly in the act of pausing, then in that of lingering, and finally in that of stepping unprecedentedly near. The thing might have been, by the distance at which it kept her, a Mahometan mosque, with which no base heretic could take a liberty; there so hung about it the vision of one's putting off one's shoes to enter, and even, verily, of one's paying with one's life if found there as an interloper. She had not, certainly, arrived at the conception of paying with her life for anything she might do; but it was nevertheless quite as if she had sounded with a tap or two one of the rare porcelain plates. She had knocked, in short — though she could scarce have said whether for admission or for what; she had applied her hand to a cool smooth spot and had waited to see what would happen. Something had happened; it was as if a sound, at her touch, after a little, had come back to her from within; a sound sufficiently suggesting that her approach had been noted.

If this image, however, may represent our young woman's consciousness of a recent change in her life — a change now but a few days old — it must at the same time be observed that she both sought and found in renewed circulation, as I have called it, a measure of relief from the idea of having perhaps to answer for what she had done. The pagoda in her blooming garden figured the arrangement — how otherwise was it to be named? — by which, so strikingly, she had been able to marry without breaking, as she liked to put it, with the past. She had surrendered herself to her husband without the shadow of a reserve or a condition, and yet she had not, all the while, given up her father — the least little inch. She had compassed the high city of seeing the two men beautifully take to each other, and nothing in her marriage had marked it as more happy than this fact of its having practically given the elder, the lonelier, a new friend. What had moreover all the while enriched the whole aspect of success was that the latter's marriage had been no more meassurably paid for than her own. His having taken the same great step in the same free way had not in the least involved the relegation of his daughter. That it was remarkable they should have been able at once so to separate and so to keep together had never for a moment, from however far back, been equivocal to her; that it was remarkable had in fact quite counted, at first and always, and for each of them equally, as part of their inspiration and their support. There were plenty of singular things they were NOT enamoured of — flights of brilliancy, of audacity, of originality, that, speaking at least for the dear man and herself, were not at all in their line; but they liked to think they had given their life this unusual extension and this liberal form, which many families, many couples, and still more many pairs of couples, would not have found workable. That last truth had been distinctly brought home to them by the bright testimony, the quite explicit envy, of most of their friends, who had remarked to them again and again that they must, on all the showing, to keep on such terms, be people of the highest amiability — equally including in the praise, of course, Amerigo and Charlotte. It had given them pleasure — as how should it not? — to find themselves shed such a glamour; it had certainly, that is, given pleasure to her father and herself, both of them distinguishably of a nature so slow to presume that they would scarce have been sure of their triumph without this pretty reflection of it. So it was that their felicity had fructified; so it was that the ivory tower, visible and admirable doubtless, from any point of the social field, had risen stage by stage. Maggie's actual reluctance to ask herself with proportionate sharpness why she had ceased to take comfort in the sight of it represented accordingly a lapse from that ideal consistency on which her moral comfort almost at any time depended. To remain consistent she had always been capable of cutting down more or less her prior term.

Moving for the first time in her life as in the darkening shadow of a false position, she reflected that she should either not have ceased to be right — that is, to be confident — or have recognised that she was wrong; though she tried to deal with herself, for a space, only as a silken-coated spaniel who has scrambled out of a pond and who rattles the water from his ears. Her shake of her head, again and again, as she went, was much of that order, and she had the resource, to which, save for the rude equivalent of his generalising bark, the spaniel would have been a stranger, of humming to herself hard as a sign that nothing had happened to her. She had not, so to speak, fallen in; she had had no accident and had not got wet; this at any rate was her pretension until after she began a little to wonder if she mightn't, with or without exposure, have taken cold. She could at all events remember no time at which she had felt so excited, and certainly none — which was another special point — that so brought with it as well the necessity for concealing excitement. This birth of a new eagerness became a high pastime, in her view, precisely by reason of the ingenuity required for keeping the thing born out of sight. The ingenuity was thus a private and absorbing exercise, in the light of which, might I so far multiply my metaphors, I should compare her to the frightened but clinging young mother of an unlawful child. The idea that had possession of her would be, by our new analogy, the proof of her misadventure, but likewise, all the while, only another sign of a relation that was more to her than anything on earth. She had lived long enough to make out for herself that any deep-seated passion has its pangs as well as its joys, and that we are made by its aches and its anxieties most richly conscious of it. She had never doubted of the force of the feeling that bound her to her husband; but to become aware, almost suddenly, that it had begun to vibrate with a violence that had some of the effect of a strain would, rightly looked at, after all but show that she was, like thousands of women, every day, acting up to the full privilege of passion. Why in the world shouldn't she, with every right — if, on consideration, she saw no good reason against it? The best reason against it would have been the possibility of some consequence disagreeable or inconvenient to others — especially to such others as had never incommoded her by the egotism of THEIR passions; but if once that danger were duly guarded against the fulness of one's measure amounted to no more than the equal use of one's faculties or the proper playing of one's part. It had come to the Princess, obscurely at first, but little by little more conceivably, that her faculties had not for a good while been concomitantly used; the case resembled in a manner that of her once-loved dancing, a matter of remembered steps that had grown vague from her ceasing to go to balls. She would go to balls again — that seemed, freely, even crudely, stated, the remedy; she would take out of the deep receptacles in which she had laid them away the various ornaments congruous with the greater occasions, and of which her store, she liked to think, was none of the smallest. She would have been easily to be figured for us at this occupation; dipping, at off moments and quiet hours, in snatched visits and by draughty candle-light, into her rich collections and seeing her jewels again a little shyly, but all unmistakably, glow. That in fact may pass as the very picture of her semi-smothered agitation, of the diversion she to some extent successfully found in referring her crisis, so far as was possible, to the mere working of her own needs.

It must be added, however, that she would have been at a loss to determine — and certainly at first — to which order, that of self-control or that of large expression, the step she had taken the afternoon of her husband's return from Matcham with his companion properly belonged. For it had been a step, distinctly, on Maggie's part, her deciding to do something, just then and there, which would strike Amerigo as unusual, and this even though her departure from custom had merely consisted in her so arranging that he wouldn't find her, as he would definitely expect to do, in Eaton Square. He would have, strangely enough, as might seem to him, to come back home for it, and there get the impression of her rather pointedly, or at least all impatiently and independently, awaiting him. These were small variations and mild manoeuvres, but they went accompanied on Maggie's part, as we have mentioned, with an infinite sense of intention. Her watching by his fireside for her husband's return from an absence might superficially have presented itself as the most natural act in the world, and the only one, into the bargain, on which he would positively have reckoned. It fell by this circumstance into the order of plain matters, and yet the very aspect by which it was, in the event, handed over to her brooding fancy was the fact that she had done with it all she had designed. She had put her thought to the proof, and the proof had shown its edge; this was what was before her, that she was no longer playing with blunt and idle tools, with weapons that didn't cut. There passed across her vision ten times a day the gleam of a bare blade, and at this it was that she most shut her eyes, most knew the impulse to cheat herself with motion and sound. She had merely driven, on a certain Wednesday, to Portland Place, instead of remaining in Eaton Square, and she privately repeated it again and again — there had appeared beforehand no reason why she should have seen the mantle of history flung, by a single sharp sweep, over so commonplace a deed. That, all the same, was what had happened; it had been bitten into her mind, all in an hour, that nothing she had ever done would hereafter, in some way yet to be determined, so count for her — perhaps not even what she had done in accepting, in their old golden Rome, Amerigo's proposal of marriage. And yet, by her little crouching posture there, that of a timid tigress, she had meant nothing recklessly ultimate, nothing clumsily fundamental; so that she called it names, the invidious, the grotesque attitude, holding it up to her own ridicule, reducing so far as she could the portee of what had followed it. She had but wanted to get nearer — nearer to something indeed that she couldn't, that she wouldn't, even to herself, describe; and the degree of this achieved nearness was what had been in advance incalculable. Her actual multiplication of distractions and suppressions, whatever it did for her, failed to prevent her living over again any chosen minute — for she could choose them, she could fix them — of the freshness of relation produced by her having administered to her husband the first surprise to which she had ever treated him. It had been a poor thing, but it had been all her own, and the whole passage was backwardly there, a great picture hung on the wall of her daily life, for her to make what she would of.

It fell, for retrospect, into a succession of moments that were WATCHABLE still; almost in the manner of the different things done during a scene on the stage, some scene so acted as to have left a great impression on the tenant of one of the stalls. Several of these moments stood out beyond the others, and those she could feel again most, count again like the firm pearls on a string, had belonged more particularly to the lapse of time before dinner — dinner which had been so late, quite at nine o'clock, that evening, thanks to the final lateness of Amerigo's own advent. These were parts of the experience — though in fact there had been a good many of them — between which her impression could continue sharply to discriminate. Before the subsequent passages, much later on, it was to be said, the flame of memory turned to an equalising glow, that of a lamp in some side-chapel in which incense was thick. The great moment, at any rate, for conscious repossession, was doubtless the first: the strange little timed silence which she had fully gauged, on the spot, as altogether beyond her own intention, but which — for just how long? should she ever really know for just how long? — she could do nothing to break. She was in the smaller drawing-room, in which she always "sat," and she had, by calculation, dressed for dinner on finally coming in. It was a wonder how many things she had calculated in respect to this small incident — a matter for the importance of which she had so quite indefinite a measure. He would be late — he would be very late; that was the one certainty that seemed to look her in the face. There was still also the possibility that if he drove with Charlotte straight to Eaton Square he might think it best to remain there even on learning she had come away. She had left no message for him on any such chance; this was another of her small shades of decision, though the effect of it might be to keep him still longer absent. He might suppose she would already have dined; he might stay, with all he would have to tell, just on purpose to be nice to her father. She had known him to stretch the point, to these beautiful ends, far beyond that; he had more than once stretched it to the sacrifice of the opportunity of dressing.

If she herself had now avoided any such sacrifice, and had made herself, during the time at her disposal, quite inordinately fresh and quite positively smart, this had probably added, while she waited and waited, to that very tension of spirit in which she was afterwards to find the image of her having crouched. She did her best, quite intensely, by herself, to banish any such appearance; she couldn't help it if she couldn't read her pale novel — ah, that, par exemple, was beyond her! but she could at least sit by the lamp with the book, sit there with her newest frock, worn for the first time, sticking out, all round her, quite stiff and grand; even perhaps a little too stiff and too grand for a familiar and domestic frock, yet marked none the less, this time, she ventured to hope, by incontestable intrinsic merit. She had glanced repeatedly at the clock, but she had refused herself the weak indulgence of walking up and down, though the act of doing so, she knew, would make her feel, on the polished floor, with the rustle and the "hang," still more beautifully bedecked. The difficulty was that it would also make her feel herself still more sharply in a state; which was exactly what she proposed not to do. The only drops of her anxiety had been when her thought strayed complacently, with her eyes, to the front of her gown, which was in a manner a refuge, a beguilement, especially when she was able to fix it long enough to wonder if it would at last really satisfy Charlotte. She had ever been, in respect to her clothes, rather timorous and uncertain; for the last year, above all, she had lived in the light of Charlotte's possible and rather inscrutable judgment of them. Charlotte's own were simply the most charming and interesting that any woman had ever put on; there was a kind of poetic justice in her being at last able, in this particular, thanks to means, thanks quite to omnipotence, freely to exercise her genius. But Maggie would have described herself as, in these connections, constantly and intimately "torn"; conscious on one side of the impossibility of copying her companion and conscious on the other of the impossibility of sounding her, independently, to the bottom. Yes, it was one of the things she should go down to her grave without having known — how Charlotte, after all had been said, really thought her stepdaughter looked under any supposedly ingenious personal experiment. She had always been lovely about the stepdaughter's material braveries — had done, for her, the very best with them; but there had ever fitfully danced at the back of Maggie's head the suspicion that these expressions were mercies, not judgments, embodying no absolute, but only a relative, frankness. Hadn't Charlotte, with so perfect a critical vision, if the truth were known, given her up as hopeless — hopeless by a serious standard, and thereby invented for her a different and inferior one, in which, as the only thing to be done, she patiently and soothingly abetted her? Hadn't she, in other words, assented in secret despair, perhaps even in secret irritation, to her being ridiculous? — so that the best now possible was to wonder, once in a great while, whether one mightn't give her the surprise of something a little less out of the true note than usual. Something of this kind was the question that Maggie, while the absentees still delayed, asked of the appearance she was endeavouring to present; but with the result, repeatedly again, that it only went and lost itself in the thick air that had begun more and more to hang, for our young woman, over her accumulations of the unanswered. They were THERE, these accumulations; they were like a roomful of confused objects, never as yet "sorted," which for some time now she had been passing and re-passing, along the corridor of her life. She passed it when she could without opening the door; then, on occasion, she turned the key to throw in a fresh contribution. So it was that she had been getting things out of the way. They rejoined the rest of the confusion; it was as if they found their place, by some instinct of affinity, in the heap. They knew, in short, where to go; and when she, at present, by a mental act, once more pushed the door open, she had practically a sense of method and experience. What she should never know about Charlotte's thought — she tossed THAT in. It would find itself in company, and she might at last have been standing there long enough to see it fall into its corner. The sight moreover would doubtless have made her stare, had her attention been more free — the sight of the mass of vain things, congruous, incongruous, that awaited every addition. It made her in fact, with a vague gasp, turn away, and what had further determined this was the final sharp extinction of the inward scene by the outward. The quite different door had opened and her husband was there.

It had been as strange as she could consent, afterwards, to think it; it had been, essentially, what had made the abrupt bend in her life: he had come back, had followed her from the other house, VISIBLY uncertain — this was written in the face he for the first minute showed her. It had been written only for those seconds, and it had appeared to go, quickly, after they began to talk; but while it lasted it had been written large, and, though she didn't quite know what she had expected of him, she felt she hadn't expected the least shade of embarrassment. What had made the embarrassment — she called it embarrassment so as to be able to assure herself she put it at the very worst — what had made the particular look was his thus distinguishably wishing to see how he should find her. Why FIRST — that had, later on, kept coming to her; the question dangled there as if it were the key to everything. With the sense of it on the spot, she had felt, overwhelmingly, that she was significant, that so she must instantly strike him, and that this had a kind of violence beyond what she had intended. It was in fact even at the moment not absent from her view that he might easily have made an abject fool of her — at least for the time. She had indeed, for just ten seconds, been afraid of some such turn: the uncertainty in his face had become so, the next thing, an uncertainty in the very air. Three words of impatience the least bit loud, some outbreak of "What in the world are you 'up to', and what do you mean?" any note of that sort would instantly have brought her low — and this all the more that heaven knew she hadn't in any manner designed to be high. It was such a trifle, her small breach with custom, or at any rate with his natural presumption, that all magnitude of wonder had already had, before one could deprecate the shadow of it, the effect of a complication. It had made for him some difference that she couldn't measure, this meeting him at home and alone instead of elsewhere and with others, and back and back it kept coming to her that the blankness he showed her before he was able to SEE might, should she choose to insist on it, have a meaning — have, as who should say, an historic value — beyond the importance of momentary expressions in general. She had naturally had on the spot no ready notion of what he might want to see; it was enough for a ready notion, not to speak of a beating heart, that he DID see, that he saw his wife in her own drawing-room at the hour when she would most properly be there. He hadn't in any way challenged her, it was true, and, after those instants during which she now believed him to have been harbouring the impression of something unusually prepared and pointed in her attitude and array, he had advanced upon her smiling and smiling, and thus, without hesitation at the last, had taken her into his arms. The hesitation had been at the first, and she at present saw that he had surmounted it without her help. She had given him no help; for if, on the one hand, she couldn't speak for hesitation, so on the other — and especially as he didn't ask her — she couldn't explain why she was agitated. She had known it all the while down to her toes, known it in his presence with fresh intensity, and if he had uttered but a question it would have pressed in her the spring of recklessness. It had been strange that the most natural thing of all to say to him should have had that appearance; but she was more than ever conscious that any appearance she had would come round, more or less straight, to her father, whose life was now so quiet, on the basis accepted for it, that any alteration of his consciousness even in the possible sense of enlivenment, would make their precious equilibrium waver. THAT was at the bottom of her mind, that their equilibrium was everything, and that it was practically precarious, a matter of a hair's breadth for the loss of the balance. It was the equilibrium, or at all events her conscious fear about it, that had brought her heart into her mouth; and the same fear was, on either side, in the silent look she and Amerigo had exchanged. The happy balance that demanded this amount of consideration was truly thus, as by its own confession, a delicate matter; but that her husband had also HIS habit of anxiety and his general caution only brought them, after all, more closely together. It would have been most beautifully, therefore, in the name of the equilibrium, and in that of her joy at their feeling so exactly the same about it, that she might have spoken if she had permitted the truth on the subject of her behaviour to ring out — on the subject of that poor little behaviour which was for the moment so very limited a case of eccentricity.

" 'Why, why' have I made this evening such a point of our not all dining together? Well, because I've all day been so wanting you alone that I finally couldn't bear it, and that there didn't seem any great reason why I should try to. THAT came to me — funny as it may at first sound, with all the things we've so wonderfully got into the way of bearing for each other. You've seemed these last days — I don't know what: more absent than ever before, too absent for us merely to go on so. It's all very well, and I perfectly see how beautiful it is, all round; but there comes a day when something snaps, when the full cup, filled to the very brim, begins to flow over. That's what has happened to my need of you — the cup, all day, has been too full to carry. So here I am with it, spilling it over you — and just for the reason that is the reason of my life. After all, I've scarcely to explain that I'm as much in love with you now as the first hour; except that there are some hours — which I know when they come, because they almost frighten me — that show me I'm even more so. They come of themselves — and, ah, they've been coming! After all, after all —!" Some such words as those were what DIDN'T ring out, yet it was as if even the unuttered sound had been quenched here in its own quaver. It was where utterance would have broken down by its very weight if he had let it get so far. Without that extremity, at the end of a moment, he had taken in what he needed to take — that his wife was TESTIFYING, that she adored and missed and desired him. "After all, after all," since she put it so, she was right. That was what he had to respond to; that was what, from the moment that, as has been said, he "saw," he had to treat as the most pertinent thing possible. He held her close and long, in expression of their personal reunion — this, obviously, was one way of doing so. He rubbed his cheek, tenderly, and with a deep vague murmur, against her face, that side of her face she was not pressing to his breast. That was, not less obviously, another way, and there were ways enough, in short, for his extemporised ease, for the good humour she was afterwards to find herself thinking of as his infinite tact. This last was partly, no doubt, because the question of tact might be felt as having come up at the end of a quarter of an hour during which he had liberally talked and she had genially questioned. He had told her of his day, the happy thought of his roundabout journey with Charlotte, all their cathedral-hunting adventure, and how it had turned out rather more of an affair than they expected. The moral of it was, at any rate, that he was tired, verily, and must have a bath and dress — to which end she would kindly excuse him for the shortest time possible. She was to remember afterwards something that had passed between them on this — how he had looked, for her, during an instant, at the door, before going out, how he had met her asking him, in hesitation first, then quickly in decision, whether she couldn't help him by going up with him. He had perhaps also for a moment hesitated, but he had declined her offer, and she was to preserve, as I say, the memory of the smile with which he had opined that at that rate they wouldn't dine till ten o'clock and that he should go straighter and faster alone. Such things, as I say, were to come back to her — they played, through her full after-sense, like lights on the whole impression;

the subsequent parts of the experience were not to have blurred their distinctness. One of these subsequent parts, the first, had been the not inconsiderable length, to her later and more analytic consciousness, of this second wait for her husband's reappearance. She might certainly, with the best will in the world, had she gone up with him, have been more in his way than not, since people could really, almost always, hurry better without help than with it. Still, she could actually hardly have made him take more time than he struck her taking, though it must indeed be added that there was now in this much-thinking little person's state of mind no mere crudity of impatience. Something had happened, rapidly, with the beautiful sight of him and with the drop of her fear of having annoyed him by making him go to and fro. Subsidence of the fearsome, for Maggie's spirit, was always, at first, positive emergence of the sweet, and it was long since anything had been so sweet to her as the particular quality suddenly given by her present emotion to the sense of possession.

XXVI

Amerigo was away from her again, as she sat there, as she walked there without him — for she had, with the difference of his presence in the house, ceased to keep herself from moving about; but the hour was filled nevertheless with the effect of his nearness, and above all with the effect, strange in an intimacy so established, of an almost renewed vision of the facts of his aspect. She had seen him last but five days since, yet he had stood there before her as if restored from some far country, some long voyage, some combination of dangers or fatigues. This unquenchable variety in his appeal to her interest, what did it mean but that — reduced to the flatness of mere statement — she was married, by good fortune, to an altogether dazzling person? That was an old, old story, but the truth of it shone out to her like the beauty of some family picture, some mellow portrait of an ancestor, that she might have been looking at, almost in surprise, after a long intermission. The dazzling person was upstairs and she was down, and there were moreover the other facts of the selection and decision that this demonstration of her own had required, and of the constant care that the equilibrium involved; but she had, all the same, never felt so absorbingly married, so abjectly conscious of a master of her fate. He could do what he would with her; in fact what was actually happening was that he was actually doing it. "What he would," what he REALLY would — only that quantity itself escaped perhaps, in the brightness of the high harmony, familiar naming and discussing. It was enough of a recognition for her that, whatever the thing he might desire, he would always absolutely bring it off. She knew at this moment, without a question, with the fullest surrender, how he had brought off, in her, by scarce more than a single allusion, a perfect flutter of tenderness. If he had come back tired, tired from his long day, the exertion had been, literally, in her service and her father's. They two had sat at home at peace, the Principino between them, the complications of life kept down, the bores sifted out, the large ease of the home preserved, because of the way the others held the field and braved the weather. Amerigo never complained — any more than, for that matter, Charlotte did; but she seemed to see to-night as she had never yet quite done that their business of social representation, conceived as they conceived it, beyond any conception of her own, and conscientiously carried out, was an affair of living always in harness. She remembered Fanny Assingham's old judgment, that friend's description of her father and herself as not living at all, as not knowing what to do or what might be done for them; and there came back to her with it an echo of the long talk they had had together, one September day at Fawns, under the trees, when she put before him this dictum of Fanny's.

That occasion might have counted for them — she had already often made the reflection — as the first step in an existence more intelligently arranged. It had been an hour from which the chain of causes and consequences was definitely traceable — so many things, and at the head of the list her father's marriage, having appeared to her to flow from Charlotte's visit to Fawns, and that event itself having flowed from the memorable talk. But what perhaps most came out in the light of these concatenations was that it had been, for all the world, as if Charlotte had been "had in," as the servants always said of extra help, because they had thus suffered it to be pointed out to them that if their family coach lumbered and stuck the fault was in its lacking its complement of wheels. Having but three, as they might say, it had wanted another, and what had Charlotte done from the first but begin to act, on the spot, and ever so smoothly and beautifully, as a fourth? Nothing had been, immediately, more manifest than the greater grace of the movement of the vehicle — as to which, for the completeness of her image, Maggie was now supremely to feel how every strain had been lightened for herself. So far as SHE was one of the wheels she had but to keep in her place; since the work was done for her she felt no weight, and it wasn't too much to acknowledge that she had scarce to turn round. She had a long pause before the fire during which she might have been fixing with intensity her projected vision, have been conscious even of its taking an absurd, fantastic shape. She might have been watching the family coach pass and noting that, somehow, Amerigo and Charlotte were pulling it while she and her father were not so much as pushing. They were seated inside together, dandling the Principino and holding him up to the windows, to see and be seen, like an infant positively royal; so that the exertion was ALL with the others. Maggie found in this image a repeated challenge; again and yet again she paused before the fire: after which, each time, in the manner of one for whom a strong light has suddenly broken, she gave herself to livelier movement. She had seen herself at last, in the picture she was studying, suddenly jump from the coach; whereupon, frankly, with the wonder of the sight, her eyes opened wider and her heart stood still for a moment. She looked at the person so acting as if this person were somebody else, waiting with intensity to see what would follow. The person had taken a decision — which was evidently because an impulse long gathering had at last felt a sharpest pressure. Only how was the decision to be applied? — what, in particular, would the figure in the picture do? She looked about her, from the middle of the room, under the force of this question, as if THERE, exactly, were the field of action involved. Then, as the door opened again, she recognised, whatever the action, the form, at any rate, of a first opportunity. Her husband had reappeared — he stood before her refreshed, almost radiant, quite reassuring. Dressed, anointed, fragrant, ready, above all, for his dinner, he smiled at her over the end of their delay. It was as if her opportunity had depended on his look — and now she saw that it was good. There was still, for the instant, something in suspense, but it passed more quickly than on his previous entrance. He was already holding out his arms. It was, for hours and hours, later on, as if she had somehow been lifted aloft, were floated and carried on some warm high tide beneath which stumbling blocks had sunk out of sight. This came from her being again, for the time, in the enjoyment of confidence, from her knowing, as she believed, what to do. All the next day, and all the next, she appeared to herself to know it. She had a plan, and she rejoiced in her plan: this consisted of the light that, suddenly breaking into her restless reverie, had marked the climax of that vigil. It had come to her as a question —"What if I've abandoned THEM, you know? What if I've accepted too passively the funny form of our life?" There would be a process of her own by which she might do differently in respect to Amerigo and Charlotte — a process quite independent of any process of theirs. Such a solution had but to rise before her to affect her, to charm her, with its simplicity, an advantageous simplicity she had been stupid, for so long, not to have been struck by; and the simplicity meanwhile seemed proved by the success that had already begun to attend her. She had only had herself to do something to see how immediately it answered. This consciousness of its having answered with her husband was the uplifting, sustaining wave. He had "met" her — she so put it to herself; met her with an effect of generosity and of gaiety, in especial, on his coming back to her ready for dinner, which she wore in her breast as the token of an escape for them both from something not quite definite, but clearly, much less good. Even at that moment, in fact, her plan had begun to work; she had been, when he brightly reappeared, in the act of plucking it out of the heart of her earnestness — plucking it, in the garden of thought, as if it had been some full-blown flower that she could present to him on the spot. Well, it was the flower of participation, and as that, then and there, she held it out to him, putting straightway into execution the idea, so needlessly, so absurdly obscured, of her SHARING with him, whatever the enjoyment, the interest, the experience might be-and sharing also, for that matter, with Charlotte.

She had thrown herself, at dinner, into every feature of the recent adventure of the companions, letting him see, without reserve, that she wished to hear everything about it, and making Charlotte in particular, Charlotte's judgment of Matcham, Charlotte's aspect, her success there, her effect traceably produced, her clothes inimitably worn, her cleverness gracefully displayed, her social utility, in fine, brilliantly exemplified, the subject of endless inquiry. Maggie's inquiry was most empathetic, moreover, for the whole happy thought of the cathedral-hunt, which she was so glad they had entertained, and as to the pleasant results of which, down to the cold beef and bread-and-cheese, the queer old smell and the dirty table-cloth at the inn, Amerigo was good-humouredly responsive. He had looked at her across the table, more than once, as if touched by the humility of this welcome offered to impressions at second-hand, the amusements, the large freedoms only of others — as if recognising in it something fairly exquisite;

and at the end, while they were alone, before she had rung for a servant, he had renewed again his condonation of the little irregularity, such as it was, on which she had ventured. They had risen together to come upstairs; he had been talking at the last about some of the people, at the very last of all about Lady Castledean and Mr. Blint; after which she had once more broken ground on the matter of the "type" of Gloucester. It brought her, as he came round the table to join her, yet another of his kind conscious stares, one of the looks, visibly beguiled, but at the same time not invisibly puzzled, with which he had already shown his sense of this charming grace of her curiosity. It was as if he might for a moment be going to say: —"You needn't PRETEND, dearest, quite so hard, needn't think it necessary to care quite so much!" — it was as if he stood there before her with some such easy intelligence, some such intimate reassurance, on his lips. Her answer would have been all ready — that she wasn't in the least pretending; and she looked up at him, while he took her hand, with the maintenance, the real persistence, of her lucid little plan in her eyes. She wanted him to understand from that very moment that she was going to be WITH him again, quite with them, together, as she doubtless hadn't been since the "funny" changes — that was really all one could call them — into which they had each, as for the sake of the others, too easily and too obligingly slipped. They had taken too much for granted that their life together required, as people in London said, a special "form" — which was very well so long as the form was kept only for the outside world and was made no more of among themselves than the pretty mould of an iced pudding, or something of that sort, into which, to help yourself, you didn't hesitate to break with the spoon. So much as that she would, with an opening, have allowed herself furthermore to observe; she wanted him to understand how her scheme embraced Charlotte too; so that if he had but uttered the acknowledgment she judged him on the point of making — the acknowledgment of his catching at her brave little idea for their case — she would have found herself, as distinctly, voluble almost to eloquence.

What befell, however, was that even while she thus waited she felt herself present at a process taking place rather deeper within him than the occasion, on the whole, appeared to require — a process of weighing something in the balance, of considering, deciding, dismissing. He had guessed that she was there with an idea, there in fact by reason of her idea; only this, oddly enough, was what at the last stayed his words. She was helped to these perceptions by his now looking at her still harder than he had yet done — which really brought it to the turn of a hair, for her, that she didn't make sure his notion of her idea was the right one. It was the turn of a hair, because he had possession of her hands and was bending toward her, ever so kindly, as if to see, to understand, more, or possibly give more — she didn't know which; and that had the effect of simply putting her, as she would have said, in his power. She gave up, let her idea go, let everything go; her one consciousness was that he was taking her again into his arms. It was not till afterwards that she discriminated as to this; felt how the act operated with him instead of the words he hadn't uttered — operated, in his view, as probably better than any words, as always better, in fact, at any time, than anything. Her acceptance of it, her response to it, inevitable, foredoomed, came back to her, later on, as a virtual assent to the assumption he had thus made that there was really nothing such a demonstration didn't anticipate and didn't dispose of, and that the spring acting within herself moreover might well have been, beyond any other, the impulse legitimately to provoke it. It made, for any issue, the third time since his return that he had drawn her to his breast; and at present, holding her to his side as they left the room, he kept her close for their moving into the hall and across it, kept her for their slow return together to the apartments above. He had been right, overwhelmingly right, as to the felicity of his tenderness and the degree of her sensibility, but even while she felt these things sweep all others away she tasted of a sort of terror of the weakness they produced in her. It was still, for her, that she had positively something to do, and that she mustn't be weak for this, must much rather be strong. For many hours after, none the less, she remained weak — if weak it was; though holding fast indeed to the theory of her success, since her agitated overture had been, after all, so unmistakably met.

She recovered soon enough on the whole, the sense that this left her Charlotte always to deal with — Charlotte who, at any rate, however SHE might meet overtures, must meet them, at the worst, more or less differently. Of that inevitability, of such other ranges of response as were open to Charlotte, Maggie took the measure in approaching her, on the morrow of her return from Matcham, with the same show of desire to hear all her story. She wanted the whole picture from her, as she had wanted it from her companion, and, promptly, in Eaton Square, whither, without the Prince, she repaired, almost ostentatiously, for the purpose, this purpose only, she brought her repeatedly back to the subject, both in her husband's presence and during several scraps of independent colloquy. Before her father, instinctively, Maggie took the ground that his wish for interesting echoes would be not less than her own — allowing, that is, for everything his wife would already have had to tell him, for such passages, between them, as might have occurred since the evening before. Joining them after luncheon, reaching them, in her desire to proceed with the application of her idea, before they had quitted the breakfast-room, the scene of their mid-day meal, she referred, in her parent's presence, to what she might have lost by delay, and expressed the hope that there would be an anecdote or two left for her to pick up. Charlotte was dressed to go out, and her husband, it appeared, rather positively prepared not to; he had left the table, but was seated near the fire with two or three of the morning papers and the residuum of the second and third posts on a stand beside him — more even than the usual extravagance, as Maggie's glance made out, of circulars, catalogues, advertisements, announcements of sales, foreign envelopes and foreign handwritings that were as unmistakable as foreign clothes. Charlotte, at the window, looking into the side-street that abutted on the Square, might have been watching for their visitor's advent before withdrawing; and in the light, strange and coloured, like that of a painted picture, which fixed the impression for her, objects took on values not hitherto so fully shown. It was the effect of her quickened sensibility; she knew herself again in presence of a problem, in need of a solution for which she must intensely work: that consciousness, lately born in her, had been taught the evening before to accept a temporary lapse, but had quickly enough again, with her getting out of her own house and her walking across half the town — for she had come from Portland Place on foot — found breath still in its lungs.

It exhaled this breath in a sigh, faint and unheard; her tribute, while she stood there before speaking, to realities looming through the golden mist that had already begun to be scattered. The conditions facing her had yielded, for the time, to the golden mist — had considerably melted away; but there they were again, definite, and it was for the next quarter of an hour as if she could have counted them one by one on her fingers. Sharp to her above all was the renewed attestation of her father's comprehensive acceptances, which she had so long regarded as of the same quality with her own, but which, so distinctly now, she should have the complication of being obliged to deal with separately. They had not yet struck her as absolutely extraordinary — which had made for her lumping them with her own, since her view of her own had but so lately begun to change; though it instantly stood out for her that there was really no new judgment of them she should be able to show without attracting in some degree his attention, without perhaps exciting his surprise and making thereby, for the situation she shared with him, some difference. She was reminded and warned by the concrete image; and for a minute Charlotte's face, immediately presented to her, affected her as searching her own to see the reminder tell. She had not less promptly kissed her stepmother, and then had bent over her father, from behind, and laid her cheek upon him; little amenities tantamount heretofore to an easy change of guard — Charlotte's own frequent, though always cheerful, term of comparison for this process of transfer. Maggie figured thus as the relieving sentry, and so smoothly did use and custom work for them that her mate might even, on this occasion, after acceptance of the pass-word, have departed without irrelevant and, in strictness, unsoldierly gossip. This was not, none the less, what happened; inasmuch as if our young woman had been floated over her first impulse to break the existing charm at a stroke, it yet took her but an instant to sound, at any risk, the note she had been privately practising. If she had practised it the day before, at dinner, on Amerigo, she knew but the better how to begin for it with Mrs. Verver, and it immensely helped her, for that matter, to be able at once to speak of the Prince as having done more to quicken than to soothe her curiosity. Frankly and gaily she had come to ask — to ask what, in their unusually prolonged campaign, the two had achieved. She had got out of her husband, she admitted, what she could, but husbands were never the persons who answered such questions ideally. He had only made her more curious, and she had arrived early, this way, in order to miss as little as possible of Charlotte's story.

"Wives, papa," she said; "are always much better reporters — though I grant," she added for Charlotte, "that fathers are not much better than husbands. He never," she smiled, "tells me more than a tenth of what you tell him; so I hope you haven't told him everything yet, since in that case I shall probably have lost the best part of it." Maggie went, she went — she felt herself going; she reminded herself of an actress who had been studying a part and rehearsing it, but who suddenly, on the stage, before the footlights, had begun to improvise, to speak lines not in the text. It was this very sense of the stage and the footlights that kept her up, made her rise higher: just as it was the sense of action that logically involved some platform — action quite positively for the first time in her life, or, counting in the previous afternoon, for the second. The platform remained for three or four days thus sensibly under her feet, and she had all the while, with it, the inspiration of quite remarkably, of quite heroically improvising. Preparation and practice had come but a short way; her part opened out, and she invented from moment to moment what to say and to do. She had but one rule of art — to keep within bounds and not lose her head; certainly she might see for a week how far that would take her. She said to herself, in her excitement, that it was perfectly simple: to bring about a difference, touch by touch, without letting either of the three, and least of all her father, so much as suspect her hand. If they should suspect they would want a reason, and the humiliating truth was that she wasn't ready with a reason — not, that is, with what she would have called a reasonable one. She thought of herself, instinctively, beautifully, as having dealt, all her life, at her father's side and by his example, only in reasonable reasons; and what she would really have been most ashamed of would be to produce for HIM, in this line, some inferior substitute. Unless she were in a position to plead, definitely, that she was jealous she should be in no position to plead, decently, that she was dissatisfied. This latter condition would be a necessary implication of the former; without the former behind it it would HAVE to fall to the ground. So had the case, wonderfully, been arranged for her; there was a card she could play, but there was only one, and to play it would be to end the game. She felt herself — as at the small square green table, between the tall old silver candlesticks and the neatly arranged counters — her father's playmate and partner; and what it constantly came back to, in her mind, was that for her to ask a question, to raise a doubt, to reflect in any degree on the play of the others, would be to break the charm. The charm she had to call it, since it kept her companion so constantly engaged, so perpetually seated and so contentedly occupied. To say anything at all would be, in fine, to have to say WHY she was jealous; and she could, in her private hours, but stare long, with suffused eyes, at that impossibility.

By the end of a week, the week that had begun, especially, with her morning hour, in Eaton Square, between her father and his wife, her consciousness of being beautifully treated had become again verily greater than her consciousness of anything else; and I must add, moreover, that she at last found herself rather oddly wondering what else, as a consciousness, could have been quite so overwhelming. Charlotte's response to the experiment of being more with her OUGHT, as she very well knew, to have stamped the experiment with the feeling of success; so that if the success itself seemed a boon less substantial than the original image of it, it enjoyed thereby a certain analogy with our young woman's aftertaste of Amerigo's own determined demonstrations. Maggie was to have retained, for that matter, more than one aftertaste, and if I have spoken of the impressions fixed in her as soon as she had, so insidiously, taken the field, a definite note must be made of her perception, during those moments, of Charlotte's prompt uncertainty. She had shown, no doubt — she couldn't not have shown — that she had arrived with an idea; quite exactly as she had shown her husband, the night before, that she was awaiting him with a sentiment. This analogy in the two situations was to keep up for her the remembrance of a kinship of expression in the two faces in respect to which all she as yet professed to herself was that she had affected them, or at any rate the sensibility each of them so admirably covered, in the same way. To make the comparison at all was, for Maggie, to return to it often, to brood upon it, to extract from it the last dregs of its interest — to play with it, in short, nervously, vaguely, incessantly, as she might have played with a medallion containing on either side a cherished little portrait and suspended round her neck by a gold chain of a firm fineness that no effort would ever snap. The miniatures were back to back, but she saw them forever face to face, and when she looked from one to the other she found in Charlotte's eyes the gleam of the momentary "What does she really want?" that had come and gone for her in the Prince's. So again, she saw the other light, the light touched into a glow both in Portland Place and in Eaton Square, as soon as she had betrayed that she wanted no harm — wanted no greater harm of Charlotte, that is, than to take in that she meant to go out with her. She had been present at that process as personally as she might have been present at some other domestic incident — the hanging of a new picture, say, or the fitting of the Principino with his first little trousers.

She remained present, accordingly, all the week, so charmingly and systematically did Mrs. Verver now welcome her company. Charlotte had but wanted the hint, and what was it but the hint, after all, that, during the so subdued but so ineffaceable passage in the breakfast-room, she had seen her take? It had been taken moreover not with resignation, not with qualifications or reserves, however bland; it had been taken with avidity, with gratitude, with a grace of gentleness that supplanted explanations. The very liberality of this accommodation might indeed have appeared in the event to give its own account of the matter — as if it had fairly written the Princess down as a person of variations and had accordingly conformed but to a rule of tact in accepting these caprices for law. The caprice actually prevailing happened to be that the advent of one of the ladies anywhere should, till the fit had changed, become the sign, unfailingly, of the advent of the other; and it was emblazoned, in rich colour, on the bright face of this period, that Mrs. Verver only wished to know, on any occasion, what was expected of her, only held herself there for instructions, in order even to better them if possible. The two young women, while the passage lasted, became again very much the companions of other days, the days of Charlotte's prolonged visits to the admiring and bountiful Maggie, the days when equality of condition for them had been all the result of the latter's native vagueness about her own advantages. The earlier elements flushed into life again, the frequency, the intimacy, the high pitch of accompanying expression — appreciation, endearment, confidence; the rarer charm produced in each by this active contribution to the felicity of the other: all enhanced, furthermore — enhanced or qualified, who should say which? — by a new note of diplomacy, almost of anxiety, just sensible on Charlotte's part in particular; of intensity of observance, in the matter of appeal and response, in the matter of making sure the Princess might be disposed or gratified, that resembled an attempt to play again, with more refinement, at disparity of relation. Charlotte's attitude had, in short, its moments of flowering into pretty excesses of civility, self-effacements in the presence of others, sudden little formalisms of suggestion and recognition, that might have represented her sense of the duty of not "losing sight" of a social distinction. This impression came out most for Maggie when, in their easier intervals, they had only themselves to regard, and when her companion's inveteracy of never passing first, of not sitting till she was seated, of not interrupting till she appeared to give leave, of not forgetting, too, familiarly, that in addition to being important she was also sensitive, had the effect of throwing over their intercourse a kind of silver tissue of decorum. It hung there above them like a canopy of state, a reminder that though the lady-inwaiting was an established favourite, safe in her position, a little queen, however, good-natured, was always a little queen and might, with small warning, remember it.

And yet another of these concomitants of feverish success, all the while, was the perception that in another quarter too things were being made easy. Charlotte's alacrity in meeting her had, in one sense, operated slightly overmuch as an intervention: it had begun to reabsorb her at the very hour of her husband's showing her that, to be all there, as the phrase was, he likewise only required — as one of the other phrases was too — the straight tip. She had heard him talk about the straight tip, in his moods of amusement at English slang, in his remarkable displays of assimilative power, power worthy of better causes and higher inspirations; and he had taken it from her, at need, in a way that, certainly in the first glow of relief, had made her brief interval seem large. Then, however, immediately, and even though superficially, there had declared itself a readjustment of relations to which she was, once more, practically a little sacrificed. "I must do everything," she had said, "without letting papa see what I do — at least till it's done!" but she scarce knew how she proposed, even for the next few days, to blind or beguile this participant in her life. What had in fact promptly enough happened, she presently recognised, was that if her stepmother had beautifully taken possession of her, and if she had virtually been rather snatched again thereby from her husband's side, so, on the other hand, this had, with as little delay, entailed some very charming assistance for her in Eaton Square. When she went home with Charlotte, from whatever happy demonstration, for the benefit of the world in which they supposed themselves to live, that there was no smallest reason why their closer association shouldn't be public and acclaimed — at these times she regularly found that Amerigo had come either to sit with his father-inlaw in the absence of the ladies, or to make, on his side, precisely some such display of the easy working of the family life as would represent the equivalent of her excursions with Charlotte. Under this particular impression it was that everything in Maggie most melted and went to pieces — every thing, that is, that belonged to her disposition to challenge the perfection of their common state. It divided them again, that was true, this particular turn of the tide — cut them up afresh into pairs and parties; quite as if a sense for the equilibrium was what, between them all, had most power of insistence; quite as if Amerigo himself were all the while, at bottom, equally thinking of it and watching it. But, as against that, he was making her father not miss her, and he could have rendered neither of them a more excellent service. He was acting in short on a cue, the cue given him by observation; it had been enough for him to see the shade of change in her behaviour; his instinct for relations, the most exquisite conceivable, prompted him immediately to meet and match the difference, to play somehow into its hands. That was what it was, she renewedly felt, to have married a man who was, sublimely, a gentleman; so that, in spite of her not wanting to translate ALL their delicacies into the grossness of discussion, she yet found again and again, in Portland Place, moments for saying: "If I didn't love you, you know, for yourself, I should still love you for HIM." He looked at her, after such speeches, as Charlotte looked, in Eaton Square, when she called HER attention to his benevolence: through the dimness of the almost musing smile that took account of her extravagance, harmless though it might be, as a tendency to reckon with. "But my poor child," Charlotte might under this pressure have been on the point of replying, "that's the way nice people ARE, all round — so that why should one be surprised about it? We're all nice together — as why shouldn't we be? If we hadn't been we wouldn't have gone far — and I consider that we've gone very far indeed. Why should you 'take on' as if you weren't a perfect dear yourself, capable of all the sweetest things? — as if you hadn't in fact grown up in an atmosphere, the atmosphere of all the good things that I recognised, even of old, as soon as I came near you, and that you've allowed me now, between you, to make so blessedly my own." Mrs. Verver might in fact have but just failed to make another point, a point charmingly natural to her as a grateful and irreproachable wife. "It isn't a bit wonderful, I may also remind you, that your husband should find, when opportunity permits, worse things to do than to go about with mine. I happen, love, to appreciate my husband — I happen perfectly to understand that his acquaintance should be cultivated and his company enjoyed."

Some such happily-provoked remarks as these, from Charlotte, at the other house, had been in the air, but we have seen how there was also in the air, for our young woman, as an emanation from the same source, a distilled difference of which the very principle was to keep down objections and retorts. That impression came back — it had its hours of doing so; and it may interest us on the ground of its having prompted in Maggie a final reflection, a reflection out of the heart of which a light flashed for her like a great flower grown in a night. As soon as this light had spread a little it produced in some quarters a surprising distinctness, made her of a sudden ask herself why there should have been even for three days the least obscurity. The perfection of her success, decidedly, was like some strange shore to which she had been noiselessly ferried and where, with a start, she found herself quaking at the thought that the boat might have put off again and left her. The word for it, the word that flashed the light, was that they were TREATING her, that they were proceeding with her — and, for that matter, with her father — by a plan that was the exact counterpart of her own. It was not from her that they took their cue, but — and this was what in particular made her sit up — from each other; and with a depth of unanimity, an exact coincidence of inspiration that, when once her attention had begun to fix it, struck her as staring out at her in recovered identities of behaviour, expression and tone. They had a view of her situation, and of the possible forms her own consciousness of it might take — a view determined by the change of attitude they had had, ever so subtly, to recognise in her on their return from Matcham. They had had to read into this small and all-but-suppressed variation a mute comment — on they didn't quite know what; and it now arched over the Princess's head like a vault of bold span that important communication between them on the subject couldn't have failed of being immediate. This new perception bristled for her, as we have said, with odd intimations, but questions unanswered played in and out of it as well — the question, for instance, of why such promptitude of harmony SHOULD have been important. Ah, when she began to recover, piece by piece, the process became lively; she might have been picking small shining diamonds out of the sweepings of her ordered house. She bent, in this pursuit, over her dust-bin; she challenged to the last grain the refuse of her innocent economy. Then it was that the dismissed vision of Amerigo, that evening, in arrest at the door of her salottino while her eyes, from her placed chair, took him in-then it was that this immense little memory gave out its full power. Since the question was of doors, she had afterwards, she now saw, shut it out; she had responsibly shut in, as we have understood, shut in there with her sentient self, only the fact of his reappearance and the plenitude of his presence. These things had been testimony, after all, to supersede any other, for on the spot, even while she looked, the warmly-washing wave had travelled far up the strand. She had subsequently lived, for hours she couldn't count, under the dizzying, smothering welter positively in submarine depths where everything came to her through walls of emerald and mother-of-pearl; though indeed she had got her head above them, for breath, when face to face with Charlotte again, on the morrow, in Eaton Square. Meanwhile, none the less, as was so apparent, the prior, the prime impression had remained, in the manner of a spying servant, on the other side of the barred threshold; a witness availing himself, in time, of the lightest pretext to re-enter. It was as if he had found this pretext in her observed necessity of comparing — comparing the obvious common elements in her husband's and her stepmother's ways of now "taking" her. With or without her witness, at any rate, she was led by comparison to a sense of the quantity of earnest intention operating, and operating so harmoniously, between her companions; and it was in the mitigated midnight of these approximations that she had made out the promise of her dawn.

It was a worked-out scheme for their not wounding her, for their behaving to her quite nobly; to which each had, in some winning way, induced the other to contribute, and which therefore, so far as that went, proved that she had become with them a subject of intimate study. Quickly, quickly, on a certain alarm taken, eagerly and anxiously, before they SHOULD, without knowing it, wound her, they had signalled from house to house their clever idea, the idea by which, for all these days, her own idea had been profiting. They had built her in with their purpose — which was why, above her, a vault seemed more heavily to arch; so that she sat there, in the solid chamber of her helplessness, as in a bath of benevolence artfully prepared for her, over the brim of which she could but just manage to see by stretching her neck. Baths of benevolence were very well, but, at least, unless one were a patient of some sort, a nervous eccentric or a lost child, one was usually not so immersed save by one's request. It wasn't in the least what she had requested. She had flapped her little wings as a symbol of desired flight, not merely as a plea for a more gilded cage and an extra allowance of lumps of sugar. Above all she hadn't complained, not by the quaver of a syllable — so what wound in particular had she shown her fear of receiving? What wound HAD she received — as to which she had exchanged the least word with them? If she had ever whined or moped they might have had some reason; but she would be hanged — she conversed with herself in strong language — if she had been, from beginning to end, anything but pliable and mild. It all came back, in consequence, to some required process of their own, a process operating, quite positively, as a precaution and a policy. They had got her into the bath and, for consistency with themselves — which was with each other — must keep her there. In that condition she wouldn't interfere with the policy, which was established, which was arranged. Her thought, over this, arrived at a great intensity — had indeed its pauses and timidities, but always to take afterwards a further and lighter spring. The ground was well-nigh covered by the time she had made out her husband and his colleague as directly interested in preventing her freedom of movement. Policy or no policy, it was they themselves who were arranged. She must be kept in position so as not to DISarrange them. It fitted immensely together, the whole thing, as soon as she could give them a motive; for, strangely as it had by this time begun to appear to herself, she had hitherto not imagined them sustained by an ideal distinguishably different from her own. Of course they were arranged — all four arranged; but what had the basis of their life been, precisely, but that they were arranged together? Amerigo and Charlotte were arranged together, but she — to confine the matter only to herself — was arranged apart. It rushed over her, the full sense of all this, with quite another rush from that of the breaking wave of ten days before; and as her father himself seemed not to meet the vaguely-clutching hand with which, during the first shock of complete perception, she tried to steady herself, she felt very much alone.

XXVII

There had been, from far back — that is from the Christmas time on — a plan that the parent and the child should "do something lovely" together, and they had recurred to it on occasion, nursed it and brought it up theoretically, though without as yet quite allowing it to put its feet to the ground. The most it had done was to try a few steps on the drawing-room carpet, with much attendance, on either side, much holding up and guarding, much anticipation, in fine, of awkwardness or accident. Their companions, by the same token, had constantly assisted at the performance, following the experiment with sympathy and gaiety, and never so full of applause, Maggie now made out for herself, as when the infant project had kicked its little legs most wildly — kicked them, for all the world, across the Channel and half the Continent, kicked them over the Pyrenees and innocently crowed out some rich Spanish name. She asked herself at present if it had been a "real" belief that they were but wanting, for some such adventure, to snatch their moment; whether either had at any instant seen it as workable, save in the form of a toy to dangle before the other, that they should take flight, without wife or husband, for one more look, "before they died," at the Madrid pictures as well as for a drop of further weak delay in respect to three or four possible prizes, privately offered, rarities of the first water, responsibly reported on and profusely photographed, still patiently awaiting their noiseless arrival in retreats to which the clue had not otherwise been given away. The vision dallied with during the duskier days in Eaton Square had stretched to the span of three or four weeks of springtime for the total adventure, three or four weeks in the very spirit, after all, of their regular life, as their regular life had been persisting; full of shared mornings, afternoons, evenings, walks, drives, "looks-in," at old places, on vague chances; full also, in especial, of that purchased social ease, the sense of the comfort and credit of their house, which had essentially the perfection of something paid for, but which "came," on the whole, so cheap that it might have been felt as costing — as costing the parent and child — nothing. It was for Maggie to wonder, at present, if she had been sincere about their going, to ask herself whether she would have stuck to their plan even if nothing had happened.

Her view of the impossibility of sticking to it now may give us the measure of her sense that everything had happened. A difference had been made in her relation to each of her companions, and what it compelled her to say to herself was that to behave as she might have behaved before would be to act, for Amerigo and Charlotte, with the highest hypocrisy. She saw in these days that a journey abroad with her father would, more than anything else, have amounted, on his part and her own, to a last expression of an ecstasy of confidence, and that the charm of the idea, in fact, had been in some such sublimity. Day after day she put off the moment of "speaking," as she inwardly and very comprehensively, called it — speaking, that is, to her father; and all the more that she was ridden by a strange suspense as to his himself breaking silence. She gave him time, gave him, during several days, that morning, that noon, that night, and the next and the next and the next; even made up her mind that if he stood off longer it would be proof conclusive that he too wasn't at peace. They would then have been, all successfully, throwing dust in each other's eyes; and it would be at last as if they must turn away their faces, since the silver mist that protected them had begun to grow sensibly thin. Finally, at the end of April, she decided that if he should say nothing for another period of twenty-four hours she must take it as showing that they were, in her private phraseology, lost; so little possible sincerity could there be in pretending to care for a journey to Spain at the approach of a summer that already promised to be hot. Such a proposal, on his lips, such an extravagance of optimism, would be HIS way of being consistent — for that he didn't really want to move, or to move further, at the worst, than back to Fawns again, could only signify that he wasn't, at heart, contented. What he wanted, at any rate, and what he didn't want were, in the event, put to the proof for Maggie just in time to give her a fresh wind. She had been dining, with her husband, in Eaton Square, on the occasion of hospitality offered by Mr. and Mrs. Verver to Lord and Lady Castledean. The propriety of some demonstration of this sort had been for many days before our group, the question reduced to the mere issue of which of the two houses should first take the field. The issue had been easily settled — in the manner of every issue referred in any degree to Amerigo and Charlotte: the initiative obviously belonged to Mrs. Verver, who had gone to Matcham while Maggie had stayed away, and the evening in Eaton Square might have passed for a demonstration all the more personal that the dinner had been planned on "intimate" lines. Six other guests only, in addition to the host and the hostess of Matcham, made up the company, and each of these persons had for Maggie the interest of an attested connection with the Easter revels at that visionary house. Their common memory of an occasion that had clearly left behind it an ineffaceable charm — this air of beatific reference, less subdued in the others than in Amerigo and Charlotte, lent them, together, an inscrutable comradeship against which the young woman's imagination broke in a small vain wave.

It wasn't that she wished she had been of the remembered party and possessed herself of its secrets; for she didn't care about its secrets — she could concern herself at present, absolutely, with no secret but her own. What occurred was simply that she became aware, at a stroke, of the quantity of further nourishment required by her own, and of the amount of it she might somehow extract from these people; whereby she rose, of a sudden, to the desire to possess and use them, even to the extent of braving, of fairly defying, of directly exploiting, of possibly quite enjoying, under cover of an evil duplicity, the felt element of curiosity with which they regarded her. Once she was conscious of the flitting wing of this last impression — the perception, irresistible, that she was something for their queer experience, just as they were something for hers — there was no limit to her conceived design of not letting them escape. She went and went, again, to-night, after her start was taken; went, positively, as she had felt herself going, three weeks before, on the morning when the vision of her father and his wife awaiting her together in the breakfast-room had been so determinant. In this other scene it was Lady Castledean who was determinant, who kindled the light, or at all events the heat, and who acted on the nerves; Lady Castledean whom she knew she, so oddly, didn't like, in spite of reasons upon reasons, the biggest diamonds on the yellowest hair, the longest lashes on the prettiest, falsest eyes, the oldest lace on the most violet velvet, the rightest manner on the wrongest assumption. Her ladyship's assumption was that she kept, at every moment of her life, every advantage — it made her beautifully soft, very nearly generous; so she didn't distinguish the little protuberant eyes of smaller social insects, often endowed with such a range, from the other decorative spots on their bodies and wings. Maggie had liked, in London, and in the world at large, so many more people than she had thought it right to fear, right even to so much as judge, that it positively quickened her fever to have to recognise, in this case, such a lapse of all the sequences. It was only that a charming clever woman wondered about her — that is wondered about her as Amerigo's wife, and wondered, moreover, with the intention of kindness and the spontaneity, almost, of surprise.

The point of view — that one — was what she read in their free contemplation, in that of the whole eight; there was something in Amerigo to be explained, and she was passed about, all tenderly and expertly, like a dressed doll held, in the right manner, by its firmly-stuffed middle, for the account she could give. She might have been made to give it by pressure of her stomach; she might have been expected to articulate, with a rare imitation of nature, "Oh yes, I'm HERE all the while; I'm also in my way a solid little fact and I cost originally a great deal of money: cost, that is, my father, for my outfit, and let in my husband for an amount of pains — toward my training — that money would scarce represent." Well, she WOULD meet them in some such way, and she translated her idea into action, after dinner, before they dispersed, by engaging them all, unconventionally, almost violently, to dine with her in Portland Place, just as they were, if they didn't mind the same party, which was the party she wanted. Oh she was going, she was going — she could feel it afresh; it was a good deal as if she had sneezed ten times or had suddenly burst into a comic song. There were breaks in the connection, as there would be hitches in the process; she didn't wholly see, yet, what they would do for her, nor quite how, herself, she should handle them; but she was dancing up and down, beneath her propriety, with the thought that she had at least begun something — she so fairly liked to feel that she was a point for convergence of wonder. It wasn't after all, either, that THEIR wonder so much signified — that of the cornered six, whom it glimmered before her that she might still live to drive about like a flock of sheep: the intensity of her consciousness, its sharpest savour, was in the theory of her having diverted, having, as they said, captured the attention of Amerigo and Charlotte, at neither of whom, all the while, did she so much as once look. She had pitched them in with the six, for that matter, so far as they themselves were concerned; they had dropped, for the succession of minutes, out of contact with their function — had, in short, startled and impressed, abandoned their post. "They're paralysed, they're paralysed!" she commented, deep within; so much it helped her own apprehension to hang together that they should suddenly lose their bearings.

Her grasp of appearances was thus out of proportion to her view of causes; but it came to her then and there that if she could only get the facts of appearance straight, only jam them down into their place, the reasons lurking behind them, kept uncertain, for the eyes, by their wavering and shifting, wouldn't perhaps be able to help showing. It wasn't of course that the Prince and Mrs. Verver marvelled to see her civil to their friends; it was rather, precisely, that civil was just what she wasn't: she had so departed from any such custom of delicate approach — approach by the permitted note, the suggested "if," the accepted vagueness — as would enable the people in question to put her off if they wished. And the profit of her plan, the effect of the violence she was willing to let it go for, was exactly in their BEING the people in question, people she had seemed to be rather shy of before and for whom she suddenly opened her mouth so wide. Later on, we may add, with the ground soon covered by her agitated but resolute step, it was to cease to matter what people they were or weren't; but meanwhile the particular sense of them that she had taken home to-night had done her the service of seeming to break the ice where that formation was thickest. Still more unexpectedly, the service might have been the same for her father; inasmuch as, immediately, when everyone had gone, he did exactly what she had been waiting for and despairing of — and did it, as he did everything, with a simplicity that left any purpose of sounding him deeper, of drawing him out further, of going, in his own frequent phrase, "behind" what he said, nothing whatever to do. He brought it out straight, made it bravely and beautifully irrelevant, save for the plea of what they should lose by breaking the charm: "I guess we won't go down there after all, will we, Mag? — just when it's getting so pleasant here." That was all, with nothing to lead up to it; but it was done for her at a stroke, and done, not less, more rather, for Amerigo and Charlotte, on whom the immediate effect, as she secretly, as she almost breathlessly measured it, was prodigious. Everything now so fitted for her to everything else that she could feel the effect as prodigious even while sticking to her policy of giving the pair no look. There were thus some five wonderful minutes during which they loomed, to her sightless eyes, on either side of her, larger than they had ever loomed before, larger than life, larger than thought, larger than any danger or any safety. There was thus a space of time, in fine, fairly vertiginous for her, during which she took no more account of them than if they were not in the room.

She had never, never treated them in any such way — not even just now, when she had plied her art upon the Matcham band; her present manner was an intenser exclusion, and the air was charged with their silence while she talked with her other companion as if she had nothing but him to consider. He had given her the note amazingly, by his allusion to the pleasantness — that of such an occasion as his successful dinner — which might figure as their bribe for renouncing; so that it was all as if they were speaking selfishly, counting on a repetition of just such extensions of experience. Maggie achieved accordingly an act of unprecedented energy, threw herself into her father's presence as by the absolute consistency with which she held his eyes; saying to herself, at the same time that she smiled and talked and inaugurated her system, "What does he mean by it? That's the question — what does he mean?" but studying again all the signs in him that recent anxiety had made familiar and counting the stricken minutes on the part of the others. It was in their silence that the others loomed, as she felt; she had had no measure, she afterwards knew, of this duration, but it drew out and out — really to what would have been called in simpler conditions awkwardness — as if she herself were stretching the cord. Ten minutes later, however, in the homeward carriage, to which her husband, cutting delay short, had proceeded at the first announcement, ten minutes later she was to stretch it almost to breaking. The Prince had permitted her to linger much less, before his move to the door, than they usually lingered at the gossiping close of such evenings; which she, all responsive, took for a sign of his impatience to modify for her the odd effect of his not having, and of Charlotte's not having, instantly acclaimed the issue of the question debated, or more exactly, settled, before them. He had had time to become aware of this possible impression in her, and his virtually urging her into the carriage was connected with his feeling that he must take action on the new ground. A certain ambiguity in her would absolutely have tormented him; but he had already found something to soothe and correct — as to which she had, on her side, a shrewd notion of what it would be. She was herself, for that matter, prepared, and she was, of a truth, as she took her seat in the brougham, amazed at her preparation. It allowed her scarce an interval; she brought it straight out.

"I was certain that was what father would say if I should leave him alone. I HAVE been leaving him alone, and you see the effect. He hates now to move — he likes too much to be with us. But if you see the effect" — she felt herself magnificently keeping it up — "perhaps you don't see the cause. The cause, my dear, is too lovely."

Her husband, on taking his place beside her, had, during a minute or two, for her watching sense, neither said nor done anything; he had been, for that sense, as if thinking, waiting, deciding: yet it was still before he spoke that he, as she felt it to be, definitely acted. He put his arm round her and drew her close — indulged in the demonstration, the long, firm embrace by his single arm, the infinite pressure of her whole person to his own, that such opportunities had so often suggested and prescribed. Held, accordingly, and, as she could but too intimately feel, exquisitely solicited, she had said the thing she was intending and desiring to say, and as to which she felt, even more than she felt anything else, that whatever he might do she mustn't be irresponsible. Yes, she was in his exerted grasp, and she knew what that was; but she was at the same time in the grasp of her conceived responsibility, and the extraordinary thing was that, of the two intensities, the second was presently to become the sharper. He took his time for it meanwhile, but he met her speech after a fashion.

"The cause of your father's deciding not to go?"

"Yes, and of my having wanted to let it act for him quietly — I mean without my insistence." She had, in her compressed state, another pause, and it made her feel as if she were immensely resisting. Strange enough was this sense for her, and altogether new, the sense of possessing, by miraculous help, some advantage that, absolutely then and there, in the carriage, as they rolled, she might either give up or keep. Strange, inexpressibly strange — so distinctly she saw that if she did give it up she should somehow give up everything for ever. And what her husband's grasp really meant, as her very bones registered, was that she SHOULD give it up: it was exactly for this that he had resorted to unfailing magic. He KNEW HOW to resort to it — he could be, on occasion, as she had lately more than ever learned, so munificent a lover: all of which was, precisely, a part of the character she had never ceased to regard in him as princely, a part of his large and beautiful ease, his genius for charm, for intercourse, for expression, for life. She should have but to lay her head back on his shoulder with a certain movement to make it definite for him that she didn't resist. To this, as they went, every throb of her consciousness prompted her — every throb, that is, but one, the throb of her deeper need to know where she "really" was. By the time she had uttered the rest of her idea, therefore, she was still keeping her head and intending to keep it; though she was also staring out of the carriage-window with eyes into which the tears of suffered pain had risen, indistinguishable, perhaps, happily, in the dusk. She was making an effort that horribly hurt her, and, as she couldn't cry out, her eyes swam in her silence. With them, all the same, through the square opening beside her, through the grey panorama of the London night, she achieved the feat of not losing sight of what she wanted;

and her lips helped and protected her by being able to be gay. "It's not to leave YOU, my dear — for that he'll give up anything; just as he would go off anywhere, I think, you know, if you would go with him. I mean you and he alone," Maggie pursued with her gaze out of her window.

For which Amerigo's answer again took him a moment. "Ah, the dear old boy! You would like me to propose him something —?"

"Well, if you think you could bear it."

"And leave," the Prince asked, "you and Charlotte alone?"

"Why not?" Maggie had also to wait a minute, but when she spoke it came clear. "Why shouldn't Charlotte be just one of MY reasons — my not liking to leave her? She has always been so good, so perfect, to me — but never so wonderfully as just now. We have somehow been more together — thinking, for the time, almost only of each other; it has been quite as in old days." And she proceeded consummately, for she felt it as consummate: "It's as if we had been missing each other, had got a little apart — though going on so side by side. But the good moments, if one only waits for them," she hastened to add, "come round of themselves. Moreover you've seen for yourself, since you've made it up so to father; feeling, for yourself, in your beautiful way, every difference, every air that blows; not having to be told or pushed, only being perfect to live with, through your habit of kindness and your exquisite instincts. But of course you've seen, all the while, that both he and I have deeply felt how you've managed; managed that he hasn't been too much alone and that I, on my side, haven't appeared, to — what you might call — neglect him. This is always," she continued, "what I can never bless you enough for; of all the good things you've done for me you've never done anything better." She went on explaining as for the pleasure of explaining — even though knowing he must recognise, as a part of his easy way too, her description of his large liberality. "Your taking the child down yourself, those days, and your coming, each time, to bring him away — nothing in the world, nothing you could have invented, would have kept father more under the charm. Besides, you know how you've always suited him, and how you've always so beautifully let it seem to him that he suits you. Only it has been, these last weeks, as if you wished — just in order to please him — to remind him of it afresh. So there it is," she wound up; "it's your doing. You've produced your effect — that of his wanting not to be, even for a month or two, where you're not. He doesn't want to bother or bore you — THAT, I think, you know, he never has done; and if you'll only give me time I'll come round again to making it my care, as always, that he shan't. But he can't bear you out of his sight."

She had kept it up and up, filling it out, crowding it in; and all, really, without difficulty, for it was, every word of it, thanks to a long evolution of feeling, what she had been primed to the brim with. She made the picture, forced it upon him, hung it before him; remembering, happily, how he had gone so far, one day, supported by the Principino, as to propose the Zoo in Eaton Square, to carry with him there, on the spot, under this pleasant inspiration, both his elder and his younger companion, with the latter of whom he had taken the tone that they were introducing Granddaddy, Granddaddy nervous and rather funking it, to lions and tigers more or less at large. Touch by touch she thus dropped into her husband's silence the truth about his good nature and his good manners; and it was this demonstration of his virtue, precisely, that added to the strangeness, even for herself, of her failing as yet to yield to him. It would be a question but of the most trivial act of surrender, the vibration of a nerve, the mere movement of a muscle; but the act grew important between them just through her doing perceptibly nothing, nothing but talk in the very tone that would naturally have swept her into tenderness. She knew more and more — every lapsing minute taught her — how he might by a single rightness make her cease to watch him; that rightness, a million miles removed from the queer actual, falling so short, which would consist of his breaking out to her diviningly, indulgently, with the last happy inconsequence. "Come away with me, somewhere, YOU — and then we needn't think, we needn't even talk, of anything, of anyone else:" five words like that would answer her, would break her utterly down. But they were the only ones that would so serve. She waited for them, and there was a supreme instant when, by the testimony of all the rest of him, she seemed to feel them in his heart and on his lips; only they didn't sound, and as that made her wait again so it made her more intensely watch. This in turn showed her that he too watched and waited, and how much he had expected something that he now felt wouldn't come. Yes, it wouldn't come if he didn't answer her, if he but said the wrong things instead of the right. If he could say the right everything would come — it hung by a hair that everything might crystallise for their recovered happiness at his touch. This possibility glowed at her, however, for fifty seconds, only then to turn cold, and as it fell away from her she felt the chill of reality and knew again, all but pressed to his heart and with his breath upon her cheek, the slim rigour of her attitude, a rigour beyond that of her natural being. They had silences, at last, that were almost crudities of mutual resistance — silences that persisted through his felt effort to treat her recurrence to the part he had lately played, to interpret all the sweetness of her so talking to him, as a manner of making love to him. Ah, it was no such manner, heaven knew, for Maggie; she could make love, if this had been in question, better than that! On top of which it came to her presently to say, keeping in with what she had already spoken: "Except of course that, for the question of going off somewhere, he'd go readily, quite delightedly, with you. I verily believe he'd like to have you for a while to himself."

"Do you mean he thinks of proposing it?" the Prince after a moment sounded.

"Oh no — he doesn't ask, as you must so often have seen. But I believe he'd go 'like a shot,' as you say, if you were to suggest it."

It had the air, she knew, of a kind of condition made, and she had asked herself while she spoke if it wouldn't cause his arm to let her go. The fact that it didn't suggested to her that she had made him, of a sudden, still more intensely think, think with such concentration that he could do but one thing at once. And it was precisely as if the concentration had the next moment been proved in him. He took a turn inconsistent with the superficial impression — a jump that made light of their approach to gravity and represented for her the need in him to gain time. That she made out, was his drawback — that the warning from her had come to him, and had come to Charlotte, after all, too suddenly. That they were in face of it rearranging, that they had to rearrange, was all before her again; yet to do as they would like they must enjoy a snatch, longer or shorter, of recovered independence. Amerigo, for the instant, was but doing as he didn't like, and it was as if she were watching his effort without disguise. "What's your father's idea, this year, then, about Fawns? Will he go at Whitsuntide, and will he then stay on?"

Maggie went through the form of thought. "He will really do, I imagine, as he has, in so many ways, so often done before; do whatever may seem most agreeable to yourself. And there's of course always Charlotte to be considered. Only their going early to Fawns, if they do go," she said, "needn't in the least entail your and my going."

"Ah," Amerigo echoed, "it needn't in the least entail your and my going?"

"We can do as we like. What they may do needn't trouble us, since they're by good fortune perfectly happy together."

"Oh," the Prince returned, "your father's never so happy as with you near him to enjoy his being so."

"Well, I may enjoy it," said Maggie, "but I'm not the cause of it."

"You're the cause," her husband declared, "of the greater part of everything that's good among us." But she received this tribute in silence, and the next moment he pursued: "If Mrs. Verver has arrears of time with you to make up, as you say, she'll scarcely do it — or you scarcely will — by our cutting, your and my cutting, too loose."

"I see what you mean," Maggie mused.

He let her for a little to give her attention to it; after which, "Shall I just quite, of a sudden," he asked, "propose him a journey?"

Maggie hesitated, but she brought forth the fruit of reflection. "It would have the merit that Charlotte then would be with me — with me, I mean, so much more. Also that I shouldn't, by choosing such a time for going away, seem unconscious and ungrateful, seem not to respond, seem in fact rather to wish to shake her off. I should respond, on the contrary, very markedly — by being here alone with her for a month."

"And would you like to be here alone with her for a month?"

"I could do with it beautifully. Or we might even," she said quite gaily, "go together down to Fawns."

"You could be so very content without me?" the Prince presently inquired.

"Yes, my own dear — if you could be content for a while with father. That would keep me up. I might, for the time," she went on, "go to stay there with Charlotte; or, better still, she might come to Portland Place."

"Oho!" said the Prince with cheerful vagueness.

"I should feel, you see," she continued, "that the two of us were showing the same sort of kindness."

Amerigo thought. "The two of us? Charlotte and I?"

Maggie again hesitated. "You and I, darling."

"I see, I see" — he promptly took it in. "And what reason shall I give — give, I mean, your father?"

"For asking him to go off? Why, the very simplest — if you conscientiously can. The desire," said Maggie, "to be agreeable to him. Just that only."

Something in this reply made her husband again reflect. "'Conscientiously?' Why shouldn't I conscientiously? It wouldn't, by your own contention," he developed, "represent any surprise for him. I must strike him sufficiently as, at the worst, the last person in the world to wish to do anything to hurt him."

Ah, there it was again, for Maggie — the note already sounded, the note of the felt need of not working harm! Why this precautionary view, she asked herself afresh, when her father had complained, at the very least, as little as herself? With their stillness together so perfect, what had suggested so, around them, the attitude of sparing them? Her inner vision fixed it once more, this attitude, saw it, in the others, as vivid and concrete, extended it straight from her companion to Charlotte. Before she was well aware, accordingly, she had echoed in this intensity of thought Amerigo's last words. "You're the last person in the world to wish to do anything to hurt him."

She heard herself, heard her tone, after she had spoken, and heard it the more that, for a minute after, she felt her husband's eyes on her face, very close, too close for her to see him. He was looking at her because he was struck, and looking hard — though his answer, when it came, was straight enough. "Why, isn't that just what we have been talking about — that I've affected you as fairly studying his comfort and his pleasure? He might show his sense of it," the Prince went on, "by proposing to ME an excursion."

"And you would go with him?" Maggie immediately asked.

He hung fire but an instant. "Per Dio!"

She also had her pause, but she broke it — since gaiety was in the air — with an intense smile. "You can say that safely, because the proposal's one that, of his own motion, he won't make."

She couldn't have narrated afterwards — and in fact was at a loss to tell herself — by what transition, what rather marked abruptness of change in their personal relation, their drive came to its end with a kind of interval established, almost confessed to, between them. She felt it in the tone with which he repeated, after her, "'Safely' —?"

"Safely as regards being thrown with him perhaps after all, in such a case, too long. He's a person to think you might easily feel yourself to be. So it won't," Maggie said, "come from father. He's too modest."

Their eyes continued to meet on it, from corner to corner of the brougham. "Oh your modesty, between you —!" But he still smiled for it. "So that unless I insist —?"

"We shall simply go on as we are."

"Well, we're going on beautifully," he answered — though by no means with the effect it would have had if their mute transaction, that of attempted capture and achieved escape, had not taken place. As Maggie said nothing, none the less, to gainsay his remark, it was open to him to find himself the next moment conscious of still another idea. "I wonder if it would do. I mean for me to break in."

"'To break in' —?"

"Between your father and his wife. But there would be a way," he said —"we can make Charlotte ask him." And then as Maggie herself now wondered, echoing it again: "We can suggest to her to suggest to him that he shall let me take him off."

"Oh!" said Maggie.

"Then if he asks her why I so suddenly break out she'll be able to tell him the reason."

They were stopping, and the footman, who had alighted, had rung at the house-door. "That you think it would be so charming?"

"That I think it would be so charming. That we've persuaded HER will be convincing."

"I see," Maggie went on while the footman came back to let them out. "I see," she said again; though she felt a little disconcerted. What she really saw, of a sudden, was that her stepmother might report her as above all concerned for the proposal, and this brought her back her need that her father shouldn't think her concerned in any degree for anything. She alighted the next instant with a slight sense of defeat; her husband, to let her out, had passed before her, and, a little in advance, he awaited her on the edge of the low terrace, a step high, that preceded their open entrance, on either side of which one of their servants stood. The sense of a life tremendously ordered and fixed rose before her, and there was something in Amerigo's very face, while his eyes again met her own through the dusky lamplight, that was like a conscious reminder of it. He had answered her, just before, distinctly, and it appeared to leave her nothing to say. It was almost as if, having planned for the last word, she saw him himself enjoying it. It was almost as if — in the strangest way in the world — he were paying her back, by the production of a small pang, that of a new uneasiness, for the way she had slipped from him during their drive.

XXVIII

Maggie's new uneasiness might have had time to drop, inasmuch as she not only was conscious, during several days that followed, of no fresh indication for it to feed on, but was even struck, in quite another way, with an augmentation of the symptoms of that difference she had taken it into her head to work for. She recognised by the end of a week that if she had been in a manner caught up her father had been not less so — with the effect of her husband's and his wife's closing in, together, round them, and of their all having suddenly begun, as a party of four, to lead a life gregarious, and from that reason almost hilarious, so far as the easy sound of it went, as never before. It might have been an accident and a mere coincidence — so at least she said to herself at first; but a dozen chances that furthered the whole appearance had risen to the surface, pleasant pretexts, oh certainly pleasant, as pleasant as Amerigo in particular could make them, for associated undertakings, quite for shared adventures, for its always turning out, amusingly, that they wanted to do very much the same thing at the same time and in the same way. Funny all this was, to some extent, in the light of the fact that the father and daughter, for so long, had expressed so few positive desires; yet it would be sufficiently natural that if Amerigo and Charlotte HAD at last got a little tired of each other's company they should find their relief not so much in sinking to the rather low level of their companions as in wishing to pull the latter into the train in which they so constantly moved. "We're in the train," Maggie mutely reflected after the dinner in Eaton Square with Lady Castledean; "we've suddenly waked up in it and found ourselves rushing along, very much as if we had been put in during sleep — shoved, like a pair of labelled boxes, into the van. And since I wanted to 'go' I'm certainly going," she might have added; "I'm moving without trouble — they're doing it all for us: it's wonderful how they understand and how perfectly it succeeds." For that was the thing she had most immediately to acknowledge: it seemed as easy for them to make a quartette as it had formerly so long appeared for them to make a pair of couples — this latter being thus a discovery too absurdly belated. The only point at which, day after day, the success appeared at all qualified was represented, as might have been said, by her irresistible impulse to give her father a clutch when the train indulged in one of its occasional lurches. Then — there was no denying it — his eyes and her own met; so that they were themselves doing active violence, as against the others, to that very spirit of union, or at least to that very achievement of change, which she had taken the field to invoke.

The maximum of change was reached, no doubt, the day the Matcham party dined in Port-land Place; the day, really perhaps, of Maggie's maximum of social glory, in the sense of its showing for her own occasion, her very own, with every one else extravagantly rallying and falling in, absolutely conspiring to make her its heroine. It was as if her father himself, always with more initiative as a guest than as a host, had dabbled too in the conspiracy; and the impression was not diminished by the presence of the Assinghams, likewise very much caught-up, now, after something of a lull, by the side-wind of all the rest of the motion, and giving our young woman, so far at least as Fanny was concerned, the sense of some special intention of encouragement and applause. Fanny, who had not been present at the other dinner, thanks to a preference entertained and expressed by Charlotte, made a splendid show at this one, in new orange-coloured velvet with multiplied turquoises, and with a confidence, furthermore, as different as possible, her hostess inferred, from her too-marked betrayal of a belittled state at Matcham. Maggie was not indifferent to her own opportunity to redress this balance — which seemed, for the hour, part of a general rectification; she liked making out for herself that on the high level of Portland Place, a spot exempt, on all sorts of grounds, from jealous jurisdictions, her friend could feel as "good" as any one, and could in fact at moments almost appear to take the lead in recognition and celebration, so far as the evening might conduce to intensify the lustre of the little Princess. Mrs. Assingham produced on her the impression of giving her constantly her cue for this; and it was in truth partly by her help, intelligently, quite gratefully accepted, that the little Princess, in Maggie, was drawn out and emphasised.

She couldn't definitely have said how it happened, but she felt herself, for the first time in her career, living up to the public and popular notion of such a personage, as it pressed upon her from all round; rather wondering, inwardly too, while she did so, at that strange mixture in things through which the popular notion could be evidenced for her by such supposedly great ones of the earth as the Castledeans and their kind. Fanny Assingham might really have been there, at all events, like one of the assistants in the ring at the circus, to keep up the pace of the sleek revolving animal on whose back the lady in short spangled skirts should brilliantly caper and posture. That was all, doubtless Maggie had forgotten, had neglected, had declined, to be the little Princess on anything like the scale open to her; but now that the collective hand had been held out to her with such alacrity, so that she might skip up into the light, even, as seemed to her modest mind, with such a show of pink stocking and such an abbreviation of white petticoat, she could strike herself as perceiving, under arched eyebrows, where her mistake had been. She had invited for the later hours, after her dinner, a fresh contingent, the whole list of her apparent London acquaintance — which was again a thing in the manner of little princesses for whom the princely art was a matter of course. That was what she was learning to do, to fill out as a matter of course her appointed, her expected, her imposed character; and, though there were latent considerations that somewhat interfered with the lesson, she was having to-night an inordinate quantity of practice, none of it so successful as when, quite wittingly, she directed it at Lady Castledean, who was reduced by it at last to an unprecedented state of passivity. The perception of this high result caused Mrs. Assingham fairly to flush with responsive joy; she glittered at her young friend, from moment to moment, quite feverishly; it was positively as if her young friend had, in some marvellous, sudden, supersubtle way, become a source of succour to herself, become beautifully, divinely retributive. The intensity of the taste of these registered phenomena was in fact that somehow, by a process and through a connexion not again to be traced, she so practised, at the same time, on Amerigo and Charlotte — with only the drawback, her constant check and second-thought, that she concomitantly practised perhaps still more on her father.

This last was a danger indeed that, for much of the ensuing time, had its hours of strange beguilement — those at which her sense for precautions so suffered itself to lapse that she felt her communion with him more intimate than any other. It COULDN'T but pass between them that something singular was happening — so much as this she again and again said to herself; whereby the comfort of it was there, after all, to be noted, just as much as the possible peril, and she could think of the couple they formed together as groping, with sealed lips, but with mutual looks that had never been so tender, for some freedom, some fiction, some figured bravery, under which they might safely talk of it. The moment was to come — and it finally came with an effect as penetrating as the sound that follows the pressure of an electric button — when she read the least helpful of meanings into the agitation she had created. The merely specious description of their case would have been that, after being for a long time, as a family, delightfully, uninterruptedly happy, they had still had a new felicity to discover; a felicity for which, blessedly, her father's appetite and her own, in particular, had been kept fresh and grateful. This livelier march of their intercourse as a whole was the thing that occasionally determined in him the clutching instinct we have glanced at; very much as if he had said to her, in default of her breaking silence first: "Everything is remarkably pleasant, isn't it? — but WHERE, for it, after all, are we? up in a balloon and whirling through space, or down in the depths of the earth, in the glimmering passages of a gold-mine?" The equilibrium, the precious condition, lasted in spite of rearrangement; there had been a fresh distribution of the different weights, but the balance persisted and triumphed: all of which was just the reason why she was forbidden, face to face with the companion of her adventure, the experiment of a test. If they balanced they balanced — she had to take that; it deprived her of every pretext for arriving, by however covert a process, at what he thought.

But she had her hours, thus, of feeling supremely linked to him by the rigour of their law, and when it came over her that, all the while, the wish, on his side, to spare her might be what most worked with him, this very fact of their seeming to have nothing "inward" really to talk about wrapped him up for her in a kind of sweetness that was wanting, as a consecration, even in her yearning for her husband. She was powerless, however, was only more utterly hushed, when the interrupting flash came, when she would have been all ready to say to him, "Yes, this is by every appearance the best time we've had yet; but don't you see, all the same, how they must be working together for it, and how my very success, my success in shifting our beautiful harmony to a new basis, comes round to being their success, above all; their cleverness, their amiability, their power to hold out, their complete possession, in short, of our life?" For how could she say as much as that without saying a great deal more? without saying "They'll do everything in the world that suits us, save only one thing — prescribe a line for us that will make them separate." How could she so much as imagine herself even faintly murmuring that without putting into his mouth the very words that would have made her quail? "Separate, my dear? Do you want them to separate? Then you want US to — you and me? For how can the one separation take place without the other?" That was the question that, in spirit, she had heard him ask — with its dread train, moreover, of involved and connected inquiries. Their own separation, his and hers, was of course perfectly thinkable, but only on the basis of the sharpest of reasons. Well, the sharpest, the very sharpest, would be that they could no longer afford, as it were, he to let his wife, she to let her husband, "run" them in such compact formation. And say they accepted this account of their situation as a practical finality, acting upon it and proceeding to a division, would no sombre ghosts of the smothered past, on either side, show, across the widening strait, pale unappeased faces, or raise, in the very passage, deprecating, denouncing hands?

Meanwhile, however such things might be, she was to have occasion to say to herself that there might be but a deeper treachery in recoveries and reassurances. She was to feel alone again, as she had felt at the issue of her high tension with her husband during their return from meeting the Castledeans in Eaton Square. The evening in question had left her with a larger alarm, but then a lull had come — the alarm, after all, was yet to be confirmed. There came an hour, inevitably, when she knew, with a chill, what she had feared and why; it had taken, this hour, a month to arrive, but to find it before her was thoroughly to recognise it, for it showed her sharply what Amerigo had meant in alluding to a particular use that they might make, for their reaffirmed harmony and prosperity, of Charlotte. The more she thought, at present, of the tone he had employed to express their enjoyment of this resource, the more it came back to her as the product of a conscious art of dealing with her. He had been conscious, at the moment, of many things — conscious even, not a little, of desiring; and thereby of needing, to see what she would do in a given case. The given case would be that of her being to a certain extent, as she might fairly make it out, MENACED — horrible as it was to impute to him any intention represented by such a word. Why it was that to speak of making her stepmother intervene, as they might call it, in a question that seemed, just then and there, quite peculiarly their own business — why it was that a turn so familiar and so easy should, at the worst, strike her as charged with the spirit of a threat, was an oddity disconnected, for her, temporarily, from its grounds, the adventure of an imagination within her that possibly had lost its way. That, precisely, was doubtless why she had learned to wait, as the weeks passed by, with a fair, or rather indeed with an excessive, imitation of resumed serenity. There had been no prompt sequel to the Prince's equivocal light, and that made for patience; yet she was none the less to have to admit, after delay, that the bread he had cast on the waters had come home, and that she should thus be justified of her old apprehension. The consequence of this, in turn, was a renewed pang in presence of his remembered ingenuity. To be ingenious with HER — what DIDN'T, what mightn't that mean, when she had so absolutely never, at any point of contact with him, put him, by as much as the value of a penny, to the expense of sparing, doubting, fearing her, of having in any way whatever to reckon with her? The ingenuity had been in his simply speaking of their use of Charlotte as if it were common to them in an equal degree, and his triumph, on the occasion, had been just in the simplicity. She couldn't — and he knew it — say what was true: "Oh, you 'use' her, and I use her, if you will, yes; but we use her ever so differently and separately — not at all in the same way or degree. There's nobody we really use together but ourselves, don't you see? — by which I mean that where our interests are the same I can so beautifully, so exquisitely serve you for everything, and you can so beautifully, so exquisitely serve me. The only person either of us needs is the other of us; so why, as a matter of course, in such a case as this, drag in Charlotte?"

She couldn't so challenge him, because it would have been — and there she was paralysed — the NOTE. It would have translated itself on the spot, for his ear, into jealousy; and, from reverberation to repercussion, would have reached her father's exactly in the form of a cry piercing the stillness of peaceful sleep. It had been for many days almost as difficult for her to catch a quiet twenty minutes with her father as it had formerly been easy; there had been in fact, of old — the time, so strangely, seemed already far away — an inevitability in her longer passages with him, a sort of domesticated beauty in the calculability, round about them, of everything. But at present Charlotte was almost always there when Amerigo brought her to Eaton Square, where Amerigo was constantly bringing her; and Amerigo was almost always there when Charlotte brought her husband to Portland Place, where Charlotte was constantly bringing HIM. The fractions of occasions, the chance minutes that put them face to face had, as yet, of late, contrived to count but little, between them, either for the sense of opportunity or for that of exposure; inasmuch as the lifelong rhythm of their intercourse made against all cursory handling of deep things. They had never availed themselves of any given quarter-of-an-hour to gossip about fundamentals; they moved slowly through large still spaces; they could be silent together, at any time, beautifully, with much more comfort than hurriedly expressive. It appeared indeed to have become true that their common appeal measured itself, for vividness, just by this economy of sound; they might have been talking "at" each other when they talked with their companions, but these latter, assuredly, were not in any directer way to gain light on the current phase of their relation. Such were some of the reasons for which Maggie suspected fundamentals, as I have called them, to be rising, by a new movement, to the surface — suspected it one morning late in May, when her father presented himself in Portland Place alone. He had his pretext — of that she was fully aware: the Principino, two days before, had shown signs, happily not persistent, of a feverish cold and had notoriously been obliged to spend the interval at home. This was ground, ample ground, for punctual inquiry; but what it wasn't ground for, she quickly found herself reflecting, was his having managed, in the interest of his visit, to dispense so unwontedly — as their life had recently come to be arranged — with his wife's attendance. It had so happened that she herself was, for the hour, exempt from her husband's, and it will at once be seen that the hour had a quality all its own when I note that, remembering how the Prince had looked in to say he was going out, the Princess whimsically wondered if their respective sposi mightn't frankly be meeting, whimsically hoped indeed they were temporarily so disposed of. Strange was her need, at moments, to think of them as not attaching an excessive importance to their repudiation of the general practice that had rested only a few weeks before on such a consecrated rightness. Repudiations, surely, were not in the air — they had none of them come to that; for wasn't she at this minute testifying directly against them by her own behaviour? When she should confess to fear of being alone with her father, to fear of what he might then — ah, with such a slow, painful motion as she had a horror of! — say to her, THEN would be time enough for Amerigo and Charlotte to confess to not liking to appear to foregather.

She had this morning a wonderful consciousness both of dreading a particular question from him and of being able to check, yes even to disconcert, magnificently, by her apparent manner of receiving it, any restless imagination he might have about its importance. The day, bright and soft, had the breath of summer; it made them talk, to begin with, of Fawns, of the way Fawns invited — Maggie aware, the while, that in thus regarding, with him, the sweetness of its invitation to one couple just as much as to another, her humbugging smile grew very nearly convulsive. That was it, and there was relief truly, of a sort, in taking it in: she was humbugging him already, by absolute necessity, as she had never, never done in her life — doing it up to the full height of what she had allowed for. The necessity, in the great dimly-shining room where, declining, for his reasons, to sit down, he moved about in Amerigo's very footsteps, the necessity affected her as pressing upon her with the very force of the charm itself; of the old pleasantness, between them, so candidly playing up there again; of the positive flatness of their tenderness, a surface all for familiar use, quite as if generalised from the long succession of tapestried sofas, sweetly faded, on which his theory of contentment had sat, through unmeasured pauses, beside her own. She KNEW, from this instant, knew in advance and as well as anything would ever teach her, that she must never intermit for a solitary second her so highly undertaking to prove that there was nothing the matter with her. She saw, of a sudden, everything she might say or do in the light of that undertaking, established connections from it with any number of remote matters, struck herself, for instance, as acting all in its interest when she proposed their going out, in the exercise of their freedom and in homage to the season, for a turn in the Regent's Park. This resort was close at hand, at the top of Portland Place, and the Principino, beautifully better, had already proceeded there under high attendance: all of which considerations were defensive for Maggie, all of which became, to her mind, part of the business of cultivating continuity.

Upstairs, while she left him to put on something to go out in, the thought of his waiting below for her, in possession of the empty house, brought with it, sharply if briefly, one of her abrupt arrests of consistency, the brush of a vain imagination almost paralysing her, often, for the minute, before her glass — the vivid look, in other words, of the particular difference his marriage had made. The particular difference seemed at such instants the loss, more than anything else, of their old freedom, their never having had to think, where they were together concerned, of any one, of anything but each other. It hadn't been HER marriage that did it; that had never, for three seconds, suggested to either of them that they must act diplomatically, must reckon with another presence — no, not even with her husband's. She groaned to herself, while the vain imagination lasted, "WHY did he marry? ah, why DID he?" and then it came up to her more than ever that nothing could have been more beautiful than the way in which, till Charlotte came so much more closely into their life, Amerigo hadn't interfered. What she had gone on owing him for this mounted up again, to her eyes, like a column of figures — — or call it even, if one would, a house of cards; it was her father's wonderful act that had tipped the house down and made the sum wrong. With all of which, immediately after her question, her "Why did he, why did he?" rushed back, inevitably, the confounding, the overwhelming wave of the knowledge of his reason. "He did it for ME, he did it for me," she moaned, "he did it, exactly, that our freedom — meaning, beloved man, simply and solely mine — should be greater instead of less; he did it, divinely, to liberate me so far as possible from caring what became of him." She found time upstairs, even in her haste, as she had repeatedly found time before, to let the wonderments involved in these recognitions flash at her with their customary effect of making her blink: the question in especial of whether she might find her solution in acting, herself, in the spirit of what he had done, in forcing her "care" really to grow as much less as he had tried to make it. Thus she felt the whole weight of their case drop afresh upon her shoulders, was confronted, unmistakably, with the prime source of her haunted state. It all came from her not having been able not to mind — not to mind what became of him; not having been able, without anxiety, to let him go his way and take his risk and lead his life. She had made anxiety her stupid little idol; and absolutely now, while she stuck a long pin, a trifle fallaciously, into her hat — she had, with an approach to irritation, told her maid, a new woman, whom she had lately found herself thinking of as abysmal, that she didn't want her — she tried to focus the possibility of some understanding between them in consequence of which he should cut loose.

Very near indeed it looked, any such possibility! that consciousness, too, had taken its turn by the time she was ready; all the vibration, all the emotion of this present passage being, precisely, in the very sweetness of their lapse back into the conditions of the simpler time, into a queer resemblance between the aspect and the feeling of the moment and those of numberless other moments that were sufficiently far away. She had been quick in her preparation, in spite of the flow of the tide that sometimes took away her breath; but a pause, once more, was still left for her to make, a pause, at the top of the stairs, before she came down to him, in the span of which she asked herself if it weren't thinkable, from the perfectly practical point of view, that she should simply sacrifice him. She didn't go into the detail of what sacrificing him would mean — she didn't need to; so distinct was it, in one of her restless lights, that there he was awaiting her, that she should find him walking up and down the drawing-room in the warm, fragrant air to which the open windows and the abundant flowers contributed; slowly and vaguely moving there and looking very slight and young and, superficially, manageable, almost as much like her child, putting it a little freely, as like her parent; with the appearance about him, above all, of having perhaps arrived just on purpose to SAY it to her, himself, in so many words: "Sacrifice me, my own love; do sacrifice me, do sacrifice me!" Should she want to, should she insist on it, she might verily hear him bleating it at her, all conscious and all accommodating, like some precious, spotless, exceptionally intelligent lamb. The positive effect of the intensity of this figure, however, was to make her shake it away in her resumed descent; and after she had rejoined him, after she had picked him up, she was to know the full pang of the thought that her impossibility was MADE, absolutely, by his consciousness, by the lucidity of his intention: this she felt while she smiled there for him, again, all hypocritically; while she drew on fair, fresh gloves; while she interrupted the process first to give his necktie a slightly smarter twist and then to make up to him for her hidden madness by rubbing her nose into his cheek according to the tradition of their frankest levity.

From the instant she should be able to convict him of intending, every issue would be closed and her hypocrisy would have to redouble. The only way to sacrifice him would be to do so without his dreaming what it might be for. She kissed him, she arranged his cravat, she dropped remarks, she guided him out, she held his arm, not to be led, but to lead him, and taking it to her by much the same intimate pressure she had always used, when a little girl, to mark the inseparability of her doll — she did all these things so that he should sufficiently fail to dream of what they might be for.

XXIX

There was nothing to show that her effort in any degree fell short till they got well into the Park and he struck her as giving, unexpectedly, the go-by to any serious search for the Principino. The way they sat down awhile in the sun was a sign of that; his dropping with her into the first pair of sequestered chairs they came across and waiting a little, after they were placed, as if now at last she might bring out, as between them, something more specific. It made her but feel the more sharply how the specific, in almost any direction, was utterly forbidden her — how the use of it would be, for all the world, like undoing the leash of a dog eager to follow up a scent. It would come out, the specific, where the dog would come out; would run to earth, somehow, the truth — for she was believing herself in relation to the truth! — at which she mustn't so much as indirectly point. Such, at any rate, was the fashion in which her passionate prudence played over possibilities of danger, reading symptoms and betrayals into everything she looked at, and yet having to make it evident, while she recognised them, that she didn't wince. There were moments between them, in their chairs, when he might have been watching her guard herself and trying to think of something new that would trip her up. There were pauses during which, with her affection as sweet and still as the sunshine, she might yet, as at some hard game, over a table, for money, have been defying him to fasten upon her the least little complication of consciousness. She was positively proud, afterwards, of the great style in which she had kept this up; later on, at the hour's end, when they had retraced their steps to find Amerigo and Charlotte awaiting them at the house, she was able to say to herself that, truly, she had put her plan through; even though once more setting herself the difficult task of making their relation, every minute of the time, not fall below the standard of that other hour, in the treasured past, which hung there behind them like a framed picture in a museum, a high watermark for the history of their old fortune; the summer evening, in the park at Fawns, when, side by side under the trees just as now, they had let their happy confidence lull them with its most golden tone. There had been the possibility of a trap for her, at present, in the very question of their taking up anew that residence; wherefore she had not been the first to sound it, in spite of the impression from him of his holding off to see what she would do. She was saying to herself in secret: "CAN we again, in this form, migrate there? Can I, for myself, undertake it? face all the intenser keeping-up and stretching-out, indefinitely, impossibly, that our conditions in the country, as we've established and accepted them, would stand for?" She had positively lost herself in this inward doubt — so much she was subsequently to remember; but remembering then too that her companion, though perceptibly perhaps as if not to be eager, had broken the ice very much as he had broken it in Eaton Square after the banquet to the Castledeans.

Her mind had taken a long excursion, wandered far into the vision of what a summer at Fawns, with Amerigo and Charlotte still more eminently in presence against that higher sky, would bring forth. Wasn't her father meanwhile only pretending to talk of it? just as she was, in a manner, pretending to listen? He got off it, finally, at all events, for the transition it couldn't well help thrusting out at him; it had amounted exactly to an arrest of her private excursion by the sense that he had begun to IMITATE — oh, as never yet! — the ancient tone of gold. It had verily come from him at last, the question of whether she thought it would be very good — but very good indeed — that he should leave England for a series of weeks, on some pretext, with the Prince. Then it had been that she was to know her husband's "menace" hadn't really dropped, since she was face to face with the effect of it. Ah, the effect of it had occupied all the rest of their walk, had stayed out with them and come home with them, besides making it impossible that they shouldn't presently feign to recollect how rejoining the child had been their original purpose. Maggie's uneffaced note was that it had, at the end of five minutes more, driven them to that endeavour as to a refuge, and caused them afterwards to rejoice, as well, that the boy's irrepressibly importunate company, in due course secured and enjoyed, with the extension imparted by his governess, a person expectant of consideration, constituted a cover for any awkwardness. For that was what it had all come to, that the dear man had spoken to her to

197

TRY her — quite as he had been spoken to himself by Charlotte, with the same fine idea. The Princess took it in, on the spot, firmly grasping it; she heard them together, her father and his wife, dealing with the queer case. "The Prince tells me that Maggie has a plan for your taking some foreign journey with him, and, as he likes to do everything she wants, he has suggested my speaking to you for it as the thing most likely to make you consent. So I do speak — see? — being always so eager myself, as you know, to meet Maggie's wishes. I speak, but without quite understanding, this time, what she has in her head. Why SHOULD she, of a sudden, at this particular moment, desire to ship you off together and to remain here alone with me? The compliment's all to me, I admit, and you must decide quite as you like. The Prince is quite ready, evidently, to do his part — but you'll have it out with him. That is you'll have it out with HER." Something of that kind was what, in her mind's ear, Maggie heard — and this, after his waiting for her to appeal to him directly, was her father's invitation to her to have it out. Well, as she could say to herself all the rest of the day, that was what they did while they continued to sit there in their penny chairs, that was what they HAD done as much as they would now ever, ever, have out anything. The measure of this, at least, had been given, that each would fight to the last for the protection, for the perversion, of any real anxiety. She had confessed, instantly, with her humbugging grin, not flinching by a hair, meeting his eyes as mildly as he met hers, she had confessed to her fancy that they might both, he and his son-inlaw, have welcomed such an escapade, since they had both been so long so furiously domestic. She had almost cocked her hat under the inspiration of this opportunity to hint how a couple of spirited young men, reacting from confinement and sallying forth arm-inarm, might encounter the agreeable in forms that would strike them for the time at least as novel. She had felt for fifty seconds, with her eyes, all so sweetly and falsely, in her companion's, horribly vulgar; yet without minding it either — such luck should she have if to be nothing worse than vulgar would see her through. "And I thought Amerigo might like it better," she had said, "than wandering off alone."

"Do you mean that he won't go unless I take him?"

She had considered here, and never in her life had she considered so promptly and so intently. If she really put it that way, her husband, challenged, might belie the statement; so that what would that do but make her father wonder, make him perhaps ask straight out, why she was exerting pressure? She couldn't of course afford to be suspected for an instant of exerting pressure; which was why she was obliged only to make answer: "Wouldn't that be just what you must have out with HIM?"

"Decidedly — if he makes me the proposal. But he hasn't made it yet."

Oh, once more, how she was to feel she had smirked! "Perhaps he's too shy!"

"Because you're so sure he so really wants my company?"

"I think he has thought you might like it."

"Well, I should —!" But with this he looked away from her, and she held her breath to hear him either ask if she wished him to address the question to Amerigo straight, or inquire if she should be greatly disappointed by his letting it drop. What had "settled" her, as she was privately to call it, was that he had done neither of these things, and had thereby markedly stood off from the risk involved in trying to draw out her reason. To attenuate, on the other hand, this appearance, and quite as if to fill out the too large receptacle made, so musingly, by his abstention, he had himself presently given her a reason — had positively spared her the effort of asking whether he judged Charlotte not to have approved. He had taken everything on himself — THAT was what had settled her. She had had to wait very little more to feel, with this, how much he was taking. The point he made was his lack of any eagerness to put time and space, on any such scale, between himself and his wife. He wasn't so unhappy with her — far from it, and Maggie was to hold that he had grinned back, paternally, through his rather shielding glasses, in easy emphasis of this — as to be able to hint that he required the relief of absence. Therefore, unless it was for the Prince himself —!

"Oh, I don't think it would have been for Amerigo himself. Amerigo and I," Maggie had said, "perfectly rub on together."

"Well then, there we are."

"I see" — and she had again, with sublime blandness, assented. "There we are."

"Charlotte and I too," her father had gaily proceeded, "perfectly rub on together." And then he had appeared for a little to be making time. "To put it only so," he had mildly and happily added —"to put it only so!" He had spoken as if he might easily put it much better, yet as if the humour of contented understatement fairly sufficed for the occasion. He had played then, either all consciously or all unconsciously, into Charlotte's hands; and the effect of this was to render trebly oppressive Maggie's conviction of Charlotte's plan. She had done what she wanted, his wife had — which was also what Amerigo had made her do. She had kept her test, Maggie's test, from becoming possible, and had applied instead a test of her own. It was exactly as if she had known that her stepdaughter would be afraid to be summoned to say, under the least approach to cross-examination, why any change was desirable; and it was, for our young woman herself, still more prodigiously, as if her father had been capable of calculations to match, of judging it important he shouldn't be brought to demand of her what was the matter with her. Why otherwise, with such an opportunity, hadn't he demanded it? Always from calculation — that was why, that was why. He was terrified of the retort he might have invoked: "What, my dear, if you come to that, is the matter with YOU?" When, a minute later on, he had followed up his last note by a touch or two designed still further to conjure away the ghost of the anomalous, at that climax verily she would have had to be dumb to the question. "There seems a kind of charm, doesn't there? on our life — and quite as if, just lately, it had got itself somehow renewed, had waked up refreshed. A kind of wicked selfish prosperity perhaps, as if we had grabbed everything, fixed everything, down to the last lovely object for the last glass case of the last corner, left over, of my old show. That's the only take-off, that it has made us perhaps lazy, a wee bit languid — lying like gods together, all careless of mankind."

"Do you consider that we're languid?" — that form of rejoinder she had jumped at for the sake of its pretty lightness. "Do you consider that we are careless of mankind? — living as we do in the biggest crowd in the world, and running about always pursued and pursuing."

It had made him think indeed a little longer than she had meant; but he came up again, as she might have said, smiling. "Well, I don't know. We get nothing but the fun, do we?"

"No," she had hastened to declare; "we certainly get nothing but the fun."

"We do it all," he had remarked, "so beautifully."

"We do it all so beautifully." She hadn't denied this for a moment. "I see what you mean."

"Well, I mean too," he had gone on, "that we haven't, no doubt, enough, the sense of difficulty."

"Enough? Enough for what?"

"Enough not to be selfish."

"I don't think YOU are selfish," she had returned — and had managed not to wail it.

"I don't say that it's me particularly — or that it's you or Charlotte or Amerigo. But we're selfish together — we move as a selfish mass. You see we want always the same thing," he had gone on —"and that holds us, that binds us, together. We want each other," he had further explained; "only wanting it, each time, FOR each other. That's what I call the happy spell; but it's also, a little, possibly, the immorality."

"'The immorality'?" she had pleasantly echoed.

"Well, we're tremendously moral for ourselves — that is for each other; and I won't pretend that I know exactly at whose particular personal expense you and I, for instance, are happy. What it comes to, I daresay, is that there's something haunting — as if it were a bit uncanny — in such a consciousness of our general comfort and privilege. Unless indeed," he had rambled on, "it's only I to whom, fantastically, it says so much. That's all I mean, at any rate — that it's sort of soothing; as if we were sitting about on divans, with pigtails, smoking opium and seeing visions. 'Let us then be up and doing' — what is it Longfellow says? That seems sometimes to ring out; like the police breaking in-into our opium den — to give us a shake. But the beauty of it is, at the same time, that we ARE doing; we're doing, that is, after all, what we went in for. We're working it, our life, our chance, whatever you may call it, as we saw it, as we felt it, from the first. We HAVE worked it, and what more can you do than that? It's a good deal for me," he had wound up, "to have made Charlotte so happy — to have so perfectly contented her. YOU, from a good way back, were a matter of course — I mean your being all right; so that I needn't mind your knowing that my great interest, since then, has rather inevitably been in making sure of the same success, very much to your advantage as well, for Charlotte. If we've worked our life, our idea really, as I say — if at any rate I can sit here and say that I've worked my share of it — it has not been what you may call least by our having put Charlotte so at her ease. THAT has been soothing, all round; that has curled up as the biggest of the blue fumes, or whatever they are, of the opium. Don't you see what a cropper we would have come if she hadn't settled down as she has?" And he had concluded by turning to Maggie as for something she mightn't really have thought of. "You, darling, in that case, I verily believe, would have been the one to hate it most."

"To hate it —?" Maggie had wondered.

"To hate our having, with our tremendous intentions, not brought it off. And I daresay I should have hated it for you even more than for myself."

"That's not unlikely perhaps when it was for me, after all, that you did it."

He had hesitated, but only a moment. "I never told you so."

"Well, Charlotte herself soon enough told me."

"But I never told HER," her father had answered.

"Are you very sure?" she had presently asked.

"Well, I like to think how thoroughly I was taken with her, and how right I was, and how fortunate, to have that for my basis. I told her all the good I thought of her."

"Then that," Maggie had returned, "was precisely part of the good. I mean it was precisely part of it that she could so beautifully understand."

"Yes — understand everything."

"Everything — and in particular your reasons. Her telling me — that showed me how she had understood."

They were face to face again now, and she saw she had made his colour rise; it was as if he were still finding in her eyes the concrete image, the enacted scene, of her passage with Charlotte, which he was now hearing of for the first time and as to which it would have been natural he should question her further. His forbearance to do so would but mark, precisely, the complication of his fears. "What she does like," he finally said, "is the way it has succeeded."

"Your marriage?"

"Yes — my whole idea. The way I've been justified. That's the joy I give her. If for HER, either, it had failed —!" That, however, was not worth talking about; he had broken off. "You think then you could now risk Fawns?"

"'Risk' it?"

"Well, morally — from the point of view I was talking of; that of our sinking deeper into sloth. Our selfishness, somehow, seems at its biggest down there."

Maggie had allowed him the amusement of her not taking this up. "Is Charlotte," she had simply asked, "really ready?"

"Oh, if you and I and Amerigo are. Whenever one corners Charlotte," he had developed more at his ease, "one finds that she only wants to know what we want. Which is what we got her for!"

"What we got her for — exactly!" And so, for a little, even though with a certain effect of oddity in their more or less successful ease, they left it; left it till Maggie made the remark that it was all the same wonderful her stepmother should be willing, before the season was out, to exchange so much company for so much comparative solitude.

"Ah," he had then made answer, "that's because her idea, I think, this time, is that we shall have more people, more than we've hitherto had, in the country. Don't you remember that THAT, originally, was what we were to get her for?"

"Oh yes — to give us a life." Maggie had gone through the form of recalling this, and the light of their ancient candour, shining from so far back, had seemed to bring out some things so strangely that, with the sharpness of the vision, she had risen to her feet. "Well, with a 'life' Fawns will certainly do." He had remained in his place while she looked over his head; the picture, in her vision, had suddenly swarmed. The vibration was that of one of the lurches of the mystic train in which, with her companion, she was travelling; but she was having to steady herself, this time, before meeting his eyes. She had measured indeed the full difference between the move to Fawns because each of them now knew the others wanted it and the pairing-off, for a journey, of her husband and her father, which nobody knew that either wanted. "More company" at Fawns would be effectually enough the key in which her husband and her stepmother were at work; there was truly no question but that she and her father must accept any array of visitors. No one could try to marry him now. What he had just said was a direct plea for that, and what was the plea itself but an act of submission to Charlotte? He had, from his chair, been noting her look, but he had, the next minute, also risen, and then it was they had reminded each other of their having come out for the boy. Their junction with him and with his companion successfully effected, the four had moved home more slowly, and still more vaguely; yet with a vagueness that permitted of Maggie's reverting an instant to the larger issue.

"If we have people in the country then, as you were saying, do you know for whom my first fancy would be? You may be amused, but it would be for the Castledeans."

"I see. But why should I be amused?"

"Well, I mean I am myself. I don't think I like her — and yet I like to see her: which, as Amerigo says, is 'rum.'"

"But don't you feel she's very handsome?" her father inquired.

"Yes, but it isn't for that."

"Then what is it for?"

"Simply that she may be THERE — just there before us. It's as if she may have a value — as if something may come of her. I don't in the least know what, and she rather irritates me meanwhile. I don't even know, I admit, why — but if we see her often enough I may find out."

"Does it matter so very much?" her companion had asked while they moved together.

She had hesitated. "You mean because you do rather like her?"

He on his side too had waited a little, but then he had taken it from her. "Yes, I guess I do rather like her."

Which she accepted for the first case she could recall of their not being affected by a person in the same way. It came back therefore to his pretending; but she had gone far enough, and to add to her appearance of levity she further observed that, though they were so far from a novelty, she should also immediately desire, at Fawns, the presence of the Assinghams. That put everything on a basis independent of explanations; yet it was extraordinary, at the same time, how much, once in the country again with the others, she was going, as they used to say at home, to need the presence of the good Fanny. It was the strangest thing in the world, but it was as if Mrs. Assingham might in a manner mitigate the intensity of her consciousness of Charlotte. It was as if the two would balance, one against the other; as if it came round again in that fashion to her idea of the equilibrium. It would be like putting this friend into her scale to make weight — into the scale with her father and herself. Amerigo and Charlotte would be in the other; therefore it would take the three of them to keep that one straight. And as this played, all duskily, in her mind it had received from her father, with a sound of suddenness, a luminous contribution. "Ah, rather! DO let's have the Assinghams."

"It would be to have them," she had said, "as we used so much to have them. For a good long stay, in the old way and on the old terms: 'as regular boarders' Fanny used to call it. That is if they'll come."

"As regular boarders, on the old terms — that's what I should like too. But I guess they'll come," her companion had added in a tone into which she had read meanings. The main meaning was that he felt he was going to require them quite as much as she was. His recognition of the new terms as different from the old, what was that, practically, but a confession that something had happened, and a perception that, interested in the situation she had helped to create, Mrs. Assingham would be, by so much as this, concerned in its inevitable development? It amounted to an intimation, off his guard, that he should be thankful for some one to turn to. If she had wished covertly to sound him he had now, in short, quite given himself away, and if she had, even at the start, needed anything MORE to settle her, here assuredly was enough. He had hold of his small grandchild as they retraced their steps, swinging the boy's hand and not bored, as he never was, by his always bristling, like a fat little porcupine, with shrill interrogation-points — so that, secretly, while they went, she had wondered again if the equilibrium mightn't have been more real, mightn't above all have demanded less strange a study, had it only been on the books that Charlotte should give him a Principino of his own. She had repossessed herself now of his other arm, only this time she was drawing him back, gently, helplessly back, to what they had tried, for the hour, to get away from — just as he was consciously drawing the child, and as high Miss Bogle on her left, representing the duties of home, was complacently drawing HER. The duties of home, when the house in Portland Place reappeared, showed, even from a distance, as vividly there before them. Amerigo and Charlotte had come in- that is Amerigo had, Charlotte, rather, having come out — and the pair were perched together in the balcony, he bare-headed, she divested of her jacket, her mantle, or whatever, but crowned with a brilliant brave hat, responsive to the balmy day, which Maggie immediately "spotted" as new, as insuperably original, as worn, in characteristic generous harmony, for the first time; all, evidently, to watch for the return of the absent, to be there to take them over again as punctually as possible. They were gay, they were amused, in the pleasant morning; they leaned across the rail and called down their greeting, lighting up the front of the great black house with an expression that quite broke the monotony, that might almost have shocked the decency, of Portland Place. The group on the pavement stared up as at the peopled battlements of a castle; even Miss Bogle, who carried her head most aloft, gaped a little, through the interval of space, as toward truly superior beings. There could scarce have been so much of the open mouth since the dingy waits, on Christmas Eve, had so lamentably chanted for pennies — the time when Amerigo, insatiable for English customs, had come out, with a gasped "Santissima Vergine!" to marvel at the depositaries of this tradition and purchase a reprieve. Maggie's individual gape was inevitably again for the thought of how the pair would be at work.

XXX

She had not again, for weeks, had Mrs. Assingham so effectually in presence as on the afternoon of that lady's return from the Easter party at Matcham; but the intermission was made up as soon as the date of the migration to Fawns — that of the more or less simultaneous adjournment of the two houses — began to be discussed. It had struck her, promptly, that this renewal, with an old friend, of the old terms she had talked of with her father, was the one opening, for her spirit, that wouldn't too much advertise or betray her. Even her father, who had always, as he would have said, "believed in" their ancient ally, wouldn't necessarily suspect her of invoking Fanny's aid toward any special inquiry — and least of all if Fanny would only act as Fanny so easily might. Maggie's measure of Fanny's ease would have been agitating to Mrs. Assingham had it been all at once revealed to her — as, for that matter, it was soon destined to become even on a comparatively graduated showing. Our young woman's idea, in particular, was that her safety, her escape from being herself suspected of suspicion, would proceed from this friend's power to cover, to protect and, as might be, even showily to represent her — represent, that is, her relation to the form of the life they were all actually leading. This would doubtless be, as people said, a large order; but that Mrs. Assingham existed, substantially, or could somehow be made prevailingly to exist, for her private benefit, was the finest flower Maggie had plucked from among the suggestions sown, like abundant seed, on the occasion of the entertainment offered in Portland Place to the Matcham company. Mrs. Assingham, that night, rebounding from dejection, had bristled with bravery and sympathy; she had then absolutely, she had perhaps recklessly, for herself, betrayed the deeper and darker consciousness — an impression it would now be late for her inconsistently to attempt to undo. It was with a wonderful air of giving out all these truths that the Princess at present approached her again; making doubtless at first a sufficient scruple of letting her know what in especial she asked of her, yet not a bit ashamed, as she in fact quite expressly declared, of Fanny's discerned foreboding of the strange uses she might perhaps have for her. Quite from the first, really, Maggie said extraordinary things to her, such as "You can help me, you know, my dear, when nobody else can;" such as "I almost wish, upon my word, that you had something the matter with you, that you had lost your health, or your money, or your reputation (forgive me, love!) so that I might be with you as much as I want, or keep you with ME, without exciting comment, without exciting any other remark than that such kindnesses are 'like' me." We have each our own way of making up for our unselfishness, and Maggie, who had no small self at all as against her husband or her father and only a weak and uncertain one as against her stepmother, would verily, at this crisis, have seen Mrs. Assingham's personal life or liberty sacrificed without a pang.

The attitude that the appetite in question maintained in her was to draw peculiar support moreover from the current aspects and agitations of her victim. This personage struck her, in truth, as ready for almost anything; as not perhaps effusively protesting, yet as wanting with a restlessness of her own to know what she wanted. And in the long run — which was none so long either — there was to be no difficulty, as happened, about that. It was as if, for all the world, Maggie had let her see that she held her, that she made her, fairly responsible for something; not, to begin with, dotting all the i's nor hooking together all the links, but treating her, without insistence, rather with caressing confidence, as there to see and to know, to advise and to assist. The theory, visibly, had patched itself together for her that the dear woman had somehow, from the early time, had a hand in ALL their fortunes, so that there was no turn of their common relations and affairs that couldn't be traced back in some degree to her original affectionate interest. On this affectionate interest the good lady's young friend now built, before her eyes — very much as a wise, or even as a mischievous, child, playing on the floor, might pile up blocks, skilfully and dizzily, with an eye on the face of a covertly-watching elder.

When the blocks tumbled down they but acted after the nature of blocks; yet the hour would come for their rising so high that the structure would have to be noticed and admired. Mrs. Assingham's appearance of unreservedly giving herself involved meanwhile, on her own side, no separate recognitions: her face of almost anxious attention was directed altogether to her young friend's so vivid felicity; it suggested that she took for granted, at the most, certain vague recent enhancements of that state. If the Princess now, more than before, was going and going, she was prompt to publish that she beheld her go, that she had always known she WOULD, sooner or later, and that any appeal for participation must more or less contain and invite the note of triumph. There was a blankness in her blandness, assuredly, and very nearly an extravagance in her generalising gaiety; a precipitation of cheer particularly marked whenever they met again after short separations: meetings during the first flush of which Maggie sometimes felt reminded of other looks in other faces; of two strangely unobliterated impressions above all, the physiognomic light that had played out in her husband at the shock — she had come at last to talk to herself of the "shock" — of his first vision of her on his return from Matcham and Gloucester, and the wonder of Charlotte's beautiful bold wavering gaze when, the next morning in Eaton Square, this old friend had turned from the window to begin to deal with her.

If she had dared to think of it so crudely she would have said that Fanny was afraid of her, afraid of something she might say or do, even as, for their few brief seconds, Amerigo and Charlotte had been — which made, exactly, an expressive element common to the three. The difference however was that this look had in the dear woman its oddity of a constant renewal, whereas it had never for the least little instant again peeped out of the others. Other looks, other lights, radiant and steady, with the others, had taken its place, reaching a climax so short a time ago, that morning of the appearance of the pair on the balcony of her house to overlook what she had been doing with her father; when their general interested brightness and beauty, attuned to the outbreak of summer, had seemed to shed down warmth and welcome and the promise of protection. They were conjoined not to do anything to startle her — and now at last so completely that, with experience and practice, they had almost ceased to fear their liability. Mrs. Assingham, on the other hand, deprecating such an accident not less, had yet less assurance, as having less control. The high pitch of her cheer, accordingly, the tentative, adventurous expressions, of the would-be smiling order, that preceded her approach even like a squad of skirmishers, or whatever they were called, moving ahead of the baggage train — these things had at the end of a fortnight brought a dozen times to our young woman's lips a challenge that had the cunning to await its right occasion, but of the relief of which, as a demonstration, she meanwhile felt no little need. "You've such a dread of my possibly complaining to you that you keep pealing all the bells to drown my voice; but don't cry out, my dear, till you're hurt — and above all ask yourself how I can be so wicked as to complain. What in the name of all that's fantastic can you dream that I have to complain OF?" Such inquiries the Princess temporarily succeeded in repressing, and she did so, in a measure, by the aid of her wondering if this ambiguity with which her friend affected her wouldn't be at present a good deal like the ambiguity with which she herself must frequently affect her father. She wondered how she should enjoy, on HIS part, such a take-up as she but just succeeded, from day to day, in sparing Mrs. Assingham, and that made for her trying to be as easy with this associate as Mr. Verver, blessed man, all indulgent but all inscrutable, was with his daughter. She had extracted from her, none the less, a vow in respect to the time that, if the Colonel might be depended on, they would spend at Fawns; and nothing came home to her more, in this connection, or inspired her with a more intimate interest, than her sense of absolutely seeing her interlocutress forbear to observe that Charlotte's view of a long visit, even from such allies, was there to be reckoned with.

Fanny stood off from that proposition as visibly to the Princess, and as consciously to herself, as she might have backed away from the edge of a chasm into which she feared to slip; a truth that contributed again to keep before our young woman her own constant danger of advertising her subtle processes. That Charlotte should have begun to be restrictive about the Assinghams — which she had never, and for a hundred obviously good reasons, been before — this in itself was a fact of the highest value for Maggie, and of a value enhanced by the silence in which Fanny herself so much too unmistakably dressed it. What gave it quite thrillingly its price was exactly the circumstance that it thus opposed her to her stepmother more actively — if she was to back up her friends for holding out — than she had ever yet been opposed; though of course with the involved result of the fine chance given Mrs. Verver to ask her husband for explanations. Ah, from the moment she should be definitely CAUGHT in opposition there would be naturally no saying how much Charlotte's opportunities might multiply! What would become of her father, she hauntedly asked, if his wife, on the one side, should begin to press him to call his daughter to order, and the force of old habit — to put it only at that — should dispose him, not less effectively, to believe in this young person at any price? There she was, all round, imprisoned in the circle of the reasons it was impossible she should give — certainly give HIM. The house in the country was his house, and thereby was Charlotte's; it was her own and Amerigo's only so far as its proper master and mistress should profusely place it at their disposal. Maggie felt of course that she saw no limit to her father's profusion, but this couldn't be even at the best the case with Charlotte's, whom it would never be decent, when all was said, to reduce to fighting for her preferences. There were hours, truly, when the Princess saw herself as not unarmed for battle if battle might only take place without spectators.

This last advantage for her, was, however, too sadly out of the question; her sole strength lay in her being able to see that if Charlotte wouldn't "want" the Assinghams it would be because that sentiment too would have motives and grounds. She had all the while command of one way of meeting any objection, any complaint, on his wife's part, reported to her by her father; it would be open to her to retort to his possible "What are your reasons, my dear?" by a lucidly-produced "What are hers, love, please? — isn't that what we had better know? Mayn't her reasons be a dislike, beautifully founded, of the presence, and thereby of the observation, of persons who perhaps know about her things it's inconvenient to her they should know?" That hideous card she might in mere logic play — being by this time, at her still swifter private pace, intimately familiar with all the fingered pasteboard in her pack. But she could play it only on the forbidden issue of sacrificing him; the issue so forbidden that it involved even a horror of finding out if he would really have consented to be sacrificed. What she must do she must do by keeping her hands off him; and nothing meanwhile, as we see, had less in common with that scruple than such a merciless manipulation of their yielding beneficiaries as her spirit so boldly revelled in. She saw herself, in this connexion, without detachment — saw others alone with intensity; otherwise she might have been struck, fairly have been amused, by her free assignment of the pachydermatous quality. If SHE could face the awkwardness of the persistence of her friends at Fawns in spite of Charlotte, she somehow looked to them for an inspiration of courage that would improve upon her own. They were in short not only themselves to find a plausibility and an audacity, but were somehow by the way to pick up these forms for her, Maggie, as well. And she felt indeed that she was giving them scant time longer when, one afternoon in Portland Place, she broke out with an irrelevance that was merely superficial.

"What awfulness, in heaven's name, is there between them? What do you believe, what do you KNOW?"

Oh, if she went by faces her visitor's sudden whiteness, at this, might have carried her far! Fanny Assingham turned pale for it, but there was something in such an appearance, in the look it put into the eyes, that renewed Maggie's conviction of what this companion had been expecting. She had been watching it come, come from afar, and now that it was there, after all, and the first convulsion over, they would doubtless soon find themselves in a more real relation. It was there because of the Sunday luncheon they had partaken of alone together; it was there, as strangely as one would, because of the bad weather, the cold perverse June rain, that was making the day wrong; it was there because it stood for the whole sum of the perplexities and duplicities among which our young woman felt herself lately to have picked her steps; it was there because Amerigo and Charlotte were again paying together alone a "week end" visit which it had been Maggie's plan infernally to promote — just to see if, this time, they really would; it was there because she had kept Fanny, on her side, from paying one she would manifestly have been glad to pay, and had made her come instead, stupidly, vacantly, boringly, to luncheon: all in the spirit of celebrating the fact that the Prince and Mrs. Verver had thus put it into her own power to describe them exactly as they were. It had abruptly occurred, in truth, that Maggie required the preliminary help of determining HOW they were; though, on the other hand, before her guest had answered her question everything in the hour and the place, everything in all the conditions, affected her as crying it out. Her guest's stare of ignorance, above all — that of itself at first cried it out. "'Between them?' What do you mean?"

"Anything there shouldn't be, there shouldn't have BEEN — all this time. Do you believe there is — or what's your idea?"

Fanny's idea was clearly, to begin with, that her young friend had taken her breath away; but she looked at her very straight and very hard. "Do you speak from a suspicion of your own?"

"I speak, at last, from a torment. Forgive me if it comes out. I've been thinking for months and months, and I've no one to turn to, no one to help me to make things out; no impression but my own, don't you see? to go by."

"You've been thinking for months and months?" Mrs. Assingham took it in. "But WHAT then, dear Maggie, have you been thinking?"

"Well, horrible things — like a little beast that I perhaps am. That there may be something — something wrong and dreadful, something they cover up."

The elder woman's colour had begun to come back; she was able, though with a visible effort, to face the question less amazedly. "You imagine, poor child, that the wretches are in love? Is that it?"

But Maggie for a minute only stared back at her. "Help me to find out WHAT I imagine. I don't know — I've nothing but my perpetual anxiety. Have you any? — do you see what I mean? If you'll tell me truly, that at least, one way or the other, will do something for me."

Fanny's look had taken a peculiar gravity — a fulness with which it seemed to shine. "Is what it comes to that you're jealous of Charlotte?"

"Do you mean whether I hate her?" — and Maggie thought. "No; not on account of father."

"Ah," Mrs. Assingham returned, "that isn't what one would suppose. What I ask is if you're jealous on account of your husband."

"Well," said Maggie presently, "perhaps that may be all. If I'm unhappy I'm jealous; it must come to the same thing; and with you, at least, I'm not afraid of the word. If I'm jealous, don't you see? I'm tormented," she went on —"and all the more if I'm helpless. And if I'm both helpless AND tormented I stuff my pocket-handkerchief into my mouth, I keep it there, for the most part, night and day, so as not to be heard too indecently moaning. Only now, with you, at last, I can't keep it longer; I've pulled it out, and here I am fairly screaming at you. They're away," she wound up, "so they can't hear; and I'm, by a miracle of arrangement, not at luncheon with father at home. I live in the midst of miracles of arrangement, half of which I admit, are my own; I go about on tiptoe, I watch for every sound, I feel every breath, and yet I try all the while to seem as smooth as old satin dyed rose-colour. Have you ever thought of me," she asked, "as really feeling as I do?"

Her companion, conspicuously, required to be clear. "Jealous, unhappy, tormented —? No," said Mrs. Assingham; "but at the same time — and though you may laugh at me for it! — I'm bound to confess that I've never been so awfully sure of what I may call knowing you. Here you are indeed, as you say — such a deep little person! I've never imagined your existence poisoned, and, since you wish to know if I consider that it need be, I've not the least difficulty in speaking on the spot. Nothing, decidedly, strikes me as more unnecessary."

For a minute after this they remained face to face; Maggie had sprung up while her friend sat enthroned, and, after moving to and fro in her intensity, now paused to receive the light she had invoked. It had accumulated, considerably, by this time, round Mrs. Assingham's ample presence, and it made, even to our young woman's own sense, a medium in which she could at last take a deeper breath. "I've affected you, these months — and these last weeks in especial — as quiet and natural and easy?"

But it was a question that took, not imperceptibly, some answering. "You've never affected me, from the first hour I beheld you, as anything but — in a way all your own — absolutely good and sweet and beautiful. In a way, as I say," Mrs. Assingham almost caressingly repeated, "just all your very own — nobody else's at all. I've never thought of you but as OUTSIDE of ugly things, so ignorant of any falsity or cruelty or vulgarity as never to have to be touched by them or to touch them. I've never mixed you up with them; there would have been time enough for that if they had seemed to be near you. But they haven't — if that's what you want to know."

"You've only believed me contented then because you've believed me stupid?"

Mrs. Assingham had a free smile, now, for the length of this stride, dissimulated though it might be in a graceful little frisk. "If I had believed you stupid I shouldn't have thought you interesting, and if I hadn't thought you interesting I shouldn't have noted whether I 'knew' you, as I've called it, or not. What I've always been conscious of is your having concealed about you somewhere no small amount of character; quite as much in fact," Fanny smiled, "as one could suppose a person of your size able to carry. The only thing was," she explained, "that thanks to your never calling one's attention to it, I hadn't made out much more about it, and should have been vague, above all, as to WHERE you carried it or kept it. Somewhere UNDER, I should simply have said — like that little silver cross you once showed me, blest by the Holy Father, that you always wear, out of sight, next your skin. That relic I've had a glimpse of" — with which she continued to invoke the privilege of humour. "But the precious little innermost, say this time little golden, personal nature of you — blest by a greater power, I think, even than the Pope — that you've never consentingly shown me. I'm not sure you've ever consentingly shown it to anyone. You've been in general too modest."

Maggie, trying to follow, almost achieved a little fold of her forehead. "I strike you as modest today — modest when I stand here and scream at you?"

"Oh, your screaming, I've granted you, is something new. I must fit it on somewhere. The question is, however," Mrs. Assingham further proceeded, "of what the deuce I can fit it on TO. Do you mean," she asked, "to the fact of our friends' being, from yesterday to tomorrow, at a place where they may more or less irresponsibly meet?" She spoke with the air of putting it as badly for them as possible. "Are you thinking of their being there alone — of their having consented to be?" And then as she had waited without result for her companion to say: "But isn't it true that — after you had this time again, at the eleventh hour, said YOU wouldn't — they would really much rather not have gone?"

"Yes — they would certainly much rather not have gone. But I wanted them to go."

"Then, my dear child, what in the world is the matter?"

"I wanted to see if they WOULD. And they've had to," Maggie added. "It was the only thing."

Her friend appeared to wonder. "From the moment you and your father backed out?"

"Oh, I don't mean go for those people; I mean go for us. For father and me," Maggie went on. "Because now they know."

"They 'know'?" Fanny Assingham quavered.

"That I've been for some time past taking more notice. Notice of the queer things in our life."

Maggie saw her companion for an instant on the point of asking her what these queer things might be; but Mrs. Assingham had the next minute brushed by that ambiguous opening and taken, as she evidently felt, a better one. "And is it for that you did it? I mean gave up the visit."

"It's for that I did it. To leave them to themselves — as they less and less want, or at any rate less and less venture to appear to want, to be left. As they had for so long arranged things," the Princess went on, "you see they sometimes have to be." And then, as if baffled by the lucidity of this, Mrs. Assingham for a little said nothing: "Now do you think I'm modest?"

With time, however; Fanny could brilliantly think anything that would serve. "I think you're wrong. That, my dear, is my answer to your question. It demands assuredly the straightest I can make. I see no "awfulness' — I suspect none. I'm deeply distressed," she added, "that you should do anything else." It drew again from Maggie a long look. "You've never even imagined anything?"

"Ah, God forbid! — for it's exactly as a woman of imagination that I speak. There's no moment of my life at which I'm not imagining something; and it's thanks to that, darling," Mrs. Assingham pursued, "that I figure the sincerity with which your husband, whom you see as viciously occupied with your stepmother, is interested, is tenderly interested, in his admirable, adorable wife." She paused a minute as to give her friend the full benefit of this — as to Maggie's measure of which, however, no sign came; and then, poor woman, haplessly, she crowned her effort. —"He wouldn't hurt a hair of your head."

It had produced in Maggie, at once, and apparently in the intended form of a smile, the most extraordinary expression. "Ah, there it is!"

But her guest had already gone on. "And I'm absolutely certain that Charlotte wouldn't either."

It kept the Princess, with her strange grimace, standing there. "No — Charlotte wouldn't either. That's how they've had again to go off together. They've been afraid not to — lest it should disturb me, aggravate me, somehow work upon me. As I insisted that they must, that we couldn't all fail — though father and Charlotte hadn't really accepted; as I did this they had to yield to the fear that their showing as afraid to move together would count for them as the greater danger: which would be the danger, you see, of my feeling myself wronged. Their least danger, they know, is in going on with all the things that I've seemed to accept and that I've given no indication, at any moment, of not accepting. Everything that has come up for them has come up, in an extraordinary manner, without my having by a sound or a sign given myself away — so that it's all as wonderful as you may conceive. They move at any rate among the dangers I speak of — between that of their doing too much and that of their not having any longer the confidence, or the nerve, or whatever you may call it, to do enough." Her tone, by this time, might have shown a strangeness to match her smile; which was still more marked as she wound up. "And that's how I make them do what I like!"

It had an effect on Mrs. Assingham, who rose with the deliberation that, from point to point, marked the widening of her grasp. "My dear child, you're amazing."

"Amazing —?"

"You're terrible."

Maggie thoughtfully shook her head. "No; I'm not terrible, and you don't think me so. I do strike you as surprising, no doubt — but surprisingly mild. Because — don't you see? — I AM mild. I can bear anything."

"Oh, 'bear'!" Mrs. Assingham fluted.

"For love," said the Princess.

Fanny hesitated. "Of your father?"

"For love," Maggie repeated.

It kept her friend watching. "Of your husband?"

"For love," Maggie said again.

It was, for the moment, as if the distinctness of this might have determined in her companion a choice between two or three highly different alternatives. Mrs. Assingham's rejoinder, at all events — however much or however little it was a choice — was presently a triumph. "Speaking with this love of your own then, have you undertaken to convey to me that you believe your husband and your father's wife to be in act and in fact lovers of each other?" And then as the Princess didn't at first answer: "Do you call such an allegation as that 'mild'?"

"Oh, I'm not pretending to be mild to you. But I've told you, and moreover you must have seen for yourself, how much so I've been to them."

Mrs. Assingham, more brightly again, bridled. "Is that what you call it when you make them, for terror as you say, do as you like?"

"Ah, there wouldn't be any terror for them if they had nothing to hide."

Mrs. Assingham faced her — quite steady now. "Are you really conscious, love, of what you're saying?"

"I'm saying that I'm bewildered and tormented, and that I've no one but you to speak to. I've thought, I've in fact been sure, that you've seen for yourself how much this is the case. It's why I've believed you would meet me half way."

"Half way to what? To denouncing," Fanny asked, "two persons, friends of years, whom I've always immensely admired and liked, and against whom I haven't the shadow of a charge to make?"

Maggie looked at her with wide eyes. "I had much rather you should denounce me than denounce them. Denounce me, denounce me," she said, "if you can see your way." It was exactly what she appeared to have argued out with herself. "If, conscientiously, you can denounce me; if, conscientiously, you can revile me; if, conscientiously, you can put me in my place for a low-minded little pig —!"

"Well?" said Mrs. Assingham, consideringly, as she paused for emphasis.

"I think I shall be saved."

Her friend took it, for a minute, however, by carrying thoughtful eyes, eyes verily portentous, over her head. "You say you've no one to speak to, and you make a point of your having so disguised your feelings — not having, as you call it, given yourself away. Have you then never seen it not only as your right, but as your bounden duty, worked up to such a pitch, to speak to your husband?"

"I've spoken to him," said Maggie.

Mrs. Assingham stared. "Ah, then it isn't true that you've made no sign."

Maggie had a silence. "I've made no trouble. I've made no scene. I've taken no stand. I've neither reproached nor accused him. You'll say there's a way in all that of being nasty enough."

"Oh!" dropped from Fanny as if she couldn't help it.

"But I don't think — strangely enough — that he regards me as nasty. I think that at bottom — for that IS," said the Princess, "the strangeness — he's sorry for me. Yes, I think that, deep within, he pities me."

Her companion wondered. "For the state you've let yourself get into?"

"For not being happy when I've so much to make me so."

"You've everything," said Mrs. Assingham with alacrity. Yet she remained for an instant embarrassed as to a further advance. "I don't understand, however, how, if you've done nothing —"

An impatience from Maggie had checked her. "I've not done absolutely 'nothing.'"

"But what then —?"

"Well," she went on after a minute, "he knows what I've done."

It produced on Mrs. Assingham's part, her whole tone and manner exquisitely aiding, a hush not less prolonged, and the very duration of which inevitably gave it something of the character of an equal recognition. "And what then has HE done?"

Maggie took again a minute. "He has been splendid."

"'Splendid'? Then what more do you want?"

"Ah, what you see!" said Maggie. "Not to be afraid."

It made her guest again hang fire. "Not to be afraid really to speak?"

"Not to be afraid NOT to speak."

Mrs. Assingham considered further. "You can't even to Charlotte?" But as, at this, after a look at her, Maggie turned off with a movement of suppressed despair, she checked herself and might have been watching her, for all the difficulty and the pity of it, vaguely moving to the window and the view of the hill street. It was almost as if she had had to give up, from failure of responsive wit in her friend — the last failure she had feared — the hope of the particular relief she had been working for. Mrs. Assingham resumed the next instant, however, in the very tone that seemed most to promise her she should have to give up nothing. "I see, I see; you would have in that case too many things to consider." It brought the Princess round again, proving itself thus the note of comprehension she wished most to clutch at. "Don't be afraid."

Maggie took it where she stood — which she was soon able to signify. "Thank-you."

It very properly encouraged her counsellor. "What your idea imputes is a criminal intrigue carried on, from day to day, amid perfect trust and sympathy, not only under your eyes, but under your father's. That's an idea it's impossible for me for a. moment to entertain."

"Ah, there you are then! It's exactly what I wanted from you."

"You're welcome to it!" Mrs. Assingham breathed.

"You never HAVE entertained it?" Maggie pursued.

"Never for an instant," said Fanny with her head very high.

Maggie took it again, yet again as wanting more. "Pardon my being so horrid. But by all you hold sacred?"

Mrs. Assingham faced her. "Ah, my dear, upon my positive word as an honest woman."

"Thank-you then," said the Princess.

So they remained a little; after which, "But do you believe it, love?" Fanny inquired.

"I believe YOU."

"Well, as I've faith in THEM, it comes to the same thing."

Maggie, at this last, appeared for a moment to think again; but she embraced the proposition. "The same thing."

"Then you're no longer unhappy?" her guest urged, coming more gaily toward her.

"I doubtless shan't be a great while."

But it was now Mrs. Assingham's turn to want more. "I've convinced you it's impossible?"

She had held out her arms, and Maggie, after a moment, meeting her, threw herself into them with a sound that had its oddity as a sign of relief. "Impossible, impossible," she emphatically, more than emphatically, replied; yet the next minute she had burst into tears over the impossibility, and a few seconds later, pressing, clinging, sobbing, had even caused them to flow, audibly, sympathetically and perversely, from her friend.

XXXI

The understanding appeared to have come to be that the Colonel and his wife were to present themselves toward the middle of July for the "good long visit" at Fawns on which Maggie had obtained from her father that he should genially insist; as well as that the couple from Eaton Square should welcome there earlier in the month, and less than a week after their own arrival, the advent of the couple from Portland Place. "Oh, we shall give you time to breathe!" Fanny remarked, in reference to the general prospect, with a gaiety that announced itself as heedless of criticism, to each member of the party in turn; sustaining and bracing herself by her emphasis, pushed even to an amiable cynicism, of the confident view of these punctualities of the Assinghams. The ground she could best occupy, to her sense, was that of her being moved, as in this connexion she had always been moved, by the admitted grossness of her avidity, the way the hospitality of the Ververs met her convenience and ministered to her ease, destitute as the Colonel had kept her, from the first, of any rustic retreat, any leafy bower of her own, any fixed base for the stale season now at hand. She had explained at home, she had repeatedly reexplained, the terms of her dilemma, the real difficulty of her, or — as she now put it — of their, position. When the pair could do nothing else, in Cadogan Place, they could still talk of marvellous little Maggie, and of the charm, the sinister charm, of their having to hold their breath to watch her; a topic the momentous midnight discussion at which we have been present was so far from having exhausted. It came up, irrepressibly, at all private hours; they had planted it there between them, and it grew, from day to day, in a manner to make their sense of responsibility almost yield to their sense of fascination. Mrs. Assingham declared at such moments that in the interest of this admirable young thing — to whom, she also declared, she had quite "come over" — she was ready to pass with all the world else, even with the Prince himself, the object, inconsequently, as well, of her continued, her explicitly shameless appreciation, for a vulgar, indelicate, pestilential woman, showing her true character in an abandoned old age. The Colonel's confessed attention had been enlisted, we have seen, as never yet, under pressure from his wife, by any guaranteed imbroglio; but this, she could assure him she perfectly knew, was not a bit because he was sorry for her, or touched by what she had let herself in for, but because, when once they had been opened, he couldn't keep his eyes from resting complacently, resting almost intelligently, on the Princess. If he was in love with HER now, however, so much the better; it would help them both not to wince at what they would have to do for her. Mrs. Assingham had come back to that, whenever he groaned or grunted; she had at no beguiled moment — since Maggie's little march WAS positively beguiling — let him lose sight of the grim necessity awaiting them. "We shall have, as I've again and again told you, to lie for her — to lie till we're black in the face."

"To lie 'for' her?" The Colonel often, at these hours, as from a vague vision of old chivalry in a new form, wandered into apparent lapses from lucidity.

"To lie TO her, up and down, and in and out — it comes to the same thing. It will consist just as much of lying to the others too: to the Prince about one's belief in HIM; to Charlotte about one's belief in HER; to Mr. Verver, dear sweet man, about one's belief in everyone. So we've work cut out — with the biggest lie, on top of all, being that we LIKE to be there for such a purpose. We hate it unspeakably — I'm more ready to be a coward before it, to let the whole thing, to let everyone, selfishly and pusillanimously slide, than before any social duty, any felt human call, that has ever forced me to be decent. I speak at least for myself. For you," she had added, "as I've given you so perfect an opportunity to fall in love with Maggie, you'll doubtless find your account in being so much nearer to her."

"And what do you make," the Colonel could, at this, always imperturbably enough ask, "of the account you yourself will find in being so much nearer to the Prince; of your confirmed, if not exasperated, infatuation with whom — to say nothing of my weak good-nature about it — you give such a pretty picture?"

To the picture in question she had been always, in fact, able contemplatively to return. "The difficulty of my enjoyment of that is, don't you see? that I'm making, in my loyalty to Maggie, a sad hash of his affection for me."

"You find means to call it then, this whitewashing of his crime, being 'loyal' to Maggie?"

"Oh, about that particular crime there is always much to say. It is always more interesting to us than any other crime; it has at least that for it. But of course I call everything I have in mind at all being loyal to Maggie. Being loyal to her is, more than anything else, helping her with her father — which is what she most wants and needs."

The Colonel had had it before, but he could apparently never have too much of it. "Helping her 'with' him —?"

"Helping her against him then. Against what we've already so fully talked of — its having to be recognised between them that he doubts. That's where my part is so plain — to see her through, to see her through to the end." Exaltation, for the moment, always lighted Mrs. Assingham's reference to this plainness; yet she at the same time seldom failed, the next instant, to qualify her view of it. "When I talk of my obligation as clear I mean that it's absolute; for just HOW, from day to day and through thick and thin, to keep the thing up is, I grant you, another matter. There's one way, luckily, nevertheless, in which I'm strong. I can perfectly count on her."

The Colonel seldom failed here, as from the insidious growth of an excitement, to wonder, to encourage. "Not to see you're lying?"

"To stick to me fast, whatever she sees. If I stick to her — that is to my own poor struggling way, under providence, of watching over them ALL — she'll stand by me to the death. She won't give me away. For, you know, she easily can."

This, regularly, was the most lurid turn of their road; but Bob Assingham, with each journey, met it as for the first time. "Easily?"

"She can utterly dishonour me with her father. She can let him know that I was aware, at the time of his marriage — as I had been aware at the time of her own — of the relations that had preexisted between his wife and her husband."

"And how can she do so if, up to this minute, by your own statement, she is herself in ignorance of your knowledge?"

It was a question that Mrs. Assingham had ever, for dealing with, a manner to which repeated practice had given almost a grand effect; very much as if she was invited by it to say that about this, exactly, she proposed to do her best lying. But she said, and with full lucidity, something quite other: it could give itself a little the air, still, of a triumph over his coarseness. "By acting, immediately with the blind resentment with which, in her place, ninety-nine women out of a hundred would act; and by so making Mr. Verver, in turn, act with the same natural passion, the passion of ninety-nine men out of a hundred. They've only to agree about me," the poor lady said; "they've only to feel at one over it, feel bitterly practised upon, cheated and injured; they've only to denounce me to each other as false and infamous, for me to be quite irretrievably dished. Of course it's I who have been, and who continue to be, cheated — cheated by the Prince and Charlotte; but they're not obliged to give me the benefit of that, or to give either of us the benefit of anything. They'll be within their rights to lump us all together as a false, cruel, conspiring crew, and, if they can find the right facts to support them, get rid of us root and branch."

This, on each occasion, put the matter so at the worst that repetition even scarce controlled the hot flush with which she was compelled to see the parts of the whole history, all its ugly consistency and its temporary gloss, hang together. She enjoyed, invariably, the sense of making her danger present, of making it real, to her husband, and of his almost turning pale, when their eyes met, at this possibility of their compromised state and their shared discredit. The beauty was that, as under a touch of one of the ivory notes at the left of the keyboard, he sounded out with the short sharpness of the dear fond stupid uneasy man. "Conspiring — so far as YOU were concerned — to what end?"

"Why, to the obvious end of getting the Prince a wife — at Maggie's expense. And then to that of getting Charlotte a husband at Mr. Verver's."

"Of rendering friendly services, yes — which have produced, as it turns out, complications. But from the moment you didn't do it FOR the complications, why shouldn't you have rendered them?"

It was extraordinary for her, always, in this connexion, how, with time given him, he fell to speaking better for her than she could, in the presence of her clear-cut image of the "worst," speak for herself. Troubled as she was she thus never wholly failed of her amusement by the way. "Oh, isn't what I may have meddled 'for' — so far as it can be proved I did meddle — open to interpretation; by which I mean to Mr. Verver's and Maggie's? Mayn't they see my motive, in the light of that appreciation, as the wish to be decidedly more friendly to the others than to the victimised father and daughter?" She positively liked to keep it up. "Mayn't they see my motive as the determination to serve the Prince, in any case, and at any price, first; to 'place' him comfortably; in other words to find him his fill of money? Mayn't it have all the air for them of a really equivocal, sinister bargain between us — something quite unholy and louche?"

It produced in the poor Colonel, infallibly, the echo. "'Louche,' love —?"

"Why, haven't you said as much yourself? — haven't you put your finger on that awful possibility?"

She had a way now, with his felicities, that made him enjoy being reminded of them. "In speaking of your having always had such a 'mash' —?"

"Such a mash, precisely, for the man I was to help to put so splendidly at his ease. A motherly mash an impartial look at it would show it only as likely to have been — but we're not talking, of course, about impartial looks. We're talking of good innocent people deeply worked upon by a horrid discovery, and going much further, in their view of the lurid, as such people almost always do, than those who have been wider awake, all round, from the first. What I was to have got from my friend, in such a view, in exchange for what I had been able to do for him — well, that would have been an equivalent, of a kind best known to myself, for me shrewdly to consider." And she easily lost herself, each time, in the anxious satisfaction of filling out the picture. "It would have been seen, it would have been heard of, before, the case of the woman a man doesn't want, or of whom he's tired, or for whom he has no use but SUCH uses, and who is capable, in her infatuation, in her passion, of promoting his interests with other women rather than lose sight of him, lose touch of him, cease to have to do with him at all. Cela s'est vu, my dear; and stranger things still — as I needn't tell YOU! Very good then," she wound up; "there is a perfectly possible conception of the behaviour of your sweet wife; since, as I say, there's no imagination so lively, once it's started, as that of really agitated lambs. Lions are nothing to them, for lions are sophisticated, are blasés, are brought up, from the first, to prowling and mauling. It does give us, you'll admit, something to think about. My relief is luckily, however, in what I finally do think."

He was well enough aware, by this time, of what she finally did think; but he was not without a sense, again, also for his amusement by the way. It would have made him, for a spectator of these passages between the pair, resemble not a little the artless child who hears his favourite story told for the twentieth time and enjoys it exactly because he knows what is next to happen. "What of course will pull them up, if they turn out to have less imagination than you assume, is the profit you can have found in furthering Mrs. Verver's marriage. You weren't at least in love with Charlotte."

"Oh," Mrs. Assingham, at this, always brought out, "my hand in that is easily accounted for by my desire to be agreeable to HIM."

"To Mr. Verver?"

"To the Prince — by preventing her in that way from taking, as he was in danger of seeing her do, some husband with whom he wouldn't be able to open, to keep open, so large an account as with his father-inlaw. I've brought her near him, kept her within his reach, as she could never have remained either as a single woman or as the wife of a different man."

"Kept her, on that sweet construction, to be his mistress?"

"Kept her, on that sweet construction, to be his mistress." She brought it out grandly — it had always so, for her own ear as well as, visibly, for her husband's, its effect. "The facilities in the case, thanks to the particular conditions, being so quite ideal."

"Down even to the facility of your minding everything so little — from your own point of view — as to have supplied him with the enjoyment of TWO beautiful women."

"Down even to THAT — to the monstrosity of my folly. But not," Mrs. Assingham added, "'two' of anything. One beautiful woman — and one beautiful fortune. That's what a creature of pure virtue exposes herself to when she suffers her pure virtue, suffers her sympathy, her disinterestedness, her exquisite sense for the lives of others, to carry her too far. Voila."

"I see. It's the way the Ververs have you."

"It's the way the Ververs 'have' me. It's in other words the way they would be able to make such a show to each other of having me — if Maggie weren't so divine."

"She lets you off?" He never failed to insist on all this to the very end; which was how he had become so versed in what she finally thought.

"She lets me off. So that now, horrified and contrite at what I've done, I may work to help her out. And Mr. Verver," she was fond of adding, "lets me off too."

"Then you do believe he knows?"

It determined in her always, there, with a significant pause, a deep immersion in her thought. "I believe he would let me off if he did know — so that I might work to help HIM out. Or rather, really," she went on, "that I might work to help Maggie. That would be his motive, that would be his condition, in forgiving me; just as hers, for me, in fact, her motive and her condition, are my acting to spare her father. But it's with Maggie only that I'm directly concerned; nothing, ever — not a breath, not a look, I'll guarantee — shall I have, whatever happens, from Mr. Verver himself. So it is, therefore, that I shall probably, by the closest possible shave, escape the penalty of my crimes."

"You mean being held responsible."

"I mean being held responsible. My advantage will be that Maggie's such a trump."

"Such a trump that, as you say, she'll stick to you."

"Stick to me, on our understanding — stick to me. For our understanding's signed and sealed." And to brood over it again was ever, for Mrs. Assingham, to break out again with exaltation. "It's a grand, high compact. She has solemnly promised."

"But in words —?"

"Oh yes, in words enough — since it's a matter of words. To keep up HER lie so long as I keep up mine."

"And what do you call 'her' lie?"

"Why, the pretence that she believes me. Believes they're innocent."

"She positively believes then they're guilty? She has arrived at that, she's really content with it, in the absence of proof?" It was here, each time, that Fanny Assingham most faltered; but always at last to get the matter, for her own sense, and with a long sigh, sufficiently straight. "It isn't a question of belief or of proof, absent or present; it's inevitably, with her, a question of natural perception, of insurmountable feeling. She irresistibly knows that there's something between them. But she hasn't 'arrived' at it, as you say, at all; that's exactly what she hasn't done, what she so steadily and intensely refuses to do. She stands off and off, so as not to arrive; she keeps out to sea and away from the rocks, and what she most wants of me is to keep at a safe distance with her — as I, for my own skin, only ask not to come nearer." After which, invariably, she let him have it all. "So far from wanting proof — which she must get, in a manner, by my siding with her — she wants DISproof, as against herself, and has appealed to me, so extraordinarily, to side against her. It's really magnificent, when you come to think of it, the spirit of her appeal. If I'll but cover them up brazenly enough, the others, so as to show, round and about them, as happy as a bird, she on her side will do what she can. If I'll keep them quiet, in a word, it will enable her to gain time — time as against any idea of her father's — and so, somehow, come out. If I'll take care of Charlotte, in particular, she'll take care of the Prince; and it's beautiful and wonderful, really pathetic and exquisite, to see what she feels that time may do for her."

"Ah, but what does she call, poor little thing, 'time'?"

"Well, this summer at Fawns, to begin with. She can live as yet, of course, but from hand to mouth; but she has worked it out for herself, I think, that the very danger of Fawns, superficially looked at, may practically amount to a greater protection. THERE the lovers — if they ARE lovers! — will have to mind. They'll feel it for themselves, unless things are too utterly far gone with them."

"And things are NOT too utterly far gone with them?"

She had inevitably, poor woman, her hesitation for this, but she put down her answer as, for the purchase of some absolutely indispensable article, she would have put down her last shilling. "No."

It made him always grin at her. "Is THAT a lie?"

"Do you think you're worth lying to? If it weren't the truth, for me," she added, "I wouldn't have accepted for Fawns. I CAN, I believe, keep the wretches quiet."

"But how — at the worst?"

"Oh, 'the worst' — don't talk about the worst! I can keep them quiet at the best, I seem to feel, simply by our being there. It will work, from week to week, of itself. You'll see."

He was willing enough to see, but he desired to provide —! "Yet if it doesn't work?"

"Ah, that's talking about the worst!"

Well, it might be; but what were they doing, from morning to night, at this crisis, but talk? "Who'll keep the others?"

"The others —?"

"Who'll keep THEM quiet? If your couple have had a life together, they can't have had it completely without witnesses, without the help of persons, however few, who must have some knowledge, some idea about them. They've had to meet, secretly, protectedly, they've had to arrange; for if they haven't met, and haven't arranged, and haven't thereby, in some quarter or other, had to give themselves away, why are we piling it up so? Therefore if there's evidence, up and down London —"

"There must be people in possession of it? Ah, it isn't all," she always remembered, "up and down London. Some of it must connect them — I mean," she musingly added, "it naturally WOULD — with other places; with who knows what strange adventures, opportunities, dissimulations? But whatever there may have been, it will also all have been buried on the spot. Oh, they've known HOW — too beautifully! But nothing, all the same, is likely to find its way to Maggie of itself."

"Because every one who may have anything to tell, you hold, will have been so squared?" And then inveterately, before she could say — he enjoyed so much coming to this: "What will have squared Lady Castledean?"

"The consciousness" — she had never lost her promptness —"of having no stones to throw at any one else's windows. She has enough to do to guard her own glass. That was what she was doing," Fanny said, "that last morning at Matcham when all of us went off and she kept the Prince and Charlotte over. She helped them simply that she might herself be helped — if it wasn't perhaps, rather, with her ridiculous Mr. Blint, that HE might be. They put in together, therefore, of course, that day; they got it clear — and quite under her eyes; inasmuch as they didn't become traceable again, as we know, till late in the evening." On this historic circumstance Mrs. Assingham was always ready afresh to brood; but she was no less ready, after her brooding, devoutly to add "Only we know nothing whatever else — for which all our stars be thanked!"

The Colonel's gratitude was apt to be less marked. "What did they do for themselves, all the same, from the moment they got that free hand to the moment (long after dinner-time, haven't you told me?) of their turning up at their respective homes?"

"Well, it's none of your business!"

"I don't speak of it as mine, but it's only too much theirs. People are always traceable, in England, when tracings are required. Something, sooner or later, happens; somebody, sooner or later, breaks the holy calm. Murder will out."

"Murder will — but this isn't murder. Quite the contrary perhaps! I verily believe," she had her moments of adding, "that, for the amusement of the row, you would prefer an explosion."

This, however, was a remark he seldom noticed; he wound up, for the most part, after a long, contemplative smoke, with a transition from which no exposed futility in it had succeeded in weaning him. "What I can't for my life make out is your idea of the old boy."

"Charlotte's too inconceivably funny husband? I HAVE no idea."

"I beg your pardon — you've just shown it. You never speak of him but as too inconceivably funny."

"Well, he is," she always confessed. "That is he may be, for all I know, too inconceivably great. But that's not an idea. It represents only my weak necessity of feeling that he's beyond me — which isn't an idea either. You see he MAY be stupid too."

"Precisely — there you are."

"Yet on the other hand," she always went on, "he MAY be sublime: sublimer even than Maggie herself. He may in fact have already been. But we shall never know." With which her tone betrayed perhaps a shade of soreness for the single exemption she didn't yearningly welcome. "THAT I can see."

"Oh, I say —!" It came to affect the Colonel himself with a sense of privation.

"I'm not sure, even, that Charlotte will."

"Oh, my dear, what Charlotte doesn't know —!"

But she brooded and brooded. "I'm not sure even that the Prince will." It seemed privation, in short, for them all. "They'll be mystified, confounded, tormented. But they won't know — and all their possible putting their heads together won't make them. That," said Fanny Assingham, "will be their punishment." And she ended, ever, when she had come so far, at the same pitch. "It will probably also — if I get off with so little — be mine."

"And what," her husband liked to ask, "will be mine?"

"Nothing — you're not worthy of any. One's punishment is in what one feels, and what will make ours effective is that we SHALL feel." She was splendid with her "ours"; she flared up with this prophecy. "It will be Maggie herself who will mete it out."

"Maggie —?"

"SHE'LL know — about her father; everything. Everything," she repeated. On the vision of which, each time, Mrs. Assingham, as with the presentiment of an odd despair, turned away from it. "But she'll never tell us."

XXXII

If Maggie had not so firmly made up her mind never to say, either to her good friend or to any one else, more than she meant about her father, she might have found herself betrayed into some such overflow during the week spent in London with her husband after the others had adjourned to Fawns for the summer. This was because of the odd element of the unnatural imparted to the so simple fact of their brief separation by the assumptions resident in their course of life hitherto. She was used, herself, certainly, by this time, to dealing with odd elements; but she dropped, instantly, even from such peace as she had patched up, when it was a question of feeling that her unpenetrated parent might be alone with them. She thought of him as alone with them when she thought of him as alone with Charlotte — and this, strangely enough, even while fixing her sense to the full on his wife's power of preserving, quite of enhancing, every felicitous appearance. Charlotte had done that — under immeasurably fewer difficulties indeed — during the numerous months of their hymeneal absence from England, the period prior to that wonderful reunion of the couples, in the interest of the larger play of all the virtues of each, which was now bearing, for Mrs. Verver's stepdaughter at least, such remarkable fruit. It was the present so much briefer interval, in a situation, possibly in a relation, so changed — it was the new terms of her problem that would tax Charlotte's art. The Princess could pull herself up, repeatedly, by remembering that the real "relation" between her father and his wife was a thing that she knew nothing about and that, in strictness, was none of her business; but she none the less failed to keep quiet, as she would have called it, before the projected image of their ostensibly happy isolation. Nothing could have had less of the quality of quietude than a certain queer wish that fitfully flickered up in her, a wish that usurped, perversely, the place of a much more natural one. If Charlotte, while she was about it, could only have been WORSE! — that idea Maggie fell to invoking instead of the idea that she might desirably have been better. For, exceedingly odd as it was to feel in such ways, she believed she mightn't have worried so much if she didn't somehow make her stepmother out, under the beautiful trees and among the dear old gardens, as lavish of fifty kinds of confidence and twenty kinds, at least, of gentleness. Gentleness and confidence were certainly the right thing, as from a charming woman to her husband, but the fine tissue of reassurance woven by this lady's hands and flung over her companion as a light, muffling veil, formed precisely a wrought transparency through which she felt her father's eyes continually rest on herself. The reach of his gaze came to her straighter from a distance; it showed him as still more conscious, down there alone, of the suspected, the felt elaboration of the process of their not alarming or hurting him. She had herself now, for weeks and weeks, and all unwinkingly, traced the extension of this pious effort; but her perfect success in giving no sign — she did herself THAT credit — would have been an achievement quite wasted if Mrs. Verver should make with him those mistakes of proportion, one set of them too abruptly, too incoherently designed to correct another set, that she had made with his daughter. However, if she HAD been worse, poor woman, who should say that her husband would, to a certainty, have been better?

One groped noiselessly among such questions, and it was actually not even definite for the Princess that her own Amerigo, left alone with her in town, had arrived at the golden mean of non-precautionary gallantry which would tend, by his calculation, to brush private criticism from its last perching-place. The truth was, in this connection, that she had different sorts of terrors, and there were hours when it came to her that these days were a prolonged repetition of that night-drive, of weeks before, from the other house to their own, when he had tried to charm her, by his sovereign personal power, into some collapse that would commit her to a repudiation of consistency. She was never alone with him, it was to be said, without her having sooner or later to ask herself what had already become of her consistency; yet, at the same time, so long as she breathed no charge, she kept hold of a remnant of appearance that could save her from attack. Attack, real attack, from him, as he would conduct it was what she above all dreaded; she was so far from sure that under that experience she mightn't drop into some depth of weakness, mightn't show him some shortest way with her that he would know how to use again. Therefore, since she had given him, as yet, no moment's pretext for pretending to her that she had either lost faith or suffered by a feather's weight in happiness, she left him, it was easy to reason, with an immense advantage for all waiting and all tension. She wished him, for the present, to "make up" to her for nothing. Who could say to what making-up might lead, into what consenting or pretending or destroying blindness it might plunge her? She loved him too helplessly, still, to dare to open the door, by an inch, to his treating her as if either of them had wronged the other. Something or somebody — and who, at this, which of them all? — would inevitably, would in the gust of momentary selfishness, be sacrificed to that; whereas what she intelligently needed was to know where she was going. Knowledge, knowledge, was a fascination as well as a fear; and a part, precisely, of the strangeness of this juncture was the way her apprehension that he would break out to her with some merely general profession was mixed with her dire need to forgive him, to reassure him, to respond to him, on no ground that she didn't fully measure. To do these things it must be clear to her what they were FOR; but to act in that light was, by the same effect, to learn, horribly, what the other things had been. He might tell her only what he wanted, only what would work upon her by the beauty of his appeal; and the result of the direct appeal of ANY beauty in him would be her helpless submission to his terms. All her temporary safety, her hand-to-mouth success, accordingly, was in his neither perceiving nor divining this, thanks to such means as she could take to prevent him; take, literally from hour to hour, during these days of more unbroken exposure. From hour to hour she fairly expected some sign of his having decided on a jump. "Ah yes, it HAS been as you think; I've strayed away, I've fancied myself free, given myself in other quantities, with larger generosities, because I thought you were different — different from what I now see. But it was only, only, because I didn't know — and you must admit that you gave me scarce reason enough. Reason enough, I mean, to keep clear of my mistake; to which I confess, for which I'll do exquisite penance, which you can help me now, I too beautifully feel, to get completely over."

That was what, while she watched herself, she potentially heard him bring out; and while she carried to an end another day, another sequence and yet another of their hours together, without his producing it, she felt herself occupied with him beyond even the intensity of surrender. She was keeping her head, for a reason, for a cause; and the labour of this detachment, with the labour of her keeping the pitch of it down, held them together in the steel hoop of an intimacy compared with which artless passion would have been but a beating of the air. Her greatest danger, or at least her greatest motive for care, was the obsession of the thought that, if he actually did suspect, the fruit of his attention to her couldn't help being a sense of the growth of her importance. Taking the measure, with him, as she had taken it with her father, of the prescribed reach of her hypocrisy, she saw how it would have to stretch even to her seeking to prove that she was NOT, all the same, important. A single touch from him — oh, she should know it in case of its coming! — any brush of his hand, of his lips, of his voice, inspired by recognition of her probable interest as distinct from pity for her virtual gloom, would hand her over to him bound hand and foot. Therefore to be free, to be free to act, other than abjectly, for her father, she must conceal from him the validity that, like a microscopic insect pushing a grain of sand, she was taking on even for herself. She could keep it up with a change in sight, but she couldn't keep it up forever; so that, really, one extraordinary effect of their week of untempered confrontation, which bristled with new marks, was to make her reach out, in thought, to their customary companions and calculate the kind of relief that rejoining them would bring. She was learning, almost from minute to minute, to be a mistress of shades since, always, when there were possibilities enough of intimacy, there were also, by that fact, in intercourse, possibilities of iridescence; but she was working against an adversary who was a master of shades too, and on whom, if she didn't look out, she should presently have imposed a consciousness of the nature of their struggle. To feel him in fact, to think of his feeling himself, her adversary in things of this fineness — to see him at all, in short, brave a name that would represent him as in opposition — was already to be nearly reduced to a visible smothering of her cry of alarm.

Should he guess they were having, in their so occult manner, a HIGH fight, and that it was she, all the while, in her supposed stupidity, who had made it high and was keeping it high — in the event of his doing this before they could leave town she should verily be lost.

The possible respite for her at Fawns would come from the fact that observation, in him, there, would inevitably find some of its directness diverted. This would be the case if only because the remarkable strain of her father's placidity might be thought of as likely to claim some larger part of his attention. Besides which there would be always Charlotte herself to draw him off. Charlotte would help him again, doubtless, to study anything, right or left, that might be symptomatic; but Maggie could see that this very fact might perhaps contribute, in its degree, to protect the secret of her own fermentation. It is not even incredible that she may have discovered the gleam of a comfort that was to broaden in the conceivable effect on the Prince's spirit, on his nerves, on his finer irritability, of some of the very airs and aspects, the light graces themselves, of Mrs. Verver's too perfect competence. What it would most come to, after all, she said to herself, was a renewal for him of the privilege of watching that lady watch her. Very well, then: with the elements after all so mixed in him, how long would he go on enjoying mere spectatorship of that act? For she had by this time made up her mind that in Charlotte's company he deferred to Charlotte's easier art of mounting guard. Wouldn't he get tired — to put it only at that — of seeing her always on the rampart, erect and elegant, with her lace-flounced parasol now folded and now shouldered, march to and fro against a gold-coloured east or west? Maggie had gone far, truly for a view of the question of this particular reaction, and she was not incapable of pulling herself up with the rebuke that she counted her chickens before they were hatched. How sure she should have to be of so many things before she might thus find a weariness in Amerigo's expression and a logic in his weariness!

One of her dissimulated arts for meeting their tension, meanwhile, was to interweave Mrs. Assingham as plausibly as possible with the undulations of their surface, to bring it about that she should join them, of an afternoon, when they drove together or if they went to look at things — looking at things being almost as much a feature of their life as if they were bazaar-opening royalties. Then there were such combinations, later in the day, as her attendance on them, and the Colonel's as well, for such whimsical matters as visits to the opera no matter who was singing, and sudden outbreaks of curiosity about the British drama. The good couple from Cadogan Place could always unprotestingly dine with them and "go on" afterwards to such publicities as the Princess cultivated the boldness of now perversely preferring. It may be said of her that, during these passages, she plucked her sensations by the way, detached, nervously, the small wild blossoms of her dim forest, so that she could smile over them at least with the spacious appearance, for her companions, for her husband above all, of bravely, of altogether frivolously, going a-maying. She had her intense, her smothered excitements, some of which were almost inspirations; she had in particular the extravagant, positively at moments the amused, sense of using her friend to the topmost notch, accompanied with the high luxury of not having to explain. Never, no never, should she have to explain to Fanny Assingham again — who, poor woman, on her own side, would be charged, it might be forever, with that privilege of the higher ingenuity. She put it all off on Fanny, and the dear thing herself might henceforth appraise the quantity. More and more magnificent now in her blameless egoism, Maggie asked no questions of her, and thus only signified the greatness of the opportunity she gave her. She didn't care for what devotions, what dinners of their own the Assinghams might have been "booked"; that was a detail, and she could think without wincing of the ruptures and rearrangements to which her service condemned them. It all fell in beautifully, moreover; so that, as hard, at this time, in spite of her fever, as a little pointed diamond, the Princess showed something of the glitter of consciously possessing the constructive, the creative hand. She had but to have the fancy of presenting herself, of presenting her husband, in a certain high and convenient manner, to make it natural they should go about with their gentleman and their lady. To what else but this, exactly, had Charlotte, during so many weeks of the earlier season, worked her up? — herself assuming and discharging, so far as might be, the character and office of one of those revolving subordinate presences that float in the wake of greatness.

The precedent was therefore established and the group normally constituted. Mrs. Assingham, meanwhile, at table, on the stairs, in the carriage or the opera-box, might — with her constant overflow of expression, for that matter, and its singularly resident character where men in especial were concerned — look across at Amerigo in whatever sense she liked: it was not of that Maggie proposed to be afraid. She might warn him, she might rebuke him, she might reassure him, she might — if it were impossible not to — absolutely make love to him; even this was open to her, as a matter simply between them, if it would help her to answer for the impeccability he had guaranteed. And Maggie desired in fact only to strike her as acknowledging the efficacy of her aid when she mentioned to her one evening a small project for the morrow, privately entertained — the idea, irresistible, intense, of going to pay, at the Museum, a visit to Mr. Crichton. Mr. Crichton, as Mrs. Assingham could easily remember, was the most accomplished and obliging of public functionaries, whom every one knew and who knew every one — who had from the first, in particular, lent himself freely, and for the love of art and history, to becoming one of the steadier lights of Mr. Verver's adventurous path. The custodian of one of the richest departments of the great national collection of precious things, he could feel for the sincere private collector and urge him on his way even when condemned to be present at his capture of trophies sacrificed by the country to parliamentary thrift. He carried his amiability to the point of saying that, since London, under pettifogging views, had to miss, from time to time, its rarest opportunities, he was almost consoled to see such lost causes invariably wander at last, one by one, with the tormenting tinkle of their silver bells, into the wondrous, the already famous fold beyond the Mississippi. There was a charm in his "almosts" that was not to be resisted, especially after Mr. Verver and Maggie had grown sure — or almost, again — of enjoying the monopoly of them; and on this basis of envy changed to sympathy by the more familiar view of the father and the daughter, Mr. Crichton had at both houses, though especially in Eaton Square, learned to fill out the responsive and suggestive character. It was at his invitation, Fanny well recalled, that Maggie, one day, long before, and under her own attendance precisely, had, for the glory of the name she bore, paid a visit to one of the ampler shrines of the supreme exhibitory temple, an alcove of shelves charged with the gold-and-brown, gold-and-ivory, of old Italian bindings and consecrated to the records of the Prince's race. It had been an impression that penetrated, that remained; yet Maggie had sighed, ever so prettily, at its having to be so superficial. She was to go back some day, to dive deeper, to linger and taste; in spite of which, however, Mrs. Assingham could not recollect perceiving that the visit had been repeated. This second occasion had given way, for a long time, in her happy life, to other occasions — all testifying, in their degree, to the quality of her husband's blood, its rich mixture and its many remarkable references; after which, no doubt, the charming piety involved had grown, on still further grounds, bewildered and faint.

It now appeared, none the less, that some renewed conversation with Mr. Crichton had breathed on the faintness revivingly, and Maggie mentioned her purpose as a conception of her very own, to the success of which she designed to devote her morning. Visits of gracious ladies, under his protection, lighted up rosily, for this perhaps most flower-loving and honey-sipping member of the great Bloomsbury hive, its packed passages and cells; and though not sworn of the province toward which his friend had found herself, according to her appeal to him, yearning again, nothing was easier for him than to put her in relation with the presiding urbanities. So it had been settled, Maggie said to Mrs. Assingham, and she was to dispense with Amerigo's company. Fanny was to remember later on that she had at first taken this last fact for one of the finer notes of her young woman's detachment, imagined she must be going alone because of the shade of irony that, in these ambiguous days, her husband's personal presence might be felt to confer, practically, on any tribute to his transmitted significance. Then as, the next moment, she felt it clear that so much plotted freedom was virtually a refinement of reflection, an impulse to commemorate afresh whatever might still survive of pride and hope, her sense of ambiguity happily fell and she congratulated her companion on having anything so exquisite to do and on being so exquisitely in the humour to do it. After the occasion had come and gone she was confirmed in her optimism; she made out, in the evening, that the hour spent among the projected lights, the annals and illustrations, the parchments and portraits, the emblazoned volumes and the murmured commentary, had been for the Princess enlarging and inspiring. Maggie had said to her some days before, very sweetly but very firmly, "Invite us to dine, please, for Friday, and have any one you like or you can — it doesn't in the least matter whom;" and the pair in Cadogan Place had bent to this mandate with a docility not in the least ruffled by all that it took for granted.

It provided for an evening — this had been Maggie's view; and she lived up to her view, in her friend's eyes, by treating the occasion, more or less explicitly, as new and strange. The good Assinghams had feasted in fact at the two other boards on a scale so disproportionate to the scant solicitations of their own that it was easy to make a joke of seeing how they fed at home, how they met, themselves, the question of giving to eat. Maggie dined with them, in short, and arrived at making her husband appear to dine, much in the manner of a pair of young sovereigns who have, in the frolic humour of the golden years of reigns, proposed themselves to a pair of faithfully-serving subjects. She showed an interest in their arrangements, an inquiring tenderness almost for their economies; so that her hostess not unnaturally, as they might have said, put it all down — the tone and the freedom of which she set the example — to the effect wrought in her afresh by one of the lessons learned, in the morning, at the altar of the past. Hadn't she picked it up, from an anecdote or two offered again to her attention, that there were, for princesses of such a line, more ways than one of being a heroine? Maggie's way to-night was to surprise them all, truly, by the extravagance of her affability. She was doubtless not positively boisterous; yet, though Mrs. Assingham, as a bland critic, had never doubted her being graceful, she had never seen her put so much of it into being what might have been called assertive. It was all a tune to which Fanny's heart could privately palpitate: her guest was happy, happy as a consequence of something that had occurred, but she was making the Prince not lose a ripple of her laugh, though not perhaps always enabling him to find it absolutely not foolish. Foolish, in public, beyond a certain point, he was scarce the man to brook his wife's being thought to be; so that there hovered before their friend the possibility of some subsequent scene between them, in the carriage or at home, of slightly sarcastic inquiry, of promptly invited explanation; a scene that, according as Maggie should play her part in it, might or might not precipitate developments. What made these appearances practically thrilling, meanwhile, was this mystery — a mystery, it was clear, to Amerigo himself — of the incident or the influence that had so peculiarly determined them.

The lady of Cadogan Place was to read deeper, however, within three days, and the page was turned for her on the eve of her young confidant's leaving London. The awaited migration to Fawns was to take place on the morrow, and it was known meanwhile to Mrs. Assingham that their party of four were to dine that night, at the American Embassy, with another and a larger party; so that the elder woman had a sense of surprise on receiving from the younger, under date of six o'clock, a telegram requesting her immediate attendance. "Please come to me at once; dress early, if necessary, so that we shall have time: the carriage, ordered for us, will take you back first." Mrs. Assingham, on quick deliberation, dressed, though not perhaps with full lucidity, and by seven o'clock was in Portland Place, where her friend, "upstairs" and described to her on her arrival as herself engaged in dressing, instantly received her. She knew on the spot, poor Fanny, as she was afterwards to declare to the Colonel, that her feared crisis had popped up as at the touch of a spring, that her impossible hour was before her. Her impossible hour was the hour of its coming out that she had known of old so much more than she had ever said; and she had often put it to herself, in apprehension, she tried to think even in preparation, that she should recognise the approach of her doom by a consciousness akin to that of the blowing open of a window on some night of the highest wind and the lowest thermometer. It would be all in vain to have crouched so long by the fire; the glass would have been smashed, the icy air would fill the place. If the air in Maggie's room then, on her going up, was not, as yet, quite the polar blast she had expected, it was distinctly, none the less, such an atmosphere as they had not hitherto breathed together. The Princess, she perceived, was completely dressed — that business was over; it added indeed to the effect of her importantly awaiting the assistance she had summoned, of her showing a deck cleared, so to speak, for action. Her maid had already left her, and she presented herself, in the large, clear room, where everything was admirable, but where nothing was out of place, as, for the first time in her life rather "bedizened." Was it that she had put on too many things, overcharged herself with jewels, wore in particular more of them than usual, and bigger ones, in her hair? — a question her visitor presently answered by attributing this appearance largely to the bright red spot, red as some monstrous ruby, that burned in either of her cheeks. These two items of her aspect had, promptly enough, their own light for Mrs. Assingham, who made out by it that nothing more pathetic could be imagined than the refuge and disguise her agitation had instinctively asked of the arts of dress, multiplied to extravagance, almost to incoherence. She had had, visibly, her idea — that of not betraying herself by inattentions into which she had never yet fallen, and she stood there circled about and furnished forth, as always, in a manner that testified to her perfect little personal processes. It had ever been her sign that she was, for all occasions, FOUND ready, without loose ends or exposed accessories or unremoved superfluities; a suggestion of the swept and garnished, in her whole splendid, yet thereby more or less encumbered and embroidered setting, that reflected her small still passion for order and symmetry, for objects with their backs to the walls, and spoke even of some probable reference, in her American blood, to dusting and polishing New England grandmothers. If her apartment was "princely," in the clearness of the lingering day, she looked as if she had been carried there prepared, all attired and decorated, like some holy image in a procession, and left, precisely, to show what wonder she could work under pressure. Her friend felt — how could she not? — as the truly pious priest might feel when confronted, behind the altar, before the festa, with his miraculous Madonna. Such an occasion would be grave, in general, with all the gravity of what he might look for. But the gravity to-night would be of the rarest; what he might look for would depend so on what he could give.

XXXIII

"Something very strange has happened, and I think you ought to know it."

Maggie spoke this indeed without extravagance, yet with the effect of making her guest measure anew the force of her appeal. It was their definite understanding: whatever Fanny knew Fanny's faith would provide for. And she knew, accordingly, at the end of five minutes, what the extraordinary, in the late occurrence, had consisted of, and how it had all come of Maggie's achieved hour, under Mr. Crichton's protection, at the Museum. He had desired, Mr. Crichton, with characteristic kindness, after the wonderful show, after offered luncheon at his incorporated lodge hard by, to see her safely home; especially on his noting, in attending her to the great steps, that she had dismissed her carriage; which she had done, really, just for the harmless amusement of taking her way alone. She had known she should find herself, as the consequence of such an hour, in a sort of exalted state, under the influence of which a walk through the London streets would be exactly what would suit her best; an independent ramble, impressed, excited, contented, with nothing to mind and nobody to talk to, and shop-windows in plenty to look at if she liked: a low taste, of the essence, it was to be supposed, of her nature, that she had of late, for so many reasons, been unable to gratify. She had taken her leave, with her thanks — she knew her way quite enough; it being also sufficiently the case that she had even a shy hope of not going too straight. To wander a little wild was what would truly amuse her; so that, keeping clear of Oxford Street and cultivating an impression as of parts she didn't know, she had ended with what she had more or less had been fancying, an encounter with three or four shops — an old bookseller's, an old printmonger's, a couple of places with dim antiquities in the window — that were not as so many of the other shops, those in Sloane Street, say; a hollow parade which had long since ceased to beguile. There had remained with her moreover an allusion of Charlotte's, of some months before — seed dropped into her imagination in the form of a casual speech about there being in Bloomsbury such "funny little fascinating" places and even sometimes such unexpected finds. There could perhaps have been no stronger mark than this sense of well-nigh romantic opportunity — no livelier sign of the impression made on her, and always so long retained, so watchfully nursed, by any observation of Charlotte's, however lightly thrown off. And then she had felt, somehow, more at her ease than for months and months before; she didn't know why, but her time at the Museum, oddly, had done it; it was as if she hadn't come into so many noble and beautiful associations, nor secured them also for her boy, secured them even for her father, only to see them turn to vanity and doubt, turn possibly to something still worse. "I believed in him again as much as ever, and I felt how I believed in him," she said with bright, fixed eyes; "I felt it in the streets as I walked along, and it was as if that helped me and lifted me up, my being off by myself there, not having, for the moment, to wonder and watch; having, on the contrary, almost nothing on my mind."

It was so much as if everything would come out right that she had fallen to thinking of her father's birthday, had given herself this as a reason for trying what she could pick up for it. They would keep it at Fawns, where they had kept it before — since it would be the twenty-first of the month; and she mightn't have another chance of making sure of something to offer him. There was always the impossibility, of course, of finding him anything, the least bit "good," that he wouldn't already, long ago, in his rummagings, have seen himself — and only not to think a quarter good enough; this, however, was an old story, and one could not have had any fun with him but for his sweet theory that the individual gift, the friendship's offering, was, by a rigorous law of nature, a foredoomed aberration, and that the more it was so the more it showed, and the more one cherished it for showing, how friendly it had been. The infirmity of art was the candour of affection, the grossness of pedigree the refinement of sympathy; the ugliest objects, in fact, as a general thing, were the bravest, the tenderest mementos, and, as such, figured in glass cases apart, worthy doubtless of the home, but not worthy of the temple — dedicated to the grimacing, not to the clear-faced, gods. She herself, naturally, through the past years, had come to be much represented in those receptacles; against the thick, locked panes of which she still liked to flatten her nose, finding in its place, each time, everything she had on successive anniversaries tried to believe he might pretend, at her suggestion, to be put off with, or at least think curious. She was now ready to try it again: they had always, with his pleasure in her pretence and her pleasure in his, with the funny betrayal of the sacrifice to domestic manners on either side, played the game so happily. To this end, on her way home, she had loitered everywhere; quite too deludedly among the old books and the old prints, which had yielded nothing to her purpose, but with a strange inconsequence in one of the other shops, that of a small antiquarian, a queer little foreign man, who had shown her a number of things, shown her finally something that, struck with it as rather a rarity and thinking it would, compared to some of her ventures, quite superlatively do, she had bought — bought really, when it came to that, for a price. "It appears now it won't do at all," said Maggie, "something has happened since that puts it quite out of the question. I had only my day of satisfaction in it, but I feel, at the same time, as I keep it here before me, that I wouldn't have missed it for the world."

She had talked, from the first of her friend's entrances coherently enough, even with a small quaver that overstated her calm; but she held her breath every few seconds, as if for deliberation and to prove she didn't pant — all of which marked for Fanny the depth of her commotion: her reference to her thought about her father, about her chance to pick up something that might divert him, her mention, in fine, of his fortitude under presents, having meanwhile, naturally, it should be said, much less an amplitude of insistence on the speaker's lips than a power to produce on the part of the listener herself the prompt response and full comprehension of memory and sympathy, of old amused observation. The picture was filled out by the latter's fond fancy. But Maggie was at any rate under arms; she knew what she was doing and had already her plan — a plan for making, for allowing, as yet, "no difference"; in accordance with which she would still dine out, and not with red eyes, nor convulsed features, nor neglected items of appearance, nor anything that would raise a question. Yet there was some knowledge that, exactly to this support of her not breaking down, she desired, she required, possession of; and, with the sinister rise and fall of lightning unaccompanied by thunder, it played before Mrs. Assingham's eyes that she herself should have, at whatever risk or whatever cost, to supply her with the stuff of her need. All our friend's instinct was to hold off from this till she should see what the ground would bear; she would take no step nearer unless INTELLIGIBLY to meet her, and, awkward though it might be to hover there only pale and distorted, with mere imbecilities of vagueness, there was a quality of bald help in the fact of not as yet guessing what such an ominous start could lead to. She caught, however, after a second's thought, at the Princess's allusion to her lost reassurance.

"You mean you were so at your ease on Monday — the night you dined with us?"

"I was very happy then," said Maggie.

"Yes — we thought you so gay and so brilliant." Fanny felt it feeble, but she went on. "We were so glad you were happy."

Maggie stood a moment, at first only looking at her. "You thought me all right, eh?"

"Surely, dearest; we thought you all right."

"Well, I daresay it was natural; but in point of fact I never was more wrong in my life. For, all the while, if you please, this was brewing."

Mrs. Assingham indulged, as nearly as possible to luxury, her vagueness. "'This' —?"

"THAT!" replied the Princess, whose eyes, her companion now saw, had turned to an object on the chimney-piece of the room, of which, among so many precious objects — the Ververs, wherever they might be, always revelled peculiarly in matchless old mantel ornaments — her visitor had not taken heed.

"Do you mean the gilt cup?"

"I mean the gilt cup."

The piece now recognised by Fanny as new to her own vision was a capacious bowl, of old-looking, rather strikingly yellow gold, mounted, by a short stem, on an ample foot, which held a central position above the fire-place, where, to allow it the better to show, a clearance had been made of other objects, notably of the Louis-Seize clock that accompanied the candelabra. This latter trophy ticked at present on the marble slab of a commode that exactly matched it in splendour and style. Mrs. Assingham took it, the bowl, as a fine thing; but the question was obviously not of its intrinsic value, and she kept off from it, admiring it at a distance. "But what has that to do —?"

"It has everything. You'll see." With which again, however, for the moment, Maggie attached to her strange wide eyes. "He knew her before — before I had ever seen him."

" 'He' knew —?" But Fanny, while she cast about her for the links she missed, could only echo it.

"Amerigo knew Charlotte — more than I ever dreamed."

Fanny felt then it was stare for stare. "But surely you always knew they had met."

"I didn't understand. I knew too little. Don't you see what I mean?" the Princess asked.

Mrs. Assingham wondered, during these instants, how much she even now knew; it had taken a minute to perceive how gently she was speaking. With that perception of its being no challenge of wrath, no heat of the deceived soul, but only a free exposure of the completeness of past ignorance, inviting derision even if it must, the elder woman felt, first, a strange, barely credible relief: she drew in, as if it had been the warm summer scent of a flower, the sweet certainty of not meeting, any way she should turn, any consequence of judgment. She shouldn't be judged — save by herself; which was her own wretched business. The next moment, however, at all events, she blushed, within, for her immediate cowardice: she had thought of herself, thought of "getting off," before so much as thinking — that is of pitifully seeing — that she was in presence of an appeal that was ALL an appeal, that utterly accepted its necessity. "In a general way, dear child, yes. But not — a — in connexion with what you've been telling me."

"They were intimate, you see. Intimate," said the Princess.

Fanny continued to face her, taking from her excited eyes this history, so dim and faint for all her anxious emphasis, of the far-away other time. "There's always the question of what one considers —!"

"What one considers intimate? Well, I know what I consider intimate now. Too intimate," said Maggie, "to let me know anything about it."

It was quiet — yes; but not too quiet for Fanny Assingham's capacity to wince. "Only compatible with letting ME, you mean?" She had asked it after a pause, but turning again to the new ornament of the chimney and wondering, even while she took relief from it, at this gap in her experience. "But here are things, my dear, of which my ignorance is perfect."

"They went about together — they're known to have done it. And I don't mean only before — I mean after."

"After?" said Fanny Assingham.

"Before we were married — yes; but after we were engaged."

"Ah, I've known nothing about that!" And she said it with a braver assurance — clutching, with comfort, at something that was apparently new to her.

"That bowl," Maggie went on, "is, so strangely — too strangely, almost, to believe at this time of day — the proof. They were together all the while — up to the very eve of our marriage. Don't you remember how just before that she came back, so unexpectedly, from America?"

The question had for Mrs. Assingham — and whether all consciously or not — the oddest pathos of simplicity. "Oh yes, dear, of course I remember how she came back from America — and how she stayed with US, and what view one had of it."

Maggie's eyes still, all the time, pressed and penetrated; so that, during a moment, just here, she might have given the little flare, have made the little pounce, of asking what then "one's" view had been. To the small flash of this eruption Fanny stood, for her minute, wittingly exposed; but she saw it as quickly cease to threaten — quite saw the Princess, even though in all her pain, refuse, in the interest of their strange and exalted bargain, to take advantage of the opportunity for planting the stab of reproach, the opportunity thus coming all of itself. She saw her — or she believed she saw her — look at her chance for straight denunciation, look at it and then pass it by; and she felt herself, with this fact, hushed well-nigh to awe at the lucid higher intention that no distress could confound and that no discovery — since it was, however obscurely, a case of "discovery" — could make less needful. These seconds were brief — they rapidly passed; but they lasted long enough to renew our friend's sense of her own extraordinary undertaking, the function again imposed on her, the answerability again drilled into her, by this intensity of intimation. She was reminded of the terms on which she was let off — her quantity of release having made its sufficient show in that recall of her relation to Charlotte's old reappearance; and deep within the whole impression glowed — ah, so inspiringly when it came to that! her steady view, clear from the first, of the beauty of her companion's motive. It was like a fresh sacrifice for a larger conquest "Only see me through now, do it in the face of this and in spite of it, and I leave you a hand of which the freedom isn't to be said!" The aggravation of fear — or call it, apparently, of knowledge — had jumped straight into its place as an aggravation above all for her father; the effect of this being but to quicken to passion her reasons for making his protectedness, or in other words the forms of his ignorance, still the law of her attitude and the key to her solution. She kept as tight hold of these reasons and these forms, in her confirmed horror, as the rider of a plunging horse grasps his seat with his knees; and she might absolutely have been putting it to her guest that she believed she could stay on if they should only "meet" nothing more. Though ignorant still of what she had definitely met Fanny yearned, within, over her spirit; and so, no word about it said, passed, through mere pitying eyes, a vow to walk ahead and, at crossroads, with a lantern for the darkness and wavings away for unadvised traffic, look out for alarms. There was accordingly no wait in Maggie's reply. "They spent together hours — spent at least a morning — the certainty of which has come back to me now, but that I didn't dream of it at the time. That cup there has turned witness — by the most wonderful of chances. That's why, since it has been here, I've stood it out for my husband to see; put it where it would meet him, almost immediately, if he should come into the room. I've wanted it to meet him," she went on, "and I've wanted him to meet it, and to be myself present at the meeting. But that hasn't taken place as yet; often as he has lately been in the way of coming to see me here — yes, in particular lately — he hasn't showed today." It was with her managed quietness, more and more, that she talked — an achieved coherence that helped her, evidently, to hear and to watch herself; there was support, and thereby an awful harmony, but which meant a further guidance, in the facts she could add together. "It's quite as if he had an instinct — something that has warned him off or made him uneasy. He doesn't quite know, naturally, what has happened, but guesses, with his beautiful cleverness, that something has, and isn't in a hurry to be confronted with it. So, in his vague fear, he keeps off."

"But being meanwhile in the house —?"

"I've no idea — not having seen him today, by exception, since before luncheon. He spoke to me then," the Princess freely explained, "of a ballot, of great importance, at a club — for somebody, some personal friend, I think, who's coming up and is supposed to be in danger. To make an effort for him he thought he had better lunch there. You see the efforts he can make" — for which Maggie found a smile that went to her friend's heart. "He's in so many ways the kindest of men. But it was hours ago."

Mrs. Assingham thought. "The more danger then of his coming in and finding me here. I don't know, you see, what you now consider that you've ascertained; nor anything of the connexion with it of that object that you declare so damning." Her eyes rested on this odd acquisition and then quitted it, went back to it and again turned from it: it was inscrutable in its rather stupid elegance, and yet, from the moment one had thus appraised it, vivid and definite in its domination of the scene. Fanny could no more overlook it now than she could have overlooked a lighted Christmas-tree; but nervously and all in vain she dipped into her mind for some floating reminiscence of it. At the same time that this attempt left her blank she understood a good deal, she even not a little shared the Prince's mystic apprehension. The golden bowl put on, under consideration, a sturdy, a conscious perversity; as a "document," somehow, it was ugly, though it might have a decorative grace. "His finding me here in presence of it might be more flagrantly disagreeable — for all of us — than you intend or than would necessarily help us. And I must take time, truly, to understand what it means."

"You're safe, as far as that goes," Maggie returned; "you may take it from me that he won't come in; and that I shall only find him below, waiting for me, when I go down to the carriage."

Fanny Assingham took it from her, took it and more. "We're to sit together at the Ambassador's then — or at least you two are — with this new complication thrust up before you, all unexplained; and to look at each other with faces that pretend, for the ghastly hour, not to be seeing it?"

Maggie looked at HER with a face that might have been the one she was preparing. "'Unexplained,' my dear? Quite the contrary — explained: fully, intensely, admirably explained, with nothing really to add. My own love" — she kept it up —"I don't want anything more. I've plenty to go upon and to do with, as it is."

Fanny Assingham stood there in her comparative darkness, with her links, verily, still missing; but the most acceptable effect of this was, singularly, as yet, a cold fear of getting nearer the fact. "But when you come home —? I mean he'll come up with you again. Won't he see it then?"

On which Maggie gave her, after an instant's visible thought, the strangest of slow headshakes. "I don't know. Perhaps he'll never see it — if it only stands there waiting for him. He may never again," said the Princess, "come into this room."

Fanny more deeply wondered, "Never again? Oh —!"

"Yes, it may be. How do I know? With THIS!" she quietly went on. She had not looked again at the incriminating piece, but there was a marvel to her friend in the way the little word representing it seemed to express and include for her the whole of her situation. "Then you intend not to speak to him —?"

Maggie waited. "To 'speak' —?"

"Well, about your having it and about what you consider that it represents."

"Oh, I don't know that I shall speak — if he doesn't. But his keeping away from me because of that — what will that be but to speak? He can't say or do more. It won't be for me to speak," Maggie added in a different tone, one of the tones that had already so penetrated her guest. "It will be for me to listen."

Mrs. Assingham turned it over. "Then it all depends on that object that you regard, for your reasons, as evidence?"

"I think I may say that I depend on it. I can't," said Maggie, "treat it as nothing now."

Mrs. Assingham, at this, went closer to the cup on the chimney — quite liking to feel that she did so, moreover, without going closer to her companion's vision. She looked at the precious thing — if precious it was — found herself in fact eyeing it as if, by her dim solicitation, to draw its secret from it rather than suffer the imposition of Maggie's knowledge. It was brave and rich and firm, with its bold deep hollow; and, without this queer torment about it, would, thanks to her love of plenty of yellow, figure to her as an enviable ornament, a possession really desirable. She didn't touch it, but if after a minute she turned away from it the reason was, rather oddly and suddenly, in her fear of doing so. "Then it all depends on the bowl? I mean your future does? For that's what it comes to, I judge."

"What it comes to," Maggie presently returned, "is what that thing has put me, so almost miraculously, in the way of learning: how far they had originally gone together. If there was so much between them before, there can't — with all the other appearances — not be a great deal more now." And she went on and on; she steadily made her points. "If such things were already then between them they make all the difference for possible doubt of what may have been between them since. If there had been nothing before there might be explanations. But it makes today too much to explain. I mean to explain away," she said.

Fanny Assingham was there to explain away — of this she was duly conscious; for that at least had been true up to now. In the light, however, of Maggie's demonstration the quantity, even without her taking as yet a more exact measure, might well seem larger than ever. Besides which, with or without exactness, the effect of each successive minute in the place was to put her more in presence of what Maggie herself saw. Maggie herself saw the truth, and that was really, while they remained there together, enough for Mrs. Assingham's relation to it. There was a force in the Princess's mere manner about it that made the detail of what she knew a matter of minor importance. Fanny had in fact something like a momentary shame over her own need of asking for this detail. "I don't pretend to repudiate," she said after a little, "my own impressions of the different times I suppose you speak of; any more," she added, "than I can forget what difficulties and, as it constantly seemed to me, what dangers, every course of action — whatever I should decide upon — made for me. I tried, I tried hard, to act for the best. And, you know," she next pursued, while, at the sound of her own statement, a slow courage and even a faint warmth of conviction came back to her —"and, you know, I believe it's what I shall turn out to have done."

This produced a minute during which their interchange, though quickened and deepened, was that of silence only, and the long, charged look; all of which found virtual consecration when Maggie at last spoke. "I'm sure you tried to act for the best."

It kept Fanny Assingham again a minute in silence. "I never thought, dearest, you weren't an angel."

Not, however, that this alone was much help! "It was up to the very eve, you see," the Princess went on —"up to within two or three days of our marriage. That, THAT, you know —!" And she broke down for strangely smiling.

"Yes, as I say, it was while she was with me. But I didn't know it. That is," said Fanny Assingham, "I didn't know of anything in particular." It sounded weak — that she felt; but she had really her point to make. "What I mean is that I don't know, for knowledge, now, anything I didn't then. That's how I am." She still, however, floundered. "I mean it's how I WAS."

"But don't they, how you were and how you are," Maggie asked, "come practically to the same thing?" The elder woman's words had struck her own ear as in the tone, now mistimed, of their recent, but all too factitious understanding, arrived at in hours when, as there was nothing susceptible of proof, there was nothing definitely to disprove. The situation had changed by — well, by whatever there was, by the outbreak of the definite; and this could keep Maggie at least firm. She was firm enough as she pursued. "It was ON the whole thing that Amerigo married me." With which her eyes had their turn again at her damnatory piece. "And it was on that — it was on that!" But they came back to her visitor. "And it was on it all that father married HER."

Her visitor took it as might be. "They both married — ah, that you must believe! — with the highest intentions."

"Father did certainly!" And then, at the renewal of this consciousness, it all rolled over her. "Ah, to thrust such things on us, to do them here between us and with us, day after day, and in return, in return —! To do it to HIM — to him, to him!"

Fanny hesitated. "You mean it's for him you most suffer?" And then as the Princess, after a look, but turned away, moving about the room — which made the question somehow seem a blunder —"I ask," she continued, "because I think everything, everything we now speak of, may be for him, really may be MADE for him, quite as if it hadn't been."

But Maggie had, the next moment faced about as if without hearing her. "Father did it for ME — did it all and only for me."

Mrs. Assingham, with a certain promptness, threw up her head; but she faltered again before she spoke. "Well —!"

It was only an intended word, but Maggie showed after an instant that it had reached her. "Do you mean that that's the reason, that that's A reason —?"

Fanny at first, however, feeling the response in this, didn't say all she meant; she said for the moment something else instead. "He did it for you — largely at least for you. And it was for you that I did, in my smaller, interested way — well, what I could do. For I could do something," she continued; "I thought I saw your interest as he himself saw it. And I thought I saw Charlotte's. I believed in her."

"And *I* believed in her," said Maggie.

Mrs. Assingham waited again; but she presently pushed on. "She believed then in herself."

"Ah?" Maggie murmured.

Something exquisite, faintly eager, in the prompt simplicity of it, supported her friend further. "And the Prince believed. His belief was real. Just as he believed in himself."

Maggie spent a minute in taking it from her. "He believed in himself?"

"Just as I too believed in him. For I absolutely did, Maggie." To which Fanny then added: "And I believe in him yet. I mean," she subjoined —"well, I mean I DO."

Maggie again took it from her; after which she was again, restlessly, set afloat. Then when this had come to an end: "And do you believe in Charlotte yet?"

Mrs. Assingham had a demur that she felt she could now afford. "We'll talk of Charlotte some other day. They both, at any rate, thought themselves safe at the time."

"Then why did they keep from me everything I might have known?"

Her friend bent upon her the mildest eyes. "Why did I myself keep it from you?"

"Oh, you weren't, for honour, obliged."

"Dearest Maggie," the poor woman broke out on this, "you ARE divine!"

"They pretended to love me," the Princess went on. "And they pretended to love HIM."

"And pray what was there that I didn't pretend?"

"Not, at any rate, to care for me as you cared for Amerigo and for Charlotte. They were much more interesting — it was perfectly natural. How couldn't you like Amerigo?" Maggie continued.

Mrs. Assingham gave it up. "How couldn't I, how couldn't I?" Then, with a fine freedom, she went all her way. "How CAN'T I, how can't I?"

It fixed afresh Maggie's wide eyes on her. "I see — I see. Well, it's beautiful for you to be able to. And of course," she added, "you wanted to help Charlotte."

"Yes" — Fanny considered it —"I wanted to help Charlotte. But I wanted also, you see, to help you — by not digging up a past that I believed, with so much on top of it, solidly buried. I wanted, as I still want," she richly declared, "to help every one."

It set Maggie once more in movement — movement which, however, spent itself again with a quick emphasis. "Then it's a good deal my fault — if everything really began so well?"

Fanny Assingham met it as she could. "You've been only too perfect. You've thought only too much."

But the Princess had already caught at the words. "Yes — I've thought only too much!" Yet she appeared to continue, for the minute, full of that fault. She had it in fact, by this prompted thought, all before her. "Of him, dear man, of HIM —!"

Her friend, able to take in thus directly her vision of her father, watched her with a new suspense. THAT way might safety lie — it was like a wider chink of light. "He believed — with a beauty! — in Charlotte."

"Yes, and it was I who had made him believe. I didn't mean to, at the time, so much; for I had no idea then of what was coming. But I did it, I did it!" the Princess declared.

"With a beauty — ah, with a beauty, you too!" Mrs. Assingham insisted.

Maggie, however, was seeing for herself — it was another matter, "The thing was that he made her think it would be so possible."

Fanny again hesitated. "The Prince made her think —?"

Maggie stared — she had meant her father. But her vision seemed to spread. "They both made her think. She wouldn't have thought without them."

"Yet Amerigo's good faith," Mrs. Assingham insisted, "was perfect. And there was nothing, all the more," she added, "against your father's."

The remark, however, kept Maggie for a moment still. "Nothing perhaps but his knowing that she knew."

"'Knew'?"

"That he was doing it, so much, for me. To what extent," she suddenly asked of her friend, "do you think he was aware that she knew?"

"Ah, who can say what passes between people in such a relation? The only thing one can be sure of is that he was generous." And Mrs. Assingham conclusively smiled. "He doubtless knew as much as was right for himself."

"As much, that is, as was right for her."

"Yes then — as was right for her. The point is," Fanny declared, "that, whatever his knowledge, it made, all the way it went, for his good faith."

Maggie continued to gaze, and her friend now fairly waited on her successive movements. "Isn't the point, very considerably, that his good faith must have been his faith in her taking almost as much interest in me as he himself took?"

Fanny Assingham thought. "He recognised, he adopted, your long friendship. But he founded on it no selfishness."

"No," said Maggie with still deeper consideration: "he counted her selfishness out almost as he counted his own."

"So you may say."

"Very well," Maggie went on; "if he had none of his own, he invited her, may have expected her, on her side, to have as little. And she may only since have found that out."

Mrs. Assingham looked blank. "Since —?"

"And he may have become aware," Maggie pursued, "that she has found it out. That she has taken the measure, since their marriage," she explained, "of how much he had asked of her — more, say, than she had understood at the time. He may have made out at last how such a demand was, in the long run, to affect her."

"He may have done many things," Mrs. Assingham responded; "but there's one thing he certainly won't have done. He'll never have shown that he expected of her a quarter as much as she must have understood he was to give."

"I've often wondered," Maggie mused, "what Charlotte really understood. But it's one of the things she has never told me."

"Then as it's one of the things she has never told me either, we shall probably never know it; and we may regard it as none of our business. There are many things," said Mrs. Assingham, "that we shall never know."

Maggie took it in with a long reflection. "Never."

"But there are others," her friend went on, "that stare us in the face and that — under whatever difficulty you may feel you labour — may now be enough for us. Your father has been extraordinary."

It had been as if Maggie were feeling her way; but she rallied to this with a rush. "Extraordinary."

"Magnificent," said Fanny Assingham.

Her companion held tight to it. "Magnificent."

"Then he'll do for himself whatever there may be to do. What he undertook for you he'll do to the end. He didn't undertake it to break down; in what — quiet, patient, exquisite as he is — did he ever break down? He had never in his life proposed to himself to have failed, and he won't have done it on this occasion."

"Ah, this occasion!" — and Maggie's wail showed her, of a sudden, thrown back on it. "Am I in the least sure that, with everything, he even knows what it is? And yet am I in the least sure he doesn't?"

"If he doesn't then, so much the better. Leave him alone."

"Do you mean give him up?"

"Leave HER," Fanny Assingham went on. "Leave her TO him."

Maggie looked at her darkly. "Do you mean leave him to HER? After this?"

"After everything. Aren't they, for that matter, intimately together now?"

"'Intimately' —? How do I know?"

But Fanny kept it up. "Aren't you and your husband — in spite of everything?"

Maggie's eyes still further, if possible, dilated. "It remains to be seen!"

"If you're not then, where's your faith?"

"In my husband —?"

Mrs. Assingham but for an instant hesitated. "In your father. It all comes back to that. Rest on it."

"On his ignorance?"

Fanny met it again. "On whatever he may offer you. TAKE that."

"Take it —?" Maggie stared.

Mrs. Assingham held up her head. "And be grateful." On which, for a minute, she let the Princess face her. "Do you see?"

"I see," said Maggie at last.

"Then there you are." But Maggie had turned away, moving to the window, as if still to keep something in her face from sight. She stood there with her eyes on the street while Mrs. Assingham's reverted to that complicating object on the chimney as to which her condition, so oddly even to herself, was that both of recurrent wonder and recurrent protest. She went over it, looked at it afresh and yielded now to her impulse to feel it in her hands. She laid them on it, lifting it up, and was surprised, thus, with the weight of it — she had seldom handled so much massive gold. That effect itself somehow prompted her to further freedom and presently to saying: "I don't believe in this, you know."

It brought Maggie round to her. "Don't believe in it? You will when I tell you."

"Ah, tell me nothing! I won't have it," said Mrs. Assingham. She kept the cup in her hand, held it there in a manner that gave Maggie's attention to her, she saw the next moment, a quality of excited suspense. This suggested to her, oddly, that she had, with the liberty she was taking, an air of intention, and the impression betrayed by her companion's eyes grew more distinct in a word of warning. "It's of value, but its value's impaired, I've learned, by a crack."

"A crack? — in the gold —?"

"It isn't gold." With which, somewhat strangely, Maggie smiled.

"That's the point."

"What is it then?"

"It's glass — and cracked, under the gilt, as I say, at that."

"Glass? — of this weight?"

"Well," said Maggie, "it's crystal — and was once, I suppose, precious. But what," she then asked, "do you mean to do with it?"

She had come away from her window, one of the three by which the wide room, enjoying an advantageous "back," commanded the western sky and caught a glimpse of the evening flush; while Mrs. Assingham, possessed of the bowl, and possessed too of this indication of a flaw, approached another for the benefit of the slowly-fading light. Here, thumbing the singular piece, weighing it, turning it over, and growing suddenly more conscious, above all, of an irresistible impulse, she presently spoke again. "A crack? Then your whole idea has a crack."

Maggie, by this time at some distance from her, waited a moment. "If you mean by my idea the knowledge that has come to me THAT —"

But Fanny, with decision, had already taken her up. "There's only one knowledge that concerns us — one fact with which we can have anything to do."

"Which one, then?"

"The fact that your husband has never, never, never —!" But the very gravity of this statement, while she raised her eyes to her friend across the room, made her for an instant hang fire.

"Well, never what?"

"Never been half so interested in you as now. But don't you, my dear, really feel it?"

Maggie considered. "Oh, I think what I've told you helps me to feel it. His having today given up even his forms; his keeping away from me; his not having come." And she shook her head as against all easy glosses. "It is because of that, you know."

"Well then, if it's because of this —!" And Fanny Assingham, who had been casting about her and whose inspiration decidedly had come, raised the cup in her two hands, raised it positively above her head, and from under it, solemnly, smiled at the Princess as a signal of intention. So for an instant, full of her thought and of her act, she held the precious vessel, and then, with due note taken of the margin of the polished floor, bare, fine and hard in the embrasure of her window, she dashed it boldly to the ground, where she had the thrill of seeing it, with the violence of the crash, lie shattered. She had flushed with the force of her effort, as Maggie had flushed with wonder at the sight, and this high reflection in their faces was all that passed between them for a minute more. After which, "Whatever you meant by it — and I don't want to know NOW — has ceased to exist," Mrs. Assingham said.

"And what in the world, my dear, did you mean by it?" — that sound, as at the touch of a spring, rang out as the first effect of Fanny's speech. It broke upon the two women's absorption with a sharpness almost equal to the smash of the crystal, for the door of the room had been opened by the Prince without their taking heed. He had apparently had time, moreover, to catch the conclusion of Fanny's act; his eyes attached themselves, through the large space allowing just there, as happened, a free view, to the shining fragments at this lady's feet. His question had been addressed to his wife, but he moved his eyes immediately afterwards to those of her visitor, whose own then held them in a manner of which neither party had been capable, doubtless, for mute penetration, since the hour spent by him in Cadogan Place on the eve of his marriage and the afternoon of Charlotte's reappearance. Something now again became possible for these communicants, under the intensity of their pressure, something that took up that tale and that might have been a redemption of pledges then exchanged. This rapid play of suppressed appeal and disguised response lasted indeed long enough for more results than one — long enough for Mrs. Assingham to measure the feat of quick self-recovery, possibly therefore of recognition still more immediate, accompanying Amerigo's vision and estimate of the evidence with which she had been — so admirably, she felt as she looked at him — inspired to deal. She looked at him and looked at him — there were so many things she wanted, on the spot, to say. But Maggie was looking too — and was moreover looking at them both; so that these things, for the elder woman, quickly enough reduced themselves to one. She met his question — not too late, since, in their silence, it had remained in the air. Gathering herself to go, leaving the golden bowl split into three pieces on the ground, she simply referred him to his wife. She should see them later, they would all meet soon again; and meanwhile, as to what Maggie had meant — she said, in her turn, from the door — why, Maggie herself was doubtless by this time ready to tell him.

XXXIV

Left with her husband, Maggie, however, for the time, said nothing; she only felt, on the spot, a strong, sharp wish not to see his face again till he should have had a minute to arrange it. She had seen it enough for her temporary clearness and her next movement — seen it as it showed during the stare of surprise that followed his entrance. Then it was that she knew how hugely expert she had been made, for judging it quickly, by that vision of it, indelibly registered for reference, that had flashed a light into her troubled soul the night of his late return from Matcham. The expression worn by it at that juncture, for however few instants, had given her a sense of its possibilities, one of the most relevant of which might have been playing up for her, before the consummation of Fanny Assingham's retreat, just long enough to be recognised. What she had recognised in it was HIS recognition, the result of his having been forced, by the flush of their visitor's attitude and the unextinguished report of her words, to take account of the flagrant signs of the accident, of the incident, on which he had unexpectedly dropped. He had, not unnaturally, failed to see this occurrence represented by the three fragments of an object apparently valuable which lay there on the floor and which, even across the width of the room, his kept interval, reminded him, unmistakably though confusedly, of something known, some other unforgotten image. That was a mere shock, that was a pain — as if Fanny's violence had been a violence redoubled and acting beyond its intention, a violence calling up the hot blood as a blow across the mouth might have called it. Maggie knew as she turned away from him that she didn't want his pain; what she wanted was her own simple certainty — not the red mark of conviction flaming there in his beauty. If she could have gone on with bandaged eyes she would have liked that best; if it were a question of saying what she now, apparently, should have to, and of taking from him what he would say, any blindness that might wrap it would be the nearest approach to a boon.

She went in silence to where her friend — never, in intention, visibly, so much her friend as at that moment — had braced herself to so amazing an energy, and there, under Amerigo's eyes, she picked up the shining pieces. Bedizened and jewelled, in her rustling finery, she paid, with humility of attitude, this prompt tribute to order — only to find, however, that she could carry but two of the fragments at once. She brought them over to the chimney-piece, to the conspicuous place occupied by the cup before Fanny's appropriation of it, and, after laying them carefully down, went back for what remained, the solid detached foot. With this she returned to the mantel-shelf, placing it with deliberation in the centre and then, for a minute, occupying herself as with the attempt to fit the other morsels. After she had squared again her little objects on the chimney, she was within an ace, in fact, of turning on him with that appeal; besides its being lucid for her, all the while, that the occasion was passing, that they were dining out, that he wasn't dressed, and that, though she herself was, she was yet, in all probability, so horribly red in the face and so awry, in many ways, with agitation, that in view of the Ambassador's company, of possible comments and constructions, she should need, before her glass, some restoration of appearances.

Amerigo, meanwhile, after all, could clearly make the most of her having enjoined on him to wait — suggested it by the positive pomp of her dealings with the smashed cup; to wait, that is, till she should pronounce as Mrs. Assingham had promised for her. This delay, again, certainly tested her presence of mind — though that strain was not what presently made her speak. Keep her eyes, for the time, from her husband's as she might, she soon found herself much more drivingly conscious of the strain on his own wit. There was even a minute, when her back was turned to him, during which she knew once more the strangeness of her desire to spare him, a strangeness that had already, fifty times, brushed her, in the depth of her trouble, as with the wild wing of some bird of the air who might blindly have swooped for an instant into the shaft of a well, darkening there by his momentary flutter the far-off round of sky. It was extraordinary, this quality in the taste of her wrong which made her completed sense of it seem rather to soften than to harden and it was the more extraordinary the more she had to recognise it; for what it came to was that seeing herself finally sure, knowing everything, having the fact, in all its abomination, so utterly before her that there was nothing else to add — what it came to was that, merely by being WITH him there in silence, she felt, within her, the sudden split between conviction and action. They had begun to cease, on the spot, surprisingly, to be connected; conviction, that is, budged no inch, only planting its feet the more firmly in the soil — but action began to hover like some lighter and larger, but easier form, excited by its very power to keep above ground. It would be free, it would be independent, it would go in-wouldn't it? — for some prodigious and superior adventure of its own. What would condemn it, so to speak, to the responsibility of freedom — this glimmered on Maggie even now — was the possibility, richer with every lapsing moment, that her husband would have, on the whole question, a new need of her, a need which was in fact being born between them in these very seconds. It struck her truly as so new that he would have felt hitherto none to compare with it at all; would indeed, absolutely, by this circumstance, be REALLY needing her for the first one in their whole connection. No, he had used her, had even exceedingly enjoyed her, before this; but there had been no precedent for that character of a proved necessity to him which she was rapidly taking on. The immense advantage of this particular clue, moreover, was that she should have now to arrange, alter, to falsify nothing; should have to be but consistently simple and straight. She asked herself, with concentration, while her back was still presented, what would be the very ideal of that method; after which, the next instant, it had all come to her and she had turned round upon him for the application. "Fanny Assingham broke it — knowing it had a crack and that it would go if she used sufficient force. She thought, when I had told her, that that would be the best thing to do with it — thought so from her own point of view. That hadn't been at all my idea, but she acted before I understood. I had, on the contrary," she explained, "put it here, in full view, exactly that you might see."

He stood with his hands in his pockets; he had carried his eyes to the fragments on the chimney-piece, and she could already distinguish the element of relief, absolutely of succour, in his acceptance from her of the opportunity to consider the fruits of their friend's violence — every added inch of reflection and delay having the advantage, from this point on, of counting for him double. It had operated within her now to the last intensity, her glimpse of the precious truth that by her helping him, helping him to help himself, as it were, she should help him to help HER. Hadn't she fairly got into his labyrinth with him? — wasn't she indeed in the very act of placing herself there, for him, at its centre and core, whence, on that definite orientation and by an instinct all her own, she might securely guide him out of it? She offered him thus, assuredly, a kind of support that was not to have been imagined in advance, and that moreover required — ah most truly! — some close looking at before it could be believed in and pronounced void of treachery. "Yes, look, look," she seemed to see him hear her say even while her sounded words were other — "look, look, both at the truth that still survives in that smashed evidence and at the even more remarkable appearance that I'm not such a fool as you supposed me. Look at the possibility that, since I AM different, there may still be something in it for you — if you're capable of working with me to get that out. Consider of course, as you must, the question of what you may have to surrender, on your side, what price you may have to pay, whom you may have to pay WITH, to set this advantage free; but take in, at any rate, that there is something for you if you don't too blindly spoil your chance for it." He went no nearer the damnatory pieces, but he eyed them, from where he stood, with a degree of recognition just visibly less to be dissimulated; all of which represented for her a certain traceable process. And her uttered words, meanwhile, were different enough from those he might have inserted between the lines of her already-spoken. "It's the golden bowl, you know, that you saw at the little antiquario's in Bloomsbury, so long ago — when you went there with Charlotte, when you spent those hours with her, unknown to me, a day or two before our marriage. It was shown you both, but you didn't take it; you left it for me, and I came upon it, extraordinarily, through happening to go into the same shop on Monday last; in walking home, in prowling about to pick up some small old thing for father's birthday, after my visit to the Museum, my appointment there with Mr. Crichton, of which I told you. It was shown me, and I was struck with it and took it — knowing nothing about it at the time. What I now know I've learned since — I learned this afternoon, a couple of hours ago; receiving from it naturally a great impression. So there it is — in its three pieces. You can handle them — don't be afraid — if you want to make sure the thing is the thing you and Charlotte saw together. Its having come apart makes an unfortunate difference for its beauty, its artistic value, but none for anything else. Its other value is just the same — I mean that of its having given me so much of the truth about you. I don't therefore so much care what becomes of it now — unless perhaps you may yourself, when you come to think, have some good use for it. In that case," Maggie wound up, "we can easily take the pieces with us to Fawns."

It was wonderful how she felt, by the time she had seen herself through this narrow pass, that she had really achieved something — that she was emerging a little, in fine, with the prospect less contracted. She had done for him, that is, what her instinct enjoined; had laid a basis not merely momentary on which he could meet her. When, by the turn of his head, he did finally meet her, this was the last thing that glimmered out of his look; but it came into sight, none the less, as a perception of his distress and almost as a question of his eyes; so that, for still another minute, before he committed himself, there occurred between them a kind of unprecedented moral exchange over which her superior lucidity presided. It was not, however, that when he did commit himself the show was promptly portentous. "But what in the world has Fanny Assingham had to do with it?"

She could verily, out of all her smothered soreness, almost have smiled: his question so affected her as giving the whole thing up to her. But it left her only to go the straighter. "She has had to do with it that I immediately sent for her and that she immediately came. She was the first person I wanted to see — because I knew she would know. Know more about what I had learned, I mean, than I could make out for myself. I made out as much as I could for myself — that I also wanted to have done; but it didn't, in spite of everything, take me very far, and she has really been a help. Not so much as she would like to be-not so much as, poor dear, she just now tried to be; yet she has done her very best for you — never forget that! — and has kept me along immeasurably better than I should have been able to come without her. She has gained me time; and that, these three months, don't you see? has been everything."

She had said "Don't you see?" on purpose, and was to feel the next moment that it had acted. "These three months'?" the Prince asked.

"Counting from the night you came home so late from Matcham. Counting from the hours you spent with Charlotte at Gloucester; your visit to the cathedral — which you won't have forgotten describing to me in so much detail. For that was the beginning of my being sure. Before it I had been sufficiently in doubt. Sure," Maggie developed, "of your having, and of your having for a long time had, TWO relations with Charlotte."

He stared, a little at sea, as he took it up. "Two —?"

Something in the tone of it gave it a sense, or an ambiguity, almost foolish — leaving Maggie to feel, as in a flash, how such a consequence, a foredoomed infelicity, partaking of the ridiculous even in one of the cleverest, might be of the very essence of the penalty of wrong-doing. "Oh, you may have had fifty — had the same relation with her fifty times! It's of the number of KINDS of relation with her that I speak — a number that doesn't matter, really, so long as there wasn't only one kind, as father and I supposed. One kind," she went on, "was there before us; we took that fully for granted, as you saw, and accepted it. We never thought of there being another, kept out of our sight. But after the evening I speak of I knew there was something else. As I say, I had, before that, my idea — which you never dreamed I had. From the moment I speak of it had more to go upon, and you became yourselves, you and she, vaguely, yet uneasily, conscious of the difference. But it's within these last hours that I've most seen where we are; and as I've been in communication with Fanny Assingham about my doubts, so I wanted to let her know my certainty — with the determination of which, however, you must understand, she has had nothing to do. She defends you," Maggie remarked.

He had given her all his attention, and with this impression for her, again, that he was, in essence, fairly reaching out to her for time — time, only time — she could sufficiently imagine, and to whatever strangeness, that he absolutely liked her to talk, even at the cost of his losing almost everything else by it. It was still, for a minute, as if he waited for something worse; wanted everything that was in her to come out, any definite fact, anything more precisely nameable, so that he too — as was his right — should know where he was. What stirred in him above all, while he followed in her face the clear train of her speech, must have been the impulse to take up something she put before him that he was yet afraid directly to touch. He wanted to make free with it, but had to keep his hands off — for reasons he had already made out; and the discomfort of his privation yearned at her out of his eyes with an announcing gleam of the fever, the none too tolerable chill, of specific recognition. She affected him as speaking more or less for her father as well, and his eyes might have been trying to hypnotise her into giving him the answer without his asking the question. "Had HE his idea, and has he now, with you, anything more?" — those were the words he had to hold himself from not speaking and that she would as yet, certainly, do nothing to make easy. She felt with her sharpest thrill how he was straitened and tied, and with the miserable pity of it her present conscious purpose of keeping him so could none the less perfectly accord. To name her father, on any such basis of anxiety, of compunction, would be to do the impossible thing, to do neither more nor less than give Charlotte away. Visibly, palpably, traceably, he stood off from this, moved back from it as from an open chasm now suddenly perceived, but which had been, between the two, with so much, so strangely much else, quite uncalculated. Verily it towered before her, this history of their confidence. They had built strong and piled high — based as it was on such appearances — their conviction that, thanks to her native complacencies of so many sorts, she would always, quite to the end and through and through, take them as nobly sparing her. Amerigo was at any rate having the sensation of a particular ugliness to avoid, a particular difficulty to count with, that practically found him as unprepared as if he had been, like his wife, an abjectly simple person. And she meanwhile, however abjectly simple, was further discerning, for herself, that, whatever he might have to take from her — she being, on her side, beautifully free — he would absolutely not be able, for any qualifying purpose, to name Charlotte either. As his father-inlaw's wife Mrs. Verver rose between them there, for the time, in august and prohibitive form; to protect her, defend her, explain about her, was, at the least, to bring her into the question — which would be by the same stroke to bring her husband. But this was exactly the door Maggie wouldn't open to him; on all of which she was the next moment asking herself if, thus warned and embarrassed, he were not fairly writhing in his pain. He writhed, on that hypothesis, some seconds more, for it was not till then that he had chosen between what he could do and what he couldn't.

"You're apparently drawing immense conclusions from very small matters. Won't you perhaps feel, in fairness, that you're striking out, triumphing, or whatever I may call it, rather too easily — feel it when I perfectly admit that your smashed cup there does come back to me? I frankly confess, now, to the occasion, and to having wished not to speak of it to you at the time. We took two or three hours together, by arrangement; it WAS on the eve of my marriage — at the moment you say. But that put it on the eve of yours too, my dear — which was directly the point. It was desired to find for you, at the eleventh hour, some small wedding-present — a hunt, for something worth giving you, and yet possible from other points of view as well, in which it seemed I could be of use. You were naturally not to be told — precisely because it was all FOR you. We went forth together and we looked; we rummaged about and, as I remember we called it, we prowled; then it was that, as I freely recognise, we came across that crystal cup — which I'm bound to say, upon my honour, I think it rather a pity Fanny Assingham, from whatever good motive, should have treated so." He had kept his hands in his pockets; he turned his eyes again, but more complacently now, to the ruins of the precious vessel; and Maggie could feel him exhale into the achieved quietness of his explanation a long, deep breath of comparative relief. Behind everything, beneath everything, it was somehow a comfort to him at last to be talking with her — and he seemed to be proving to himself that he COULD talk. "It was at a little shop in Bloomsbury — I think I could go to the place now. The man understood Italian, I remember; he wanted awfully to work off his bowl. But I didn't believe in it, and we didn't take it."

Maggie had listened with an interest that wore all the expression of candour. "Oh, you left it for me. But what did you take?"

He looked at her; first as if he were trying to remember, then as if he might have been trying to forget. "Nothing, I think — at that place."

"What did you take then at any other? What did you get me — since that was your aim and end — for a wedding-gift?"

The Prince continued very nobly to bethink himself. "Didn't we get you anything?"

Maggie waited a little; she had for some time, now, kept her eyes on him steadily; but they wandered, at this, to the fragments on her chimney. "Yes; it comes round, after all, to your having got me the bowl. I myself was to come upon it, the other day, by so wonderful a chance; was to find it in the same place and to have it pressed upon me by the same little man, who does, as you say, understand Italian. I did 'believe in it,' you see — must have believed in it somehow instinctively; for I took it as soon as I saw it. Though I didn't know at all then," she added, "what I was taking WITH it."

The Prince paid her for an instant, visibly, the deference of trying to imagine what this might have been. "I agree with you that the coincidence is extraordinary — the sort of thing that happens mainly in novels and plays. But I don't see, you must let me say, the importance or the connexion —"

"Of my having made the purchase where you failed of it?" She had quickly taken him up; but she had, with her eyes on him once more, another drop into the order of her thoughts, to which, through whatever he might say, she was still adhering. "It's not my having gone into the place, at the end of four years, that makes the strangeness of the coincidence; for don't such chances as that, in London, easily occur? The strangeness," she lucidly said, "is in what my purchase was to represent to me after I had got it home; which value came," she explained, "from the wonder of my having found such a friend."

" 'Such a friend'?" As a wonder, assuredly, her husband could but take it.

"As the little man in the shop. He did for me more than he knew — I owe it to him. He took an interest in me," Maggie said; "and, taking that interest, he recalled your visit, he remembered you and spoke of you to me."

On which the Prince passed the comment of a sceptical smile. "Ah but, my dear, if extraordinary things come from people's taking an interest in you —"

"My life in that case," she asked, "must be very agitated? Well, he liked me, I mean — very particularly. It's only so I can account for my afterwards hearing from him — and in fact he gave me that today," she pursued, "he gave me it frankly as his reason."

"To-day?" the Prince inquiringly echoed.

But she was singularly able — it had been marvellously "given" her, she afterwards said to herself — to abide, for her light, for her clue, by her own order.

"I inspired him with sympathy — there you are! But the miracle is that he should have a sympathy to offer that could be of use to me. That was really the oddity of my chance," the Princess proceeded —"that I should have been moved, in my ignorance, to go precisely to him."

He saw her so keep her course that it was as if he could, at the best, but stand aside to watch her and let her pass; he only made a vague demonstration that was like an ineffective gesture. "I'm sorry to say any ill of your friends, and the thing was a long time ago; besides which there was nothing to make me recur to it. But I remember the man's striking me as a decided little beast."

She gave a slow headshake — as if, no, after consideration, not THAT way were an issue. "I can only think of him as kind, for he had nothing to gain. He had in fact only to lose. It was what he came to tell me — that he had asked me too high a price, more than the object was really worth. There was a particular reason, which he hadn't mentioned, and which had made him consider and repent. He wrote for leave to see me again — wrote in such terms that I saw him here this afternoon."

"Here?" — it made the Prince look about him.

"Downstairs — in the little red room. While he was waiting he looked at the few photographs that stand about there and recognised two of them. Though it was so long ago, he remembered the visit made him by the lady and the gentleman, and that gave him his connexion. It gave me mine, for he remembered everything and told me everything. You see you too had produced your effect; only, unlike you, he had thought of it again — he HAD recurred to it. He told me of your having wished to make each other presents — but of that's not having come off. The lady was greatly taken with the piece I had bought of him, but you had your reason against receiving it from her, and you had been right. He would think that of you more than ever now," Maggie went on; "he would see how wisely you had guessed the flaw and how easily the bowl could be broken. I had bought it myself, you see, for a present — he knew I was doing that. This was what had worked in him — especially after the price I had paid."

Her story had dropped an instant; she still brought it out in small waves of energy, each of which spent its force; so that he had an opportunity to speak before this force was renewed. But the quaint thing was what he now said. "And what, pray, WAS the price?"

She paused again a little. "It was high, certainly — for those fragments. I think I feel, as I look at them there, rather ashamed to say."

The Prince then again looked at them; he might have been growing used to the sight. "But shall you at least get your money back?"

"Oh, I'm far from wanting it back — I feel so that I'm getting its worth." With which, before he could reply, she had a quick transition. "The great fact about the day we're talking of seems to me to have been, quite remarkably, that no present was then made me. If your undertaking had been for that, that was not at least what came of it."

"You received then nothing at all?" The Prince looked vague and grave, almost retrospectively concerned.

"Nothing but an apology for empty hands and empty pockets; which was made me — as if it mattered a mite! — ever so frankly, ever so beautifully and touchingly."

This Amerigo heard with interest, yet not with confusion. "Ah, of course you couldn't have minded!" Distinctly, as she went on, he was getting the better of the mere awkwardness of his arrest; quite as if making out that he need SUFFER arrest from her now — before they should go forth to show themselves in the world together — in no greater quantity than an occasion ill-chosen at the best for a scene might decently make room for. He looked at his watch; their engagement, all the while, remained before him. "But I don't make out, you see, what case against me you rest —"

"On everything I'm telling you? Why, the whole case — the case of your having for so long so successfully deceived me. The idea of your finding something for me — charming as that would have been — was what had least to do with your taking a morning together at that moment. What had really to do with it," said Maggie, "was that you had to: you couldn't not, from the moment you were again face to face. And the reason of that was that there had been so much between you before — before I came between you at all."

Her husband had been for these last moments moving about under her eyes; but at this, as to check any show of impatience, he again stood still. "You've never been more sacred to me than you were at that hour — unless perhaps you've become so at this one."

The assurance of his speech, she could note, quite held up its head in him; his eyes met her own so, for the declaration, that it was as if something cold and momentarily unimaginable breathed upon her, from afar off, out of his strange consistency. She kept her direction still, however, under that. "Oh, the thing I've known best of all is that you've never wanted, together, to offend us. You've wanted quite intensely not to, and the precautions you've had to take for it have been for a long time one of the strongest of my impressions. That, I think," she added, "is the way I've best known."

"Known?" he repeated after a moment.

"Known. Known that you were older friends, and so much more intimate ones, than I had any reason to suppose when we married. Known there were things that hadn't been told me — and that gave their meaning, little by little, to other things that were before me."

"Would they have made a difference, in the matter of our marriage," the Prince presently asked, "if you HAD known them?"

She took her time to think. "I grant you not — in the matter of OURS." And then as he again fixed her with his hard yearning, which he couldn't keep down: "The question is so much bigger than that. You see how much what I know makes of it for me." That was what acted on him, this iteration of her knowledge, into the question of the validity, of the various bearings of which, he couldn't on the spot trust himself to pretend, in any high way, to go. What her claim, as she made it, represented for him — that he couldn't help betraying, if only as a consequence of the effect of the word itself, her repeated distinct "know, know," on his nerves. She was capable of being sorry for his nerves at a time when he should need them for dining out, pompously, rather responsibly, without his heart in it; yet she was not to let that prevent her using, with all economy, so precious a chance for supreme clearness. "I didn't force this upon you, you must recollect, and it probably wouldn't have happened for you if you hadn't come in."

"Ah," said the Prince, "I was liable to come in, you know."

"I didn't think you were this evening."

"And why not?"

"Well," she answered, "you have many liabilities — of different sorts." With which she recalled what she had said to Fanny Assingham. "And then you're so deep."

It produced in his features, in spite of his control of them, one of those quick plays of expression, the shade of a grimace, that testified as nothing else did to his race. "It's you, cara, who are deep."

Which, after an instant, she had accepted from him; she could so feel at last that it was true. "Then I shall have need of it all."

"But what would you have done," he was by this time asking, "if I HADN'T come in?"

"I don't know." She had hesitated. "What would you?"

"Oh; io — that isn't the question. I depend upon you. I go on. You would have spoken tomorrow?"

"I think I would have waited."

"And for what?" he asked.

"To see what difference it would make for myself. My possession at last, I mean, of real knowledge."

"Oh!" said the Prince.

"My only point now, at any rate," she went on, "is the difference, as I say, that it may make for YOU. Your knowing was — from the moment you did come in-all I had in view." And she sounded it again — he should have it once more. "Your knowing that I've ceased —"

"That you've ceased —?" With her pause, in fact, she had fairly made him press her for it.

"Why, to be as I was. NOT to know."

It was once more then, after a little, that he had had to stand receptive; yet the singular effect of this was that there was still something of the same sort he was made to want. He had another hesitation, but at last this odd quantity showed. "Then does any one else know?"

It was as near as he could come to naming her father, and she kept him at that distance. "Any one —?"

"Any one, I mean, but Fanny Assingham."

"I should have supposed you had had by this time particular means of learning. I don't see," she said, "why you ask me."

Then, after an instant — and only after an instant, as she saw — he made out what she meant; and it gave her, all strangely enough, the still further light that Charlotte, for herself, knew as little as he had known. The vision loomed, in this light, it fairly glared, for the few seconds — the vision of the two others alone together at Fawns, and Charlotte, as one of them, having gropingly to go on, always not knowing and not knowing! The picture flushed at the same time with all its essential colour — that of the so possible identity of her father's motive and principle with her own. HE was "deep," as Amerigo called it, so that no vibration of the still air should reach his daughter; just as she had earned that description by making and by, for that matter, intending still to make, her care for his serenity, or at any rate for the firm outer shell of his dignity, all marvellous enamel, her paramount law. More strangely even than anything else, her husband seemed to speak now but to help her in this. "I know nothing but what you tell me."

"Then I've told you all I intended. Find out the rest —!"

"Find it out —?" He waited.

She stood before him a moment — it took that time to go on. Depth upon depth of her situation, as she met his face, surged and sank within her; but with the effect somehow, once more, that they rather lifted her than let her drop. She had her feet somewhere, through it all — it was her companion, absolutely, who was at sea. And she kept her feet; she pressed them to what was beneath her. She went over to the bell beside the chimney and gave a ring that he could but take as a summons for her maid. It stopped everything for the present; it was an intimation to him to go and dress. But she had to insist. "Find out for yourself!"

Part Fifth

XXXV

After the little party was again constituted at Fawns — which had taken, for completeness, some ten days — Maggie naturally felt herself still more possessed, in spirit, of everything that had last happened in London. There was a phrase that came back to her from old American years: she was having, by that idiom, the time of her life — she knew it by the perpetual throb of this sense of possession, which was almost too violent either to recognise or to hide. It was as if she had come out — that was her most general consciousness; out of a dark tunnel, a dense wood, or even simply a smoky room, and had thereby, at least, for going on, the advantage of air in her lungs. It was as if she were somehow at last gathering in the fruits of patience; she had either been really more patient than she had known at the time, or had been so for longer: the change brought about by itself as great a difference of view as the shift of an inch in the position of a telescope. It was her telescope in fact that had gained in range — just as her danger lay in her exposing herself to the observation by the more charmed, and therefore the more reckless, use of this optical resource. Not under any provocation to produce it in public was her unremitted rule; but the difficulties of duplicity had not shrunk, while the need of it had doubled. Humbugging, which she had so practised with her father, had been a comparatively simple matter on the basis of mere doubt; but the ground to be covered was now greatly larger, and she felt not unlike some young woman of the theatre who, engaged for a minor part in the play and having mastered her cues with anxious effort, should find herself suddenly promoted to leading lady and expected to appear in every act of the five. She had made much to her husband, that last night, of her "knowing"; but it was exactly this quantity she now knew that, from the moment she could only dissimulate it, added to her responsibility and made of the latter all a mere question of having something precious and precarious in charge. There was no one to help her with it — not even Fanny Assingham now; this good friend's presence having become, inevitably, with that climax of their last interview in Portland Place, a severely simplified function. She had her use, oh yes, a thousand times; but it could only consist henceforth in her quite conspicuously touching at no point whatever — assuredly, at least with Maggie — the matter they had discussed. She was there, inordinately, as a value, but as a value only for the clear negation of everything. She was their general sign, precisely, of unimpaired beatitude — and she was to live up to that somewhat arduous character, poor thing, as she might. She might privately lapse from it, if she must, with Amerigo or with Charlotte — only not, of course, ever, so much as for the wink of an eye, with the master of the house. Such lapses would be her own affair, which Maggie at present could take no thought of. She treated her young friend meanwhile, it was to be said, to no betrayal of such wavering; so that from the moment of her alighting at the door with the Colonel everything went on between them at concert pitch. What had she done, that last evening in Maggie's room, but bring the husband and wife more together than, as would seem, they had ever been? Therefore what indiscretion should she not show by attempting to go behind the grand appearance of her success? — which would be to court a doubt of her beneficent work. She knew accordingly nothing but harmony and diffused, restlessly, nothing but peace — an extravagant, expressive, aggressive peace, not incongruous, after all, with the solid calm of the place; a kind of helmetted, trident-shaking pax Britannica.

The peace, it must be added, had become, as the days elapsed, a peace quite generally animated and peopled — thanks to that fact of the presence of "company" in which Maggie's ability to preserve an appearance had learned, from so far back, to find its best resource. It was not inconspicuous, it was in fact striking, that this resource, just now, seemed to meet in the highest degree every one's need: quite as if every one were, by the multiplication of human objects in the scene, by the creation, by the confusion, of fictive issues, hopeful of escaping somebody else's notice. It had reached the point, in truth, that the collective bosom might have been taken to heave with the knowledge of the descent upon adjacent shores, for a short period, of Mrs. Rance and the Lutches, still united, and still so divided, for conquest: the sense of the party showed at least, oddly enough, as favourable to the fancy of the quaint turn that some near "week-end" might derive from their reappearance. This measured for Maggie the ground they had all travelled together since that unforgotten afternoon of the none so distant year, that determinant September Sunday when, sitting with her father in the park, as in commemoration of the climax both of their old order and of their old danger, she had proposed to him that they should "call in" Charlotte — call her in as a specialist might be summoned to an invalid's chair. Wasn't it a sign of something rather portentous, their being ready to be beholden, as for a diversion, to the once despised Kitty and Dotty? That had already had its application, in truth, to her invocation of the Castledeans and several other members, again, of the historic Matcham week, made before she left town, and made, always consistently, with an idea — since she was never henceforth to approach these people without an idea, and since that lurid element of their intercourse grew and grew for her with each occasion. The flame with which it burned afresh during these particular days, the way it held up the torch to anything, to everything, that MIGHT have occurred as the climax of revels springing from traditions so vivified — this by itself justified her private motive and reconsecrated her diplomacy. She had already produced by the aid of these people something of the effect she sought — that of being "good" for whatever her companions were good for, and of not asking either of them to give up anyone or anything for her sake. There was moreover, frankly, a sharpness of point in it that she enjoyed; it gave an accent to the truth she wished to illustrate — the truth that the surface of her recent life, thick-sown with the flower of earnest endeavour, with every form of the unruffled and the undoubting, suffered no symptom anywhere to peep out. It was as if, under her pressure, neither party could get rid of the complicity, as it might be figured, of the other; as if, in a word, she saw Amerigo and Charlotte committed, for fear of betrayals on their own side, to a kind of wan consistency on the subject of Lady Castledean's "set," and this latter group, by the same stroke, compelled to assist at attestations the extent and bearing of which they rather failed to grasp and which left them indeed, in spite of hereditary high spirits, a trifle bewildered and even a trifle scared.

They made, none the less, at Fawns, for number, for movement, for sound — they played their parts during a crisis that must have hovered for them, in the long passages of the old house, after the fashion of the established ghost, felt, through the dark hours as a constant possibility, rather than have menaced them in the form of a daylight bore, one of the perceived outsiders who are liable to be met in the drawing-room or to be sat next to at dinner. If the Princess, moreover, had failed of her occult use for so much of the machinery of diversion, she would still have had a sense not other than sympathetic for the advantage now extracted from it by Fanny Assingham's bruised philosophy. This good friend's relation to it was actually the revanche, she sufficiently indicated, of her obscured lustre at Matcham, where she had known her way about so much less than most of the others. She knew it at Fawns, through the pathless wild of the right tone, positively better than any one, Maggie could note for her; and her revenge had the magnanimity of a brave pointing out of it to every one else, a wonderful irresistible, conscious, almost compassionate patronage. Here was a house, she triumphantly caused it to be noted, in which she so bristled with values that some of them might serve, by her amused willingness to share, for such of the temporarily vague, among her fellow-guests, such of the dimly disconcerted, as had lost the key to their own. It may have been partly through the effect of this especial strain of community with her old friend that Maggie found herself, one evening, moved to take up again their dropped directness of reference. They had remained downstairs together late; the other women of the party had filed, singly or in couples, up the "grand" staircase on which, from the equally grand hall, these retreats and advances could always be pleasantly observed; the men had apparently taken their way to the smoking-room; while the Princess, in possession thus of a rare reach of view, had lingered as if to enjoy it. Then she saw that Mrs. Assingham was remaining a little — and as for the appreciation of her enjoyment; upon which they stood looking at each other across the cleared prospect until the elder woman, only vaguely expressive and tentative now, came nearer. It was like the act of asking if there were anything she could yet do, and that question was answered by her immediately feeling, on this closer view, as she had felt when presenting herself in Portland Place after Maggie's last sharp summons. Their understanding was taken up by these new snatched moments where that occasion had left it.

"He has never told her that I know. Of that I'm at last satisfied." And then as Mrs. Assingham opened wide eyes: "I've been in the dark since we came down, not understanding what he has been doing or intending — not making out what can have passed between them. But within a day or two I've begun to suspect, and this evening, for reasons — oh, too many to tell you! — I've been sure, since it explains. NOTHING has passed between them — that's what has happened. It explains," the Princess repeated with energy; "it explains, it explains!" She spoke in a manner that her auditor was afterwards to describe to the Colonel, oddly enough, as that of the quietest excitement; she had turned back to the chimney-place, where, in honour of a damp day and a chill night, the piled logs had turned to flame and sunk to embers; and the evident intensity of her vision for the fact she imparted made Fanny Assingham wait upon her words. It explained, this striking fact, more indeed than her companion, though conscious of fairly gaping with good-will, could swallow at once. The Princess, however, as for indulgence and confidence, quickly filled up the measure. "He hasn't let her know that I know — and, clearly, doesn't mean to. He has made up his mind; he'll say nothing about it. Therefore, as she's quite unable to arrive at the knowledge by herself, she has no idea how much I'm really in possession. She believes," said Maggie, "and, so far as her own conviction goes, she knows, that I'm not in possession of anything. And that, somehow, for my own help seems to me immense."

"Immense, my dear!" Mrs. Assingham applausively murmured, though not quite, even as yet, seeing all the way. "He's keeping quiet then on purpose?"

"On purpose." Maggie's lighted eyes, at least, looked further than they had ever looked. "He'll NEVER tell her now."

Fanny wondered; she cast about her; most of all she admired her little friend, in whom this announcement was evidently animated by an heroic lucidity. She stood there, in her full uniform, like some small erect commander of a siege, an anxious captain who has suddenly got news, replete with importance for him, of agitation, of division within the place. This importance breathed upon her comrade. "So you're all right?"

"Oh, ALL right's a good deal to say. But I seem at least to see, as I haven't before, where I am with it."

Fanny bountifully brooded; there was a point left vague. "And you have it from him? — your husband himself has told you?"

"'Told' me —?"

"Why, what you speak of. It isn't of an assurance received from him then that you do speak?"

At which Maggie had continued to stare. "Dear me, no. Do you suppose I've asked him for an assurance?"

"Ah, you haven't?" Her companion smiled. "That's what I supposed you MIGHT mean. Then, darling, what HAVE you —?"

"Asked him for? I've asked him for nothing."

But this, in turn, made Fanny stare. "Then nothing, that evening of the Embassy dinner, passed between you?"

"On the contrary, everything passed."

"Everything —?"

"Everything. I told him what I knew — and I told him how I knew it."

Mrs. Assingham waited. "And that was all?"

"Wasn't it quite enough?"

"Oh, love," she bridled, "that's for you to have judged!"

"Then I HAVE judged," said Maggie —"I did judge. I made sure he understood — then I let him alone."

Mrs. Assingham wondered. "But he didn't explain —?"

"Explain? Thank God, no!" Maggie threw back her head as with horror at the thought, then the next moment added: "And I didn't, either."

The decency of pride in it shed a cold little light — yet as from heights at the base of which her companion rather panted. "But if he neither denies nor confesses —?"

"He does what's a thousand times better — he lets it alone. He does," Maggie went on, "as he would do; as I see now that I was sure he would. He lets me alone."

Fanny Assingham turned it over. "Then how do you know so where, as you say, you 'are'?"

"Why, just BY that. I put him in possession of the difference; the difference made, about me, by the fact that I hadn't been, after all — though with a wonderful chance, I admitted, helping me — too stupid to have arrived at knowledge. He had to see that I'm changed for him — quite changed from the idea of me that he had so long been going on with. It became a question then of his really taking in the change — and what I now see is that he is doing so."

Fanny followed as she could. "Which he shows by letting you, as you say, alone?"

Maggie looked at her a minute. "And by letting her."

Mrs. Assingham did what she might to embrace it — checked a little, however, by a thought that was the nearest approach she could have, in this almost too large air, to an inspiration. "Ah, but does Charlotte let HIM?"

"Oh, that's another affair — with which I've practically nothing to do. I dare say, however, she doesn't." And the Princess had a more distant gaze for the image evoked by the question. "I don't in fact well see how she CAN. But the point for me is that he understands."

"Yes," Fanny Assingham cooed, "understands —?"

"Well, what I want. I want a happiness without a hole in it big enough for you to poke in your finger."

"A brilliant, perfect surface — to begin with at least. I see."

"The golden bowl — as it WAS to have been." And Maggie dwelt musingly on this obscured figure. "The bowl with all our happiness in it. The bowl without the crack."

For Mrs. Assingham too the image had its force, and the precious object shone before her again, reconstituted, plausible, presentable. But wasn't there still a piece missing? "Yet if he lets you alone and you only let him —?"

"Mayn't our doing so, you mean, be noticed? — mayn't it give us away? Well, we hope not — we try not — we take such care. We alone know what's between us — we and you; and haven't you precisely been struck, since you've been here," Maggie asked, "with our making so good a show?"

Her friend hesitated. "To your father?"

But it made her hesitate too; she wouldn't speak of her father directly. "To everyone. To her — now that you understand."

It held poor Fanny again in wonder. "To Charlotte — yes: if there's so much beneath it, for you, and if it's all such a plan. That makes it hang together it makes YOU hang together." She fairly exhaled her admiration. "You're like nobody else — you're extraordinary."

Maggie met it with appreciation, but with a reserve. "No, I'm not extraordinary — but I AM, for every one, quiet."

"Well, that's just what is extraordinary. 'Quiet' is more than I am, and you leave me far behind." With which, again, for an instant, Mrs. Assingham frankly brooded. "'Now that I understand,' you say — but there's one thing I don't understand." And the next minute, while her companion waited, she had mentioned it. "How can Charlotte, after all, not have pressed him, not have attacked him about it? How can she not have asked him — asked him on his honour, I mean — if you know?"

"How can she 'not'? Why, of course," said the Princess limpidly, "she MUST!"

"Well then —?"

"Well then, you think, he must have told her? Why, exactly what I mean," said Maggie, "is that he will have done nothing of the sort; will, as I say, have maintained the contrary."

Fanny Assingham weighed it. "Under her direct appeal for the truth?"

"Under her direct appeal for the truth."

"Her appeal to his honour?"

"Her appeal to his honour. That's my point."

Fanny Assingham braved it. "For the truth as from him to her?"

"From him to any one."

Mrs. Assingham's face lighted. "He'll simply, he'll insistently have lied?"

Maggie brought it out roundly. "He'll simply, he'll insistently have lied."

It held again her companion, who next, however, with a single movement, throwing herself on her neck, overflowed. "Oh, if you knew how you help me!"

Maggie had liked her to understand, so far as this was possible; but had not been slow to see afterwards how the possibility was limited, when one came to think, by mysteries she was not to sound. This inability in her was indeed not remarkable, inasmuch as the Princess herself, as we have seen, was only now in a position to boast of touching bottom. Maggie lived, inwardly, in a consciousness that she could but partly open even to so good a friend, and her own visitation of the fuller expanse of which was, for that matter, still going on. They had been duskier still, however, these recesses of her imagination — that, no doubt, was what might at present be said for them. She had looked into them, on the eve of her leaving town, almost without penetration: she had made out in those hours, and also, of a truth, during the days which immediately followed, little more than the strangeness of a relation having for its chief mark — whether to be prolonged or not — the absence of any "intimate" result of the crisis she had invited her husband to recognise. They had dealt with this crisis again, face to face, very briefly, the morning after the scene in her room — but with the odd consequence of her having appeared merely to leave it on his hands. He had received it from her as he might have received a bunch of keys or a list of commissions — attentive to her instructions about them, but only putting them, for the time, very carefully and safely, into his pocket. The instructions had seemed, from day to day, to make so little difference for his behaviour — that is for his speech or his silence; to produce, as yet, so little of the fruit of action. He had taken from her, on the spot, in a word, before going to dress for dinner, all she then had to give — after which, on the morrow, he had asked her for more, a good deal as if she might have renewed her supply during the night; but he had had at his command for this latter purpose an air of extraordinary detachment and discretion, an air amounting really to an appeal which, if she could have brought herself to describe it vulgarly, she would have described as cool, just as he himself would have described it in any one else as "cheeky"; a suggestion that she should trust him on the particular ground since she didn't on the general. Neither his speech nor his silence struck her as signifying more, or less, under this pressure, than they had seemed to signify for weeks past; yet if her sense hadn't been absolutely closed to the possibility in him of any thought of wounding her, she might have taken his undisturbed manner, the perfection of his appearance of having recovered himself, for one of those intentions of high impertinence by the aid of which great people, les grands seigneurs, persons of her husband's class and type, always know how to re-establish a violated order.

It was her one purely good fortune that she could feel thus sure impertinence — to HER at any rate — was not among the arts on which he proposed to throw himself; for though he had, in so almost mystifying a manner, replied to nothing, denied nothing, explained nothing, apologised for nothing, he had somehow conveyed to her that this was not because of any determination to treat her case as not "worth" it. There had been consideration, on both occasions, in the way he had listened to her — even though at the same time there had been extreme reserve; a reserve indeed, it was also to be remembered, qualified by the fact that, on their second and shorter interview, in Portland Place, and quite at the end of this passage, she had imagined him positively proposing to her a temporary accommodation. It had been but the matter of something in the depths of the eyes he finally fixed upon her, and she had found in it, the more she kept it before her, the tacitly-offered sketch of a working arrangement. "Leave me my reserve; don't question it — it's all I have, just now, don't you see? so that, if you'll make me the concession of letting me alone with it for as long a time as I require, I promise you something or other, grown under cover of it, even though I don't yet quite make out what, as a return for your patience." She had turned away from him with some such unspoken words as that in her ear, and indeed she had to represent to herself that she had spiritually heard them, had to listen to them still again, to explain her particular patience in face of his particular failure. He hadn't so much as pretended to meet for an instant the question raised by her of her accepted ignorance of the point in time, the period before their own marriage, from which his intimacy with Charlotte dated. As an ignorance in which he and Charlotte had been personally interested — and to the pitch of consummately protecting, for years, each other's interest — as a condition so imposed upon her the fact of its having ceased might have made it, on the spot, the first article of his defence. He had vouchsafed it, however, nothing better than his longest stare of postponed consideration. That tribute he had coldly paid it, and Maggie might herself have been stupefied, truly, had she not had something to hold on by, at her own present ability, even provisional, to make terms with a chapter of history into which she could but a week before not have dipped without a mortal chill. At the rate at which she was living she was getting used hour by hour to these extensions of view; and when she asked herself, at Fawns, to what single observation of her own, in London, the Prince had had an affirmation to oppose, she but just failed to focus the small strained wife of the moments in question as some panting dancer of a difficult step who had capered, before the footlights of an empty theatre, to a spectator lounging in a box.

Her best comprehension of Amerigo's success in not committing himself was in her recall, meanwhile, of the inquiries he had made of her on their only return to the subject, and which he had in fact explicitly provoked their return in order to make. He had had it over with her again, the so distinctly remarkable incident of her interview at home with the little Bloomsbury shopman. This anecdote, for him, had, not altogether surprisingly, required some straighter telling, and the Prince's attitude in presence of it had represented once more his nearest approach to a cross-examination. The difficulty in respect to the little man had been for the question of his motive — his motive in writing, first, in the spirit of retraction, to a lady with whom he had made a most advantageous bargain, and in then coming to see her so that his apology should be personal. Maggie had felt her explanation weak; but there were the facts, and she could give no other. Left alone, after the transaction, with the knowledge that his visitor designed the object bought of him as a birthday-gift to her father — for Maggie confessed freely to having chattered to him almost as to a friend — the vendor of the golden bowl had acted on a scruple rare enough in vendors of any class, and almost unprecedented in the thrifty children of Israel. He hadn't liked what he had done, and what he had above all made such a "good thing" of having done; at the thought of his purchaser's good faith and charming presence, opposed to that flaw in her acquestion which would make it, verily, as an offering to a loved parent, a thing of sinister meaning and evil effect, he had known conscientious, he had known superstitious visitings, had given way to a whim all the more remarkable to his own commercial mind, no doubt, from its never having troubled him in other connexions. She had recognised the oddity of her adventure and left it to show for what it was. She had not been unconscious, on the other hand, that if it hadn't touched Amerigo so nearly he would have found in it matter for some amused reflection. He had uttered an extraordinary sound, something between a laugh and a howl, on her saying, as she had made a point of doing: "Oh, most certainly, he TOLD me his reason was because he 'liked' me" — though she remained in doubt of whether that inarticulate comment had been provoked most by the familiarities she had offered or by those that, so pictured, she had had to endure. That the partner of her bargain had yearned to see her again, that he had plainly jumped at a pretext for it, this also she had frankly expressed herself to the Prince as having, in no snubbing, no scandalised, but rather in a positively appreciative and indebted spirit, not delayed to make out. He had wished, ever so seriously, to return her a part of her money, and she had wholly declined to receive it; and then he had uttered his hope that she had not, at all events, already devoted the crystal cup to the beautiful purpose she had, so kindly and so fortunately, named to him. It wasn't a thing for a present to a person she was fond of, for she wouldn't wish to give a present that would bring ill luck. That had come to him — so that he couldn't rest, and he should feel better now that he had told her. His having led her to act in ignorance was what he should have been ashamed of; and, if she would pardon, gracious lady as she was, all the liberties he had taken, she might make of the bowl any use in life but that one.

It was after this that the most extraordinary incident of all, of course, had occurred — his pointing to the two photographs with the remark that those were persons he knew, and that, more wonderful still, he had made acquaintance with them, years before, precisely over the same article. The lady, on that occasion, had taken up the fancy of presenting it to the gentleman, and the gentleman, guessing and dodging ever so cleverly, had declared that he wouldn't for the world receive an object under such suspicion. He himself, the little man had confessed, wouldn't have minded — about THEM; but he had never forgotten either their talk or their faces, the impression altogether made by them, and, if she really wished to know, now, what had perhaps most moved him, it was the thought that she should ignorantly have gone in for a thing not good enough for other buyers. He had been immensely struck — that was another point — with this accident of their turning out, after so long, friends of hers too: they had disappeared, and this was the only light he had ever had upon them. He had flushed up, quite red, with his recognition, with all his responsibility — had declared that the connexion must have had, mysteriously, something to do with the impulse he had obeyed. And Maggie had made, to her husband, while he again stood before her, no secret of the shock, for herself, so suddenly and violently received. She had done her best, even while taking it full in the face, not to give herself away; but she wouldn't answer — no, she wouldn't — for what she might, in her agitation, have made her informant think. He might think what he would — there had been three or four minutes during which, while she asked him question upon question, she had doubtless too little cared. And he had spoken, for his remembrance, as fully as she could have wished; he had spoken, oh, delightfully, for the "terms" on which his other visitors had appeared to be with each other, and in fact for that conviction of the nature and degree of their intimacy under which, in spite of precautions, they hadn't been able to help leaving him. He had observed and judged and not forgotten; he had been sure they were great people, but no, ah no, distinctly, hadn't "liked" them as he liked the Signora Principessa. Certainly — she had created no vagueness about that — he had been in possession of her name and address, for sending her both her cup and her account. But the others he had only, always, wondered about — he had been sure they would never come back. And as to the time of their visit, he could place it, positively, to a day — by reason of a transaction of importance, recorded in his books, that had occurred but a few hours later. He had left her, in short, definitely rejoicing that he had been able to make up to her for not having been quite "square" over their little business by rendering her, so unexpectedly, the service of this information. His joy, moreover, was — as much as Amerigo would! — a matter of the personal interest with which her kindness, gentleness, grace, her charming presence and easy humanity and familiarity, had inspired him. All of which, while, in thought, Maggie went over it again and again — oh, over any imputable rashness of her own immediate passion and pain, as well as over the rest of the straight little story she had, after all, to tell — might very conceivably make a long sum for the Prince to puzzle out.

There were meanwhile, after the Castledeans and those invited to meet them had gone, and before Mrs. Rance and the Lutches had come, three or four days during which she was to learn the full extent of her need not to be penetrable; and then it was indeed that she felt all the force, and threw herself upon all the help, of the truth she had confided, several nights earlier, to Fanny Assingham. She had known it in advance, had warned herself of it while the house was full: Charlotte had designs upon her of a nature best known to herself, and was only waiting for the better opportunity of their finding themselves less companioned. This consciousness had been exactly at the bottom of Maggie's wish to multiply their spectators; there were moments for her, positively, moments of planned postponement, of evasion scarcely less disguised than studied, during which she turned over with anxiety the different ways — there being two or three possible ones — in which her young stepmother might, at need, seek to work upon her. Amerigo's not having "told" her of his passage with his wife gave, for Maggie, altogether a new aspect to Charlotte's consciousness and condition — an aspect with which, for apprehension, for wonder, and even, at moments, inconsequently enough, for something like compassion, the Princess had now to reckon. She asked herself — for she was capable of that — what he had MEANT by keeping the sharer of his guilt in the dark about a matter touching her otherwise so nearly; what he had meant, that is, for this unmistakably mystified personage herself. Maggie could imagine what he had meant for her — all sorts of thinkable things, whether things of mere "form" or things of sincerity, things of pity or things of prudence: he had meant, for instance, in all probability, primarily, to conjure away any such appearance of a changed relation between the two women as his father-inlaw might notice and follow up. It would have been open to him however, given the pitch of their intimacy, to avert this danger by some more conceivable course with Charlotte; since an earnest warning, in fact, the full freedom of alarm, that of his insisting to her on the peril of suspicion incurred, and on the importance accordingly of outward peace at any price, would have been the course really most conceivable. Instead of warning and advising he had reassured and deceived her; so that our young woman, who had been, from far back, by the habit, if her nature, as much on her guard against sacrificing others as if she felt the great trap of life mainly to be set for one's doing so, now found herself attaching her fancy to that side of the situation of the exposed pair which involved, for themselves at least, the sacrifice of the least fortunate.

She never, at present, thought of what Amerigo might be intending, without the reflection, by the same stroke, that, whatever this quantity, he was leaving still more to her own ingenuity. He was helping her, when the thing came to the test, only by the polished, possibly almost too polished surface his manner to his wife wore for an admiring world; and that, surely, was entitled to scarcely more than the praise of negative diplomacy. He was keeping his manner right, as she had related to Mrs. Assingham; the case would have been beyond calculation, truly, if, on top of everything, he had allowed it to go wrong. She had hours of exaltation indeed when the meaning of all this pressed in upon her as a tacit vow from him to abide without question by whatever she should be able to achieve or think fit to prescribe. Then it was that, even while holding her breath for the awe of it, she truly felt almost able enough for anything. It was as if she had passed, in a time incredibly short, from being nothing for him to being all; it was as if, rightly noted, every turn of his head, every tone of his voice, in these days, might mean that there was but one way in which a proud man reduced to abjection could hold himself. During those of Maggie's vigils in which that view loomed largest, the image of her husband that it thus presented to her gave out a beauty for the revelation of which she struck herself as paying, if anything, all too little. To make sure of it — to make sure of the beauty shining out of the humility, and of the humility lurking in all the pride of his presence — she would have gone the length of paying more yet, of paying with difficulties and anxieties compared to which those actually before her might have been as superficial as headaches or rainy days.

The point at which these exaltations dropped, however, was the point at which it was apt to come over her that if her complications had been greater the question of paying would have been limited still less to the liabilities of her own pocket. The complications were verily great enough, whether for ingenuities or sublimities, so long as she had to come back to it so often that Charlotte, all the while, could only be struggling with secrets sharper than her own. It was odd how that certainty again and again determined and coloured her wonderments of detail; the question, for instance, of HOW Amerigo, in snatched opportunities of conference, put the haunted creature off with false explanations, met her particular challenges and evaded — if that was what he did do! — her particular demands. Even the conviction that Charlotte was but awaiting some chance really to test her trouble upon her lover's wife left Maggie's sense meanwhile open as to the sight of gilt wires and bruised wings, the spacious but suspended cage, the home of eternal unrest, of pacings, beatings, shakings, all so vain, into which the baffled consciousness helplessly resolved itself. The cage was the deluded condition, and Maggie, as having known delusion — rather! — understood the nature of cages. She walked round Charlotte's — cautiously and in a very wide circle; and when, inevitably, they had to communicate she felt herself, comparatively, outside, on the breast of nature, and saw her companion's face as that of a prisoner looking through bars. So it was that through bars, bars richly gilt, but firmly, though discreetly, planted, Charlotte finally struck her as making a grim attempt; from which, at first, the Princess drew back as instinctively as if the door of the cage had suddenly been opened from within.

XXXVI

They had been alone that evening — alone as a party of six, and four of them, after dinner, under suggestion not to be resisted, sat down to "bridge" in the smoking-room. They had passed together to that apartment, on rising from table, Charlotte and Mrs. Assingham alike indulgent, always, to tobacco, and in fact practising an emulation which, as Fanny said, would, for herself, had the Colonel not issued an interdict based on the fear of her stealing his cigars, have stopped only at the short pipe. Here cards had with inevitable promptness asserted their rule, the game forming itself, as had often happened before, of Mr. Verver with Mrs. Assingham for partner and of the Prince with Mrs. Verver. The Colonel, who had then asked of Maggie license to relieve his mind of a couple of letters for the earliest post out on the morrow, was addressing himself to this task at the other end of the room, and the Princess herself had welcomed the comparatively hushed hour — for the bridge-players were serious and silent — much in the mood of a tired actress who has the good fortune to be "off," while her mates are on, almost long enough for a nap on the property sofa in the wing. Maggie's nap, had she been able to snatch forty winks, would have been of the spirit rather than of the sense; yet as she subsided, near a lamp, with the last salmon-coloured French periodical, she was to fail, for refreshment, even of that sip of independence.

There was no question for her, as she found, of closing her eyes and getting away; they strayed back to life, in the stillness, over the top of her Review; she could lend herself to none of those refinements of the higher criticism with which its pages bristled; she was there, where her companions were, there again and more than ever there; it was as if, of a sudden, they had been made, in their personal intensity and their rare complexity of relation, freshly importunate to her. It was the first evening there had been no one else. Mrs. Rance and the Lutches were due the next day; but meanwhile the facts of the situation were upright for her round the green cloth and the silver flambeaux; the fact of her father's wife's lover facing his mistress; the fact of her father sitting, all unsounded and unblinking, between them; the fact of Charlotte keeping it up, keeping up everything, across the table, with her husband beside her; the fact of Fanny Assingham, wonderful creature, placed opposite to the three and knowing more about each, probably, when one came to think, than either of them knew of either. Erect above all for her was the sharp-edged fact of the relation of the whole group, individually and collectively, to herself — herself so speciously eliminated for the hour, but presumably more present to the attention of each than the next card to be played.

Yes, under that imputation, to her sense, they sat — the imputation of wondering, beneath and behind all their apparently straight play, if she weren't really watching them from her corner and consciously, as might be said, holding them in her hand. She was asking herself at last how they could bear it — for, though cards were as nought to her and she could follow no move, so that she was always, on such occasions, out of the party, they struck her as conforming alike, in the matter of gravity and propriety, to the stiff standard of the house. Her father, she knew, was a high adept, one of the greatest — she had been ever, in her stupidity, his small, his sole despair; Amerigo excelled easily, as he understood and practised every art that could beguile large leisure; Mrs. Assingham and Charlotte, moreover, were accounted as "good" as members of a sex incapable of the nobler consistency could be. Therefore, evidently, they were not, all so up to their usual form, merely passing it off, whether for her or for themselves; and the amount of enjoyed, or at least achieved, security represented by so complete a conquest of appearances was what acted on her nerves, precisely, with a kind of provocative force. She found herself, for five minutes, thrilling with the idea of the prodigious effect that, just as she sat there near them, she had at her command; with the sense that if she were but different — oh, ever so different! — all this high decorum would hang by a hair. There reigned for her, absolutely, during these vertiginous moments, that fascination of the monstrous, that temptation of the horribly possible, which we so often trace by its breaking out suddenly, lest it should go further, in unexplained retreats and reactions.

After it had been thus vividly before her for a little that, springing up under her wrong and making them all start, stare and turn pale, she might sound out their doom in a single sentence, a sentence easy to choose among several of the lurid — after she had faced that blinding light and felt it turn to blackness, she rose from her place, laying aside her magazine, and moved slowly round the room, passing near the card-players and pausing an instant behind the chairs in turn. Silent and discreet, she bent a vague mild face upon them, as if to signify that, little as she followed their doings, she wished them well; and she took from each, across the table, in the common solemnity, an upward recognition which she was to carry away with her on her moving out to the terrace, a few minutes later. Her father and her husband, Mrs. Assingham and Charlotte, had done nothing but meet her eyes; yet the difference in these demonstrations made each a separate passage — which was all the more wonderful since, with the secret behind every face, they had alike tried to look at her THROUGH it and in denial of it.

It all left her, as she wandered off, with the strangest of impressions — the sense, forced upon her as never yet, of an appeal, a positive confidence, from the four pairs of eyes, that was deeper than any negation, and that seemed to speak, on the part of each, of some relation to be contrived by her, a relation with herself, which would spare the individual the danger, the actual present strain, of the relation with the others. They thus tacitly put it upon her to be disposed of, the whole complexity of their peril, and she promptly saw why because she was there, and there just as she was, to lift it off them and take it; to charge herself with it as the scapegoat of old, of whom she had once seen a terrible picture, had been charged with the sins of the people and had gone forth into the desert to sink under his burden and die. That indeed wasn't THEIR design and their interest, that she should sink under hers; it wouldn't be their feeling that she should do anything but live, live on somehow for their benefit, and even as much as possible in their company, to keep proving to them that they had truly escaped and that she was still there to simplify. This idea of her simplifying, and of their combined struggle, dim as yet but steadily growing, toward the perception of her adopting it from them, clung to her while she hovered on the terrace, where the summer night was so soft that she scarce needed the light shawl she had picked up. Several of the long windows of the occupied rooms stood open to it, and the light came out in vague shafts and fell upon the old smooth stones. The hour was moonless and starless and the air heavy and still — which was why, in her evening dress, she need fear no chill and could get away, in the outer darkness, from that provocation of opportunity which had assaulted her, within, on her sofa, as a beast might have leaped at her throat.

Nothing in fact was stranger than the way in which, when she had remained there a little, her companions, watched by her through one of the windows, actually struck her as almost consciously and gratefully safer. They might have been — really charming as they showed in the beautiful room, and Charlotte certainly, as always, magnificently handsome and supremely distinguished — they might have been figures rehearsing some play of which she herself was the author; they might even, for the happy appearance they continued to present, have been such figures as would, by the strong note of character in each, fill any author with the certitude of success, especially of their own histrionic. They might in short have represented any mystery they would; the point being predominantly that the key to the mystery, the key that could wind and unwind it without a snap of the spring, was there in her pocket — or rather, no doubt, clasped at this crisis in her hand and pressed, as she walked back and forth, to her breast. She walked to the end and far out of the light; she returned and saw the others still where she had left them; she passed round the house and looked into the drawing-room, lighted also, but empty now, and seeming to speak the more, in its own voice, of all the possibilities she controlled. Spacious and splendid, like a stage again awaiting a drama, it was a scene she might people, by the press of her spring, either with serenities and dignities and decencies, or with terrors and shames and ruins, things as ugly as those formless fragments of her golden bowl she was trying so hard to pick up.

She continued to walk and continued to pause; she stopped afresh for the look into the smoking-room, and by this time — it was as if the recognition had of itself arrested her —

she saw as in a picture, with the temptation she had fled from quite extinct, why it was she had been able to give herself so little, from the first, to the vulgar heat of her wrong. She might fairly, as she watched them, have missed it as a lost thing; have yearned for it, for the straight vindictive view, the rights of resentment, the rages of jealousy, the protests of passion, as for something she had been cheated of not least: a range of feelings which for many women would have meant so much, but which for HER husband's wife, for HER father's daughter, figured nothing nearer to experience than a wild eastern caravan, looming into view with crude colours in the sun, fierce pipes in the air, high spears against the sky, all a thrill, a natural joy to mingle with, but turning off short before it reached her and plunging into other defiles. She saw at all events why horror itself had almost failed her; the horror that, foreshadowed in advance, would, by her thought, have made everything that was unaccustomed in her cry out with pain; the horror of finding evil seated, all at its ease, where she had only dreamed of good; the horror of the thing HIDEOUSLY behind, behind so much trusted, so much pretended, nobleness, cleverness, tenderness. It was the first sharp falsity she had known in her life, to touch at all, or be touched by; it had met her like some bad-faced stranger surprised in one of the thick-carpeted corridors of a house of quiet on a Sunday afternoon; and yet, yes, amazingly, she had been able to look at terror and disgust only to know that she must put away from her the bitter-sweet of their freshness. The sight, from the window, of the group so constituted, TOLD her why, told her how, named to her, as with hard lips, named straight AT her, so that she must take it full in the face, that other possible relation to the whole fact which alone would bear upon her irresistibly. It was extraordinary: they positively brought home to her that to feel about them in any of the immediate, inevitable, assuaging ways, the ways usually open to innocence outraged and generosity betrayed, would have been to give them up, and that giving them up was, marvellously, not to be thought of. She had never, from the first hour of her state of acquired conviction, given them up so little as now; though she was, no doubt, as the consequence of a step taken a few minutes later, to invoke the conception of doing that, if might be, even less. She had resumed her walk — stopping here and there, while she rested on the cool smooth stone balustrade, to draw it out; in the course of which, after a little, she passed again the lights of the empty drawing-room and paused again for what she saw and felt there.

It was not at once, however, that this became quite concrete; that was the effect of her presently making out that Charlotte was in the room, launched and erect there, in the middle, and looking about her; that she had evidently just come round to it, from her card-table, by one of the passages — with the expectation, to all appearance, of joining her stepdaughter. She had pulled up at seeing the great room empty — Maggie not having passed out, on leaving the group, in a manner to be observed. So definite a quest of her, with the bridge-party interrupted or altered for it, was an impression that fairly assailed the Princess, and to which something of attitude and aspect, of the air of arrested pursuit and purpose, in Charlotte, together with the suggestion of her next vague movements, quickly added its meaning. This meaning was that she had decided, that she had been infinitely conscious of Maggie's presence before, that she knew that she would at last find her alone, and that she wanted her, for some reason, enough to have presumably called on Bob Assingham for aid. He had taken her chair and let her go, and the arrangement was for Maggie a signal proof of her earnestness; of the energy, in fact, that, though superficially commonplace in a situation in which people weren't supposed to be watching each other, was what affected our young woman, on the spot, as a breaking of bars. The splendid shining supple creature was out of the cage, was at large; and the question now almost grotesquely rose of whether she mightn't by some art, just where she was and before she could go further, be hemmed in and secured. It would have been for a moment, in this case, a matter of quickly closing the windows and giving the alarm — with poor Maggie's sense that, though she couldn't know what she wanted of her, it was enough for trepidation that, at these firm hands, anything should be to say nothing of the sequel of a flight taken again along the terrace, even under the shame of the confessed feebleness of such evasions on the part of an outraged wife. It was to this feebleness, none the less, that the outraged wife had presently resorted; the most that could be said for her being, as she felt while she finally stopped short, at a distance, that she could at any rate resist her abjection sufficiently not to sneak into the house by another way and safely reach her room. She had literally caught herself in the act of dodging and ducking, and it told her there, vividly, in a single word, what she had all along been most afraid of.

She had been afraid of the particular passage with Charlotte that would determine her father's wife to take him into her confidence as she couldn't possibly as yet have done, to prepare for him a statement of her wrong, to lay before him the infamy of what she was apparently suspected of. This, should she have made up her mind to do it, would rest on a calculation the thought of which evoked, strangely, other possibilities and visions. It would show her as sufficiently believing in her grasp of her husband to be able to assure herself that, with his daughter thrown on the defensive, with Maggie's cause and Maggie's word, in fine, against her own, it wasn't Maggie's that would most certainly carry the day. Such a glimpse of her conceivable idea, which would be founded on reasons all her own, reasons of experience and assurance, impenetrable to others, but intimately familiar to herself — such a glimpse opened out wide as soon as it had come into view; for if so much as this was still firm ground between the elder pair, if the beauty of appearances had been so consistently preserved, it was only the golden bowl as Maggie herself knew it that had been broken. The breakage stood not for any wrought discomposure among the triumphant three — it stood merely for the dire deformity of her attitude toward them. She was unable at the minute, of course, fully to measure the difference thus involved for her, and it remained inevitably an agitating image, the way it might be held over her that if she didn't, of her own prudence, satisfy Charlotte as to the reference, in her mocking spirit, of so much of the unuttered and unutterable, of the constantly and unmistakably implied, her father would be invited without further ceremony to recommend her to do so. But ANY confidence, ANY latent operating insolence, that Mrs. Verver should, thanks to her large native resources, continue to be possessed of and to hold in reserve, glimmered suddenly as a possible working light and seemed to offer, for meeting her, a new basis and something like a new system. Maggie felt, truly, a rare contraction of the heart on making out, the next instant, what the new system would probably have to be-and she had practically done that before perceiving that the thing she feared had already taken place. Charlotte, extending her search, appeared now to define herself vaguely in the distance; of this, after an instant, the Princess was sure, though the darkness was thick, for the projected clearness of the smoking-room windows had presently contributed its help. Her friend came slowly into that circle — having also, for herself, by this time, not indistinguishably discovered that Maggie was on the terrace. Maggie, from the end, saw her stop before one of the windows to look at the group within, and then saw her come nearer and pause again, still with a considerable length of the place between them.

Yes, Charlotte had seen she was watching her from afar, and had stopped now to put her further attention to the test. Her face was fixed on her, through the night; she was the creature who had escaped by force from her cage, yet there was in her whole motion assuredly, even as so dimly discerned, a kind of portentous intelligent stillness. She had escaped with an intention, but with an intention the more definite that it could so accord with quiet measures. The two women, at all events, only hovered there, for these first minutes, face to face over their interval and exchanging no sign; the intensity of their mutual look might have pierced the night, and Maggie was at last to start with the scared sense of having thus yielded to doubt, to dread, to hesitation, for a time that, with no other proof needed, would have completely given her away. How long had she stood staring? — a single minute or five? Long enough, in any case, to have felt herself absolutely take from her visitor something that the latter threw upon her, irresistibly, by this effect of silence, by this effect of waiting and watching, by this effect, unmistakably, of timing her indecision and her fear. If then, scared and hanging back, she had, as was so evident, sacrificed all past pretences, it would have been with the instant knowledge of an immense advantage gained that Charlotte finally saw her come on. Maggie came on with her heart in her hands; she came on with the definite prevision, throbbing like the tick of a watch, of a doom impossibly sharp and hard, but to which, after looking at it with her eyes wide open, she had none the less bowed her head. By the time she was at her companion's side, for that matter, by the time Charlotte had, without a motion, without a word, simply let her approach and stand there, her head was already on the block, so that the consciousness that everything had now gone blurred all perception of whether or no the axe had fallen. Oh, the "advantage," it was perfectly enough, in truth, with Mrs. Verver; for what was Maggie's own sense but that of having been thrown over on her back, with her neck, from the first, half broken and her helpless face staring up? That position only could account for the positive grimace of weakness and pain produced there by Charlotte's dignity.

"I've come to join you — I thought you would be here."

"Oh yes, I'm here," Maggie heard herself return a little flatly. "It's too close indoors."

"Very — but close even here." Charlotte was still and grave — she had even uttered her remark about the temperature with an expressive weight that verged upon solemnity; so that Maggie, reduced to looking vaguely about at the sky, could only feel her not fail of her purpose. "The air's heavy as if with thunder — I think there'll be a storm." She made the suggestion to carry off an awkwardness — which was a part, always, of her companion's gain; but the awkwardness didn't diminish in the silence that followed. Charlotte had said nothing in reply; her brow was dark as with a fixed expression, and her high elegance, her handsome head and long, straight neck testified, through the dusk, to their inveterate completeness and noble erectness. It was as if what she had come out to do had already begun, and when, as a consequence, Maggie had said helplessly, "Don't you want something? won't you have my shawl?" everything might have crumbled away in the comparative poverty of the tribute. Mrs. Verver's rejection of it had the brevity of a sign that they hadn't closed in for idle words, just as her dim, serious face, uninterruptedly presented until they moved again, might have represented the success with which she watched all her message penetrate. They presently went back the way she had come, but she stopped Maggie again within range of the smoking-room window and made her stand where the party at cards would be before her. Side by side, for three minutes, they fixed this picture of quiet harmonies, the positive charm of it and, as might have been said, the full significance — which, as was now brought home to Maggie, could be no more, after all, than a matter of interpretation, differing always for a different interpreter. As she herself had hovered in sight of it a quarter-of-an-hour before, it would have been a thing for her to show Charlotte — to show in righteous irony, in reproach too stern for anything but silence. But now it was she who was being shown it, and shown it by Charlotte, and she saw quickly enough that, as Charlotte showed it, so she must at present submissively seem to take it.

The others were absorbed and unconscious, either silent over their game or dropping remarks unheard on the terrace; and it was to her father's quiet face, discernibly expressive of nothing that was in his daughter's mind, that our young woman's attention was most directly given. His wife and his daughter were both closely watching him, and to which of them, could he have been notified of this, would his raised eyes first, all impulsively, have responded; in which of them would he have felt it most important to destroy — for HIS clutch at the equilibrium — any germ of uneasiness? Not yet, since his marriage, had Maggie so sharply and so formidably known her old possession of him as a thing divided and contested. She was looking at him by Charlotte's leave and under Charlotte's direction; quite in fact as if the particular way she should look at him were prescribed to her; quite, even, as if she had been defied to look at him in any other. It came home to her too that the challenge wasn't, as might be said, in his interest and for his protection, but, pressingly, insistently, in Charlotte's, for that of HER security at any price. She might verily, by this dumb demonstration, have been naming to Maggie the price, naming it as a question for Maggie herself, a sum of money that she, properly, was to find. She must remain safe and Maggie must pay — what she was to pay with being her own affair.

Straighter than ever, thus, the Princess again felt it all put upon her, and there was a minute, just a supreme instant, during which there burned in her a wild wish that her father would only look up. It throbbed for these seconds as a yearning appeal to him — she would chance it, that is, if he would but just raise his eyes and catch them, across the larger space, standing in the outer dark together. Then he might be affected by the sight, taking them as they were; he might make some sign — she scarce knew what — that would save her; save her from being the one, this way, to pay all. He might somehow show a preference — distinguishing between them; might, out of pity for her, signal to her that this extremity of her effort for him was more than he asked. That represented Maggie's one little lapse from consistency — the sole small deflection in the whole course of her scheme. It had come to nothing the next minute, for the dear man's eyes had never moved, and Charlotte's hand, promptly passed into her arm, had already, had very firmly drawn her on — quite, for that matter, as from some sudden, some equal perception on her part too of the more ways than one in which their impression could appeal. They retraced their steps along the rest of the terrace, turning the corner of the house, and presently came abreast of the other windows, those of the pompous drawing-room, still lighted and still empty. Here Charlotte again paused, and it was again as if she were pointing out what Maggie had observed for herself, the very look the place had of being vivid in its stillness, of having, with all its great objects as ordered and balanced as for a formal reception, been appointed for some high transaction, some real affair of state. In presence of this opportunity she faced her companion once more; she traced in her the effect of everything she had already communicated; she signified, with the same success, that the terrace and the sullen night would bear too meagre witness to the completion of her idea. Soon enough then, within the room, under the old lustres of Venice and the eyes of the several great portraits, more or less contemporary with these, that awaited on the walls of Fawns their final far migration — soon enough Maggie found herself staring, and at first all too gaspingly, at the grand total to which each separate demand Mrs. Verver had hitherto made upon her, however she had made it, now amounted.

"I've been wanting — and longer than you'd perhaps believe — to put a question to you for which no opportunity has seemed to me yet quite so good as this. It would have been easier perhaps if you had struck me as in the least disposed ever to give me one. I have to take it now, you see, as I find it." They stood in the centre of the immense room, and Maggie could feel that the scene of life her imagination had made of it twenty minutes before was by this time sufficiently peopled. These few straight words filled it to its uttermost reaches, and nothing was now absent from her consciousness, either, of the part she was called upon to play in it. Charlotte had marched straight in, dragging her rich train; she rose there beautiful and free, with her whole aspect and action attuned to the firmness of her speech. Maggie had kept the shawl she had taken out with her, and, clutching it tight in her nervousness, drew it round her as if huddling in it for shelter, covering herself with it for humility. She looked out as from under an improvised hood — the sole headgear of some poor woman at somebody's proud door; she waited even like the poor woman; she met her friend's eyes with recognitions she couldn't suppress. She might sound it as she could —"What question then?" — everything in her, from head to foot, crowded it upon Charlotte that she knew. She knew too well — that she was showing; so that successful vagueness, to save some scrap of her dignity from the imminence of her defeat, was already a lost cause, and the one thing left was if possible, at any cost, even that of stupid inconsequence, to try to look as if she weren't afraid. If she could but appear at all not afraid she might appear a little not ashamed — that is not ashamed to be afraid, which was the kind of shame that could be fastened on her, it being fear all the while that moved her. Her challenge, at any rate, her wonder, her terror — the blank, blurred surface, whatever it was that she presented became a mixture that ceased to signify; for to the accumulated advantage by which Charlotte was at present sustained her next words themselves had little to add.

"Have you any ground of complaint of me? Is there any wrong you consider I've done you? I feel at last that I've a right to ask you."

Their eyes had to meet on it, and to meet long; Maggie's avoided at least the disgrace of looking away. "What makes you want to ask it?"

"My natural desire to know. You've done that, for so long, little justice."

Maggie waited a moment. "For so long? You mean you've thought —?"

"I mean, my dear, that I've seen. I've seen, week after week, that YOU seemed to be thinking — of something that perplexed or worried you. Is it anything for which I'm in any degree responsible?"

Maggie summoned all her powers. "What in the world SHOULD it be?"

"Ah, that's not for me to imagine, and I should be very sorry to have to try to say! I'm aware of no point whatever at which I may have failed you," said Charlotte; "nor of any at which I may have failed any one in whom I can suppose you sufficiently interested to care. If I've been guilty of some fault I've committed it all unconsciously, and am only anxious to hear from you honestly about it. But if I've been mistaken as to what I speak of — the difference, more and more marked, as I've thought, in all your manner to me — why, obviously, so much the better. No form of correction received from you could give me greater satisfaction."

She spoke, it struck her companion, with rising, with extraordinary ease; as if hearing herself say it all, besides seeing the way it was listened to, helped her from point to point. She saw she was right — that this WAS the tone for her to take and the thing for her to do, the thing as to which she was probably feeling that she had in advance, in her delays and uncertainties, much exaggerated the difficulty. The difficulty was small, and it grew smaller as her adversary continued to shrink; she was not only doing as she wanted, but had by this time effectively done it and hung it up. All of which but deepened Maggie's sense of the sharp and simple need, now, of seeing her through to the end. "'If' you've been mistaken, you say?" — and the Princess but barely faltered. "You HAVE been mistaken."

Charlotte looked at her splendidly hard. "You're perfectly sure it's ALL my mistake?"

"All I can say is that you've received a false impression."

"Ah then — so much the better! From the moment I HAD received it I knew I must sooner or later speak of it — for that, you see, is, systematically, my way. And now," Charlotte added, "you make me glad I've spoken. I thank you very much."

It was strange how for Maggie too, with this, the difficulty seemed to sink. Her companion's acceptance of her denial was like a general pledge not to keep things any worse for her than they essentially had to be; it positively helped her to build up her falsehood — to which, accordingly, she contributed another block. "I've affected you evidently — quite accidentally — in some way of which I've been all unaware. I've NOT felt at any time that you've wronged me."

"How could I come within a mile," Charlotte inquired, "of such a possibility?"

Maggie, with her eyes on her more easily now, made no attempt to say; she said, after a little, something more to the present point. "I accuse you — I accuse you of nothing."

"Ah, that's lucky!"

Charlotte had brought this out with the richness, almost, of gaiety; and Maggie, to go on, had to think, with her own intensity, of Amerigo — to think how he, on his side, had had to go through with his lie to her, how it was for his wife he had done so, and how his doing so had given her the clue and set her the example. He must have had his own difficulty about it, and she was not, after all, falling below him. It was in fact as if, thanks to her hovering image of him confronted with this admirable creature even as she was confronted, there glowed upon her from afar, yet straight and strong, a deep explanatory light which covered the last inch of the ground. He had given her something to conform to, and she hadn't unintelligently turned on him, "gone back on" him, as he would have said, by not conforming. They were together thus, he and she, close, close together — whereas Charlotte, though rising there radiantly before her, was really off in some darkness of space that would steep her in solitude and harass her with care. The heart of the Princess swelled, accordingly, even in her abasement; she had kept in tune with the right, and something, certainly, something that might be like a rare flower snatched from an impossible ledge, would, and possibly soon, come of it for her. The right, the right — yes, it took this extraordinary form of her humbugging, as she had called it, to the end. It was only a question of not, by a hair's breadth, deflecting into the truth. So, supremely, was she braced. "You must take it from me that your anxiety rests quite on a misconception. You must take it from me that I've never at any moment fancied I could suffer by you." And, marvellously, she kept it up — not only kept it up, but improved on it. "You must take it from me that I've never thought of you but as beautiful, wonderful and good. Which is all, I think, that you can possibly ask."

Charlotte held her a moment longer: she needed — not then to have appeared only tactless — the last word. "It's much more, my dear, than I dreamed of asking. I only wanted your denial."

"Well then, you have it."

"Upon your honour?"

"Upon my honour:"

And she made a point even, our young woman, of not turning away. Her grip of her shawl had loosened — she had let it fall behind her; but she stood there for anything more and till the weight should be lifted. With which she saw soon enough what more was to come. She saw it in Charlotte's face, and felt it make between them, in the air, a chill that completed the coldness of their conscious perjury. "Will you kiss me on it then?"

She couldn't say yes, but she didn't say no; what availed her still, however, was to measure, in her passivity, how much too far Charlotte had come to retreat. But there was something different also, something for which, while her cheek received the prodigious kiss, she had her opportunity — the sight of the others, who, having risen from their cards to join the absent members of their party, had reached the open door at the end of the room and stopped short, evidently, in presence of the demonstration that awaited them. Her husband and her father were in front, and Charlotte's embrace of her — which wasn't to be distinguished, for them, either, she felt, from her embrace of Charlotte — took on with their arrival a high publicity.

XXXVII

Her father had asked her, three days later, in an interval of calm, how she was affected, in the light of their reappearance and of their now perhaps richer fruition, by Dotty and Kitty, and by the once formidable Mrs. Rance; and the consequence of this inquiry had been, for the pair, just such another stroll together, away from the rest of the party and off into the park, as had asserted its need to them on the occasion of the previous visit of these anciently more agitating friends — that of their long talk, on a sequestered bench beneath one of the great trees, when the particular question had come up for them the then purblind discussion of which, at their enjoyed leisure, Maggie had formed the habit of regarding as the "first beginning" of their present situation. The whirligig of time had thus brought round for them again, on their finding themselves face to face while the others were gathering for tea on the terrace, the same odd impulse quietly to "slope" — so Adam Verver himself, as they went, familiarly expressed it — that had acted, in its way, of old; acted for the distant autumn afternoon and for the sharpness of their since so outlived crisis. It might have been funny to them now that the presence of Mrs. Rance and the Lutches — and with symptoms, too, at that time less developed — had once, for their anxiety and their prudence, constituted a crisis; it might have been funny that these ladies could ever have figured, to their imagination, as a symbol of dangers vivid enough to precipitate the need of a remedy. This amount of entertainment and assistance they were indeed disposed to extract from their actual impressions; they had been finding it, for months past, by Maggie's view, a resource and a relief to talk, with an approach to intensity, when they met, of all the people they weren't really thinking of and didn't really care about, the people with whom their existence had begun almost to swarm; and they closed in at present round the spectres of their past, as they permitted themselves to describe the three ladies, with a better imitation of enjoying their theme than they had been able to achieve, certainly, during the stay, for instance, of the Castledeans. The Castledeans were a new joke, comparatively, and they had had — always to Maggie's view — to teach themselves the way of it; whereas the Detroit, the Providence party, rebounding so from Providence, from Detroit, was an old and ample one, of which the most could be made and as to which a humorous insistence could be guarded.

Sharp and sudden, moreover, this afternoon, had been their well-nigh confessed desire just to rest together, a little, as from some strain long felt but never named; to rest, as who should say, shoulder to shoulder and hand in hand, each pair of eyes so yearningly — and indeed what could it be but so wearily? — closed as to render the collapse safe from detection by the other pair. It was positively as if, in short, the inward felicity of their being once more, perhaps only for half-an-hour, simply daughter and father had glimmered out for them, and they had picked up the pretext that would make it easiest. They were husband and wife — oh, so immensely! — as regards other persons; but after they had dropped again on their old bench, conscious that the party on the terrace, augmented, as in the past, by neighbours, would do beautifully without them, it was wonderfully like their having got together into some boat and paddled off from the shore where husbands and wives, luxuriant complications, made the air too tropical. In the boat they were father and daughter, and poor Dotty and Kitty supplied abundantly, for their situation, the oars or the sail. Why, into the bargain, for that matter — this came to Maggie — couldn't they always live, so far as they lived together, in a boat? She felt in her face, with the question, the breath of a possibility that soothed her; they needed only KNOW each other, henceforth, in the unmarried relation. That other sweet evening, in the same place, he had been as unmarried as possible — which had kept down, so to speak, the quantity of change in their state. Well then, that other sweet evening was what the present sweet evening would resemble; with the quite calculable effect of an exquisite inward refreshment. They HAD, after all, whatever happened, always and ever each other; each other — that was the hidden treasure and the saving truth — to do exactly what they would with: a provision full of possibilities. Who could tell, as yet, what, thanks to it, they wouldn't have done before the end?

They had meanwhile been tracing together, in the golden air that, toward six o'clock of a July afternoon, hung about the massed Kentish woods, several features of the social evolution of her old playmates, still beckoned on, it would seem, by unattainable ideals, still falling back, beyond the sea, to their native seats, for renewals of the moral, financial, conversational — one scarce knew what to call it — outfit, and again and for ever reappearing like a tribe of Wandering Jewesses. Our couple had finally exhausted, however, the study of these annals, and Maggie was to take up, after a drop, a different matter, or one at least with which the immediate connection was not at first apparent. "Were you amused at me just now — when I wondered what other people could wish to struggle for? Did you think me," she asked with some earnestness —"well, fatuous?"

"'Fatuous'?" — he seemed at a loss.

"I mean sublime in OUR happiness — as if looking down from a height. Or, rather, sublime in our general position — that's what I mean." She spoke as from the habit of her anxious conscience something that disposed her frequently to assure herself, for her human commerce, of the state of the "books" of the spirit. "Because I don't at all want," she explained, "to be blinded, or made 'sniffy,' by any sense of a social situation." Her father listened to this declaration as if the precautions of her general mercy could still, as they betrayed themselves, have surprises for him — to say nothing of a charm of delicacy and beauty; he might have been wishing to see how far she could go and where she would, all touchingly to him, arrive. But she waited a little — as if made nervous, precisely, by feeling him depend too much on what she said. They were avoiding the serious, standing off, anxiously, from the real, and they fell, again and again, as if to disguise their precaution itself, into the tone of the time that came back to them from their other talk, when they had shared together this same refuge. "Don't you remember," she went on, "how, when they were here before, I broke it to you that I wasn't so very sure we, ourselves had the thing itself?"

He did his best to do so. "Had, you mean a social situation?"

"Yes — after Fanny Assingham had first broken it to me that, at the rate we were going, we should never have one."

"Which was what put us on Charlotte?" Oh yes, they had had it over quite often enough for him easily to remember.

Maggie had another pause — taking it from him that he now could both affirm and admit without wincing that they had been, at their critical moment, "put on" Charlotte. It was as if this recognition had been threshed out between them as fundamental to the honest view of their success. "Well," she continued, "I recall how I felt, about Kitty and Dotty, that even if we had already then been more 'placed,' or whatever you may call what we are now, it still wouldn't have been an excuse for wondering why others couldn't obligingly leave me more exalted by having, themselves, smaller ideas. For those," she said, "were the feelings we used to have."

"Oh yes," he responded philosophically —"I remember the feelings we used to have."

Maggie appeared to wish to plead for them a little, in tender retrospect — as if they had been also respectable. "It was bad enough, I thought, to have no sympathy in your heart when you HAD a position. But it was worse to be sublime about it — as I was so afraid, as I'm in fact still afraid of being — when it wasn't even there to support one." And she put forth again the earnestness she might have been taking herself as having outlived; became for it — which was doubtless too often even now her danger — almost sententious. "One must always, whether or no, have some imagination of the states of others — of what they may feel deprived of. However," she added, "Kitty and Dotty couldn't imagine we were deprived of anything. And now, and now —!" But she stopped as for indulgence to their wonder and envy.

"And now they see, still more, that we can have got everything, and kept everything, and yet not be proud."

"No, we're not proud," she answered after a moment. "I'm not sure that we're quite proud enough." Yet she changed the next instant that subject too. She could only do so, however, by harking back — as if it had been a fascination. She might have been wishing, under this renewed, this still more suggestive visitation, to keep him with her for remounting the stream of time and dipping again, for the softness of the water, into the contracted basin of the past. "We talked about it — we talked about it; you don't remember so well as I. You too didn't know — and it was beautiful of you; like Kitty and Dotty you too thought we had a position, and were surprised when *I* thought we ought to have told them we weren't doing for them what they supposed. In fact," Maggie pursued, "we're not doing it now. We're not, you see, really introducing them. I mean not to the people they want."

"Then what do you call the people with whom they're now having tea?"

It made her quite spring round. "That's just what you asked me the other time — one of the days there was somebody. And I told you I didn't call anybody anything."

"I remember — that such people, the people we made so welcome, didn't 'count'; that Fanny Assingham knew they didn't." She had awakened, his daughter, the echo; and on the bench there, as before, he nodded his head amusedly, he kept nervously shaking his foot. "Yes, they were only good enough — the people who came — for US. I remember," he said again: "that was the way it all happened."

"That was the way — that was the way. And you asked me," Maggie added, "if I didn't think we ought to tell them. Tell Mrs. Rance, in particular, I mean, that we had been entertaining her up to then under false pretences."

"Precisely — but you said she wouldn't have understood."

"To which you replied that in that case you were like her. YOU didn't understand."

"No, no — but I remember how, about our having, in our benighted innocence, no position, you quite crushed me with your explanation."

"Well then," said Maggie with every appearance of delight, "I'll crush you again. I told you that you by yourself had one — there was no doubt of that. You were different from me — you had the same one you always had."

"And THEN I asked you," her father concurred, "why in that case you hadn't the same."

"Then indeed you did." He had brought her face round to him before, and this held it, covering him with its kindled brightness, the result of the attested truth of their being able thus, in talk, to live again together. "What I replied was that I had lost my position by my marriage. THAT one — I know how I saw it — would never come back. I had done something TO it — I didn't quite know what; given it away, somehow, and yet not, as then appeared, really got my return. I had been assured — always by dear Fanny — that I COULD get it, only I must wake up. So I was trying, you see, to wake up — trying very hard."

"Yes — and to a certain extent you succeeded; as also in waking me. But you made much," he said, "of your difficulty." To which he added: "It's the only case I remember, Mag, of you ever making ANYTHING of a difficulty."

She kept her eyes on him a moment. "That I was so happy as I was?"

"That you were so happy as you were."

"Well, you admitted" — Maggie kept it up — "that that was a good difficulty. You confessed that our life did seem to be beautiful."

He thought a moment. "Yes — I may very well have confessed it, for so it did seem to me." But he guarded himself with his dim, his easier smile. "What do you want to put on me now?"

"Only that we used to wonder — that we were wondering then — if our life wasn't perhaps a little selfish." This also for a time, much at his leisure, Adam Verver retrospectively fixed. "Because Fanny Assingham thought so?"

"Oh no; she never thought, she couldn't think, if she would, anything of that sort. She only thinks people are sometimes fools," Maggie developed; "she doesn't seem to think so much about their being wrong — wrong, that is, in the sense of being wicked. She doesn't," the Princess further adventured, "quite so much mind their being wicked."

"I see — I see." And yet it might have been for his daughter that he didn't so very vividly see. "Then she only thought US fools?"

"Oh no — I don't say that. I'm speaking of our being selfish."

"And that comes under the head of the wickedness Fanny condones?"

"Oh, I don't say she CONDONES —!" A scruple in Maggie raised its crest. "Besides, I'm speaking of what was."

Her father showed, however, after a little, that he had not been reached by this discrimination; his thoughts were resting for the moment where they had settled. "Look here, Mag," he said reflectively —"I ain't selfish. I'll be blowed if I'm selfish."

Well, Maggie, if he WOULD talk of that, could also pronounce. "Then, father, I am."

"Oh shucks!" said Adam Verver, to whom the vernacular, in moments of deepest sincerity, could thus come back. "I'll believe it," he presently added, "when Amerigo complains of you."

"Ah, it's just he who's my selfishness. I'm selfish, so to speak, FOR him. I mean," she continued, "that he's my motive — in everything."

Well, her father could, from experience, fancy what she meant. "But hasn't a girl a right to be selfish about her husband?"

"What I DON'T mean," she observed without answering, "is that I'm jealous of him. But that's his merit — it's not mine."

Her father again seemed amused at her. "You COULD be-otherwise?"

"Oh, how can I talk," she asked, "of otherwise? It ISN'T, luckily for me, otherwise. If everything were different" — she further presented her thought —"of course everything WOULD be." And then again, as if that were but half: "My idea is this, that when you only love a little you're naturally not jealous — or are only jealous also a little, so that it doesn't matter. But when you love in a deeper and intenser way, then you are, in the same proportion, jealous; your jealousy has intensity and, no doubt, ferocity. When, however, you love in the most abysmal and unutterable way of all — why then you're beyond everything, and nothing can pull you down."

Mr. Verver listened as if he had nothing, on these high lines, to oppose. "And that's the way YOU love?"

For a minute she failed to speak, but at last she answered: "It wasn't to talk about that. I do FEEL, however, beyond everything — and as a consequence of that, I dare say," she added with a turn to gaiety, "seem often not to know quite WHERE I am."

The mere fine pulse of passion in it, the suggestion as of a creature consciously floating and shining in a warm summer sea, some element of dazzling sapphire and silver, a creature cradled upon depths, buoyant among dangers, in which fear or folly, or sinking otherwise than in play, was impossible — something of all this might have been making once more present to him, with his discreet, his half shy assent to it, her probable enjoyment of a rapture that he, in his day, had presumably convinced no great number of persons either of his giving or of his receiving. He sat awhile as if he knew himself hushed, almost admonished, and not for the first time; yet it was an effect that might have brought before him rather what she had gained than what he had missed.

Besides, who but himself really knew what he, after all, hadn't, or even had, gained? The beauty of her condition was keeping him, at any rate, as he might feel, in sight of the sea, where, though his personal dips were over, the whole thing could shine at him, and the air and the plash and the play become for him too a sensation. That couldn't be fixed upon him as missing; since if it wasn't personally floating, if it wasn't even sitting in the sand, it could yet pass very well for breathing the bliss, in a communicated irresistible way — for tasting the balm. It could pass, further, for knowing — for knowing that without him nothing might have been: which would have been missing least of all.

"I guess I've never been jealous," he finally remarked. And it said more to her, he had occasion next to perceive, than he was intending; for it made her, as by the pressure of a spring, give him a look that seemed to tell of things she couldn't speak.

But she at last tried for one of them. "Oh, it's you, father, who are what I call beyond everything. Nothing can pull YOU down."

He returned the look as with the sociability of their easy communion, though inevitably throwing in this time a shade of solemnity. He might have been seeing things to say, and others, whether of a type presumptuous or not, doubtless better kept back. So he settled on the merely obvious. "Well then, we make a pair. We're all right."

"Oh, we're all right!" A declaration launched not only with all her discriminating emphasis, but confirmed by her rising with decision and standing there as if the object of their small excursion required accordingly no further pursuit. At this juncture, however — with the act of their crossing the bar, to get, as might be, into port — there occurred the only approach to a betrayal of their having had to beat against the wind. Her father kept his place, and it was as if she had got over first and were pausing for her consort to follow. If they were all right; they were all right; yet he seemed to hesitate and wait for some word beyond. His eyes met her own, suggestively, and it was only after she had contented herself with simply smiling at him, smiling ever so fixedly, that he spoke, for the remaining importance of it, from the bench; where he leaned back, raising his face to her, his legs thrust out a trifle wearily and his hands grasping either side of the seat. They had beaten against the wind, and she was still fresh; they had beaten against the wind, and he, as at the best the more battered vessel, perhaps just vaguely drooped. But the effect of their silence was that she appeared to beckon him on, and he might have been fairly alongside of her when, at the end of another minute, he found their word. "The only thing is that, as for ever putting up again with your pretending that you're selfish —!"

At this she helped him out with it. "You won't take it from me?"

"I won't take it from you."

"Well, of course you won't, for that's your way. It doesn't matter, and it only proves —! But it doesn't matter, either, what it proves. I'm at this very moment," she declared, "frozen stiff with selfishness."

He faced her awhile longer in the same way; it was, strangely, as if, by this sudden arrest, by their having, in their acceptance of the unsaid, or at least their reference to it, practically given up pretending — it was as if they were "in" for it, for something they had been ineffably avoiding, but the dread of which was itself, in a manner, a seduction, just as any confession of the dread was by so much an allusion. Then she seemed to see him let himself go. "When a person's of the nature you speak of there are always other persons to suffer. But you've just been describing to me what you'd take, if you had once a good chance, from your husband."

"Oh, I'm not talking about my husband!"

"Then whom, ARE you talking about?"

Both the retort and the rejoinder had come quicker than anything previously exchanged, and they were followed, on Maggie's part, by a momentary drop. But she was not to fall away, and while her companion kept his eyes on her, while she wondered if he weren't expecting her to name his wife then, with high hypocrisy, as paying for his daughter's bliss, she produced something that she felt to be much better. "I'm talking about YOU."

"Do you mean I've been your victim?"

"Of course you've been my victim. What have you done, ever done, that hasn't been FOR me?"

"Many things; more than I can tell you — things you've only to think of for yourself. What do you make of all that I've done for myself?"

" 'Yourself'? —" She brightened out with derision.

"What do you make of what I've done for American City?"

It took her but a moment to say. "I'm not talking of you as a public character — I'm talking of you on your personal side."

"Well, American City — if 'personalities' can do it — has given me a pretty personal side. What do you make," he went on, "of what I've done for my reputation?"

"Your reputation THERE? You've given it up to them, the awful people, for less than nothing; you've given it up to them to tear to pieces, to make their horrible vulgar jokes against you with."

"Ah, my dear, I don't care for their horrible vulgar jokes," Adam Verver almost artlessly urged.

"Then there, exactly, you are!" she triumphed. "Everything that touches you, everything that surrounds you, goes on — by your splendid indifference and your incredible permission — at your expense."

Just as he had been sitting he looked at her an instant longer; then he slowly rose, while his hands stole into his pockets, and stood there before her. "Of course, my dear, YOU go on at my expense: it has never been my idea," he smiled, "that you should work for your living. I wouldn't have liked to see it." With which, for a little again, they remained face to face. "Say therefore I HAVE had the feelings of a father. How have they made me a victim?"

"Because I sacrifice you."

"But to what in the world?"

At this it hung before her that she should have had as never yet her opportunity to say, and it held her for a minute as in a vise, her impression of his now, with his strained smile, which touched her to deepest depths, sounding her in his secret unrest. This was the moment, in the whole process of their mutual vigilance, in which it decidedly most hung by a hair that their thin wall might be pierced by the lightest wrong touch. It shook between them, this transparency, with their very breath; it was an exquisite tissue, but stretched on a frame, and would give way the next instant if either so much as breathed too hard. She held her breath, for she knew by his eyes, the light at the heart of which he couldn't blind, that he was, by his intention, making sure — sure whether or no her certainty was like his. The intensity of his dependence on it at that moment — this itself was what absolutely convinced her so that, as if perched up before him on her vertiginous point and in the very glare of his observation, she balanced for thirty seconds, she almost rocked: she might have been for the time, in all her conscious person, the very form of the equilibrium they were, in their different ways, equally trying to save. And they were saving it — yes, they were, or at least she was: that was still the workable issue, she could say, as she felt her dizziness drop. She held herself hard; the thing was to be done, once for all, by her acting, now, where she stood. So much was crowded into so short a space that she knew already she was keeping her head. She had kept it by the warning of his eyes; she shouldn't lose it again; she knew how and why, and if she had turned cold this was precisely what helped her. He had said to himself "She'll break down and name Amerigo; she'll say it's to him she's sacrificing me; and its by what that will give me — with so many other things too — that my suspicion will be clinched." He was watching her lips, spying for the symptoms of the sound; whereby these symptoms had only to fail and he would have got nothing that she didn't measure out to him as she gave it. She had presently in fact so recovered herself that she seemed to know she could more easily have made him name his wife than he have made her name her husband. It was there before her that if she should so much as force him just NOT consciously to avoid saying "Charlotte, Charlotte" he would have given himself away. But to be sure of this was enough for her, and she saw more clearly with each lapsing instant what they were both doing. He was doing what he had steadily been coming to; he was practically OFFERING himself, pressing himself upon her, as a sacrifice — he had read his way so into her best possibility; and where had she already, for weeks and days past, planted her feet if not on her acceptance of the offer? Cold indeed, colder and colder she turned, as she felt herself suffer this close personal vision of his attitude still not to make her weaken. That was her very certitude, the intensity of his pressure; for if something dreadful hadn't happened there wouldn't, for either of them, be these dreadful things to do. She had meanwhile, as well, the immense advantage that she could have named Charlotte without exposing herself — as, for that matter, she was the next minute showing him.

"Why, I sacrifice you, simply, to everything and to every one. I take the consequences of your marriage as perfectly natural."

He threw back his head a little, settling with one hand his eyeglass. "What do you call, my dear, the consequences?"

"Your life as your marriage has made it."

"Well, hasn't it made it exactly what we wanted?" She just hesitated, then felt herself steady — oh, beyond what she had dreamed. "Exactly what *I* wanted — yes."

His eyes, through his straightened glasses, were still on hers, and he might, with his intenser fixed smile, have been knowing she was, for herself, rightly inspired. "What do you make then of what I wanted?"

"I don't make anything, any more than of what you've got. That's exactly the point. I don't put myself out to do so — I never have; I take from you all I can get, all you've provided for me, and I leave you to make of your own side of the matter what you can. There you are — the rest is your own affair. I don't even pretend to concern myself —!"

"To concern yourself —?" He watched her as she faintly faltered, looking about her now so as not to keep always meeting his face.

"With what may have REALLY become of you. It's as if we had agreed from the first not to go into that — such an arrangement being of course charming for ME. You can't say, you know, that I haven't stuck to it."

He didn't say so then — even with the opportunity given him of her stopping once more to catch her breath. He said instead: "Oh, my dear — oh, oh!"

But it made no difference, know as she might what a past — still so recent and yet so distant — it alluded to; she repeated her denial, warning him off, on her side, from spoiling the truth of her contention. "I never went into anything, and you see I don't; I've continued to adore you — but what's that, from a decent daughter to such a father? what but a question of convenient arrangement, our having two houses, three houses, instead of one (you would have arranged for fifty if I had wished!) and my making it easy for you to see the child? You don't claim, I suppose, that my natural course, once you had set up for yourself, would have been to ship you back to American City?"

These were direct inquiries, they quite rang out, in the soft, wooded air; so that Adam Verver, for a minute, appeared to meet them with reflection. She saw reflection, however, quickly enough show him what to do with them. "Do you know, Mag, what you make me wish when you talk that way?" And he waited again, while she further got from him the sense of something that had been behind, deeply in the shade, coming cautiously to the front and just feeling its way before presenting itself. "You regularly make me wish that I had shipped back to American City. When you go on as you do —" But he really had to hold himself to say it.

"Well, when I go on —?"

"Why, you make me quite want to ship back myself. You make me quite feel as if American City would be the best place for us."

It made her all too finely vibrate. "For 'us' —?"

"For me and Charlotte. Do you know that if we should ship, it would serve you quite right?" With which he smiled — oh he smiled! "And if you say much more we WILL ship."

Ah, then it was that the cup of her conviction, full to the brim, overflowed at a touch! THERE was his idea, the clearness of which for an instant almost dazzled her. It was a blur of light, in the midst of which she saw Charlotte like some object marked, by contrast, in blackness, saw her waver in the field of vision, saw her removed, transported, doomed. And he had named Charlotte, named her again, and she had MADE him — which was all she had needed more: it was as if she had held a blank letter to the fire and the writing had come out still larger than she hoped. The recognition of it took her some seconds, but she might when she spoke have been folding up these precious lines and restoring them to her pocket. "Well, I shall be as much as ever then the cause of what you do. I haven't the least doubt of your being up to that if you should think I might get anything out of it; even the little pleasure," she laughed, "of having said, as you call it, 'more.' Let my enjoyment of this therefore, at any price, continue to represent for you what *I* call sacrificing you."

She had drawn a long breath; she had made him do it ALL for her, and had lighted the way to it without his naming her husband. That silence had been as distinct as the sharp, the inevitable sound, and something now, in him, followed it up, a sudden air as of confessing at last fully to where she was and of begging the particular question. "Don't you think then I can take care of myself?"

"Ah, it's exactly what I've gone upon. If it wasn't for that —!"

But she broke off, and they remained only another moment face to face. "I'll let you know, my dear, the day *I* feel you've begun to sacrifice me."

"'Begun'?" she extravagantly echoed.

"Well, it will be, for me, the day you've ceased to believe in me."

With which, his glasses still fixed on her, his hands in his pockets, his hat pushed back, his legs a little apart, he seemed to plant or to square himself for a kind of assurance it had occurred to him he might as well treat her to, in default of other things, before they changed their subject. It had the effect, for her, of a reminder — a reminder of all he was, of all he had done, of all, above and beyond his being her perfect little father, she might take him as representing, take him as having, quite eminently, in the eyes of two hemispheres, been capable of, and as therefore wishing, not — was it? — illegitimately, to call her attention to. The "successful," beneficent person, the beautiful, bountiful, original, dauntlessly wilful great citizen, the consummate collector and infallible high authority he had been and still was — these things struck her, on the spot, as making up for him, in a wonderful way, a character she must take into account in dealing with him either for pity or for envy. He positively, under the impression, seemed to loom larger than life for her, so that she saw him during these moments in a light of recognition which had had its brightness for her at many an hour of the past, but which had never been so intense and so almost admonitory. His very quietness was part of it now, as always part of everything, of his success, his originality, his modesty, his exquisite public perversity, his inscrutable, incalculable energy; and this quality perhaps it might be-all the more too as the result, for the present occasion, of an admirable, traceable effort — that placed him in her eyes as no precious a work of art probably had ever been placed in his own. There was a long moment, absolutely, during which her impression rose and rose, even as that of the typical charmed gazer, in the still museum, before the named and dated object, the pride of the catalogue, that time has polished and consecrated. Extraordinary, in particular, was the number of the different ways in which he thus affected her as showing. He was strong — that was the great thing. He was sure — sure for himself, always, whatever his idea: the expression of that in him had somehow never appeared more identical with his proved taste for the rare and the true. But what stood out beyond everything was that he was always, marvellously, young — which couldn't but crown, at this juncture, his whole appeal to her imagination. Before she knew it she was lifted aloft by the consciousness that he was simply a great and deep and high little man, and that to love him with tenderness was not to be distinguished, a whit, from loving him with pride. It came to her, all strangely, as a sudden, an immense relief. The sense that he wasn't a failure, and could never be, purged their predicament of every meanness — made it as if they had really emerged, in their transmuted union, to smile almost without pain. It was like a new confidence, and after another instant she knew even still better why. Wasn't it because now, also, on his side, he was thinking of her as his daughter, was TRYING her, during these mute seconds, as the child of his blood? Oh then, if she wasn't with her little conscious passion, the child of any weakness, what was she but strong enough too? It swelled in her, fairly; it raised her higher, higher: she wasn't in that case a failure either — hadn't been, but the contrary; his strength was her strength, her pride was his, and they were decent and competent together. This was all in the answer she finally made him.

"I believe in you more than any one."

"Than any one at all?"

She hesitated, for all it might mean; but there was — oh a thousand times! — no doubt of it. "Than any one at all." She kept nothing of it back now, met his eyes over it, let him have the whole of it; after which she went on: "And that's the way, I think, you believe in me."

He looked at her a minute longer, but his tone at last was right. "About the way — yes."

"Well then —?" She spoke as for the end and for other matters — for anything, everything, else there might be. They would never return to it.

"Well then —!" His hands came out, and while her own took them he drew her to his breast and held her. He held her hard and kept her long, and she let herself go; but it was an embrace that, august and almost stern, produced, for all its intimacy, no revulsion and broke into no inconsequence of tears.

XXXVIII

Maggie was to feel, after this passage, how they had both been helped through it by the influence of that accident of her having been caught, a few nights before, in the familiar embrace of her father's wife. His return to the saloon had chanced to coincide exactly with this demonstration, missed moreover neither by her husband nor by the Assinghams, who, their card-party suspended, had quitted the billiard-room with him. She had been conscious enough at the time of what such an impression, received by the others, might, in that extended state, do for her case; and none the less that, as no one had appeared to wish to be the first to make a remark about it, it had taken on perceptibly the special shade of consecration conferred by unanimities of silence. The effect, she might have considered, had been almost awkward — the promptitude of her separation from Charlotte, as if they had been discovered in some absurdity, on her becoming aware of spectators. The spectators, on the other hand — that was the appearance — mightn't have supposed them, in the existing relation, addicted to mutual endearments; and yet, hesitating with a fine scruple between sympathy and hilarity, must have felt that almost any spoken or laughed comment could be kept from sounding vulgar only by sounding, beyond any permitted measure, intelligent. They had evidently looked, the two young wives, like a pair of women "making up" effusively, as women were supposed to do, especially when approved fools, after a broil; but taking note of the reconciliation would imply, on her father's part, on Amerigo's, and on Fanny Assingham's, some proportionate vision of the grounds of their difference. There had been something, there had been but too much, in the incident, for each observer; yet there was nothing any one could have said without seeming essentially to say: "See, see, the dear things — their quarrel's blissfully over!" "Our quarrel? What quarrel?" the dear things themselves would necessarily, in that case, have demanded; and the wits of the others would thus have been called upon for some agility of exercise. No one had been equal to the flight of producing, off-hand, a fictive reason for any estrangement — to take, that is, the place of the true, which had so long, for the finer sensibility, pervaded the air; and every one, accordingly, not to be inconveniently challenged, was pretending, immediately after, to have remarked nothing that any one else hadn't.

Maggie's own measure had remained, all the same, full of the reflection caught from the total inference; which had acted, virtually, by enabling every one present — and oh Charlotte not least! — to draw a long breath. The message of the little scene had been different for each, but it had been this, markedly, all round, that it reinforced — reinforced even immensely — the general effort, carried on from week to week and of late distinctly more successful, to look and talk and move as if nothing in life were the matter. Supremely, however, while this glass was held up to her, had Maggie's sense turned to the quality of the success constituted, on the spot, for Charlotte. Most of all, if she was guessing how her father must have secretly started, how her husband must have secretly wondered, how Fanny Assingham must have secretly, in a flash, seen daylight for herself — most of all had she tasted, by communication, of the high profit involved for her companion. She FELT, in all her pulses, Charlotte feel it, and how publicity had been required, absolutely, to crown her own abasement. It was the added touch, and now nothing was wanting — which, to do her stepmother justice, Mrs. Verver had appeared but to desire, from that evening, to show, with the last vividness, that she recognised. Maggie lived over again the minutes in question — had found herself repeatedly doing so; to the degree that the whole evening hung together, to her aftersense, as a thing appointed by some occult power that had dealt with her, that had for instance — animated the four with just the right restlessness too, had decreed and directed and exactly timed it in them, making their game of bridge — however abysmal a face it had worn for her — give way, precisely, to their common unavowed impulse to find out, to emulate Charlotte's impatience; a preoccupation, this latter, attached detectedly to the member of the party who was roaming in her queerness and was, for all their simulated blindness, not roaming unnoted.

If Mrs. Verver meanwhile, then, had struck her as determined in a certain direction by the last felicity into which that night had flowered, our young woman was yet not to fail of appreciating the truth that she had not been put at ease, after all, with absolute permanence. Maggie had seen her, unmistakably, desire to rise to the occasion and be magnificent — seen her decide that the right way for this would be to prove that the reassurance she had extorted there, under the high, cool lustre of the saloon, a twinkle of crystal and silver, had not only poured oil upon the troubled waters of their question, but had fairly drenched their whole intercourse with that lubricant. She had exceeded the limit of discretion in this insistence on her capacity to repay in proportion a service she acknowledged as handsome. "Why handsome?" Maggie would have been free to ask; since if she had been veracious the service assuredly would not have been huge. It would in that case have come up vividly, and for each of them alike, that the truth, on the Princess's lips, presented no difficulty. If the latter's mood, in fact, could have turned itself at all to private gaiety it might have failed to resist the diversion of seeing so clever a creature so beguiled. Charlotte's theory of a generous manner was manifestly to express that her stepdaughter's word, wiping out, as she might have said, everything, had restored them to the serenity of a relation without a cloud. It had been, in short, in this light, ideally conclusive, so that no ghost of anything it referred to could ever walk again. What was the ecstasy of that, however, but in itself a trifle compromising? — as truly, within the week, Maggie had occasion to suspect her friend of beginning, and rather abruptly, to remember. Convinced as she was of the example already given her by her husband, and in relation to which her profession of trust in his mistress had been an act of conformity exquisitely calculated, her imagination yet sought in the hidden play of his influence the explanation of any change of surface, any difference of expression or intention. There had been, through life, as we know, few quarters in which the Princess's fancy could let itself loose; but it shook off restraint when it plunged into the figured void of the detail of that relation. This was a realm it could people with images — again and again with fresh ones; they swarmed there like the strange combinations that lurked in the woods at twilight; they loomed into the definite and faded into the vague, their main present sign for her being, however, that they were always, that they were duskily, agitated. Her earlier vision of a state of bliss made insecure by the very intensity of the bliss — this had dropped from her; she had ceased to see, as she lost herself, the pair of operatic, of high Wagnerian lovers (she found, deep within her, these comparisons) interlocked in their wood of enchantment, a green glade as romantic as one's dream of an old German forest. The picture was veiled, on the contrary, with the dimness of trouble; behind which she felt, indistinguishable, the procession of forms that had lost, all so pitifully, their precious confidence. Therefore, though there was in these days, for her, with Amerigo, little enough even of the imitation, from day to day, of unembarrassed references — as she had foreseen, for that matter, from the first, that there would be-her active conception of his accessibility to their companion's own private and unextinguished right to break ground was not much less active than before. So it was that her inner sense, in spite of everything, represented him as still pulling wires and controlling currents, or rather indeed as muffling the whole possibility, keeping it down and down, leading his accomplice continually on to some new turn of the road. As regards herself Maggie had become more conscious from week to week of his ingenuities of intention to make up to her for their forfeiture, in so dire a degree, of any reality of frankness — a privation that had left on his lips perhaps a little of the same thirst with which she fairly felt her own distorted, the torment of the lost pilgrim who listens in desert sands for the possible, the impossible, plash of water. It was just this hampered state in him, none the less, that she kept before her when she wished most to find grounds of dignity for the hard little passion which nothing he had done could smother. There were hours enough, lonely hours, in which she let dignity go; then there were others when, clinging with her winged concentration to some deep cell of her heart, she stored away her hived tenderness as if she had gathered it all from flowers. He was walking ostensibly beside her, but in fact given over, without a break, to the grey medium in which he helplessly groped; a perception on her part which was a perpetual pang and which might last what it would — for ever if need be-but which, if relieved at all, must be relieved by his act alone. She herself could do nothing more for it; she had done the utmost possible. It was meantime not the easier to bear for this aspect under which Charlotte was presented as depending on him for guidance, taking it from him even in doses of bitterness, and yet lost with him in devious depths. Nothing was thus more sharply to be inferred than that he had promptly enough warned her, on hearing from her of the precious assurance received from his wife, that she must take care her satisfaction didn't betray something of her danger. Maggie had a day of still waiting, after allowing him time to learn how unreservedly she had lied for him — of waiting as for the light of she scarce knew what slow-shining reflection of this knowledge in his personal attitude. What retarded evolution, she asked herself in these hours, mightn't poor Charlotte all unwittingly have precipitated? She was thus poor Charlotte again for Maggie even while Maggie's own head was bowed, and the reason for this kept coming back to our young woman in the conception of what would secretly have passed. She saw her, face to face with the Prince, take from him the chill of his stiffest admonition, with the possibilities of deeper difficulty that it represented for each. She heard her ask, irritated and sombre, what tone, in God's name — since her bravery didn't suit him — she was then to adopt; and, by way of a fantastic flight of divination, she heard Amerigo reply, in a voice of which every fine note, familiar and admirable, came home to her, that one must really manage such prudences a little for one's self. It was positive in the Princess that, for this, she breathed Charlotte's cold air — turned away from him in it with her, turned with her, in growing compassion, this way and that, hovered behind her while she felt her ask herself where then she should rest. Marvellous the manner in which, under such imaginations, Maggie thus circled and lingered — quite as if she were, materially, following her unseen, counting every step she helplessly wasted, noting every hindrance that brought her to a pause.

A few days of this, accordingly, had wrought a change in that apprehension of the instant beatitude of triumph — of triumph magnanimous and serene — with which the upshot of the night-scene on the terrace had condemned our young woman to make terms. She had had, as we know, her vision of the gilt bars bent, of the door of the cage forced open from within and the creature imprisoned roaming at large — a movement, on the creature's part, that was to have even, for the short interval, its impressive beauty, but of which the limit, and in yet another direction, had loomed straight into view during her last talk under the great trees with her father. It was when she saw his wife's face ruefully attached to the quarter to which, in the course of their session, he had so significantly addressed his own — it was then that Maggie could watch for its turning pale, it was then she seemed to know what she had meant by thinking of her, in she shadow of his most ominous reference, as "doomed." If, as I say, her attention now, day after day, so circled and hovered, it found itself arrested for certain passages during which she absolutely looked with Charlotte's grave eyes. What she unfailingly made out through them was the figure of a little quiet gentleman who mostly wore, as he moved, alone, across the field of vision, a straw hat, a white waistcoat and a blue necktie, keeping a cigar in his teeth and his hands in his pockets, and who, oftener than not, presented a somewhat meditative back while he slowly measured the perspectives of the park and broodingly counted (it might have appeared) his steps. There were hours of intensity, for a week or two, when it was for all the world as if she had guardedly tracked her stepmother, in the great house, from room to room and from window to window, only to see her, here and there and everywhere, TRY her uneasy outlook, question her issue and her fate. Something, unmistakably, had come up for her that had never come up before; it represented a new complication and had begotten a new anxiety — things, these, that she carried about with her done up in the napkin of her lover's accepted rebuke, while she vainly hunted for some corner where she might put them safely down. The disguised solemnity, the prolonged futility of her search might have been grotesque to a more ironic eye; but Maggie's provision of irony, which we have taken for naturally small, had never been so scant as now, and there were moments while she watched with her, thus unseen, when the mere effect of being near her was to feel her own heart in her throat, was to be almost moved to saying to her: "Hold on tight, my poor dear — without TOO MUCH terror — and it will all come out somehow."

Even to that indeed, she could reflect, Charlotte might have replied that it was easy to say; even to that no great meaning could attach so long as the little meditative man in the straw hat kept coming into view with his indescribable air of weaving his spell, weaving it off there by himself. In whatever quarter of the horizon the appearances were scanned he was to be noticed as absorbed in this occupation; and Maggie was to become aware of two or three extraordinary occasions of receiving from him the hint that he measured the impression he produced. It was not really till after their recent long talk in the park that she knew how deeply, how quite exhaustively, they had then communicated — so that they were to remain together, for the time, in consequence, quite in the form of a couple of sociable drinkers who sit back from the table over which they have been resting their elbows, over which they have emptied to the last drop their respective charged cups. The cups were still there on the table, but turned upside down; and nothing was left for the companions but to confirm by placid silences the fact that the wine had been good. They had parted, positively, as if, on either side, primed with it — primed for whatever was to be; and everything between them, as the month waned, added its touch of truth to this similitude. Nothing, truly, WAS at present between them save that they were looking at each other in infinite trust; it fairly wanted no more words, and when they met, during the deep summer days, met even without witnesses, when they kissed at morning and evening, or on any of the other occasions of contact that they had always so freely celebrated, a pair of birds of the upper air could scarce have appeared less to invite each other to sit down and worry afresh. So it was that in the house itself, where more of his waiting treasures than ever were provisionally ranged, she sometimes only looked at him — from end to end of the great gallery, the pride of the house, for instance — as if, in one of the halls of a museum, she had been an earnest young woman with a Baedeker and he a vague gentleman to whom even Baedekers were unknown. He had ever, of course, had his way of walking about to review his possessions and verify their condition; but this was a pastime to which he now struck her as almost extravagantly addicted, and when she passed near him and he turned to give her a smile she caught — or so she fancied — the greater depth of his small, perpetual hum of contemplation. It was as if he were singing to himself, sotto voce, as he went — and it was also, on occasion, quite ineffably, as if Charlotte, hovering, watching, listening, on her side too, kept sufficiently within earshot to make it out as song, and yet, for some reason connected with the very manner of it, stood off and didn't dare.

One of the attentions she had from immediately after her marriage most freely paid him was that of her interest in his rarities, her appreciation of his taste, her native passion for beautiful objects and her grateful desire not to miss anything he could teach her about them. Maggie had in due course seen her begin to "work" this fortunately natural source of sympathy for all it was worth. She took possession of the mound throughout its extent; she abounded, to odd excess, one might have remarked, in the assumption of its being for her, with her husband, ALL the ground, the finest, clearest air and most breathable medium common to them. It had been given to Maggie to wonder if she didn't, in these intensities of approbation, too much shut him up to his province; but this was a complaint he had never made his daughter, and Charlotte must at least have had for her that, thanks to her admirable instinct, her range of perception marching with his own and never falling behind, she had probably not so much as once treated him to a rasping mistake or a revealing stupidity. Maggie, wonderfully, in the summer days, felt it forced upon her that that was one way, after all, of being a genial wife; and it was never so much forced upon her as at these odd moments of her encountering the sposi, as Amerigo called them, under the coved ceilings of Fawns while, so together, yet at the same time so separate, they were making their daily round. Charlotte hung behind, with emphasised attention; she stopped when her husband stopped, but at the distance of a case or two, or of whatever other succession of objects; and the likeness of their connection would not have been wrongly figured if he had been thought of as holding in one of his pocketed hands the end of a long silken halter looped round her beautiful neck. He didn't twitch it, yet it was there; he didn't drag her, but she came; and those indications that I have described the Princess as finding extraordinary in him were two or three mute facial intimations which his wife's presence didn't prevent his addressing his daughter — nor prevent his daughter, as she passed, it was doubtless to be added, from flushing a little at the receipt of. They amounted perhaps only to a wordless, wordless smile, but the smile was the soft shake of the twisted silken rope, and Maggie's translation of it, held in her breast till she got well away, came out only, as if it might have been overheard, when some door was closed behind her. "Yes, you see — I lead her now by the neck, I lead her to her doom, and she doesn't so much as know what it is, though she has a fear in her heart which, if you had the chances to apply your ear there that I, as a husband, have, you would hear thump and thump and thump. She thinks it MAY be, her doom, the awful place over there — awful for HER; but she's afraid to ask, don't you see? just as she's afraid of not asking; just as she's afraid of so many other things that she sees multiplied round her now as portents and betrayals. She'll know, however — when she does know."

Charlotte's one opportunity, meanwhile, for the air of confidence she had formerly worn so well and that agreed so with her firm and charming type, was the presence of visitors, never, as the season advanced, wholly intermitted — rather, in fact, so constant, with all the people who turned up for luncheon and for tea and to see the house, now replete, now famous, that Maggie grew to think again of this large element of "company" as of a kind of renewed water-supply for the tank in which, like a party of panting gold-fish, they kept afloat. It helped them, unmistakably, with each other, weakening the emphasis of so many of the silences of which their intimate intercourse would otherwise have consisted. Beautiful and wonderful for her, even, at times, was the effect of these interventions — their effect above all in bringing home to each the possible heroism of perfunctory things. They learned fairly to live in the perfunctory; they remained in it as many hours of the day as might be; it took on finally the likeness of some spacious central chamber in a haunted house, a great overarched and overglazed rotunda, where gaiety might reign, but the doors of which opened into sinister circular passages. Here they turned up for each other, as they said, with the blank faces that denied any uneasiness felt in the approach; here they closed numerous doors carefully behind them — all save the door that connected the place, as by a straight tented corridor, with the outer world, and, encouraging thus the irruption of society, imitated the aperture through which the bedizened performers of the circus are poured into the ring. The great part Mrs. Verver had socially played came luckily, Maggie could make out, to her assistance; she had "personal friends" — Charlotte's personal friends had ever been, in London, at the two houses, one of the most convenient pleasantries — who actually tempered, at this crisis, her aspect of isolation; and it wouldn't have been hard to guess that her best moments were those in which she suffered no fear of becoming a bore to restrain her appeal to their curiosity. Their curiosity might be vague, but their clever hostess was distinct, and she marched them about, sparing them nothing, as if she counted, each day, on a harvest of half crowns. Maggie met her again, in the gallery, at the oddest hours, with the party she was entertaining; heard her draw out the lesson, insist upon the interest, snub, even, the particular presumption and smile for the general bewilderment — inevitable features, these latter, of almost any occasion — in a manner that made our young woman, herself incurably dazzled, marvel afresh at the mystery by which a creature who could be in some connexions so earnestly right could be in others so perversely wrong. When her father, vaguely circulating, was attended by his wife, it was always Charlotte who seemed to bring up the rear; but he hung in the background when she did cicerone, and it was then perhaps that, moving mildly and modestly to and fro on the skirts of the exhibition, his appearance of weaving his spell was, for the initiated conscience, least to be resisted. Brilliant women turned to him in vague emotion, but his response scarce committed him more than if he had been the person employed to see that, after the invading wave was spent, the cabinets were all locked and the symmetries all restored.

There was a morning when, during the hour before luncheon and shortly after the arrival of a neighbourly contingent — neighbourly from ten miles off — whom Mrs. Verver had taken in charge, Maggie paused on the threshold of the gallery through which she had been about to pass, faltered there for the very impression of his face as it met her from an opposite door. Charlotte, half-way down the vista, held together, as if by something almost austere in the grace of her authority, the semi-scared (now that they were there!) knot of her visitors, who, since they had announced themselves by telegram as yearning to inquire and admire, saw themselves restricted to this consistency. Her voice, high and clear and a little hard, reached her husband and her step-daughter while she thus placed beyond doubt her cheerful submission to duty. Her words, addressed to the largest publicity, rang for some minutes through the place, every one as quiet to listen as if it had been a church ablaze with tapers and she were taking her part in some hymn of praise. Fanny Assingham looked rapt in devotion — Fanny Assingham who forsook this other friend as little as she forsook either her host or the Princess or the Prince or the Principino; she supported her, in slow revolutions, in murmurous attestations of presence, at all such times, and Maggie, advancing after a first hesitation, was not to fail of noting her solemn, inscrutable attitude, her eyes attentively lifted, so that she might escape being provoked to betray an impression. She betrayed one, however, as Maggie approached, dropping her gaze to the latter's level long enough to seem to adventure, marvellously, on a mute appeal. "You understand, don't you, that if she didn't do this there would be no knowing what she might do?" This light Mrs. Assingham richly launched while her younger friend, unresistingly moved, became uncertain again, and then, not too much to show it — or, rather, positively to conceal it, and to conceal something more as well — turned short round to one of the windows and awkwardly, pointlessly waited. "The largest of the three pieces has the rare peculiarity that the garlands, looped round it, which, as you see, are the finest possible vieux Saxe, are not of the same origin or period, or even, wonderful as they are, of a taste quite so perfect. They have been put on at a later time, by a process of which there are very few examples, and none so important as this, which is really quite unique — so that, though the whole thing is a little baroque, its value as a specimen is, I believe, almost inestimable."

So the high voice quavered, aiming truly at effects far over the heads of gaping neighbours; so the speaker, piling it up, sticking at nothing, as less interested judges might have said, seemed to justify the faith with which she was honoured. Maggie meanwhile, at the window, knew the strangest thing to be happening: she had turned suddenly to crying, or was at least on the point of it — the lighted square before her all blurred and dim. The high voice went on; its quaver was doubtless for conscious ears only, but there were verily thirty seconds during which it sounded, for our young woman, like the shriek of a soul in pain. Kept up a minute longer it would break and collapse — so that Maggie felt herself, the next thing, turn with a start to her father. "Can't she be stopped? Hasn't she done it ENOUGH?" — some such question as that she let herself ask him to suppose in her. Then it was that, across half the gallery — for he had not moved from where she had first seen him — he struck her as confessing, with strange tears in his own eyes, to sharp identity of emotion. "Poor thing, poor thing" — it reached straight — "ISN'T she, for one's credit, on the swagger?" After which, as, held thus together they had still another strained minute, the shame, the pity, the better knowledge, the smothered protest, the divined anguish even, so overcame him that, blushing to his eyes, he turned short away. The affair but of a few muffled moments, this snatched communion yet lifted Maggie as on air — so much, for deep guesses on her own side too, it gave her to think of. There was, honestly, an awful mixture in things, and it was not closed to her aftersense of such passages — we have already indeed, in other cases, seen it open — that the deepest depth of all, in a perceived penalty, was that you couldn't be sure some of your compunctions and contortions wouldn't show for ridiculous. Amerigo, that morning, for instance, had been as absent as he at this juncture appeared to desire he should mainly be noted as being; he had gone to London for the day and the night — a necessity that now frequently rose for him and that he had more than once suffered to operate during the presence of guests, successions of pretty women, the theory of his fond interest in whom had been publicly cultivated. It had never occurred to his wife to pronounce him ingenuous, but there came at last a high dim August dawn when she couldn't sleep and when, creeping restlessly about and breathing at her window the coolness of wooded acres, she found the faint flush of the east march with the perception of that other almost equal prodigy. It rosily coloured her vision that — even such as he was, yes — her husband could on occasion sin by excess of candour. He wouldn't otherwise have given as his reason for going up to Portland Place in the August days that he was arranging books there. He had bought a great many of late, and he had had others, a large number, sent from Rome — wonders of old print in which her father had been interested. But when her imagination tracked him to the dusty town, to the house where drawn blinds and pale shrouds, where a caretaker and a kitchenmaid were alone in possession, it wasn't to see him, in his shirtsleeves, unpacking battered boxes.

She saw him, in truth, less easily beguiled — saw him wander, in the closed dusky rooms, from place to place, or else, for long periods, recline on deep sofas and stare before him through the smoke of ceaseless cigarettes. She made him out as liking better than anything in the world just now to be alone with his thoughts. Being herself connected with his thoughts, she continued to believe, more than she had ever been, it was thereby a good deal as if he were alone with HER. She made him out as resting so from that constant strain of the perfunctory to which he was exposed at Fawns; and she was accessible to the impression of the almost beggared aspect of this alternative. It was like his doing penance in sordid ways — being sent to prison or being kept without money; it wouldn't have taken much to make her think of him as really kept without food. He might have broken away, might easily have started to travel; he had a right — thought wonderful Maggie now — to so many more freedoms than he took! His secret was of course that at Fawns he all the while winced, was all the while in presences in respect to which he had thrown himself back, with a hard pressure, on whatever mysteries of pride, whatever inward springs familiar to the man of the world, he could keep from snapping. Maggie, for some reason, had that morning, while she watched the sunrise, taken an extraordinary measure of the ground on which he would have HAD to snatch at pretexts for absence. It all came to her there — he got off to escape from a sound. The sound was in her own ears still — that of Charlotte's high coerced quaver before the cabinets in the hushed gallery; the voice by which she herself had been pierced the day before as by that of a creature in anguish and by which, while she sought refuge at the blurred window, the tears had been forced into her eyes. Her comprehension soared so high that the wonder for her became really his not feeling the need of wider intervals and thicker walls. Before THAT admiration she also meditated; consider as she might now, she kept reading not less into what he omitted than into what he performed a beauty of intention that touched her fairly the more by being obscure. It was like hanging over a garden in the dark; nothing was to be made of the confusion of growing things, but one felt they were folded flowers, and their vague sweetness made the whole air their medium. He had to turn away, but he wasn't at least a coward; he would wait on the spot for the issue of what he had done on the spot. She sank to her knees with her arm on the ledge of her window-seat, where she blinded her eyes from the full glare of seeing that his idea could only be to wait, whatever might come, at her side. It was to her buried face that she thus, for a long time, felt him draw nearest; though after a while, when the strange wail of the gallery began to repeat its inevitable echo, she was conscious of how that brought out his pale hard grimace.

XXXIX

The resemblance had not been present to her on first coming out into the hot, still brightness of the Sunday afternoon — only the second Sunday, of all the summer, when the party of six, the party of seven including the Principino, had practically been without accessions or invasions; but within sight of Charlotte, seated far away, very much where she had expected to find her, the Princess fell to wondering if her friend wouldn't be affected quite as she herself had been, that night on the terrace, under Mrs. Verver's perceptive pursuit. The relation, today, had turned itself round; Charlotte was seeing her come, through patches of lingering noon, quite as she had watched Charlotte menace her through the starless dark; and there was a moment, that of her waiting a little as they thus met across the distance, when the interval was bridged by a recognition not less soundless, and to all appearance not less charged with strange meanings, than that of the other occasion. The point, however, was that they had changed places; Maggie had from her window, seen her stepmother leave the house — at so unlikely an hour, three o'clock of a canicular August, for a ramble in garden or grove — and had thereupon felt her impulse determined with the same sharpness that had made the spring of her companion's three weeks before. It was the hottest day of the season, and the shaded siesta, for people all at their ease, would certainly rather have been prescribed; but our young woman had perhaps not yet felt it so fully brought home that such refinements of repose, among them, constituted the empty chair at the feast. This was the more distinct as the feast, literally, in the great bedimmed dining-room, the cool, ceremonious semblance of luncheon, had just been taking place without Mrs. Verver. She had been represented but by the plea of a bad headache, not reported to the rest of the company by her husband, but offered directly to Mr. Verver himself, on their having assembled, by her maid, deputed for the effect and solemnly producing it.

Maggie had sat down, with the others, to viands artfully iced, to the slow circulation of precious tinkling jugs, to marked reserves of reference in many directions — poor Fanny Assingham herself scarce thrusting her nose out of the padded hollow into which she had withdrawn. A consensus of languor, which might almost have been taken for a community of dread, ruled the scene — relieved only by the fitful experiments of Father Mitchell, good holy, hungry man, a trusted and overworked London friend and adviser, who had taken, for a week or two, the light neighbouring service, local rites flourishing under Maggie's munificence, and was enjoying, as a convenience, all the bounties of the house. HE conversed undiscouraged, Father Mitchell — conversed mainly with the indefinite, wandering smile of the entertainers, and the Princess's power to feel him on the whole a blessing for these occasions was not impaired by what was awkward in her consciousness of having, from the first of her trouble, really found her way without his guidance. She asked herself at times if he suspected how more than subtly, how perversely, she had dispensed with him, and she balanced between visions of all he must privately have guessed and certitudes that he had guessed nothing whatever. He might nevertheless have been so urbanely filling up gaps, at present, for the very reason that his instinct, sharper than the expression of his face, had sufficiently served him — made him aware of the thin ice, figuratively speaking, and of prolongations of tension, round about him, mostly foreign to the circles in which luxury was akin to virtue. Some day in some happier season, she would confess to him that she hadn't confessed, though taking so much on her conscience; but just now she was carrying in her weak, stiffened hand a glass filled to the brim, as to which she had recorded a vow that no drop should overflow. She feared the very breath of a better wisdom, the jostle of the higher light, of heavenly help itself; and, in addition, however that might be, she drew breath this afternoon, as never yet, in an element heavy to oppression. Something grave had happened, somehow and somewhere, and she had, God knew, her choice of suppositions: her heart stood still when she wondered above all if the cord mightn't at last have snapped between her husband and her father. She shut her eyes for dismay at the possibility of such a passage — there moved before them the procession of ugly forms it might have taken. "Find out for yourself!" she had thrown to Amerigo, for her last word, on the question of who else "knew," that night of the breaking of the Bowl; and she flattered herself that she hadn't since then helped him, in her clear consistency, by an inch. It was what she had given him, all these weeks, to be busy with, and she had again and again lain awake for the obsession of this sense of his uncertainty ruthlessly and endlessly playing with his dignity. She had handed him over to an ignorance that couldn't even try to become indifferent and that yet wouldn't project itself, either, into the cleared air of conviction. In proportion as he was generous it had bitten into his spirit, and more than once she had said to herself that to break the spell she had cast upon him and that the polished old ivory of her father's inattackable surface made so absolute, he would suddenly commit some mistake or some violence, smash some windowpane for air, fail even of one of his blest inveteracies of taste. In that way, fatally, he would have put himself in the wrong — blighting by a single false step the perfection of his outward show.

These shadows rose and fell for her while Father Mitchell prattled; with other shadows as well, those that hung over Charlotte herself, those that marked her as a prey to equal suspicions — to the idea, in particular, of a change, such a change as she didn't dare to face, in the relations of the two men. Or there were yet other possibilities, as it seemed to Maggie; there were always too many, and all of them things of evil when one's nerves had at last done for one all that nerves could do; had left one in a darkness of prowling dangers that was like the predicament of the night-watcher in a beast-haunted land who has no more means for a fire. She might, with such nerves, have supposed almost anything of any one; anything, almost, of poor Bob Assingham, condemned to eternal observances and solemnly appreciating her father's wine; anything, verily, yes, of the good priest, as he finally sat back with fat folded hands and twiddled his thumbs on his stomach. The good priest looked hard at the decanters, at the different dishes of dessert — he eyed them, half-obliquely, as if THEY might have met him today, for conversation, better than any one present. But the Princess had her fancy at last about that too; she was in the midst of a passage, before she knew it, between Father Mitchell and Charlotte — some approach he would have attempted with her, that very morning perhaps, to the circumstance of an apparent detachment, recently noted in her, from any practice of devotion. He would have drawn from this, say, his artless inference — taken it for a sign of some smothered inward trouble and pointed, naturally, the moral that the way out of such straits was not through neglect of the grand remedy. He had possibly prescribed contrition — he had at any rate quickened in her the beat of that false repose to which our young woman's own act had devoted her at her all so deluded instance. The falsity of it had laid traps compared to which the imputation of treachery even accepted might have seemed a path of roses. The acceptance, strangely, would have left her nothing to do — she could have remained, had she liked, all insolently passive; whereas the failure to proceed against her, as it might have been called, left her everything, and all the more that it was wrapped so in confidence. She had to confirm, day after day, the rightness of her cause and the justice and felicity of her exemption — so that wouldn't there have been, fairly, in any explicit concern of Father Mitchell's, depths of practical derision of her success?

The question was provisionally answered, at all events, by the time the party at luncheon had begun to disperse — with Maggie's version of Mrs. Verver sharp to the point of representing her pretext for absence as a positive flight from derision. She met the good priest's eyes before they separated, and priests were really, at the worst, so to speak, such wonderful people that she believed him for an instant on the verge of saying to her, in abysmal softness: "Go to Mrs. Verver, my child — YOU go: you'll find that you can help her." This didn't come, however; nothing came but the renewed twiddle of thumbs over the satisfied stomach and the full flush, the comical candour, of reference to the hand employed at Fawns for mayonnaise of salmon. Nothing came but the receding backs of each of the others — her father's slightly bent shoulders, in especial, which seemed to weave his spell, by the force of habit, not less patiently than if his wife had been present. Her husband indeed was present to feel anything there might be to feel — which was perhaps exactly why this personage was moved promptly to emulate so definite an example of "sloping." He had his occupations — books to arrange perhaps even at Fawns; the idea of the siesta, moreover, in all the conditions, had no need to be loudly invoked.

Maggie, was, in the event, left alone for a minute with Mrs. Assingham, who, after waiting for safety, appeared to have at heart to make a demonstration. The stage of "talking over" had long passed for them; when they communicated now it was on quite ultimate facts; but Fanny desired to testify to the existence, on her part, of an attention that nothing escaped. She was like the kind lady who, happening to linger at the circus while the rest of the spectators pour grossly through the exits, falls in with the overworked little trapezist girl — the acrobatic support presumably of embarrassed and exacting parents — and gives her, as an obscure and meritorious artist, assurance of benevolent interest. What was clearest, always, in our young woman's imaginings, was the sense of being herself left, for any occasion, in the breach. She was essentially there to bear the burden, in the last resort, of surrounding omissions and evasions, and it was eminently to that office she had been today abandoned — with this one alleviation, as appeared, of Mrs. Assingham's keeping up with her. Mrs. Assingham suggested that she too was still on the ramparts — though her gallantry proved indeed after a moment to consist not a little of her curiosity. She had looked about and seen their companions beyond earshot.

"Don't you really want us to go —?"

Maggie found a faint smile. "Do you really want to —?"

It made her friend colour. "Well then — no. But we WOULD, you know, at a look from you. We'd pack up and be off — as a sacrifice."

"Ah, make no sacrifice," said Maggie. "See me through."

"That's it — that's all I want. I should be too base —! Besides," Fanny went on, "you're too splendid."

"Splendid?"

"Splendid. Also, you know, you ARE all but 'through.' You've done it," said Mrs. Assingham. But Maggie only half took it from her.

"What does it strike you that I've done?"

"What you wanted. They're going."

Maggie continued to look at her. "Is that what I wanted?"

"Oh, it wasn't for you to say. That was his business."

"My father's?" Maggie asked after an hesitation.

"Your father's. He has chosen — and now she knows. She sees it all before her — and she can't speak, or resist, or move a little finger. That's what's the matter with HER," said Fanny Assingham.

It made a picture, somehow, for the Princess, as they stood there — the picture that the words of others, whatever they might be, always made for her, even when her vision was already charged, better than any words of her own. She saw, round about her, through the chinks of the shutters, the hard glare of nature — saw Charlotte, somewhere in it, virtually at bay, and yet denied the last grace of any protecting truth. She saw her off somewhere all unaided, pale in her silence and taking in her fate. "Has she told you?" she then asked.

Her companion smiled superior. "*I* don't need to be told — either! I see something, thank God, every day." And then as Maggie might appear to be wondering what, for instance: "I see the long miles of ocean and the dreadful great country, State after State — which have never seemed to me so big or so terrible. I see THEM at last, day by day and step by step, at the far end — and I see them never come back. But NEVER — simply. I see the extraordinary 'interesting' place — which I've never been to, you know, and you have — and the exact degree in which she will be expected to be interested."

"She WILL be," Maggie presently replied. "Expected?"

"Interested."

For a little, after this, their eyes met on it; at the end of which Fanny said: "She'll be-yes — what she'll HAVE to be. And it will be-won't it? for ever and ever." She spoke as abounding in her friend's sense, but it made Maggie still only look at her.

These were large words and large visions — all the more that now, really, they spread and spread. In the midst of them, however, Mrs. Assingham had soon enough continued. "When

I talk of 'knowing,' indeed, I don't mean it as you would have a right to do. You know because you see — and I don't see HIM. I don't make him out," she almost crudely confessed.

Maggie again hesitated. "You mean you don't make out Amerigo?"

But Fanny shook her head, and it was quite as if, as an appeal to one's intelligence, the making out of Amerigo had, in spite of everything, long been superseded. Then Maggie measured the reach of her allusion, and how what she next said gave her meaning a richness. No other name was to be spoken, and Mrs. Assingham had taken that, without delay, from her eyes — with a discretion, still, that fell short but by an inch. "You know how he feels."

Maggie at this then slowly matched her headshake. "I know nothing."

"You know how YOU feel."

But again she denied it. "I know nothing. If I did —!"

"Well, if you did?" Fanny asked as she faltered.

She had had enough, however. "I should die," she said as she turned away.

She went to her room, through the quiet house; she roamed there a moment, picking up, pointlessly, a different fan, and then took her way to the shaded apartments in which, at this hour, the Principino would be enjoying his nap. She passed through the first empty room, the day nursery, and paused at an open door. The inner room, large, dim and cool, was equally calm; her boy's ample, antique, historical, royal crib, consecrated, reputedly, by the guarded rest of heirs-apparent, and a gift, early in his career, from his grandfather, ruled the scene from the centre, in the stillness of which she could almost hear the child's soft breathing. The prime protector of his dreams was installed beside him; her father sat there with as little motion — with head thrown back and supported, with eyes apparently closed, with the fine foot that was so apt to betray nervousness at peace upon the other knee, with the unfathomable heart folded in the constant flawless freshness of the white waistcoat that could always receive in its armholes the firm prehensile thumbs. Mrs. Noble had majestically melted, and the whole place signed her temporary abdication; yet the actual situation was regular, and Maggie lingered but to look. She looked over her fan, the top of which was pressed against her face, long enough to wonder if her father really slept or if, aware of her, he only kept consciously quiet. Did his eyes truly fix her between lids partly open, and was she to take this — his forebearance from any question — only as a sign again that everything was left to her? She at all events, for a minute, watched his immobility — then, as if once more renewing her total submission, returned, without a sound, to her own quarters.

A strange impulse was sharp in her, but it was not, for her part, the desire to shift the weight. She could as little have slept as she could have slept that morning, days before, when she had watched the first dawn from her window. Turned to the east, this side of her room was now in shade, with the two wings of the casement folded back and the charm she always found in her seemingly perched position — as if her outlook, from above the high terraces, was that of some castle-tower mounted on a rock. When she stood there she hung over, over the gardens and the woods — all of which drowsed below her, at this hour, in the immensity of light. The miles of shade looked hot, the banks of flowers looked dim; the peacocks on the balustrades let their tails hang limp and the smaller birds lurked among the leaves. Nothing therefore would have appeared to stir in the brilliant void if Maggie, at the moment she was about to turn away, had not caught sight of a moving spot, a clear green sunshade in the act of descending a flight of steps. It passed down from the terrace, receding, at a distance, from sight, and carried, naturally, so as to conceal the head and back of its bearer; but Maggie had quickly recognised the white dress and the particular motion of this adventurer — had taken in that Charlotte, of all people, had chosen the glare of noon for an exploration of the gardens, and that she could be betaking herself only to some unvisited quarter deep in them, or beyond them, that she had already marked as a superior refuge. The Princess kept her for a few minutes in sight, watched her long enough to feel her, by the mere betrayal of her pace and direction, driven in a kind of flight, and then understood, for herself, why the act of sitting still had become impossible to either of them. There came to her, confusedly, some echo of an ancient fable — some vision of Io goaded by the gadfly or of Ariadne roaming the lone sea-strand. It brought with it all the sense of her own intention and desire; she too might have been, for the hour, some far-off harassed heroine — only with a part to play for which she knew, exactly, no inspiring precedent. She knew but that, all the while — all the while of her sitting there among the others without her — she had wanted to go straight to this detached member of the party and make somehow, for her support, the last demonstration. A pretext was all that was needful, and Maggie after another instant had found one. She had caught a glimpse, before Mrs. Verver disappeared, of her carrying a book — made out, half lost in the folds of her white dress, the dark cover of a volume that was to explain her purpose in case of her being met with surprise, and the mate of which, precisely, now lay on Maggie's table. The book was an old novel that the Princess had a couple of days before mentioned having brought down from Portland Place in the charming original form of its three volumes. Charlotte had hailed, with a specious glitter of interest, the opportunity to read it, and our young woman had, thereupon, on the morrow, directed her maid to carry it to Mrs. Verver's apartments. She was afterwards to observe that this messenger, unintelligent or inadvertent, had removed but one of the volumes, which happened not to be the first. Still possessed, accordingly, of the first while Charlotte, going out, fantastically, at such an hour, to cultivate romance in an arbour, was helplessly armed with the second, Maggie prepared on the spot to sally forth with succour. The right volume, with a parasol, was all she required — in addition, that is, to the bravery of her general idea. She passed again through the house, unchallenged, and emerged upon the terrace, which she followed, hugging the shade, with that consciousness of turning the tables on her friend which we have already noted. But so far as she went, after descending into the open and beginning to explore the grounds, Mrs. Verver had gone still further — with the increase of the oddity, moreover, of her having exchanged the protection of her room for these exposed and shining spaces. It was not, fortunately, however, at last, that by persisting in pursuit one didn't arrive at regions of admirable shade: this was the asylum, presumably, that the poor wandering woman had had in view — several wide alleys, in particular, of great length, densely overarched with the climbing rose and the honeysuckle and converging, in separate green vistas, at a sort of umbrageous temple, an ancient rotunda, pillared and statued, niched and roofed, yet with its uncorrected antiquity, like that of everything else at Fawns, conscious hitherto of no violence from the present and no menace from the future. Charlotte had paused there, in her frenzy, or what ever it was to be called; the place was a conceivable retreat, and she was staring before her, from the seat to which she appeared to have sunk, all unwittingly, as Maggie stopped at the beginning of one of the perspectives.

It was a repetition more than ever then of the evening on the terrace; the distance was too great to assure her she had been immediately seen, but the Princess waited, with her intention, as Charlotte on the other occasion had waited — allowing, oh allowing, for the difference of the intention! Maggie was full of the sense of THAT — so full that it made her impatient; whereupon she moved forward a little, placing herself in range of the eyes that had been looking off elsewhere, but that she had suddenly called to recognition. Charlotte had evidently not dreamed of being followed, and instinctively, with her pale stare, she stiffened herself for protest. Maggie could make that out — as well as, further, however, that her second impression of her friend's approach had an instant effect on her attitude. The Princess came nearer, gravely and in silence, but fairly paused again, to give her time for whatever she would. Whatever she would, whatever she could, was what Maggie wanted — wanting above all to make it as easy for her as the case permitted. That was not what Charlotte had wanted the other night, but this never mattered — the great thing was to allow her, was fairly to produce in her, the sense of highly choosing. At first, clearly, she had been frightened; she had not been pursued, it had quickly struck her, without some design on the part of her pursuer, and what might she not be thinking of in addition but the way she had, when herself the pursuer, made her stepdaughter take in her spirit and her purpose? It had sunk into Maggie at the time, that hard insistence, and Mrs. Verver had felt it and seen it and heard it sink; which wonderful remembrance of pressure successfully applied had naturally, till now, remained with her. But her stare was like a projected fear that the buried treasure, so dishonestly come by, for which her companion's still countenance, at the hour and afterwards, had consented to serve as the deep soil, might have worked up again to the surface, to be thrown back upon her hands. Yes, it was positive that during one of these minutes the Princess had the vision of her particular alarm. "It's her lie, it's her lie that has mortally disagreed with her; she can keep down no longer her rebellion at it, and she has come to retract it, to disown it and denounce it — to give me full in my face the truth instead." This, for a concentrated instant, Maggie felt her helplessly gasp — but only to let it bring home the indignity, the pity of her state. She herself could but tentatively hover, place in view the book she carried, look as little dangerous, look as abjectly mild, as possible; remind herself really of people she had read about in stories of the wild west, people who threw up their hands, on certain occasions, as a sign they weren't carrying revolvers. She could almost have smiled at last, troubled as she yet knew herself, to show how richly she was harmless; she held up her volume, which was so weak a weapon, and while she continued, for consideration, to keep her distance, she explained with as quenched a quaver as possible. "I saw you come out — saw you from my window, and couldn't bear to think you should find yourself here without the beginning of your book. THIS is the beginning; you've got the wrong volume, and I've brought you out the right."

She remained after she had spoken; it was like holding a parley with a possible adversary, and her intense, her exalted little smile asked for formal leave. "May I come nearer now?" she seemed to say — as to which, however, the next minute, she saw Charlotte's reply lose itself in a strange process, a thing of several sharp stages, which she could stand there and trace. The dread, after a minute, had dropped from her face; though, discernibly enough, she still couldn't believe in her having, in so strange a fashion, been deliberately made up to. If she had been made up to, at least, it was with an idea — the idea that had struck her at first as necessarily dangerous. That it wasn't, insistently wasn't, this shone from Maggie with a force finally not to be resisted; and on that perception, on the immense relief so constituted, everything had by the end of three minutes extraordinarily changed. Maggie had come out to her, really, because she knew her doomed, doomed to a separation that was like a knife in her heart; and in the very sight of her uncontrollable, her blinded physical quest of a peace not to be grasped, something of Mrs. Assingham's picture of her as thrown, for a grim future, beyond the great sea and the great continent had at first found fulfilment. She had got away, in this fashion — burning behind her, almost, the ships of disguise — to let her horror of what was before her play up without witnesses; and even after Maggie's approach had presented an innocent front it was still not to be mistaken that she bristled with the signs of her extremity. It was not to be said for them, either, that they were draped at this hour in any of her usual graces; unveiled and all but unashamed, they were tragic to the Princess in spite of the dissimulation that, with the return of comparative confidence, was so promptly to operate. How tragic, in essence, the very change made vivid, the instant stiffening of the spring of pride — this for possible defence if not for possible aggression. Pride indeed, the next moment, had become the mantle caught up for protection and perversity; she flung it round her as a denial of any loss of her freedom. To be doomed was, in her situation, to have extravagantly incurred a doom, so that to confess to wretchedness was, by the same stroke, to confess to falsity. She wouldn't confess, she didn't — a thousand times no; she only cast about her, and quite frankly and fiercely, for something else that would give colour to her having burst her bonds. Her eyes expanded, her bosom heaved as she invoked it, and the effect upon Maggie was verily to wish she could only help her to it. She presently got up — which seemed to mean "Oh, stay if you like!" and when she had moved about awhile at random, looking away, looking at anything, at everything but her visitor; when she had spoken of the temperature and declared that she revelled in it; when she had uttered her thanks for the book, which, a little incoherently, with her second volume, she perhaps found less clever than she expected; when she had let Maggie approach sufficiently closer to lay, untouched, the tribute in question on a bench and take up obligingly its superfluous mate:

when she had done these things she sat down in another place, more or less visibly in possession of her part. Our young woman was to have passed, in all her adventure, no stranger moments; for she not only now saw her companion fairly agree to take her then for the poor little person she was finding it so easy to appear, but fell, in a secret, responsive ecstasy, to wondering if there were not some supreme abjection with which she might be inspired. Vague, but increasingly brighter, this possibility glimmered on her. It at last hung there adequately plain to Charlotte that she had presented herself once more to (as they said) grovel; and that, truly, made the stage large. It had absolutely, within the time, taken on the dazzling merit of being large for each of them alike.

"I'm glad to see you alone — there's something I've been wanting to say to you. I'm tired," said Mrs. Verver, "I'm tired —!"

"Tired —?" It had dropped the next thing; it couldn't all come at once; but Maggie had already guessed what it was, and the flush of recognition was in her face.

"Tired of this life — the one we've been leading. You like it, I know, but I've dreamed another dream." She held up her head now; her lighted eyes more triumphantly rested; she was finding, she was following her way. Maggie, by the same influence, sat in sight of it; there was something she was SAVING, some quantity of which she herself was judge; and it was for a long moment, even with the sacrifice the Princess had come to make, a good deal like watching her, from the solid shore, plunge into uncertain, into possibly treacherous depths. "I see something else," she went on; "I've an idea that greatly appeals to me — I've had it for a long time. It has come over me that we're wrong. Our real life isn't here."

Maggie held her breath. "'Ours' —?"

"My husband's and mine. I'm not speaking for you."

"Oh!" said Maggie, only praying not to be, not even to appear, stupid.

"I'm speaking for ourselves. I'm speaking," Charlotte brought out, "for HIM."

"I see. For my father."

"For your father. For whom else?" They looked at each other hard now, but Maggie's face took refuge in the intensity of her interest. She was not at all even so stupid as to treat her companion's question as requiring an answer; a discretion that her controlled stillness had after an instant justified. "I must risk your thinking me selfish — for of course you know what it involves. Let me admit it — I AM selfish. I place my husband first."

"Well," said Maggie smiling and smiling, "since that's where I place mine —!"

"You mean you'll have no quarrel with me? So much the better then; for," Charlotte went on with a higher and higher flight, "my plan is completely formed."

Maggie waited — her glimmer had deepened; her chance somehow was at hand. The only danger was her spoiling it; she felt herself skirting an abyss. "What then, may I ask IS your plan?"

It hung fire but ten seconds; it came out sharp. "To take him home — to his real position. And not to wait."

"Do you mean — a — this season?"

"I mean immediately. And — I may as well tell you now — I mean for my own time. I want," Charlotte said, "to have him at last a little to myself; I want, strange as it may seem to you" — and she gave it all its weight "to KEEP the man I've married. And to do so, I see, I must act."

Maggie, with the effort still to follow the right line, felt herself colour to the eyes. "Immediately?" she thoughtfully echoed.

"As soon as we can get off. The removal of everything is, after all, but a detail. That can always be done; with money, as he spends it, everything can. What I ask for," Charlotte declared, "is the definite break. And I wish it now." With which her head, like her voice rose higher. "Oh," she added, "I know my difficulty!"

Far down below the level of attention, in she could scarce have said what sacred depths, Maggie's inspiration had come, and it had trembled the next moment into sound. "Do you mean I'M your difficulty?"

"You and he together — since it's always with you that I've had to see him. But it's a difficulty that I'm facing, if you wish to know; that I've already faced; that I propose to myself to surmount. The struggle with it — none too pleasant — hasn't been for me, as you may imagine, in itself charming; I've felt in it at times, if I must tell you all, too great and too strange, an ugliness. Yet I believe it may succeed."

She had risen, with this, Mrs. Verver, and had moved, for the emphasis of it, a few steps away; while Maggie, motionless at first, but sat and looked at her. "You want to take my father FROM me?"

The sharp, successful, almost primitive wail in it made Charlotte turn, and this movement attested for the Princess the felicity of her deceit. Something in her throbbed as it had throbbed the night she stood in the drawing-room and denied that she had suffered. She was ready to lie again if her companion would but give her the opening. Then she should know she had done all. Charlotte looked at her hard, as if to compare her face with her note of resentment; and Maggie, feeling this, met it with the signs of an impression that might pass for the impression of defeat. "I want really to possess him," said Mrs. Verver. "I happen also to feel that he's worth it."

Maggie rose as if to receive her. "Oh — worth it!" she wonderfully threw off.

The tone, she instantly saw, again had its effect: Charlotte flamed aloft — might truly have been believing in her passionate parade. "You've thought YOU'VE known what he's worth?"

"Indeed then, my dear, I believe I have — as I believe I still do."

She had given it, Maggie, straight back, and again it had not missed. Charlotte, for another moment, only looked at her; then broke into the words — Maggie had known they would come — of which she had pressed the spring. "How I see that you loathed our marriage!"

"Do you ASK me?" Maggie after an instant demanded.

Charlotte had looked about her, picked up the parasol she had laid on a bench, possessed herself mechanically of one of the volumes of the relegated novel and then, more consciously, flung it down again: she was in presence, visibly, of her last word. She opened her sunshade with a click; she twirled it on her shoulder in her pride. "'Ask' you? Do I need? How I see," she broke out, "that you've worked against me!"

"Oh, oh, oh!" the Princess exclaimed.

Her companion, leaving her, had reached one of the archways, but on this turned round with a flare. "You haven't worked against me?"

Maggie took it and for a moment kept it; held it, with closed eyes, as if it had been some captured fluttering bird pressed by both hands to her breast. Then she opened her eyes to speak. "What does it matter — if I've failed?"

"You recognise then that you've failed?" asked Charlotte from the threshold.

Maggie waited; she looked, as her companion had done a moment before, at the two books on the seat; she put them together and laid them down; then she made up her mind. "I've failed!" she sounded out before Charlotte, having given her time, walked away. She watched her, splendid and erect, float down the long vista; then she sank upon a seat. Yes, she had done all.

Part Sixth

XL

"I'll do anything you like," she said to her husband on one of the last days of the month, "if our being here, this way at this time, seems to you too absurd, or too uncomfortable, or too impossible. We'll either take leave of them now, without waiting — or we'll come back in time, three days before they start. I'll go abroad with you, if you but say the word; to Switzerland, the Tyrol, the Italian Alps, to whichever of your old high places you would like most to see again — those beautiful ones that used to do you good after Rome and that you so often told me about."

Where they were, in the conditions that prompted this offer, and where it might indeed appear ridiculous that, with the stale London September close at hand, they should content themselves with remaining, was where the desert of Portland Place looked blank as it had never looked, and where a drowsy cabman, scanning the horizon for a fare, could sink to oblivion of the risks of immobility. But Amerigo was of the odd opinion, day after day, that their situation couldn't be bettered; and he even went at no moment through the form of replying that, should their ordeal strike her as exceeding their patience, any step they might take would be for her own relief. This was, no doubt, partly because he stood out so wonderfully, to the end, against admitting, by a weak word at least, that any element of their existence WAS, or ever had been, an ordeal; no trap of circumstance, no lapse of "form," no accident of irritation, had landed him in that inconsequence. His wife might verily have suggested that he was consequent — consequent with the admirable appearance he had from the first so undertaken, and so continued, to present — rather too rigidly at HER expense; only, as it happened, she was not the little person to do anything of the sort, and the strange tacit compact actually in operation between them might have been founded on an intelligent comparison, a definite collation positively, of the kinds of patience proper to each. She was seeing him through — he had engaged to come out at the right end if she WOULD see him: this understanding, tacitly renewed from week to week, had fairly received, with the procession of the weeks, the consecration of time; but it scarce needed to be insisted on that she was seeing him on HIS terms, not all on hers, or that, in other words, she must allow him his unexplained and uncharted, his one practicably workable way. If that way, by one of the intimate felicities the liability to which was so far from having even yet completely fallen from him, happened handsomely to show him as more bored than boring (with advantages of his own freely to surrender, but none to be persuadedly indebted to others for,) what did such a false face of the matter represent but the fact itself that she was pledged? If she had questioned or challenged or interfered — if she had reserved herself that right — she wouldn't have been pledged; whereas there were still, and evidently would be yet a while, long, tense stretches during which their case might have been hanging, for every eye, on her possible, her impossible defection. She must keep it up to the last, mustn't absent herself for three minutes from her post: only on those lines, assuredly, would she show herself as with him and not against him.

It was extraordinary how scant a series of signs she had invited him to make of being, of truly having been at any time, "with" his wife: that reflection she was not exempt from as they now, in their suspense, supremely waited — a reflection under the brush of which she recognised her having had, in respect to him as well, to "do all," to go the whole way over, to move, indefatigably, while he stood as fixed in his place as some statue of one of his forefathers. The meaning of it would seem to be, she reasoned in sequestered hours, that he HAD a place, and that this was an attribute somehow indefeasible, unquenchable, which laid upon others — from the moment they definitely wanted anything of him — the necessity of taking more of the steps that he could, of circling round him, of remembering for his benefit the famous relation of the mountain to Mahomet. It was strange, if one had gone into it, but such a place as Amerigo's was like something made for him beforehand by innumerable facts, facts largely of the sort known as historical, made by ancestors, examples, traditions, habits; while Maggie's own had come to show simply as that improvised "post" — a post of the kind spoken of as advanced — with which she was to have found herself connected in the fashion of a settler or a trader in a new country; in the likeness even of some Indian squaw with a papoose on her back and barbarous bead-work to sell. Maggie's own, in short, would have been sought in vain in the most rudimentary map of the social relations as such. The only geography marking it would be doubtless that of the fundamental passions. The "end" that the Prince was at all events holding out for was represented to expectation by his father-inlaw's announced departure for America with Mrs. Verver; just as that prospective event had originally figured as advising, for discretion, the flight of the younger couple, to say nothing of the withdrawal of whatever other importunate company, before the great upheaval of Fawns. This residence was to be peopled for a month by porters, packers and hammerers, at whose operations it had become peculiarly public — public that is for Portland Place — that Charlotte was to preside in force; operations the quite awful appointed scale and style of which had at no moment loomed so large to Maggie's mind as one day when the dear Assinghams swam back into her ken besprinkled with sawdust and looking as pale as if they had seen Samson pull down the temple. They had seen at least what she was not seeing, rich dim things under the impression of which they had retired; she having eyes at present but for the clock by which she timed her husband, or for the glass — the image perhaps would be truer — in which he was reflected to her as HE timed the pair in the country. The accession of their friends from Cadogan Place contributed to all their intermissions, at any rate, a certain effect of resonance; an effect especially marked by the upshot of a prompt exchange of inquiries between Mrs. Assingham and the Princess. It was noted, on the occasion of that anxious lady's last approach to her young friend at Fawns, that her sympathy had ventured, after much accepted privation, again to become inquisitive, and it had perhaps never so yielded to that need as on this question of the present odd "line" of the distinguished eccentrics.

"You mean to say really that you're going to stick here?" And then before Maggie could answer: "What on earth will you do with your evenings?"

Maggie waited a moment — Maggie could still tentatively smile. "When people learn we're here — and of course the papers will be full of it! — they'll flock back in their hundreds, from wherever they are, to catch us. You see you and the Colonel have yourselves done it. As for our evenings, they won't, I dare say, be particularly different from anything else that's ours. They won't be different from our mornings or our afternoons — except perhaps that you two dears will sometimes help us to get through them. I've offered to go anywhere," she added; "to take a house if he will. But THIS — just this and nothing else — is Amerigo's idea. He gave it yesterday" she went on, "a name that, as he said, described and fitted it. So you see" — and the Princess indulged again in her smile that didn't play, but that only, as might have been said, worked —"so you see there's a method in our madness."

It drew Mrs. Assingham's wonder. "And what then is the name?"

"'The reduction to its simplest expression of what we ARE doing' — that's what he called it. Therefore as we're doing nothing, we're doing it in the most aggravated way — which is the way he desires." With which Maggie further said: "Of course I understand."

"So do I!" her visitor after a moment breathed. "You've had to vacate the house — that was inevitable. But at least here he doesn't funk."

Our young woman accepted the expression. "He doesn't funk."

It only, however, half contented Fanny, who thoughtfully raised her eyebrows. "He's prodigious; but what is there — as you've 'fixed' it — TO dodge? Unless," she pursued, "it's her getting near him; it's — if you'll pardon my vulgarity — her getting AT him. That," she suggested, "may count with him."

But it found the Princess prepared. "She can get near him here. She can get 'at' him. She can come up."

"CAN she?" Fanny Assingham questioned.

"CAN'T she?" Maggie returned.

Their eyes, for a minute, intimately met on it; after which the elder woman said: "I mean for seeing him alone."

"So do I," said the Princess.

At which Fanny, for her reasons, couldn't help smiling. "Oh, if it's for THAT he's staying —!"

"He's staying — I've made it out — to take anything that comes or calls upon him. To take," Maggie went on, "even that." Then she put it as she had at last put it to herself. "He's staying for high decency."

"Decency?" Mrs. Assingham gravely echoed.

"Decency. If she SHOULD try —!"

"Well —?" Mrs. Assingham urged.

"Well, I hope —!"

"Hope he'll see her?"

Maggie hesitated, however; she made no direct reply. "It's useless hoping," she presently said. "She won't. But he ought to." Her friend's expression of a moment before, which had been apologised for as vulgar, prolonged its sharpness to her ear — that of an electric bell under continued pressure. Stated so simply, what was it but dreadful, truly, that the feasibility of Charlotte's "getting at" the man who for so long had loved her should now be in question? Strangest of all things, doubtless, this care of Maggie's as to what might make for it or make against it; stranger still her fairly lapsing at moments into a vague calculation of the conceivability, on her own part, with her husband, of some direct sounding of the subject. Would it be too monstrous, her suddenly breaking out to him as in alarm at the lapse of the weeks: "Wouldn't it really seem that you're bound in honour to do something for her, privately, before they go?" Maggie was capable of weighing the risk of this adventure for her own spirit, capable of sinking to intense little absences, even while conversing, as now, with the person who had most of her confidence, during which she followed up the possibilities. It was true that Mrs. Assingham could at such times somewhat restore the balance — by not wholly failing to guess her thought. Her thought, however, just at present, had more than one face — had a series that it successively presented. These were indeed the possibilities involved in the adventure of her concerning herself for the quantity of compensation that Mrs. Verver might still look to. There was always the possibility that she WAS, after all, sufficiently to get at him — there was in fact that of her having again and again done so. Against this stood nothing but Fanny Assingham's apparent belief in her privation — more mercilessly imposed, or more hopelessly felt, in the actual relation of the parties; over and beyond everything that, from more than three months back, of course, had fostered in the Princess a like conviction. These assumptions might certainly be baseless — inasmuch as there were hours and hours of Amerigo's time that there was no habit, no pretence of his accounting for; inasmuch too as Charlotte, inevitably, had had more than once, to the undisguised knowledge of the pair in Portland Place, been obliged to come up to Eaton Square, whence so many of her personal possessions were in course of removal. She didn't come to Portland Place — didn't even come to ask for luncheon on two separate occasions when it reached the consciousness of the household there that she was spending the day in London. Maggie hated, she scorned, to compare hours and appearances, to weigh the idea of whether there hadn't been moments, during these days, when an assignation, in easy conditions, a snatched interview, in an air the season had so cleared of prying eyes, mightn't perfectly work. But the very reason of this was partly that, haunted with the vision of the poor woman carrying off with such bravery as she found to her hand the secret of her not being appeased, she was conscious of scant room for any alternative image. The alternative image would have been that the secret covered up was the secret of appeasement somehow obtained, somehow extorted and cherished; and the difference between the two kinds of hiding was too great to permit of a mistake. Charlotte was hiding neither pride nor joy — she was hiding humiliation; and here it was that the Princess's passion, so powerless for vindictive flights, most inveterately bruised its tenderness against the hard glass of her question.

Behind the glass lurked the WHOLE history of the relation she had so fairly flattened her nose against it to penetrate — the glass Mrs. Verver might, at this stage, have been frantically tapping, from within, by way of supreme, irrepressible entreaty. Maggie had said to herself complacently, after that last passage with her stepmother in the garden of Fawns, that there was nothing left for her to do and that she could thereupon fold her hands. But why wasn't it still left to push further and, from the point of view of personal pride, grovel lower? — why wasn't it still left to offer herself as the bearer of a message reporting to him their friend's anguish and convincing him of her need?

She could thus have translated Mrs. Verver's tap against the glass, as I have called it, into fifty forms; could perhaps have translated it most into the form of a reminder that would pierce deep. "You don't know what it is to have been loved and broken with. You haven't been broken with, because in your RELATION what can there have been, worth speaking of, to break? Ours was everything a relation could be, filled to the brim with the wine of consciousness; and if it was to have no meaning, no better meaning than that such a creature as you could breathe upon it, at your hour, for blight, why was I myself dealt with all for deception? why condemned after a couple of short years to find the golden flame — oh, the golden flame! — a mere handful of black ashes?" Our young woman so yielded, at moments, to what was insidious in these foredoomed ingenuities of her pity, that for minutes together, sometimes, the weight of a new duty seemed to rest upon her — the duty of speaking before separation should constitute its chasm, of pleading for some benefit that might be carried away into exile like the last saved object of price of the emigre, the jewel wrapped in a piece of old silk and negotiable some day in the market of misery.

This imagined service to the woman who could no longer help herself was one of the traps set for Maggie's spirit at every turn of the road; the click of which, catching and holding the divine faculty fast, was followed inevitably by a flutter, by a struggle of wings and even, as we may say, by a scattering of fine feathers. For they promptly enough felt, these yearnings of thought and excursions of sympathy, the concussion that couldn't bring them down — the arrest produced by the so remarkably distinct figure that, at Fawns, for the previous weeks, was constantly crossing, in its regular revolution, the further end of any watched perspective. Whoever knew, or whoever didn't, whether or to what extent Charlotte, with natural business in Eaton Square, had shuffled other opportunities under that cloak, it was all matter for the kind of quiet ponderation the little man who so kept his wandering way had made his own. It was part of the very inveteracy of his straw hat and his white waistcoat, of the trick of his hands in his pockets, of the detachment of the attention he fixed on his slow steps from behind his secure pince-nez. The thing that never failed now as an item in the picture was that gleam of the silken noose, his wife's immaterial tether, so marked to Maggie's sense during her last month in the country. Mrs. Verver's straight neck had certainly not slipped it; nor had the other end of the long cord — oh, quite conveniently long! — disengaged its smaller loop from the hooked thumb that, with his fingers closed upon it, her husband kept out of sight. To have recognised, for all its tenuity, the play of this gathered lasso might inevitably be to wonder with what magic it was twisted, to what tension subjected, but could never be to doubt either of its adequacy to its office or of its perfect durability. These reminded states for the Princess were in fact states of renewed gaping. So many things her father knew that she even yet didn't!

All this, at present, with Mrs. Assingham, passed through her in quick vibrations. She had expressed, while the revolution of her thought was incomplete, the idea of what Amerigo "ought," on his side, in the premises, to be capable of, and then had felt her companion's answering stare. But she insisted on what she had meant. "He ought to wish to see her — and I mean in some protected and independent way, as he used to — in case of her being herself able to manage it. That," said Maggie with the courage of her conviction, "he ought to be ready, he ought to be happy, he ought to feel himself sworn — little as it is for the end of such a history! — to take from her. It's as if he wished to get off without taking anything."

Mrs. Assingham deferentially mused. "But for what purpose is it your idea that they should again so intimately meet?"

"For any purpose they like. That's THEIR affair."

Fanny Assingham sharply laughed, then irrepressibly fell back to her constant position. "You're splendid — perfectly splendid." To which, as the Princess, shaking an impatient head, wouldn't have it again at all, she subjoined: "Or if you're not it's because you're so sure. I mean sure of HIM."

"Ah, I'm exactly NOT sure of him. If I were sure of him I shouldn't doubt —!" But Maggie cast about her.

"Doubt what?" Fanny pressed as she waited.

"Well, that he must feel how much less than she he pays — and how that ought to keep her present to him."

This, in its turn, after an instant, Mrs. Assingham could meet with a smile. "Trust him, my dear, to keep her present! But trust him also to keep himself absent. Leave him his own way."

"I'll leave him everything," said Maggie. "Only — you know it's my nature — I THINK."

"It's your nature to think too much," Fanny Assingham a trifle coarsely risked.

This but quickened, however, in the Princess the act she reprobated. "That may be. But if I hadn't thought —!"

"You wouldn't, you mean, have been where you are?"

"Yes, because they, on their side, thought of everything BUT that. They thought of everything but that I might think."

"Or even," her friend too superficially concurred, "that your father might!"

As to this, at all events, Maggie discriminated. "No, that wouldn't have prevented them; for they knew that his first care would be not to make me do so. As it is," Maggie added, "that has had to become his last."

Fanny Assingham took it in deeper — for what it immediately made her give out louder. "HE'S splendid then." She sounded it almost aggressively; it was what she was reduced to — she had positively to place it.

"Ah, that as much as you please!"

Maggie said this and left it, but the tone of it had the next moment determined in her friend a fresh reaction. "You think, both of you, so abysmally and yet so quietly. But it's what will have saved you."

"Oh," Maggie returned, "it's what — from the moment they discovered we could think at all — will have saved THEM. For they're the ones who are saved," she went on. "We're the ones who are lost."

"Lost —?"

"Lost to each other — father and I" And then as her friend appeared to demur, "Oh yes," Maggie quite lucidly declared, "lost to each other much more, really, than Amerigo and Charlotte are; since for them it's just, it's right, it's deserved, while for us it's only sad and strange and not caused by our fault. But I don't know," she went on, "why I talk about myself, for it's on father it really comes. I let him go," said Maggie.

"You let him, but you don't make him."

"I take it from him," she answered.

"But what else can you do?"

"I take it from him," the Princess repeated. "I do what I knew from the first I SHOULD do. I get off by giving him up."

"But if he gives you?" Mrs. Assingham presumed to object. "Doesn't it moreover then," she asked, "complete the very purpose with which he married — that of making you and leaving you more free?"

Maggie looked at her long. "Yes — I help him to do that."

Mrs. Assingham hesitated, but at last her bravery flared. "Why not call it then frankly his complete success?"

"Well," said Maggie, "that's all that's left me to do."

"It's a success," her friend ingeniously developed, "with which you've simply not interfered." And as if to show that she spoke without levity Mrs. Assingham went further. "He has made it a success for THEM —!"

"Ah, there you are!" Maggie responsively mused. "Yes," she said the next moment, "that's why Amerigo stays."

"Let alone it's why Charlotte goes." that Mrs. Assingham, and emboldened, smiled "So he knows —?"

But Maggie hung back. "Amerigo —?" After which, however, she blushed — to her companion's recognition.

"Your father. He knows what YOU know? I mean," Fanny faltered — "well, how much does he know?" Maggie's silence and Maggie's eyes had in fact arrested the push of the question — which, for a decent consistency, she couldn't yet quite abandon. "What I should rather say is does he know how much?" She found it still awkward. "How much, I mean, they did. How far" — she touched it up —"they went."

Maggie had waited, but only with a question. "Do you think he does?"

"Know at least something? Oh, about him I can't think. He's beyond me," said Fanny Assingham.

"Then do you yourself know?"

"How much —?"

"How much."

"How far —?"

"How far."

Fanny had appeared to wish to make sure, but there was something she remembered — remembered in time and even with a smile. "I've told you before that I know absolutely nothing."

"Well — that's what *I* know," said the Princess.

Her friend again hesitated. "Then nobody knows —? I mean," Mrs. Assingham explained, "how much your father does."

Oh, Maggie showed that she understood. "Nobody."

"Not — a little — Charlotte?"

"A little?" the Princess echoed. "To know anything would be, for her, to know enough."

"And she doesn't know anything?"

"If she did," Maggie answered, "Amerigo would."

"And that's just it — that he doesn't?"

"That's just it," said the Princess profoundly.

On which Mrs. Assingham reflected. "Then how is Charlotte so held?"

"Just by that."

"By her ignorance?"

"By her ignorance." Fanny wondered. "A torment —?"

"A torment," said Maggie with tears in her eyes.

Her companion a moment watched them. But the Prince then —?"

"How is HE held?" Maggie asked.

"How is HE held?"

"Oh, I can't tell you that!" And the Princess again broke off.

XLI

A telegram, in Charlotte's name, arrived early —"We shall come and ask you for tea at five, if convenient to you. Am wiring for the Assinghams to lunch." This document, into which meanings were to be read, Maggie promptly placed before her husband, adding the remark that her father and his wife, who would have come up the previous night or that morning, had evidently gone to an hotel. The Prince was in his "own" room, where he often sat now alone; half-a-dozen open newspapers, the "Figaro" notably, as well as the "Times," were scattered about him; but, with a cigar in his teeth and a visible cloud on his brow, he appeared actually to be engaged in walking to and fro. Never yet, on thus approaching him — for she had done it of late, under one necessity or another, several times — had a particular impression so greeted her; supremely strong, for some reason, as he turned quickly round on her entrance. The reason was partly the look in his face — a suffusion like the flush of fever, which brought back to her Fanny Assingham's charge, recently uttered under that roof, of her "thinking" too impenetrably. The word had remained with her and made her think still more; so that, at first, as she stood there, she felt responsible for provoking on his part an irritation of suspense at which she had not aimed. She had been going about him these three months, she perfectly knew, with a maintained idea — of which she had never spoken to him; but what had at last happened was that his way of looking at her, on occasion, seemed a perception of the presence not of one idea, but of fifty, variously prepared for uses with which he somehow must reckon. She knew herself suddenly, almost strangely, glad to be coming to him, at this hour, with nothing more abstract than a telegram; but even after she had stepped into his prison under her pretext, while her eyes took in his face and then embraced the four walls that enclosed his restlessness, she recognised the virtual identity of his condition with that aspect of Charlotte's situation for which, early in the summer and in all the amplitude of a great residence, she had found, with so little seeking, the similitude of the locked cage. He struck her as caged, the man who couldn't now without an instant effect on her sensibility give an instinctive push to the door she had not completely closed behind her. He had been turning twenty ways, for impatiences all his own, and when she was once shut in with him it was yet again as if she had come to him in his more than monastic cell to offer him light or food. There was a difference none the less, between his captivity and Charlotte's — the difference, as it might be, of his lurking there by his own act and his own choice; the admission of which had indeed virtually been in his starting, on her entrance, as if even this were in its degree an interference. That was what betrayed for her, practically, his fear of her fifty ideas, and what had begun, after a minute, to make her wish to repudiate or explain. It was more wonderful than she could have told; it was for all the world as if she was succeeding with him beyond her intention. She had, for these instants, the sense that he exaggerated, that the imputation of purpose had fairly risen too high in him. She had begun, a year ago, by asking herself how she could make him think more of her; but what was it, after all, he was thinking now? He kept his eyes on her telegram; he read it more than once, easy as it was, in spite of its conveyed deprecation, to understand; during which she found herself almost awestruck with yearning, almost on the point of marking somehow what she had marked in the garden at Fawns with Charlotte — that she had truly come unarmed. She didn't bristle with intentions — she scarce knew, as he at this juncture affected her, what had become of the only intention she had come with. She had nothing but her old idea, the old one he knew; she hadn't the ghost of another. Presently in fact, when four or five minutes had elapsed, it was as if she positively, hadn't so much even as that one. He gave her back her paper, asking with it if there were anything in particular she wished him to do.

She stood there with her eyes on him, doubling the telegram together as if it had been a precious thing and yet all the while holding her breath. Of a sudden, somehow, and quite as by the action of their merely having between them these few written words, an extraordinary fact came up. He was with her as if he were hers, hers in a degree and on a scale, with an intensity and an intimacy, that were a new and a strange quantity, that were like the irruption of a tide loosening them where they had stuck and making them feel they floated. What was it that, with the rush of this, just kept her from putting out her hands to him, from catching at him as, in the other time, with the superficial impetus he and Charlotte had privately conspired to impart, she had so often, her breath failing her, known the impulse to catch at her father? She did, however, just yet, nothing inconsequent — though she couldn't immediately have said what saved her; and by the time she had neatly folded her telegram she was doing something merely needful. "I wanted you simply to know — so that you mayn't by accident miss them. For it's the last," said Maggie.

"The last?"

"I take it as their good-bye." And she smiled as she could always smile. "They come in state — to take formal leave. They do everything that's proper. Tomorrow," she said, "they go to Southampton."

"If they do everything that's proper," the Prince presently asked, "why don't they at least come to dine?"

She hesitated, yet she lightly enough provided her answer. "That we must certainly ask them. It will be easy for you. But of course they're immensely taken —!"

He wondered. "So immensely taken that they can't — that your father can't — give you his last evening in England?"

This, for Maggie, was more difficult to meet; yet she was still not without her stop-gap. "That may be what they'll propose — that we shall go somewhere together, the four of us, for a celebration — except that, to round it thoroughly off, we ought also to have Fanny and the Colonel. They don't WANT them at tea, she quite sufficiently expresses; they polish them off, poor dears, they get rid of them, beforehand. They want only us together; and if they cut us down to tea," she continued, "as they cut Fanny and the Colonel down to luncheon, perhaps it's for the fancy, after all, of their keeping their last night in London for each other."

She said these things as they came to her; she was unable to keep them back, even though, as she heard herself, she might have been throwing everything to the winds. But wasn't that the right way — for sharing his last day of captivity with the man one adored? It was every moment more and more for her as if she were waiting with him in his prison — waiting with some gleam of remembrance of how noble captives in the French Revolution, the darkness of the Terror, used to make a feast, or a high discourse, of their last poor resources. If she had broken with everything now, every observance of all the past months, she must simply then take it so — take it that what she had worked for was too near, at last, to let her keep her head. She might have been losing her head verily in her husband's eyes — since he didn't know, all the while, that the sudden freedom of her words was but the diverted intensity of her disposition personally to seize him. He didn't know, either, that this was her manner — now she was with him — of beguiling audaciously the supremacy of suspense. For the people of the French Revolution, assuredly, there wasn't suspense; the scaffold, for those she was thinking of, was certain — whereas what Charlotte's telegram announced was, short of some incalculable error, clear liberation. Just the point, however, was in its being clearer to herself than to him; her clearnesses, clearances — those she had so all but abjectly laboured for — threatened to crowd upon her in the form of one of the clusters of angelic heads, the peopled shafts of light beating down through iron bars, that regale, on occasion, precisely, the fevered vision of those who are in chains. She was going to know, she felt, later on — was going to know with compunction, doubtless, on the very morrow, how thumpingly her heart had beaten at this foretaste of their being left together: she should judge at leisure the surrender she was making to the consciousness of complications about to be bodily lifted. She should judge at leisure even that avidity for an issue which was making so little of any complication but the unextinguished presence of the others; and indeed that she was already simplifying so much more than her husband came out for her next in the face with which he listened. He might certainly well be puzzled, in respect to his father-in-law and Mrs. Verver, by her glance at their possible preference for a concentrated evening. "But it isn't — is it?" he asked —"as if they were leaving each other?"

"Oh no; it isn't as if they were leaving each other. They're only bringing to a close — without knowing when it may open again — a time that has been, naturally, awfully interesting to them." Yes, she could talk so of their "time" — she was somehow sustained; she was sustained even to affirm more intensely her present possession of her ground. "They have their reasons — many things to think of; how can one tell? But there's always, also, the chance of his proposing to me that we shall have our last hours together; I mean that he and I shall. He may wish to take me off to dine with him somewhere alone — and to do it in memory of old days. I mean," the Princess went on, "the real old days; before my grand husband was invented and, much more, before his grand wife was: the wonderful times of his first great interest in what he has since done, his first great plans and opportunities, discoveries and bargains. The way we've sat together late, ever so late, in foreign restaurants, which he used to like; the way that, in every city in Europe, we've stayed on and on, with our elbows on the table and most of the lights put out, to talk over things he had that day seen or heard of or made his offer for, the things he had secured or refused or lost! There were places he took me to — you wouldn't believe! — for often he could only have left me with servants. If he should carry me off with him to-night, for old sake's sake, to the Earl's Court Exhibition, it will be a little — just a very, very little — like our young adventures." After which while Amerigo watched her, and in fact quite because of it, she had an inspiration, to which she presently yielded. If he was wondering what she would say next she had found exactly the thing. "In that case he will leave you Charlotte to take care of in our absence. You'll have to carry her off somewhere for your last evening; unless you may prefer to spend it with her here. I shall then see that you dine, that you have everything, quite beautifully. You'll be able to do as you like."

She couldn't have been sure beforehand, and had really not been; but the most immediate result of this speech was his letting her see that he took it for no cheap extravagance either of irony or of oblivion. Nothing in the world, of a truth, had ever been so sweet to her, as his look of trying to be serious enough to make no mistake about it. She troubled him — which hadn't been at all her purpose; she mystified him — which she couldn't help and, comparatively, didn't mind; then it came over her that he had, after all, a simplicity, very considerable, on which she had never dared to presume. It was a discovery — not like the other discovery she had once made, but giving out a freshness; and she recognised again in the light of it the number of the ideas of which he thought her capable. They were all, apparently, queer for him, but she had at least, with the lapse of the months, created the perception that there might be something in them; whereby he stared there, beautiful and sombre, at what she was at present providing him with. There was something of his own in his mind, to which, she was sure, he referred everything for a measure and a meaning; he had never let go of it, from the evening, weeks before, when, in her room, after his encounter with the Bloomsbury cup, she had planted it there by flinging it at him, on the question of her father's view of him, her determined "Find out for yourself!" She had been aware, during the months, that he had been trying to find out, and had been seeking, above all, to avoid the appearance of any evasions of such a form of knowledge as might reach him, with violence or with a penetration more insidious, from any other source. Nothing, however, had reached him; nothing he could at all conveniently reckon with had disengaged itself for him even from the announcement, sufficiently sudden, of the final secession of their companions. Charlotte was in pain, Charlotte was in torment, but he himself had given her reason enough for that; and, in respect to the rest of the whole matter of her obligation to follow her husband, that personage and she, Maggie, had so shuffled away every link between consequence and cause, that the intention remained, like some famous poetic line in a dead language, subject to varieties of interpretation. What renewed the obscurity was her strange image of their common offer to him, her father's and her own, of an opportunity to separate from Mrs. Verver with the due amount of form — and all the more that he was, in so pathetic a way, unable to treat himself to a quarrel with it on the score of taste. Taste, in him, as a touchstone, was now all at sea; for who could say but that one of her fifty ideas, or perhaps forty-nine of them, wouldn't be, exactly, that taste by itself, the taste he had always conformed to, had no importance whatever? If meanwhile, at all events, he felt her as serious, this made the greater reason for her profiting by it as she perhaps might never be able to profit again. She was invoking that reflection at the very moment he brought out, in reply to her last words, a remark which, though perfectly relevant and perfectly just, affected her at first as a high oddity. "They're doing the wisest thing, you know. For if they were ever to go —!" And he looked down at her over his cigar.

If they were ever to go, in short, it was high time, with her father's age, Charlotte's need of initiation, and the general magnitude of the job of their getting settled and seasoned, their learning to "live into" their queer future — it was high time that they should take up their courage. This was eminent sense, but it didn't arrest the Princess, who, the next moment, had found a form for her challenge. "But shan't you then so much as miss her a little? She's wonderful and beautiful, and I feel somehow as if she were dying. Not really, not physically," Maggie went on — "she's so far, naturally, splendid as she is, from having done with life. But dying for us — for you and me; and making us feel it by the very fact of there being so much of her left."

The Prince smoked hard a minute. "As you say, she's splendid, but there is — there always will be-much of her left. Only, as you also say, for others."

"And yet I think," the Princess returned, "that it isn't as if we had wholly done with her. How can we not always think of her? It's as if her unhappiness had been necessary to us — as if we had needed her, at her own cost, to build us up and start us."

He took it in with consideration, but he met it with a lucid inquiry. "Why do you speak of the unhappiness of your father's wife?"

They exchanged a long look — the time that it took her to find her reply. "Because not to —!"

"Well, not to —?"

"Would make me have to speak of him. And I can't," said Maggie, "speak of him."

"You 'can't' —?"

"I can't." She said it as for definite notice, not to be repeated. "There are too many things," she nevertheless added. "He's too great."

The Prince looked at his cigar-tip, and then as he put back the weed: "Too great for whom?" Upon which as she hesitated, "Not, my dear, too great for you," he declared. "For me — oh, as much as you like."

"Too great for me is what I mean. I know why I think it," Maggie said. "That's enough."

He looked at her yet again as if she but fanned his wonder; he was on the very point, she judged, of asking her why she thought it. But her own eyes maintained their warning, and at the end of a minute he had uttered other words. "What's of importance is that you're his daughter. That at least we've got. And I suppose that, if I may say nothing else, I may say at least that I value it."

"Oh yes, you may say that you value it. I myself make the most of it."

This again he took in, letting it presently put forth for him a striking connection. "She ought to have known you. That's what's present to me. She ought to have understood you better."

"Better than you did?"

"Yes," he gravely maintained, "better than I did. And she didn't really know you at all. She doesn't know you now."

"Ah, yes she does!" said Maggie.

But he shook his head — he knew what he meant. "She not only doesn't understand you more than I, she understands you ever so much less. Though even I —!"

"Well, even you?" Maggie pressed as he paused. "Even I, even I even yet —!" Again he paused and the silence held them.

But Maggie at last broke it. "If Charlotte doesn't understand me, it is that I've prevented her. I've chosen to deceive her and to lie to her."

The Prince kept his eyes on her. "I know what you've chosen to do. But I've chosen to do the same."

"Yes," said Maggie after an instant —"my choice was made when I had guessed yours. But you mean," she asked, "that she understands YOU?"

"It presents small difficulty!"

"Are you so sure?" Maggie went on.

"Sure enough. But it doesn't matter." He waited an instant; then looking up through the fumes of his smoke, "She's stupid," he abruptly opined.

"O — oh!" Maggie protested in a long wail.

It had made him in fact quickly change colour. "What I mean is that she's not, as you pronounce her, unhappy." And he recovered, with this, all his logic. "Why is she unhappy if she doesn't know?"

"Doesn't know —?" She tried to make his logic difficult.

"Doesn't know that YOU know."

It came from him in such a way that she was conscious, instantly, of three or four things to answer. But what she said first was: "Do you think that's all it need take?" And before he could reply, "She knows, she knows!" Maggie proclaimed.

"Well then, what?"

But she threw back her head, she turned impatiently away from him. "Oh, I needn't tell you! She knows enough. Besides," she went on, "she doesn't believe us."

It made the Prince stare a little. "Ah, she asks too much!" That drew, however, from his wife another moan of objection, which determined in him a judgment. "She won't let you take her for unhappy."

"Oh, I know better than any one else what she won't let me take her for!"

"Very well," said Amerigo, "you'll see."

"I shall see wonders, I know. I've already seen them, and I'm prepared for them." Maggie recalled — she had memories enough. "It's terrible" — her memories prompted her to speak. "I see it's ALWAYS terrible for women."

The Prince looked down in his gravity. "Everything's terrible, cara, in the heart of man. She's making her life," he said. "She'll make it."

His wife turned back upon him; she had wandered to a table, vaguely setting objects straight. "A little by the way then too, while she's about it, she's making ours." At this he raised his eyes, which met her own, and she held him while she delivered herself of some thing that had been with her these last minutes.

"You spoke just now of Charlotte's not having learned from you that I 'know.' Am I to take from you then that you accept and recognise my knowledge?"

He did the inquiry all the honours — visibly weighed its importance and weighed his response. "You think I might have been showing you that a little more handsomely?"

"It isn't a question of any beauty," said Maggie; "it's only a question of the quantity of truth."

"Oh, the quantity of truth!" the Prince richly, though ambiguously, murmured.

"That's a thing by itself, yes. But there are also such things, all the same, as questions of good faith."

"Of course there are!" the Prince hastened to reply. After which he brought up more slowly: "If ever a man, since the beginning of time, acted in good faith!" But he dropped it, offering it simply for that.

For that then, when it had had time somewhat to settle, like some handful of gold-dust thrown into the air — for that then Maggie showed herself, as deeply and strangely taking it. "I see." And she even wished this form to be as complete as she could make it. "I see."

The completeness, clearly, after an instant, had struck him as divine. "Ah, my dear, my dear, my dear —!" It was all he could say.

She wasn't talking, however, at large. "You've kept up for so long a silence —!"

"Yes, yes, I know what I've kept up. But will you do," he asked, "still one thing more for me?"

It was as if, for an instant, with her new exposure, it had made her turn pale. "Is there even one thing left?"

"Ah, my dear, my dear, my dear!" — it had pressed again in him the fine spring of the unspeakable. There was nothing, however, that the Princess herself couldn't say. "I'll do anything, if you'll tell me what."

"Then wait." And his raised Italian hand, with its play of admonitory fingers, had never made gesture more expressive. His voice itself dropped to a tone —! "Wait," he repeated. "Wait."

She understood, but it was as if she wished to have it from him. "Till they've been here, you mean?"

"Yes, till they've gone. Till they're away."

She kept it up. "Till they've left the country?" She had her eyes on him for clearness; these were the conditions of a promise — so that he put the promise, practically, into his response. "Till we've ceased to see them — for as long as God may grant! Till we're really alone."

"Oh, if it's only that —!" When she had drawn from him thus then, as she could feel, the thick breath of the definite — which was the intimate, the immediate, the familiar, as she hadn't had them for so long — she turned away again, she put her hand on the knob of the door. But her hand rested at first without a grasp; she had another effort to make, the effort of leaving him, of which everything that had just passed between them, his presence, irresistible, overcharged with it, doubled the difficulty. There was something — she couldn't have told what; it was as if, shut in together, they had come too far — too far for where they were; so that the mere act of her quitting him was like the attempt to recover the lost and gone. She had taken in with her something that, within the ten minutes, and especially within the last three or four, had slipped away from her — which it was vain now, wasn't it? to try to appear to clutch or to pick up. That consciousness in fact had a pang, and she balanced, intensely, for the lingering moment, almost with a terror of her endless power of surrender. He had only to press, really, for her to yield inch by inch, and she fairly knew at present, while she looked at him through her cloud, that the confession of this precious secret sat there for him to pluck. The sensation, for the few seconds, was extraordinary; her weakness, her desire, so long as she was yet not saving herself, flowered in her face like a light or a darkness. She sought for some word that would cover this up; she reverted to the question of tea, speaking as if they shouldn't meet sooner. "Then about five. I count on you."

On him too, however, something had descended; as to which this exactly gave him his chance. "Ah, but I shall see you —! No?" he said, coming nearer.

She had, with her hand still on the knob, her back against the door, so that her retreat, under his approach must be less than a step, and yet she couldn't for her life, with the other hand, have pushed him away. He was so near now that she could touch him, taste him, smell him, kiss him, hold him; he almost pressed upon her, and the warmth of his face — frowning, smiling, she mightn't know which; only beautiful and strange — was bent upon her with the largeness with which objects loom in dreams. She closed her eyes to it, and so, the next instant, against her purpose, she had put out her hand, which had met his own and which he held. Then it was that, from behind her closed eyes, the right word came. "Wait!" It was the word of his own distress and entreaty, the word for both of them, all they had left, their plank now on the great sea. Their hands were locked, and thus she said it again. "Wait. Wait." She kept her eyes shut, but her hand, she knew, helped her meaning — which after a minute she was aware his own had absorbed. He let her go — he turned away with this message, and when she saw him again his back was presented, as he had left her, and his face staring out of the window. She had saved herself and she got off.

XLII

Later on, in the afternoon, before the others arrived, the form of their reunion was at least remarkable: they might, in their great eastward drawing-room, have been comparing notes or nerves in apprehension of some stiff official visit. Maggie's mind, in its restlessness, even played a little with the prospect; the high cool room, with its afternoon shade, with its old tapestries uncovered, with the perfect polish of its wide floor reflecting the bowls of gathered flowers and the silver and linen of the prepared tea-table, drew from her a remark in which this whole effect was mirrored, as well as something else in the Prince's movement while he slowly paced and turned. "We're distinctly bourgeois!" she a trifle grimly threw off, as an echo of their old community; though to a spectator sufficiently detached they might have been quite the privileged pair they were reputed, granted only they were taken as awaiting the visit of Royalty. They might have been ready, on the word passed up in advance, to repair together to the foot of the staircase — the Prince somewhat in front, advancing indeed to the open doors and even going down, for all his princedom, to meet, on the stopping of the chariot, the august emergence. The time was stale, it was to be admitted, for incidents of magnitude; the September hush was in full possession, at the end of the dull day, and a couple of the long windows stood open to the balcony that overhung the desolation — the balcony from which Maggie, in the springtime, had seen Amerigo and Charlotte look down together at the hour of her return from the Regent's Park, near by, with her father, the Principino and Miss Bogle. Amerigo now again, in his punctual impatience, went out a couple of times and stood there; after which, as to report that nothing was in sight, he returned to the room with frankly nothing else to do. The Princess pretended to read; he looked at her as he passed; there hovered in her own sense the thought of other occasions when she had cheated appearances of agitation with a book. At last she felt him standing before her, and then she raised her eyes.

"Do you remember how, this morning, when you told me of this event, I asked you if there were anything particular you wished me to do? You spoke of my being at home, but that was a matter of course. You spoke of something else," he went on, while she sat with her book on her knee and her raised eyes; "something that makes me almost wish it may happen. You spoke," he said, "of the possibility of my seeing her alone. Do you know, if that comes," he asked, "the use I shall make of it?" And then as she waited: "The use is all before me."

"Ah, it's your own business now!" said his wife. But it had made her rise.

"I shall make it my own," he answered. "I shall tell her I lied to her."

"Ah no!" she returned.

"And I shall tell her you did."

She shook her head again. "Oh, still less!"

With which therefore they stood at difference, he with his head erect and his happy idea perched, in its eagerness, on his crest. "And how then is she to know?"

"She isn't to know."

"She's only still to think you don't —?"

"And therefore that I'm always a fool? She may think," said Maggie, "what she likes."

"Think it without my protest —?"

The Princess made a movement. "What business is it of yours?"

"Isn't it my right to correct her —?"

Maggie let his question ring — ring long enough for him to hear it himself; only then she took it up. "'Correct' her?" — and it was her own now that really rang. "Aren't you rather forgetting who she is?" After which, while he quite stared for it, as it was the very first clear majesty he had known her to use, she flung down her book and raised a warning hand. "The carriage. Come!"

The "Come!" had matched, for lucid firmness, the rest of her speech, and, when they were below, in the hall, there was a "Go!" for him, through the open doors and between the ranged servants, that matched even that. He received Royalty, bareheaded, therefore, in the persons of Mr. and Mrs. Verver, as it alighted on the pavement, and Maggie was at the threshold to welcome it to her house. Later on, upstairs again, she even herself felt still more the force of the limit of which she had just reminded him; at tea, in Charlotte's affirmed presence — as Charlotte affirmed it — she drew a long breath of richer relief. It was the strangest, once more, of all impressions; but what she most felt, for the half-hour, was that Mr. and Mrs. Verver were making the occasion easy. They were somehow conjoined in it, conjoined for a present effect as Maggie had absolutely never yet seen them; and there occurred, before long, a moment in which Amerigo's look met her own in recognitions that he couldn't suppress. The question of the amount of correction to which Charlotte had laid herself open rose and hovered, for the instant, only to sink, conspicuously, by its own weight; so high a pitch she seemed to give to the unconsciousness of questions, so resplendent a show of serenity she succeeded in making. The shade of the official, in her beauty and security, never for a moment dropped; it was a cool, high refuge, like the deep, arched recess of some coloured and gilded image, in which she sat and smiled and waited, drank her tea, referred to her husband and remembered her mission. Her mission had quite taken form — it was but another name for the interest of her great opportunity — that of representing the arts and the graces to a people languishing, afar off, in ignorance. Maggie had sufficiently intimated to the Prince, ten minutes before, that she needed no showing as to what their friend wouldn't consent to be taken for; but the difficulty now indeed was to choose, for explicit tribute of admiration, between the varieties of her nobler aspects. She carried it off, to put the matter coarsely, with a taste and a discretion that held our young woman's attention, for the first quarter-of-an-hour, to the very point of diverting it from the attitude of her overshadowed, her almost superseded companion. But Adam Verver profited indeed at this time, even with his daughter, by his so marked peculiarity of seeming on no occasion to have an attitude; and so long as they were in the room together she felt him still simply weave his web and play out his long fine cord, knew herself in presence of this tacit process very much as she had known herself at Fawns. He had a way, the dear man, wherever he was, of moving about the room, noiselessly, to see what it might contain; and his manner of now resorting to this habit, acquainted as he already was with the objects in view, expressed with a certain sharpness the intention of leaving his wife to her devices. It did even more than this; it signified, to the apprehension of the Princess, from the moment she more directly took thought of him, almost a special view of these devices, as actually exhibited in their rarity, together with an independent, a settled appreciation of their general handsome adequacy, which scarcely required the accompaniment of his faint contemplative hum.

Charlotte throned, as who should say, between her hostess and her host, the whole scene having crystallised, as soon as she took her place, to the right quiet lustre; the harmony was not less sustained for being superficial, and the only approach to a break in it was while Amerigo remained standing long enough for his father-inlaw, vaguely wondering, to appeal to him, invite or address him, and then, in default of any such word, selected for presentation to the other visitor a plate of petits fours. Maggie watched her husband — if it now could be called watching — offer this refreshment; she noted the consummate way — for "consummate" was the term she privately applied — in which Charlotte cleared her acceptance, cleared her impersonal smile, of any betrayal, any slightest value, of consciousness; and then felt the slow surge of a vision that, at the end of another minute or two, had floated her across the room to where her father stood looking at a picture, an early Florentine sacred subject, that he had given her on her marriage. He might have been, in silence, taking his last leave of it; it was a work for which he entertained, she knew, an unqualified esteem. The tenderness represented for her by his sacrifice of such a treasure had become, to her sense, a part of the whole infusion, of the immortal expression; the beauty of his sentiment looked out at her, always, from the beauty of the rest, as if the frame made positively a window for his spiritual face: she might have said to herself, at this moment, that in leaving the thing behind him, held as in her clasping arms, he was doing the most possible toward leaving her a part of his palpable self. She put her hand over his shoulder, and their eyes were held again, together, by the abiding felicity; they smiled in emulation, vaguely, as if speech failed them through their having passed too far; she would have begun to wonder the next minute if it were reserved to them, for the last stage, to find their contact, like that of old friends reunited too much on the theory of the unchanged, subject to shy lapses.

"It's all right, eh?"

"Oh, my dear — rather!"

He had applied the question to the great fact of the picture, as she had spoken for the picture in reply, but it was as if their words for an instant afterwards symbolised another truth, so that they looked about at everything else to give them this extension. She had passed her arm into his, and the other objects in the room, the other pictures, the sofas, the chairs, the tables, the cabinets, the "important" pieces, supreme in their way, stood out, round them, consciously, for recognition and applause. Their eyes moved together from piece to piece, taking in the whole nobleness — quite as if for him to measure the wisdom of old ideas. The two noble persons seated, in conversation, at tea, fell thus into the splendid effect and the general harmony: Mrs. Verver and the Prince fairly "placed" themselves, however unwittingly, as high expressions of the kind of human furniture required, esthetically, by such a scene. The fusion of their presence with the decorative elements, their contribution to the triumph of selection, was complete and admirable; though, to a lingering view, a view more penetrating than the occasion really demanded, they also might have figured as concrete attestations of a rare power of purchase. There was much indeed in the tone in which Adam Verver spoke again, and who shall say where his thought stopped? "Le compte y est. You've got some good things."

Maggie met it afresh —"Ah, don't they look well?" Their companions, at the sound of this, gave them, in a spacious intermission of slow talk, an attention, all of gravity, that was like an ampler submission to the general duty of magnificence; sitting as still, to be thus appraised, as a pair of effigies of the contemporary great on one of the platforms of Madame Tussaud. "I'm so glad — for your last look."

With which, after Maggie — quite in the air — had said it, the note was struck indeed; the note of that strange accepted finality of relation, as from couple to couple, which almost escaped an awkwardness only by not attempting a gloss. Yes, this was the wonder, that the occasion defied insistence precisely because of the vast quantities with which it dealt — so that separation was on a scale beyond any compass of parting. To do such an hour justice would have been in some degree to question its grounds — which was why they remained, in fine, the four of them, in the upper air, united in the firmest abstention from pressure. There was no point, visibly, at which, face to face, either Amerigo or Charlotte had pressed; and how little she herself was in danger of doing so Maggie scarce needed to remember. That her father wouldn't, by the tip of a toe — of that she was equally conscious: the only thing was that, since he didn't, she could but hold her breath for what he would do instead. When, at the end of three minutes more, he had said, with an effect of suddenness, "Well, Mag — and the Principino?" it was quite as if that were, by contrast, the hard, the truer voice.

She glanced at the clock. "I 'ordered' him for half-past five — which hasn't yet struck. Trust him, my dear, not to fail you!"

"Oh, I don't want HIM to fail me!" was Mr. Verver's reply; yet uttered in so explicitly jocose a relation to the possibilities of failure that even when, just afterwards, he wandered in his impatience to one of the long windows and passed out to the balcony, she asked herself but for a few seconds if reality, should she follow him, would overtake or meet her there. She followed him of necessity — it came, absolutely, so near to his inviting her, by stepping off into temporary detachment, to give the others something of the chance that she and her husband had so fantastically discussed. Beside him then, while they hung over the great dull place, clear and almost coloured now, coloured with the odd, sad, pictured, "old-fashioned" look that empty London streets take on in waning afternoons of the summer's end, she felt once more how impossible such a passage would have been to them, how it would have torn them to pieces, if they had so much as suffered its suppressed relations to peep out of their eyes. This danger would doubtless indeed have been more to be reckoned with if the instinct of each — she could certainly at least answer for her own — had not so successfully acted to trump up other apparent connexions for it, connexions as to which they could pretend to be frank.

"You mustn't stay on here, you know," Adam Verver said as a result of his unobstructed outlook. "Fawns is all there for you, of course — to the end of my tenure. But Fawns so dismantled," he added with mild ruefulness, "Fawns with half its contents, and half its best things, removed, won't seem to you, I'm afraid, particularly lively."

"No," Maggie answered, "we should miss its best things. Its best things, my dear, have certainly been removed. To be back there," she went on, "to be back there —!" And she paused for the force of her idea.

"Oh, to be back there without anything good —!" But she didn't hesitate now; she brought her idea forth. "To be back there without Charlotte is more than I think would do." And as she smiled at him with it, so she saw him the next instant take it — take it in a way that helped her smile to pass all for an allusion to what she didn't and couldn't say. This quantity was too clear — that she couldn't at such an hour be pretending to name to him what it was, as he would have said, "going to be," at Fawns or anywhere else, to want for HIM. That was now — and in a manner exaltedly, sublimely — out of their compass and their question; so that what was she doing, while they waited for the Principino, while they left the others together and their tension just sensibly threatened, what was she doing but just offer a bold but substantial substitute? Nothing was stranger moreover, under the action of Charlotte's presence, than the fact of a felt sincerity in her words. She felt her sincerity absolutely sound — she gave it for all it might mean. "Because Charlotte, dear, you know," she said, "is incomparable." It took thirty seconds, but she was to know when these were over that she had pronounced one of the happiest words of her life. They had turned from the view of the street; they leaned together against the balcony rail, with the room largely in sight from where they stood, but with the Prince and Mrs. Verver out of range. Nothing he could try, she immediately saw, was to keep his eyes from lighting; not even his taking out his cigarette-case and saying before he said anything else: "May I smoke?" She met it, for encouragement, with her "My dear!" again, and then, while he struck his match, she had just another minute to be nervous — a minute that she made use of, however, not in the least to falter, but to reiterate with a high ring, a ring that might, for all she cared, reach the pair inside: "Father, father — Charlotte's great!"

It was not till after he had begun to smoke that he looked at her. "Charlotte's great."

They could close upon it — such a basis as they might immediately feel it make; and so they stood together over it, quite gratefully, each recording to the other's eyes that it was firm under their feet. They had even thus a renewed wait, as for proof of it; much as if he were letting her see, while the minutes lapsed for their concealed companions, that this was finally just why — but just WHY! "You see," he presently added, "how right I was. Right, I mean, to do it for you."

"Ah, rather!" she murmured with her smile. And then, as to be herself ideally right: "I don't see what you would have done without her."

"The point was," he returned quietly, "that I didn't see what you were to do. Yet it was a risk."

"It was a risk," said Maggie —"but I believed in it. At least for myself!" she smiled.

"Well NOW," he smoked, "we see."

"We see."

"I know her better."

"You know her best."

"Oh, but naturally!" On which, as the warranted truth of it hung in the air — the truth warranted, as who should say, exactly by the present opportunity to pronounce, this opportunity created and accepted — she found herself lost, though with a finer thrill than she had perhaps yet known, in the vision of all he might mean. The sense of it in her rose higher, rose with each moment that he invited her thus to see him linger; and when, after a little more, he had said, smoking again and looking up, with head thrown back and hands spread on the balcony rail, at the grey, gaunt front of the house, "She's beautiful, beautiful!" her sensibility reported to her the shade of a new note. It was all she might have wished, for it was, with a kind of speaking competence, the note of possession and control; and yet it conveyed to her as nothing till now had done the reality of their parting. They were parting, in the light of it, absolutely on Charlotte's VALUE — the value that was filling the room out of which they had stepped as if to give it play, and with which the Prince, on his side, was perhaps making larger acquaintance. If Maggie had desired, at so late an hour, some last conclusive comfortable category to place him in for dismissal, she might have found it here in its all coming back to his ability to rest upon high values. Somehow, when all was said, and with the memory of her gifts, her variety, her power, so much remained of Charlotte's! What else had she herself meant three minutes before by speaking of her as great? Great for the world that was before her — that he proposed she should be: she was not to be wasted in the application of his plan. Maggie held to this then — that she wasn't to be wasted. To let his daughter know it he had sought this brief privacy. What a blessing, accordingly, that she could speak her joy in it! His face, meanwhile, at all events, was turned to her, and as she met his eyes again her joy went straight. "It's success, father."

"It's success. And even this," he added as the Principino, appearing alone, deep within, piped across an instant greeting — "even this isn't altogether failure!"

They went in to receive the boy, upon whose introduction to the room by Miss Bogle Charlotte and the Prince got up — seemingly with an impressiveness that had caused Miss Bogle not to give further effect to her own entrance. She had retired, but the Principino's presence, by itself, sufficiently broke the tension — the subsidence of which, in the great room, ten minutes later, gave to the air something of the quality produced by the cessation of a sustained rattle. Stillness, when the Prince and Princess returned from attending the visitors to their carriage, might have been said to be not so much restored as created; so that whatever next took place in it was foredoomed to remarkable salience. That would have been the case even with so natural, though so futile, a movement as Maggie's going out to the balcony again to follow with her eyes her father's departure. The carriage was out of sight — it had taken her too long solemnly to reascend, and she looked awhile only at the great grey space, on which, as on the room still more, the shadow of dusk had fallen. Here, at first, her husband had not rejoined her; he had come up with the boy, who, clutching his hand, abounded, as usual, in remarks worthy of the family archives; but the two appeared then to have proceeded to report to Miss Bogle. It meant something for the Princess that her husband had thus got their son out of the way, not bringing him back to his mother; but everything now, as she vaguely moved about, struck her as meaning so much that the unheard chorus swelled. Yet THIS above all — her just being there as she was and waiting for him to come in, their freedom to be together there always — was the meaning most disengaged: she stood in the cool twilight and took in, all about her, where it lurked, her reason for what she had done. She knew at last really why — and how she had been inspired and guided, how she had been persistently able, how, to her soul, all the while, it had been for the sake of this end. Here it was, then, the moment, the golden fruit that had shone from afar; only, what were these things, in the fact, for the hand and for the lips, when tested, when tasted — what were they as a reward? Closer than she had ever been to the measure of her course and the full face of her act, she had an instant of the terror that, when there has been suspense, always precedes, on the part of the creature to be paid, the certification of the amount. Amerigo knew it, the amount; he still held it, and the delay in his return, making her heart beat too fast to go on, was like a sudden blinding light on a wild speculation. She had thrown the dice, but his hand was over her cast.

He opened the door, however, at last — he hadn't been away ten minutes; and then, with her sight of him renewed to intensity, she seemed to have a view of the number. His presence alone, as he paused to look at her, somehow made it the highest, and even before he had spoken she had begun to be paid in full. With that consciousness, in fact, an extraordinary thing occurred; the assurance of her safety so making her terror drop that already, within the minute, it had been changed to concern for his own anxiety, for everything that was deep in his being and everything that was fair in his face. So far as seeing that she was "paid" went, he might have been holding out the money-bag for her to come and take it. But what instantly rose, for her, between the act and her acceptance was the sense that she must strike him as waiting for a confession. This, in turn, charged her with a new horror: if that was her proper payment she would go without money. His acknowledgment hung there, too monstrously, at the expense of Charlotte, before whose mastery of the greater style she had just been standing dazzled. All she now knew, accordingly, was that she should be ashamed to listen to the uttered word; all, that is, but that she might dispose of it on the spot forever.

"Isn't she too splendid?" she simply said, offering it to explain and to finish.

"Oh, splendid!" With which he came over to her.

"That's our help, you see," she added — to point further her moral.

It kept him before her therefore, taking in-or trying to — what she so wonderfully gave. He tried, too clearly, to please her — to meet her in her own way; but with the result only that, close to her, her face kept before him, his hands holding her shoulders, his whole act enclosing her, he presently echoed: "'See'? I see nothing but you." And the truth of it had, with this force, after a moment, so strangely lighted his eyes that, as for pity and dread of them, she buried her own in his breast.

CPSIA information can be obtained
at www.ICGtesting.com
Printed in the USA
LVHW080132110522
718468LV00013B/643

9 788027 330799